D1146063

Destiny

Elizabeth Haydon

BCA

LONDON   NEW YORK   SYDNEY   TORONTO

This edition published 2002
by BCA
by arrangement with Gollancz
an imprint of Orion Publishing Group

CN 100281

The right of Elizabeth Haydon to be identified as the
author of this work has been asserted by her in accordance
with the Copyright, Designs and Patents Act 1988.

Typeset in Plantin Light
at The Spartan Press Ltd, Lymington, Hants

Printed in Great Britain by
Omnia Books Limited, Glasgow

This book is dedicated to the other half of my soul
My traveling companion for eternity
My co-parent, best friend, dream-come-true
And general all around favorite person
The heartless lout
Who scratches out some of my favorite dialogue
Deletes whole passages I worked very *hard on*
Believes 'yeah, it's fine,' to be the ultimate compliment
And keeps it Real
Without whom none of these books would exist
To Bill
with love
throughout Time

Acknowledgments

Many thanks to the usual suspects, the fine folks at Tor, especially Jim Minz and Jodi Rosoff, and the great Tom Doherty. And to Richard Curtis, as always.

Sincere appreciation to the Henry Mercer Museum and Tile Foundry, the Comparative Literature Department of SMU, the International Maritime Museum and the chiefs and clan mothers of the Onondaga Nation.

Thanks to Glynn Gomes for the hydrogeological review.

My deepest gratitude to Aidan Rose, MJ Urist, Rebecca Caballo, Diane Rogers, Az-Kim, the Weltman Clan, and the Friedmans, for your endless support.

With love to my parents, for everything you taught me and the world you showed me.

And Bill and the kids, my world now.

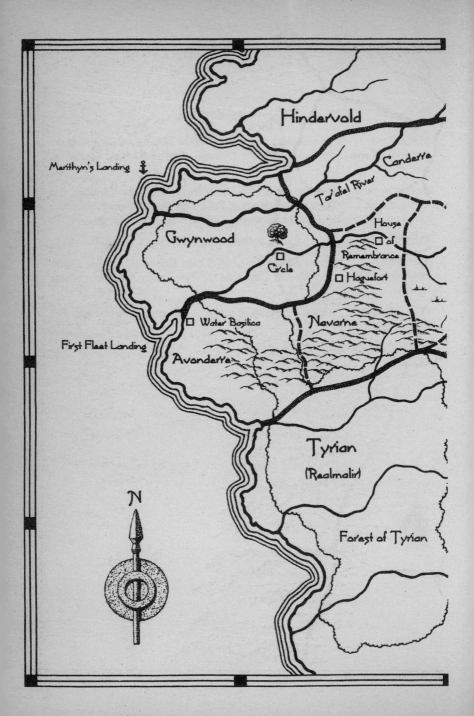

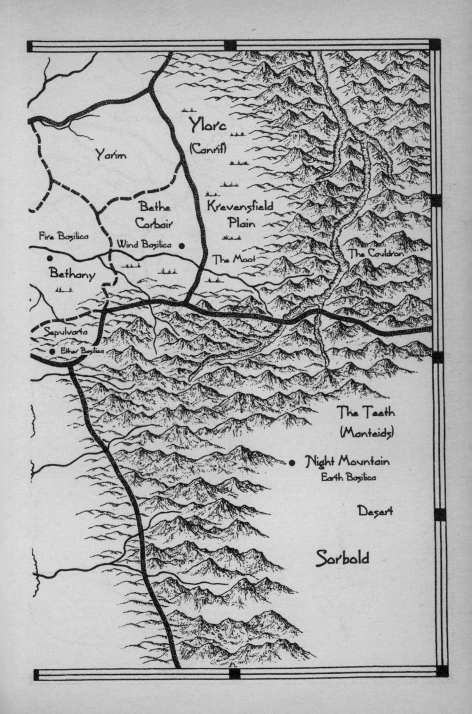

THE PROPHECY OF THE THREE

The Three shall come, leaving early, arriving late,
The lifestages of all men:
Child of Blood, Child of Earth, Child of the Sky.

Each man, formed in blood and born in it,
Walks the Earth and sustained by it,
Reaching to the sky, and sheltered beneath it,
He ascends there only in his ending, becoming part of the stars.
Blood gives new beginning, Earth gives sustenance,
The Sky gives dreams in life – eternity in death.
Thus shall the Three be, one to the other.

THE PROPHECY OF THE UNINVITED GUEST

Among the last to leave, among the first to come,
Seeking a new host, uninvited, in a new place.
The power gained in being the first,
Was lost in being the last.
Hosts shall nurture it, unknowing,
Like the guest wreathed in smiles
While secretly poisoning the larder.
Jealously guarded of its own power,
Ne'er has, nor ever shall its host bear or sire children,
Yet ever it seeks to procreate.

THE PROPHECY OF THE SLEEPING CHILD

The Sleeping Child, the youngest born
Lives on in dreams, though Death has come
To write her name within his tome
And no one yet has thought to mourn.

The middle child, who sleeping lies,
'Twixt watersky and shifting sands
Sits silent, holding patient hands
Until the day she can arise.

The eldest child rests deep within
The ever-silent vault of earth,
Unborn as yet, but with its birth
The end of Time Itself begins.

THE PROPHECY OF THE LAST GUARDIAN

Within a Circle of Four will stand a Circle of Three
Children of the Wind all, and yet none
The hunter, the sustainer, the healer,
Brought together by fear, held together by love,
To find that which hides from the Wind.

Hear, oh guardian, and look upon your destiny:
The one who hunts also will stand guard
The one who sustains also will abandon,
The one who heals also will kill
To find that which hides from the Wind.

Listen, oh Last One, to the wind:
The wind of the past to beckon her home
The wind of the earth to carry her to safety
The wind of the stars to sing the mother's-song most known to her soul
To hide the Child from the Wind.

From the lips of the Sleeping Child will come the words of ultimate
  wisdom:
Beware the Sleepwalker
For blood will be the means
To find that which hides from the Wind.

THE PROPHECY OF THE KING OF SOLDIERS

As each life begins, Blood is joined, but is spilled as well; it divides too easily
  to heal the rift.

The Earth is shared by all, but it too is divided, generation into generation.

Only the Sky encompasses all, and the sky cannot be divided; thus shall it be
  the means by which peace and unity will come.

If you seek to mend the rift, General, guard the Sky, lest it fall.

First you must heal the rift within yourself. With Gwylliam's death you now
  are the king of soldiers, but until you find the slightest of your kinsmen
  and protect that helpless one, you are unworthy of forgiveness. And so it
  shall be until you either are redeemed, or die unabsolved.

THE KINSMAN CALL

By the Star, I will wait, I will watch, I will call and will be heard.

Destiny

The Order of the Filids

LLAURON THE INVOKER

Chief Priests:
Khaddyr, Llauron's Tanist [successor] and Healer
Lark, Herbalist
Gavin, Chief Forester
Ilyana, Chief of Agriculture

The Circle [lower level Priests and foresters]

The Patrician Religion of Sepulvarta

THE PATRIARCH, SILINEUS

The Benisons:
The Blesser of Avonderre-Navarne, Philabet Griswold
The Blesser of Sorbold, Nielash Mousa
The Blesser of Bethe Corbair, Lanacan Orlando
The Blesser of Canderre-Yarim, Ian Steward
The Blesser of the Nonaligned States, Colin Abernathy

The Elemental Basilicas
Ether   Lianta'ar, Sepulvarta
Fire   Vrackna, Bethany
Water   Abbat Mythlinis, Avonderre
Air   Ryles Cedelian, Bethe Corbair
Earth   Terreanfor, Sorbold

Finale

At the Edge of the Krevensfield Plain

Time was growing short, Meridion knew.

The seven-and-a-half-foot-tall monster in ring mail threw back his head, bared tusklike fangs, and roared. The bellowing howl of rage rang through the darkness that clung to the toothlike, mountainous crags, sending loose shale stone and clods of snow tumbling down into the canyon a mile or more below.

Achmed the Snake, king of the Firbolg, exchanged a glance with Rhapsody and Krinsel, the Bolg midwife who was helping her pack for their journey. He returned to his sorting, hiding a smile behind his face-veil at the shock in the Singer's enormous green eyes.

'What's upsetting Grunthor now?' she asked, handing the midwife a sack of roots. Krinsel sniffed it, then shook her head, and Rhapsody set the sack down again.

'He's apparently displeased with the quartermaster and his regiment,' Achmed answered as a stream of Bolgish profanities rumbled over the heath.

'I think he's more perturbed that he can't go with us,' Rhapsody said, looking through the gray light of foredawn with sympathy at the terrified soldiers and their leader, who were doing their best to stand at attention, withering under the Sergeant-Major's violent dressing-down. The midwife handed her a pouch, and she smiled.

'Undoubtedly, but it can't be helped.' Achmed cinched a leather sack and wedged it into his saddlebag. 'The Bolglands are not in any state to be left without a leader at the moment. Do you have everything you need for the delivery?'

The Singer's smile vanished. 'Thank you, Krinsel. Be well while I'm away, and look in on my grandchildren for me, will you?' The Bolg woman nodded, bowed perfunctorily to the king, and then made a cautious exit, disappearing into one of the Cauldron's many exit tunnels.

'I have no idea what I'm going to need for this delivery,' she said in a low voice with a terse edge to it. 'I've never delivered a child who is demon-spawn before. Have you?'

Achmed's dark, mismatched eyes stared at her for a moment above the veil, then looked away as he went back to his packing.

Rhapsody brushed back a strand of her golden hair, exhaled, and rested a hand gently on the Bolg king's forearm. 'I'm sorry for being churlish. I'm nervous about this journey.'

Achmed hoisted the snow-encrusted saddlebag over his shoulder. 'I know,' he said evenly. 'You should be. We are still agreed about these children, I take it? You understand the conditions under which my help is given?'

Rhapsody returned his piercing stare with one that was milder but every bit as determined. 'Yes.'

'Good. Then let's go rescue the quartermaster from Grunthor's wrath.'

The newly fallen snow of winter's earliest days crunched below their feet as they tramped over the dark heath. Rhapsody paused for a moment, turning away from the western foothills and the wide Krevensfield Plain to the black eastern horizon beyond the peaks of the Teeth, lightening now at its jagged rim with the paler gray that preceded daybreak.

An hour, maybe less, before sunrise, she thought, trying to gauge when she and Achmed would be departing. It was important to be in a place where she could greet the dawn with the ritual songs that were the morning prayers of the Liringlas, her mother's race. She inhaled the clear, cold air, and watched as it passed back out with her exhalation, frozen clouds in the bitter wind.

'Achmed,' she called to the king, twenty or more paces ahead of her. He turned around and waited silently as she caught up with him. 'I am grateful for your help in this matter; I really am.'

'Don't be, Rhapsody,' he said seriously. 'I'm not doing this to help you spare the spawn of the F'dor from damnation. My motives are entirely selfish. You should know that by now.'

'If your motives were entirely selfish, you would not have agreed to accompany me on this mission to find them, you would have gone alone and hunted them down,' she said, untangling the strap of her pack. 'Let's strike a bargain: I won't pretend your intentions are altruistic, and you won't pretend they're selfish. Agreed?'

'I'll agree to whatever makes you hurry up and get ready. If we don't leave before full-sun we run the risk of being seen.'

She nodded, and the two of them hurried over the remainder of the heath and down to the lower tier of battlements, where Grunthor and the quartermaster's troops were waiting.

'You're a disgrace to this regiment, the whole lot of you,' Grunthor was snarling at the trembling Bolg soldiers. 'One more missed instruction, I'm going to flay you, fillet you, and fry you in fat for my supper, every last one of you. And you, Hagraith, *you* will be dessert.'

Achmed cleared his throat. 'Are the horses ready, Sergeant-Major?'

''Bout as ready as can be expected,' Grunthor grumbled. 'Provisions will be in place momentarily, as soon as Corporal Hagraith here gets his head out of his arse, cleans the *hrekin* out of his ears, and gets them rolled bandages I requested *two hours ago.*' The soldier took off in a dead run.

Rhapsody waited in respectful silence as Grunthor dismissed the rest of the supply troops, then came up behind him and wound her arms around his massive waist, a sensation similar to encircling a full-grown tree trunk.

'I'm going to miss your troops tromping by my chamber and singing me awake,' she said jokingly. 'Dawn just won't be the same without a few choruses of "Leave No Limb Unbroken."'

The giant's leathery features relaxed into a fond grin. 'Well, you could always stay, then,' he said, mussing her glistening locks, which shone with the brilliance of the sun.

It never failed to amaze him, looking at her thus, how much she resembled the Great Fire they had passed through together, in that journey so long ago. While crawling along the root of Sagia the World Tree, that had wound itself around the centerline of the Earth, he had come to respect this tiny woman, even though his own race had preyed on hers in the old world.

Rhapsody sighed. 'How I wish I could.' She watched his amber eyes darken sadly. 'Will you be all right, Grunthor?'

A sharp sound of annoyance came from over her shoulder. 'Safeguarding the mountain is child's play to Grunthor.'

'No. I vaguely recall enjoying child's play. Don't like this at all,' the Firbolg giant muttered, his fearsome face wreathed in a terrifying scowl. 'We almost lost *you* once to a bastard child of the demon; I don't especially want you risking your life – and your *afterlife* – again, miss. Wish you'd reconsider.'

She patted his arm. 'I can't. We have to do this; it's the only way to get the blood we need for Achmed to finally track and find the host of the F'dor.'

'*He* may need to do it, then,' Grunthor said. 'No need for you to go along, Duchess. His Majesty works best alone, anyway. We've already lost Jo; I don't see no reason to risk losing you as well.'

The reference to the death of the street child she had adopted as her sister made Rhapsody's eyes sting, but outwardly she betrayed no sign of sorrow. She had sung Jo's final dirge a few days before, along with the laments for the others they had lost along the way. She bit back a bitter answer, remembering that Grunthor had loved Jo almost as much as she had.

'Jo was little more than a child. I'm a trained warrior, trained by the best. Between you and Oelendra I believe I am fully capable of defending myself. Besides, since you're "The Ultimate Authority, to Be Obeyed at All Costs," you can just command me to live, and I suppose I will have to do so. I wouldn't want to risk your wrath by dying against orders.'

Grunthor surrendered to a smile. 'All right, consider it a command, then, miss.' He encircled her warmly in his massive arms. 'Take care of yourself, Your Ladyship.'

'I shall.' Rhapsody glanced over at Achmed, who was securing the saddles of the horses Grunthor had ordered provisioned for them. 'Are you ready, Achmed?'

'Before we set out, there's something I want you to see,' the king answered, checking the cinches.

'What? I thought you wished to be gone ere full-sun.'

'This will only take a few moments, but it should be worth the delay. I want to be in the observatory at dawn.'

Delight splashed over her face, making it shine as brightly as the sun soon would. 'The observatory? The restoration of the stairway is finished?'

'Yes. And if you hurry we can get an overlook of the Inner Teeth and the Krevensfield Plain before we try to cross it.' He turned and gestured to the entrance to the Cauldron, the dark network of tunnels, barracks, and rooms of state that was his seat of power in Ylorc.

Rhapsody gave Grunthor a final squeeze, then gently broke loose of his embrace and followed the king through the dismal, windowless hallways, past the ancient statuary that was only now being cleaned and restored by Bolg artisans to its former glory from the Cymrian Age thirteen centuries before, when Ylorc, then known as Canrif, had been built.

They entered the Great Hall through its large double doors wrought in gold and inscribed with intricate symbols, and crossed the enormous expanse of the round throne room, where Bolg masons were carefully cleaning centuries of grime off the blue-black marble of the room's twenty-four pillars, one marking each of the hours in the day.

'The renovation is coming along nicely,' Rhapsody commented as they hurried through the patches of dusty gray light, filtering down from the glass blocks that had been embedded in the circular ceiling centuries before, affording not only illumination but glimpses of the peaks of the Inner Teeth above them. 'This place was a mass of rubble the last time I was here.'

Achmed circumvented an enormous, star-shaped mosaic on the floor; the last of a series of celestial representations wrought in multicolored marble, cloudily visible beneath a layer of construction grit. 'Mind your step here. If I recall, the last time you were in here you succumbed to a vision on this spot.'

Rhapsody shuddered and picked up her pace. The gift of prescience had been hers for as long as she could remember. Nonetheless, each time she was assailed by a memory that was not her own, a vision that related something significant in the Past or, worse, warned of something coming in the Future, it caught her off guard, especially if it caused her to relive the intense emotions that remained behind like the smoky residue of a long-dead forest fire.

Her nightmares had returned to plague her as well, now that Ashe was no longer there to keep them at bay. At the thought, Rhapsody felt her throat go dry, and she struggled to banish the memory of her former lover from her mind by walking even faster. Their time together was over; he had his own responsibilities, chief among them seeking out the First Generation Cymrian woman he planned to marry, to rule with him as Lady, as the Ring of Wisdom had advised. They both had known from the beginning that their romance would only last a short time, but that knowledge had not made its passing any less painful.

Achmed had disappeared through an open doorway behind the dais on which stood the thrones of the Lord and Lady Cymrian, some of the few antiquities that had survived the Bolg rout of Canrif at the end of the Cymrian War intact.

'Hurry up.' His voice echoed through the circular room.

'I'm coming as fast as I can,' Rhapsody retorted as she hastened through the doorway. 'You're a head taller than I am, Achmed; your stride is longer.' She fell silent, admiring the beauty of the restored stairway to the observatory, high within one of the peaks of the Teeth.

On one side of the room, a twisting staircase of polished hespera wood, dark and rich with a blue undertone, curved in many spirals up to the opening of the tower high above. On the other, a strange apparatus rested on the floor, apparently still being renovated. It resembled a small, hexagonal room with glass panes.

'It's a form of vertical trolley, a funicular of sorts like we use in the mining tunnels,' Achmed explained, reading her mind. 'Another of Gwylliam's inventions. He'd written precise plans for its construction and maintenance. Apparently it ferried courtiers and the like who were too sedentary to climb the stairs. Clever design.'

'Interesting. I'd prefer to walk, however, even if it were operational. I don't like the idea of riding in a glass room above a stone floor.'

Achmed hid a smile. 'As you wish.'

They climbed the polished stairway, ascending higher and higher within the hollow mountain peak. As they neared the top Achmed reached into his boot and pulled out a large brass key. Rhapsody cast a glance over the railing at the distant floor and shuddered slightly.

'I'm certainly impressed with your renovations, Achmed, but why couldn't this tour wait until our return? Surely the view of the Krevensfield Plain is panoramic enough from the Heath, or from the tower in Grivven Post. Then at least we would be moving westward.'

The Firbolg king inserted the key into the lock, and twisted it, causing an audible *klink*. 'You may be able to see something from the observatory that you couldn't from the Heath or Grivven Tower.'

The heavy door, bound in long-rusted iron, swung open on recently oiled hinges with a groan, revealing the domed room beyond. Rhapsody caught her breath. The observatory had not been renovated yet; white cloths, frosted with layers of dust, were draped heavily, covering what appeared to be furniture and freestanding equipment. They gleamed in the diffuse light of the room like ghosts in the darkness.

Achmed's strong hand encircled her arm; he drew her into the room and closed the door quickly behind them.

The room itself was square, with a ceiling that arched into a buttressed dome. It had been carved into the peak of the mountain crag itself, the walls burnished smooth as marble. Each of the four walls contained an enormous window, sealed shut, forgotten by Time. Ancient telescopes stood at each of the windows, oddly jointed, with wide eyepieces. Magic and history hung, static, in the air of the long-sealed chamber. It had a bitter taste, the taste of dust from the crypt, of shining hope long abandoned.

Rhapsody surveyed the rest of the room quickly – shelves of ancient log-books and maps, intricate frescoes on the quartered ceiling, depicting the four elements of water, air, fire, and earth at each directional point, with the fifth, ether, represented by a covered globe suspended from the apex in the center. She would have loved the opportunity to examine the room thoroughly, but Achmed was gesturing impatiently from in front of the western window.

'Here,' he said, and pointed at the vast, panoramic horizon stretching in all directions below them. 'Have a look.'

She came to the window and gazed out at the land coming awake with First-light. The view was more breathtaking than any other she had ever seen; here, in the tower-top pinnacle of the highest crag in the Teeth, she felt suspended in the air itself, perched above the whispering clouds below, with the world quite literally at her feet. *Small wonder the Cymrians thought themselves akin to gods,* she mused in awe. *They stood in the heavens and looked down at the Earth, by the work of their own hands. It must have been a very long fall.*

Once this observatory looked out over the realm of Canrif, the marvel of the Age, a kingdom of all the races of men, built from the unforgiving mountains by the sheer will of the Cymrian Lord, Gwylliam, sometimes called the Visionary, known of late by less flattering epithets. Now, centuries after the war in which the Cymrians destroyed themselves and the dominion they had held over the continent, their ancient mountainous cities, their observatories and libraries, vaults and storerooms, palaces and roadways were the domain of the Bolg, the descendants of the marauding tribes that overran Canrif at the end of the bloody Cymrian War.

The gray light of early morning flattened the panorama of the Teeth into thick shards of semi-darkness. As the sun rose it would illuminate the breathtaking sight, glittering on the millions of crags and fissures, the abundance of canyons and high forests, and the ruins of the ancient city of Canrif, the expansive edifice of a civilization that had been carved out of the face of the multicolored mountains. Now, however, with but moments of night remaining, the jagged range appeared flat and stolid, silent and dead in the sight of the world.

Rhapsody watched as the first tentative rays of morning sun cracked the black vault of night, favoring certain mountaintops with its purest light, a light that made the ever-present icecaps on the peaks of the Teeth glisten encouragingly. *An interesting metaphor for the Bolg,* she mused.

In the minds of the men of the surrounding realms, this primitive culture was considered monstrous, only demi-human, a scattered swarm of cannibalistic predators roving the mountains, preying on all living things. She had believed those myths herself once, long ago, before she had met Grunthor and Achmed, who by birth were half-Bolg.

Now she saw the Bolg as they really were. The tendencies for which they were feared were not totally unfounded – Firbolg were fierce and warlike, and, without the guiding hand of a strong leader, resorted to whatever means necessary to survive, including the consumption of human flesh. Given that strong leader, however, she had seen and come to admire, and eventually love, this simple race, these primitive survivors, the outcasts of Nature and of man who nonetheless kept their values and legends alive, even in the harshest of realities.

They were a simple people, beautiful and uncomplicated in their interactions, with a disdain for self-pity and a single-mindedness about fostering the continuation of their society. Bloodied warriors could lie on the battlefield and die of non-mortal wounds while medical attention was directed to a laboring woman, in the belief that the infant was the Future, while the soldier was merely the Present. Anything that was the Past did not matter, save for a few stories and the all-encompassing need to survive.

The first long rays of sun crested the horizon, making the thin snow-blanket of the Krevensfield Plain twinkle with the brilliance of a diamond sea. The light reflected off the brightening sky, revealing the many layers of the mountains in all their splendor. Silver streams of artesian water rippled in cascading ribbons down the faces of the crags, pooling into the deep canyon river. Dawn coming to the Teeth was a sight that always took Rhapsody's breath away.

Softly she began her aubade, the morning love song to the rising sun that had been chanted at dawn by the Liringlas throughout the ages from the beginning of Time. The melody vibrated against the window, hovering in the frosty air beyond the glass, then dissipated on the wind as if scattered like flax over the wide fields and foothills below her.

When her song came to an end she felt Achmed's hand on her shoulder. 'Close your eyes,' he said quietly. Rhapsody obeyed, listening to the silence of the hills and the song of the wind that danced through them. Achmed's hand left her shoulder. She waited for him to speak again, but after a few moments heard nothing more.

'Well?' she said, eyes still closed. When no reply came, her voice took on a note of irritation. 'Achmed?'

Hearing nothing still, Rhapsody opened her eyes. The irritation that had flushed her cheeks was swallowed by the horror of the sight in the valley below.

The wide expanse of the Krevensfield Plain, the undulating prairie that led from the feet of the Teeth westward through the province of Bethe Corbair all the way to Bethany, was rolling in waves of blood. The red tide began to surge up the side of the valley below them, splashing like a churning sea of gore against the rocky steppes and foothills that bordered the mountains.

Rhapsody gasped, and her eyes darted to the mountains themselves. The glistening waterfalls that scored the mountainsides were flowing red as well, raining bloody tears onto the heath and the canyon below. With trembling hands she gripped the sill of the window and closed her eyes again.

It was a vision, she knew; the gift of prescience had been hers even before she and the two Bolg left the old world and came here to this new and mysterious place, where the history was a paean to great aspirations destroyed by wanton foolishness.

What she did not know was what the vision meant; whether she was seeing the Past, or, far more frighteningly, the Future.

Slowly she opened her eyes once more. The valley was no longer crimson, but gray, as if in the aftermath of a devastating fire. But now, rather than the wide-open expanse that had been there a moment before, she saw the hilly farm country half a world away, the wide meadows of Serendair, where she had been born. A place in her youth she had called the Patchworks.

The hayfields and villages of her childhood were scorched, the pasture-land smoldering, the farmhouses and outbuildings in ashes. The ground was razed and ash reached from the Teeth to the horizon. This was a sight she had seen in many a dream; nightmares had been a curse as long as prescience had been a gift. Rhapsody began to shake violently. She knew from experience what was coming next.

Around her she could feel intense heat, hear the crackling of flames. The fire was not the warm and pure element through which she and her companions had passed on their way here in their trek through the center of the Earth; it was a dark and ravenous inferno, the sign of the F'dor, the demon that they hunted, that was undoubtedly hunting them as well.

The walls and windows of the observatory were gone. Now she stood in a village or encampment consumed by black fire, while soldiers rode through the streets, slaying everyone in sight. A crescendo of screaming filled her ears. In the distance at the edge of the horizon she saw eyes, tinged in red, laughing silently at her amid the wailing chorus of death.

In the thunder of horses' hooves, she turned, as she always had in this dream. He was there as he always was, the bloodstained warrior atop a raging steed, riding down on her, his eyes lifeless.

Rhapsody looked up into the smoke-fouled sky above her. Always in this part of the dream she was lifted up in the air in the claw of a great copper dragon that appeared through the blackening clouds to rescue her.

But now there was nothing above her but the unbroken firmament of rolling black clouds and showers of flaming sparks ripping through the sooty air.

The pounding clamor was louder now. Rhapsody turned back.

The horseman was upon her.

A broken sword, dripping with gore and black flame, was in his hand. He raised it above his head.

With the speed born of her training by Oelendra, the Lirin champion, Rhapsody drew Daystar Clarion, the sword of elemental fire and ethereal light that she wielded as the Iliachenva'ar. It was in her hands as she inhaled; with the release of her breath she slashed the gleaming blade across the warrior's chest, unbalancing him from the warhorse. Blood that smoked like acid splashed her forehead, searing her eyes.

Shakily the warrior rose, steadying his dripping weapon. Time slowed as he hovered over her, striding at her with a great gaping wound bisecting his chest. Within his eye sockets was darkness, and nothing more.

Rhapsody inhaled and willed herself calm again. She calculated the trajectory of his attack, and as it came, with excruciating slowness, she dodged heavily out of his way. Her limbs felt as if they were made of marble. With tremendous effort she raised her arms and brought Daystar Clarion down on the back of the sightless man's neck, aiming her strike at the seam of his cuirass. The flash of light as intense as a star exploding signaled her connection.

A geyser of steaming blood shot skyward, spattering her again and burning hideously. The warrior's neck dangled awkwardly; then his head rolled forward, separated from the broken flesh of his shoulders, before thudding to the ground at her feet. The sightless eyes stared up at her; within them she could see tiny flames of dark fire fizzle, then burn out.

Rhapsody stood, hunched over and panting, her hands resting on her knees. In the light of Daystar Clarion's flames she watched the headless body list to one side, preparing to topple.

Then, as she watched, it righted itself.

The headless corpse turned toward her again, sword in hand, and began to walk toward her once more. As it lifted its sword purposefully, she heard Achmed's voice far away, as though calling from the other side of Time.

Rhapsody.

She turned to see him standing behind her, watching her from inside the observatory tower, then quickly glanced over her shoulder again.

The headless soldier was gone. Nothing remained of the vision.

She exhaled deeply and put a hand to her forehead. A moment later the Firbolg king was beside her.

'What did you see?'

'I'm fine, thank you, really I am,' she muttered distantly, too spent to muster much sarcasm.

Achmed took her by the shoulders and gave her a firm shake. 'Tell me, by the gods,' he hissed. *'What did you see?'*

Rhapsody's eyes narrowed to emerald slits. 'You did this intentionally, didn't you? You brought me up here, into this place heavy with magic and ancient memories, intending to spark a vision, didn't you? That's what you meant when you said I might see something I couldn't from the Heath or Grivven Tower. You unspeakable bastard.'

'I need to know what you saw,' he said impatiently. 'This is the highest vista in the Teeth, the best possible place to see an attack coming. And one *is* coming, Rhapsody; I know it, and you know it. I need to know where it's coming from.' His unnaturally strong hands tightened their grip ever so slightly.

She slapped them away and wrested free from his grasp. 'I am not your personal vizier. Ask first next time. You have no idea what these visions cost me.'

'I know that ultimately without them the cost may be your life, at the very least,' Achmed snarled. 'That, of course, is if you are lucky. The alternatives are far more likely, and far worse. And far more widespread. Now stop acting the petulant brat and *tell me what I need to know.* Where is the attack coming from?'

Rhapsody looked back out the window at the glistening plain, the mountains coming to rosy life in the light of dawn. She stood silently for a moment, breathing the frosty air and listening to the silence broken only by the occasional whine of a bitter wind turning ever colder.

'Everywhere,' she said. 'I think it's coming from everywhere.'

High off, from his vantage point in the Future, hanging between the threads of Time in his glass globe observatory, Meridion stared in dismay at the people he had changed history to bring to this place in the hope that they would avert the fiery death that was now consuming what was left of the Earth.

He put his head down on the instrument panel of the Time Editor and wept.

Light was breaking over the whole of the Krevensfield Plain as Achmed and Rhapsody departed, cloaked, gloved, and hooded, riding the mounts Grunthor had provisioned for them through the light snow that had come on the morning wind.

The path that led down from the foothills to the steppes was a rocky one, and necessitated a slow passage. Rhapsody scanned the sky thoughtfully, her thoughts darker than the hour before dawn. It was impossible not to notice that she had grown quiet and pensive, and finally Achmed broke the silence.

'What's troubling you?'

Rhapsody turned her emerald gaze on him; her walk through the pure Fire at the Earth's core had caused her to absorb the element, making her hypnotically attractive, like the element itself. When she was excited, she was breathtaking; with an undercurrent of worry in her features she was absolutely captivating. Achmed exhaled. The time was coming when his theories about the power of her beauty would be put to the test.

'Do you think the Earthchild will be all right while we're gone?' she asked finally.

Achmed looked into her anxious face, considering the question solemnly.

'Yes,' he said, after a moment. 'The tunnel to the Loritorium is finished and all the other entrances sealed. Grunthor is moving out of the barracks while I'm away and sleeping in my chambers to guard the entranceway.'

'Good,' Rhapsody said. She had stood at the tunnel entrance in the darkness of early morning and sung to the Sleeping Child, the rare and beautiful creature formed from Living Stone that slumbered perpetually in the vault miles below Achmed's chambers. It had been hard to keep her voice steady, knowing that the F'dor they were seeking was in turn seeking the Child.

Let that which sleeps within the Earth rest undisturbed, the Dhracian sage had said. *Its awakening heralds eternal night.* Of all the things she had learned in the time they had been in this new world, one that frightened her the most was that such prophecies often had more than one meaning.

Yarim, she thought miserably, *why did the first demon-spawn have to be in Yarim?* The province lay to the northwest, on the leeward hollow of the arid plain that abutted the northern Teeth. She had been to the rotting, desolate city once before, with Ashe, looking for answers in the crumbling temple of Manwyn, the Seer of the Future. Those answers had led them to the journey they were now undertaking. Rhapsody shook her head to clear her memory of the madwoman's maniacal laugh.

'Are you ready?' Achmed's voice shattered her thoughts.

Rhapsody looked around; they had reached the steppes, the rocky footlands at the base of the mountains. She clucked to her horse.

'Yes,' she said. 'Let's finish this.'

Together they eased their horses into a steady canter. They didn't look back as the multicolored peaks of their mountainous home faded into the distance behind them like a memory.

In the shadows of Grivven, one of the highest peaks of the Teeth and the westernmost military outpost, four sets of Bolg eyes, night eyes of a race of men who had risen up from the caves, followed the horses until they had crested the steppes and had disappeared into the vastness of the Orlandan Plateau.

When the Bolg king could no longer be seen, one turned to the others and nodded slowly. Four men exchanged a final glance, then disappeared into the mountains, traveling in four different directions.

Meridion watched them go as well, struggling to contain his despair.

Light from the Time Editor, the now-dormant machine before him, spilled over the glass walls of his spherical tower, suspended here among the stars. Below, the world was growing dark, the black fire that was consuming it nearly at land's end.

Soon it would consume him as well. In light of the rest of the devastation, that hardly mattered.

He leaned back against his aurelay, the vibrational field generated by his namesong, shaped now like a cushioned chair, and folded his hands, trying to remain calm. All around him the lights of his laboratory gleamed, standing ready.

Meridion sighed. There was nothing more for him to do. He reached forward and snapped the lever that closed off the blinding light of the machine's power source from the Editor's main bay. Nothing more.

In the new dark he could see only the viewing screen, the ghostly projection of the last strands of the timefilm he had cobbled together, using threads from the Past. He had spliced them, hoping to avert the disaster that loomed below him. It never occurred to him, in the face of the coming nightmare, that his solution might be even worse than the original problem.

13

How could I have known? he mused. Total destruction of the Earth in blood and black fire had seemed absolute, as horrific as any fate could have been. It never occurred to him that taking the paths he had might doom it to an even greater devastation, one that survived death, that lingered into Eternity.

Please, he whispered silently. *Open your eyes and see. Please.*

Even as he watched, the Time-strand grew filmy, changing from the Past to the Present. Soon it would be the Future. Whatever came to pass, he could no longer intervene; the thread would never again be solid enough to manipulate.

Meridion settled back into the humming chair and closed his eyes, to wait.

Please . . .

I

Yarim Paar, Province of Yarim

In winter the dry red earth that had given Yarim its name was akin to desert sand. Granular specks of it hung heavy in the air of the decaying province, sweeping it like a vengeful wind demon, stinging with cold.

That blood-red clay-sand glistened in the first light of morning, sprinkled with a thin coating of crystalline frost. The frost painted the dilapidated stone buildings and neglected streets, dressing them for a moment in a shining finery that Yarim's capital had no doubt known long ago, an elegance that now existed only in memory, and for a few fleeting moments in the rosy haze of sunrise.

Achmed reined his horse to a stop at the crest of a rolling hill that led down into the crumbling city below him. He stared down into the valley as Rhapsody came to a halt beside him, musing. Looking down at Yarim from above gave him the opposite sensation to looking up at Canrif from the steppes at the edge of the Krevensfield Plain. While the Bolg were reclaiming the mountain, reaching skyward along with the peaks, Yarim sat broken, fetid, all but forgotten, at the bottom of this hill like dried mud left behind where a pond had been. Where once there had been greatness now there was not only decay, but diffidence, as if even the Earth were oblivious of the state of ruin that was Yarim. It seemed a pity.

Rhapsody dismounted first, walking to the edge of the hill's crest. 'Pretty in the light of first sun,' she said absently, staring off beyond the city's walls.

'Like the beauty of youth; it's fleeting,' Achmed said, descending himself. 'The mist will burn off momentarily, and the sparkle will be gone, leaving nothing but a vast carcass rotting in the sun. Then we'll see her for the aged hag she really is.' He would be glad to see the glistening vapor go; mist such as this hung wet in the air, masking vibration. It might hide the signature of

the ancient blood that surged in the veins of the F'dor's spawn hidden somewhere amid all that standing rubble.

An inexplicable shiver ran through him, and he turned to Rhapsody. 'Did
you feel that?'

She shook her head. 'Nothing unusual. What was it?'

Achmed closed his eyes, waiting for the vibration to return. He felt
nothing now but the calm, cold gusts of the wind. 'A tingle on the surface of
my skin,' he said after a moment, when he could not reclaim the sensation.

'Perhaps you're feeling Manwyn,' Rhapsody suggested. 'Sometimes
when a dragon is examining something with its senses, there's a chill of
sorts; a presence. It's almost like a – a hum; it tickles.'

Achmed shielded his eyes. 'I had wondered what you could have possibly
seen in Ashe,' he said sourly, gazing down into the morning shadows as they
began to stretch west of the city. 'Now I know. Manwyn knows we're here,
then.' He gritted his teeth; they had hoped to avoid the notice of the mad
Seer, the unpredictable dragonchild who wielded her Seren father's ancient
power of vision and her dragon mother's control over the elements.

Rhapsody shook her head. 'Manwyn knew we were coming before we got
here. If someone asked her a week, or a day, or even a moment ago, she
could have told him so. But now that we're here, it's the Present. Manwyn
can see only the Future. I think the moment has passed. We're gone from
her awareness.'

'Let's hope you're right.' Achmed glanced around, looking for a high rise
of ground or other summit on which to stand. He spied a jutting outcropping of rock to the east. He set his pack on the ground, pulling forth
a scrap of fabric that had once been soaked in the blood of the Rakshas,
now dried to the same color as the earth in Yarim. 'That's the place. Wait
here.'

Rhapsody nodded, and drew her cloak closer as she watched Achmed
lope over to the small hilly rise. She had witnessed his Hunting ritual once
before, and knew that he required absolute silence and stillness of movement to be able to discern a flickering heartbeat on the wind. She clucked
softly to the horses, hoping to gentle them into a quiet contentment.

Achmed climbed to the top of the outcropping and stood with nothing
but the wind surrounding him on all sides, staring down into the skeletal
city. Somewhere amid its broken buildings a tainted soul was hiding, one of
the nine children spawned of the ancient evil through a systematic campaign of rape and propagation. The blood in his own veins burned at the
thought.

With a single, smooth motion he pulled away the veils that shielded his
skin-web, the network of sensitive nerves and exposed veins that scored his
neck and face, casting a final glance back at Rhapsody. She smiled but did
not move otherwise. Achmed turned away.

He knew Rhapsody was aware that because of his Dhracian heritage he
was predisposed to disposal, not rescue, of anything that contained the
blood of F'dor. This undertaking, should it prove successful, would

undoubtedly be the first time one of his race would hunt a creature spawned of the F'dor and not exterminate it immediately upon capture.

The natural detachment that the Dhracians felt when confronting the malignant filth had deserted him, leaving him shaking with hatred. It was all he could do to remain calm, to keep from allowing his racial proclivities to roar forth, launching him into a blood rage that would culminate in the efficient, traceless slaughter of this demon-child and all its misbegotten siblings. He swallowed and began to breathe shallowly, trying to keep focused on the greater outcome.

That ancient blood, which pulsed softly now in the distance like a trace of perfume across a crowded bazaar, could eventually help him find the F'dor itself.

Achmed closed his eyes and willed the landscape from his mind, emptying it of conscious thought, concentrating on the rhythm of his own pulse. As always, when this moment of the hunt came, he could almost smell the odor of candle wax in the monastery where he was raised, could hear his mentor speak again in his memory.

Child of Blood, Father Halphasion had intoned softly in his fricative voice. *Brother to all men, akin to none.* The Dhracian sage, dead more than a thousand years now.

The hunt required of him a tremendous sacrifice, both mental and spiritual. It was in the power of those words that he had been able to divert his *kirai,* the Seeking vibration inherent in all Dhracians, to home onto the heartbeats of non-F'dor, his own unique gift. *Brother to all men.* He had been known only as the Brother most of his life, a deadly relative to his victims, whose pulses had briefly shared a rhythm with his.

Let your identity die, the Grandmother had instructed him; the ancient guardian and mentor so recently gone. It was more than his identity, however. At the moment when he subdued his own vibration, even that part of him which might be called a soul disappeared without a trace, replaced by the distant, thudding rhythm of his target.

He once wondered casually what would happen if instead of emerging the victorious stalker, he were to die while following his *kirai.* The place to which his identity went while in the throes of the hunt was undoubtedly the Void, the great emptiness of space, the opposite of Life. He suspected, when he allowed himself to think about it, that should luck turn against him and his victim instead overpower and kill him, everything that had been part of his identity would dissipate instantly, shattering in that empty space into tiny particles that would burn out forever like firesparks, robbing him of any existence in the Afterlife.

It was a risk he could abide.

All thought receded, replaced by a distant thudding that grew ever louder with each breath.

The pulse was at the same time alien and familiar to him. There was a hint of the old world, a hum that had beat in the veins of every soul born on Seren soil; the deep magic in the Island of Serendair had a unique ring to it, and it permeated the blood of those whose lives had been brought into existence there. But this was only the slightest trace in the rhythm that made up the rest of the heartbeat.

When he had first learned to listen to his skin, he had heard a roar of drums. Countless chaotic, cacophonous rhythms had thundered directly into him, threatened to overwhelm him, to drown him like the echoes of waves in a canyon. Here he heard barely a whisper.

Because the blood that pumped through the demon-spawn's heart was almost totally of this world, he could not discern its rhythm, could not track it. The blood of the new world swirled around the evanescent flutter from the old world like ocean waves, like a windstorm of dried leaves in the last vestiges of autumn; and occasionally he could taste some of its traits. He chased them with his breath, tasted the mix and dip of tones, looking for the deep shadow tone he was hunting.

There would be warmth in a pulse-wave that broke over him – that must be from the child's unknown mother – followed by the chill of ice; bequeathed by its father, the Rakshas, the artificial being that had sired all these cursed progeny of its demonic master. There was something feral in there as well, something with red eyes and a wild, brutal nature. Rhapsody had said the F'dor used the blood of wolves and other night creatures when it constructed the Rakshas. Perhaps that was it.

Still, each passing moment the ancient rhythm grew slightly louder, a bit clearer. Achmed opened his left hand and held it aloft, allowing the gusts of wind to dance over his palm.

Each intake of breath became slower, deeper, each exhalation measured. When the pattern of his breathing matched that of the distant beating heart, he turned his attention to his own heart, to the pressure it exerted on the vessels and pathways through which his blood flowed. He willed it to slow, lowering his pulse to a level barely able to sustain his life. He drove all stray thoughts from his mind, leaving it blank except for the color red. Everything else faded, leaving nothing but the vision of blood before his mind's eye.

Blood will be the means, the prophecy had said.

Child of Blood. Brother to all men, akin to none.

Achmed held absolutely still, remained utterly silent. He loosed the pulse of his own heart, willing it to match the distant heartbeat. Like trying to catch a flywheel in motion, he could only synchronize with one beat in every five, then every two, until each beat matched perfectly. He clung to the tiny burr of the ancient blood, followed it through distant veins, chased its flow, gathered its ebb until from that whisper of a handhold he crawled into his victim's rhythm. Their heartbeats locked.

And then, as the trail became clear, as his prey became unerringly linked to him, another tiny, discordant rhythm shattered the cadence. Achmed clutched his chest and staggered back as pain exploded like a volcano inside him.

Over his agonized groan he could hear Rhapsody gasp. His body rolled down the rocky outcropping, battering his limbs against the frozen rock ledge. Achmed struggled to find consciousness, catching intermittent glimpses of it from moment to moment, then fading into darkness between. The two heartbeats he had found wrestled inside his own; breath failed him. He clenched his teeth. The sky swam in blue circles, then went black.

He felt warmth surround him. The wind that tickled his nostrils was suddenly sweeter. Achmed opened his eyes to see Rhapsody's face swimming among the circles.

'Gods! What happened?' Her voice vibrated strangely.

Achmed gestured dizzily and curled into a tight ball, lying sideways on the ground. He took several deliberate, measured breaths, the cold wind stinging his burning chest. He noted absently that Rhapsody was still beside him, but had refrained from touching him. *She's learning*, he thought, strangely pleased.

With the grind of sand in his teeth and a painful growl, he forced himself into a crouch. They sat in silence on the windy hilltop above the crumbling city. When the sun was overhead and the shadows shifted, Achmed finally looked up. He exhaled deeply, then rose to a shaky stand, waving away the offer of her hand.

'What happened?' Her voice was calm.

Slowly he shook the sand from his clothes, retied his veils, staring down at Yarim below. The city had come to life of a sort while he had been coming back to himself, and now human and animal traffic shuffled through the unkempt streets, filling the distant air with sound.

'There's another one here,' he said.

'Another child?'

Achmed nodded slowly. 'Another heartbeat. Another spawn of some sort.'

Rhapsody went back to the horses and pulled open one of the saddlebags. She drew forth an oilcloth journal and brought it back to the rim of the hill.

'Rhonwyn said there was only one in Yarim,' she said, rifling through the pages. 'Here it is – one in Sorbold – the gladiator – two in the Hintervold, one in Yarim, one in the easternmost province of the Nonaligned States, one in Bethany, one in Navarne, one in Zafhiel, one in Tyrian, and the unborn baby, in the Lirin fields to the south of Tyrian. Are you certain the second heartbeat belongs to one of the children?'

'No, of course I'm not certain,' Achmed spat crossly, shaking more grit from his hair and cloak. 'And perhaps it's not another child. But somewhere near here is another pulse with the same taint to it, the same clouded blood.'

Rhapsody pulled her cloak even closer. 'Perhaps it's the F'dor itself.'

2

Keltar'sid, Sorbold Border, Southeast of Sepulvarta

The inside of the carriage was a haven from the blistering sun, dark and reasonably cool. He longed to disembark, to feel the wheels roll to a final stop, so that he could at last step out into the light and searing heat of the Sorboldian desert, where the earth held the fiery warmth of the sun even at the onset of winter.

From the sound of it, that moment was almost upon him.

He stretched the arms of the aged body he now occupied, the human vessel that had been his host for many decades, feeling the weakness that time had rendered upon him.

But not for much longer.

Soon he would be changing hosts again, would be taking on a newer, younger body. There would be a bit of an adjustment, as there always was, a transition he recalled clearly even though he had not made one in a very long time. Just the thought of it made his arthritic hands itch with excitement.

With that excitement came the burning, the flare of the fire that was the core of him. It was the primordial element from which all of his kind had come, and to which they would one day return.

All in good time.

It was best not to contemplate it at the moment, he knew. Once the spark of anticipation had ignited it became more difficult to hide his nether side, the dark and destructive spirit of chaos that was his true form, clinging to the flesh and bone of the human body only out of necessity. It was at moments of excitement that the malodor was strongest, the stench that clung to him and the others of his race, the smell of flesh in fire. And in the thrill of expectation the color of blood would rise to the edges of his eyes, rimming them red.

He willed himself to be calm again. It would not do to be discovered on so important a mission. It would not do to be seen as anything other than the pious religious leader that he was.

He leaned forward as the carriage came to a shuddering halt, then sat back against the pillowed seat, breathing shallowly.

The door opened, spilling blindingly bright light into the dark chamber, along with arid heat.

'Your Grace. We have arrived in Keltar'sid. His Grace, the Blesser of Sorbold, has an honor regiment here to greet you.'

He blinked as his eyes adjusted to the sunlight. Keltar'sid was the northern capital of Sorbold, the mustering ground for the Sorboldian armies that fortified the northern and western fringes of the Teeth. It was a city-state of soldiers, a most intimidating place unless one was traveling under the banner of a church or religious sect.

It was exactly where he wanted to be.

'How very kind,' he said. The cultured voice of his human host felt silky to his ears. His demon voice, the one that spoke internally, without traveling on the wind, was much harsher, like the crackle of an ominous flame. 'Express our thanks while I alight, please.'

He smiled and waved away the hands extended in the offer of assistance and stepped out of the carriage; his was a somewhat elderly body, but spry and still with some remnant of youth's vigor. He had to shield his eyes from the gleam of the sunlight. Though fire was his life's essence, it was a dark fire, a primordial element that burned black as death, not bright and cheery as bastard fire did in the air of the world above. He could tolerate the sunlight, but he did not like it.

A contingent of ten Sorbold guardsmen stood at a respectful distance, their swarthy faces set in masks of somber attention. He smiled beneficently at them, then raised his hand in a gesture of blessing. He struggled to appear nonchalant. This moment was, after all, what he had come for.

Softly he whispered the words of ensnarement, the sub-audible chant that would bind the men to his will, if only temporarily. Anything more long-lasting would require more extensive eye contact, more direct interaction, than would be appropriate between a visiting holy man and a troop of foreign guardsmen. To ensnare one permanently he would need to take some of the soldier's blood, but all of them appeared healthy and without wounds that needed a healer's blessing. Ah, well.

The threads of the snare, invisible to all eyes but his own, wafted toward him on the warm wind, anchored shallowly within each of his new servants. He caught the threads with a subtle gesture that seemed nothing more than the hand motions of his blessing. He could see that the thrall had taken hold in their eyes; the glimmer of dark fire within them that his prayer had summoned was evident in the glint of the sun. He smiled again.

This was, after all, the sole outcome of the visit to Sorbold he had intended. Anything else that resulted from the long and arduous journey was a boon.

He already had what he wanted.

A column leader approached, followed by four men bearing the poles of a white linen canopy – Sorbold was known for its linen – and another low-level aide-de-camp carrying a tray with a water flask and a goblet.

The soldier bowed from the waist.

'Welcome, Your Grace.' With a gesture he directed the other armsmen around the visiting holy leader. They immediately raised the canopy to shield him from the sun, eliciting a warm smile and a twinkle in blue eyes without even a trace of red.

He accepted the goblet of water and drank gratefully, then returned it to the tray. The soldier carrying it withdrew a few steps to be out of the way, but near enough if the guest of state had need of it.

'I'm afraid I bear awkward news,' said the column leader haltingly.

'Oh?'

'His Grace, the Blesser of Sorbold, has been detained at the sickbed of Her Serenity, the Dowager Empress. The benison extends his fervent apologies, and directs me to offer you escort to the basilica at Night Mountain, where he will be returning once the empress is no longer in need of his aid. I am directed to make you and your retinue comfortable.'

The soldier's black eyes glittered nervously, and the holy man suppressed a laugh. The Sorboldian tongue had little familiarity with the language of courtly and religious etiquette, primarily because the culture itself had little familiarity with such concepts. The Sorbolds were a rude and plainspoken people. The column leader doubtless had undergone intense study to be able to communicate in this manner, and was uncertain about his fluency in it.

'You are most kind, but I'm afraid that is quite impossible. This was only to be the briefest of visits, as I need to return to my own lands shortly. The winter solstice approaches, and I am planning to attend the carnival in Navarne.'

'His sincerest apologies for any inconvenience,' the column leader stuttered again. 'Please instruct me in how I may accommodate you. I am at your disposal, Your Grace.'

The holy man's eyes gleamed in the filtered light of the canopy. 'Ah, you are? How very generous. What is your name, my son?'

'Mildiv Jephaston, leader of the Third Western Face Column, Your Grace.'

'Well, Mildiv Jephaston, I am exceedingly glad to know that you are at my disposal, and I will indeed take you up on that very gracious offer, but at the moment there is nothing I require save escort back to the Sorbold-Roland border.'

'As you wish, Your Grace. The benison will be most disappointed that he missed your visit.'

'As am I, I assure you, Mildiv Jephaston.' He patted the soldier's shoulder compassionately, then blessed him as he had the others.

In the distance he could see the infinitesimal flicker of black fire, repeated many hundred times over in a sea of dark eyes, as all who were bound by oath to this column leader were now in his thrall as well. Armies were his favorite prey, just because of their myriad ranks of fealty – ensnare the leader, and all his followers, and their followers, were yours as well. *Ah, loyalty is a wonderful thing, a mindless snare of steel, so very easily manipulated,* he thought jubilantly. *Though so difficult to overcome when not offered freely.*

'He had hoped to show you the basilica at Night Mountain.' The soldier swallowed dryly. 'He knew you had not seen it.' The tone carried his real meaning. The benison's offer of entrance into the most secret of the elemental temples, Terreanfor, the Cymrian word meaning *Lord God, King of the Earth*, the basilica of Living Stone, was a great and prestigious honor, one that had only been made rarely.

Hidden deep within the Night Mountain, a place of consummate darkness in this realm of endless sun, the basilica was doubtless the most mystical of the holy shrines, a place where the Earth was still alive from the days of Creation. His refusal of the tour, no matter how polite, was dumbfounding to the Sorboldian soldiers. He choked back another laugh.

Fools, he thought contemptuously. *Your nation's generous offers be damned, as you will soon be.* He could not visit the temple even if he wanted to. The basilica was blessed ground.

His kind could not broach blessed ground.

'I am extraordinarily sorry to be unable to take advantage of the Blesser's invitation,' he said again, nodding to his own guards. His retinue returned to their carriages and mounts in preparation for leaving. 'Night Mountain is many days to the south of here, I believe. A visit would delay me too greatly. So again, I thank you, but I'm afraid I must decline. But please do extend my best wishes to the benison, and to Her Serenity for a speedy recovery.'

He turned briskly and hurried back into the dark silence of the coach. The Sorboldian soldiers stared after him in dismay as his footman shut the door briskly and the carriage began to roll out of sight. The enormous linen canopy that had shielded their visitor a moment before hung flaccidly in the breezeless air, like a dispirited flag of surrender.

3

Haguefort, Province of Navarne

The winter carnival was a tradition in Navarne, held in honor of the solstice and coinciding with holy days in both the Patriarchal religion of Sepulvarta and the order of the Filids, the nature priests of the Circle in Gwynwood. The duke of the province, Lord Stephen Navarne, was an adherent to the former but a well-loved friend of the latter, and so at his example the populace of the province, divided almost equally between the two faiths, put aside religious acrimony and differences to make merry at the coming of snow.

In earlier years the festival had sprawled as far as the eye could see over the wide rolling hills of Narvarne. Haguefort, Lord Stephen's keep and the site of the celebration, was located atop a gentle rise at the western forest's edge with a panoramic vista of farms and meadowlands stretching to the horizon in all three other directions. Some of the other Orlandan provinces, notably Canderre, Bethany, Avonderre, and even faraway Bethe Corbair, had long since given up their own solstice celebrations in order to combine their festivities with Lord Stephen's revels, largely because Stephen was unsurpassed as a merrymaker.

For two decades the young duke, whose Cymrian lineage was far removed but still granted him some of the exceptional vigor of youth enjoyed by the refugees of Serendair, had opened his lands at the first sign of winter, decreeing the contests and prizes for that year's festival amid trumpet calls and flourish not often seen in Roland during this age. The Cymrian War had brought the pageantry of the First Age, the age of building and enlightenment, to a shattering end, leaving this, the Second Age, colorless and dreary, as most struggles for survival and rebuilding tend to be. Lord Stephen's revels were the only regular exception to that dull tendency.

Like his father before him, Stephen understood the need for color and traditional secular celebration in the hardscrabble lives of the peasantry of his duchy. To that end he devoted his attention first to the safeguarding of his subjects' lands and lives, then to that of their spirits, believing that a dearth of joy had been largely responsible for the troubles the land had suffered in the first place.

Each annual festival proffered a new contest: a treasure quest, a poetry competition, a footrace with a unique handicap, along with the traditional games of chance and sport, awards for the best singing – Lord Stephen was an enthusiastic patron of good singing – recitation and dance, sleigh races, snow sculpting, and performances by magicians capped by a great bonfire that warmed the wintry night and sent such sparks skyward as to challenge the stars.

It was small wonder that even travelers from the distant, warm lands of Yarim, Roland's easternmost province, and Sorbold, the arid nation of mountains and deserts to the south, made their way to the inland province of Navarne to enjoy the wintersport of Lord Stephen's carnival, as did many of the Lirin of Tyrian, at least in better days. Recent acts of terror and violence had begun to diminish the festival's attendance as traveling overland grew more hazardous. As times worsened, the festivities became more of a local celebration than one enjoyed by much of the continent.

The expected diminution of attendance this year would be both unfortunate and fortuitous in Lord Stephen's eyes. He had recently completed the building of a vast wall, a protective rampart more than two men's heights high and similarly thick, that encircled all of Haguefort's royal lands and much of the nearby village and surrounding farmlands as well. This undertaking had almost consumed his every waking moment for the better part of two years, but it was a project he saw as critical to ensuring the safety of his subjects and his children.

Now, as he stood on the balcony beyond the windows of his vast library, Stephen observed the new masonry border he had erected with silent dismay. The once-unbroken landscape was now divided by the ugly structure with its severe guard towers and battlements, the formerly pristine meadows scarred by the construction of it. Instead of the wide, glittering horizon of snow there was a defined and muddy limit to the lands surrounding his keep. He had known when he began the undertaking that this would be the result. It was one thing to know with one's mind, he mused sadly, another altogether to see with one's eyes.

The winter festival would need to adapt to the new reality of Roland and its neighbors, the grim knowledge that violence, inexplicable and unpredictable, was escalating far and wide. The sheer madness of it had scarred more than Stephen's fields; it had rent his life as well, taking his young wife and his best friend, Gwydion of Manosse, in its insanity, along with the lives of many of his subjects and his sense of well-being. It had been five years since Stephen had experienced a restful night's sleep.

Daytime was easy enough; there was an endless stream of tasks awaiting his attention, as well as the time he devoted to his son and daughter. They provided in his life a genuine delight that was as vital to his happiness, his very existence, as sunlight or air. It was no longer the struggle to be happy it had been when Lydia died.

It was only at night now that he felt somber, downhearted, in the long hours after he had tucked his children beneath their quilts of warmest eiderdown, waiting by Melly's bedside until she fell asleep, answering Gwydion's questions about life and manhood in the comfortable darkness.

Each night the questions finally came to an end, replaced by the sound of soft, rhythmic breathing, and the scent of a boy's sweet exhalations becoming the saltier breath of a young man on the threshold of adulthood. Stephen cherished that moment when sleep finally took his son to whatever adventures he was dreaming of; he would rise reluctantly and bend to kiss Gwydion's smooth brow, knowing the time he would be able to do so was coming to an end.

A melancholy invariably washed over him as he made his way back to his own chambers, to the room where he and Lydia had slept, had made love and plans and their own unique happiness. Gerald Owen, his chamberlain, had gently offered to outfit another of Haguefort's many bedchambers for him after the bloody Lirin ambush that had ripped her from his life, but Stephen had declined in the same graciousness with which he always comported himself. How could Owen know what he was asking? His faithful chamberlain could never understand how much of Lydia was there in that room still, in the damask curtains at the window, in the canopy of the bed, in the looking-glass beside her dressing table, the silver hairbrush atop it. It was all he had left of her now, all save memories and their children. He lay there, night after night, in that bed, beneath that canopy, hearing the voices of ghosts until restless sleep finally came.

The sound of childish voices swelled behind Lord Stephen as the library doors opened. Melisande, who had turned six on the first day of spring, ran to him as he turned and threw her arms around his leg, planting a kiss on his cheek as he lifted her high.

'Snow, Father, snow!' she squealed gleefully; the sound dragged a broad grin to the corners of Stephen's face.

'You must have been *rolling* in it,' he said with a mock wince, brushing the chilly clumps of frozen white powder from his doublet as he set her down, then slung an arm over Gwydion's shoulders. Melly nodded excitedly. After a moment her smile faded to a look of disapproval.

24

'How ugly it is,' she said, pointing over her father's lands to the endless wall that encircled them.

'And it will be uglier still, once the people start rebuilding their homes inside it,' Stephen said, pulling Gwydion closer for a moment. 'Enjoy the tranquillity for what moments more you may, children; come next winter festival, it will be a town.'

'But why, Father? Why would people want to give up their lovely lands and move inside of an ugly wall?'

'For safety's sake,' Gwydion said solemnly. He ran his forefinger and thumb along his hairless chin in the exact gesture his father used when pondering something. 'They'll be within the protection of the keep.'

'It won't be all bad, Melly,' Stephen said, tousling the little girl's golden curls, smiling at the sparkle that had returned to her black eyes. 'There will be more children for you to play with.'

'Hurray!' she shouted, dancing in excitement through the thin snow on the balcony floor.

Stephen nodded to the children's governess as she appeared at the balcony doors. 'Just wait a few more days, Sunbeam. The winter carnival will be set up, with so many brightly colored banners and flags that you will think it is snowing rainbows. Now, run along. Rosella is waiting for you.' He gave Gwydion's shoulder another squeeze and kissed his daughter as she ran by, then turned once more to contemplate the changing times.

4

Yarim Paar, Province of Yarim

The lore of Entudenin

Unlike the capitals of Bethany, Bethe Corbair, Navarne, and the other provinces of Roland, the capital city of Yarim had not been built by Cymrians; it was far more ancient than that.

Yarim Paar, the second word meaning *camp* in the language of the people indigenous to the continent, had been constructed in the midst of the great dustbowl that formed the majority of the province's central lands, hemmed in between the dry winds of the peaks of the northern Teeth to the east and the ice of the Hintervold to the north. Farther west, nearer to Canderre and Bethany, the lands grew more fertile, but the majority of the province was a dry land of scrub and red clay, baking in the cold sun.

Yarim's neighbors, the hidden lands east of the Teeth, were fertile and forested; it was as if the mountains had reached into the sky itself and wrung precious rain from the thin clouds hovering around their peaks. The sea winds swept the continent from the west, carrying moisture as well, endowing the coastal realms of Gwynwood and Tyrian and the near inland provinces with robes of deep green forest and field. By the time those winds had made their way east to Yarim, however, there was little relief left to give; the clouds had expended the bulk of the rain on their more favored children. In especially dry years, Yarim grew little more than dust as a crop.

At one time, a tributary of the Tar'afel River had run down from the glaciers of the frozen wasteland of the Hintervold, mixing with what the early dwellers had called the Erim Rus, or Blood River, a muddy red watercourse tainted by the mineral deposits that caked the face of the mountains. It was at the confluence of these two rare waterways that the village of Yarim Paar had had its birth.

For all that the area had seemed a wasteland to the early inhabitants of the continent, nothing could be further from the truth. A king whose name had long been forgotten smugly referred to the lands of Yarim as the chamber pot of the iceworld and the eastern mountains. There was some unintentional wisdom in those words.

Its spot on the continental divide had left Yarim rich in mineral deposits and, more important, salt beds. Beneath its unassuming exterior skin ran wide veins of manganese and iron ore against the eastern faces of the mountains, with a great underground sea of brine farther west. Finally, as if these earthly treasures were not enough for the area to be seen as richly blessed, the windy steppes were pocketed with vast opal deposits containing stones of myriad colors, like frozen rainbows extracted from the earth. One of the opal mining camps, Zbekaglou, bore the name, in the indigenous language, Rainbow's End, or where the skycolors touch the earth.

So Yarim's eastern mountains gave the province great hoards of manganese and copper, iron ore and rysin, a blueish metal valued highly by the Nain; its wide western fields provided the greatly prized commodity of salt, which was pumped from the earth through shallow wells that vented into the underground ocean of brine and potash, then was spread out in wide stone beds to allow the sun to evaporate the water, leaving the precious preservative behind; its central-eastern steppes produced gems of priceless value.

Yarim Paar, by contrast, was endowed with no mineral deposits to speak of, no brine sea, no fertile farmlands. It was a barren waste of dry red clay. But it was the poor south-central area of Yarim Paar which made all of the province's wealth possible, because Yarim Paar had received one gift from the Creator that none of the other areas of the province had been given – the gift of water.

Even more than the riverhead of the Erim Rus and the Tar'afel tributary that joined it, themselves great watery riches in an arid, thirsty land, Yarim Paar was also the site of Entudenin, a marvel whose name was commonly translated later as the Wellspring. It was more often known as the Fountain Rock or simply the Wonder – the Yarimese had few examples of Nature's artistry to marvel at, and so expended many names on the one they did have – but a more exact meaning of the word in the ancient language would have been the Artery.

In the time when it was named, Entudenin had been a towering geyser spraying forth from an obelisk of minerals deposited over the centuries in ever taller layers. At its pinnacle the obelisk was twice the height of a man, or perhaps even twice Grunthor, and as broad as a two-team oxcart at the base, tapering up to a narrower, angled shaft.

Even without its miraculous gift of water in near-desert, Entudenin would have been a wonder to behold. The dissolved solid minerals in the runoff that had formed the obelisk were myriad, and had stained the enormous formation with a variety of rich colors, hues of vermilion and rose, deep russet and aqua, sulfurous yellow and a wide stripe of rich earth-brown that teased the sandy red clay on which the huge waterspout stood. The mineral formation glistened in the light of the sun, gleaming with an effect similar to the glaze on sugared marzipan.

Unlike the hot springs rumored to have been the center of the mythic city of Kurimah Milani, an ancient center of culture said to have been built at the desert's edge that one day vanished into the sand without a trace, the water that shot forth from the mouth of Entudenin was cool and clear, though heavy in mineral sediment. The legend of Kurimah Milani told of how the hot springs there had endowed those fortunate enough to have bathed in them or drunk from them with special powers of healing and other magics, derived, no doubt, from the rich mineral slough contained within them. The inhabitants of Yarim Paar did not covet those healing springs – the cool, life-giving water welling forth from Entudenin was magic enough for them.

The discovery of the marvelous geyser in the middle of nowhere prompted the building of an outpost near it that later became a camp, then a village, then a town, and finally a city. With the ready availability of water came construction for function and expansion for form. Great hanging gardens were built, elegant fountains and outdoor statuary museums with quiet reflecting pools as well, transforming the ramshackle little camp into a glorious example of lush desert architecture. Within a few centuries Entudenin was supplying not only the vast amounts of water necessary to maintain this sparkling jewel of a capital city, but all the water to the outlying cities, villages, outposts, and mining camps as well.

In its living time the Fountain Rock was roughly attuned to the cycles of the moon. At the onset of the cycle a great blast of ferocious furor would rage forth from the Wellspring, spraying sparkling water skyward, showering the thirsty ground. The sound that accompanied the event welled from a deep roar to a glad shout as the torrent surged from the darkness of the Earth's depths into the air and light.

For a full week of the cycle, the water flowed copiously. On the first day of the blast, known as the Awakening, the townspeople would gather to thank the All-God in ritual prayer but refrained from actually drinking or collecting the Wellspring's liquid bounty. Part of this was a sacrificial abstinence in thanks to the Creator, but part of it was the rule of common sense as well; initially, the force of the water rushing forth from Entudenin was similar to a raging rapid, more than sufficient to break a man's back.

27

Within one turn of day the water flow would subside to a voluminous spray. The legends said that there was a noticeable change in the Wellspring's attitude, from anger to placidity. Once this change had occurred, the people of Yarim Paar and eventually its neighbors would quickly begin harvesting the water, storing it in cisterns that ranged from the enormous fountainbed that had been built at the obelisk's base to the small vessels carried by the town's children on their heads. The spray that filled the air at the outskirts of the waterspout rained down in a wide sweep, and was used by the townspeople as a public bath.

After the Week of Plenty came the Week of Rest. Entudenin subsided from its joyful shower into a calmer, bubbling flow. The more patient townspeople who had planned ahead and therefore could wait until the second week to obtain their water benefited from their forbearance, because this was the time when the water was said to be the sweetest, purged of the sour minerals that had built up during its sleeping time.

The third week, the Week of Loss, still saw water coming forth from Entudenin, but it had dwindled to a mere trickle. During this time only those with desperate illness in their households were allowed to collect water from the Fountain Rock. Unlike the raucous harvest of the first two weeks, any such collection was done reverently, with great humility, and at considerable expense in the form of a donation of food or coinage to the priestesses who guarded Entudenin.

Finally, the trickle would vanish. The Fountain Rock would go dry, and this week, the Week of Slumber, was a time when a sense of apprehension bordering on dread would come over Yarim Paar, at least according to the legends. Though the geyser had been erupting cyclically with its gift for as long as anyone could remember, there was always an unspoken fear that each time might be the last. And while the Yarimese had managed to trust the sun and moon to follow the patterns the All-God had laid out for them without a second thought, there was always a fear that Entudenin might change her mind, might abandon her children to the dust of the wasteland around them if anything gave her offense.

The task of tending to the Wellspring was entrusted to a clan known as the Shanouin, a band of former nomads that were said to have come originally from Kurimah Milani. The Shanouin water-priestesses were accorded the highest social status in Yarim, second only to the line of the duke and the benison that Yarim shared with the neighboring province of Canderre. Because Entudenin followed a monthly cycle it was believed to have a female outlook, and so only the Shanouin women were allowed the actual task of cleaning and maintaining the obelisk in its rest, as well as managing the access of the townspeople to the Wellspring. The men and children of the clan were accorded the tasks of basin-building and water delivery to the more important households; the Shanouin carter who brought monthly water vessels to the house of the duke was accorded a position even higher than that of the royal chamberlain.

When centuries passed and the Erim Rus became contaminated with the

Blood Fever, and the tributary of the Tar'afel went dry, Entudenin remained stalwart, constant, nurturing the dry realm with the elixir of life, twenty days out of every moon-cycle. The verdant desert gardens that had grown up in Yarim Paar were allowed to wither in order to divert some of the Wellspring's water to the outlying towns and villages, and the opal outposts and mineral mining camps as well. The paradise that Yarim Paar had become settled into a more staid, sensible city, a comely matron taking the place of the once ravishingly beautiful bride.

And so it went, month after month, year after year, century after century for millennia uncounted until the day that Entudenin went to sleep and did not awaken.

At first the Shanouin had cautioned composure. The Wellspring had not been perfect in the marking of its cycles, though no one at the time could remember it ever deviating from its routine by more than three days. When the fourth day passed, then the fifth, however, the Blesser of Canderre-Yarim was summoned by avian messenger from his basilica in Bethany to Yarim Paar, in the hope that perhaps his divine wisdom, endowed by the Creator through the Patriarch, would be able to determine the cause of Entudenin's silence, and perhaps make amends for whatever offense had been committed.

The benison came in all due haste, riding his desert stallion in the company of but eight guards, rather than resorting to the slower method of the royal caravan. By the time he arrived from Bethany the Wellspring had been dry for ten days, and there was widespread consternation bordering on panic, not only in Yarim Paar, but in the other Yarimese cities and outposts as well, since all of them depended upon the water of Entudenin for sustenance. That panic soon had spread to the other provinces of Roland, because many of the Orlandan dukes had holdings and financial interests in Yarim.

When the benison was unable to summon the life back into the Wellspring with his prayers to the Patriarch, much of the population of Yarim began reverting from the monotheistic practices of the religion of Sepulvarta, the Patriarch, and his benisons back to the pagan polytheism that had been their creed before the Cymrians came. Sacrifices, both public and private, benign and malevolent, were offered to the goddess of the Earth, to the Lord of the Sea, to the god of water, to any and every possible deity that might have taken offense, in the hope that whatever divine entity would listen might call off the curse of thirst. The pleas fell on deaf ears all the way around.

Finally the finger pointed. Word swept through the town that it was the Shanouin who were to blame; Entudenin's handmaidens had displeased her, had caused her to withdraw from her people. The water-priestesses and the rest of their clan escaped Yarim Paar by night as the brushy scrub for their pyres was being collected. But even with the departure of the Shanouin, Entudenin still remained unmoved, still refused to open her heart.

When murderous rioting broke out over control of the drying cisterns, the city of Yarim Paar, under the hand of the duke, settled back into sullen silence and contemplated how it would survive now that the water was gone. A halfhearted attempt at well-digging was made, then quickly abandoned; no one alive had ever undertaken such a task, so no one knew how, having lived all their lives with Entudenin tending to their water needs like a generous wet-nurse. In addition, even if they had known how to pierce the dry earth, doing it in a place that would produce water was as likely as finding a specific grain of flax in a ten-stone sack. What water there might be crept so far beneath the sand that it might as well be on the other side of the earth for all the tunneling required to reach it.

At last it occurred to the duke that the Shanouin, while they might have displeased the Wellspring, were the repository of knowledge about water in this arid climate. He sent forth his army to round up the entire tribe and had them herded back to Yarim, where they then met in council with him, the magistrate of Yarim Paar, the supervisors of the various mining camps, and the officials of the other Yarimese cities.

At this meeting the duke of Yarim promised the Shanouin free citizenship again, and the protection of the Yarimese army, if they would find a way to bring forth water from the dry clay to sustain life in the province's thirsty cities.

And so the Shanouin slowly regained their social status over the centuries, establishing successful water camps that fed the province of Yarim, though never again as abundantly as it had been in its glory days. Though they were now without the Artery that brought forth life from the heart of the Earth, there were still any number of small veins running near the surface, which the former priestesses of Entudenin were able to divine. The work was difficult and chancy, but somehow Yarim survived its apocalypse. The once-glorious capital of Yarim Paar withered in the heat, drying out in the sun and cracking as it did.

As for Entudenin, it continued to stand, stalwartly rising toward the sky, but silent now. The great marble basin around it dried out as well and crumbled away. The obelisk baked in the heat, losing its luster, its colors, until finally it was as dry and red as the rest of the clay that had built Yarim. It was visited from time to time by pilgrims from across the desert, who stood at its base, gazing up at the carcass of the dead Fountain Rock, shaking their heads either at the overwhelming sadness of its loss, or the exaggeration of the stories they had heard about it in the first place.

When darkness fell each night, however, just as twilight was leaving the sky, someone watching the ancient formation might note the tiniest glimmer of gold, the silvery sheen of fragile mica, forever forged in the heat into the dark, spindling rock, pointing the way to the stars.

'I take it Ashe never brought you to this place when the two of you visited Yarim?'

'No. Why?'

Achmed stared up at the tall, thinning shaft of the towering obelisk. 'I would think this giant phallus would only reinforce his feelings of inadequacy. Justifiable feelings, I might add.'

Beneath the veils of the pilgrim disguise that shielded her face from sight, Rhapsody smiled but said nothing. Instead she waited until the three elderly women, draped as she was in flowing white ghodins with their faces shielded behind veils, finished their prayers and moved on. She then moved closer to the ancient formation.

Entudenin was smaller than she had envisioned, and thinner; it had the appearance of frailty to it. They had, in fact, walked past it twice, because it stood in the midst of the central town square like an unappreciated statue, while oxcarts and cattle caravans rumbled past and around it as if it were not there. The three women who had just walked away were the only people in all of the busy traffic of Yarim Paar that had stopped to look at the obelisk that morning.

The deposits of mineral sediment that had once formed it now had solidified into hard red rock, pocked and scarred with deep gouges and holes. Rhapsody observed that it looked vaguely like a dismembered arm balanced on the ground, missing the hand as well.

She cast a glance around the busy town square, then quickly averted her eyes as a cadre of Yarimese soldiers, distinguished by their horned helmets, rode past. When she could no longer hear the sounds of the horses' hooves, she looked back at Achmed. He was staring off toward the south.

'What do you think happened to the water? Why did Entudenin go dry?'

Achmed smirked. 'Are you mistaking me for Manwyn just because we're in the same city?'

'Hardly. She's ever so much more pleasant than you are.' Rhapsody shuddered, remembering the Oracle's hideous laughter, her unprovoked taunting of Ashe, her ugly prophecies.

I see an unnatural child born of an unnatural act. Rhapsody, you should beware of childbirth: the mother shall die, but the child shall live.

Ashe had been furious at his aunt's words. When he demanded an explanation, Manwyn had thrown puzzling words at him as well.

Gwydion ap Llauron, thy mother died in giving birth to thee, but thy children's mother shall not die giving birth to them.

There had been something else, but Rhapsody could not remember what it was, almost as if it had been plucked from her memory.

She blinked and found Achmed's mismatched eyes staring at her. Rhapsody shook her head to drive the memory away.

'If I wanted to ask a Seer about what happened to Entudenin, it would have to be Anwyn,' she said. 'She's the one who sees the Past. I think I'll pass, thank you. I'd rather ask you, even if you can only give your opinion. What offense do you think was committed that caused the Fountain Rock to run dry?'

Beneath his veils she could tell he was smiling. He turned and stared up at

Entudenin. 'The offense of a mineral clog, or a shifting of strata within the Earth.'

'Really? That's all?'

'That's all, at least in my opinion. Have you ever noticed, Rhapsody, that when something miraculous and good happens it's a gift from the All-God, but when something baleful or terrible takes it away, it was man's fault? Perhaps everything that happens, good and bad, is just random chance.'

'Perhaps,' she said hastily. She pulled out the journal and began thumbing through it. 'Rhonwyn said the child's location was *Yarim Paar, below Entudenin*, didn't she?'

Achmed nodded, not looking away from the fossilized geyser. 'Listening to you pry the names, ages, and locations of those demon brats out of that lunatic Seer was torture.'

Rhapsody chuckled. 'I'm sorry. It's not easy to get information from someone who can't remember who you are from moment to moment, because she can only see the Present. A heartbeat later the Present becomes the Past and she can't remember what she said, let alone what *you* said. And if you think Rhonwyn was bad, be glad you didn't meet Manwyn.' She leaned forward and tried to peer over the domes of the buildings toward the Oracle's crumbling temple, but could not see the minaret. 'The fountain square is the direct center of the city. Do you think "below" meant south of the square?'

The Firbolg king shrugged, trying to concentrate. The heartbeats were muffled now, swallowed by the hum of human traffic, the whine of the winter wind through the narrow alleys, the haggling of the women, the cacophony of merchants in the marketplace shouting their wares. Added to this was the muffling of the veils that were worn by almost everyone in Yarim to keep the blowing dirt from the eyes and nose.

His chest was still aching from the shock of the arrhythmia, the jolt of dissonance that his heart's rhythm had experienced when the second pulse had ricocheted off it. He understood what Rhapsody meant about name-songs, songs of one's self; the way that she could attune her music to something's true name. Her musical lore worked in much the same way that his tracking ability did, locking both of them to the unique vibrations that each individual emitted. He had always known how vulnerable he was when matching his own heartbeat to another's. It made him wonder what her exposure was as well.

He could still hear both rhythms, distantly. There was such an infinitesimal amount of blood from the old world in the makeup of the children that he hardly should be able to hear it at all. One of the heartbeats was fainter and more intermittent than the other.

'One of them – the first one – is at the southeastern edge of the city,' he said finally. 'As for the other one, it could be anywhere.'

Rhapsody adjusted the veil in front of her face nervously. 'That doesn't inspire great confidence.'

'I'm sorry.'

'Don't be angry. It's just that your ability to track these children is the only hope we have of finding them.'

Achmed took her elbow and drew her away from the dry fountain. He led her to a sheltered alcove in a side alley, and after checking to be certain they were alone, leaned close to her ear.

'I should have explained this to you long ago,' he said in a voice so low as to be barely above a whisper. 'You do not understand the difficulty in what you are asking.

'On the Island, I could find and follow any man's heartbeat easily. Like finding my way through a familiar forest, there was uncertainty, there were perils, but I knew where they were, and how to cope with them. That ability vanished, and with the exception of those who were also born on Serendair, I can no longer do that. I can match heartbeats with you, and Grunthor, and a handful of First Generation Cymrians. That's all.'

His voice dropped even lower. 'Hunting F'dor was always more difficult and rare; as you know, I've never held a real one in thrall before. It's a combination of my blood-gift, and the racial ability of the Dhracians, that may – I repeat, *may* – allow me to do it this time, assuming we can extract the demon's blood from these children.

'Whenever a F'dor spirit came forth from its broken vault within the Earth, it took an initial host. It had to be a fairly powerless one, like a child, or a weak man, because it can only subsume a host weaker than itself, or at best as powerful as it is, and when it is first out in the air of the world it is weak. Blood is spilled – perhaps just a drop, but there is a bond of blood each time. It needs that blood to tie it to a living entity. That blood becomes the demon's own. Even as it grows, that blood remains its own, though it is mixed and tainted and diluted with the blood of each new host it takes on.

'The F'dor who fathered these children was a spirit from the old world. It doubtless had many hosts on Serendair. We know it has had even more since it has been here.' He stopped, and they both turned their heads at the sound of giggling. A group of children, mistaking them for lovers nuzzling in a back alley, stared for a moment, then scattered at the ferocious look in Achmed's eyes, the only of his features visible. He scowled, then returned his lips to her ear.

'Given how powerful we know it is now, it has doubtless masked what might have begun as one drop of blood with the blood of hundreds, perhaps thousands of other hosts. Then it made the Rakshas. It mixed the blood of feral animals with that of its human host. The Rakshas impregnated the mothers of these children, diluting the content of the F'dor's blood even further.

'So understand – to me, the signature of the F'dor's blood in the veins of these children is like a whiff of perfume I have smelled only once before. You are asking me to find that odor in the air of this town, amid all the other scents here. And the person who wore that perfume wore it a month ago.'

'Well, he probably hasn't bathed in the intervening time, if that helps,'

Rhapsody said lightly. Her green eyes sparkled, then grew solemn. 'I'm sorry to put so much weight on your shoulders. What shall we do next?'

Achmed sighed and leaned away, standing upright again. 'We'll head southeast, and see what we find. And if we can't find this child, or any of the others, we'll have to make do with the one or ones we can find, even if it's only the baby we know will be born in Tyrian nine weeks hence. You have the exact time, date, and place for that one. All I need is a small amount of pure demon's blood.'

'And abandon the others to their damnation? To the Void?'

Achmed didn't blink. 'Yes.'

'You would really do that?'

'In a heartbeat, so to speak. Now, come. Our chance to find this thing grows slimmer with every moment that passes.' Achmed put out his hand, gloved in a thin leather sheath, and Rhapsody took it. Together they crossed the alley and disappeared into the depths of Yarim Paar.

5

Tile Foundry, Yarim Paar

Omet did not like the new apprentice.

Under normal circumstances, Omet was busy enough that he would be hard pressed to have even noticed the new apprentice. As an apprentice himself in the tile foundry, two years away from his journeyman's year, work was endless and life sleepless. He didn't have time for opinions, or sentiments, or anything else that might distract him from remembering to check the temperature of the slip as it cooked, or getting up every two hours to stoke the fires of the ovens through the night with peat and coal, dung, and, sparingly, wood.

The red clay of Yarim had been of little use for raising crops, but it made wonderful tile. In its heyday Yarim had produced most of the utilitarian drainage and paving stones that built the great Cymrian cities, as well as the mosaics and ceramic tiles that decorated them. Yarim had adorned itself in the grandest pieces, from the glistening fountainbeds that surrounded the duke's palace to the walls of the Oracle's temple. Even now, in its declining years, with the availability of the water necessary to make it limited, Yarim still produced both tile and pottery for export.

The enormous foundry was the city's largest building outside of the various government facilities and the temple of the Oracle. It stood, partially empty, at the outskirts of the city to the southeast, near the largest interprovince thoroughfare. Caustic black smoke from the fires that burned night and day hung heavy in the air above and around the building and the nearby streets, making it difficult to breathe, so there were few other buildings, and no residences near it.

When Omet's mother had apprenticed him to the proprietor of the tileworks, she had known full well the life to which she was sentencing her son. The foundry's owner, a diminutive woman of mixed human and Lirin blood by the name of Esten, was known by sight or name or reputation not only through all of the province of Yarim, but west in Canderre and south in Bethe Corbair as well.

Esten's small physical stature was in direct opposition to her social one; publicly she was the owner and operator of Yarim's largest foundry. Even more commonly known was her position as chief of the bloodthirsty Raven's Guild, a coterie of blacksmiths, thugs, and professional thieves that ruled the dark hours in Yarim.

Despite her ferocious reputation, Esten's face was a pretty one, an exotic countenance with angular lines and high cheekbones, probably owing to her Lirin blood. That anyone had even seen it at all was a testament to her status in and of itself, since most women in Yarim took the veil. Most striking of all that face's features were the eyes, dark and inquisitive like that of the bird her guild had been named for. Those eyes always held a hint of amusement, even when they were black with anger, and were more piercing in their stare than an ice pick. Omet had decided at the meeting where he was chosen as an apprentice that he would always avoid their gaze if at all possible. The few seconds he had been the target of it had made him fear he would lose his water onto the floor at her feet. It was of little surprise to him that his mother had not come to visit him once in the five years since then.

For the most part he had managed to avoid Esten's notice. She came every new moon to check the progress of the tunnel, and when she did he made certain he was busy feeding the slave children or stoking the ovens so as to eliminate any encounter but a chance one.

Perhaps his decision to remain away from her notice had been an error in judgment. Ever since Vincane, the new apprentice, had been pulled from the tunnel and promoted to work beside Omet and the others, he had gone out of his way to endear himself to Esten, to curry her favor in a dozen slavish, obvious ways that had turned Omet's stomach. Those antics had seemed to have turned Esten's head as well; now she favored Vincane, brought him small treats and tousled his hair, laughing and teasing him. There was something in Vincane's eyes, something dark and inquisitive that mirrored Esten's own, and it served to place him in a position as her pet.

It was not this favored status that bothered Omet. Rather, it was the cruel streak that Vincane displayed without reprimand, occasionally toward Omet and the other apprentices, but mostly toward the slave children.

For the most part, no one saw much of those children. Food and water were handed down the shaft several times a day, always as a reward for making their quota of clay. Fifty buckets of clay came up, one pail of water was lowered down. One hundred buckets of clay came up, one box of food went down. Up, down, up, down. Such was the life of a fifth-year apprentice, hauling the hook-stick up out of the well, dumping the clay, tossing the pail back down again, occasionally bestowing a little bread and broth on the small dark beings that scrambled like rats at the bottom of the shaft and in the tunnel beyond. In between they handed down the hods of finished tiles and mortar, all the while minding the furnace and the ovens, checking the huge vats of clay slip as it baked in the sweltering heat, ringing the bell to summon the journeymen from the separate annex in which they lived and worked when their special firings were finished.

Vincane had been one of those slave children himself until recently. A ragtag orphan like all the others, purchased or stolen from wherever he had come from, he had shown remarkable stamina in the digging, and more – he had a resistance to pain that seemed almost inhuman. Omet had seen him once put his hand directly into the kiln itself and pull forth a rack of greenware tiles without flinching as his hand grasped the red-hot wire. That, and a willingness to betray the small secrets of his fellow slaves – they had widened the tunnel a few hands' widths for extra sleeping room, they had hidden the broken pieces of a trowel instead of turning it in – had endeared him to Esten, and had given him the singular opportunity to escape the tunnel and come to work for her as an apprentice.

At first the journeymen had feared the slave children would begin turning on each other to see if they could obtain the same promotion, and that chaos would disrupt the digging, but Esten had nipped that possibility in the bud easily. Any uproar whatsoever would result in Vincane coming back down into the tunnel, she had announced sweetly during the slave children's monthly airing. And he would be allowed to bring some of his toys. The slaves had eaten their meal even more quietly than the moment before she spoke, their all-but-blind eyes glimmering in terror.

Omet felt no particular compassion toward the plight of the slave children – his own life was nothing to be envied, after all – but even he was appalled at the cruelties Vincane employed. A pallet of food would be handed down, eagerly clutched at by two dozen filthy hands, to be discovered to contain only two hard rolls and scraps of rope left over from the packing area. Vincane's high, shrieking laugh at the bloody riot that ensued had caused Omet to go cold, even in the reflected heat of the ovens.

It seemed whenever Vincane was responsible for hoisting the hods that dragged the diggers up for their monthly feeding and airing, at least half of them would be bloodied in the process, battered against the tiled walls of the well or accidentally dropped out of the hod and stepped upon. Anguished wails or fisticuffs would break out whenever he was in the midst of passing out the monthly rations, to Vincane's wide-eyed protestations of innocence, followed by self-righteous accusations. It bothered Omet greatly that Vincane's eyes glittered even more excitedly while watching the accused slave child being thrashed after his indictment, bothered him so greatly in fact that he sometimes considered knocking Vincane backward down the shaft when the new apprentice was off his guard.

Vincane had even gone so far as to cut Omet's hair as he slept as a joke; he had tossed in the throes of horrific dreams all the long night, visions of Vincane hovering over him with a knife, grinning, to wake in a loose mane of his own hair, slashed in uneven swaths across his pate. Omet had thought about giving Vincane the beating he deserved, but decided that, even if he were to emerge victorious, it would attract Esten's notice, and that was something Omet sought never to do. So he swallowed his fury and shaved the rest of his head completely bald, finding it cooler in the heat of the furnaces anyway.

The only misstep he had seen Vincane make was the time he had chosen to urinate in the drinking water bucket before handing it down, thinking this to be great fun. He had his back to the doorway, and had not noticed that Esten had arrived early for her monthly inspection of the tunnel. The wasting of water was a crime in Yarim Paar, and though Esten chose to disregard a number of common laws herself on a daily basis, apparently this was one about which she felt strongly.

She had seized Vincane by the ears from behind and twisted them violently, almost ripping them free of his head in the process, following the action up with a resounding box on both sides of his bleeding head. Vincane had learned from that experience and had not repeated his joke, at least as far as Omet had noticed, though he had not seemed to even notice the pain.

Even those things that could be seen as positive attributes about Vincane somehow or another always turned fetid. Unlike the other apprentices, Vincane had no compunction about hauling out the bodies of the slave-child miners who died in the tunnels, dragging them out of the hod and back to the furnace in the wing of the foundry where the journeymen slept.

Esten had decreed that the secondary furnace, the journeymen's furnace, would be used as a crematorium since the unfortunate day when one of the slave boys had made the mistake of attempting escape during the monthly airing. Esten had hurled him into the largest main kiln and slammed the door shut. The stench afterward had been minimal, but the slip had been affected by the additional moisture; six racks of tiles were ruined, and so from that time on Vincane would use only the furnace in the far wing for disposal of slave-child bodies. Omet had once gone back to see what had taken him so long, and had retched upon discovering what Vincane's ritual before cremation had been.

Blessedly, only one of the current crew had died recently; this batch appeared to be fairly hardy. No one spoke of the tunnel; it was forbidden, under pain of death, to do so outside the tileworks. The tileworks itself was merely a front for the digging, which took place all hours of the day and night.

The front of the foundry, known as the anteroom, held a small forge and some ceramic kilns for firing the tiles and pottery which was sold throughout Yarim and Roland. The first- and second-year apprentices served there, learning to mix and measure the slip, to trim the molds and shovel the heavy pallets of tile from the smaller furnaces.

The real work took place in the rear, behind the great double doors, in the firing room where the larger ovens and vats were. The third-, fourth-, and fifth-year apprentices lived and worked in this place, pouring and baking drainage tiles and paving stones. The more artistic work was done in the foundry's wings, where the journeymen lived and worked. Sixth-year apprentices, as well as sevens in their journeyman year, spent their days serving the end of their training under the masters of the craft, learning the delicate intricacies of architectural drawing and hand-painted porcelain.

For a brief time in his fourth year, Omet had served an overseer's rotation among the first- and second-year apprentices, supervising their work. Quickly he had learned the most important lesson of supervision: put the whip to those lower than you on the ladder. It had been an easy few months, and he looked forward to returning to the indolence of supervision when his journeyman year was over. Once the profession in which he was training had been a vocation, an artistic calling. Now Omet hated tile, hated the hard work of pouring and baking, trimming and hauling, hated the red clay that stained his hands and arms the color of dried blood.

And Omet hated the new apprentice.

Esten's voice reverberated up from the well shaft.

'Done.'

Omet continued to gather the battered tin plates from the filthy hands of the diggers, watching silently out of the corner of his eye as two of the journeymen dashed to the well and lowered down the hook-stick.

Esten's head appeared a moment later; one of the journeymen offered her a hand and hauled her over the edge of the well shaft. She brushed the loose clay from her dark clothing, the same plain black shirt and trousers she always wore on her monthly inspections, and shook her long, black braid. Her face molded into a glittering smile as she turned to the small group of a dozen ragged souls, huddled against the far wall of the foundry, surrounded by the armed journeymen.

'Well done, boys; you're doing very well,' she said soothingly. The eyes of the children, the only thing visible in the fireshadows from the open kilns, blinked in their dark red faces.

She strode to the bag she had left by the door, snatched it up, and returned to the group. Almost every thin limb retracted as the boys recoiled at her approach. Esten opened the sack and dug deep, then drew forth a handful of sweetmeats and tossed them into the trembling crew. Instantly cacophony erupted, and she laughed in delight.

'Aren't they sweet?' she said to the journeymen, then crouched down to get a better look at the individuals of the group. 'Omet, where's Tidd?'

Omet felt his throat go drier than Entudenin. 'Dead, mum,' he said. The words came out in a croak.

'Tidd, dead? Dear me.' The glittering smile vanished, and Esten surveyed the group more closely. 'What a shame. He had a fine sense of direction. Hmmm, now, who can we make chief?'

A forest of sapling limbs shot up and began waving desperately, accompanied by thin cries for selection. Esten's smile returned, and she stood.

'That's my boys! Such an enthusiastic lot. Let's see, Haverill, Avery, no, you're blind as a bat, aren't you, dear? Jyn, Collin, no; Gume, hmmm, not you, either; you're always doing everyone else's work; much too soft-hearted. Hello, Vincane, who have we here?' She stopped in front of a small, yellow-haired boy, with large eyes and an angled face, trembling violently, his arms wrapped around spindly bent knees.

'That's Aric,' Vincane crowed importantly. 'He's new – in for Tidd.'

'Well, you weren't much of a trade, were you, lad?' Esten turned again and smiled down at a tall boy whose hair had once been white-blond, but now bore the same red filth as the others. 'Ernst – what about you? Would you like to be crew chief?'

The tall boy smiled broadly, showing the few remaining teeth he had. 'Yes, mum.'

'Good, good! Then come, lad, and we'll go back to the tunnel and discuss the direction I want you to take this month.'

After Esten had returned from the well shaft, and the child miners had been lowered back in, she went to the door and took her coat from the peg rack near it, then left through the double doors without a backward glance. Omet caught fragments of her parting words to the journeyman in the anteroom.

'Have you seen how tall Ernst has gotten? What are you feeding him?'

'Same as the others. They scrap for it. We don't dole it out or nothin'.'

'Hmmm. Well, that might be a problem soon. Tell the apprentices to be certain to guard that well shaft and to keep listening. We'll decide what to do next month – if we haven't broken through yet.' Her smile glittered in the dark shadows of the firing room. 'I suspect it's a moot issue. Have the journeymen summon me immediately when the time comes.'

'Yes, mum.'

In the distance Omet heard the door open, and the whine of the winter wind that lingered after it slammed shut. After a moment, he realized that the soft keening was no longer the voice of the wind, but came from the well shaft. Then it was gone.

6

From a distance it was difficult to tell whether the tile foundry was in full operation or all but abandoned. Smoke rose from the open chimneys near the center of the building, but after two hours of observation, no one came or left the complex. As night began to fall the furnaces continued to fire, but still no one came.

'Strange,' Rhapsody commented from behind the broken wall where they had set up their observation. 'Do you think it's a foundry run by ghosts?'

Achmed waved her to silence, trying to follow the pattern of the tainted heartbeat within the brick-and-mortar building. Though he could only feel it intermittently, he could sense that it was slowing somewhat, as if preparing for sleep.

The sky was dark now in the grip of winter; the wind had grown cold with the coming of night. Rhapsody pulled the edges of her ghodin closer to keep them from flapping in the high breeze.

Smoke from the fires still rolled heavily in the air, but now dispersed somewhat, chased by the insistent wind. The cloud-covered sky reflected the light of the fire which flickered now in distant inner windows.

Achmed rose from his crouch and unslung the cwellan. 'Stay here. I'm going to scout around. Remain watchful.' He waited until Rhapsody nodded her understanding, then disappeared into the flickering shadows.

The anterior wing of the building was dark and silent. Achmed edged his way along the southeastern wall, the side of the foundry that did not abut the longer wings. Slatted windows whose use was solely ventilation were the only openings in the long mudbrick wall.

There was a small service door on the other side of the building, closer to the long wings. Achmed eased through it quietly and closed it quickly behind him.

The anteroom of the foundry was unoccupied. Two large kilns stood, open and cold, with racks of fired bisque pots and bowls. Long tables, thick with ceramic dust, bore other pottery in various stages of completion. Vats of paint and covered barrels of lacquer filled the room with an unhealthy stench. Achmed could tell without difficulty that the wares in the room could not possibly be the sole output from the constantly burning furnaces.

Carefully he skirted the heavy tables, being vigilant not to leave footprints in the dust that covered the floor, and sidled up to the heavy brass-bound door he had seen in the shadows at the back of the anteroom. The door was solidly closed; Achmed rested his hand on the roughhewn wood and felt heat beyond it. Light flickered in the space beneath it.

Achmed took off one of his gloves. His fingers studied the heavy iron hinges in the dark and found them corroded and heavy with rust. *They will undoubtedly groan upon opening,* he thought. He leaned against the door and exhaled.

The path lore he had gained crawling within the bowels of the Earth had given him a second sight of sorts, a disorienting vision of the given direction he was seeking. He had not made the attempt to use it to track a heartbeat until now.

Achmed closed his eyes and loosed his second sight. The room around him appeared in his mind's eye, the tables covered with greenware and fired bisque, the pots of paint gleaming dully in the dark.

The heartbeat of the demon-spawn swelled in his ears and throbbed in his skin. His stomach clenched, nauseated, preparing for the jolt as his vision sped away, turning from the room, and through the door, tilting at a strange angle as it did. The search did not take long.

His inner sight blazed into the room beyond the door, a cavernous chamber, obviously a firing room, with three enormous ovens, burning low and steady, before which rested numerous wire racks, empty now. A sizable cast-iron bell was attached to the wall past the open door. With a shuddering lurch the vision stopped.

Achmed inhaled shakily, trying to hang on to the vision. The shadows from the open kilns spun crazily around and about, flickering over the landscape of the room. The floor beyond the doorway was littered with pails and poles with hooks, coils of rope, molds and various tools. The vast room held five enormous vats of thick liquid, each suspended between stone columns and bubbling over piles of firecoals, next to which were mounds of red dirt. Near the vats were three cots, on which, under blankets, lay three bodies, spent in sleep. One was in the process of rolling over.

The vision jolted again, and the color of blood filled his mind as the alien pulse that his own now matched rose to a heavy crescendo in his ears. As if his head and shoulders were being turned by invisible hands, his perspective shifted to the cot to the left of a dark alcove, and moved in closely to see a dark head beneath a thin blanket, as the thudding grew louder. The color of blood appeared before him, dousing his view in a red haze. Then the vision vanished.

Weakly Achmed mopped the beads of cold perspiration from his brow, took several deep breaths, then crossed the room silently and slipped back out the door into the night.

Rhapsody studied his face as he drank from the waterskin for a moment, then rummaged in her pack for her tinderbox. She struck the flint and steel until it sparked, then lighted a short wick, which she held up before her eyes as she looked him over.

'You don't look well. Are you all right?'

Achmed wiped the water from his lips. 'Yes. Are you ready?'

'Yes. I've got some anise oil; it should soothe those angry hinges.'

He capped the skin and returned it to his pack. 'There are ropes you can use to tie up the apprentices – if that's what they are. Get the spawn first. He's the one on the cot to the left of the alcove in the back, the one with the black hair. I'll take care of the other two – the blond brat and the one with no hair.' Rhapsody nodded. 'And Rhapsody – if he causes you a moment's danger, kill him, or I will. That was the bargain. Is it still understood?'

'Yes.'

Achmed studied her face for signs of distress, but saw none. It made him breathe easier than the moment before. Ever since the death of Jo she had seemed more reserved, more pragmatic, as if the role of the Iliachenva'ar, the bearer of the ancient sword of starfire, was beginning to weigh less heavily on her. Still, there was something behind her eyes he could not fathom, almost as if something was missing. He pulled up his hood and unslung his cwellan.

He was still feeling weak from the vision, possibly even from the arrhythmia, but he had to get through this, had to finish it, for all their sakes.

41

At the slight nod of his head, Rhapsody pulled up the hood of her cape and followed him into the dark foundry.

The door into the back section opened without a whisper of sound. Rhapsody had oiled the hinges and whispered the name of silence in a soft roundelay as Achmed lifted the latch and eased the heavy wooden panel into the chamber.

The fires of the kilns roared in greeting, shining off Rhapsody's face. The leaping flames cast sheets of bright light around the room for a moment, illuminating its contents.

Racks of tiles and sacks of grout stood against the walls. There were shelves of supplies and foodstuffs in the far corner, forming a labyrinth of shadows in the room. A deep alcove was recessed in the wall at the back, behind the cots of the three apprentices.

Rhapsody held up the length of cloth Achmed had given her to use as a gag, signaling her readiness, and received a nod in return.

Like quicksilver Achmed glided through the flickering shadows to the cots of the two apprentices who slept to the right of the alcove. A coil of rope lay near the beds; he whisked it from the floor, slashed it into pieces and tossed one to Rhapsody, then turned to the task of binding the sleeping boys.

He bent over the first, a tall, thin lad with wiry blond hair, and pressed a finger against the artery in his neck. As the boy's eyes flew open and he opened his mouth in a gasp for breath Achmed wedged the gag in, pushing it roughly but not enough to cause choking. Before the apprentice could exhale his hands were tied behind his back.

'Don't move,' Achmed murmured to the other apprentice, a bald boy whose eyes had opened at the sound from across the room. He was concentrating on finishing his task, but could tell from the noise behind him that the demon-spawn was giving Rhapsody some difficulty.

'Ow! Hold still, you brat – augh! You *bit* me!' Achmed whirled in time to see Rhapsody, struggling with the ropes as the boy on the cot scratched at her, pull back and deliver the haymaker blow that Grunthor had been the admiring victim of once before. She used it with similar effect now; the dark-haired apprentice fell back onto the cot with an *uuumph!* as a sickening *crack* rent the air. The boy Achmed was binding cringed.

Rhapsody was rubbing the side of her hand. 'If you want to keep your teeth, don't try that again,' she said through clenched jaws.

Achmed took her hand, pulled off the glove and examined it in the inconstant light. 'Did he draw blood?' he asked in Bolgish.

'No, but I believe I did.' They glanced back at the apprentice on the cot, sneering through a bleeding mouth.

'Don't spill that – I need it,' Achmed said, still in the tongue of the Bolg. Rhapsody smiled as she put her glove back on.

The bleeding apprentice struggled to rise, and as he did, Rhapsody belted him again, then sat down on him as she finished tying the ropes.

'Hog-tie – like this,' Achmed called as he bound the blond apprentice's hands and feet together behind him.

Rhapsody winced. 'Is that really necessary? It looks painful.'

'Yes. I've seen all three of them glance at that bell more than once. Undoubtedly it would summon reinforcements.'

'What's in the alcove?' Rhapsody asked as she finished binding the demon's child, struggling to ignore the deadly look in his piercing black eyes.

Achmed put his finger against the throat of the other apprentice, who was trembling like a leaf in a high wind.

'What's in the alcove?' he asked in the Orlandan tongue.

The bald boy struggled to speak, but nothing came out. He swallowed and tried again.

'The tunnel,' he whispered.

'Tunnel to where?'

'I – I don't know.' The boy went white at the expression on Achmed's face.

'I think he's telling the truth,' Rhapsody interjected hastily, seeing that the pressure on the boy's neck artery had been increased. 'The tones in his voice suggest that he is. Here, let me finish tying him and you can look into it.'

Achmed rose in disgust as Rhapsody bent down in front of the bald apprentice. He walked slowly into the dark alcove, empty except for an enormous disk of contoured metal that was propped up against one of the walls, and looked down the hole in the floor.

It appeared to be a tiled shaft, like a that of a well, as deep as two men and narrow, perhaps as wide around as his outstretched arm-span. At the bottom was a dark hole in the southern wall, from which a small intermittent stream flowed. Broken pallets and buckets littered the wet floor. He could see little else in the reflected fires of the open kilns.

Rhapsody bound the apprentice's hands as gently as she could.

'What's your name?'

'Omet.'

'Who would come if you rang the bell, Omet?' she asked.

The boy's expression went slack as he examined her face; then he blinked. 'The journeymen. They live in the next wing.'

She nodded. 'Why is there a tunnel in your workroom?'

'It's where the slave boys dig.'

'Slave boys?'

Her question went unanswered as Achmed dropped woozily to the floor.

7

'What happened? Are you all right?'

Achmed reached up and shoved Rhapsody aside impatiently, clearing his line of sight to the child of the Rakshas. The dark-haired apprentice was still hog-tied, glaring furiously, struggling in his bonds.

'Don't turn away from him, even for an instant,' he snarled.

Rhapsody looped the rope length in her hand, then snapped it suddenly with a whiplike action. It struck the struggling apprentice on the bare leg and elicited a muted howl of anger. The apprentice's body jerked under the snap of the rope, then lay still.

'What happened?' she whispered again.

'The other heartbeat is down there.'

'In the well?'

'No, deeper within.' Achmed mopped his brow, his face gray in the reflected light of the kiln fires. 'This vertical shaft, the well, is just an entranceway. There is a long horizontal tunnel at the bottom – tiled, more than half a league long, a catacomb of some sort. Heads northwest.' He had loosed his sight, and it sped along in the dark, confined space, the vision making him feel claustrophobic, but not as much as the sight of what he had seen at the end of the tunnel.

'Lie still,' Rhapsody ordered the demon-spawn. The child struggled within his bonds, hissing and making gargled threats. She ignored him and walked to the edge of the well. 'Why the secrecy? What are they doing?'

'There are human rats down there, undoubtedly the "slave boys" that one just mentioned. One of them is the other tainted heartbeat, but it's hard to distinguish between them because they are swathed in mud and up to their ankles in water. I would guess they are digging the tunnel themselves; probably laying the tile, too.' He turned to the blond apprentice, whose eyes stared in wide terror above the gag in his mouth. 'What do you think? Does that sound plausible to you?' The boy nodded, glassy-eyed and terrified. 'What a cooperative young whelp you are. I think I may let you live after all.'

'But why are they tiling the tunnel?' Rhapsody asked, leaning down in the attempt to peer into the horizontal hole at the bottom of the shaft. 'And if they are merely digging for clay to make into slip for the tileworks, wouldn't it make more sense for them not to build so narrow a tunnel? Have less distance to haul the clay?'

'Perhaps our new friend here can tell us,' the Firbolg king suggested. 'Any thoughts?' The apprentice shook his head violently, shrugging his shoulders in exaggerated motions. Achmed exhaled in disgust. 'They are deep in, Rhapsody – some of them asleep halfway up the tunnel, more of them at the terminus half a league away. You won't be able to see anything from up here.'

'How many are there?'

Achmed blotted the sweat from his forehead with the back of his arm. Slowly he eased his arrhythmic pulse to disconnect from the heartbeat of the glowering apprentice who still struggled in his bonds, glancing from the two of them to the bell beside the open kiln. 'Hard to say. They're masked by water. You know how much I *love* water.'

Rhapsody nodded and stepped away from the alcove. Achmed watched as her face went suddenly pale in the flickering light of the ovens; the kiln fires roared to sudden life as terror came over her face.

'Gods,' she whispered. She walked quickly over to Achmed and spoke softly in his ear. 'Water. *Below* Entudenin. That's what they're doing here – *they're tunneling to the artery that once was Entudenin.*'

Achmed cast a glance at the enormous metal disk leaning against the alcove's wall.

'It's a well – an aqueduct,' he said. 'They're building an aqueduct to harness the water from the wellspring that once fed the geyser. A sensible idea; should be incredibly lucrative if they plan to sell the water, though I can't imagine that the duke would allow such a thing.'

'Which must be why they are doing it in secret,' Rhapsody added, glancing nervously over her shoulder at the bound apprentices; the blond boy and Omet looked at her hopefully in return, while the demon-spawn snarled and spat around the edges of his gag.

'It might also have something to do with the fact that they are employing slave children to do the digging,' Achmed said curtly, rolling the dark-haired apprentice over on his face with a swift kick. The demon-spawn only grew more angry, spitting and cursing at the floor. 'No one else would undertake the project; much too risky.'

Rhapsody was trembling. 'Once they break through to the artery, those children are dead,' she said. 'The force of Entudenin was said to be strong enough to shatter a man's back on the first day of the water cycle; imagine the power it will have blasting through the first crack in the clay.'

Achmed walked back over to the alcove and peered down into the well shaft. 'If there's water now, then they've already broached the water table. They were fortunate to find it in its fallow part of the cycle – whatever it was you said the lore called it, the time of Slumber. When the Awakening happens again, the water will roar forth. It could happen at any time, judging by the waterflow down there already. We'd best get the other child out now, then.'

'Child? You mean *children*. Achmed, we have to get all of them out of there.'

The Firbolg king rolled his eyes. He drew his long, thin sword of Seren steel and handed it to her.

'Gag the bald one. If any of them move so much as a hairsbreadth while I'm gone, cut their throats,' he said in the Orlandan vernacular to be certain each of the apprentices understood him.

He waited until he was certain that Rhapsody was watching all three apprentices at the same time before lowering himself into the well shaft. The tiles were smooth and slippery, and Achmed had to fully extend both legs, then both arms, bracing himself against the sides of the shaft, inching down the vertical tunnel with agonizing slowness.

At the bottom of the well shaft he gingerly removed one foot, then the

45

other, from the walls, and dropped carefully into the debris of broken pallets and mudfilth that coated the tiled floor. He bent and stared into the dark horizontal passageway that tunneled away into even blacker darkness.

A few moments later he hoisted himself back out and came back to where Rhapsody stood in the pulsing light of the kiln fires. The logs under the huge vats of clay slip were burning down to coals, unattended, and now the slip was beginning to thicken in heavy clumps within the viscous liquid.

'There's nothing to be done; I can't fit down the aqueduct,' he said, brushing the mud from his cloak.

He watched her face carefully in the inconstant light, knowing what she would say.

'Can I fit?'

'You can.' His voice was quiet, his words considered. 'It would be much like crawling along the Root again.'

He had expected her to shudder, but instead she just nodded and began to remove her pack.

'Narrower, perhaps,' he added.

'I understand. Can you lower me down? My arms aren't long enough to climb down as you did.'

Achmed cast a glance around the firing room of the foundry. The demon-spawn had settled into seething quiet, and was still lying facedown on the dirt floor, his countenance contorted by the twisting shadows cast by the firecoals beneath the cooling vats of slip. The other two apprentices lay near him, frozen with fear, watching Achmed apprehensively. He pointed at the nearest vat of hot slip.

'If you ever wanted to be the subject of a statue, just move.'

He turned and picked up a pole with a hook on it that was obviously used to lower and raise up buckets of clay from the bottom of the well shaft. Achmed held it at an angle and Rhapsody stepped on to the hook, grasping it with both hands. Her eyes were calm, though they were shining brightly.

'Are you certain you want to do this?' he asked quietly in Bolgish.

'Is there another option? Besides, I'm the Iliancheva'ar. It's my duty to bring light into a dark place.'

Achmed snorted and began to lower the pole into the shaft.

'Perhaps you should wedge your blade squarely inside my head, then. There has been no illumination burning in there for a long time; it's been utterly absent of reason ever since I allowed myself to get caught up in this ridiculous crusade of yours. Hurry. And remember, if there's a moment's hesitation, or threat, kill the little bastards. That was the agreement.'

'Yes. That was the agreement.' Her smile shone as brightly as her eyes for a moment, then disappeared into the murky blackness at the bottom of the well shaft.

A moment later the dark vertical tunnel filled with a brilliant pulse of light, and a hum that rang like a silvery horn being sounded. Achmed glanced over the edge of the tunnel. Rhapsody stared up at him from the bottom of the well shaft, Daystar Clarion in her hand. The sword of melded element fire and starlight burned brightly, sending glistening waves of illumination over fetid water on the shaft's floor. She smiled again, then waded to the tiled hole in the well-shaft wall and crawled inside the horizontal tunnel, holding the sword before her like a torch.

Achmed watched as the blazing light from Daystar Clarion receded into a faint glow inside the tunnel. He turned around just in time to see the child of the Rakshas lurch to the side, rolling into the firecoals that burned beneath one of the steaming vats of hot slip.

Achmed lunged with the hooked pole, but it was too late. A shower of burning coals sprayed at him as the demon-spawn, now free of the leg ropes that had incinerated in the fire, kicked the coal logs and burning dung out from under the vat, scrambling beneath the hot metal of the cauldron's base to the other side. He could hear the apprentices' muffled cries behind him, probably more from fear than pain, as the sparks hit the dirt floor and burned out in puffs of dusty smoke.

Beneath the vat he could see the boy plunging his hands into the fiery coals, burning free of those bindings as well. Then the apprentice retreated even farther behind the cauldron of slip, apparently unharmed by the fire.

Achmed swept the long pole under the vat, trying to catch the leg of the boy, but barely had time to leap clear as the child pulled the chain on the cauldron, upending the enormous vessel and sending its boiling contents spilling out in a great steaming mudslide onto the floor of the room.

Swiftly Achmed swung the hooked pole at the nearer of the two apprentices, the bald boy to the right of the alcove, catching the ropes by which his hands were bound and hauling him clear of the river of hot mud. The other apprentice, directly in the pathway of the boiling slip, was buried in the ton of slag within seconds; the blond wisps of his hair disappeared into the steaming dirt as the muddy liquid swallowed his body, filling his mouth, then nose, then eyes in fragments of a second, drowning him instantly.

With a violent shake Achmed loosed the trembling apprentice from the end of the pole, leaving the bound boy gasping in fear behind a stack of broken pallets. He turned back in time to see the demon-spawn, now standing on the far side of the tipped vat closest to the oven, hurl a mold at the cast-iron bell. The heavy weight collided with the bell and reverberated loudly; the ripples of sound tore across Achmed's skin and eyelids, sending waves of pain through his body to the roots of his hair.

He swallowed his fury, leapt across the space between them, and lunged, slamming the hooked end of the pole into the boy's shoulder as his arm was coming down from tossing the weight. He could hear the *crack* as the collarbone snapped; the black-eyed apprentice gasped aloud, the first time Achmed had witnessed him experience pain, though a moment later he determined it might just have been shock. The boy glanced in the direction of the journeymen's wing, then turned back and stared at him, readying a lunge, but he barely had time to parry a second swing of the staff. The heavy iron hook shattered his wrist and pushed him off balance.

47

The insolent look in the demon-spawn's eyes had cleared, leaving nothing behind but panic. His arms and legs stiffened for a moment; then he dashed toward the empty wire racks, desperately searching for cover. But Achmed was too fast for him; he arced the pole in the other direction, catching the apprentice in the ribs with sufficient force to break the shaft. The Bolg king drove the end of the pole into the boy's shoulder again, then shoved him, full force, into the base of the open kiln. Before the boy could catch his breath, Achmed was upon him, grabbing his rope belt and singed shirt to lift and heave him through the opening. The broken wrist and shoulder offered little resistance. Achmed firmly closed the door and wedged the latch closed before he brushed the still-hot ash and embers from his gloves.

He listened. A moment later he could hear them coming, footfalls and sounds of alarm approaching from the journeymen's quarters.

Achmed looked quickly around the room, gauging the shadows. A deep one hovered near the farthest kiln, next to which stood rows of pottery in various stages of firing, forming a dark labyrinth. He ducked into the shadow as the pounding of boots drew nearer.

Into the room spilled a cadre of men, more than a dozen, many heavyset, most of them trying to adjust sleep-blind eyes to the destruction in the firing room. Those at the head of the group exclaimed in shock at the upended cauldron and the oozing hill of hardening slip that had been dumped onto the floor. From their initial exchanges Achmed could tell that they believed they had been summoned because of what seemed to be a disastrous accident.

Then they discovered Omet, bound and gagged behind the broken pallets.

During the pause that followed while the journeymen, now armed, searched the room, Achmed reached behind his back and silently drew his cwellan, the asymmetrical crossbow-like weapon of his own design, loading it with disks without a sound. He slid quietly along the wall near the maze of shelves, wanting to be in position as soon as the cadre realized he was there.

It took longer than he expected. Almost a full minute passed before the muttering came to an abrupt halt, and one of the thinner men made a dash for the bell.

Achmed stepped out of the shadow and fired, sending three razor-sharp disks, thin as butterfly wings but made of serrated steel, through the back of the would-be messenger's neck, severing his spine and all but decapitating him. The body spun in a half-circle to the ground, the blade he carried clattering against some of the stone molds on the dirt floor. Two more of the journeymen died a moment later, felled by the deadly disks. Then Achmed stepped back into the shadows once again.

Like rats when a lantern is suddenly unhooded the journeymen scattered, fleeing to all corners of the firing room. Achmed counted them silently; he had seen thirteen come in, and had dispatched three. Ten remained for him to deal with.

Odds he liked.

He crept quietly through the shadows that writhed on the wall leading up to the alcove, passing the place where the bound apprentice still remained behind the pallets. Achmed paused long enough to stare down at the boy, still hog-tied – the journeymen had not bothered to release him – and held a finger to his lips. The apprentice did not move or cry out, but merely blinked, signaling his understanding.

Slowly Achmed circumvented where the boy Rhapsody had called Omet sat, stepping around the broken pallets and the outer reaches of the new hill of mud. The shadow of a man with a long knife lurked in the opening of the alcove, waiting for Achmed to pass so he could stab from behind.

Achmed leaned against the outer wall, listening to the ragged breathing of the journeyman on the other side of it. He measured the shadows from the fires of the four remaining vats of slip and the two open kilns, waiting until one particularly bright one flickered against the wall. As the light surged he passed his fist through it, casting an elongated shadow into the alcove.

As he expected, the journeyman lunged, taking a wide swipe at the shadow, missing any solid target but encountering Achmed's swift kick in the shins instead. The man stumbled, then teetered on the edge of the well shaft, his eyes bulging wide. His arms circled wildly; then, losing his battle against the forces of gravity, he toppled headfirst into the well shaft. A shriek embarrassingly void of male characteristics followed him down, ending in an impressive crescendo of clattering pails and shattering pallets.

Rhapsody's voice echoed up the well shaft, distant.

'What's happening up there?'

Achmed pivoted and fired the cwellan into the far corner by the double doors, sending silvery disks spinning through the fireshadows, catching the light. A heavyset body slumped in the doorframe.

'Dropped something,' he called down the well. 'Sorry. Keep going.'

'Try to be quieter,' the faraway voice echoed. 'Someone will hear you.'

Achmed stepped back over the bound apprentice and took cover behind the second kiln's open door near the labyrinth of shadows where he knew more of the journeymen lurked.

'Wouldn't want that,' he said under his breath.

A growl of anger erupted behind him. Achmed ducked and dodged the charging man's attack, knocking him unconscious with a blow to the head.

He crouched behind a wire rack, waiting, stilling his breathing until it was almost nonexistent. These opponents posed so little challenge that he turned his mind to avoiding the waste of supplies. He would wait, patient, until the remaining seven were all positioned in simultaneous view.

One round for the rest of them, at the most two, he thought. *Conserves disks that way.*

8

When Rhapsody first crawled into the tunnel she felt no harkening back to their passage along the Root at all. Unlike the dank darkness of Sagia's sheath, which was uneven in its height and full of stringy, hairlike minor roots called radix, the catacomb had been carefully and evenly tiled, more closely resembling one of the aqueducts in Canrif, part of the enormous ventilation and water-collection system Gwylliam had designed and built into the mountain. In addition, the warm glow of Daystar Clarion's flames, burning low and steady above the murky water through which she was crawling, made the tunnel walls shine as bright as day.

She pushed all thoughts of confinement and depth out of her mind, concentrating instead on the ethereal light below the flames of the sword. So focused was she on the sword, so intent on keeping her panic in check, that she barely caught sight of the two glittering eyes in the distant darkness up ahead.

As soon as she saw them she stopped; the flames of the sword, deeply bonded to her through her tie to elemental fire, roared to life with her excitement.

A shriek of pain and fear echoed up the catacomb as the slave child, night blind from digging and living in the endless dark, covered his eyes and scurried away, sobbing in horror.

Quickly Rhapsody sheathed the sword, dousing the light, feeling remorse for not realizing what dread the glowing radiance might be bringing to those who lived in this place of endless night.

'It's all right,' she called softly up the tunnel. 'It's all right. I'm sorry.'

Only silence and the sound of trickling water answered her.

Now blind herself, she felt along the tiled floor, conscious now of the rats that skittered along the edge of the tunnel, the snakes that swirled in the deepest parts of the flow, the worms. In the absence of the light the vermin began to return.

The smooth skin of a snake that darted over her hand put her in mind of the sluglike, carnivorous larvae that infested the root of Sagia, calling forth a deep shudder from within her memory. Rhapsody swallowed and crawled forward, struggling to see in the absolute blackness. Ahead of her she heard scuffling movements, larger than rats, she thought, but perhaps not just large rats.

Her internal bond to the sword, now housed in its scabbard of black ivory, seemed tentative, distant. Black ivory was an impenetrable material; no vibration passed through it, preventing anything held within a vessel made of the material from being scryed upon, an important measure of safety for the Iliachenva'ar. The disadvantage was that the power of the sword did not reach her, did not tie its strength to her, as it did when Daystar Clarion was unsheathed in her grasp.

Tentatively Rhapsody passed a hand through the murky water on the floor ahead of her, shuddering inwardly again, and pressed forward. The walls of the tiled tunnel began to feel closer, tighter than they had in the light; in her ear she could hear her own voice whispering her confession to the giant Sergeant-Major, then a stranger, now one of her dearest friends, in the dank tunnel along the tree root.

I'm Lirin. We don't do well underground.

I can see that.

Her stomach rushed into her mouth, and she fought down her gorge as the world around her began to spin.

How did it feel to you? Elynsynos, the ancient dragon, had queried in her sonorous, multitoned voice. *Were you, Lirin as you are, comfortable there, within the Earth, separated from the sky?*

Her own reply came out in a whisper now, as it had then.

It was like a living death.

Her arms began to tremble. Balanced as she was on her hands and knees, her elbows shuddered under the strain, then buckled for a moment, causing her to lurch forward and splash, chest-first, into the fetid water, banging her chin on the wet tunnel floor.

Hurriedly she righted herself again. She wanted to shout to Achmed, as she had when the sword was still lighting the passageway, just to hear his voice, but realized immediately that she could not panic and call for help. The slave children hovering somewhere beyond her in the dark tunnel were still, for the moment, perhaps as frightened of her as she was of the catacomb, the snakes, the rats. One sign of weakness on her part, however, and they might take the opportunity to attack her as a group, pressing a clear advantage on this home turf, this dark land that they inhabited. She had no doubt that they were hard, brutal, toughened by the cruel life they were forced to lead.

They could tear her to pieces.

Her heart began to race. She thought desperately of Grunthor and his tie to the earth, wishing mindlessly that he were there. *Child of Earth*, Manwyn's prophecy had declared him.

> The Three shall come, leaving early, arriving late,
> The lifestages of all men:
> Child of Blood, Child of Earth, Child of the Sky.

If their speculation was right, and she, Achmed and Grunthor were the Three in the divination, then she was the Child of the Sky – the term Lirin used to describe themselves. *It's wrong, wrong for me to be here*, she thought woozily, fighting growing nausea. She should be out in the open air, beneath the stars, singing her aubades and vespers to the sky.

Death was in the air; she could feel it hovering, squalid, thick. Had a child died in this place, perhaps many of them, succumbing to the backbreaking work, the vile conditions, the lack of air? Or was it her own death she could feel coming for her? She could sense the children closer now. Had they summoned the courage to come for her?

Coward, she thought as her trembling grew stronger. *The Iliachenva'ar, the bringer of light into darkness. Struggling to keep from curling up like a babe in the womb. Mama – my dreams are chasing me. Come to my bed; bring the light.*

The words of the Liringlas aubade, the morning love song to the sky, found themselves in her mouth. Shakily she began to sing, softly chanting the words her mother had taught her, words she had sung for many days with Oelendra, her mentor, words born in a place deep in her soul that was old as the ages.

In that deep place she felt a flicker of warmth, a pulse of light, as if she had physically touched the bond she had to the sword. The thought gave her courage, and she began to sing a little more strongly, loud enough to hear the notes echo slightly off the black tunnel walls ahead of her.

Then, a moment later, she heard another echo, softer than the first, and in a different voice, a voice that was familiar but not recognizable. A high voice, a frightened voice.

A child's voice.

Mimen?

The word rang in her ears; it had come forth, spoken haltingly in Ancient Lirin, the language of the Liringlas, her mother's people. Its meaning was unmistakable.

Mama?

Rhapsody raised her head up. In the tunnel ahead of her she could almost make out the silhouette of a head, shoulders – thin they seemed; scraggly. Or perhaps it was just her imagination; the darkness was so complete that her eyes could not focus. She felt a great exhalation of air come out of her, breath she had not known she had been holding.

'Nay,' she said softly. 'Hamimen.' *Grandmother.*

'Hamimen?'

'Aye,' she replied, louder, a little more clearly, still in the ancient tongue of the Liringlas. 'What be your name, child?'

'Aric.' The outline of the head vibrated in the dark.

'May I bring the light, Aric? Dimmer this time?'

A scuffling sound; the head retreated.

'Nay! Nay!'

Beyond him, in the tunnel ahead, a rustle of movement.

'Aric, wait! I've come to take you out of the darkness – all of you.'

Silence.

Desperation was beginning to claw at her throat. 'Aric?'

There was no reply.

Rhapsody slid her hand over the hilt of the sword. She gripped it tightly, then gently pulled, loosing the blade from the scabbard just a little. She exhaled slowly, gathering control of herself; with the return of her calm, the sword burned evenly, and only the slightest of flickers issued forth from the scabbard.

The nightmares of the tunnel receded, leaving just the tiled aqueduct once more in dimmer light than before. Up ahead at the edge of the glow, two even smaller tunnels branched out, no doubt the area in which Achmed had said the children were sleeping.

She inched forward slowly, keeping the sword by her side, and peered into the branching tunnels. They ended in alcoves, where dirty scraps of cloth, perhaps used at one time for blankets, now floated in the filthy water. Rhapsody tried not to recoil from the overwhelming stench of sewage.

Huddled at the end of the alcove was a yellow-haired child, long of bone and translucent of skin, trembling in fear. Rhapsody's throat went dry in memory; it was the same ethereal complexion, the same slender angles that had once graced her mother's face. And yet there was something more, something almost feral, a hint of his inhuman father.

'Aric,' she said gently, 'come to me.'

The child shook his head and turned his face toward the wall.

Rhapsody crept forward another few paces, then looked down at her arms. The water on the floor of the tunnel was now up to her elbows.

Impatience, spurred by fear, took over. 'Aric, come now!' The child only quivered more violently.

A thought suddenly occurred to her. She pulled back out of the alcove and began to move backward on her hands and knees; once she was a short way away she began to sing a children's song from Serendair, a tune with which she had once jokingly serenaded Grunthor.

> Wake, Little Man
> Let the sun fill your eyes
> The day beckons you to come and play

She continued to back away, weaving her call into the lyrics and tones of the traditional song.

> Come hither, come whither, come follow!
> Come hither, come whither, come follow!

At the edge of the tiny sword flame's glow, Rhapsody could hear movement, could see a few faces appear. She nodded slightly and kept backing away, still singing.

> Run, Little Man,
> To the end of the skies
> Where the night meets the cusp of the day

> Come hither, come whither, come follow!
> Come hither, come whither, come follow!

Deeper down the tunnel more faces appeared, haggard, like the wraiths that sometimes stalked her dreams, blinking in the weak light. She continued to crawl backward, singing her song of summoning.

> Play, Little Man,
> Before you grow wise,
> Chasing your dreams while you may

Come hither, come thither, come follow!
Come hither, come thither, come follow!

By the time Rhapsody reached the well shaft, a small herd, perhaps a score in all, of ragged boys, all heights, all thin, had crawled along after her, filling the tunnel until she could not see anything past them, just more heads, more faces, sallow beneath their smeared masks of red dirt, bulging, cloudy eyes, all but naked – human rats, Achmed had called them. She had had no idea how apt the name was.

A ramp of a sort had been constructed in the well shaft to take the place of the hook – she wouldn't find out until later that it hid the body of the journeyman who had fallen down the shaft headfirst – from broken pallets and other debris of the firing room. Achmed's face glared down at her from above. He took one look at the seemingly endless line of filthy children, exhaled, picked up a nearby rope, and threw one end of it down the well shaft to her.

'What's taken so long? Here, start passing the brats up; we have to get out of here.'

Rhapsody took hold of the dirty Liringlas child, who shrank from her touch but didn't pull away, and grabbed the rope that Achmed had tossed down to her.

'Did you have any trouble with the demon-spawn?' she asked as she looped the rope around Aric's waist and helped him onto the ramp, holding on to him until Achmed began to haul him out of the shaft.

'Only a bit,' he said nonchalantly. 'He's in the kiln.'

Rhapsody whirled around from sorting out the other slave boys and stared up the well shaft. '*In the kiln?*'

'Sit there,' Achmed directed the first child, pointing to Omet, still hog-tied but back on his cot. He leaned over the well shaft again. 'Yes, in the kiln. Like you, and some other accursed minions of his demonic father, he appears to be impervious to the effects of fire; has quite a tolerance for pain as well. But he should be all right, as long as his air holds out.'

With a new urgency Rhapsody pulled the next youth forward and looped him with the rope. 'How long has he been in there?' she asked nervously.

Achmed yanked on the rope, dragging the child rapidly up the ramp. 'A while. I'd hurry if you want to get him out before he turns into a vase.'

One by one the children, utterly silent, ascended the ramp. Finally, when the last one was out, Achmed tossed the rope down one last time and hauled Rhapsody back up the shaft and into the alcove.

'What on Earth happened?' she said, looking around the firing room in dismay at the mountain of hardening slip and the neat stack of bodies by the outside wall of the alcove. Her voice dropped to a whisper. 'Couldn't you at least have hidden those? Look at how frightened the children are.'

'Good; that was the point. You'll notice none of them bothered me or made any noise while I was hauling you out.' He sliced through Omet's bonds with his dagger, then came next to her and pointed at the doorway through which the journeymen had come. 'There are close to one hundred more where these came from, sleeping in shifts in the barracks beyond that entrance. In addition I would suspect that someone is watching this place very closely, given how near they are to their goal. We have no time to sort these children out – they're witnesses, and I would guess whoever owns this place is not going to be particularly pleased with our emancipation of them.

'Now that you know our situation, let me suggest that you pull the demon-spawn out of the oven – he should be nicely browned by now – and we'll leave with all due haste. The chance of any of us making it out of here alive grows slimmer with each passing second. And I mean that, Rhapsody – you know I am not given to hyperbole.'

Rhapsody nodded and hurried to the closed kiln, pulled the bolt, and swung the door wide open. The demon-spawn was slumped at the back, unconscious, breathing shallowly. Those slave children whose eyes had adjusted to the flickering light watched in amazement as she climbed into the red-hot oven, seized the boy, and pulled him by his feet out of the kiln. She checked him perfunctorily, then dragged him over to Omet's cot, where the slaves were huddled together.

'Don't touch him unless you need to; he's hot and you'll burn yourselves, at least until he cools down,' she said to the boys in the Orlandan dialect. 'But if he moves at all, please jump on him, all of you, and sit on his back.' She looked back at Achmed. 'How are we getting out of here?' she asked in Bolgish.

'The same service door through which we came. We can go down the inner alley – there are no windows on that side of the building – and get out of the city through the backstreets. We can take them to the northern outposts of Ylorc—' He raised a hand to silence her protest. 'We can argue about this later. There's no time now.'

'Agreed. But I have to do one more thing before I can go – I have to close the tunnel. Otherwise they're just going to round up a new group of slaves, and send them down again, until they break through, if they haven't already. I don't want them to get away with drowning a bunch of boys for their own selfish purposes.'

Achmed walked over to the demon-spawn, bent down, and gauged his body temperature. He roughly bound him hand and foot, ignoring the dangling wrist and uneven shoulder, then picked him up and slung him over his shoulder.

'And exactly how do you propose to do that? Grunthor's not here.'

'I know. Give me exactly five minutes – I promise that's the longest I will take.'

Achmed shook his head as he beckoned to the slave children, who leapt from the cot and lined up next to him.

'We may not have that long.'

'Then go – I'll catch up to you. Go.'

She ignored the hard look he gave her, then ran to the door and spoke the word of silence again. The door opened without a sound. The passage of the slave boys through it was equally silent, but that was due to the terror that the look on Achmed's face was apparently inspiring in them.

Once they were all out into the antechamber of the foundry, Rhapsody went back into the firing room. She stared for a moment at the carnage before her, then strode to the first of the four remaining vats and upended it, dumping the contents onto the floor, where it ran like a muddy river into the alcove. She then went to the next vat, and the next, pulling the chains grimly, staying clear of the landslide of burning mud.

When enough had swelled into the alcove to fill the well shaft to the brim and more, she drew her sword. The flames of Daystar Clarion danced in the shadowy darkness, shining with a firm authority, burning a million times brighter than the fires that had now reduced to sleepy coals beneath the great vats in the firing ovens.

Rhapsody closed her eyes amid the lakes of slip, searching her soul for her bond to the sword, for her tie to elemental fire, now the core of her being as it had been ever since she passed through the wall of fire at the heart of the Earth. She concentrated on the well shaft, now gurgling with its burden of slip, and raised the sword slowly until it pointed where she knew the alcove was.

'Luten,' she said with a ringing authority. *Bake.*

An arc of flame shot forth from the sword, blasting the alcove with a heat far more intense than the kilns, hotter and brighter than the light of the sun. Rhapsody felt a thrill run through her as the fire soared into the alcove, firing the clay solid in a matter of seconds, filling the shaft with an unyielding plug as hard as the ceramic columns of Manwyn's temple. The top of the well shaft glowed red, then settled into the dull color of fired clay.

That's the most I can do, she thought as she sheathed her sword, hurrying to catch up with Achmed and the boys. *For the boys, and for Entudenin.*

When they slipped out of Yarim Paar that night, past the Yarimese guards in their horned helmets, through the alleys of a city that slept like a drunken wastrel or a hibernating bear, she took a moment in their flight and cast a glance back at the dry fountain, the dead wellspring obelisk. *May you return to life one day,* she thought, *and make Yarim bloom again.*

Though she was many street corners away, she was certain she saw, in the dull red clay, a momentary shimmer, like a wink from a star.

9

On the Krevensfield Plain, Southern Bethany

The holy man stood with his face to the sun, on the edge of winter and the Krevensfield Plain. The mountains of Sorbold had receded into the southeastern distance like a grim nightmare. Now an endless vista of low, frosty plateau lay at his feet, the sky stretching out to the blue edge of the horizon all around, no longer broken by fanglike mounds of earth.

Night was coming earlier with the advent of the season of the moon; a red sun burned at the world's rim, bathing the edge of the meadows in bloody light that spread slowly eastward as it set. He smiled. How prophetic.

His retinue of guards was encamped around a small fire in the frozen grass some distance away, preparing their supper. He had begged their indulgence and walked slowly to the edge of a deep swale, presumably to take the air, and now stood alone, undisturbed, watching the western horizon grow ever more crimson in the grip of coming night.

For almost three hundred years these lands lay fallow, a wide, fertile stretch of pastureland dotted in later centuries by the occasional farming community. These intrepid homesteaders came in groups consisting of four to six families, braving the bitter winds of winter, the brushfires of high summer, to live beneath the endless sky. Without exception those homesteaders were newlanders, immigrants from the south or west that did not share a drop of Cymrian blood between them. For if they had, they would never have even thought to put the first stake into the ground here, let alone build their homes and rear their children on this haunted soil.

Time had erased most of the visible scars of the Cymrian War. In Tyrian and Sorbold, great battles had devolved into heinous slaughter and reckless carnage, streaking the earth red beneath the bodies of the innumerable fallen. With the passage of the centuries, however, the forest had reclaimed in Tyrian the places no Lirin soul would have thought to rest his head in sleep. The song of the wind in the new trees' leaves had drowned out the whispers of battlefield ghosts, except on nights when the breeze was high. Then Lirin fathers drew their progeny around the warm hearths of their longhouses and told them stories of war hags, spirits of widows long dead who walked the slaughtering grounds still, eternally mourning their soldier spouses, even longer dead.

In Sorbold to the south, the mountains had taken back the battlefield passes as well. It was said that in the north the blood of the dead had stained Yarim's clay its rubeous hue, had made its river run scarlet with gore. Anyone surviving from the First Generation knew this to be a myth. Yarim's soil and river had always been red in the memory of men, colored by the runoff from great deposits of manganese and copper in the foothills of the northern Teeth. In all the lands that ringed Roland, it was neither Anwyn nor Gwylliam but Time that had been victorious. Time had at last covered the memory of grim pandemic death, even if other scars, the wounds of souls and memory, remained.

But here, in the bowl of the continent, the center lands betwixt the sea and the mountains, the blood of the multitudes who had died in that glorious war had pooled, had sunk into the ground, making the soil fertile and the pall of death heavy in the air, so heavy that even the strongest wind, the most driving rain, could not wash it away. This truly was the realm of ghosts, irrespective of the fact that the Bolg had purloined that name for Kraldurge, their own place of restless spirits within the mountains.

It was almost time. A few more sunsets, a few more days, a season, maybe two, and it would finally be at hand. After all the centuries he had waited, his patience was about to be rewarded.

Soon he would have the army. Then he would take the mountain. Then he would have the Child. Once he possessed her, the ultimate goal was assured. The rib of her body, formed as she was from Living Stone, would open the vault deep within the Earth, the prison in which his kind had been held since the Before-Time. The thoughts of destruction that raced through his mind had to be reined back, or he would give himself away in his excitement.

The day was coming soon. All in good time.

He glanced over his shoulder casually at the guards, who were laughing and passing a flask between them, then turned westward again with a smile.

With a sudden violence he bit down hard on the back of his tongue, puncturing the surface and drawing blood into his mouth. He then opened that mouth ever so slightly.

The holy man inhaled the evening air, stinging his nostrils with chill and the scent of dried grass in fire. Softly he began to chant into the wind, keeping his voice low so that it had no chance of being overheard by the drunken oafs who called themselves his escort.

Had his retinue been paying attention they would have heard the cleric whispering the names of ancient battles, moments of carnage frozen in time, inhaling their names into his mouth and breathing them back out again, coated with the taste and vibration of blood. But the day had been long and uneventful, as had the rest of the journey thus far, and the soldiers were too engaged in their banter, too involved in their games of dice and throw-spikes to notice.

In fairness to the guards, they felt safe here, the holy man noted in the back of his mind. After all, there was virtually no chance that they would be attacked, here in the middle of the endless meadow, with the plain stretching for leagues to the horizon. There was no place for an enemy to hide in all that space, no opportunity for surprise.

He chuckled in amusement at the inaccuracy of supposition.

The wind grew colder. As he spoke the words formed evanescent clouds of frozen steam and hovered before him in the crimson sky, as if too heavy with grief to rise on the breeze now.

The raid on Farrow's Down, he whispered. *The siege of Bethe Corbair. The Death March of the Cymrian Nain, the burning of the western villages. Kesel Tai, Tomingorllo, Lingen Swale.* One by one, a litany of death and disgrace, spoken softly into the wind. *The slaughter at Wynnarth Keep, the rape of the Yarimese water camp. The assault on the Southeastern Face. The evisceration of the fourth column. The mass execution of the First Fleet farming settlements.*

Only the snow answered him, and even it did not appear to be listening.

Flakes of ice blew about in the stiff breeze, masking his words and the frosty breath that uttered them.

He felt the flush of excitement begin to creep over him, starting in his groin and radiating outward with each beat of his failing heart. The spirits of the dead called out in the wind, as they had for centuries, the anguish of their cries vibrating over his skin in delicious ecstasy. It was the sound, or more accurately, the feel, of brutal suffering, of violence, that remained in the earth and the air, dissipated only slightly over time when the memory was recalled, like blood pooled at the bottom of a deep bowl. Even those without his unique abilities could feel the noise of it, could sense the agony that was extant in the place, and hurried to be away from here. He, of course, could more than feel it. In a way, he could take credit for it.

The holy man inhaled the vibrations of suffering from the wind, tasted the death in his mouth, savoring it. His inner demon shouted for the joy of it, roiled in the orgiastic pleasure of the destruction that had occurred here, and would occur again soon. It was all he could do to keep from being carried away on an orgasm of bloody memory.

Now, Mildiv Jephaston, he whispered into the wind.

'Your Grace?' The lieutenant was standing directly behind him.

He spun quickly around, struggling to mask his annoyance. 'Yes, my son?'

'Is everything all right, Your Grace?'

He struggled to set his features in a smile. 'Yes, of course, my son,' he said, sliding his hands into the sleeves of his robe. 'And how kind of you to be concerned. Is the fire going well?'

'Fairly well, Your Grace,' said the young soldier as the two began to head back. 'The wood's a trifle wet to really catch thoroughly.'

The holy man smiled as he returned with the young armsman to the camp. 'Perhaps I can be of assistance,' he said. 'I've always had a touch with fire.'

By the time they reached the rocky swales that lay east of the city of Yarim Paar it was clear to Achmed that the lives of the slave children had been purchased at the cost of gathering at least one of the additional demon-spawn. Given his dislike of people in general and children in particular, he was not particularly aggrieved at the development, but he suspected that Rhapsody would be.

Nine living brats of the Rakshas and one yet to be born, scattered all the way across the continent – it would be a daunting task in a season without snow, when time was not working against them. Now, entering winter, with but nine weeks before the birth of the last child, and taking on this new problem, her plan to obtain all of them seemed very much in doubt.

He did not know how many tainted children it would require to extract the necessary amount of blood for him to find the F'dor, or if this insane quest for it would even work at all. *Blood will be the means to find that which hides from the Wind,* the ancient Dhracian prophecy had said. Rhapsody had interpreted it, had set the plan in place, arranging with her Lirin mentor, Oelendra, to take the children in as they found each of them, and guard them until all had been found. Then Rhapsody would take them, assuming she could find it, to the Veil of Hoen, a place she said was legendary for healing.

With each passing day Achmed had grown more impatient, more uncertain, both of the plan's potential success and of the likelihood of their own survival. Rhapsody was certain that the Lord and Lady Rowan, the mysterious figures who dwelt beyond the Veil of Hoen, would be the ones to separate out the blood without killing the children. *They healed Ashe when his soul was torn asunder,* she had argued. *The Lady is the Keeper of Dreams, the Guardian of Sleep, Yl Breudiwyr. The Lord is the Hand of Mortality, the Peaceful Death, Yl Angaulor. They are the only ones I can think of who can take out the demon's blood without killing the children. It's the place to do this, I know it is. If I can just make it there in time – time passes differently in that place; I know, because Oelendra told me. If anyone can help it is they.*

He had not had time to discuss the change of plans with her; it had been a mad race to escape before dawn broke over Yarim Paar. Behind them in the distance he could hear the faint ringing of alarms, or at least he thought he could – perhaps it was more a matter of imagination and fear. After all, they had only stolen slave children who were being illegally used. And what thief reports the theft of his own stolen property?

Those of the ratty children who were willing to endure human contact had gravitated to Rhapsody as they fled; the others had tried to stay as far away from both of them as would be allowed. Twenty-two in all; some of them took turns riding in pairs on the horses, while others preferred to walk the entire journey. Two pairs had had to be tied together to keep them with the group but away from the frailer boys and the apprentices, whose maltreatment of them in their captivity was deeply resented. It made for excruciatingly slow traveling, but Rhapsody did not seem to mind.

She spent a good deal of her walking time talking with the bald apprentice named Omet, and most of her resting time comforting the yellow-haired child whose mother had been Liringlas, whose leg was infected, bordering on septic, singing her healing songs and music to keep the children compliant, applying her medicinal herbs. Now, as they made camp at sunset, breaking open the rations intended for the longer journey to feed so many starving mouths, Achmed looked east, musing silently.

It was another two days' travel to the Bakhran Pass, the second northernmost Firbolg outpost in the Teeth. They had agreed to leave the children there, in the hands of the Bolg army garrison, all but the two demon-spawn. Every child they had rescued except the apprentice was an orphan, and Omet had assured Rhapsody that he was leaving behind nothing in Yarim Paar.

Seeing Rhapsody now, sitting near the crackling flames of the campfire with the boy named Aric in her lap, Achmed felt a shiver of a sort pass through him. The child, like Rhapsody herself, was rosy of skin with golden hair; there were definite racial similarities. Still, there was a fae air to him that made him seem alien, a feral aspect that made Achmed nervous. It was almost as if Rhapsody were cuddling a blanket-wrapped badger in her lap, cooing over it as if it were a Liringlas baby, oblivious of its deeper, threatening nature.

It did not bode well in his mind for the times ahead.

Many leagues to the south, at the northernmost edge of the mountains of Sorbold, the watch had just changed. The third column of the Western Face had returned only half a sun's span ago from maneuvers in Otar, a distant city-state famous primarily for the linens of Otar'sid, the capital.

It was had been a fairly light rotation, guarding the underbenisons who were making their annual pilgrimage to Sepulvarta to deliver new white robes to the Patriarch for the Blessing of the Year ceremony that would take place half a year hence, at the vernal equinox.

The mission had been completed without event, and now the soldiers were encamped along the lee of the Western Face, their campfires beginning to catch in the thin, cold air, forming a bright sea of ground-torches in the growing darkness. Morning would find them, after a brief march, back in base camp at Keltar'sid. The ground forces were especially eager to return to the city-state of soldiers, looking forward to further training with the strange weapons of Bolg manufacture that they had been outfitted with before departing for Otar. Mildiv Jephaston, the column leader, was coming off watch, preparing for supper and sleep, when he heard the voice, warm on the winter wind, tickling his ear.

Now, Mildiv Jephaston.

The soldier shook his head; he was accustomed to hearing strange things in the wind, especially after a long march, but never before had the breeze spoken so clearly.

And it had never before called his name.

He stopped in his tracks, rubbed his ear, shook his head again, brushing the imaginary summoning aside, and sat down by the larger of the two campfires, taking his plate of stew from the column's cook as he passed by. He was almost comfortable, almost ready to eat, when he heard it again, softer.

Now, Mildiv Jephaston.

Warmer and softer than he could have said it in his own head himself.

Jephaston looked around at the column, encamped by unit – five hundred sleeping, three hundred on watch, with all one hundred twenty of the cavalry quartered in the field with their mounts. 'Who is calling me?' he asked the other commander, sitting next to him. The man looked up over his stew, glanced around, then shook his head.

The column leader listened once more, but heard nothing. He decided to ignore it and returned to his supper.

Perhaps it was the sound of his own mastication, the grinding of his teeth, the clatter of the spoon against the metal plate, the crackling of the fire, the

61

conversation of the men, the hooting, cheering, and cursing that cut through the night at each toss of the bones. Perhaps one or more of these noises was responsible for the masking of the change, camouflaging the silent words that crept into his brain through his ear and found a connection there, lying dormant, planted but a short time ago, awaiting the arrival of the demon's command.

And while the change was a subtle one, he did feel it, even if he was unaware of what was occurring. Like waves it came over him, endless waves of the sea, waves of pulsing heat from a fire, waves of blood from a beating heart, lulling him, sinking into him, absorbing only into the surface of his soul, because there had been no blood pact, no permanent bond; he was not bound to the demon eternally.

But, unlike the others who lay about their own fires, succumbing to their own waves of heat, their own internal summonses, Mildiv Jephaston had given the F'dor his name.

He was perfectly comfortable with the new elongation of focus, so that all objects, whatever their distance, were equally clear, as if the world had flattened. His own arms and legs appeared comfortably distant, and the aches in his back relaxed and slipped away. He felt intensely light, and strong, as if he were drawing air and warmth from all around, and ineffably calm.

And as the command ensnared his conscious mind, it spread unconsciously to those who had sworn fealty to him, who followed his commands without hesitation.

So when he decisively stood up, packed his gear, mounted his war horse, and issued the call for the column to fall out, there was never even an eyebrow raised, not a single question considered. The column mustered out and followed him, in two divisions, four-fifths of the soldiers in the first, the remainder in the second riding a day behind them, battle-ready, down from the Western Face, into the biting wind of the Krevensfield Plain.

On their way to Navarne.

10

Border, Eastern Yarim, Northern Ylorc

The Firbolg soldiers manning the guard post in the northern wastes of the Bakhran Pass took the slave children into their custody without comment. The slave children were bundled up with Firbolg army blankets and packed aboard a pair of wagons scheduled to depart for Canrif with the second-week caravan, which arrived in time.

Achmed gave lengthy instructions to the Bolg soldiers who were to guard the slave children until they were delivered to Grunthor. The children would be cared for in Ylorc until he and Rhapsody returned, when they would either be allowed to remain or travel to Navarne to live. The boys were in high spirits; one look at the strange weapons and armor of the Bolg had caused excitement to roar through the group like wildfire. Only the bald apprentice seemed reserved, eyeing the Bolg soldiers apprehensively.

As the caravan prepared to depart for the Cauldron, Rhapsody took Omet aside.

'Will you be all right?'

The apprentice smiled wanly. 'I hope so. I don't expect I'd make much of a meal, being on the thin side.'

'The stories about cannibalism are greatly exaggerated,' she said, running her fingertips affectionately over the fuzz that was beginning to darken his pate. 'You will be safe among the Bolg. Ask to see Grunthor, and tell him I said to put you to work. Look him in the eye and stand your ground – he'll respect you for it. Don't limit the uses of your skill and imagination. I believe that you could become one of the great artisans of the Rebuilding.'

'Thank you.'

'But if you are uneasy, or you find living within the mountain is not to your liking, when I return I will see that you are escorted to wherever you wish to go.' Omet nodded. 'In the meantime, please look after the boys for me.'

'I will.'

She turned him toward the southeast, where a trace of pink was just cresting the blue horizon.

'Somewhere in those mountains greatness is taking hold,' she said. 'You can be a part of it. Go carve your name into the ageless rock for history to see.' Omet nodded, then climbed into the wagon with the slave boys, and rode away over the rocky snow amid a tumble of waving hands and shouted goodbyes.

Dusk found the travelers, four now in total, camped on a bluff overlooking the banks of Mislet Stream, a red tributary of the Blood River. The water was frozen now, cloudy pink in the coming darkness.

The campfire crackled in the bitter wind, filling the cold air with sparks. Rhapsody drew her winter cloak around her, seeking to hold the wind and the desolation at bay.

How much longer will it be like this? she wondered, stirring the fire with a long, thin reed, dry and cracked from winter's cold. *How many more nights must I spend wandering? When will it end? Will it end?*

Nine living children of the F'dor, and one yet to be born. They had two. In a little more than eight weeks the baby would be born south of Tyrian. *How can we possibly find them all in time?* Rhapsody struggled to keep the panic from gripping her as her stomach knotted. The knowledge that Oelendra was waiting for them at the border of Canderre to take possession of the children they had found, and had been for three days, only made the queasy sensation worse.

A light, shaking sigh matched the whine of the wind, and she looked up from her contemplation. Aric had chosen to sleep near the horses, away from the adults and Vincane, who now dozed in herb-induced slumber near the fire. Rhapsody rose, feeling the cold in her bones, and went to the child, bending beside him to check his festering leg. She crooned a soft tune, aimed at easing his pain in sleep, then came back to her place near the fire beside Achmed.

He was staring into the western distance, his face shielded, his eyes clouded with thought. Rhapsody waited for him to speak. It was not until the bottom of the sun had sunk below the rim of the horizon that he did.

'We can't make it to the carnival, or to Sorbold now before the birth of the last child.'

Rhapsody exhaled. As always, Achmed was giving practical voice to her thoughts. The oldest child of the Rakshas was a young man, a gladiator in the nation of the Sorbold, in the northwestern city-state of Jakar. Achmed had never been thrilled with the prospect of attempting a rescue of this child, but Rhapsody had been insistent, and finally he had granted the possibility as long as the timing allowed. Prior to their diversion back to Ylorc, had they followed the schedule, the gladiator, whose name was Constantin, could have been found outside Sorbold, at the winter carnival of Navarne. By the time they got there now, however, the carnival would be over and Constantin would have returned to Sorbold. It seemed the rescue of the additional slave children had been bought at the price of the gladiator's damnation.

'The baby is due to be born in the Lirin fields to the south of Tyrian forest,' she said mildly, watching the sunset herself. 'We'll be in the area. We could go to Sorbold after Oelendra takes the baby off our hands.'

'No.' Achmed tossed some frozen grass into the fire. 'It's too much of a risk. If I'm caught while in Sorbold secretly, stealing as valuable a commodity as a gladiator, it will be an act of war. This mission, as I've told you from the beginning, was to gather these children for the blood we could get out of them, not to save their souls.'

'Perhaps for you.' Rhapsody's gaze didn't move. 'How ironic,' she said, with a bitter tinge in her voice. 'I suppose that means we are no better than the Rakshas, tying children up like swine and slaughtering them in the House of Remembrance. I guess blood is the means, whether you are well-intentioned or not.'

'Perspective is everything, Rhapsody.'

'I'm going after him,' she said mildly, still not moving her eyes from the vanishing sun. 'I appreciate all that you have done, and will do, but I am not abandoning him. I understand your predicament, and I can't ask you to risk your kingdom for this. But I'm going into Sorbold, even if I have to go in alone.'

Achmed exhaled. 'I'd advise against it.'

'I can ask Llauron for help.'

'I'd advise against that even more.'

'You're not leaving me many choices,' Rhapsody said, searching the sky for the earliest stars, waiting for their appearance to begin her evening devotions.

'Leave him. When this is over I will hunt him down and put him out of his misery; you know as a Dhracian I cannot abide anything tainted with F'dor blood being left alive.'

'You'll be damning him to the Vault of the Underworld.' Her comment was rote; they had argued unproductively about this many nights before this one.

Achmed shrugged. 'If you like I will sprinkle holy water on the cinders of his corpse for you.'

'Thank you, no.'

'Well, there's always Ashe. He could round up the rest of them. You called him on the wind once, and he came.'

Rhapsody shuddered. 'Yes, I did, but I was standing in the gazebo at Elysian, which is a natural amplifier. I don't know if it would work in the open air. Besides, you know very well that I don't want to tell Ashe about these children until I'm back from the Veil of Hoen.'

Achmed's fists clenched more tightly, but his face did not move. 'He doesn't deserve the protection you are always wrapping around him like a child's blanket,' he said bitterly. 'Perhaps it would do him some good to fight his own battles, to be responsible for wiping his own arse once in a while. It is making me ill to watch you be his arse-rag.'

The light of the setting sun filled her eyes, making them sting with memory. 'Why do you hate him?'

Achmed didn't look at her. 'Why do you love him?'

She stared silently over the endless fields to the horizon, darkening now. The rosy glow of sunset was deserting the clouds, leaving only hazy gray where a moment before there had been glory. Finally she spoke, her voice soft.

'There is no reason for love. It just is. And when it's there, it endures, even when it shouldn't. Even when you try to make it go away. It's hard to make it die. I've learned it's also unnecessary – and unwise. It only lessens you for it. So you accept it. You lock it away. You let it stay. You don't deliberately kill love. You just don't act on it.'

She glanced his way, noting his eyes fixed beyond the rim of the world, his folded hands resting on his lips, lost in thought. 'But hate is different. If you're going to hate, you should at least have a reason.'

Achmed inhaled the cold wind of the coming night, then let his breath out slowly.

'I don't hate. I have given up hate. But I disdain Ashe's promises, his misplaced loyalty, his weakness.'

Rhapsody ran her hand over a dry stalk of highgrass, blanched and frozen, that jutted forth from the snow.

'He's no longer weak. I've seen what he's endured, Achmed. Even in his agony, his isolation, he spent his time protecting the innocent, struggling to find the very demon that held his soul captive. He's whole now. He's strong.'

'You misuse the word; I thought Namers were more selective in their use of accurate language. He's been mended. Mending him did not make a god of him. He will betray you again, fail you, lose his grasp while you hang in the balance, arrive moments too late. I have seen it before.' He glanced at her and their eyes met. 'So have you.'

She pulled the stalk of grass from the frozen ground. 'You don't know what you're talking about.'

'I believe I do.'

The grains of the seedpod slid between her fingers, then scattered onto the snow. 'It's easy to criticize something you think of as a weakness, something you've never had. But if you've never been in love yourself, never had to balance it against duty, never been totally *lost* in it, you can't—'

'Stop!' The word came forth violently enough to make Rhapsody drop the remains of the grass stalk. 'How do you know what I have had? How do you know I can't understand from personal experience how weak love can make you? How dare you presume that I would condemn anyone, even him, without having walked those paths myself?'

Achmed's eyes finally turned on her, and they were blazing with dark light. 'I know everything about the promises of youth. I know that stupid surrender, that need to save the unsavable that love makes you believe is possible. That's what I despise most about Ashe – that he has made you expect that he can save you, or you him. That he has made you believe you need saving. That *he* was worth saving at the cost you paid to do it.'

He broke his gaze away and stared out into the new darkness at the horizon's edge. Rhapsody watched him for a moment, then looked westward herself.

'Who was she?'

The Firbolg king exhaled, then lowered his gaze. 'Please. This is lore that will remain lost. Consider this my own Sleeping Child, better left alone.'

Rhapsody nodded. 'Does Grunthor know?'

'He knows all, because he doesn't judge, or remind. You could ask his opinion of Ashe if you really wish to have an objective analysis.'

She rose and stretched her arms. 'I don't. It doesn't matter. He's gone.'

'He'll be back.'

'No, he won't. He's off to propose to a First Generation Cymrian woman, someone the Patriarch's ring of wisdom confirmed as a good choice for his Lady.'

Achmed leaned back and stared into the fire. 'Proof again of what I said earlier about his weakness and misplaced loyalty.'

'I don't think his loyalty is misplaced,' Rhapsody said. 'We knew from the beginning that this was his destiny. He was born to be the Lord Cymrian, Achmed, whether he wants it that way or not. He needs a noble bride. I knew it before I fell in love with him – I knew it *when* I fell in love with him. I know it now. Nothing has changed. He has gone to fulfill his destiny, just like we will one day fulfill ours.'

'Well, that's good to hear, but I still suspect we'll see him again eventually.'

'It still doesn't matter. It's over.' She scanned the deep blue of the sky, looking for the evenstar, but mist clouded the horizon, making it hard to find. 'At least he gave me that.'

'What?'

'An ending. It's what I want more than anything with these events that have been unfolding ever since we met, you and I. I'm tired, Achmed.' She turned and looked at him, and her eyes had lost their inner spark, fueled now only by weariness. 'I'm tired of looking for a hidden demon. I'm tired of living in anticipation that each person we meet could be the host of the F'dor. I want to know who it is, and to kill it, once and for all, with you holding its spirit in thrall so that it can't escape.' She turned away toward the setting sun again. 'I'm tired of the nightmares. I want to finish this; I want it to be over. I want to sleep peacefully for once.'

A choked laugh went up in the darkness behind her.

'That won't happen. I'm sorry.'

'Why not?' A cold wind blew through her hair, chilling the sweat that had appeared at his words.

Achmed's voice was soft.

'You do know that if we aren't destroyed outright there is a good chance that we will never die – at least not for thousands of years? You, Grunthor, and I – like the First Generation Cymrians, we seem to have cheated Time with our little trek within the Earth. That lovely blessing of immortality comes at a cost.

'You want it to be over – it will never be over, Rhapsody. Just as the Grandmother stood for centuries guarding the Sleeping Child, ours will be lives of endless vigilance. After you've seen what hibernates within the Earth, and know that there are demons out there that seek nothing more than to release it, how can you ever sleep peacefully again? Only the ignorant and the oblivious sleep well. Only the hopelessly naive believe it will ever be over.'

With a sudden, angry sweep she drew the sword; Daystar Clarion roared forth, blazing, from the scabbard of black ivory, burning deeply in the cold air, reflecting its pulsing light off the snow. Rhapsody turned to face him.

'Fine. Then I'll be ignorant and oblivious; I'll be hopelessly naive. I don't think you understand, Achmed. I have to believe it will one day be over. I have to, or I can't go on.'

She turned away and walked to the crest of the nearest swale, searching the sky again. The evenstar winked from behind a frosty patch of cloud. Rhapsody cleared her mind and began to sing her evening devotions.

Achmed smiled slightly as the clear notes caught the wind.

'Trust me, you'll find you can,' he said, more to himself than aloud.

II

On the Border, Northwestern Bethany, Southeastern Canderre

Rhapsody heard Oelendra before she saw her.

Achmed had declared that their earlier misadventure made it hazardous to travel long through Yarim, and so they rode back through the province as quickly and minimally as they could. They found themselves after three days in the somewhat more wooded terrain at the northern tip of Bethany and eastern edge of Canderre's lush farmlands.

Achmed, who had traveled the entire journey with his strong, clawlike grip on the back of Vincane's neck, nodded at the end of a long day of riding, reining his horse to a gentle halt at the middle rise of a softly sloping hill. Rhapsody dismounted quickly and put her arms out to Aric, lifting the child carefully from the saddle to avoid hurting his sore leg.

The sun was beginning to set as they made camp; a single star appeared in the patch of sky above the leafless trees. Rhapsody stood and brushed the dirt from her trousers, looking around for a place to sing her evening vespers. Just as she did, she heard a voice in the distance begin the ancient chant.

It was a voice of the ages, warm and ragged in its tone, singing with the power and pain of one who had seen worlds end and begin, who had lived through the worst of nightmarish battles to still rise, victorious but not triumphant, continuing on with the light of each new dawn.

Tears of excitement sprang into Rhapsody's eyes. She grabbed Achmed's arm.

'Oelendra! That's Oelendra!'

Achmed nodded curtly, and continued to truss Vincane to a tree in a position where the demon-spawn could be seen at all times, but still have access to food and warmth. He already knew she was there; he had followed the ancient Lirin warrior's heartbeat to this place. She was one of a few thousand living souls born on the Island of Serendair he could still track with his blood lore.

'She's near enough. Perhaps you should go to meet her.'

He glanced back over his shoulder. Rhapsody was already gone.

The glade of trees in which they were encamped grew thinner to the east, stretching up the side of the large hill. Rhapsody ran to the top, ignoring the slippage of snowy dead leaves underfoot, the crumbling rock and roots of the hillside, spurred on by an urgency deep within her heart.

At the crest of the hill she stopped, frozen by the sight of her mentor singing, arms outstretched before her, palms up in supplication to the stars. The tears of excitement blurred into ones of poignant fondness; in the gray light of dusk, and from the side, Oelendra looked for all the world like her own mother, singing the lauds she had taught her a lifetime ago. Rhapsody had not been able to see her mother in her dreams for a long time; she swallowed and joined in singing the lauds, blending her voice in a high harmony.

Oelendra turned as the devotions ended and smiled. Rhapsody no longer saw her mother but her friend and mentor, the Lirin champion, still in fighter's trim with shoulders as broad as Achmed's. Her long, thin braid of gray hair was tied neatly up at the nape of her neck, and her large silver eyes lit up with a fond light as soon as she saw Rhapsody.

The two women, the present Ilianchenva'ar and one who had carried Daystar Clarion a lifetime before, embraced on the windy hilltop.

'You are tired,' the Lirin champion observed, brushing a lock of golden hair out of Rhapsody's eyes.

Rhapsody smiled. 'I am also late,' she replied, smiling. 'And sorry for it.'

Oelendra nodded. 'What delayed you?'

Rhapsody put her arm around her mentor's waist. 'Come with me and I'll show you.'

Achmed had his back to the women as they approached. Night had come into its fullness, and the sky was dark as they sheltered Oelendra's mounts, two roan mares, beneath a small copse of trees near Rhapsody and Achmed's horses.

Rhapsody's eyes were shining as she brought her mentor over to the fire to meet her friend.

'Achmed, this is Oelendra. Oelendra, His Majesty, King Achmed, Warlord of the realm of Ylorc.'

Achmed rose slowly and turned in the fireshadows, his two-colored gaze coming to rest fully upon the Lirin champion, who met it serenely. A moment later the look in her eyes hardened somewhat, then relaxed again, keeping an aspect of reservation.

For his part the Firbolg king looked the Lirin champion over cursorily, then turned away. He reached down with his gloved hand and pulled a pot from the campfire.

'Hungry?'

Oelendra continued to study him. Rhapsody's glance traveled from one to the other as the silence deepened. Finally she took Oelendra's hand.

'Well, I am. Why don't you ladle it out, Achmed?' She led her mentor to the other side of the fire, where the young Lirin boy cowered, and bent down beside him. 'This is Aric, Oelendra. Aric, Oelendra is my friend – she won't hurt you.'

She turned to the Lirin champion, who was staring intensely at the boy. 'Yes,' Rhapsody said, reading her thoughts. 'His mother was obviously Liringlas.'

'Aye.' Oelendra ran a hand over her mouth. 'Do you understand what this means?'

'That there are other Liringlas here on the continent that you and Rial were not aware of?'

'Perhaps.' Oelendra stared into the fire for a moment. 'Or it could mean that the Rakshas crossed the sea to Manosse, or perhaps Gaematria, the Isle of the Sea Mages – there are Liringlas there, or at least there were. If that's the case, who knows how many women he has impregnated?'

Rhapsody shuddered, but shook her head. 'No – Rhonwyn said that there were but nine living, and only one yet to be born. And the Rakshas was dead by the time we asked her.'

Oelendra exhaled. 'Good. I'd forgotten that. Good.' A slow smile came over her face and she looked thoughtfully at the child. 'Hello, Aric,' she said in the Liringlas tongue. 'Have they treated you well?'

The child was trembling. 'Aye,' he whispered in return.

Oelendra turned to Rhapsody. 'He knows the language of our people, and yet he was obviously not raised by Liringlas. What does that tell you?'

Rhapsody patted the child's head. 'Do you think he is a natural Singer?'

Achmed handed both women tankards of soup, and a battered steel mug to Aric. Oelendra nodded her thanks, then lifted it to her lips. She took a long sip, then studied the child again.

'You would know better than I,' she said at last. 'But it seems the likeliest answer.'

'Well, there's one way to find out,' Rhapsody said. She sat down, cross-legged, next to the child. 'Aric, would you please pull down your stocking and show Oelendra your leg? She won't touch it, I promise,' she said hurriedly, watching the panic come over the child's face. Oelendra nodded in agreement.

Slowly, with faltering hands, the boy pulled back the knit sock. In the firelight the festering leg was black, with healing skin visible around the outer edges, and smelled faintly of thyme.

'I've been applying herbs since we got him, so it's beginning to improve; it was gangrenous at first,' Rhapsody said to Oelendra. She turned back to the boy. 'Can you sing your name for me, Aric?'

'Pardon, miss?' the young child asked nervously.

'Pick any note that sounds right to you, and sing your name, like this.' Rhapsody intoned his name: *Aric*.

The boy swallowed, then complied. *Aric*, he sang softly.

Rhapsody looked at Oelendra. '*Sol*,' she said. 'His Naming note is *sol*, the fifth note of the scale. He probably has older siblings somewhere. If he were firstborn, like you are, Oelendra, the natural note for him would have been *ut*.' She did not glance back at Achmed, who was also a firstborn. Oelendra nodded grimly.

'So somewhere on this continent there are other Liringlas children, now motherless.'

Rhapsody exhaled. 'Yes.' She looked closely at the leg; it had not changed. 'Try again, please, Aric. Just think about wanting your leg to be better.'

The child sang the note again, to no noticeable avail. Oelendra shrugged. Rhapsody sighed silently; then a thought occurred.

'His mother probably didn't live to see him,' she said quietly to Oelendra. 'The children of the Rakshas are all orphans, their mothers died at their births. Perhaps Aric isn't his true name.'

'Perhaps. But how can you know what the true name is?'

Rhapsody patted the boy and sat back, letting the fire warm her shoulders.

'Discovery of such a thing is a long and arduous process if the person doesn't know what name they were given,' she said, musing. 'It would take far more time than we have, and involves a good deal of trial and error. I'm not even certain the mother would have named her baby – she may have given birth alone, or died before she could name him.'

'Alas, you are probably right. He may have been named by a Filidic priest, or a Liringlas Namer, if there are indeed any still alive. Or a passing stranger, even an enemy, since he ended up a slave.'

The heat that radiated across Rhapsody's back reminded her of childhood baths before the roaring hearth. She closed her eyes, trying to picture her mother's face, failing.

'Perhaps she would just call him "baby," since she may have been too weak to even have known if the child was a boy or a girl.' She finished her soup, waited for the boy to finish his own, then leaned forward again.

'Aric, will you sing another word for me?' The child nodded. 'Good! Listen to the word I am going to say, and then sing it however it feels best to you. Here it is: *pippin*.' She gave the child an encouraging smile, and saw the warmth reflect in his clear blue eyes.

Aric inhaled deeply, wincing with the pain, then sang the word *pippin* on the note *sol*.

Oelendra and Rhapsody listened raptly; after a moment they examined his leg intently, then looked at each other. There was no visible change.

The Lirin champion patted the child's shoulder gently and began to rise, but Rhapsody signaled her to wait.

'That was very good, Aric. I'm going to take my sword out a little bit – it's all right,' she added hastily as the child's clear blue eyes clouded over with fear. 'Just a little, so that I can touch it. I promise it won't be any brighter than the campfire. Agreed?'

The child, entranced with the light in her green eyes, nodded again, as if hypnotized. Rhapsody gripped Daystar Clarion's hilt just below the crosspiece, and slowly slid it out of the black ivory scabbard, willing herself calm and sending the same thought to the sword.

The tiny flame that came forth licked quietly, burning low in response to her command. The elemental bond of fire deep within her blazed, and she was one again with the sword; its song filled her soul as her mind cleared.

She looked at the child again, trying to imagine his tragic birth, the hasty exit of his mother's tortured soul to the light as his came forward, some eight or nine years before, if she had gauged correctly. Tears of sympathetic anger sprang to her eyes and she imagined the woman writhing in the grip of the agony she no doubt felt, an agony that had begun with her violation a year or more before, and had no doubt been with her through each day of the fourteen-month Liringlas gestation.

Her hands began to tremble, though she didn't know why, and she heard the harsh, multitoned voice of Manwyn speak in her ear yet again.

I see an unnatural child born of an unnatural act. Rhapsody, you should beware of childbirth: the mother shall die, but the child shall live.

What did the wyrmkin mean? Rhapsody wondered hazily. Was this the child? Or was it the Lirin baby not yet born? Or did Manwyn's prophecy have something to do with her?

Concentrate on the child before you.

Rhapsody shook her head, clearing it instantly. In the depth of her being she had heard a voice, one she had never heard before. Perhaps it was the voice of the sword itself; Oelendra had told her many months before, during her training, that when she bore the sword it had a voice, a voice that was silenced when the sword and Seren, the star it was formed from, were parted forever. Perhaps, however, it was just the voice of her own reason speaking to her, refocusing her.

She smiled at Aric again. 'One more? Will you try one more for me, Aric?'

'Aye.' His voice was almost inaudible.

'Good. Now, sing this for me: Y pippin.' *My baby.*

Y pippin, the boy sang, his voice breaking.

Both women examined the leg again. At the edge of the festering wound, where the skin had been red, the inflammation receded before their eyes, the pus-filled center clearing to a darker red, the black changing to pink. The wound was still there, but even in the weak light of the campfire it was obvious that it was better than it had been.

'Well, would you look at that,' Oelendra murmured.

'I knew he was special when we first found him,' Rhapsody said fondly. 'Proof that out of the most evil of moments, good can still come.'

Oelendra patted the child and stood abruptly. She stared across the fire ring to the tree where Achmed had tethered Vincane.

'And what do we have here?' she asked.

'Two whores and the ugliest bastard in the world,' the boy replied with a sneer.

With exaggerated slowness Oelendra walked across the clearing and crouched down in front of Vincane, leveling her gaze into his eyes. The muscles of her back rippled with threat as she studied his face. Even from where she stood Rhapsody could see Vincane wilt under the Lirin champion's stare; she chuckled, having been the recipient on more than one occasion of that martial glance, a deathly calm, intent look that pierced to the soul from gray eyes that had seen more destruction than the imagination could allow.

'Pardon me,' Oelendra said steadily. 'I'm afraid I didn't hear you. What did you say?'

The boy tried to scoot back even farther into the tree, his insolence gone, panic taking hold.

'Your name,' Oelendra said.

'Vincane,' the boy said; his voice cracked a little.

'Well, how very nice to meet you, Vincane. I am sure we are going to make fine traveling companions. I trust I will not have to take you to task during our journey, now, will I?'

'No,' the boy said hastily.

'I thought not.' She returned to the fire, where Rhapsody was tucking a camp blanket around Aric, and nodded toward Achmed, who joined them after checking Vincane's bonds.

'You are off to get the others, then?' Oelendra asked.

'Yes,' Rhapsody replied.

'As many as we have time for,' Achmed interjected, shifting into ancient Lirin after a meaningful glance at the captive. 'We had hoped to capture the gladiator at or after the winter festival, but that is impossible now.'

Oelendra nodded. 'Where are you off to next?'

Rhapsody cast a glance at both children; Aric was fast asleep, and Vincane appeared to be dozing lightly, but it was hard to tell if he was merely pretending.

'The Hintervold,' she replied. 'Rhonwyn said that there were two children there, and one in Zafhiel. The others are in Roland and the Nonaligned States, closer to you. We should be able to get all of them but the oldest before the baby is born; we'll determine what to do to obtain the gladiator after that.'

Achmed exhaled in annoyance. He spoke little Ancient Lirin, but he had been expecting her words.

'We may not even get all the others. Winter is deepening daily. A few more complications like we had in Yarim, and we will have to abandon one, possibly more.'

'No,' Rhapsody said firmly. 'We are going to get them all. We have to. Someone has to. They're just children.'

'They are not children, they're abominations,' Oelendra interjected. Both Rhapsody and Achmed looked at her in surprise. 'I cannot believe this is not clear to you, Rhapsody. Look at them – whether they are sweet and shy, or nasty and brutish, they are half-demon – can't you see it?'

Achmed smiled slightly. 'Thank you.' He turned to Rhapsody. 'Perhaps now that you have heard this from someone other than me you will listen.'

'I'm dumbfounded,' Rhapsody murmured after a moment. 'This is something I've come to expect from Achmed, but never from you, Oelendra. How can you curse these children with the association of their father, any more than they already are cursed? They're just children, like they would be if their father were a thief or a murderer. Look at Aric. He's *Liringlas*, for gods' sake!'

'His mother was Liringlas,' Oelendra said seriously. '*He* is an abomination with Liringlas ancestry; 'tis not the same. Somewhere in the veins of both those children runs the blood of the demon, Rhapsody, a F'dor. You apparently do not grasp what this means.

'In the old days there were far more F'dor, but their numbers were finite. A whole pantheon of them existed, with the most powerful of them even being catalogued in old manuscripts by name and tendencies. Upworld, or in the vault of the netherworld, if they were killed by a Dhracian while in corporeal form, 'twas one fewer to plague the world.

'Now, however, one very clever F'dor has found a way for its blood to reproduce without having to diminish its power by breaking open any of its own to do so. 'Tis a most disturbing turn of events. Through the Rakshas the F'dor has perpetuated its demonic line, which opens a very dangerous door to the future, and what we may have to face one day very soon.

'I know when you look at them you see children. You must learn to look deeper, and see what is really there, lurking beneath the surface, even in the sweetest of them. Otherwise you may be caught unaware.'

Rhapsody exhaled. 'Please tell me I am not making a mistake entrusting them to you,' she said, her voice calm but her eyes shining with intensity. 'We need to stay the course, to follow the plan. If we can get them to the Lord and Lady Rowan, and if they can separate out the demon blood, we will not only have the means to find the demon, but the children should be freed from whatever evil taint they now carry. They will be saved from the damnation of the vault, of being eternally demonic. But I need you to be honest with me, Oelendra; can you keep a cool head about this? Because if you can't, I need to come up with another plan. I will not allow your hatred of the F'dor to jeopardize their safety.'

Anger burned in the Lirin champion's eyes. 'Am I to imagine that you just questioned my ability to keep a cool head?'

Rhapsody exhaled and crossed her arms.

Oelendra pressed again, her body tensing. 'Say what you mean, Rhapsody.'

'I just did,' Rhapsody replied tonelessly. 'You hate the F'dor to the exclusion of all other motivations. I need you to see your part in this as not just assisting Achmed to find the demon, but to help shelter and protect these children as well. They may be demon-spawn, but they were born of innocent women, and they have immortal souls. I need you to remember that. You cannot allow them to be the target of your hatred of their father. Elsewise we are no better than the demon itself.' A humorous twinkle entered her eyes. 'There is my answer to your question. If it would help you hear it better I could set it to music and play it on my lute – oh, wait. Now, what happened to that lute again?'

Oelendra blinked, then winced, then succumbed to a guilty chuckle, remembering how she had smashed the instrument into kindling in a rage over the demon. Rhapsody laughed and put her arms around her mentor.

'Forgive me?' she asked as she embraced Oelendra.

'For speaking the truth?' Oelendra replied. 'No one, especially a Namer, should apologize for that. And you have my vow, Iliachenva'ar – I will protect them with my life.'

'I know you will,' Rhapsody whispered in her ear. She gave Oelendra's broad shoulders a final squeeze, then turned back to Achmed as Oelendra went to ready her horses.

'Did you feed Vincane?'

'To what?'

'Not humorous. Oelendra needs to leave forthwith, and we have to be on our way as well.'

'He wasn't particularly cooperative, but he has inhaled soup through various holes in his head. I was tempted to make a few more.'

'Well, it probably won't hurt for him to be hungry until Oelendra makes camp again.'

While Achmed tied the apprentice across one of the roans' saddles, Oelendra came back to Rhapsody and handed her a small cage made of reeds. In it a black winterbird fluttered, then settled into a curious stare.

'Here's another avian messenger for you. I will bring one to you at each meeting place, so you can tell me where you will be.'

'Thank you,' Rhapsody said, embracing Oelendra again. 'Please know that I do appreciate all that you are doing to help us, and regret the danger in which we are putting you. But you were the only one I knew that would be able to accomplish this successfully.'

'I am honored by the trust of the Iliachenva'ar,' Oelendra replied, smiling as Achmed hoisted Aric over her own mount to ride with her, far away from Vincane. 'Look after yourself, Rhapsody – I fear that there may be eyes on these children.'

'There are. And they are the best eyes that they could ever wish to be watching over them. Travel safely. I will notify you when we have the next two.'

Oelendra nodded, then looked up into Achmed's face again. They stared at each other for another moment; then Oelendra nodded, mounted, and rode off, holding the reins of Vincane's horse tightly as she went.

'By the way,' she called to Achmed over her shoulder as she left, 'once this is over I expect you to repay me by sending her to help unite the divisive factions of the Lirin kingdom again. We will need every Lirin soul ready for what is to come.'

Achmed hid a smile as Rhapsody waved back. What the Lirin champion did not know was that he had already repaid her a lifetime ago by not accepting any of the multitudinous contracts on her life he was offered back in the old world.

12

The Old Cymrian Forges, Ylorc

Grunthor rounded the bend in the dark corridor with his two aides-de-camp, whistling cheerfully. He was in fine fettle on this particular morning; the watches had all gone well, the recruits were coming nicely to heel, the reinforcements in the Hidden Realm and the great watchtower of Grivven Post were performing to expectation. He was on his way to his last stops on his morning inspection tour, the two enormous forges where the weapons were produced for export and for the armament of the Firbolg army.

The former was the first stop; this was a commercial smithy, and the product it put forth was confined to the less sophisticated designs that he and Achmed had decided were safe to allow into the hands of their trading partners in Roland. *If they were anything that resembled a threat I might not have considered giving them access to even these crude weapons,* Achmed had recounted to him and to Rhapsody over a bottle of wine provided by Lord Stephen as a gift to celebrate the trade agreement last spring. *But as far as I can see, Roland won't pose a problem until it unites, and even then, they'd break themselves on the mountain before we'd have to teach them another lesson. Putting these inferior weapons into the trade stream may make them overconfident, give them a false idea of what we are capable of making.* The king had spun his wine in his glass, then downed it. *No, I'm not worried about Roland,* he had said, gazing through the glass at the fire. *Sorbold, on the other hand, will always worry me.*

The better of the weapons, those made in the second forge, were Achmed's original designs: a heavy but well-balanced throwing knife with three blades; short, compact crossbows with extra recoil for use in the tunnels of Ylorc; split arrowheads and heavy darts for blowguns, balanced and designed for deeper penetration; midnight-blue steel drawknives which were really razor-edged hooks that replaced the makeshift close-combat weapons of many Bolg; and of course the disks of his own cwellan, the strange, asymmetrical weapon he had crafted back on the Island of Serendair and had used to ply his trade of assassination very successfully so long ago.

Grunthor smiled at the blast of heat that slapped his face as he came into the first of the weapons foundries. He looked up with pride at the half-dozen tiered galleries of anvils and fires. Long-dead Gwylliam had designed the smithy complex as if he thought to work there himself. The forges were attached to a central ventilation system that drew the soot gently rumbling through the cacophony, high toward the peaks where the heat was made use of elsewhere before it escaped. The damper system allowed the individual forges to be controlled by teams of only two or three workers each, supported by some few dozen water carriers and coal-hod bearers. In addition to the natural bellows of the flume, each forge had its own crank bellows, the action of which also drew cooler air for the general circulation, and made the place seem less like an inferno and more like the practice hall for some genius if lunatic orchestra.

The forgemaster handed him the inventory records, and watched anxiously as Grunthor reviewed them, then checked the lines of artisans who were smelting and hammering, filing and tempering. He counted each of the finished weapons against the inventory list, and found all accounted for. In addition, the number of culls had dropped considerably from where it had been during training; they were learning.

Satisfied, he returned the inventory to the forgemaster and turned to the craftsmen.

'All right, gents, good work. Keep it up, eh?'

He returned the salute of the forgemaster and strode off with his aides-de-camp, singing a tavern song as he left. His ringing bass echoed up the mountain hall before him, warning the next group of smiths of his imminent arrival.

> She 'as eyes as big as two fried eggs
> And skin as green as the sea
> If you open your coin purse, she'll open her legs,
> She's my girl in Ter-i-lee.

As the sound of his voice drifted away, three of the Bolg forge handlers exchanged a quick glance, then returned to their work in the flickering shadows of the pure, intense fire that came directly from the heart of the Earth.

Nimeth, Northwestern Sorbold

The bell that signaled the back door had opened jangled sharply. Old Ned the tinker had closed up shop several hours before, and had settled down before the fire grate with a pint of stout and a bowl of lamb stew. Immediately he reached next to the fire for one of his hammers. He rose with a creak and patted the hammer before hiding it within the folds of his stained leather apron; Old Ned was in his twilight years, but still possessed of muscular arms and a strong grip.

'Who is ye? Who be there?'

In the weak fireshadows cast by the coals in the grate two faces appeared near the back door. Even in the dark they appeared hirsute and coarse, though not as coarse as one might have expected the faces of Bolg to be, or at least so Old Ned thought. They stared at Ned thoughtfully, as they always did, serious but not threatening.

Old Ned smiled and put down the hammer.

'Well, good evening, my lads,' he said, rubbing the chill from his hands. 'Reckon 'tis been at least a month since last you came. Have ya brought me the last of the goods?'

The men exchanged a glance without taking their eyes off him, then pulled forth an oilskin sack tied with string from the darkness between them. They dropped it onto the planks against the back wall that served as a counter, then retreated to a safe distance back into the shadows.

Old Ned hobbled nimbly over to the counter, undid the string, and pulled the sack open eagerly. Impatient, he upended it onto the planks and cackled aloud with glee at its contents.

A strange, circular, three-bladed throwing knife, similar to the small ones they had brought a few months before but much heftier; a pair of long, broad swords with splayed, layered metal tips; and a shiny disk, thin as a butterfly's wing but sharp as a razor.

Weapons of Bolg manufacture.

'Ha!' shouted Old Ned, unable to contain his excitement. 'Beauties, boys, beauties! They'll fetch a fine price indeed.' His eyes were glowing with avarice as they searched the shadows to find the dark faces once more. He picked up the whisper-thin circle.

'I'll need but two more of these, and then we will have a bargain fulfilled, yes we will.'

'No.' The word spat forth from one of the shadows deeper in the room than he expected; Old Ned turned and saw the eyes in one angular face glaring back at him. 'Now. Give.'

Old Ned drew himself up to his full height and picked up the hammer again. He focused on the eyes in the dark, staring the man down like a stag or a rat in the gutter.

'Sod off,' he snarled. '*I* set the price, and *I* decide when it's eno—'

His voice choked off as a blade, thin as a ribbon and curved, was pressed against his neck from behind by the second Bolg.

'Geep – auck—' Old Ned sputtered. 'Please—'

'Give now,' his captor intoned in a harsh voice. 'You have weapons. Give now.'

'Yes!' Old Ned squeaked, coughing raggedly. 'I will! I will! Let go!'

He lurched forward as the Bolg released him, then staggered to the counter, which he gripped with both hands and leaned his head over, panting.

'It's – it's back here,' he muttered, walking behind the counter. He reached beneath it, making sure to be able to see both Bolg, then drew forth a battered metal pot, plain of design, with a broken handle. He tossed it weakly to the Bolg who had held him captive.

'Don' know what ya want it fer,' he mumbled. 'Ugly as sin. Not worth nothin'.'

The Bolg who held the pot examined it quickly, checking the inside, then nodded quickly to the other. They slipped into the shadows, making no sound with the jangling chimes as they disappeared out the back door.

Old Ned muttered a fine string of curses as he rubbed his neck, then turned his attention to the Bolg weapons. He could not imagine for all the world why anyone would be willing to trade such unique, finely made armaments for a pot that was no more than a piece of rubbish. *Proof of what is said about the Bolg,* he thought as he held the shiny disk up to the dying fire's light.

Not a grain of sense among them, but they sure make fine weapons.

13

Winter Festival, Haguefort, Province of Navarne

The line of carriages outside the rosy brown gates of Haguefort stretched for as far as the eye could see. A great convergence of wagons choked the entrance to Haguefort, squeezing in between the two slender bell towers that marked the beginning of Stephen Navarne's lands, slowing the coaches to a crawl.

The holy man sighed inwardly and sipped his cordial. *Patience,* he reminded himself, glancing out the carriage window at the billowing banners of colored silk that adorned the bell towers, flapping merrily in the icy breeze. His constant admonition to his inner demonic voice, wheedling and restless. *Patience.*

He had chosen to remain in his wheeled coach, rather than switch to one of the sleighs proffered at the eastern border of Navarne by the duke's servants, under the theory that Stephen's well-maintained roads and thoroughfares would provide swifter passage to Haguefort than the thin snowpack crusting the fields and rolling hills. He had misjudged the temperature, which had remained warm through a full day of intense snowfall followed by rain, and then dropped overnight, freezing the fields of the province into a sheet of glare ice that would have been well suited to a horse-drawn glider.

Now he was caught amid a great mass of carriages, wagons, and foot traffic. The braying of animals being brought to the carnival along with the clamor of human voices raised in excitement was enough to make him gulp his brandy in the hope that it would drown out the cacophony of merriment all around him. *Patience.*

Soon all things would be set in motion. Soon his wait would be over.

Soon his patience would be rewarded.

Lord Stephen Navarne squinted in the sun, then shielded his eyes and followed the outstretched finger of Quentin Baldasarre, the Duke of Bethe Corbair. Baldasarre was pointing from where they stood at the hillside height of the castle gates down the vast lines of sight to the road below.

'There! I think I see Tristan's coach – it's logjammed in the middle there, right between your two bell towers out front,' Quentin said, dropping his arm when Stephen nodded in agreement. 'Poor bastard – I'll wager he's trapped in there with Madeleine.'

'Gods. Poor Tristan,' said Dunstin Baldasarre, Quentin's younger brother.

Stephen suppressed a smile. 'Shame on you both. Isn't Madeleine your cousin?'

Dunstin sighed comically. 'Too true, I'm afraid to say,' he said, shielding his face in feigned shame. 'But please, gentle lord, do not judge our family too harshly for producing her. No one save the All-God is perfect.'

'Though some of us are less so than others,' said Quentin, draining his mug of spiced rum.

The carriages were discharging their passengers slowly now to keep them from being trampled by the wagons of townsfolk. Stephen motioned to Gerald Owen, his chamberlain.

'Owen, send the third regiment to see if they can direct some of the wagon traffic to the forest road and through the western gates,' he said. He waited until Owen had nodded his understanding and departed, then turned to the Baldasarre brothers.

'If Tristan has his way, one day Madeleine will be our queen,' he said seriously. 'Perhaps it is best not to joke so much at her expense.'

'My, we're a grumpy old sod today, Navarne,' said Dunstin thickly. 'You apparently haven't had enough of this lovely mulled wine.'

'That's because you finished off a legion's worth all by your rotten self and there's none left for another living soul,' Quentin retorted before Stephen could say anything. 'Next time perhaps we should just fill a trough with it and let you guzzle with your snout in the trench. Souse.'

'Well, Cedric is here, at last,' said Stephen hastily as Dunstin gave Quentin an angry shove. 'His carriage is unloading now, along with the ale wagons of the count.'

'Huzzah!' bellowed Dunstin. 'Can you see which one is Andrew's?'

Stephen looked into the sun again and spied a tall young man, lean and darkly bearded, directing a quartet of wagons loaded with wooden barrels. 'The one in the front, taking to the forest road now – there, can you see him?' He waved to the man, and received a quick wave in return. Lord Stephen smiled.

Cedric Canderre, the Baldasarres' uncle and father of Madeleine Canderre, the Lord Roland's intended, was duke and regent of the province that bore his name. Though his lands were not as politically powerful as most of the other provinces, Cedric's arrival was always anticipated greatly at the winter carnival.

The reason for this was twofold. First, Cedric Canderre was a merry-maker of great reputation, a portly, jolly man with an appetite for all of the finer things in life and the excesses they could lead to. When Madeleine's mother was alive, some of those appetites had been a source of great consternation and occasional embarrassment to the family. Her untimely death had left the door open for Cedric to delight in his indulgences, and he did so now with a vigor that was enjoyable to be around, especially at a festival.

The second, and probably more pressing, reason was the bounty of his province that came with him in the wagons. Canderre was a realm that produced luxury items, amenities that were known throughout the world for their unsurpassed quality, in particular various types of alcohol, wines, cordials, brandies, and other distillations. Cedric's merchants charged high prices for these goods, and paid no tariffs to his interprovincial trading partners, so the free distribution of these rare and pricey treasures at Stephen's carnival was always anticipated with great excitement.

Sir Andrew Canderre, the Viscount of Paige, the northeastern region of Canderre that lay at the borders of Yarim and the Hintervold, was Cedric's eldest son and primary councilor, and a good friend of Stephen Navarne.

Count Andrew was the diametric opposite of his father; where Cedric was stout and moved with a portly man's gait, Andrew was lean and nimble, often working long hours beside the merchants and carters of his province. He was also known to participate in the manual labor that sustained his holdings; the stables and barns of the nobleman were legendary for their cleanliness. Where Cedric was self-indulgent, humorous, and quick-tempered, Andrew was wry, generous, and patient. Between them the House of Canderre was well regarded, in Roland, across the sea, and around much of the sea-trading world.

Stephen shielded his eyes again as his smile broadened; Sir Andrew was making his way toward them, having arranged his caravan's passage through the keep's gates.

'Looks to be another good one, Stephen,' he said, extending his hand.

'Well met, Andrew,' Lord Stephen answered, shaking it.

'Well, there he is, the Ale Count, the Baron of the Brewery, the Lord of Libations,' slurred Dunstin, extending a tankard to him. 'Impeccable timing, as always, Sir Jrew. You're just in time to spare us from this inferior swill of Stephen's. Have a swig and you'll see what I mean.'

'As always, a pleasure to see you as well, Dunstin,' said Sir Andrew dryly. 'Quentin.'

'Jrew, you're looking well; good winter to you,' said Quentin. 'How's your intended, Lady Jecelyn of Bethe Corbair?'

'Good health to you, sir, and may next year's solstice find you the same,' replied Andrew. 'Jecelyn is well, thank you. Stephen, may I impose on your time for a moment? I want to make certain the carters deliver the casks to where you want them.'

'Of course. Gentlemen, please excuse us.' Stephen bowed politely to the Baldasarre brothers, took Andrew's elbow, and led him down the path to the buttery of the keep where the forest road entered.

'Thank you,' he said to Andrew as soon as they were out of earshot.

'My pleasure.'

Llauron, the Invoker of the Filids, smiled as he watched the Patriarch's benisons exit their carriages to the lilting strains of Stephen's court orchestra carried on the wind. The various Blessers had arrived as much as five hours apart, yet some had remained in their carriages all that time in order to ensure that they made a proper entrance. Word from Sepulvarta had indicated that the Patriarch was in his last days, and rumors were flying hot and fierce among the nobility and the clergy alike as to who the successor would be.

The first to leave his carriage was Ian Steward, brother of Tristan Steward, the Lord Roland. He was the Blesser of the provinces of Canderre and Yarim, though his basilica, Vrackna, the ringed temple of elemental fire, was located in the province of Bethany. Bethany, the capital seat, sent some of its faithful to worship in the basilica of the Star, Lianta'ar, the Patriarch's own basilica in the holy city-state of Sepulvarta.

Despite Tristan's influence, it was unlikely in Llauron's opinion that the Patriarch would choose Ian as his successor. While a likable man of seemingly good heart, Ian Steward was fairly young and inexperienced to be given such a tremendous responsibility. Still, he might be the Patriarch's choice just for that youth. Several of the other benisons were almost as old as the Patriarch, and would bring an inescapable instability when they themselves passed on to their rewards in the Afterlife a few years hence.

Two of the best examples of this problem were the next to disembark, and they did so together, leaning on each other for support. Lanacan Orlando, the heartier of the two, was the Blesser of Bethe Corbair, and held services in his city beneath the holy bell tower in the beautiful basilica of Ryles Cedelian, the cathedral dedicated to the wind. Quiet and unassuming, Lanacan was known as a talented healer, perhaps as talented as Khaddyr, but he was nervous around crowds and not particularly charismatic. Llauron did not judge him to be a likely successor, either, and was fairly certain that Lanacan would be relieved to see himself off the list as well.

Colin Abernathy, the Blesser of the Nonaligned States, to the south, who leaned on Lanacan as they made their way across the icy path, was older and frailer than his friend, but more politically powerful. He had no basilica in which to hold services, a fact that often occurred to Llauron as he ruminated on who the host of the F'dor might be. A demonic spirit would not be able to stand in a place of blessed ground, and each of the basilicas were the holiest of blessed ground. The five elements themselves consecrated the ground on which they were built. Even a F'dor of tremendous power should not be able to stand in such a place.

But Colin Abernathy didn't have to. His services were held in an enormous arena, an unblessed basilica, where he tended a congregation of many diverse groups of followers – Lirin from the plains, Sorbold citizens too far from their own cathedral to make the pilgrimage, seafarers in the fishing villages ever farther south, and a general population of malcontents.

Abernathy had been the second choice to succeed the last Patriarch, losing out to the current one, and so was long known to grumble about the leadership of the church. If he was the F'dor's host, he would be looking around to find a younger host body soon, Llauron knew. But the Invoker was more inclined to believe that the beast clung not to a member of the clergy, but to one of the provincial leaders, which opened the possibility of it even being his dear friend Stephen Navarne.

The fourth benison chose a moment of great fanfare to disembark from his carriage. Philabet Griswold, the Blesser of Avonderre-Navarne, who held sway over the great water basilica Abbat Mythlinis, was younger than either of the two elderly benisons, while still old enough to claim the wisdom of advanced years. He was pompous and self-important; Llauron found his arrogance alternately infuriating and amusing. Griswold had made no secret of his desire to be Patriarch, and had waited until the holy anthem of Sepulvarta was being played to alight from his carriage. His timing was impeccable; it seemed as if the anthem were playing in his honor.

The dark face of Nielash Mousa, the Blesser of Sorbold, resembled a thundercloud as he stepped out of his coach a moment behind Griswold. Their rivalry for the Patriarchy, long kept secret for political purposes, was now all but an open contest for the clerical throne of Sepulvarta. Mousa had come up from his arid land, braving the snow and bad traveling conditions for the opportunity to gain exposure at the winter carnival. His basilica was the only one of the five elemental cathedrals not within the territory of Roland; Terreanfor, the temple of earth, lay deep within the southern Teeth in Sorbold, hidden within the Night Mountain. His candidacy for the Patriarchy was an uphill battle, and Llauron knew it. The contest between Mousa and Griswold was shaping up to be a bloody one.

'Ah, Your Grace, I see you've arrived safely! Welcome!' Stephen's voice carried tones of genuine pleasure, and Llauron turned, smiling, to greet the young duke.

'Good solstice, my son,' he said, clasping Stephen's hand. He surveyed the festival grounds, with their bright pageantry set against the pristine field of virgin snow under a clear blue sky. 'It looks to be a marvelous fete, as always. What is the official snow sculpture this year?'

'They've done a scale model of the Judiciary of Yarim, Your Grace.'

Llauron nodded approvingly. 'A beautiful building, to be certain. I shall be fascinated to see how they managed to make the snow hold up in minarets.'

'May I offer you a brandy? Count Andrew Canderre has brought a fine supply, and a special cask in particular.' Stephen held out a silver snifter. 'I saved you some of the reserve.'

The Invoker's face lit up, and he took the brandy happily. 'Bless him, and you, my son. Nothing like a little warmth in the depth of winter.'

'I see your chiefs are here as well; very good,' said Stephen, waving to Khaddyr as the healer came into sight from behind the white guest tents. 'Is it possible that I actually see Gavin among them?'

Llauron laughed. 'Yes, indeed, the planets must be aligned this solstice, and Gavin's schedule allows him to be here; amazing, isn't it?'

'Indeed! There he is, behind Lark. And Ilyana, there with Brother Aldo. I'm so glad you all could make it.'

Llauron leaned forward and whispered conspiratorially into Stephen's ear. 'Well, the place is *crawling* with benisons. I had to bring all the Filidic leaders just to prevent a possible mass conversion away from the True Faith.'

Tristan Steward extended his hand to his fiancée and assisted her gently down from their carriage, struggling to keep from losing control and tossing her, face-first, into the deepest snowbank he could find.

I've died, and the Underworld looks exactly like this one, only I am doomed to spend Eternity in the constant presence of this soul-sucking witch, he thought wearily. *What damnable evils could I have possibly committed to deserve this?* He had learned a new skill, the skill of half-listening, on the trip from Bethany to Stephen's keep, and since Madeleine's endless nattering had shown no sign of abating, even as she descended the steps of the coach, he employed it now.

He glanced about the ground of Haguefort and the fields beyond, glistening in the fair light of midmorning. Nature and Stephen had done well by each other. Sparkling jewels of ice, left over from the storm of the previous night, adorned the branches of the trees that lined the pathways of the keep, frosted with cottony clouds of fresh snow. Stephen, in turn, had decorated Haguefort's twin guardian bell towers with shining white and silver banners proclaiming the symbol of his House, and had dressed the tall lampposts that were carefully placed throughout the keep's courtyard and walkways with long spirals of white ribbons, which spun slowly like sedate maypoles in the stiff breeze. The effect was enchanting.

In the distance the fields had been groomed for the sleigh races and other contests of wintersport, with large tents erected to house the cookfires and the thousands of common folk from outside the province. Bright banners in every color of the rainbow adorned the rolling fields down to the newly built wall that his cousin hoped would offer protection to his lands and subjects. Tristan could see the enormous bonfire pit being stocked with dry brush for the celebratory blaze that would take place on the last evening, a conflagration for which the festival's host was famous.

The bite of the fresh winter wind stung his nose, and he caught the scent of hickory chips burning. It was a smell that reminded him of childhood, and the festivals of Stephen's father. As boys he and his cousin and their friends, Andrew Canderre, the Baldasarre brothers, Gwydion of Manosse, dead twenty years now, and a host of others had looked forward to the solstice each year with an excitement unmatched by any other event. His eyes burned with the poignant memory.

More painful than any other in their sweetness were the memories of Prudence. His childhood friend, his first lover, a laughing peasant girl with strawberry curls and a wicked sense of humor, his confessor, his conscience. In the days of his youth she was part of the Wolf Pack, as he and his friends were called, participating with them in the sled races and the tugs-of-war, the pie eatings and the snow battles. Matching them, besting them. Stealing the hearts of his mates. Prudence. How he had loved her then, with a young boy's innocence blossoming into something deeper.

84

Tristan's throat caught as he and Madeleine passed Haguefort's main portico, the place where in those days Prudence had waited for him at night to slip away from his family's guest rooms within the keep, where the nobility stayed. He could always spy her from the balcony, a glint of shining red-blond curls in the torchlight, waiting for him, and him alone. Even years later, when the dukedom passed to him, and she was his servant, she still awaited him in the portico, watching furtively, giggling madly when he finally slipped away to her, finding a hiding place to make secret love among the thousands of drunken revelers, celebrating their youth, their bond, their lives.

How he loved her still. Her brutal death at the hands of the Bolg had taken the joy out of him, joy he had never realized really always belonged to Prudence, that he was merely borrowing. Without her his days were filled with melancholy and guilt, because it was his own selfishness that had brought about her death. He had sent her into the jaws of the monsters, and she had never returned.

None of his friends and fellow dukes, not even Stephen, believed that her murder was the work of the Bolg, no matter how hard he had tried to convince them. *But that will be over soon*, he thought grimly. Soon the arguments would end.

'Tristan?'

He blinked, and forced a smile as he looked down into Madeleine's unpleasantly angular face.

'Yes, dearest?'

His fiancée exhaled in annoyance. 'You haven't heard a thing I've said, have you?'

Rotely Tristan lifted her gloved hand to his lips and kissed it.

'Darling, I've been hanging on your every word.'

For all that the elite and influential of Roland utilized Stephen's festival to make public shows and secret bargains, it was the common folk for whom it was actually held. Winter was a harsh and difficult time in most of Roland, a season in which the average citizen withdrew into his dwelling, having battened it down as much as possible, and struggled to survive the bitter months. The carnival gave them an opportunity to celebrate the season before winter gave them reason to rue it, as it did every year.

Stephen counted on the annual pattern of weather to allow the carnival to take place at the mildest part of early winter, and with one exception in twenty years, he had been successful. His friendship with the Invoker of the Filids, the religious order that worshiped nature, granted him access to their information about upcoming storms and thaws, freezing winds and snowfalls, so their impressive ability to predict the weather ensured a successful event. Indeed, it was commonly believed that the Filidic order not only studied and predicted the weather, but had it in their power to control it as well, especially the Invoker. If that was the case, they exercised a good deal of largesse on Stephen's behalf, judging by the consistently fine weather his solstice festival enjoyed.

The first two days of the festival were marked by the pageantry of it, with games and races, contests and performances, dancing and merrymaking fueled by excesses of fine food and drink.

The third and final day was the religious observance of the solstice, with ceremonies in both canons. It was here that the religious posturing went on, Filid against Patrician, all very subtle, and worse since the Patriarch had begun to decline. In years when the Invoker predicted a storm or harsh weather before the solstice and better weather following it, the order of events at the carnival was switched, and the religious observances were held first, with the festival in the two days following. When this occurred the carnival was invariably spoiled, so Stephen was pleased that the weather had cooperated this year, allowing the festivities to happen first.

Now he sat on the reviewing platform with Tristan, Madeleine, and the religious leaders, who were all talking among themselves, watching the various races and games, occasionally joining in one himself.

His son, Gwydion Navarne, had proven adept at Snow Snakes, a contest where long smooth sticks were launched through icy channels hollowed out in the snow. Stephen had abandoned royal protocol and had danced excitedly at the fringes of the competition, hooting and cheering Gwydion through the semifinals and consoling him at his loss in the end. The boy had not really needed any consolation; he had broken into a sincere smile at the announcement of the winner, a redheaded farm lad named Scoutin, and extended a gracious hand of congratulations.

As the lads shook, it was all Stephen could do to hold back tears of pride and loss. *How like Gwydion of Manosse and me they look,* he thought, thinking back to his childhood friend, Llauron's only son. He glanced behind him at the Invoker, who must have been sharing the thought by the smile and nod that he gave Stephen.

He was now anxiously awaiting the outcome of Melisande's race, a comical contest where small sleds, on which a fat sheep was placed, were tied to the participants' waists with a rope. The object of the race required both child and sheep to make it across the finish line together, but this afternoon the sheep had other plans. Melly's merry giggle was unmistakable; it wafted over his head on the steamy air as she toppled into the snow yet again, then set off back toward the starting gate, chasing a bleating ewe.

She came reluctantly into her father's arms and was swathed in a rough wool blanket handed to him by Rosella, her governess.

'Father, *please!* I'm not cold, and we're going to miss the making of the snow candy!'

'Snow candy?' Tristan asked, smiling. 'That brings back memories, Navarne.' Madeleine raised an eyebrow, and the Lord Roland turned her way. 'You must try some, darling, it's marvelous. The cooks heat enormous vats of caramel sugar to boiling, then drizzle it in squiggles onto the snow where it hardens in the cold; then they dip it in chocolate and almond cream. It becomes quite the melee to see who can get some of the first batch.'

'On the *snow?*' Madeleine asked in horror.

'Not on the ground, m'lady,' said Stephen quickly, tousling Melisande's hair in the attempt to shake the look of surprise at Madeleine's reaction from her face. 'Clean snow is gathered and laid out on large cooking boards.'

'Nonetheless, it sounds repulsive,' Madeleine said.

Stephen rose as Tristan looked away and sighed.

'Come along, Melly. If we hurry we might get some of the first batch.' He tried to avoid Tristan's face; he couldn't help but notice that his cousin wore the look of a man who had lost the whole world.

On this, the feast of the longest night of the year, darkness came early, and none too soon. As the light left the sky the merrymakers and revelers moved on to the celebratory dining, an event in and of itself.

Rosella stood in the shadow of the cook tent, watching the festivities with delight. Melisande and Gwydion were chasing around beside their father near the open-air pit where four oxen were roasting over the gleaming coals, filling the frosty air with merry laughter and joyful shrieking. While the children were in his company the duke had dismissed her from her duties, suggesting she take in some of the glorious sights of the festival. She had obeyed. Standing hidden, she was observing the glorious sight that most delighted her heart.

From the day four years ago when she had been brought to Haguefort in her late teens to tend to the children of the recently widowed duke, Rosella had been enamored of Lord Stephen. Unlike Lord MacAlwaen, the baron to whom her father had originally indentured her, Lord Stephen was kind and considerate, and treated her like a member of his family rather than as the servant that she was. He was distantly pleasant at first; his young wife, the Lady Lydia Navarne, had been brutally murdered a few weeks before, and Lord Stephen wandered around for a long time in a daze, tending to the responsibilities of his duchy and family with the efficiency of one whose mind is engaged but whose soul is elsewhere.

As time passed, the duke became more alive, as if waking from a long sleep, spurred mostly by the need to be an effective father to his motherless children. Rosella's fondness for him continued to grow as she witnessed his affectionate ministrations to Melisande and Gwydion, whom she loved as if they were her own. Her daydreams were filled with the silly romantic impossibilities of class warfare, of the unspannable chasm between lord and servant crumbling away, leaving a shining bridge between their two lives. The fact that Lord Stephen was oblivious of her feelings allowed her the freedom to imagine as she would, free of the guilt that a different reality might bring.

'Good solstice, my child.'

Rosella started and backed into the fluttering fabric of the cook tent at the sound of the sonorous voice. The rich scent of roasting meat filled her nose, along with a sour hint of burning flesh in fire.

'Good solstice, Your Grace.' Her heart pounded desperately against her ribs. She had not seen the religious leader step out of the firepit's shadows. It was almost as if he had been part of the dancing flames the moment before he had made himself known to her.

Lord Stephen's close ties to the religious leaders of both faiths, the Patriarchal canon and that of the Filids, had made the presence of holy men common around the keep. Rosella, raised from childhood as a Partriarchal adherent, was equally uncomfortable around both types of clergymen.

The holy man smiled, and put out his hand. Almost as if her hand had its own will, she felt her palm rotate upward and her fingers open slowly. She could not tear her gaze away from the glistening eyes that reflected the flames of the cookfire.

A tiny bag of soft cloth was dropped into her open palm.

'I assume you know what to do with this, my child.'

Rosella didn't, but her mouth answered for her.

'Yes, Your Grace.'

The holy man's eyes gleamed red in the firelight. 'Good, good. May your winter be blessed and healthy; may spring find you the same.'

'Thank you, Your Grace.'

'Rosella?'

Rosella looked down to see Melisande tugging impatiently at her skirt. She glanced toward the roasting oxen where the duke of Navarne and his son were watching her quizzically.

'Come, Rosella, come! The ox is ready to be carved, and Father said to invite you to sup with us!'

Rosella nodded dumbly, then turned back to where the holy man had stood, but he was gone.

The campfires crackled in the darkness, sending tendrils of smoke skyward, mixed with the raucous sounds of drunken singing and merry laughter echoing across the frosty fields of Haguefort. The noise of celebration, wild and chaotic; it scratched against Tristan Steward's eardrums like a nail. He shook his head, leaned back against the cold wall of the dark portico in which he was sitting, and took another swig from the bottle of reserve port Cedric Canderre had slipped to him after the singing competition that evening.

Once the orgiastic sounds of the winter festival had been sweet music to his ears. There was a sense of sheer abandon that filled the air during the solstice, a heady, reckless excitement that stirred his blood. Now, without Prudence there to share the thrill, the passion of it, it was nothing but cacophony. He was drinking the port in great gulping swigs, hoping to drown out the din, or at least reduce it to a dull roar.

More than the noise of celebration, he was trying to silence the voice in his head. Tristan had long been unable to escape the whisper, or identify the one who had first spoken the words to him.

He vaguely recalled the day he first heard it. He thought it might have been after the awful meeting in summer when he had summoned all the Orlandan clergy and nobility together in the vain attempt to convince them to consolidate their armies and wreak vengeance on the Bolg, ostensibly for their attack on his guards, but in truth retaliation for Prudence's brutal death. His fellow regents had thought him out of his mind, had refused unanimously to support him, even his cousin, Stephen Navarne, who was as close to a brother as Tristan had ever had.

It seemed to him that after that meeting someone had sought to console him – Stephen perhaps? *No*, he thought as he shook his head foggily. *Not Stephen.* Someone older, with kindly eyes that seemed to burn a bit at the edges. A holy man, he thought, but whether he was of Sepulvarta or Gwynwood Tristan had no idea. He struggled to make his mind bend around the image, to fill in the spaces around those disembodied eyes, but his brain refused to listen. He was left with nothing more than the same words, repeated over and over again whenever he was lost in silence.

You may be the one after all.

Tristan felt suddenly cold. It was a sensation he had remembered when he first heard the words, a chill that belied the warmth in the holy man's eyes. He drew his greatcloak closer to him and shifted on the cold stone bench, trying to warm his chilling legs.

The one for what? he had asked.

The one to return peace and security to Roland. The one to have the courage to put an end to the chaos that is the royal structure of this land and assume the throne. If you had dominion over all of Roland, not just Bethany, you would control all of the armies you sought in vain to bring together today. Your fellows, the dukes, can say no to the Lord Regent. They could not refuse the king. Your lineage is as worthy as any of the others, Tristan, more so than most.

Acid burned now in the back of his throat, as it had then, the bitter taste of humiliation, of rejection. Tristan took another swig from the bottle, wiping his mouth with the back of his hand.

I am not the one in need of convincing, Your Grace, he had replied sourly. *In case this morning's fiasco didn't prove it, let me assure you that my fellow regents do not see the clarity of the succession scenario that you do.*

The eyes had smiled. *Leave that to me, m'lord. Your time will come. Just be certain that you are ready when it does. And m'lord?*

Yes?

You will think about what I said, hmmm?

Tristan remembered nodding numbly. He had been true to his word; the voice had repeated itself endlessly in his mind, in his dreams, whenever he was alone or in silence.

They could not refuse the king.

Tristan took another blind swig, wiping the spillage off with the back of his greatcloak's coarse sleeve.

In the distance a woman laughed; Tristan looked up dully from his inebriated reverie. He could see across the courtyard a pair of lovers running from pillar to post, hiding, laughing softly, crazily, shushing each other in tipsy merriment. The woman's blond hair gleamed in the lamplight for a moment, then disappeared with them into the shadows.

Like a fever breaking, the voice fell silent as Tristan's thoughts turned to his other obsession. He had been bitterly disappointed when Stephen told him that none of the invited guests from the Bolglands had come. The one respite from the torturous reality of having to spend the festival with Madeleine had been the knowledge that Rhapsody would be there, too. Heat flushed through him, tightening in his groin and spreading to his sweating palms, as he thought about her, leaving him almost sick with disappointment that he had been misinformed.

Whenever his thoughts turned to her, the voice fell silent. It was almost as if she had claimed his mind first, had set her imprint into his brain, staking it as her own. Whatever later spell had been cast upon him, forcing him to constantly consider the softly spoken words, had not been powerful enough to overturn his longings for her.

Slowly Tristan rose from the stone bench and stepped unsteadily out of the portico. Dawn would come soon, and with it the early festivities of the carnival's second day. He left the empty bottle on the bench and hurried out of the chill night air into the smoky warmth of Stephen's keep to his sleeping chambers.

The wind howled around him as he left.

Deep past the part of the night when any reveler still stood, two robed figures separately slipped out to the fields. Hooded, the elder waited at the edge of the huge shadows cast by the waning bonfires. Also hooded, the other man was forced into a vigorous walk, drawn to the meeting, a meeting of two holy men on a holy night for an unholy purpose.

Clouds flickered overhead, doubling the darkness where neither moon nor firelight shone. At the edge of Stephen Navarne's territory the light from the distant fires cast long shadows over the snowy field, illuminating the woods. The eyes of the first cleric, the man who had stood waiting, reflected a similar light, with a hint of red at the rims. He waited patiently while the other man caught his breath.

'My words resonated with you, I see. Thank you for meeting me, Your Grace.'

The other man nodded.

'Until now you have not understood what you have been asked to do. You have merely followed the compulsion, hmm?'

The second man's whisper was hoarse. 'Yes.'

'But now, now you are ready to understand, aren't you, Your Grace? Ready to participate in your own destiny? I am so pleased that you have decided to accept my offer. And you are doing so of your own free will? You understand what I am asking, and what I offer?'

'I believe I do, Your Grace.' The words were thick.

'Now, now, Your Grace, I meant no offense. I merely mean to ensure that you are aware of the power that awaits you, in this world and the Afterlife.'

'Yes.' His voice had dropped to a whisper.

The reply was a whisper as well. 'Unquestioned authority. Invulnerability. And Life unending.'

'Yes.'

'Good, good.' In the darkness the tiny blade glittered.

The second man swallowed heavily and pulled back the sleeve of his robe, his eyes shining as brightly as the blade.

'Just a drop to seal the bargain; then your position at the head of your order is secured.'

The second man nodded, trembling, but not from the cold. The thin, needle-like blade punctured the skin of his forearm swiftly, causing no pain. A crimson drop appeared, tiny at first, then welled to the size of a bead of rain.

A gray head bent over his arm, and he shuddered as the first man placed his lips, warm and eager, against the flesh of his forearm, then greedily inhaled the drop of blood. He felt a surge, a flash of fire that rolled through him like a sexual climax, something that he was forbidden by the rules of the order.

The pit of his stomach had been boiling all night. The burning acid in his stomach abated miraculously, leaving him dizzy and light-headed with relief. The sensation that had been twisting his stomach dissipated out through his skull, leaving him feeling excited and strangely alive.

The first holy man smiled warmly.

'Welcome, my son. Welcome to the *true* faith. Once we have removed any impediments, you may do with it as you will.'

14

The slaughter began just at the moment when the prizes for the sledge races were being awarded.

One of the most prestigious and hotly contested events of the winter carnival, the sledge races pitted the sheer brute strength and speed of four-man teams against each other for the coveted prizes of a full-cask of reserve Canderian whiskey, a salted roast ox, a hammered gold medallion, and bragging rights throughout Roland.

Teams for the event were usually comprised of family members, and were awarded their booty personally by Lord Stephen in a humorous ceremony full of pomp and pageantry, capped with a grandiose procession around the festival grounds. The winning contestants sat in the place of honor atop their heavy sledge, which was pulled by the members of the losing teams, to the triumphant strains of a ceremonial march, amid tremendous fanfare, up to the base of the reviewing stand, where the winners received their prizes.

The sledge races had long been one of Stephen Navarne's favorite events, and he stood now, whistling and cheering along with the masses, as the winners tormented their opponents by hurling snow and hay from their lofty perch at the losers as they dragged the sledge around the festival grounds. A good-natured snow fight had broken out at the turn, and Stephen laughed uproariously as the losing teams began rocking the sledge back and forth, toppling the winners into the snowdrifts.

There was something immensely freeing to be watching an event outside of his new ramparts for the first and only time during the carnival, Stephen decided. The wall had hampered the festival, had ensured that the snow within the sheltered lands had become packed and tramped under the thousands of boots that had trod upon it. The sledge races had required more room, and fresh snow, so the attendees had ventured outside the wall through the eastern gate, and now stood in a wide, loose oval, encircling the pristine snow of the back lands, the area past the wall. The freshness of the place was the perfect venue for this last event. Once the prizes had been awarded the crowd would return inside the ramparts and the feast would begin, culminating in what would surely be the best of his famous bonfires.

As he listened to the merry laughter of his children blending into the delayed roar of the crowd's mirth, Stephen looked down for a moment at the medallion in his hand. The gold caught the light of the winter sun and sent it reflecting around the vast open arena, coming to rest for a moment on Melisande's hair, making her tresses gleam brightly. His eye was drawn to the medal once again, and then to the roasted ox, wrapped in heavy burlap, smelling of rich spice and hickory smoke. A minor wave of surprise rippled through him. The full-cask of whiskey was missing.

The duke cast a glance around for Cedric Canderre and spotted him, laughing, his arm draped loosely around the waist of a local tavern wench. He shook his head and searched for Canderre's son instead.

'Andrew!' Stephen shouted to the Ale Count. Sir Andrew heard and turned from watching the revelry. 'The full-cask – it's not here.'

Sir Andrew glanced up to the reviewing stand from his place nearby where he had been watching the games, then nodded his understanding. He turned back to summon one of his manservants to fetch the cask, but saw they were shouting encouragement to the snow-fight participants, whistling and hooting with glee as the sledge capsized, tossing the head of the winning clan face-first into the snow. Unwilling to interrupt their revelry, Andrew smiled and started toward the front gate of Haguefort to the east-west thoroughfare, where the alewagon had been left.

Satisfied that the prize was on its way, Stephen turned his attentions back to the snow war unfolding between the winners and losers of the sledge-race competition and their extended families. He rested his hand on Melly's shoulder, winding his fingers through her bright curls, unknowingly savoring the last few moments of her innocence.

'Hie, Jrew! Wait!'

Andrew sighed. Dunstin's voice was heavy with the sound of drink – ale, from the high tone of it, calling to him from across Haguefort's inner courtyard.

Keenly mindful that the festival's host was about to award a prize that he didn't have in his possession, Sir Andrew kept up the trot he had been maintaining, and waved to the younger Baldasarre brother.

'Can't, cousin,' he shouted in return. 'I have to get Stephen's prize for the sledge race.'

'The full-cask?' Dustin called back as he struggled in vain to keep up, sliding on the slippery courtyard. 'Wait up! I'll help you! You can't lift it alone.'

Sir Andrew smiled to himself but didn't slow his pace. Despite his slight build he was strong and hearty, fit from the heavy lifting work he routinely did in his own stables and cellars. He could hear Dunstin, more used to a life of leisure as the wastrel brother of a duke, puffing behind him as he hurried on.

'Wait, you sod!' the younger Baldasarre bellowed, causing Andrew to slow to a walk as he came to the central gate, exhaling with irritation. 'What's the matter – you're worried I'm going to liberate your prize whiskey? You blackguard! Do I look like a highwayman to you?'

'No, Dunstin, you look like a petulant, drunken brat,' Andrew replied, knocking the snow off that had wedged about the heels of his boots. 'It grieves me to know how much of my fine ale is sloshing around in your fat belly at this moment.'

Dunstin's red face showed no sign of being stricken by the soft-spoken count's unusually harsh words as he came to a halt beside him in the gateway.

'I am *not* petulant,' he said, resting his hands on his knees and bending over slightly to catch his breath. 'And it *is* fine ale, I'll grant you, too fine to be wasted on the likes of *that*.' He inclined his head behind them to the east where the once-boundless vista of Navarne's fields was black with the thousands of festivalgoers and grinned. 'Let them drink Navarne's bilge-water, or perhaps Bethany's. You should be saving the Canderian liquor for the nobility anyway.'

'Only if that nobility is the winner of the sledge race, which I believe actually went to a family of smiths from Yarim,' Andrew retorted, starting down the long, wide set of stairs that led down to the thoroughfare beyond. He nodded to the guards as he passed through the gate. The keep and its surrounding battlements were all but empty, with the entire population of the duke's holdings in the back lands, watching the races with much of the rest of Roland. 'And by the way, Dunstin, if another of my stablehands complains that you have been fornicating his adolescent daughter I will give him my blessing to skewer you with the burning end of his branding iron. I may even hold you down while he does it. Family loyalty can only tolerate so much, and you are a far ways past the limit.'

'Ah, I understand now,' said Dunstin, trotting down the stone stairs behind the count. 'Lady Jecelyn is still keeping you at bay, is she? Well, don't fret, old boy. The wedding isn't too far off – in fact, aren't you planning it for just before Tristan's, a month or so hence?'

'Yes,' said Andrew shortly. He came to a halt at the bottom of the steps and stared off to the south, then shook his head and continued to cross the wide field that was the threshold of Stephen's keep.

'What is it?' Dunstin asked, finally beside him now, keeping pace.

They had reached the alewagon, unguarded except for the solitary driver. Andrew shrugged.

'I thought I saw something at the southern horizon, but it must have just been the sun.' He nodded to the guard and pulled back the canvas covering, revealing the full-cask, gilded with gold paint and sealed with a matching signet. He shouldered the cask and turned to go back to the fields, now distant, when the gleam he had seen caught his eye again.

Dunstin had seen it, too; he was staring off to the south, his florid face suddenly pale.

'What is that?' he murmured, more to himself than to Andrew.

The bright sun glinted at the horizon's blue rim, flashing for a moment, reflecting a thousand times over against a swirl of rising snow. A moment later that horizon darkened with the presence of a full mounted column of Sorbold soldiers, cavalry, heavy lance infantry, and crossbowmen, galloping and marching over the hill at the meadow's edge, dragging five wagons with steaming catapults.

The snow shattered below the pounding hoofs, flying up into the sky and cloaking the advancing army in swirls of white gauze. The earth beneath the alewagon began to tremble, causing the horses to dance fearfully.

'Sweet All-God,' Andrew whispered as the second line of the contingent crested the horizon. There could be no mistaking the intent of the soldiers, nor their intended destination.

They were heading, full-tilt, for the festival fields outside Stephen's protective wall.

The full-cask of whiskey shattered against the ground, splattering the back wheel of the alewagon. In unison Andrew and Dunstin looked behind them at the distant keep, where but a handful of guards stood watch, then back to the approaching column, where a third battle line, then a fourth, was now over the hillside and descending toward the back lands. Stephen's wall would not hold them, nor would it fend off the assault from the burning vats that rested on the levers of the catapults. It would merely serve to mask the attack until the column was upon them.

Caught between the Sorbolds and the keep, Andrew and Dunstin stared off to the south simultaneously. Ahead of them a considerable distance away were the two bell towers of Haguefort, largely decorative carillons draped in fluttering banners. The towers had been part of a larger rampart in the days of the Cymrian War. With peace came the dismantling of the outer rampart and the conversion of the towers from guard posts into slim, freestanding aesthetic spires hung with bells that rang the hours and played occasional musical pieces.

The towers stood between them and the approaching army.

The two young noblemen exchanged a glance, a nod that carried with it a grim hint of a shared smile, then split, Dunstin taking the left, Andrew the right. They dashed forward across the thoroughfare through the brown snow trodden into muck by the feet, hooves, and wagon and carriage wheels of thousands of guests, into the jaws of the conflict, Sir Andrew shouting to the alewagon's driver.

'To the gate! Warn the guards!'

They were each a thousand paces from their destinations when the Sorbolds saw them. The left flank of the column's third line peeled off, now charging the keep and its bell towers while the rest of the contingent hastened to the back lands and the festival fields.

Dunstin heard the tail end of the crossbow bolt's screaming whistle before it shattered his shoulder, sending him spinning to the ground. The impact knocked him backward; he struggled to his feet and staggered forward, fighting the shock of the injury and the panic that blazed through him from the shaking ground beneath his feet as the horizon darkened and swam before his eyes with galloping movement.

He clutched his shoulder as he ran, his fingers warm from the oozing blood. The tower was in his view, its ancient stones shining in the morning sun beneath the flapping banners. He could feel his breath grow ragged as the pain began to radiate through his chest; his exhalations formed icy clouds that shimmered against his face as he ran through them.

The horsemen were closer now. Dunstin cut right and ran at an angle across their field of vision, his boyhood training coming back to him as death loomed. Bolts from the approaching line shrieked through the air around him. He stumbled and lurched forward, catching himself before he fell, praying that Andrew was faster, more surefooted, that his own proximity to the advancing soldiers would buy his cousin enough time. It seemed little enough to ask in return for what he knew he was about to pay.

Within the black storm that was raging at the horizon before him he could hear a thick, metallic sound as a catapult was trained and loaded. He was almost to the bell tower, but nonetheless the sound reached into his bones, paralyzing his muscles, causing him to freeze where he stood. The metallic sound clinked again, ratcheting against the groan of splintering wood.

A surge of power blasted through Dunstin. He bolted forward, running with all the speed he could muster, keeping his eyes focused on the tower that was growing larger, nearer, with each step, each difficult breath. There was a small door in the back, a caretaker's entrance, no doubt, and Dunstin fixed his eyes on it, willed himself to reach it, pushing, pushing, trying to ignore the agony in his shoulder and chest and the blood that was pulsing from them now.

His hand was on the handle, cold steel stinging his palm and fingers, when the world dissolved in fire and thudding shards of stone around him.

Dunstin's tumbling consciousness could feel the rain of stones as the tower exploded, could tell that his skin was ripping away in the oily flames that were consuming him. The dust of the broken tower walls, spilt now across the frosty field like breadcrumbs scattered for the winterbirds, filled his bleeding nostrils, and as darkness closed in at the edges of his foggy vision he remembered the blackness of his childhood nightmares, and wanted his mother to come with the candle.

The force of his fall carried Dunstin over onto his side. As death took the nobleman it granted him two last boons.

Above the crumbling of the remnants of walls, and the crackling of the flames, he could hear the wild ringing of the bells from Andrew's tower, the call to arms that would warn Stephen. Despite his agony, Dunstin's blackened lips pulled back into a smile at the sound.

He was gone from the world and on his way to the light, and thus spared the sight of Andrew falling from the tower.

15

The clamor of the carillon bells initially surprised only Stephen. When they first began to ring, the populace, still cheering the victors of the sledge races, assumed that the tumultuous noise was merely an additional part of the celebration.

The Duke of Navarne, however, had been involved in the planning of the carillon program, and knew that the bells were out of schedule. He looked up from the reviewing stand at the precise moment when the Sorbold column crested the last of the undulating hills that led up to the east-west thoroughfare and the keep's entrance. He rose shakily, his hands gripping the arms of his chair.

'Sweet All-God,' he said. His lips moved. The words did not come out.

Stephen glanced quickly around the festival fields, assessing the situation between beats of his pounding heart.

His mind went first to his children; both of them were with him, along with Gerald Owen and Rosella, their governess.

The clergy, both the benisons of Sepulvarta and the Filidic Invoker and his high priests, were seated with him and the other dukes on a makeshift dais that served as a reviewing stand, composed of raised wooden pallets cordoned off with rope. The reviewing stand was just outside the eastern gate of the walled rampart and faced east onto the open land that had served as the venue for the sledge races. The dignitaries would be fairly easy to evacuate.

Stephen's focus shifted immediately to the festival attendees, certainly more than ten thousand of them, gathered in a loose oval that extended more than a league's distance to the east, out in the open, rolling lands of central Navarne. The minor nobility and the landed gentry were closest to the reviewing stand. With the decline of social position distance was added, leaving the poorest of the peasantry farthest away. As always, the ones most likely to die.

His stomach lurched.

In a heartbeat Stephen had leapt from his place on the reviewing stand, dragging Melisande with him.

'To the gate!' he shouted to the dignitaries. 'Run!' He swiveled and caught the eye of his captain of the guard, pointing to the advancing column. 'Sound the alarm!'

He estimated there were about one hundred horsemen, another seven hundred on foot, with several long catapults in tow. As they advanced they seemed to be splitting, the horsemen gravitating toward the wall behind him, the infantry veering off to the east, toward the bulk of the merry-makers.

Tristan was at his side, gripping his elbow.

'They're riding the wall!' the Lord Regent shouted above the din of the crowd, which was still in the throes of celebration. 'They'll cut off access to the gate—'

'— and slaughter everyone,' Stephen finished. The horns blared the alert as Stephen's guard began rallying to the captain's call. The duke turned to the elderly chamberlain behind him.

'Owen! Get my children to safety!'

The chamberlain, pale as milk, nodded, then seized both children by the arms, eliciting a shriek of protest from each of them.

'Quentin!' Tristan Steward shouted to the Duke of Bethe Corbair. 'Take Madeleine with you. Go!' He gestured wildly at the gate, then turned and seized the arm of his brother, Ian Steward, the benison of Canderre-Yarim, averting his eyes from his fiancée's terrified face as Baldasarre dragged her over the ropes off the back of the reviewing stand and to the gate.

A thundering of hooves could be heard from the western barracks as a contingent of Stephen's soldiers rode forth, scattering merrymakers and bales of hay that had delineated the racetrack before them. By now most of the crowd had heard the commotion and turned to see the black lines of Sorbold soldiers descending the hill, sweeping across the snow in the distance, riding and marching relentlessly forward. A great gasp rent the air, followed by a discordant chorus of screams.

A furious wave of panic swept through the crowd, followed by a human tide surging forward toward the gate in the rampart, hurrying back inside the protection of Stephen's wall. Within seconds the access was clogged, and violence broke out, great cries of anguish and wails of terror as people were crushed into each other and up against the unforgiving stone of the wall.

'M'lord!' shouted Gerald Owen. 'The children will never survive the press!'

Stephen stared in despair at the throng of people pushing in a great swell toward the only opening in the rampart. Owen was right; Gwydion and Melisande would easily be crushed to death in the throng.

Over his head he heard shouted orders and the slamming of doors in the guard towers atop the wall as the archers took up their posts. As one broad young man made ready his arrows, Stephen was struck with an idea.

'You!' he shouted to the archer up on the wall. 'Stand ready!' He snatched the ropes from the reviewing stand and ripped them from their posts, hauling them over to the wall away from the gate. 'Owen! Come with me!'

Stephen stood back from the wall and heaved with all his might, silently thanking the All-God that he had purchased the ropes from the king of the Firbolg some months back. The Bolg had discovered a manufacturing process that had reduced the weight of rope products while increasing their tensile strength. A normal rope would have been far too heavy to toss in this way. After two tries the archer atop the wall caught the frayed end and signaled his success. Behind him Stephen could hear his soldiers riding past on their way to interdict the mounted assault.

'Rosella, hold on to Melisande,' Stephen said to the frightened servant. 'Don't let go.' Rosella nodded mutely as Stephen wrapped the rope end twice about her waist. 'All right, my girl, up you go!' He nodded to the archer, and turned Rosella toward the wall, rudely grasping her hindquarters, helping her ascend in a flurry of scattered stone and torn cloth. He tried to smile encouragingly at Melisande, who was wailing in terror.

'All right, son, you're next,' he said to Gwydion. The lad nodded, and grasped the rope as it was lowered from the top of the wall above him, twice again his height.

'I can climb, Father.'

Stephen looped the boy's waist with the rope's end as Gwydion grasped the length. 'I know you can, son – hold on, now.'

The archer pulled as Gwydion scaled the wall. Stephen sighed in relief as the lad's long legs disappeared on the other side of the rampart. He turned to Gerald Owen.

'You're next, Owen.'

The elderly chamberlain shook his head.

'M'lord, I should stay until you are inside as well.'

'I'm not going inside, not until it's finished.' Stephen raised his voice to be heard over the building pandemonium. Out of the corner of his eye he could see that Tristan had heard his declaration and had made note of it. 'Now get my children away from the wall, and as many more as can be hauled over. You up there!' he shouted to the archer who had manned the rope.

'Yes, m'lord?'

'Maintain this post. One less archer will not be missed, and they're not in range yet anyway. Pull as many people to safety as you can.' He reached out and grabbed the shoulder of a burly peasant man hurrying with his children to the gate. 'Here, man, pass those children up, then stay and round up others – women, the old, anyone who needs help getting over the wall.'

'Yes, m'lord.'

'Inside, Owen. Try and quell the panic. Move those inside back from the wall – the Sorbolds have catapults.' He cast a glance over his shoulder at the resolutely approaching column, then turned back to Gerald Owen.

'Tell the Master of the Wall to prepare to maintain bow fire to cover the evacuation of the people, and then the troops once the Sorbolds are in range. And find the commanders of the third and fourth divisions inside – tell them to watch for a charge from the west, and hold the north gate.'

The chamberlain nodded his understanding, then grasped the rope and was hauled over the rampart, out of the fray that was turning bloody beneath him.

Tristan was shouting orders to the commander of his personal retinue.

'Sweep as many of those people as you can around the wall to the north – there's another gate there, and it's out of sight.'

A shock rang through him as he was jolted from behind, rammed into by several people fleeing the fields in panic in the face of the coming horsemen. Tristan, a strong man with a solid frame, maintained his balance and stepped out of the way of another oncoming wave of villagers, their faces set in masks of terror, eyes glazed. In the distance near the wall he could hear Madeleine's shrill voice shrieking his name.

'Set up two fronts,' he shouted to his commander. He pointed to the approaching column that was marching forward at the east to flank the festivalgoers. 'Set up a picket of pikemen and foot soldiers, and any peasants you can find – give them anything, sticks, haybales, balehooks – and form a line in front of the crossbowmen to set against the infantry charge. Stephen's cavalry can engage the horses riding the wall until they come within bowshot of those archers on the rampart.' The chaos swelled around him. He looked to find his cousin as the commander saluted and began calling orders.

At the wall Stephen was utilizing one of the rampart archers to pull some of the people gathering near the bulwark over the top to safety. Once the process was working the Duke of Navarne stepped back from the wall, shielded his eyes for a moment, and shouted something to the soldiers atop the rampart. One disappeared, returning a moment later with a handful of weapons, which he tossed clear of the wall.

Stephen scooped the blades from the snowy ground and began quickly passing them out to the men and women standing in wait. He trotted over to Tristan and tossed him a longsword.

'I guess we'll see if Oelendra's training stayed with us, cousin,' he said calmly, though his eyes gleamed. Tristan nodded, turning once more to the oncoming column.

With a thunderous roar a second wave of cavalrymen from Navarne's northern barracks came into sight, joining with the tail end of the first wave from the eastern quarters. The two mounted lines galloped forth, charging to engage the Sorbold horsemen while Stephen's foot soldiers hurried, amid a furious clanking of armor and clanging weapons, to interpose themselves between the oncoming infantry. Scattered huddles of men and women stood, armed with whatever they could scrounge and frozen in panic, watching the ebb and flow of the mob struggling to squeeze through the eastern gate, the last desperate line of defense between the townspeople and the wall.

'I'll face the charge,' Tristan shouted to Stephen. 'You rally the people – there are hundreds of able-bodied who can defend the wall.'

Stephen nodded and the two noblemen parted, Tristan running forward toward the oncoming column, Stephen toward the makeshift dais upon which he had been sitting only a few moments before.

'You!' the duke called to a clump of heavyset men, sledge-race participants most likely, hovering near the wall, axes and spades in hand, steeling themselves for the coming charge. 'Seize those platforms! Throw a few obstacles in their way – set up some barricades!'

Like a spell shattering, the trance in which they had been rooted vanished. With a swell of shouting, the men took hold of the makeshift dais and splintered it apart, smashing the bracing boards with axes, barrels, bare fists, whatever was within reach. In moments the enormous platform was broken into sections of pallets, which the townsfolk hauled forward and planted at the wall's edge and across the field, directly in the path of the line of thundering chargers riding the wall.

The randomly strewn pallets served as partial cover for the hailstorm of arrows and crossbow bolts slamming forth now from the Sorbold force. The air was rent with the screams of the missiles as they tore forward in waves. A sickening staccato of popping and thudding sounds erupted, followed by cries of agony or shuddering gasps as the bodies of the festivalgoers began to fall rapidly, littering the once-pristine racing field.

'Halt – hold your position!' Tristan shouted to the double line of foot soldiers from Stephen's northern barracks, the pikes in front, the bowmen in back. 'Train your crossbows on the front line and wait until they crest the field. Pikemen – keep down! Hold this line against the charge!' He looked away, his stomach turning at the looks on the faces of the conscripted peasants as realization took hold of what they were facing.

Stephen felt the wind grow colder; it stung his cheeks and eyes, kicking up a veil of sharp snowy crystals from the ground. He glanced in the direction of the two gates in his wall; the throng was still clamoring to move inside, but it was thinning as the soldiers Tristan had assigned to manage the crowd maintained a fragile order. Children were running in terror, following adults dashing blindly around the wall to the northern gate. The snow-devils in the wind spun around them, hurling some of them to the ground.

He turned and looked toward the oncoming army. Like a smoothly flowing river the Sorbold soldiers marched forward, relentlessly, unhurried. One catapult came to a halt in an unlikely place and began training on the scattered crowd of defenders manning the wall. Stephen's brow furrowed, and then his throat closed in the realization that the enemy was not positioning to attack the keep, but rather to wreak as much death among the attendees as possible.

Behind him the wind grew sharper, more insistent. Stephen shielded his eyes and turned. The look of consternation on his face melted in astonishment.

Llauron the Invoker stood in the middle of the field that had been the sledge arena, atop the small rise of packed snow where the timekeeper had stood to start the races. He was alone in the distance except for Gavin, his chief forester, who was crouched on one knee, his heavy bow far out of range of the advancing army, positioned to defend Llauron, standing as his only guard.

The Invoker seemed unaware of the cacophony all around him. His expression was calm, almost serene, his arms at his sides, the white oaken staff of his office in one hand. Llauron's eyes were closed, his face turned toward the late-afternoon sun, which would soon vanish into the long darkness of night.

Llauron raised his empty hand; Stephen looked above. The wind picked up strongly, shrieking with a moaning howl across the wide fields, whisking more sheets of frozen crystals into the swirling air. The duke closed his eyes against the blast of cold that stung his face as the wind slapped him hard.

He put his hand to his brow and looked to Tristan. The Lord Roland had not noticed the Invoker; he was instead struggling to stand and keep his soldiers trained on the approaching column.

The light of day surged, then diminished quickly. Dark clouds formed over the sun; suddenly, the hazy light of afternoon vanished into the gray of dusk as the snow began to fall rapidly stronger, coating the air thickly, rising and falling in twisting patterns on the moaning wind.

The Invoker raised his other hand, holding his staff high. The gold leaf atop the white wood gleamed like a beacon in the coming darkness. Stephen thought he could hear Llauron chanting an invocation, but the sound of it was lost in the keening music that screamed in his ears. He looked to Tristan again, who now stood erect, staring directly in front of him. Stephen ran to his cousin, pulling the front of the hood of his cape down to shield his eyes from the bite of the wind.

'What is it?' he shouted.

The Lord Roland said nothing. Stephen followed his gaze to the approaching horsemen riding Navarne's wall.

Alongside the galloping steeds the snow swirled menacingly, the wind howling wild and shrill. From within the clouds of twisting white a staccato growling sound emerged, echoing over the field, in a thousand earsplitting barks.

The snow itself rose up, took form. The men of Roland watched in amazement as it slapped at the legs of the horses like a claw, snapped like a snout, growled.

First one, then a dozen, then a score, then a hundred of them, ephemeral wolves white as winter seemed to form from the snow itself, rise up and slash at the legs of the now-frightened horses. The wind screamed in deafening, feral howls; one of the Sorbold soldiers yanked back on the reins as his horse reared in fright.

A shattering blast of air blew through again, spinning the ice crystals of snow aloft. As it rose more lupine forms rose with it, rampant, angry, snapping, tearing at the Sorbold chargers. The frosty blanket of white that had cloaked the meadow swirled viciously into a thousand more feral wolves, clawing and savaging the horses and foot soldiers in a horrific chorus of snarling howls that matched the screaming wind. A contrapuntal cry of fear blazed up from the startled army, wailing discordantly in the wind.

'Dearest All-God,' the Lord Roland whispered.

The Sorbold cavalry charge broke into chaos as the horses reared frantically, twisting and dodging to escape the phantom wolves. The prince and the duke stared as soldiers were thrown, some into the rampart itself, tossed on the boiling sea of confusion and trampling hooves.

On the eastern flank the neat lines of the column crumpled into jagged rows. Tristan laughed harshly in amazement as the oncoming infantry broke ranks, some ignoring the biting snow that tore at their heels, others succumbing to the Invoker's magic and giving in to the frenzy around them, swatting and slashing at the swirling snow-devils in lupine form. Navarne's cavalry charged in, slashing ferociously.

The Lord Roland squeezed Stephen's arm tightly.

'He's done it! Stephen, he's *done it*! Llauron's broken the charge!'

The gruesome sound of ratcheting metal broke through the keening of the wind. A moment later the air was rent by the repeated noise of catapults firing, and the lines of defending bowmen and foot soldiers erupted in caustic fire. Stephen and Tristan were blown back by the impact as clouds of oily smoke exploded in front of them, followed immediately by shrieks of agony and the bright flash of fire as it consumed the impacted soldiers.

Tristan gripped Stephen's arm violently as a scarlet shower of blood sprayed into the air. He struggled to his feet, coughing. 'Hold the line!' he screamed at the peasants frantically rolling their burning comrades in the snow.

He turned toward the wall as shattering explosions tore through the air and into the rampart, the impact of the catapults sending shards of stone flying in all directions. His throat constricted in horror at the sight of Stephen desperately trying to extinguish the fire on a peasant woman who had stood with the defenders and was now being consumed in the pitch flames. The clothes on Stephen's back were on fire as well.

'Stephen! Drop!'

As he lunged toward his cousin Tristan caught a glimmer of gold out of the corner of his eye. The wind screamed; with a howl a pocket of the storm broke loose, drenching him and those around him with icy rain. A blast of sleet in frozen sheets poured down from above. In a twinkling the flames all round them were snuffed, leaving behind no fire but roiling clouds of thick, oily smoke. Through his soaked hair and lashes Tristan looked behind him at the sledge arena, where Llauron stood. The Invoker was pointing the golden oak-leaf staff at Stephen; he stumbled forward slightly into Gavin and leaned on the forester's shoulder, shaken, then lowered the staff, grasping it with both hands. The cloudburst abated as quickly as it had come.

A clarion call of retreat rang forth over Navarne's wall; both Cymrian noblemen looked westward. The vast bulk of the crowd had been pulled within the walls of the keep, or shepherded around the rampart to the northern gate. The Master of the Wall was signaling that what people could be saved had been taken into shelter. The archers were in place.

'All right; horsemen, fall back!' Tristan called to his commander. The man raised a horn to his lips and blew the retreat. The horse soldiers of Navarne, locked in heated battle with the Sorbold cavalry, struggled to break free, leaving behind the bodies of their dead, the riderless horses, and the enemy dodging the snow wolves that tore at their mounts. As the horse soldiers galloped around the broken barricades and the common people standing in wait behind them, Stephen's archers atop the wall let fly a windstorm of arrows into the Sorbold lines, covering their retreat.

The numbness that was giving Tristan clarity was starting to recede. 'Fire!' he shouted at his broken line of crossbowmen. The soldiers loosed their bolts into the jagged lines of the Sorbold infantry, many of which whom were now writhing on the ground, battling the attacks of the wolf spectres. The wind picked up, fanning the heavy smoke and filling the air with stinging sleet that fell like needles.

'To the gate!' Stephen shouted. 'Withdraw, Tristan! The archers will cover you!'

Ten score and five men now lined the top of the rampart, methodically raining arrows down at the two flanks of the Sorbold column. Tristan signaled frantically to the leaders, the calm of training beginning to give way to the horror of the reality around him.

'Fall back! Fall back! Get inside the wall!' he screamed. In the distance he could hear the sound of the catapults being reloaded.

Time became suspended; everything around him seemed to move with painful slowness. His limbs were suddenly heavy, his head thick with sound and a mad buzzing in his ears. Tristan shook his head to try to clear his mind.

All around him lay bodies of the dead and dying, soldiers, but more often mere citizens of Roland, and even of Sorbold, children and old people, men and women, moaning in agony or lying silent, their blood staining the snow a rosy pink, their flesh burned away. Tristan coughed, trying to clear the taste of pitch from his mouth, only to find that in his flight he had inhaled some poor dying bastard's blood, and it was clotting in his throat. His stomach lurched, rushed into his mouth, and he retched, falling to his knees in the gory snow.

His head lurched as Stephen seized his arm and dragged him violently to his feet.

'Tristan, come! *Come!*'

Behind them a high pile of haybales ripped into flame and torched fiery orange with thin lines of black withering straw, like mountains of burning birdcages. The heat sent waves of shock through the Lord Roland, and he felt a sudden burst of energy as his cousin dragged him toward the gate in the rampart. Distantly he was aware of the rhythmic twang of bowstrings in unison; he saw Gavin dragging the exhausted Invoker inside the rampart ahead of them. The last of the conscripted peasantry, the common folk who stood to defend the wall and let the others make their escape, were hurrying inside to safety now. Tristan felt a surge of fondness as he saw them go. *Good people*, he thought as Stephen pulled him around the battered barricades that had only a short time ago been the comfort of a reviewing stand for the nobility. *My people.*

The gates loomed before his eyes, large chunks of stone in the nearby walls missing from the impact of the catapults, but still sound. Tristan closed his eyes and pulled free of Stephen's grasp.

'Unhand me,' he said sternly. 'I can make it on my own.'

Once inside the shelter of the walls Stephen waded through the crowd, shouting.

'Out of the way! Back, get back from the wall!'

He shut out the ferocious noise all around him – the moaning of the injured, the cries of joy from family members reunited, the frantic calls of parents searching for lost children, the shouted orders from the various regimental captains, the scream of wood and metal as the enormous gates were closed – and quickly scaled the rampart, pulling himself atop the wall next to a guard tower that had been shattered by a catapult blast.

Outside the wall what remained of the Sorbold column, now unfettered by Llauron's intervention of wolves and weather, was marching, walking, limping, crawling resolutely forward, one by one, into the rain of arrows from the archers atop the wall. Stephen shuddered at the utter lifelessness of their eyes, the relentlessness of their intentions. Only a few dozen remained of the attacking force; the cavalry had been decimated by the archers, and a hundred riderless horses were milling about aimlessly on the bloody field.

The Master of the Wall made his way to Stephen's side, and stood silently, staring, as the duke did, out onto the field beyond the wall.

After a moment Stephen found his voice; his throat was dry and tight, so it sounded young and frightened to his ears. He coughed, and spoke again.

'Command half your men to rescue what stragglers they can – lower down pikes, anything, just get the few that remain inside the wall.'

'Why aren't they retreating?' the Master of the Wall wondered aloud. 'They are marching right into the flights of arrows.'

Stephen shuddered, fighting back grisly memories. 'They will continue to do so, I fear, until the last man is dead. Tell your archers to train their arrows on the catapults, and pick off as many as you can there. I will have the commander of the third regiment send a force out to capture them. In the meantime, instruct the archers to aim to injure, not to kill. We need to capture some of the Sorbolds alive and try to make some sense of this nightmare.' The Master of the Wall nodded, and disappeared from Stephen's peripheral vision as he continued to stare out over the atrocity that only a moment ago had been the solstice festival. The bright colored banners still flapped, tattered, in the stiff, smoky breeze, the glistening maypole ribbons continued to spin merrily in the wind, black with soot.

He already knew what the Sorbolds would say.

Why?

I don't know, m'lord. I don't remember.

16

The library at Haguefort was enormous, with high ceilings that reflected the slightest sound. Footsteps echoed on the marble floor, swallowed intermittently by the silk rugs. A slight cough or the clearing of the throat could be heard in all corners of the vast room.

Despite those sensitive acoustics, not a sound was audible now save for the crackling of the fire and the ticking of the clock.

Cedric Canderre sat heavily on one of the leather sofas near the fireplace, staring blankly into the flames, his face decades older than it had been that morning. Beside him sat Quentin Baldasarre, Duke of Bethe Corbair, Dunstin's brother. His silence was very different; his eyes were gleaming with a light that barely contained its wrath, and even his silent breathing was tinged with fury. Lanacan Orlando, the benison of his province, who sat in the wing chair next to him awkwardly patting his hand in an attempt to comfort him, was growing more nervous by the moment. When Quentin finally waved him away angrily, Orlando seemed almost relieved.

Ihrman Karsrick, the Duke of Yarim, poured himself another full glass of brandy, noting that Stephen's decanter was in sorry need of refilling. He alone among the dukes of Roland had not suffered the loss of a relative or close friend, though the head of the winning sledge team, a popular guild member in his province and his personal blacksmith, had died in the attack.

The holy men had been inept at dispensing comfort, in Karsrick's opinion; Colin Abernathy had been unable to stop weeping for more than a few moments. Lanacan Orlando, generally considered a great healer and source of consolation, was clearly irritating his duke far more than he was helping him. Philabet Griswold, the pompous Blesser of Avonderre-

Navarne, had begun pontificating about Sorbold and the need for an immediate retaliation earlier but was glared into silence by Stephen Navarne, a member of his own See. Stephen was currently elsewhere looking in on his children and the makeshift hospital wards that had been set up within his holdings to tend to the wounded. Nielash Mousa, the Blesser of Sorbold, was sitting isolated in a corner, his dark skin pale and clammy. Only Ian Steward seemed calm.

The door of the library opened and Tristan Steward entered, closing it quietly behind him. He had excused himself to look in on Madeleine and the wounded from his province, and had been meeting in the courtyard below with the captains of his regiments. His face was a mask of calm as he entered the room, but Karsrick could tell from the look in his eye that he was planning something, biding his time to reveal it.

Martin Ivenstrand, the Duke of Avonderre, stood up as Tristan passed. 'The casualties, Tristan – how bad?'

'Over four hundred dead, twice that many more injured,' Tristan said, coming to a stop before the wooden stand that contained Stephen's prized atlas from Serendair. The ancient manuscript was covered with a glass dome in order to protect the fragile pages of the charts that depicted the long-dead island from the ravages of time. *Ironic,* Tristan thought absently. *A carefully preserved map of a world that died a thousand years ago. Directions to nowhere.*

'Sweet All-God,' murmured Nielash Mousa, the Blesser of Sorbold.

'Is that a benediction, or a plea for forgiveness?' snapped Philabet Griswold, the Blesser of Avonderre-Navarne.

Karsrick's eyes, along with all the others in the room, riveted onto the two holy men, bitter enemies and hostile contenders behind the scenes for the sole right to wear the Patriarch's Ring of Wisdom, white robes, and star-shaped talisman. With word coming out of Sepulvarta that the Patriarch was in his last days, the feud between the two men had heated to boiling. Throughout the festival they had gibed and sniped at each other, preening and positioning themselves with various nobles, speaking in furtive discussions, meeting secretly.

All the posturing was certainly a waste of time as far as Karsrick understood. The Patriarch could name his own successor, and pass his ring on to the benison of his choice, though the declaration did not seem to be forthcoming. If he did not do so, the great scales of Jierna Tal, the Place of Weight, would decide, with the ancient Ring of Wisdom balancing on one of the plates and the man it was judging on the other. Either way, the efforts of the two holy men to consolidate power seemed futile.

At the festival Griswold had appeared to have the upper hand. He was by far the most powerful benison in Roland, a fact that was magnified because the carnival taking place was within his See. Insiders at the Patriarch's manse, however, whispered rumors that Mousa, the only non-Cymrian benison, and the Blesser of an entire country, was the Patriarch's favored choice. In addition, if the decision of ascendancy were to go to the scales, it would certainly not weigh against Mousa that Jierna Tal was in Sorbold.

Whatever favor Mousa might have held before the festival, and whatever pleasure he might have drawn from those rumors, was gone now. While no one had broken the silence in the library in deference to the grief of Cedric Canderre and Quentin Baldasarre, it was clear by the almost-visible frost in the air where the clergy and nobility of Roland placed the blame for the attack. The Blesser of Sorbold, a normally unflappable man with dusky skin and a bland expression, had gone gray in the face. That face was puckered in worried lines and dotted with anxious perspiration.

He rose slowly now from his seat as Griswold approached.

'This – this was an inexplicable act,' he said, resting his hand on the table beside him for balance. 'Sorbold – the Crown, that is – knows nothing of this, I'm certain.' He anxiously fingered the holy amulet around his neck, its talisman shaped like the earth.

Griswold crossed his arms over his chest, causing the amulet he wore, with its talisman shaped like a drop of water, to clink soundly. 'It would certainly seem that an action involving an entire column of royal soldiers might have at least a suggestion of permission from the prince or the empress,' he said haughtily. 'Particularly one that violates peace treaties and commits atrocities upon the citizens of a neighboring land – a formerly allied nation.' He came to a halt in front of his nemesis as the Blesser of Sorbold drew himself up to his full height and turned to face the others.

'I can assure you that this heinous attack was *not* sanctioned by the government of Sorbold,' Mousa said, his voice betraying none of the anxiety apparent in his features. 'Let me state emphatically that Sorbold wishes no hostility with Roland, nor with any of its other neighbors. And even if it did, the Crown Prince has been keeping vigil at the sickbed of his mother, Her Serenity, the Dowager Empress, and would certainly not have chosen this time to attack.'

'How can you say that for certain?' sneered Griswold.

'*I* am *here*, for the love of the All-God!' Mousa growled. 'Do you think they would risk the life of their only benison this way?'

'Perhaps the Crown Prince is trying to tell you something,' Griswold suggested.

Mousa's dusky face flushed with dark anger. 'Void take you, Griswold! If you don't choose to believe in my worth to my See, let me at least assure you that if Sorbold had decided to attack Roland, we would have done so with one hundred times the force you saw today! You fool! Our own people were here at the festival! You have excused away all of the assaults that have been perpetrated on citizens of Tyrian and other Orlandan provinces by your own people as "random" or "inexplicable" – you've never taken responsibility for any of *that* violence! Yet you cannot accept that this is exactly the same?'

'It's not the same,' said Stephen Navarne quietly. The others turned to see the master of Haguefort standing in the open doorway. He had entered so silently that none had heard him come in.

The Duke of Navarne crossed the enormous room and came to stand directly in front of Nielash Mousa, who had gone pale again at his words. Stephen brought his hand awkwardly to rest on the benison's upper arm and found it to be trembling.

'It's not the same, because hithertofore there have been no incursions from Sorbold – this is the first I know of. The fact that whatever madness has been causing these attacks has spread to Sorbold is most disturbing, though not altogether unexpected. Up until now it limited itself to Tyrian and Roland.'

'And Ylorc,' said Tristan Steward firmly. 'I told you last summer that the Bolg had attacked my citizens, and you all chose to disregard me.'

'King Achmed denied it,' said Quentin Baldasarre.

Tristan's eyes blazed. He reached into his boot and pulled forth a small, three-bladed throwing knife, and threw it at Baldasarre's feet, where it clanged against the stone floor.

'He also denied selling weapons to Sorbold. See how much his word is worth.' The Lord Roland regarded Baldasarre coldly. 'In your case, Quentin, you purchased that worthless word at the cost of your brother's life.'

Baldasarre was off the leather couch and halfway across the room as the last words came from Tristan's mouth, his muscles coiled in fury. Lanacan Orlando had managed to grasp the duke's arm and was pulled along with the force of his stride, and now interposed himself between Tristan and Quentin.

'Please,' the benison whispered. 'No more violence; please. Do not desecrate your brother's memory in your anger, my son.'

'He is in the warmth of the Afterlife, having saved us all,' said Ian Steward.

'Dunstin Baldasarre died a hero's death,' Philabet Griswold intoned.

'As did Andrew Canderre,' Ian Steward added quickly.

Cedric Canderre opened his mouth to speak, but his words were stifled by the creak of the double doors as they opened, admitting Llauron, the Invoker of the Filids. The Invoker's chiefs had been lending aid to Stephen's forces, Khaddyr tending to the wounded alongside the healers of Navarne, while Gavin led the reconnaissance that was assessing the Sorbold attack. Llauron nodded to Stephen, then made his way quietly to the sideboard beside Ihrman Karsrick and poured himself a last finger of brandy, emptying the decanter.

When Cedric Canderre found his voice, it was steady, belying the pain in his eyes.

'I don't wish to debate this further,' he said flatly. 'Madeleine and I need to return to my lands, to prepare for Andrew's interment, and to comfort the Lady Jecelyn.' He cleared his throat, and cast a pointed glance at his fellow dukes, then looked to Ian Steward, the benison of Canderre-Yarim. 'She is going to need much support and consolation, Your Grace. She expects Andrew's child in autumn.'

A heavy silence fell, echoing through the library, as the holy men and regents looked at each other. Finally Tristan Steward spoke.

'Have no fear, Cedric. Madeleine and I will see to the child's needs and education as if it were Andrew's right-born heir.'

Canderre's head snapped back as if he had been struck. Stephen Navarne felt his fists unconsciously clench in anger at Tristan's words; the Lord Roland had just named the child as Andrew's bastard. The implication was lost on none of the men present: by right of succession Madeleine, and by extension, upon their marriage, Tristan, was now heir to Canderre, not Andrew's unborn child.

Quentin Baldasarre, Andrew's cousin, already furious at Tristan, stepped forward angrily again, only to have his arm caught by Lanacan Orlando, his benison.

'The child *will* be Sir Andrew's right-born heir, my son,' Orlando said calmly to Tristan, his voice no longer quaking as it had the moment before. He turned to the clergy and the provincial leaders. 'I presided over the marriage of Sir Andrew and Lady Jecelyn in secret last summer. Their union was blessed; the Unification ritual was performed. As result, any child of their union is legitimate, and the right-born heir of Cedric Canderre.' The firelight glinted off the chain around his neck, which bore no talisman in representation of the wind.

Stephen glanced at Llauron, but the Invoker showed no sign of surprise, or even interest; rather, he inhaled the bouquet of his brandy and took a sip from the snifter. Andrew had said nothing of his marriage to Stephen.

Tristan seemed shocked, while his brother, Ian, normally placid, grew red in the face. The spiral of red jewels in the sun-shaped talisman around his neck flashed angrily in the firelight as well.

'Why did he come to you, Your Grace?' Ian Steward demanded. 'He is a member of my See, not yours.'

The benison of Bethe Corbair opened his hands mildly in a gesture of reconciliation. 'And Lady Jecelyn is a member of mine. It was a romantic impulse, no doubt. It seemed too long for them to wait to be together, though they both looked forward to the more important, formal ceremony over which you would have presided next month, Your Grace. I imagine they did not wish to impose on you twice.'

The dukes exchanged a glance. It was apparent to them that Lanacan Orlando was probably offering a gracious cover for Andrew Canderre's difficult situation, though the benison maintained a steady gaze. Tristan Steward exhaled deeply, but otherwise betrayed no annoyance that his attempt to place himself in Canderre's line of succession had been thwarted. Finally Cedric spoke.

'I am grateful to you, Your Grace, for whatever blessings you have afforded my son.' He turned to his fellow regents. 'I will take my leave of you now. I have dead to bury, as do you all.'

'You'll have more, unless you listen a moment longer,' said Tristan Steward.

The curt tone drew the attention of all present in the room. The Lord Roland's blue eyes burned with fire that smoldered within a fragile control. He regarded them seriously, almost contemptuously, then lingered for a moment, staring at Nielash Mousa.

'Take your leave now, Your Grace,' he said, his tone barely civil. 'Return to His Highness, the Crown Prince, and tell him what has occurred. Inform him that I will be contacting him shortly. My retinue will see you to the border.'

The Blesser of Sorbold stared at him for a moment, then nodded reluctantly. He turned to the dukes.

'I do apologize most deeply on behalf of my countrymen for what has befallen your subjects,' he said, then looked to his fellow benisons. 'I pray you remember, my brothers in grace, that we are all children of the All-God, sons of the Creator. Whatever evil has been causing this tragic violence amongst Orlandan citizens and the Lirin of Tyrian has now spread to Sorbold, but it is not in any way condoned by the Crown. Please keep this in mind, and keep cool heads. I assure you, the prince will make restitution for this, and do everything he can to see that it does not occur again.'

He waited for a response, but the dukes and benisons of Roland stood silent in the wake of his words. After a few moments of awkwardness he bowed and left the library.

Tristan Steward waited until the door had closed behind Mousa, then turned back with barely disguised wrath to confront the regents and the clergymen.

'I have been warning you all for some time that this was coming, that we needed to take action, but you spurned those warnings, every last one of you.' He glared pointedly at Stephen. 'Now the winter solstice has been cursed, stained with the blood of citizens from each of our provinces, and even from the realm of Sorbold. I will tolerate this reckless lack of preparedness no longer. If you wish to remain blind to what is happening around you, fine. But I will no longer stand by while Orlandan subjects are slaughtered.

'Therefore, I invoke my rights as high regent and prince of the capital province. I declare sovereignty over the *all* the armies of Roland, and am assuming command thereof. It is high time to end this madness and combine our forces under a sole leadership – *my* leadership. Any province who opposes me will be cast out of the Orlandan alliance, and will no longer be under the protection of Bethany.'

'You are declaring yourself king, then?' demanded Ihrman Karsrick.

'Not yet, though that may follow as the natural progression.' Tristan's gaze went from face to face, assessing the reactions of the various dukes and benisons. 'My title is not important. The survival of Roland is. The Cymrian War fragmented this land into a ridiculous arrangement of egos and agendas, teetering on a precipice of disaster. No more! Too long we have bowed and scraped to each other, dancing gingerly around this issue to salve your fragile self-importance. My army protects your regions now. It has been Bethany's soldiers, Bethany's supply troops, that have maintained the peace throughout Roland for years now—'

'—with the aid of a considerable amount of taxes,' finished Martin Ivenstrand, the Duke of Avonderre. 'Any one of us could have built the forces that you have had they been given the assessments from which you have benefited.'

'Be that as it may, none of you have had the stomach, or the loin-pouch, to do so,' retorted Tristan angrily. 'It is my right, as high regent, to claim command, and I do so now. Those who oppose me will no longer be under my protection. I will end all trade agreements with renegade provinces, and will sever any and all diplomatic ties as well.'

'You can't be serious,' sputtered Quentin Baldasarre.

'I am completely serious. I will strip your provinces from the mail caravan, tear up your grain treaties, ostracize you so completely that you will be for all intents a foreign land. I have had enough – more than enough – of this nightmare. It has cost me far more than I am willing to continue paying.' His words faltered as he thought of Prudence, her dismembered corpse strewn about the grass of Gwylliam's Great Moot in Ylorc. 'Now decide – are you with me? Or are you out?'

The other dukes stared at each other in dismay. Tristan's voice was deep with power; his shoulders trembled with rage. The air in the room had gone as dry as a Yarim summer. Stephen thought he could taste blood in the back of his mouth.

The silence thudded heavily through the library, punctuated by the threat of the fire's crackle, the accusatory ticking of the clock.

Finally Colin Abernathy, the Blesser of the Nonaligned States, turned to Tristan.

'I will take my leave now, my son,' he said pleasantly. 'It is not fitting that I be privy to these discussions, as my See is not within the realm of Roland. Let me say, for what it is worth, however, that your plan seems the right one to me. It is high time, in my opinion, that Roland sort out its lines of succession, and unify behind one royal house. As a foreign national I can assure you the clarity will benefit both Roland and its allies.'

For the first time since he had entered the room, Tristan smiled slightly. 'Thank you, Your Grace.'

Abernathy bowed shakily to Stephen Navarne. 'I will make arrangements to collect the remains of our people who have died this day on your soil with your chamberlain, my son.'

'Thank you, Your Grace,' Stephen replied. 'He has been told to stand ready.'

'Very good. Well, then, farewell, my brothers in grace, and m'lord regents. I wish you wisdom in your discussions, and in your decisions.' Abernathy stood tall as he bowed to the clergy and the nobility, then crossed the library and closed the door soundly behind him.

Tristan turned back to the other regents of Roland.

'Sometimes it is easier to see the wisdom of an undertaking from the outside,' he said. He turned to Stephen Navarne, waving his hand to silence the other dukes as they prepared to speak.

'Let us cut to the chase. You, Stephen – you, my own cousin – you opposed me when I made a call for unity before. See where your folly has led? Four hundred dead, maybe twice that by the time the injured succumb. At your hands, Stephen – their blood is on *your* hands, because you failed to heed my warnings. You thought your pathetic wall could save you – it couldn't even protect your keep against the peasant revolt last spring from which I had to rescue you. What is it going to take to convince you? Wasn't the decapitation of your own wife enough?'

A collective gasp echoed through the room.

'M'lord!' Philabet Griswold choked.

'Your tongue is flapping dangerously, Tristan,' said Quentin Baldasarre acidly, pulling free from Lanacan Orlando's nervous clutches and interposing himself between Stephen and the Lord Roland. 'Best batten it down before you swallow it.'

'If you wish to call him out, Stephen, I will happily stand as your second,' added Martin Ivenstrand angrily.

'No,' Stephen said, pushing Quentin out of the way and locking his gaze on to Tristan's. Silence fell over the room again.

'No,' Stephen repeated. 'He's right.'

Tristan's nostrils flared, and he exhaled deeply. His fists unclenched at his sides.

'Will you stand with me now, then?' he demanded.

Stephen could feel the eyes of the others trained on him. Tristan had confronted him first deliberately, he knew, because the other dukes would align themselves with Stephen either way. Finally he nodded, still holding Tristan's gaze.

'Yes,' he said.

The collective intake of breath swallowed the air in the room, making it difficult for Stephen to breathe.

'You would support him as king?' Ivenstrand asked Stephen incredulously.

'Not as yet,' Stephen said, watching Tristan's face. 'But it is not the crown he is claiming, at least not at this time.' He turned to the others, whose faces were frozen in various expressions ranging from dismay to horror. 'How can I deny the truth of what he says? Twenty years ago Gwydion of Manosse, the best among us, the best hope for a new age and my best friend, had the life ripped out of him near the House of Remembrance – in my own lands. My wife—' His voice faltered, and his gaze fell to the floor. 'My wife, the children of my province, now these, the invited guests of my festival, Dunstin, Andrew – countless others – how can I deny that Tristan is right? How can any of us?'

'You would return us to the hand of one lord, one king?' Ihrman Karsrick asked skeptically. 'Have you, the Cymrian historian, forgotten what that led to the last time – the full-scale genocide waged by the *last* power-hungry maniacs who insisted on having "sole leadership"?' His eye caught that of Llauron, who was standing next to him, and Karsrick's voice disappeared as he realized that he was insulting the Invoker's parents. Llauron merely smiled, saluted him with the last of the brandy in his snifter, and took a sip.

'I would see us at peace,' Stephen said heavily. 'I would see this madness at an end. Obviously whatever is causing this bloody mayhem has grown too powerful, too ever-present. It is only getting stronger. It is now beyond my abilities to protect even my own people. And we still don't even know *what* it is. It is long past time that we found out.' He turned and looked back at his cousin. 'Tristan believes he can do it if we unite in support of him. I say we let him try.'

The other regents of Roland, Cedric Canderre, Quentin Baldasarre, Martin Ivenstrand, and Ihrman Karsrick, looked one to another as Stephen and Tristan continued their joint stare. Finally Cedric lowered his eyes and shook his head.

'All right, then, Tristan. I shall send my knight marshal to you upon my return to High Tower. You can work out the arrangements with him.' Tristan nodded appreciatively, breaking his glance for the first time from Stephen's. Cedric turned to Quentin Baldasarre.

'I hope you will choose to follow my lead, nephew, and end this acrimonious exchange. This has been a tragic day for our family; now all I desire is to bury my son and grieve. I suggest you commit your forces to Tristan's command, and tend to your brother as well.'

Baldasarre stared at Tristan for a moment, then nodded reluctantly, looking suddenly older and ashen.

'I will, Tristan, but be warned: do not misuse them. If you commit this new army to another foolish undertaking, like the Spring Cleaning exercise wherein you fed two thousand of your own soldiers to the Bolg, you will surely be sentencing Roland to certain death. Understand this.'

'I do,' said Tristan testily. 'And I will not have you questioning my command, Quentin. Either you acknowledge my authority, or Bethe Corbair will be forced to secede from the kingdom and defend itself. Is that clear?'

'Yes,' Baldasarre spat.

'Good. Now, what say you, Ihrman? Martin? Are you with me, or are you out?'

Martin Ivenstrand looked to Philabet Griswold, who nodded reluctantly, then to Stephen Navarne. He let loose a deep sigh.

'Avonderre is with you, Tristan. I will yield you command of my army, but not of the naval forces. I am the only province with a coastline and a shipping interest to protect.'

'That will suffice, for now,' Tristan said, walking to the sideboard and picking up the brandy decanter, which he found to be empty. He set it down again. 'And you, Ihrman? Are you casting Yarim's lot in with Roland?'

'Yes,' said Karsrick icily.

'Good. Then go home to your own lands, all of you, and send me your commanders forthwith after the state funerals. Please schedule those ceremonies so that I may attend both, as both Andrew and Dunstin were Madeleine's kinsmen.' Cedric Canderre and Quentin Baldasarre, already numbly gathering their belongings, merely nodded.

Tristan waved his hand in the direction of the benisons.

'I'd be grateful, Your Graces, if you would be so kind as to offer up some prayers to the Patriarch on my behalf, that I might lead with the All-God's granted wisdom.'

'And, of course, for the souls of the deceased as well,' said Llauron.

The Lord Roland caught the gaze of the Invoker of the Filids, and cleared his throat.

'Of course,' he said hastily. He looked into the Invoker's blue eyes and found a mild expression in them. 'Thank you for your assistance today, Your Grace. How fortunate it was for us that the chief priest of nature was among us at this time.' Llauron nodded casually, then took a final sip of brandy, draining his glass. 'I imagine this must be a poignant moment for you,' Tristan said.

Llauron smiled slightly. 'It has been a more than poignant day, my son,' he said pleasantly.

'No doubt. There was a time when we all thought that Gwydion might be the one to unite Roland into one realm again. I'm sure this brings back painful memories.'

Llauron turned so that Tristan could not see his face as he answered and set his brandy snifter on the sideboard.

'Indeed,' he said.

Hours later, within the depths of his carriage as it traveled rockily over the frozen roads back to his lands, the holy man smiled.

All in all, things had gone rather well.

17

Krevensfield Plain, South of Sepulvarta

Achmed had judged his mount to be capable of a long steady canter since the last time it had rested, and so rode steadily east through the frozen grasslands of the Krevensfield Plain, bending slightly over the horse's neck to avoid the buffeting currents of air, sprinkled occasionally with crystals of ice that whipped through from time to time from the south.

The wind had grown noticeably colder since he and Rhapsody had parted at the northern edge of the Forest of Tyrian. Perhaps that was due to winter's deepening, or maybe it was only that her fire lore made her a warm presence, even in its depth.

Nine of the demon-spawn had been successfully obtained. The information that the mad Seer of the Present had provided had been only partially helpful, and only slightly accurate; by the time they had located every child, three of them, including the Liringlas named Aric, had moved from where they had been on the day they had visited Rhonwyn in her crumbling abbey tower. Nonetheless, they had chased all of them down and caught them, some easily, some with more bloodshed, but finally each that could be had was theirs.

It had been almost painful tracking them; his Dhracian blood lore screamed in his veins each time he had caught the whiff of the Rakshas's blood, burning him as he matched the beat of his heart to the beat of the heart pumping in the demon-spawn. It had been a battle each time to disengage from his inbred command to destroy, to rid the Earth of any trace of F'dor, but he managed each time to remind himself that his prey were needed alive, so that the pure, primordial blood of the demon within their veins could be harvested and used to find it. Rhapsody's admonitions that the prey were only children had meant less than nothing to him.

Finally, with all but the last in hand, they had said goodbye at the forest's edge, Rhapsody with the remaining two children to take to Oelendra, and he on his way back to his kingdom.

It had been a difficult parting. He had made one final attempt to get her to see the folly in going after the eldest, the gladiator named Constantin, especially now that the winter carnival in Navarne was over; the visitors from Sorbold had no doubt returned to their lands, and the gladiator to the security of the arena compound in Jakar where he lived. She had refused, as always, in her maddeningly resolute manner, and so he had become resigned to the fact that they might be parting for the last time as he bade her goodbye on the doorstep of Tyrian.

Now as he rode the wide plain on his way back to the Cauldron in Ylorc he let the gusts of wind clear his mind, carrying away whatever worry they could. The icy flakes that rode the air currents stung as they impacted his skin, but he could tolerate them, concentrating on avoiding them when he could, keeping his mind busy.

He was unprepared, therefore, when the wind that slapped him at the bowl of the Krevensfield Plain carried with it a strong taste of salt.

Achmed slowed his canter and opened his mouth to allow the salty air to swirl in and around it. He spat on the ground.

The breeze contained the salty taste of sweat and blood; somewhere around here a battle was being fought.

In addition, the salt water on the wind had the unmistakable tang of the sea. Achmed spat again in disgust. Since the sea was a thousand leagues away, it could only mean one thing.

Ashe was here somewhere.

Moments later he could hear the voice of Llauron's son, calling from a swale to the south.

'Achmed! Achmed! Here! Come!'

Achmed exhaled and nudged his mount forward slowly to the upper edge of the swale, looking into the small valley below.

Even before he crested the swale he could taste the carnage on the wind. The smell of pitch mingled with fire and blood was still burning in the air, sending up tendrils of sour smoke toward the wintry sky.

Once he reached the top, Achmed winced involuntarily at the sight. The dip of the swale was strewn with bodies, some scorched from the burning pitch that still smoked on the snowy ground. Riderless horses wandered aimlessly, some still bearing their human burden slumped across their backs. The remains of a wagon burned dully in the midst of the scene. By quick count there had been a score or so horses bearing the colors of Sorbold, and another dozen in dull green or brown, with no standard displayed on their blankets. The Sorbold contingent had numbered, from the look of it, one hundred or so foot soldiers along with the twenty horsemen.

Their victims had been a smaller party, perhaps a dozen in total, apparently ambushed at the bottom of the swale, most of them brawny men, older, with an assortment of armor and weaponry, but no apparent common standard. They had held their own for a while, it appeared, but now their corpses were scattered about on the floor of the swale, their blood staining the ground a rosy pink.

In the middle of this butchery Ashe, his features obscured by the swaths of his hooded cloak of mist, was standing guard over a remaining soldier clad in motley clothing, defending the injured man from the seven remaining Sorbolds, one of whom lay at the ground at his feet. Achmed's eyes riveted on that soldier; he was swiping at Ashe with a hooked weapon that looked suspiciously like the ones used in the tunnels of Ylorc.

From a distance he judged Ashe to have the upper hand despite being outnumbered; a moment later he was proven right as Ashe, fighting with Kirsdarke, the elemental sword of water, in his left hand, and the wooden shaft of a broken wagon brake in the other, swept three of the Sorbolds down with the shaft and eviscerated a fourth in a flash of streaming blue. He looked over his shoulder at Achmed, who remained motionless atop his mount. Though his face was obscured by the hood of his cloak, the relief in his voice was unmistakable.

'Achmed! Thank the gods you're here!'

He turned again, reinvigorated, and stabbed the Sorbold with the hook through the chest, parrying the attack from the two that remained standing with the wooden shaft.

Achmed jumped down from his mount and hurried down the face of the hill, stopping halfway. He crouched in the bloody snow and picked up a short sword that lay next to the body of a dead Sorbold soldier; it gleamed in the morning light with a blue sheen as dark as midnight, its razor-sharp inner edge glinting dangerously. It was one of the Firbolg-made draw-knives, a weapon restricted to use by Achmed's elite Bolg regiment. His hands, thin and strong within their leather sheaths, began to shake with anger.

Ashe pulled his sword from the fallen Sorbold's chest, then spun out of his parry, landing a solid blow to the temple of the rightmost Sorbold. He slashed the one on the left across the neck with Kirsdarke, slamming both their heads together with crushing force. He leapt over the bodies in time to avoid the charge from the last three remaining Sorbold soldiers, looking around for Achmed.

But the Firbolg king was walking from body to body, gathering weapons, cursing under his breath.

Ashe returned to his task, quickly dispatching the remaining Sorbolds in a flurry of thrusts from the glowing water sword. He bent down and checked the fallen man he had been protecting, then turned in annoyance and shouted to the Firbolg king, who was picking up a whisper-thin disk from the ground.

'Thanks for the help,' he called sarcastically as Achmed came nearer.

'You didn't say "help," ' Achmed said, not looking up from the weapons he was examining. 'You said "come." I came. Be more specific next time.'

Ashe sighed and returned to the injured man, covering him with a saddle blanket from a riderless horse.

A moment later Achmed was beside him; he dropped the weapons with a clang onto the snowy ground, all but the cwellan disk.

'What happened here?' he asked sharply.

Ashe's eyes glared up at him from within his hood. 'Have a little respect. Do you know who this man is?'

'No, and unless he can answer my question, I can't say as I care.'

'It was an ambush of some sort,' Ashe said, checking the unconscious man's breathing. 'It appears to be part of a Sorbold column that may have broken off from the rest. I don't know what happened to the remainder of the column – there are two sets of tracks, separated by half a day or more. Undoubtedly more of the same violence the land has experienced for twenty years, but the first I've heard of on the part of the Sorbolds.'

Achmed folded his arms, reflecting silently. He had seen large, spread-out caravans making their way back to various lands on his way through the province of Navarne, though he had stayed at a distance. It seemed to him at the time that they were somber for revelers who had just attended a festival – mournful, in fact. He took a deep breath at the thought of what might have been in the wagons they were following.

'If you are headed to Navarne, you might want to have a look in on Stephen,' he said, 'if you can do it from a distance. I can see you are still in hiding, though I can't imagine why.'

'Gods – the winter solstice festival,' Ashe said softly.

'It would also help if you leave one alive for questioning next time.'

'No good – they're thralls of the demon. They never remember anything.'

Achmed nodded sullenly. 'Who is this man?'

Ashe looked down at the bloodless face. 'His name is Shrike,' he said after a moment. 'He is a First Generation Cymrian, sworn at one time to Gwylliam, and now to Anborn.'

'And you think this information would somehow interest me?'

Ashe rechecked the twine he had bound around Shrike's bleeding arm, and pulled out his waterskin.

'No, I suppose it wouldn't,' he said bitterly. 'He is merely one of the last of your kind, someone who trod the same soil on the other side of the world that you trod, that shares your history. One of the few to live that long and still keep his sanity. He is merely a human being, bleeding his life onto the ground below him. I apologize most sincerely; why on Earth would any of that interest you?'

Achmed picked up the drawknife from the top of the pile and thrust it under Ashe's nose. 'Do you know what this is?'

'It's a chicken leg.' Ashe poured the water from the skin onto a bloodstained handkerchief and placed it across Shrike's forehead. 'Or perhaps a long-stemmed daisy.'

'This chicken leg is a Bolg weapon that has no trade agreement to allow it out of the mountain,' Achmed snarled. 'These designs are secret – being in Sorbold hands means it has been *stolen,* or planted here in the attempt to cast blame for this atrocity on Ylorc, just as was attempted last summer when chewed-upon bodies were tossed into the Moot!' He threw the weapon down on the pile again and glared off to the south, to the foothills of the southern Teeth that formed the northern border of Sorbold.

Ashe shaded his eyes and looked up in the same direction.

'Seems as if someone wants to start a war with you.'

'So it seems.'

Ashe leaned down and put an ear to the injured man's chest. 'He's going to die if we don't get him to a healer.'

Achmed began gathering up the weapons again. 'So that seems as well.'

'That's rather callous, even for you. I have no horse; will you help me get him to Sepulvarta?'

Achmed glared at him and gestured to the field. 'There are two score of them running around here. Take one, and take him yourself.' He looked down at the face of the soldier; it was an old face, worn and weathered like a sailor's, with a cruel wound across the eyes. 'But I wouldn't waste my time at the basilica in Sepulvarta if I were you. When Rhapsody was injured to the point of dying in autumn I took her there; the Patriarch and his priests were less than useless.' He eyed Ashe's finger. 'That, of course, was because Rhapsody gave *you* his Ring of Wisdom to heal you. You carry the office now; the Patriarch is just a figurehead. Why don't you try to heal him yourself?'

The hooded man stared off into the wind, silent. A moment later he pulled off the leather glove that protected his left hand and took hold of the ring on the third finger. The ring was a plain one, a clear, smooth stone set in a simple platinum setting. Inside the stone, as though internally inscribed, were two symbols on opposite sides of the oval gemstone, resembling the symbols for positive and negative. Gently he took the hand of the injured man; it was a soldier's hand, rough, thick-fingered and bloody. With great care he slid the ring on the smallest finger.

Both men watched intently for a moment. The dragon nature within Ashe's blood hummed, curious, below the surface of his skin; he struggled to keep it at bay while trying to learn what it could discern. The dragon only felt a few small changes, a tiny improvement, not enough to keep the First Generation Cymrian alive much longer. Ashe judged that he might survive for a few days if he was kept sheltered, but not much more after that. Carefully he removed the ring from Shrike's finger and returned it to his own, pulling on his glove again.

'The ring is not by essence a ring of healing, but of wisdom,' he said, rising. 'It endows its wearer with the knowledge to enhance what one is already born to. The Patriarch, by study, and aptitude, and office, was a healer. He gave it to Rhapsody, who by nature and training is a healer, too. She was able to heal me with it. I am not a healer. It imparts to me wisdom in other matters.'

Achmed chuckled wryly. 'Ah, yes, that's right. It will advise you in your decisions as the Lord Cymrian if there is ever another Council called, as your father is hoping. And it has made you aware of the First Generation Cymrians still blessing us with their presence in this world – is that how you knew this man?'

'No. I have known him since boyhood. He is a great man, a kind man. He must be saved.' Ashe looked west across the Krevensfield Plain. 'If there is no one to help him in Sepulvarta, the next nearest place is Bethe Corbair. There's a basilica there, and the benison, Lanacan Orlando, is a renowned healer. Could you take him there? It is on the way to the Bolglands.'

Achmed bent and gathered the purloined weapons, fury blazing in his eyes. 'No. I will not be diverted – actually I have already been delayed far more than I can tolerate. There is nothing more essential than for me to return to Ylorc and find out what is going on in my kingdom, if I still have one left. Take him yourself – or, better yet, take him to Gwynwood to your father's Tanist. Khaddyr is said to be one of the greatest healers on the continent. If he can't help this man, I doubt anyone can.'

'He'll never make it to Gwynwood – it's too far.'

'Then take him to Bethe Corbair yourself – I will support your hiding no longer. You've been healed, and your soul has been returned to you. What else do you want? One might think it more than a bit craven of you to continue walking the world in the luxury of anonymity when your friend here is dying.'

'With your permission,' came a growl from beneath them, 'I would like to be taken to Anborn, if you please. And I'm not dying; that would be against orders.' A racking wheeze broke off his words as the old man slipped back into unconsciousness.

Achmed and Ashe stared down at the battered man at their feet, then looked to one another.

'Well, it appears the ring has given him wisdom in his lot as well, hasn't it. Do you know where to find Anborn?' Achmed asked, wrapping the weapons in a pitch-stained saddle blanket from a dead war horse. Ashe considered for a moment, then nodded. 'Sounds like a good plan. Well, I'll leave you to your journey then.' He started back to his mount.

'Wait,' Ashe called. Achmed exhaled in annoyance and turned back once more. 'Rhapsody – is she all right?'

'She told me that you were no longer keeping company,' Achmed retorted impatiently. 'If so, her condition, and all other information about her, is no longer your concern. Forget her. She has forgotten you.' He mounted, slinging the bundle of weapons before him in the saddle, and spurred the horse to a gallop. A moment later he had ascended the swale to the west and was gone from sight.

Ashe waited for a moment, as if suspended in Time, then captured a passing gelding and brought it over to where Shrike lay, breathing shallowly.

'Do not fear,' he said to the unconscious man as he lifted him into the saddle. 'I will see to it that you make it there.'

18

Eastern Avonderre, Near the Border of Navarne

Shattered blasts of freshening snow rose into the air beneath the pounding of the gelding's hooves. As it swirled up it blended with the clouds of mist emanating from Ashe's cloak, forming a fragile white screen around him and his galloping mount. From a distance he and it appeared as little more than a gust of wind whipping the snow before him.

The southern forest rim crossed the borders of Navarne and Avonderre, areas that had seen some of the greatest bloodshed from random eruptions of violence. When Ashe had traveled through this place alone, it was always silently, on foot, carefully skirting whatever living beings registered on his dragon senses.

Now, with his body restored, his soul his own once more, he braved their notice, focusing all his attention on the wounded man sprawled before him across the horse's back, and on locating his commander.

Shrike moaned intermittently as they traveled, whispering incoherently from time to time, otherwise lying silent across Ashe's knees. Occasionally the dragon in Ashe's blood felt the man's pulse ebb, his breathing grow shallow. When this happened he rested his hand, with the Patriarch's ring, near Shrike's heart, wordlessly encouraging him to hang on to life long enough to reach Anborn.

The ring's power seemed to be sufficient to sustain the man's essence, to keep it trapped within its earthly shell, at least for the moment. Ashe shielded his eyes from the sting of the wind and the burn of ice crystals slapping his face, remembering the last time he had seen a First Generation Cymrian struggle with death.

Talthea, the Gracious One, sometimes known as the Widow.

The woman had been under the care of Khaddyr, the great healer of the Filids, who was also his father's Tanist, his future successor. She lay, writhing in agony, locked in ferocious combat with the forces of this life and the next, on the Altar of the Ultimate Sacrifice, the ancient stump of a long-dead tree of massive girth, in the midst of the Circle, the center of the Filidic order.

Ashe, still a child, had stood by helplessly, dwarfed by the mourning crowd, muttering rote prayers he knew by heart but that made no sense to him and wishing desperately that she would be all right, despite never having seen her before. The wisdom of memory made him realize, more than a century later, that the anguish he felt then was mostly a reflection of the rest of the Filidic order's grief, a palpable sorrow that was raging all around him. He had not been able to understand, then or now, why her gruesome fight was not to live, but to die.

Khaddyr worked tirelessly to save her, to keep her on this side of the Gate of Life, but in the end she succumbed to wounds that should never have been mortal. Ashe had been but a young boy at the time, and had watched, devastated, as Khaddyr had bowed his head over the woman's body, then collapsed, weeping.

He could still feel the comforting grip of his father's hand on his shoulder, Llauron's voice speaking in his ear, as it did now in his memory.

She wanted to go, Gwydion. She did not wish to remain in this life any longer, and took the earliest excuse it offered her to leave.

Why? he had asked as the Filid priests gently led Khaddyr away. He stared at the corpse's alabaster face, wreathed in the death grimace of one who had lost a fierce battle.

Llauron's grip had tightened slightly; then his arm slid around Gwydion's shoulder. *Longevity that borders on immortality is as much a curse as a blessing, my boy, maybe even more so. She may appear youthful, but only because she was a young woman when she came to this new land. She left her heart behind in Serendair, a homeland that was rich in magic. After she left, both her heart and her home came to rest, silent, beneath the waves of the sea; she lost much in the passage as well. She has lived half again a thousand years, bearing witness to much suffering in that time, none greater than her own. Now finally she is where she has wanted to be all along.*

Why does she look so unhappy, then, Father? he had asked, staring at the contorted features, the furrows of pain frozen forever on her otherwise-beautiful face, her glassy eyes blindly reflecting the filtered light of the sun above the canopy of leaves.

It was a grim battle. It cost her dearly to leave this life behind.

But why?

The hand had patted his shoulder roughly, then released him. *Because she was a Cymrian, as are we. Time holds on to us all, Gwydion. Khaddyr is a compassionate man, and a great healer, but he cannot see the mortal wound within Talthea that has only festered with the passage of the centuries, because he is not Cymrian. He, like all mortal men subject to the whims of Time, struggles to stave off death as long as possible, because he does not know it for the blessing it sometimes can be. Now come, it is time to return to your lessons. For you, and for me, Time goes on.*

Ashe shook off the memory; it had come to him, stronger than it should have, with a clarity that belied ordinary recall, an almost tangible image. The scent of the funeral pyre, the grip of his father's hand, the taste of bitter bile that had been in his mouth as he watched Talthea die – all the sensations that had been part of the experience were with him again. He blinked to clear his eyes of the childish tears that had welled in them, as they had a century before.

He wasn't remembering the moment. He was reliving it.

A surge of heat on his hand shot up his forearm, making the muscles contract slightly as the power traveled up to his brain. Each tiny nerve in his fingers winced as the Patriarch's ring hummed, imparting wisdom from ages past. Ashe tightened the grip with which his knees were holding on to the gelding, bracing himself to receive the surge of enlightenment from the ancient artifact.

As though being slapped and enfolded in the swell of an ocean wave, the knowledge wrapped around him, permeating his awareness. Silver sparks brightened the air before Ashe's eyes, then illuminated a glistening path between his mind and Shrike, lying in grimacing semiconsciousness before him. His mind expanded, and he understood, at least partially, what the ring was trying to tell him.

The intense clarity of the memory was somehow connected to the man before him in the saddle.

Ashe looked down into Shrike's face, watching him wince at the jolts and lurches in the rough forest road. There seemed a flicker of fear there as well, the aspect of a man who did not yet wish to pass through Life's gate. It was all Ashe needed to spur him faster to find his uncle, a man he had seen rarely in life, and never since his all-but-death.

Time holds on to us all, Gwydion.

His thoughts remained with Shrike as his eyes returned to the road. *May it hold on to you just a little longer, Shrike,* he thought.

The wind picked up at sunset, a biting chill that penetrated the blankets within which he had wrapped the unconscious man. Ashe could feel the onset of the tremors even before Shrike began shivering violently. Against his will he finally had to concede that Shrike needed warmth and rest he was not getting, and might die without it.

He slowed the gelding to a walk and a gentle halt, then dismounted and hauled the ancient Cymrian's body off its back, allowing the animal to wander away and stretch. A bower of large mondrian bushes made a suitable shelter from the wind; they alone among fruit-bearing branches native to the western forests were resistant to the flames of the fire he would need to build. Ashe settled Shrike into a soft snowbank beneath his cache of trail blankets and began to gather fuel.

Later, once the fire caught, he found himself staring into it as if entranced. The crackling flames brought a warmth and light to the frozen darkness that reminded him painfully of Rhapsody. She was never far from his thoughts as it was; now, alone in the shelter of brambles save for the unconscious Cymrian and the howling wind, she came to him again in the fire's glow, smiling as she had in the light of their campfires when first they had traveled overland together. In the loneliest of times his mind always returned to thoughts of their journey to find the dragon Elynsynos. He had fallen ever more deeply in love with her as they traveled together through a land wakening into the sweetest spring in his memory.

Ashe shook his head, trying to dispel the thought. If he allowed himself to muse about her for more than a moment the emptiness would come back, haunting him in the depths of barren winter, the agonizing knowledge that when her memories were her own, she had consented to be his wife, had forgiven him the duplicity for which he could not forgive himself.

Now her memories were no longer her own. And by his own doing she was lost to him. It was more than he could bear to think about and still remain sane.

Shrike moaned in his sleep, snapping Ashe from his painful reverie. He uncapped his waterskin and held it to the wounded man's lips, supporting his head as he drank weakly. As he recapped the skin he felt a distant prickle on his skin, an infinitesimal hum that felt at once alien and familiar.

He had caught a taste, a breath, of Anborn on the wind.

The once-Lord Marshal of the Cymrians was miles away still, but near enough for the dragon to sense. His was a vibrational signature heavy with power and threat. Ashe exhaled deeply, his breath forming evanescent clouds of steamy vapor that lingered for a moment in the darkness and firelight, then vanished on the wind.

'Hold a little while longer, Grandfather,' he said softly to Shrike, using the Cymrian term of respect accorded to elders in Serendair long ago. 'You shall be back with your fellows and your commander ere dawn.'

The tangy scent of burning hickory cinders filled Ashe's nose as the last vestige of light left the sky. To any other nose it would have been impossible to discern, miles away, but the senses of the dragon were keen enough to detect even infinitesimal changes on the wind or in the earth, and so he closed his eyes and followed the odor to its genesis.

Through the earth he could feel the source of warmth that had spawned the crisp scent, small but intense flames burning unsteadily in the winter wind. *Torches*, he mused. There must be a small hamlet or town deep within these woods. He would undoubtedly find Anborn there.

As if reading his mind, the unconscious Cymrian stirred. Shrike's body shuddered as he came awake. Ashe patted his shoulder reassuringly as the man's eyes opened, shot with blood from his injuries, the irises black and gleaming in the fire's light.

'Rest easy, Grandfather,' he said in the Old Cymrian tongue. Shrike's bloody eyes opened wider.

'Who are you?' he rasped.

'Your protector, for the moment,' Ashe replied, glancing behind him into the dark sheets of snow undulating on the stinging wind. 'Your escort shortly. You asked me to bring you to Anborn. We are not far from him, I believe.'

Shrike blinked rapidly, as if fending off the falling snow with his eyelids. 'Who are you?' he repeated weakly.

'Does it matter?'

The ancient Cymrian struggled to sit up beneath his blankets and managed to raise himself, unaided, against the rotten trunk of a fallen tree. 'Yes, it does,' he muttered testily. 'Not to me, but it will to Anborn. And to you, if you wish recompense from me.'

Ashe chuckled. 'I've asked none such.'

Shrike closed his eyes. 'Then you're a fool, and deserve none such.' A flash of pain wrinkled his face. 'I must have offended the All-God more than I had imagined, that he would curse me to spend my last hours in the company of a coward who hides both his face and his name.' He lapsed back into weary silence.

The wintry air grew dry as the dragon bristled at the insult. Ashe took a deep breath and expelled it slowly, willing himself to be calm as his face flushed hot beneath the hood of his reviled mist cloak.

The Cymrian's words had struck deep. He knew that those who had suffered at the hands of F'dor would resent anyone who seemed to hide his identity, since that was the demon's stock-in-trade. More, to be named a coward by one who had witnessed the Cataclysm, had survived the War and all that had followed it, rang truer than he could bear. He was whole now. Even if Shrike was the demon's host himself, there was no longer any reason to hide. He reached up and took down his hood.

The light of the metallic curls of his hair, shining copper-gold in the fire's glow, reflected off the ancient man's face. Shrike felt the light and opened his tattered eyes again. The astonishment in them, tinged with horror, reflected back at Ashe.

'Impossible,' Shrike murmured. His face grew even paler.

Ashe smiled, and reached into the pocket of his cloak. He drew forth a small pouch, loosened the drawstring, and shook something small out into his hand. It caught the light of the fire in the same manner his hair had. He held it up before Shrike's eyes. It was a thirteen-sided coin, struck in copper, oddly shaped.

'Do you remember this?' he asked. 'You gave it to me years ago, when I was just a lad, to jolly me out of my boredom on a Day of Convening.'

The ancient man craned his neck with great effort, then collapsed back against the tree trunk again. 'I remember.' He pulled the rough blanket up over his shoulder with fingers that trembled. 'I can recall each time I have beheld you, Lord Gwydion, because it gave me endless joy to do so. Each time – I – looked at you I saw your grandfather, Gwylliam, at his – noblest, your grandmother, Anwyn, at her most wise. You were our hope, Gwydion, the promise – of – a brighter future for a war-torn people. Our solace. Your death was the end of hope for me – and for all the Cymrians.' The strain of speech overwhelmed him, and Shrike coughed, then went silent.

'Forgive me, Grandfather,' Ashe said softly. 'I have carried the knowledge of the injury my deception has caused my family and friends. I regret any pain it has caused you as well.'

Shrike coughed again, this time more violently. 'Why, then?'

'It was not of my doing, at first. Then it was out of necessity. I cannot explain it past that. But you are right; to continue to hide now is cowardly. I will do it no more.'

Shrike smiled wanly. 'You intend to remove the shield from your face, then?'

Ashe smiled in turn, and rested his forearms on his knees. 'When it suits me.'

'Does it suit you now?'

Ashe laughed. 'Can you see me?'

The ancient man snorted with annoyance and pain. 'Bugger you for toying with me in my last moments. Are you willing to stand in the sight of Time, and let your name be on the wind, or not?'

Ashe's face grew solemn, and his dragonesque pupils contracted.

'Yes,' he said.

Shrike inched up a little higher against the tree and smiled.

'Then I have recompense to offer you after all, Lord Gwydion.'

19

The night seemed to grow darker around the small fire. Shrike's eyes gleamed more brightly; it was as if he had drawn the light out of the air into himself, and now sat, staring into the flames, lost in thought.

Ashe waited silently, observing him closely. Though the ancient man's damaged eyes had taken on new life, his skin was growing grayer. The dragon in his blood could feel Shrike's body waning, his life ebbing away slowly, even as his soul grew stronger in the fire's light.

Finally, when the wind had died down and the night had become silent enough that the snow itself could be heard falling in soft whispers on the frozen ground, Shrike spoke.

'My sword,' he said quietly. 'Is it still here?'

Ashe rose and went to the gelding, standing twenty paces away in a copse of trees, blanketed against the snow. He unbound the curved scabbard from the saddlebag and brought it back to Shrike, putting it carefully into his hands. The old man's heart beat stronger as he touched it.

'Thank the gods,' he murmured. With great effort he eased the weapon from its sheath and held it up before his eyes. It was an ancient blade of modest manufacture and without ornamentation, old and battered as its bearer. Ashe recognized the curve of it; it was a sailor's cutlass, shortened in the same manner as the swords from the Cymrian ships that lay in the dusty display cases of Stephen's museum.

Shrike watched the fire's reflection in the dark steel a moment longer, then turned back to Ashe.

'Listen closely, son of Llauron, and I will repay your kindness.

'I met your grandsire, King Gwylliam, on the – day – the last ship of the Third Fleet set sail. I was a hand on the *Serelinda*, the vessel which – carried the king away from the Island for the last time.' Shrike leaned against the rotten trunk and closed his eyes, exerted by the effort of the speech.

'Rest, Grandfather,' said Ashe gently. 'I'm certain there will be at least a moment to talk once we reach lodging and patch you up a bit. Surely Anborn won't throw me out right away; you can tell me your story when you are feeling better.'

Shrike's eyes snapped open, blazing with intense fire. 'You're a bigger fool than I thought, Gwydion ap Llauron,' he muttered. 'What know you of moments?' He struggled to sit up taller and glared at Ashe. 'I am the Lord of the Last Moment, the Guardian of That Which None Shall See Again, so – named – by your own grandsire. Are you saying that there is none such in your own past? Nothing you would – give your very soul to see again, just once?'

Ashe's strange blue eyes blinked in shock at the harsh response. 'No,' he said after a moment, 'I would certainly not say that. There are any number of things I can think of that I would give a great deal to change if I could.' He looked away from the fire and out into the darkness, broken only by the ebb and flow of waves of crystalline snow.

Shrike snorted contemptuously. 'I said nothing of change,' he muttered, breathing more heavily. 'I cannot alter Time for you, Lord Gwydion, any more than I could for your grandsire.' He leaned back on one elbow, and brushed the snow from his head. 'Now, do you wish to hear my tale or not?'

'Forgive my rudeness. I am listening.'

The old man exhaled deeply, and drew in a ragged breath. He tilted the sword to reflect the firelight again, then looked off into the sky above him, his eyes looking past the falling snow to another night, another sky.

'Your grandsire was a man given to changeable moods, Lord Gwydion,' he said finally. 'Even before he had his vision foretelling the destruction of Serendair, the sailors told stories of his famous temper, his ready laugh that could turn to fury or despair in a heartbeat, then back again a moment later. Given that he was about to lose his birthright, and all that set him apart from any other mortal man, 'twas not surprising that he was in the clutches of a thick gloom the day we set sail, leaving the Island behind forever.' Shrike paused, and Ashe handed him the waterskin, from which he took a deep drink. Shrike capped it and handed it back, finally looking at his listener again.

'The seas were boiling, the fire beneath them raging, in the heat building from the Sleeping Child,' he said, his eyes darkening in memory. 'We were sore afraid that we would not make it out in time, all but His Majesty, who only leaned despondently on the stern rail and watched morosely as we pulled out of port for the last time, the *Serelinda* pitching fore and aft like a cork on the sea. 'Twas a miracle we were not torn apart in the crosscurrent.' Ashe, a sailor himself, nodded.

'No one dared beckon the king away from the rail, though there was word passed among the crew that his retinue feared he might go over the side. His greatest friend, Lord Hague, remained ever at his side, talking with him, keeping him tranquil; there never was a man with more of a gift for calming your grandsire than he, Gwydion.'

Ashe smiled and nodded silently. Hague had been a direct ancestor of Stephen Navarne, his best friend in life when life was still his own. Perhaps more than blue eyes ran in Cymrian royal families.

He took in breath as silently as he could so as not to distract the ancient Cymrian from his tale; Shrike's breathing had grown stronger, his lapses between words less frequent, as if the tale, and the memory it told, was sustaining him. There was a power in his voice that filled Ashe with awe, as if he was hearing history relate itself.

'As we neared the rim of the horizon, the king became even more anxious, pacing the deck and wringing his hands. He kept his eyes to the south, watching the Island ebb and return with the fallowing of the ship, panicking each time he thought it was gone from his sight forever. Even its return a moment later did not seem to calm him. 'Twas painful to watch.

'Finally, when he lost sight of it, with no return on the upwave, he grew hysterical. Madness was in his eyes, Gwydion. A score of sailors and noblemen hovered nearby, awaiting his pitch, for surely it was coming. Hague rested his hand on the king's shoulder, and Gwylliam collapsed in despair.

'I was a lookout in those days. These eyes were once sharp enough to pick out a tern in the sun a hundred leagues away; they're still a damned sight finer than most men's, I can assure you. I was standing watch in the crow's nest, and it was from there that I watched all the carryings-on.

'Gwylliam was moaning like a man on his deathbed, ranting at Lord Hague. "I've had my last sight of it, Hague; it's gone, gone forever now. What I would give to see it just once more, Hague, just once more!" Sad it is, to see a man suffer the death of all he has been, had ever hoped to be. Couldn't watch it; I had to look away, and as I did, I caught the sight of

127

Balatron's highest peak, on the north side of that purple mountain range, gleaming in the rays of the setting sun.

'I called down to your grandsire, Gwydion, shouted the bearings for him to see it again. The first mate handed him a spyglass, and evidently the king was able to sight it, too, for he grew most excited and joyful, rising out of that pit of hopelessness like a seagull on an updraft.

'He stared into the distance a good long time, becoming contemplative again, and when at last he lowered the spyglass he looked up to the crow's nest. His bright blue eyes sighted on me, and he called from the deck, "Ho, my fine man, come down so that I may thank you!" And when your king calls you so, you scurry down with all due haste.' Shrike chuckled, lost in the pleasant memory, and Ashe smiled. He could almost feel the salt spray, smell the scent of the waves, hear the creak of the decks, watching the excitement in the old man's eyes.

'When I reached the deck the king was smiling again, something I had not seen since he boarded, had never seen, in fact, since I had not had occasion to meet him, or even see him before. I confess his first words to me gave me pause – "Have you a sword, my good man?" Given his wild swings of mood and temper, I was fearful for a moment that my life was in danger, that he was somehow angry with me. Nonetheless, I surrendered my cutlass to him, as one does when the king commands.

'He asked my name, and I give it to him. "Kneel, Shrike," he says, and I prepared for my beheading. Imagine my surprise when instead he taps me lightly on both shoulders, and dubs me "the Lord of the Last Moment, the Guardian of That Which None Shall See Again," with his thanks. Coulda knocked me over with a breath, lad.'

'I can imagine,' Ashe said, chuckling. He shook the accumulation of snow from his cloak.

Shrike's face lost its smile. 'I believe when he said it he was making jest, Lord Gwydion. But it was a strange moment, not just because of his own unpredictable mood, but because of the time we were caught up in. We were at the end of an age, the last age of the first place where Time began, being flung about on a boiling sea beneath which a star was rising. And even if all that weren't the case, a king's word is a strange and powerful thing. At the time it was said in jest, but later I came to realize that an oath, no matter how it is given, has the ability to command Destiny.'

Ashe's face lost its smile. He thought back to all the times when Rhapsody had patiently explained to him the need for a Namer to speak only the truth, to be wary of what was said, even in jest, because words could become reality.

Shrike began to wheeze again. 'The long and the short of it is that I am, in fact, Lord of the Last Moment, Lord Gwydion, the guardian of – that which none will ever see again. I found over the years that I could show your grandsire that momentary glimpse of our homeland again, and again, because he had given me the power to do so. It gave him great solace in his darkest times.' He pulled the blanket closer to his neck, his hands trembling. 'Your grandmother, now, she didn't appreciate my doing so. She felt only she should be able to look back into the Past, that being her domain.'

'I'm not surprised,' Ashe said dryly. 'Anwyn is a dragon; she believes everything on Earth is hers exclusively.'

'She learned otherwise.'

'At incalculable expense,' Ashe muttered, then stopped as he saw the pain on Shrike's face. 'Forgive me, Grandfather. I'm certain your efforts brought Gwylliam great comfort, and I am glad you were able to give him sight into his lost moment.'

Shrike gave in to a racking cough, then turned his tattered eyes once on Ashe. 'And I can do so with you as well. Now, do you still wish to wait until I have been returned to Anborn?'

'If you can show me the last sight of Serendair, it would be most interesting,' Ashe said. 'But I would not risk your health further for such a vision.'

'*Your* last moment, you idiot,' Shrike growled. 'Something lost to *you*, that you have seen, that none will ever see again. Do you have such a moment in your memory?'

Ashe sat up straighter in the fire's light. Silence reigned for a time in the hidden woodland camp, broken intermittently by Shrike's heavy breath and coughing. When Ashe spoke again, his voice was soft.

'Yes,' he said slowly. 'I believe I do.'

Shrike nodded, then gestured weakly toward the low-burning fire. 'Then move me nearer, lad.'

Ashe rose, setting his waterskin down on the frozen ground. He slid his forearms gently beneath Shrike's arms, and carefully pushed him closer to the burning coals. Shrike grunted his approval when he was near enough, and Ashe returned to the log on which he had been sitting, watching the old man intently.

With great effort the ancient Cymrian raised his battered cutlass and held it so that it reflected the firelight.

'Look into the fire, Gwydion ap Llauron ap Gwylliam tuatha d'Anwynan o Manosse.'

Quickly Ashe's outstretched hand shot out. 'Wait, Grandfather; if you are to show me something in the fire, desist. I'll forgo the sight.'

'Why?'

Ashe laughed bitterly. 'Suffice to say that I don't trust the element. I would not wish any memory of mine to be visible to its denizens.'

Shrike coughed deeply, then shuddered. 'I cannot show you the Past without reflecting it to you in one of the Five Gifts, the primordial elements. In their power alone can something as fleeting as old – memory be held for a moment. We are nowhere near the sea; the stars are hidden by the snow, and the Earth – sleeps now. Fire is the only element readily handy.'

'What about a pond? Could you show it to me in such a surface?'

Shrike shook his head. 'Yes, but it's winter. Any pond would be frozen; it would distort an already hazy image too greatly.'

Ashe stood and drew his sword. Kirsdarke came forth from its sheath, the elemental water of its blade rippling like the waves of the sea. In the blue light that filled the small glade Shrike's eyes grew wide.

'Kirsdarke,' he whispered. 'Small wonder you were able to survive alone, eluding whatever was hunting you all this time.'

'Indeed.' With a smooth sweep, Ashe drew a circle in the burnt, frozen grass of the fire ring. The campfire snuffed instantly as clouds of billowing steam rose, folding in upon themselves in the moisture-heavy air, then dissipated into a wide, thin fog that hung low to the ground. Where the fire had been was a small puddle of clear water, deep and rippleless.

'Will this do?'

Shrike nodded, still watching the vapor as the wind took it, blending it into the falling snow. He turned and stared into the newly made pond.

'Very well, we'll try again. Look into the *water*, Gwydion ap Llauron ap Gwylliam tuatha d'Anwynan o Manosse.'

Ashe sheathed the water sword smoothly, extinguishing the light in the glade. He bent over the pond and stared into its darkness, snowflakes falling lightly on its surface.

For a long time he saw nothing but the all-encompassing blackness of the water, reflecting the dark sky. He shook his head, and was about to look back at Shrike when a flicker of movement in the pond caught his eye.

He could see that what a moment before had been the white mantle of falling snow now was the reflection of moonlight, diffuse and hazy in the heat of a long-ago summer. Its radiance pooled in the flax-colored hair of a young woman, still a child, really, who had sat next to him on a summer hillside, in the sweet darkness of a summer night. The flicker of movement had been the blink of her eye, wide with wonder, shining with a light brighter than the moon. She smiled at him in the dark, and Ashe could feel his knees weaken now, as they had so long ago.

Sam?

Yes? he murmured now, as he had then. His light baritone sounded much younger to his ears, filled with anxious excitement, on the verge of cracking.

Do you think we might see the ocean? Someday, I mean.

He remembered feeling that he could have truthfully promised her anything she asked of him. *Of course. We can even live there if you want. Haven't you ever seen it?*

I've never left the farmlands, Sam, never in my whole life. I've always longed to see the ocean, though. My grandfather is a sailor, and all my life he has promised me that he would take me to sea one day. Until recently I believed it. But I've seen his ship.

How can that be, if you've never seen the sea?

She had looked so wise, so sensible as she smiled at him on this, the eve of her fourteenth birthday. *Well, when he's in port, it's actually very tiny – about as big as my hand. And he keeps it on his mantel, in a bottle.*

Ashe choked on the knot that had formed in his throat, fighting back the stinging at the edge of his eyes. Rhapsody had been so beautiful then. Her face did not bear the awe-inspiring magnificence that she now kept covered with a hood, but rather the simple, dewy innocence of the spirited young girl that she was, the girl her family had called Emily. He never had the chance to see her in daylight; whatever Fate had thrown him back in Time had only allowed him one night with her, one blissful night in the hilly farmlands of Serendair where she had been born, more than thirteen centuries before his own birth.

The moment Shrike had shown him had been the moment when he had come to realize who she really was, and why Time had been altered so; she was the other half of his soul, born a world and many lifetimes away, but possessing a magic so strong that it could defy time and distance to bring them together.

Ashe's stomach turned violently as the irony clutched at him. They had spent those few moments together, only to be separated by events and trials of gruesome proportion. Fate, more cruel than kind, had brought them together for a second time, and they had fallen in love once more, only to be separated yet again.

This time, however, the one that had robbed them of the chance to be together had been Ashe himself.

The pain was becoming too much to bear; Ashe's breathing was labored. The image in the newly formed pool was beginning to fade. He whispered what he had said to her one more time as it blurred into the reflected moonlight and disappeared.

'You are the most wonderful girl in the world.'

The only answer was the whine of the winter wind. Ashe looked up, his eyes sore with unspent tears.

Shrike lay beneath the camp blanket in the dark, breathing shallowly. Ashe's dragon sense warned him immediately that the ancient man had taken a bad turn and was struggling to hold on to life once more. He stood quickly and drew the blanket tightly around Shrike, then lifted him off the ground and carried him to the horse.

'No fear, Grandfather; we are almost to Anborn,' he said as he mounted behind Shrike's hunched body. 'Lean on me and rest. We will be there very soon, and you will find solace of your own.'

Shrike could only nod, then collapsed in a fit of labored coughing. Ashe spurred the gelding onward, following the vibrations he had caught of Anborn in the distance.

'Thank you for showing me,' he said softly.

Shrike did not hear him.

20

Ashe caught the scent of the cinders first, stronger now, wafting on the wind from the west. Shrike had fallen into unconsciousness, his skin gray and dappled with cold sweat, his breathing shallow. He was clinging to life by the slightest of threads, and Ashe knew there were at least two leagues more to cover before he would reach the burning brands that had sent the cinders skyward.

His dragon sense expanded as he neared the inn where he would find Anborn. For a distance of five leagues in every direction, all aspects of information washed over him like an ocean wave, indiscriminate: the fluctuations in the heartbeat of his galloping mount, the varying weights of snow on each evergreen branch in the wide forest, the soot on the feathers of the snowwren that circled above him on a chilly updraft. Ashe swallowed and honed his concentration, willing the dragon in his blood to focus on what he sought.

He felt it instantly. A small inn, made from the rotting timber of the forest, slathered between post and beam with dried mud and mortar, a story and a half, joined by a staircase of questionable sturdiness. Thatched roof, and floor of matted thresh. Paint peeled from the sign in front of the establishment, which had once borne a fair depiction of a crowing rooster and nothing more. Eight firebrands – two recently lit, five half-spent, one on the verge of snuffing out – lighted the path in front of the inn; Ashe could tell the length of time they had been burning by the amount of melted snow he could sense pooled around their unburned bases.

Shrike groaned unconsciously as Ashe spurred the gelding onward. Four riders were approaching them, all from the northwest. He knew Anborn was aware of his presence as well, though doubtless did not know who he was; his hood was up, and the mist cloak shielded him still. He began shouting as soon as his dragon sense told him their ears could hear him, timing his call to coincide with the fading whine of the wind.

'Help! Help me! I have wounded!'

The riders, hearing his words above the howl, turned eastward in his direction and began to gallop as fast as the muddy forest path would allow. Ashe slowed his mount, wishing to be stationary when Anborn's men arrived.

It seemed an eternity before they did, a mismatched group of soldiers clad in various types of armor, bearing the standard of no royal house. Ashe recognized three of the men, Knapp, Garth, and Solarrs; they had been Anborn's compatriots for all the time Ashe had known his uncle. The Patriarch's Ring of Wisdom that he wore on his right hand told him that, like Shrike, both Knapp and Solarrs were Cymrians of the First Generation. The fourth man he did not recognize.

'Hie, in the name of Anborn ap Gwylliam!' he called. The riders slowed their mounts. Each carried a heavy crossbow that was trained on him. 'I have Shrike! He is wounded!'

Three riders reined their mounts to a halt, while Solarrs, Anborn's head scout, rode forward cautiously. He lowered his crossbow; the others remained pointed at Ashe.

'Shrike?' Solarrs shouted.

'He's dying,' Ashe shouted back into the wind. 'Take me to Anborn if you value his life.'

'You'd best not be responsible for his injuries, if you value yours,' Solarrs replied. He turned and signaled to the others. Knapp and the man Ashe didn't recognize waited while he and Solarrs passed, joined as they did by Garth. The other two brought up the rear, and the group made with all due haste toward the inn, whose glowing brands could now be seen by human eyes in the distance, blotted occasionally by the falling snow.

When the five horsemen arrived at the inn, Ashe reined to a halt and waited for the others to come and collect Shrike. Anborn's men dismounted hastily; Solarrs and Knapp rushed to him, easing the dying Cymrian from his lap and carrying him gingerly toward the inn.

At their arrival the inn door slammed open, and the flickering light of a roaring fire spilled into the snowy darkness. Several more shadows ran into the frigid night, each sliding an arm or a hand under one of Shrike's limbs or his torso, easing his transport.

The light from the doorway was snuffed a moment later as a shadow filled it, blocking the fire's illumination. Ashe inhaled deeply.

Anborn.

The ancient warrior cast a back glance toward Ashe, his face lighted by the firebrand nearest the door. Anborn signaled brusquely for him to come into the inn, then turned his attention to Shrike as the soldiers carried the wounded man over the threshold.

Ashe dismounted and tossed the reins over the horse's back, patting it gratefully on the flank. He looked up for a moment into the blackening sky; a storm was coming, though it would pass before dawn. He took a deep breath, allowing the clear air to fill his lungs, stinging his nose and throat with the burning cinders. When the noise of the soldiers had abated, he walked up the short path made of trodden snow and came into the inn.

The innkeeper looked nervously at him as he closed the door. They were alone in the inn's common room; Anborn and the soldiers were nowhere to be seen. The man gestured anxiously toward the rickety staircase, above which two doors were visible, and Ashe nodded. He took off his sodden gloves and draped them over the fire iron to dry.

Finally the innkeeper cleared his throat. 'Canna get ye some ale, sir?'

Ashe nodded, kicking the snow from his boots against the hearth as the steam from his mist cloak surrounded him. 'Thank you.'

The innkeeper scurried away behind the staircase, returning a moment later with a battered tankard filled with a thin brew. Ashe accepted the mug and returned to the fire, where he drained it. He turned to hand it back to the innkeeper, but the man had vanished.

In his stead stood the Cymrian general, the Lord Marshal of Gwylliam's ignominious army. Anborn's face was blank, and he did not look directly at Ashe. Ashe bowed slightly.

'Lord Marshal.'

'I am such no longer.' Anborn crossed his arms. 'What befell Shrike?' He sat down at a table near the staircase. A moment later three men came down the shuddering stairs; Anborn looked up questioningly, and one of them nodded. The man went back up the stairs while the other two joined Anborn at the table where tankards and a pitcher waited.

In the light of the hearth Ashe took a moment to look his uncle over with his eyes; it was always interesting to note the things his dragon sense had missed, or could not discern.

Anborn's face had not changed noticeably since the last time Ashe had seen him, twenty or more years before. It was the face of a middle-aged man, though his muscular body was more suited to a man of late youth. His hair and beard, black as night, bore a few more silver streaks than Ashe remembered. He wore the same black mail shirt he always had, its dark rings interlaced with bands of gleaming silver, and beautifully crafted steel epaulets from which a heavy black cloak once hung. Ashe knew that the cloak was now upstairs, wrapped securely around Shrike's body, giving him warmth. The general's azure eyes gleamed ferociously in an otherwise nonchalant expression. He was staring at the fire.

'I found him at the edge of the Krevensfield Plain, dying,' Ashe said. He approached the table where the men sat and set the empty mug down. 'He had been ambushed, along with his retinue, by soldiers of Sorbold.'

The men looked up, startled, at his words, and exchanged a glance, but Anborn merely nodded, his attention still on the fire.

'Why didn't you take him to Sepulvarta or Bethe Corbair to be healed?' one of Anborn's men asked. 'You risked his life further traveling with him so far in such grave condition.'

'He asked to be brought to you. He was most insistent.'

Anborn nodded again. 'You have my gratitude. If you know anything of me you know that's a valuable thing to have.'

'Indeed.'

'If you need to call in the favor, remind any of my men of your rescue of Shrike, and they will seek to aid you.' The warrior rose from the chair, but Ashe did not move. After a few moments of silently standing still, impatience darkened Anborn's countenance.

'Be off with you, then, man. I've wounded to tend to.'

'Very well.' Ashe retrieved his gloves from the fire iron, then went to the door and opened it. 'I just thought that perhaps you might wish to ask my name.'

Anborn's eyes, clear as the azure sky, grew suddenly dark. His gaze came to rest on Ashe for the first time. After a moment he motioned to his followers. 'Leave us,' he said to the men at the table without breaking his gaze away. 'Tend to Shrike.' Hurriedly the armsmen climbed the stairs and disappeared into the room at the top, the last one up closing the door resoundingly.

When the men were gone, Anborn allowed his glance to wander over the curtain of mist that shrouded Ashe from normal sight.

'Close the door,' he commanded. Ashe complied. 'I dislike games of the mind and the men who play them,' the general muttered darkly. 'I assumed you were trying to keep your identity hidden, and offered you the respect of allowing you to do so. It is rare that anyone toys with me, and even more than rare, it is unwise. Who are you?'

'Your nephew.'

Anborn snorted. 'I have none such.'

Beneath his hood, Ashe smiled. 'My name is Gwydion ap Llauron ap Gwylliam tuatha d'Anwynan o Manosse,' he said patiently. 'But you may address me as "Useless," if you'd prefer; you generally did.'

Anborn's sword was in his hand; the movement that put it there was invisible to Ashe's eyes, though the dragon in his blood sensed it and could follow the arc of electric sparks the motion left hanging in the air.

'Reveal yourself.'

Carefully Ashe took the edge of his hood in hand. He pulled it back slowly, watching the reflection from his shining copper hair catch the firelight and reflect in Anborn's widening eyes. Almost as quickly the azure eyes narrowed again, retaining the gleaming light. He did not sheathe his sword.

Ashe could feel the weight of Anborn's gaze as it assessed his face, could feel the same dragon sense that ran in his own blood, tiny pinpricks of energy where Anborn's inner nature made note of the changes in his nephew's physiology. The examination lingered longest in his eyes, eyes that had taken on reptilian pupils since the last time his uncle had beheld him. He stood as still as he could, waiting for Anborn to finish, trying to ignore the panic his own dragon sense felt at the intrusion. Finally the ancient Cymrian warrior spoke.

'Your father has been claiming for twenty years that you were dead,' he said in a tone touched with menace. 'My wife's mourning dress for your funeral was encrusted with a king's ransom of pearls to honor the tragic passing of the Heir Presumptive; the cost of the blasted thing damn near beggared me.'

'Sorry about that.'

'How woefully inadequate. I suppose your inadequacy should be no surprise. You are, after all, spawned of Llauron. What transformed you thus?'

Ashe shook off the sting of the slight. 'That matters not. What does matter is that I am here, and though I choose not to be foolhardy, I will hide no more. Not from any man, nor any demon.'

'Cocksure as always. I guess even death, or its proximate, cannot change a reckless fool.' Finally Anborn sheathed his sword. He returned to the table, where he took up his tankard and downed the contents, then looked back at Ashe again. He refilled the mug.

'I'd be a little more wary than that if I were you, Gwydion. Your newly won wyrmdom will make you all the more savory a target than you were before.'

135

'It also makes me a more formidable one.'

Anborn laughed harshly and took another drink, but said nothing. Ashe stood by silently, waiting for his uncle to speak again. Finally Anborn gestured at the door.

'Well, then, what keeps you? Be off.'

Ashe was taken aback, but gave no outward sign of it. He watched Anborn's gaze grow in fierce intensity as he wiped the ale roughly from his lips with the back of his forearm. The air in the room became warmer, drier, with an undertone of threat.

'Did you want something else?' Anborn demanded.

'I thought perhaps we could put aside old enmities and talk.'

'Why?' Anborn slammed the empty tankard down. 'I have nothing to say to you, whelp of my once-brother. Why would I waste another moment in fruitless conversation when my supper's growing cold, my man-at-arms needs looking in on, and there's a bedwench upstairs, awaiting my attention?'

Ashe took hold of the door cord. 'I can't imagine.' He pulled his hood back up.

Anborn's eyebrows drew together as his nephew opened the door. He reached hurriedly into his pocket and drew forth a small cloth sack, which he tossed at Ashe's feet.

'There. That should pay you for your trouble.'

With a sweep of his foot Ashe kicked it back to him. The air in the room hissed on the verge of cracking.

'Keep it. Your offer of it disappoints me.'

Anborn laughed menacingly. 'Not enough? I'd forgotten you would know the contents of the sack, down to the last coin, with your inner sense. Name your price, then, so that I may be rid of you.'

Ashe struggled to keep his voice calm, though the jeering tone had enflamed the dragon, and its wrath pounded behind his eyes. 'You may be rid of me by the mere request of it. Not precisely the warm family reunion I had pictured, but I will depart if that is what you wish, Uncle.'

'What did you expect, Gwydion – a lawn fete held in your honor? You and your accursed father have been lying to me for a score of years.' The general drained the tankard.

'It was necessary.'

'That may be. Further contact with you, however, is not. The truth be told, nephew, while I bear you no enmity, I felt little sorrow at the loss of you. Your return may bring joy to your confederates, to Navarne, to your mother's House in Manosse, but to me it means nothing. I couldn't care less what happens to you now. I am in your debt for the return of my man-at-arms. If you have a boon to ask, do so, and I will grant it if I can. Other than that, I have no need of your company. Be on your way.'

Ashe pulled up his hood. 'As you wish, Uncle,' he said simply. 'You deserved to know the truth about me, and now you do. Goodbye.' He opened the door and disappeared into the snowy mist.

★

Anborn waited until he could no longer hear the hoofbeats of Gwydion's horse, then took another long draught from the tankard. He watched silently as the fire burned down to coals, snapping and hissing in impotent fury. Then he rose slowly, wiped the ale from his lips, and made his way up the rickety staircase to the room above.

In the pale light of a rusty lantern his men stood around the hay mattress, quietly tending to his armsman and friend. Shrike's tattered eyes opened when Anborn came to the foot of his bed, darting quickly from man to man until their gaze came to rest on the general. He winced in pain as he turned to his fellow armsmen.

'Leave us,' Shrike said, his voice a ragged whisper.

The armsmen looked questioningly to Anborn, and he nodded silently. They quickly gathered the basin and the bloody cloths that had served as bandages, and quietly left the room.

The general took a clean cloth and soaked it in the water of the pitcher on the floor. He crouched down beside Shrike's bed and gently wiped the dried blood from his eyes. Shrike turned, and fixed his failing gaze on his commander.

'Thank the gods I lived to see you again,' he said haltingly.

'Indeed I shall,' Anborn replied, smiling slightly.

'Get – the – cutlass.'

'Later,' Anborn said. 'Rest now.'

'Bugger later,' Shrike scowled. 'It may never come. This may be the last time I can show you, m'lord – Anborn. Would you pass up that opportunity?'

Anborn fell silent for a moment as he dabbed the cool cloth on the wounded man's gray face.

'No,' he finally admitted, reluctance in his voice.

'Get it, then.'

Anborn rose wearily and strode to the corner where Shrike's belongings had been hastily tossed. He searched quickly and found the battered cutlass; he held it for a moment before bringing it back to the bedside.

'This can wait until you're stronger,' he said to Shrike, who scowled again.

'Void take you. Look into the lantern.'

Anborn reached out a hand that trembled visibly, and plucked the tarnished lantern from the bedside table. He held it up before his eyes.

Shrike watched as those azure eyes, the hallmark of Cymrian royalty, began to shine. He lay back against the hay pillow and closed his own, breathing raggedly.

21

Deep Within the Tunnels of Ylorc

The lore of the Finders

From the very oldest of days, in the very darkest corners of Firbolg history, there had been Finders.

The Bolg of Canrif had no recorded legends, no traditions immortalized in a permanent fashion; they were as a race illiterate, or at least had been until Achmed, himself of their bloodline by half, appeared as if by magic from the other side of the world and took the mountain almost by the mere demand of it.

Subduing the mountain had been a simple undertaking, really. One of the first places that the Three had found in the abandoned ruin which had once been Gwylliam's seat of power was the royal library, the heart of Canrif. It contained an endless collection of maps, plans, and manuscripts, some brought from the Lost Island of Serendair, all carefully catalogued and preserved in scroll tubes of marble and ancient ivory, stored under the watchful eyes of the enormous red-gold dragon fresco sprawling across the domed ceiling, its silver-gilt claws poised in mute threat.

The library also guarded the entranceways to the deeper treasure vaults and reliquaries in which items of great value to the long-dead king had been kept. It had even contained the body of the long-dead king himself; they had discovered Gwylliam's mummified corpse sprawled on its back amid the rotting fabric of his robes of state, his shriveled chest cruelly sundered. His simple crown of purest gold lay on its side next to him, testament to exactly how the mighty had fallen.

But the items in the library of most value to Achmed's conquest of Ylorc were the apparatuses the Cymrian king had built to track movement within the labyrinth, and the series of listening and speaking tubes that ran throughout the mountains, some visible, some hidden, most of them still operational, all of them useful. It had only been a matter of manipulating these inventions, along with the ventilation system that brought heat and fresh air into Canrif, to convince the current inhabitants that they were outmatched in their own land.

The Bolg surrendered more or less willingly to their new warlord, someone who could return the mountainous cities of the 'Willums,' as they called the Cymrians, to their former glory, this time under the hand of a leader who was half-Firbolg. They knew nothing of his other nature, the Dhracian side, which sought above all things to find any of the F'dor demon-spirits that might have escaped the great Vault of Living Stone which the dragons had built to imprison them in the Before-Time. It was a blood vow far more ancient than any he swore to them as their new king, but the Firbolg were utterly ignorant of it.

Once Achmed's reign had begun in Ylorc, Rhapsody had insisted that educating the Bolg in lessons other than warfare was necessary if they were to be able to stand on their own and not only hold the mountain against the bloodthirsty men of Roland, but build a culture that would hold currency outside the mountain. Until this year those men had participated in an annual genocide known as Spring Cleaning, a ritual of butchery in which the Bolg had offered up their old, weak, and ill in exchange for being left alone for the rest of the year.

This past spring, however, a new wind was blowing through the peaks of the Teeth. The soldiers of Roland had come as usual, this time two thousand strong at the insistence of Tristan Steward. They had discovered, much to their woe, that the monsters they were used to dispatching with indifference had been learning the lessons of slaughter that they themselves had inadvertently taught. Achmed had delivered the news of the Orlandan brigade's massacre at the hands of the Bolg to the Lord Roland personally, waking him from his sleep in his own bedchamber with the ultimatum that would lead to a reluctant peace treaty ten days later.

I'm the Eye, the Claw, the Heel and the Stomach of the Mountain. I have come to tell you that your army is gone.

The Lord Roland had risen shakily from his slumber, trembling as he listened to the sandy voice that seemed to be part of the darkness itself.

You have ten days to draft a trade agreement and to sue for peace. My emissary will be waiting at the present border of my realm and Bethe Corbair on the tenth day. On the eleventh day the border will begin to move closer, so as to facilitate our meeting. If the inclement weather discourages you from traveling, you can wait a fortnight and hold the meeting right here at the new border.

Tristan Steward, his cousin, Stephen Navarne, duke of the province that bore his family name, and Tristan's brother Ian Steward, the benison of Canderre-Yarim, had indeed appeared at the border, the first two prepared to pursue political ends, the benison religious ones. They had all been easily bested in their negotiations by Rhapsody, who had charmed them into trade agreements generous to the Bolg and peace accords restrictive to Roland with little more than an unconscious blink of her green eyes. Tristan Steward had returned home to his central province and his unpleasant fiancée with the disturbing sense that he had handed over both his birthright and his soul to Ylorc.

What Tristan Steward could not have known was the nature of the fuse his misguided decision to send a full brigade against Achmed's troops had lighted.

The natural process of establishing diplomatic ties with a new regime is traditionally a long one for good reason. It takes time for a freshly crowned monarch to learn everything he needs to know about his kingdom from his newly ascended throne, to sort out the positive and negative aspects of having a relationship of any kind with neighbors, allies, and enemies.

The destruction of Tristan's army had hastened that legitimizing process. The horror of it rippled like wildfire through the provinces of Roland and the outlying continental lands of Sorbold to the south, Gwynwood to the west, the Hintervold to the north, and even the nations beyond the Teeth to the east. Only the Lirin realm of Tyrian, the vast forest that abutted the southwestern seacoast, sent no ambassador to Ylorc, gave no indication that the ascension of a Firbolg warlord to Gwylliam's throne had made any impression upon them at all.

With that exception, all the neighboring realms of Ylorc were eager to press for whatever accords they could to ensure the continuation of peace with the Bolg and to perhaps engender a little bit of commerce on the side.

Particular interest existed in Sorbold, the arid realm of sun that had once been part of the Cymrian empire but now stood alone, an independent nation tied to Roland only through the common religious connection to the elderly Patriarch of Sepulvarta, the head of the religion of both lands. The Sorbolds craved access to the fine weapons being produced in the fires of the Firbolg forges. There were few natural resources in their land, and steel production there was expensive and difficult.

They pressed the issue through Syn Crote, their ambassador, who was noted for his persuasiveness. But Achmed, while signing trade treaties for other goods, withheld the sale of armaments to Sorbold, reasoning that it was singularly unwise to outfit a bordering nation, no matter how friendly its ambassador, with the weapons of his own arsenal. The Crown Prince of Sorbold bit his tongue and smiled painfully, but any fool could see that the resentment of this arrangement would sooner or later lead to, at bare minimum, renewed discussions, and probably worse. For the moment, however, peace reigned.

Once the trade agreements were set in place, King Achmed drafted a plan to protect those transactions and other correspondence from the random and inexplicable violence that had been a staple of this new land since he, Rhapsody, and Grunthor had crawled out of the Root into this place.

A series of guarded caravans, accompanied at weekly intervals by two score and ten of Tristan Steward's soldiers, made the rounds of all the interconnected lands of the middle continent – Ylorc to Bethe Corbair to Sorbold to Sepulvarta, across the Krevensfield Plain to Bethany and Navarne, then on to Tyrian to Avonderre to Gwynwood and Canderre, north to the frozen Hintervold, then east to the heat of Yarim and back, at last, to Ylorc. The route was a fairly easy one, though it traveled through varied terrain, making use of the old Cymrian road system that had been built in the empire's heyday.

With the return of relatively safe mail and selective travel came at last some relief from the sense of isolation the different realms of the continent had felt over the last twenty or so years, since the violence had escalated to its terrifying level. Those traveling in carriages and merchant carts would schedule journeys, when possible, to coincide with the weekly caravans, grateful for the opportunity to benefit from their protection.

For one group, however, one unknown, secret group in a little known land, the mail caravans provided something completely different. To the

Finders, it was an opportunity, the first in history, to seek something in a distant place that might help bring the Voice to them again at last.

Even the Bolg populace that shared the same mountains, held the same watches, and had inhabited the same realm for five centuries knew nothing of the existence of the Finders who lived among them. It was a society that was secret, membership seeming to pass inconsistently through certain clans, its lineage unclear. The harsh reality of Firbolg existence coupled with a decided lack of sophistication when it came to genealogy tended to prevent a trend from being recognized. Even within families the secret was kept – it was not spoken of from father to son, or between mates. No one knew of the Finders except the Finders themselves, and even they did not seek to know the names of all who felt the calling.

And it was a calling in the strictest sense that brought them together. They had nothing else in common that they could discern – no physical attributes that they could see as similar. Part of the reason for this was the widespread pollution of the Bolg bloodline; they were a truly bastard race, adulterated with the blood traits of every other race they had contacted, and so no pure Bolg racial characteristics existed. Another reason, however, was that they met in the dark, and therefore could not see what others might have – that there was a unique aspect to most of them, a slightly more human, or perhaps just slightly more refined, appearance than the other Bolg.

Appearance, however, was not the main trait the Finders had in common. Had Bolg life been less treacherous, less prone to early demise, it might have been noted that the Finders had a tendency toward longevity, at least by Firbolg standards. But since the day-to-day reality of Ylorc was a harsh one, there was often such early mortality that this trait never grew into a trend, either. Even the new warlord's party of four, which had arrived and taken the mountain the previous winter, had been reduced by one; the Second Woman, the yellow-haired teenager called Jo that the Bolg believed to be King Achmed's less favored courtesan, had died as the leaves had begun to fall, less than one turn of the seasons after they had come.

So, though the Finders did not recognize a common physical similarity among themselves, nor notice their disposition for a somewhat longer life span, they did observe one very specific ability to be unique among the members of their unspoken fellowship – they had a sense of the where-abouts of Willum objects, especially those marked with the Sign.

The Bolg as a race were not given to storytelling, and so the tales of their history were inconsistent as well as few and far between. But one piece of history was more or less common knowledge among all the clans of the Bolg: the Eyes, the mountaintop-dwelling spies; the Claws, those Bolg that inhabited the western areas of Ylorc that ended with the vast, dry canyon and the Blasted Heath above it; and the Guts, the fierce, war-prone clans of the Hidden Realm, the deep lands beyond the canyon.

Regardless of clan, all the Bolg knew the story of their taking of the mountain from the Willum king.

Before they inhabited Canrif, once one of the wonders of the world, ruined for centuries and now, slowly, undergoing reconstruction, the Bolg had been cave dwellers, a subhuman population barely more manlike than the cave bears and subterranean wolves that preyed upon them, and that they in turn preyed upon. They had lived in endless darkness, and bred with whatever small enclaves of outsiders they could subdue. Firbolg as a race lived all over the world, but the individual members would never have known that, because their concept of the world was limited to the caverns and hillsides in which they scratched out a hard and sometimes brutal living.

At least, that is, until the Willums came. The Firbolg had made note of the Cymrians almost from the moment the wayfarers from Serendair arrived in the Teeth; the ragtag caravan of storm-tossed survivors of the Third Fleet's tumultuous crossing had at first looked like prime targets for attack – vulnerable, exhausted, utterly without hope, or so it seemed; Bolg could smell such a thing. When, however, their numbers became clear – there were more than fifty thousand of them – the Bolg slunk back to the shadow of their caves. They watched as the newcomers transformed the mountains into towering cities, sprawling farmlands, well-tended forests, and deep labyrinths, the empire Gwylliam named Canrif, the Cymrian word for century, because he had vowed that within a hundred years' time it would be the marvel of the world.

And so, as the Cymrian empire grew and expanded, the Bolg disappeared deeper and deeper into the earth, moved farther back into the wastelands to the east, until the War came.

Gwylliam's battle with his wife and queen, Anwyn, the half-dragon daughter of the wyrm Elynsynos, had started as the result of what the Cymrians called the Grievous Blow, a strike across her face resulting from a marital spat of unknown cause. The resulting war decimated both the continent and the Cymrian population, which had split in twain, some choosing to follow Anwyn, others remaining loyal to Gwylliam. It was a bloody conflict that tore families asunder, even pitting Anwyn and Gwylliam's own sons, Llauron and Anborn, against one another, and causing the eldest son, Edwyn Griffyth, to abandon the family altogether.

The Bolg knew none of the details. They did know, however, that the once impenetrable fortress in the Teeth was crumbling at the edges; the border patrols that had held an iron grip on the mountains were scarcely seen at all after the first two centuries of the seven-hundred-years-long war. Five hundred years into the conflict, the Bolg finally worked up the courage to begin to take advantage of the situation.

Slowly at first, and then, encouraged by their success, with a bolder outlook, a few clans began to establish small enclaves at the outskirts of Gwylliam's vast realm. The Lord Cymrian had been too engaged to care that a ratty population of cave dwellers found its way across the eastern steppes and into some of the older sections of his vast labyrinth. Minor reports of lost Cymrian patrols or stores unaccounted for were hidden in the greater and bloodier balance sheets of the battles against Anwyn. His indifference proved to be his kingdom's undoing in the end.

As Anwyn's army was approaching, preparing to launch their last in a series of unsuccessful assaults on the mountain, the Bolg took the opportunity to overrun Canrif. Gwylliam had disappeared, and Anborn, Gwylliam's youngest son and his general, was faced with the grim decision to evacuate while he could, or try and fight the battle on two fronts, from within the mountain as well as from without. He calculated wisely that he could not hold both, and that, in fact, the mountain was already lost to the Firbolg. Canrif, the crown jewel of the Cymrian empire, which had stretched from the mountains to the western seacoast, encompassed great provincial cities, built and maintained thousands of leagues of roadways and aqueducts, basilicas of visionary architecture, and harbors sheltering a thousand ships at a time, crumbled like sand and fell forever into the eagerly outstretched hands of a populace the humans considered to be monsters.

With the overrunning of Canrif came looting, of course, and all the treasures left behind – at least those things not hidden within the library's vaults, because the library had been fitted with a musical lock that the Bolg had never been able to open – were gathered, split, battled over, or destroyed. So much of what the Cymrians valued – writings, art, maps and artifacts of the old world, museum pieces and items of technological invention – were of little or no use to the Bolg, and ended up as spurned booty. An entire private library of ancient manuscripts became fuel for a celebratory bonfire.

What the Cymrians left behind that the Bolg did value was joyfully divided or viciously fought over, sometimes again and again. Livestock, textiles, weapons and armor, and food stores were seized and carried off. Jewelry was prized as well. Even now, five centuries later, it was not uncommon to see the most ragged of Bolg women or even men, their bodies hard and leathery from lack of clothing and exposure to the elements, walking the corridors of Canrif wearing ornate necklaces on their heads like circlets or earrings clipped in their hair.

Gold coins, while initially interesting because of their shine, quickly were discarded by most of the Bolg. The culture had no concept of currency, though they did grasp the idea of barter, but only in that they knew how to trade useful goods for other useful goods. Shiny, heavy metal, while pretty, but too soft to make a reasonable weapon, had no real value, and thus was left, discarded, when the Bolg scavenged the abandoned hallways and chambers where the Cymrian populace had once lived.

But these coins did have value to the Finders, because they bore the Sign.

The sign was common in the Willum city. It was a symbol that meant nothing to the Bolg, and, in fact, contained pictures of things they had never seen before. In the foreground of the image was a star shining over the heads of a rampant lion and a griffin, beasts the Bolg had never seen nor even could have imagined. Behind those beasts was an image of the Earth,

143

an oak tree growing on it, with roots that pierced through the bottom; again, nothing recognizable to such a primitive culture.

The Finders valued anything Willum they could find, but in order to have a place in this secret brotherhood, a man or woman had to prove himself or herself to be a true recipient of the call by finding something that bore the Sign.

In the early days after the Willums had been driven from the mountain this had been a relatively easy thing to do. But as the centuries wore on, anything that had been lost in the melee had most likely been found, or had fallen so deep into the ruin of the underground city that discovering it was sheer luck. Each new discovery was cause for great excitement, because perhaps it was the item the Voice had demanded be brought to it. Over the centuries a vast hoard of items had been found, but none had proven to be the right one. Eventually, it seemed that everything that could be found within the mountain, or across the Heath in the Hidden Realm, had been found.

Still, the late-generation Finders did feel the presence of a few trinkets here and there in distant places. Most were within the realm of Roland, and therefore 'finding' them would be out of the question. A few items, however, had been sensed by many generations to be in Sorbold, but until the trade agreements and the great caravans made it possible, there was no way to broach the mountains to get them.

Until now.

The coming of the Dark Man, one who called himself the Snake King, to the mountain had provided the means for the Finders to finally obtain their treasure.

And his leaving had provided the opportunity for them to do so.

Hagraith waited in the shadows of the barracks fire, the stew in his battered metal plate growing cold, untouched. As the soldiers of his regiment, selected from the heartier of Eye and Claw clans of the Inner Teeth, chortled and ate greedily in the flickering light, he was watching, listening for the sign only he knew was coming.

At first he almost didn't hear it. It was muffled by the clanging of metal plates, the grunting and scuffling. But deep and distinct, repeated twice, he heard the tones, five together, chanted twice. He lowered his eyes into his mug.

Tonight the meeting place would be at the Hand.

In the darkest corridors of the part of the labyrinth known as Sigreed, the Crypt, or more literally the Village of the Dead, four men met in secret. In the distance they could hear the ringing of the ancient forges pounding out new weapons, new armor, new steel for the Rebuilding, a hollow, clanging sound that was more than a little unnerving. If the Bolg had been literate they might also have found it unnerving to be hiding among row upon row of burial plaques that lined the walls of the corridors, marking the tombs of

144

viceroys and chancellors, confessors and advisors of the Cymrian Age long gone, their wisdom now buried deep.

Hagraith crouched nervously in the Thumb of the Hand, the eastern tunnel that led to the central area known as the Palm, where four other tunnels also met. Tucked beneath his jerkin was a bundle wrapped in tanned leather, his prize for admission to the brotherhood. He had discovered it quite by accident when on maneuvers deep within the Hidden Realm, and had felt its call intensely. Buried within a rotten crate in a peat bog that had once been the ruins of a Lirin city, the porcelain plate he was hiding in his jerkin was a miracle for many reasons; it not only bore the Sign quite clearly, but it was as yet unbroken, unmarred by Time. If he could will himself to stop shaking, it might remain that way long enough to be presented.

Krinsel, one of the most powerful of the Finders, and one of the First Woman's favored midwives, nodded to him in the dark. She was holding a wick of candle tallow at the end of which a tiny spark burned, the only light in the consuming darkness. Krinsel sat cross-legged in the Palm, where she could see the other Finders who cowered in the other Finger tunnels which fed into the central area. Near her left foot were the ropes that would seal each tunnel if any sound came near other than the clanging of the forges in the distance above them.

When Hagraith did not move Krinsel's eyes narrowed, becoming slits in the darkness.

'Give.'

Trying to keep his hands from shaking, Hagraith crept to the opening where the Thumb joined the Palm and carefully pulled the leather package from beneath his jerkin. He held it out to Krinsel, who took it with steady hands, the hands that had caught a generation of infants and more than a few treasures that bore the Sign. He skittered back to the recesses of the Thumb, panting.

With great delicacy Krinsel unwrapped the plate, holding it in one hand as she held the low-burning tallow up to examine it. Her eyes widened, and her face relaxed into a slight smile.

'It is the Sign,' she said reverently. After a moment she turned her dark gaze on Hagraith. 'Finder you are.'

Hagraith bowed his head in relief, feeling the tightness in his abdomen abate. Sweat that had been held back by fear now poured from his brow.

He could keep his testicle, the price of misinterpreting the Sign or presenting a false find.

Krinsel held the plate aloft in both hands and closed her eyes.

'This one it is, Voice?' she asked quietly. The other Bolg crouched in the Fingers closed their eyes, listening intently, but they heard nothing but the noise of the smithy, the hammers ringing steadily, slowly.

After a moment she opened her eyes and shook her head stoically. 'For the hoard this is. Good, Hagraith. Finder you are.' She turned to the tunnel that lay in the place of the Smallest Finger. 'Give.'

One by one she examined the objects – a coin like the thousands of others in the hoard, the badly scarred lid to a box made of wood with a blue undertone to it, and finally a pot that had been brought all the way from Sorbold with the Sign inscribed inside. Each item Krinsel pronounced as genuine, and held high for the Voice to recognize.

As always, there was no answer.

Smoothly Krinsel rose and nodded to the empty tunnel in the place of the Pointing Finger that led down an endless corridor to the hoard. The Finders followed her, bearing their treasures to the place such things were housed.

22

The Cauldron, Ylorc

Night had fallen when Achmed returned to the Cauldron. The lamps had been lighted, filling the brightening hallways with thick smoke and the rancid smell of burning fat, which seeped quickly into his sensitive sinuses and nasal cavities. It made his bad mood even blacker.

The chandeliers in the Great Hall had been lighted as well; the renovations were almost finished. He took a moment, even in his fury, to stop and look around at the awesome sight of the polished marble columns, the newly restored symbols of the star Seren, the Earth, the moon, and the sun meticulously inlaid in the floor. Above him the domed ceiling was a dark cerulean blue, studded with tiny crystals that reflected the light of a mirrored device in the center of the floor, making it look like the firmament of the sky sprinkled with stars.

The illumination from the firepit in the floor that lighted those mock stars was the only light in the vast room, leaving many corners of it dark. Achmed stepped into a shadow, breathing evenly to slow his wrath.

Grunthor was sitting in one of the ancient marble thrones on the dais, one enormous leg slung over the arm of the stone chair. He was singing one of his favorite chanteys, fueled, no doubt, by the contents of the large flask that sat in a place of honor on the other throne.

> When the sounds of grim battle
> Have long stopped their rattle
> And the sweet smell of entrails and gore
> Pass away on the wind
> Salute me, my friend,
> For I'll go a-roving no more.
>
> I'll no longer tarry on
> And leave to the carrion
> The glory of well-wa-ged war,
> When the killing's all done

146

What's the point? Where's the fun?
Oh, I shall go roving no more.

On that bittersweet day
With no more foes to slay
Our martial life naught but a bore,
We'll make us some thrones
Of their skulls and their bones,
And we'll go a-roving no more.

The fury exploded behind Achmed's eyes. Angrily he strode down the long aisle leading up to the dais.

Grunthor heard him coming at the beginning of the next song he was preparing to sing. He stopped, stood quickly to attention, and broke into a wide grin, which disappeared as the king came to a halt before the dais, slamming down his bundle of weapons on the floor. The crash of steel and the clang of metal jangled harshly.

Grunthor looked at him in amazement. 'What's all this, then?' he asked.

Achmed crossed his arms.

'When I asked you to watch over the throne, I had not meant that you should be warming it with your considerable arse while someone sells the kingdom out from under me.'

Grunthor, still standing at attention, went even more rigid. The muscles in his tree-trunk arms began to tremble with anger, and his face solidified into a mask of blind fury. Achmed waved at him dispassionately.

'At ease, Sergeant. I'd rather snarl at you as my friend than berate you as my Supreme Commander.'

Grunthor assumed parade rest, his face now a stoic mask within which two eyes filled with fire burned.

'What's all this, then?' he repeated steadily. 'Sir.'

'A cache of weapons I found among the bodies of a quarter-column of dead Sorbold soldiers,' Achmed said, pushing the weapons around with the toe of his boot. 'They're culls, fortunately – the Sorbolds are such mindless imbeciles that they cannot even see the flaws, the lack of balance. But they had them – any thoughts as to how *that* might have happened?'

'No, sir,' the Sergeant replied rigidly.

Achmed watched Grunthor for a moment, then turned his back to him. It was time for the longtime ritual.

'Permission to speak freely?' said Grunthor rotely.

'Granted.'

'I proffer my resignation, sir.'

'Refused.'

'Permission to speak freely?' the Sergeant repeated.

'Granted.'

He listened, his back still turned, for the great relaxation of military discipline, for the enormous inhalation that came whenever Grunthor crossed from the realm of loyal soldier into the one of enraged equal. He braced himself as the great rush of air surged in through Grunthor's huge, flat nose.

The Sergeant-Major threw back his head and roared at the top of his lungs. The sound echoed through the Great Hall, making the columns vibrate.

A moment later from behind Achmed there came a rending of carpet and the cracking of iron bolts. One of the ancient thrones of Anwyn and Gwylliam, formed from solid marble and weighing in excess of three men in full armor, sailed through the air over Achmed's head and bounced off the polished stone floor, skidding over the image of the star and coming to a halt, with a tremendous thud, on its side. Silence reverberated in the Great Hall.

Achmed turned back to Grunthor.

'Feel better?'

The Sergeant was mopping his gray-green brow. 'Yes sir, a bit.'

'Good. Now, let me hear your thoughts.'

'When I find out who broke faith, I'm going to stick every one of those weapons in his eyes, then roast him over sagebrush and serve him to the troops for the holidays on a bed of potatoes with an apple up his arse.'

'Rhapsody does always say that you should celebrate special occasions by having friends for supper. Any other thoughts?'

The giant Bolg nodded. 'It's got to be someone on the third shift – that's when the culls are destroyed.'

'More than likely. But there are two thousand men on the third shift, and it will take an egregiously long time to discover which few are responsible. Agreed?'

'Yeah, but we have to root out the traitors.'

'Yes, but we have other, greater concerns. In the months I've been gone our most secret weaponry has made its way into the hands of a neighboring army. If Sorbold is to be the staging ground of the attack on Ylorc, they have far more knowledge of our workings than I am comfortable with. We have to respond quickly.'

Grunthor nodded. 'Am I still under the banner of "permission to speak freely," sir?'

Achmed glanced over his shoulder at the throne of Gwylliam, sideways on its arm. 'Yes.'

'Then I say if we're going to be in for this, let's be ready.'

'Details, please.'

Grunthor began to pace, concentrating. 'If we're going to war, let's go to war. Conscript every able-bodied adult and youth. Suspend the school, and train the brats to carry water, roll bandages, sling rations. Muster out every village, every enclave, women, men, *everyone*.' He stopped long enough to meet Achmed's eye. 'The Duchess isn't going like it.'

'Does that concern you?'

'Not in the least, sir.'

'Good. What else?'

'Put the smithy on triple shift. Put the mountain guard on patrol there, minding the inventory and the cull pile. Belay the specialty stuff – concentrate on long-range missile weapons and heavy armaments for the crag catapults. Tap the anthracite veins more deeply; mine the coal shale in all-day, all-night shifts. Boil down an ocean of pitch. Take off the mantle of "men" and let's go back to being monsters. If we're going to be in for this, let's make a stand that'll have them writing dirges for centuries to come. I want my name to be set to mournful music and sung sadly by widows all the way to Avonderre.'

A small smile came to Achmed's face. 'Now, won't that be a beautiful thing. All right, Sergeant; gear up. Make the mountain impenetrable. We've known from the start this day would come. Whoever this damned demon is, if he wants Ylorc, if he wants the Sleeping Child, I want him to have to come through me to get them. But before he gets to me, let us make the mountains fall on everyone else who came with him.'

Grunthor nodded, saluted, then strode out of the room, his rage converted to an even more deadly form – purposeful vengeance.

The voice of the Grandmother echoed in his ear.

You must be both hunter and guardian. It is foretold.

He pulled the pillow over his head and spoke the words of reply he had spoken then.

Bugger foretold.

A voice even older, Father Halphasion's voice, the mentor of his youth on the other side of the world, in a place that slept now beneath the waves of a restless sea.

The one who hunts will also stand guard.

Achmed blinked in the darkness.

Were you the one who spoke the prophecy into the wind? he asked hazily in his mind. *All those years before – was it you, Father?*

Nothing but the darkness answered.

Achmed had resolved centuries ago to avoid caretakership. Over the course of his long, strange existence he had found that love, life, and loyalty were ephemeral. Therefore, choosing to protect or preserve anything, an eternally sleeping child, even a mountain, was a guarantee of failure, ruin.

He lay now on his silk-draped bed, the one true luxury he had allowed himself. The slippery softness of the bedsheets soothed the eternal itch, the irritating burn of his skin; that, coupled with the solid basalt walls, kept the vibrations of the world around him at bay, or at least they had once. Now, with the forges already ringing in frenetically accelerated rhythm, with the constant sound of running bootsteps passing by his doorway, there was no peace to be had in the advent of war.

Achmed rose slowly and slid into his clothes. He waited in the doorway of his bedchamber until the heavy footfalls died away, listening in the near-distance to the noise of martial buildup awakening in his orderly mountain.

He did not have to hear the sound of the Sergeant-Major's voice bellowing commands to feel their results; the smooth ripples of air that routinely caressed the sensitive nerves in his skin-web had been replaced already by bristling shocks, frenetic energy that signaled the coming of war. He sighed deeply, feeling the work of Time upon his body and spirit for the first time since he had come to this dark and all-but-silent place.

He pushed open the sides of the the plainly fashioned cedar chest at the end of his bed and stepped into the hidden passageway, leaving the edges of the sheets to trail in the dirt at the edges of the tunnel beneath the bed for a moment. Then he closed the portal behind him.

He allowed himself a sigh as he crept through the secret bedchamber passageway, ruminating on the mysteries of guardianship. Grunthor had no need of his protection, or his scolding. Rhapsody was refreshingly, if maddeningly, independent and had absolutely no expectation of him being her protector.

Half his life had been spent in training to be the perfect guardian, and the other half spent on proving that nothing anywhere was safe. The king shook his head as he made the early turns toward what remained of the Loritorium; he was not at all certain which half had been wasted.

The people of these mountains, and the secrets, which once he thought to be his armor against an old nemesis, were weighing now upon him like armor, armor that sometimes protects but can be a hindrance or even a danger. He had fallen into a river from horseback once wearing such armor; the current had pulled him under, the armor dragging him down into the water that he so despised. His responsibility to the Bolg weighed on him similarly now. It was taking every speck of his resolve to stay here and build a battlement around those for whom he felt responsible. If his way were to be had, he would be out, alone, cwellan in hand, until it was over.

Achmed picked his way through the ashes and rubble to the remains of Gwylliam's great crypt. Little of value remained, some melted metal sconces, a few small shards of tile from the never-finished mosaics – all else had been destroyed in the conflagration that Rhapsody had lighted to destroy the demon-vine, the bastardized root of the Great White Tree that the F'dor had utilized to violate, to broach the mountain in its attempt to snatch the Sleeping Child from the colony of long-dead Dhracians who had sought to protect her.

He jumped down from a high pile of debris to find himself standing beneath the great dome of the Loritorium, the smoothly ascending arch where a case had once been built to house the fire from the star of the old world, Seren, itself. In the wide circle of what had once been planned to be the central courtyard he could see the altar of Living Stone and the large, reclining shadow atop it.

The child's body was as tall as his own, yet still there was a frailty about it, despite being formed from the living earth itself. She lay, supine, slumbering beneath Grunthor's greatcloak, which he had covered her with when last they were in this place. From the side she looked like a death statue on a catafalque. The sweet contours of her face were that of a child, and her skin shone with the cold luster of polished gray stone. Below the surface of filmy skin her flesh was darker, in muted hues of brown and green, purple and dark red, twisted together like thin strands of colored clay. Her features were at once coarse and smooth, as if her face had been carved with blunt tools, then polished carefully over a lifetime.

Achmed approached the altar slowly, careful not to disturb the child. *Let that which sleeps within the Earth rest undisturbed,* the Grandmother, the last survivor of the Dhracian settlement and the child's guardian had warned. *Its awakening heralds eternal night.*

He came alongside her and stopped. As he looked down at her from above he noted she was trembling beneath the greatcoat.

There were tears on the lashes that appeared formed from blades of dry grass, matching the texture of her long, grainy hair. Since he had last seen her that hair had gone from the gold of frost-bleached wheat to white, even at the roots which had once hinted at the grass of spring, mirroring the blanket of snow that now enveloped the earth.

Achmed swallowed heavily.

'Shhhh, now,' he whispered in his dry voice, the words barely passing through his lips. The Earthchild was frightened; he could feel it in his skin, in the depths of his bones. The earth around her was thundering with the anvil blows, the shouted orders, the horrific cacophony of the buildup to war.

Achmed crouched down beside her and gently pulled the greatcoat up over the child's shoulders. He cleared his throat.

'Hrrhhhhrmmmm – er, don't worry,' he said. His winced at the inadequacy in his own voice, and so bent closer, running a careful finger over the Earthchild's hand.

He closed his eyes and concentrated on the rapidity of her breathing, matching his own to it, and then willing it to slow.

'I know you can feel the earth being rent right now,' he said as gently as he could. 'And I'm sure it pains you. But do not be afraid. Do not fear the noise; it is there for your protection. You are safe, I swear it.'

A single tear welled up from under the child's closed eyelid and crept down her face. Achmed ran a nervous hand through his hair and leaned even closer.

'I will be your guardian,' he said softly, barely giving voice to the words. 'Yours, and yours alone.'

He rose and bent over her. His sensitive lips brushed her smooth forehead.

'Sleep now,' he said. 'Rest easy. I am standing watch.'

The child sighed in her sleep; her trembling stopped, leaving her as still as a statue amid gentle tides of breath.

Achmed smoothed the greatcoat, afraid to touch her again. He turned and left, heading back to the large pile of rubble he had scaled by the tunnel entrance. As he prepared to ascend, he stopped suddenly and stared at the blackened wall before him.

The soot-marred stone of the wall was permuting, rising like bread dough in places. Achmed drew in a sharp, silent breath as the wall seemed to liquefy, then twist into a convex relief of a left hand.

He looked back at the child, but she had not moved; she had, if anything, fallen into a deeper sleep.

His gaze returned again to the hand on the wall. The stone held the shape for a moment. Then, as he watched, each finger and the thumb elongated, stretched outward, until they formed channels that resembled long, thin tunnels running off in different directions. The palm of the hand relief remained constant, even as the finger tunnels withered away to deep, dark lines, then disappeared.

It was a map, though of what he did not know.

Achmed took off his glove, reached out, and touched the wall. The image was gone; the basalt surface had returned to its former shape without any trace left behind.

'Thank you,' he whispered.

He scaled the rubble and hurried back up the tunnel toward the frenzied buildup that was spreading like a brushfire through the mountain and over the Heath to the deepest reaches of the Hidden Realm.

23

Near Tyrian City, Forest of Tyrian

A birdcall went up from the border watchers of Tyrian as they rode out to meet the chestnut mare and its riders. Oelendra listened to the trill: *One rider, with a child.* She smiled to hear the code names they were using: *It's the goddess, without Sin.* She left the tent and headed out to greet Rhapsody.

A small brown-skinned boy rode before her on the mare, a child with gleaming black hair and enormous dark eyes. He was staring around and above him with the awe of a desert dweller who had never been in a forest before. Rhapsody spoke to him intermittently in a gentle voice that seemed to reassure him. In her arm, hidden from sight behind his back, was a bundle that Oelendra assumed was the infant; a shriek went up a moment later, confirming her guess. Oelendra chuckled as the birdcalls immediately began changing the tally on the number of children arriving with the rider.

Four Lirin guards met her, as they had each time before, at the edge of the Inner Forest border. One took the bridle she threw down to him as the other removed the saddlebags she pointed to, carrying them to Oelendra's house. The other two border watchers retraced her path to ensure that she was not followed as the first returned the bridle to her. They were all becoming accustomed to this drill; this was the third time Rhapsody had brought children to Oelendra to keep in her care.

It was the first time she had come alone, however. On each previous occasion she had arrived with Achmed, and the Lirin had treated the Firbolg king deferentially, as Rhapsody's guest, but had not accorded him the royal pomp that they otherwise might have. This was the arrangement they had all agreed to when setting the strategy by which the children of the F'dor would be located and collected. Oelendra was enjoying looking after the growing passel of them until Rhapsody could return to ferry them over to the Lord and Lady Rowan.

As initially hesitant as Oelendra had been to take in the spawn of the demon she hated more than anything, in the end she had relented and been glad of it. Although some were rambunctious, and one in particular was obnoxious in the extreme, she was beginning to acknowledge that, at least on some level, despite the demonic aspect of their makeup, they were just children like any others. In the intervening time between Rhapsody's visits she had grown quite fond of all of them, even Vincane, who vexed her more than any child she had ever met.

Rhapsody had taken to them as well. Most had been found in dire circumstances, as all were orphans, and she tried to spend at least a few days helping them get comfortable in the forest before she and Achmed left to find the others. It would have been impossible to locate them without his ability to find the blood from the old world, Rhapsody had told Oelendra, and she was right; aside from whatever unseen signature Achmed was aware of, and the occasionally feral look that came into their eyes, they were indistinguishable from other children.

Rhapsody clicked to the horse and the mare walked forward, seeming tired and in need of water. A nanny goat, hidden from sight by the horse, was tied to the saddle and followed behind. Oelendra could see the Singer's smile brighten as she noticed her standing there. Rhapsody began untying something from around her belt as Oelendra came alongside her.

'I'm glad you're back; it took longer than we had expected.'

'The weather held me up in Zafhiel. The snowstorm was worse than the one in the Hintervold when we got Anya and Mikita. Did that salve heal their frostbite?'

'Aye, they're much better.'

'And Aric?'

'He's still having some trouble with his leg,' Oelendra answered as Rhapsody pulled her sword and scabbard loose from her belt with one hand. 'Otherwise, he's fine.'

'I'll take a look at it this afternoon, when things settle down. I thought of something else to try on it a day or so ago. And now that we have at least a piece of his real name we may be able to heal it altogether.'

'Marl has stopped stealing food; I believe the ready availability of it has removed his need to do so. And Ellis made something for you.' The Lirin warrior watched her friend's face as she heard about the children; it was glowing with delight.

Rhapsody held the sword away from the mare. 'Here, Oelendra,' she said, passing Daystar Clarion to her in its sheath. 'Guard this for me, will you? If I die alone inside Sorbold in the attempt to steal a prized gladiator, I don't want it to fall into their hands. It might bring war onto Tyrian.'

Oelendra watched her for a moment, then nodded. She seemed to hesitate for a moment, then reached for Daystar Clarion.

Rhapsody put the sword in her mentor's palm. 'I had best give it to you now, or I may forget; it's become an unconscious extension of me.'

' 'Tis as it should be.' Oelendra took the scabbard and slid it through her belt, gave the mare a gentle pat to steady her, then reached out her arms to the child. He pulled back, a look of alarm on his brown face, and clung to Rhapsody.

The Singer leaned forward and spoke softly to the boy, speaking in the dialect of the far western provinces. 'It's all right, Jecen. This is Oelendra; she's my friend, and she's very nice. She'll help you down; don't be afraid.' The fear in the child's dark eyes dissipated under the warmth of her smile, and he turned to Oelendra and extended chubby arms.

'What a nice little man. You must be hungry,' the gray-haired woman said, shifting him to her hip and taking the saddlebag Rhapsody held out to her. 'Noonmeal is almost ready. Can you make it down with the baby, Rhapsody?'

'Yes,' Rhapsody replied, cradling the infant in her left arm and holding on to the saddle with her right. She swung down off the horse and slung her pack over one shoulder as one of the Lirin guards took hold of the reins and bridle again. 'Thank you,' she said to the man, receiving a giddy stare in return. She ran her hand up the mare's chestnut brow. 'Good girl,' she said softly. 'Go get some lunch and a nap. You deserve it.' The mare whinnied as if she agreed. Rhapsody patted the nanny goat's head and scratched its ears before the animals were led away.

'Let us see this little one,' Oelendra said, peering into the baby's face. Wrapped in the leather bunting was the singularly ugliest Lirin newborn Oelendra ever remembered seeing, but Rhapsody was beaming down at it with a tender look that transformed her face into something radiantly maternal.

'Isn't she beautiful?' she cooed. 'She's been so patient on this long trip. You're going to love this one, Oelendra. She's so good.' Oelendra couldn't help but smile.

The guards led the horse away, and the two women carried the children toward Oelendra's quarters, Oelendra feeding Jecen some of the kiran berries she carried in her pocket. 'Any problems on the trip?' she asked as the child gobbled the fruit in her hand and then proceeded to raid her pockets.

'Not unless you count this little one constantly trying to nurse,' Rhapsody laughed. 'I suppose that's one of the reasons I like her so much; she's the first person in the world who thought I had something of substance under my camisole.'

Oelendra smiled again. 'Somehow I doubt that.'

'I wish I could have accommodated her, poor baby. I got used to riding with the two of them, the nanny, and a waterskin full of clarified goat's milk sticking out of my shirt. Thankfully no one stopped me.' Oelendra began to laugh, and opened the flap of the shelter for them to enter.

At the opening they met Quan Li, the oldest of the children Rhapsody had brought to Oelendra. The Singer's face lit up as she saw the girl. They embraced, and Rhapsody brushed a quick kiss on the side of her head. 'How are you, Quan Li?' she asked as Oelendra lowered Jecen to the ground. Rhapsody took his hand and transferred it to the girl. 'This is Jecen, and he's very hungry. Do you think you could take him inside and set him a place for noonmeal? Go with Quan Li, Jecen. I'll be right in; I want to speak with Oelendra for a moment.' Jecen waved as he was led away, and she waved back.

The women waited until the children were inside the shelter, then walked a few feet away. 'How was the birth?' Oelendra asked, running her hand gently over the baby's pointed head.

'If Fate is kind I will never will have to witness anything like that again,' Rhapsody said, paling at the memory. 'I tried to ease the mother's suffering as best I knew how, but it was all I could do just to deliver her baby and keep the mother alive long enough to get to hold her.' She drew the infant to her cheek and kissed her. 'I shudder to imagine what the others have been like, without a healer there to help. They probably didn't even get to see their children. It makes me ill to think about it.' Her eyes grew misty, and Oelendra put an arm around her shoulder.

'Well, at least 'twas the last one,' she said.

'Not quite,' Rhapsody corrected grimly. 'I still have to go get the eldest. With any luck Llauron will have some good ideas about that one. Achmed has gone back to Ylorc already, and I'm not looking forward to going in without him. His help was invaluable in getting the first nine.'

'If you have the right reinforcements, you'll be fine,' said Oelendra. 'Sorbold gladiators are dangerous in the ring and one-on-one, but they are unaccustomed to fighting multiple adversaries. Just make sure you don't go in alone. And remember, if you get into an untenable situation, kill him. 'Tis all very well and good to want to save him, but 'tis not worth your life.'

'No, it's not,' Rhapsody agreed. The baby stretched and yawned, eliciting a delighted response from both women.

'You're right about her,' Oelendra said. 'She's beautiful.'

'She's a fighter,' Rhapsody said fondly. 'She really did come through an unspeakable nightmare. I wish you could have seen her mother's face as she held her. She couldn't speak, but—' Her voice broke, and she bowed her head. When she looked up again, her expression was grim. 'This demon really has given me motive to rip his heart out,' she said, without emotion. 'It will be returning the favor.'

'Let your hatred pass; he will use it against you,' Oelendra said. She ran her long fingers through the baby's black hair. 'Your reason for destroying him should be this child's future, not her past. If you keep that fixed in your mind, you will do it because 'tis the right thing to do, not out of revenge. There is more power in the former than the latter. 'Tis something I cannot do; my hatred is too entrenched, but you, Rhapsody, you have the chance to set things right. Don't let the atrocity of his actions ruin your focus.'

'When you talk like that, you sound just like my mother did,' Rhapsody said, smiling. 'I often wonder if the two of you were related.'

'She and I have some things in common,' Oelendra said, returning her smile. 'Now, what are we going to name this little one?' She watched the scowl on the infant's face deepen as her lips protruded in her sleep, making suckling motions.

'There she goes again,' Rhapsody laughed. 'Some funny things come to mind, but I think I'd like to call her Aria.' She caressed the baby's tiny hand, the memory of Ashe rising up in her heart. She felt the loss of him acutely, each time she was reminded of how things would never be the same, like the way she would never hear him call her by that name again. She thought about the future that was coming closer every day, a future that he would not be a part of, and she ran her finger over the tiny knuckles, thinking that these children might be some consolation when it finally came to pass.

Oelendra had her own memory of the name. 'Perfect,' she said softly, thinking back on it.

'My first gift to her was a song, the song that gave her mother a few moments with her,' Rhapsody said, blinking back tears. 'If it's not too presumptuous, someday I'd like to give each child in Tyrian the same gift; a song that is theirs and theirs alone. Maybe even before they're born, and then it can be their first lullaby. Do you think that's silly?'

'No,' said Oelendra, smiling fondly at her. 'In Serendair the queen I served did something very similar, but with a different kind of gift. You would be perpetuating a fine tradition. Come on, let's go see the others, I know they're waiting eagerly for you.' She pulled the tent flap back again for Rhapsody to enter, hearing the chorus of excited greetings as the children swarmed around her, all talking at once. She watched the Singer's face glow with delight as she bent down to hug them and show them the baby, knowing that it would not be the only tradition of the Seren queen's that Rhapsody would one day repeat.

'You're off to Llauron's, then?' Oelendra asked as she put the sleeping infant into the cradle. She covered her with a spun-wool blanket and gave her back a gentle rub before sitting down in her chair.

Rhapsody nodded. She was rocking two of the smallest children in the willow chair before Oelendra's hearth, the firelight playing off her face. 'He knows more about Sorboldian culture than anyone I know. Even though that country lies on Achmed's border, he doesn't have much knowledge of it.'

'Mountains do have a way of keeping information out, along with enemies,' Oelendra said. 'Are you certain you can trust Llauron in this?'

'Are you saying I shouldn't?'

'No.' The Lirin champion picked up her mug of spiced mead and lifted it to her lips. After she had swallowed, she looked back to find Rhapsody's emerald eyes fixed on her, reflecting the flickering firelight. 'Do you remember the Kinsman call I taught you when you first came to me for training?'

Rhapsody nodded, but her gaze did not wane. 'Yes. *By the Star, I will wait, I will watch, I will call and will be heard.*' Oelendra nodded. 'I was on horseback, preparing to leave for Sepulvarta to defend the Patriarch, so I do not recall much beyond that. What does it have to do with Llauron?'

'It has nothing to do with Llauron; we'll get back to him in a moment. It's important that you remember the call. You said you heard a whispering sound in your ear that night in Sepulvarta when you stood vigil and fought for the Patriarch?'

'Yes.'

The older woman's face took on the glow of the firelight. 'I believe you are a Kinsman now yourself, Rhapsody. In the old land, the Kinsmen were a brotherhood of warriors, masters of the craft of fighting, dedicated to the wind and the star you were born beneath. They were accepted into the brotherhood for two things: incredible skill forged over a lifetime of soldiering, and a selfless act of service to others, protecting an innocent at the threat of one's own life. I believe your protection of the Patriarch from the Rakshas in the basilica that night vested you as one of the order.'

'But that was in the old world,' Rhapsody said, nuzzling Jecen's neck. The child sighed in his sleep. 'Are there any Kinsmen still alive? Is the brotherhood still in existence?'

'I have never met one in this new land,' Oelendra answered, rocking Aria's cradle gently. 'I know not if the brotherhood still exists. But if it does, a Kinsman who hears you will always answer your cry for help on the wind if you are one yourself. Just as you must answer if you should hear the call.'

'I will,' Rhapsody promised. 'Now, please, can we go back to Llauron? What is your concern? Achmed has long suspected he might be the host of the F'dor. Do you think so as well?'

'Nay,' said Oelendra shortly. There was a finality to her tone that made Rhapsody look away into the fire. Oelendra was silent for a moment, studying her face. 'Are you worried Llauron might tell Gwydion – er, Ashe – about the children?'

'Not really,' Rhapsody answered, kissing the slumbering heads. 'Llauron isn't above withholding things from his son if he thinks they might keep him from his assigned tasks. You should see the letters he sent me in Ylorc, politely accusing me of not spending enough time accomplishing the Cymrian reunification. Once Ashe told him about the two of us, they became even worse, demanding to know if I had something to do with the fact his son wasn't around much anymore. All written in obscure dialects of

Ancient Serenne and couched in code. Besides, the only reason I didn't tell Ashe about the children yet is because I don't want to hurt him. He will be devastated when he realizes the acts his soul witnessed resulted in this situation. He'll think it's his fault.'

Oelendra was staring into the fire. 'No, 'tis certainly not his fault,' she said distantly. Rhapsody looked at her, waiting for her to elaborate, but she did not.

'You know, given how diverse these children are, it's surprising that one of them doesn't have copper-colored hair.'

'Why would they?' Oelendra asked, snapping out of her musings. 'The Rakshas may have looked like Gwydion, but its blood was that of the F'dor. There is no blood tie there.'

'I know; but it will still feel that way to Ashe,' Rhapsody said, caressing Mikita as she whimpered in her sleep. 'The fragment of his soul that gave power to the Rakshas witnessed many unspeakable things, and Ashe has fragments of those memories. Beyond the logic of reason he feels some guilt, some complicity for those acts. I'm glad none of them resemble him in any way.'

'Well, the dragon in him will know they're not his,' said Oelendra. 'Speaking of Ashe, where be he now?'

'I have no idea,' Rhapsody said, still rocking. 'He was headed south of the Krevensfield Plain when we parted; I think there was a flare-up of hostility between a human outpost and the Sorbold watchguards there. We made plans to meet in Bethany at the Lord Roland's wedding; maybe I'll see him there. Who knows?'

'Strange,' Oelendra commented.

'Yes, well, it's all strange. Hopefully it will be over soon.'

'I was referring to your face when you said you had no idea about Ashe. You miss him, do you not?'

'Yes. Why?'

'You don't show it.'

Rhapsody sighed. 'I knew all along he could never be mine, Oelendra. It was what you said about Pendaris and you that gave me the ability to love him at all. I guess in our short time together, we loved a lifetime's worth, too.'

Oelendra smiled. 'The difference, Rhapsody, is that you're both still alive. Don't ever assess a lifetime's worth until it's done.' The fire crackled in agreement, and the two women sat before it in companionable silence until it burned down to coals in the darkness of the cabin.

24

The Circle, Gwynwood

Llauron threw another log onto the fire and stood for a moment, watching it begin to catch and burn. She would be down in a moment, and it was always interesting to see the way the fire changed in proximity to her, matching itself to her mood. It was an innate ability, one that Llauron looked forward to possessing himself, though on a somewhat grander scale.

In the darkness of his study Llauron felt a sense of peace descend, a rare feeling in these last days. He leaned against the doorframe. The time was coming, and soon the waiting, and all the unpleasantness associated with uncertainty, would be over.

Rhapsody appeared at the top of the stairs. She was no longer in the dusty garments she had worn when traveling, but had attired herself in a delicate white blouse of Canderian linen, embroidered with lacy patterns in white thread, and a rich, full skirt of wine-colored wool. Her hair had been brushed and was bound merrily up in a large bow that matched her skirt.

Llauron's eyes glittered in affectionate warmth as she came down to greet him. He took both of the hands she held out to him, and kissed her on the cheek, then tucked her arm into the curve of his own as he led her to his study.

'You look fetching, my dear,' he said gallantly, holding the door for her.

'Thank you,' she answered, smiling. 'It's amazing how far a bath and a change of clothes goes in making you feel civilized again.'

'Yes, well, Vera has brought us a nice tray with our supper on it, and somewhere around here I have a lovely bottle of brandy I thought we could use to celebrate.'

Rhapsody leaned against the horsehair sofa in front of the fire, casting a hungry glance over at the tray. 'Celebrate? What are we celebrating?'

'Well, I generally feel like celebrating when you're around, my dear, even if you're here on business that is less than pleasant, and particularly if you are here without your, ah, compatriots.' He pulled a bottle from inside his liquor chest and rummaged around, eventually producing two dusty-looking brandy snifters. 'I wonder how your absence is affecting Gwydion. How do you suppose he is getting on without you?'

Rhapsody was surprised at his candid reference to Ashe. 'I'm sure he's fine,' she said, discomfort at the subject creeping into her face. 'Actually I haven't seen him in a long time.'

'Good; that's good to know,' Llauron said, pulling the cork and setting the snifters on the sideboard. 'Perhaps he is actually getting some of his work done, then, and attending to his responsibilities.' He poured a generous splash of the dark golden liquid into each glass.

Rhapsody could feel her face growing warmer as he spoke. 'I hope you don't think I'm trying to keep Ashe from his duties,' she said uncomfortably, wishing that for once she had chosen to remain silent. 'If anything, the steps we've taken, Achmed and Grunthor and I, should put him in a far better position to deal with his responsibilities.'

The venerable gentleman lifted the glasses off the sideboard. 'Those steps being – well, now, what would those steps be? Are you referring to the undoubtedly pleasant distraction you provided for so much of the summer, hiding him in some lovers' nook and keeping him from the tasks I assigned him? I have no doubt that he enjoyed the duties you gave him far more than mine.'

'I don't think you understand what I have been doing with Ashe at all, Llauron,' Rhapsody answered, struggling to swallow the offense she felt. 'I've not kept him locked away anywhere; I've been working very hard to improve his situation.'

Llauron swirled the brandy in the snifters, then came back across the room.

'I do understand, my dear, that my son is very fond of you. And I'm glad; he has excellent taste. I am not unaware that he has physical needs that have to be met.'

Rhapsody felt her throat constrict under her mentor's twinkling look; his words made her stomach turn. She fought to keep the insult she felt from coming through in her voice.

'Then you are also aware, Llauron, that by far the most pressing physical need your son had was the need to heal his wounded chest. And the physical aspect of that need was insignificant in comparison to its other factors.'

'Yes, yes, of course,' the old man said, smiling. He handed her a glass and sat down in his chair. 'And I am eternally grateful to you and the others for the part you played in mending that situation. He will owe you quite a debt when he ascends to the seat of Lord Cymrian.'

'He owes me nothing, and I want nothing from him. Achmed and Grunthor's aid was freely given as well. Ashe will have no debts to us because we did what was right.'

'That's very magnanimous of you, my dear. Actually, it doesn't surprise me where you're concerned; you are a lovely girl and I knew from the moment I saw you that you had a noble heart. But do you really feel you can speak for your Firbolg companions? How do you know this?'

Rhapsody fell silent, looking into the brandy snifter and breathing in the bouquet of the liquid. 'That was the agreement. I made sure of it from the beginning.'

'And what guarantees this agreement?'

She was beginning to lose patience. 'My friendship with them. When all this is over, that is something Achmed will not compromise by betraying his word. Besides, I think Ashe will be more than capable of taking care of himself, even if Achmed were to press an old advantage. Our help has come without strings, Llauron. I know this is a foreign concept to you, but you are just going to have to trust me about this.'

She went to the window and looked out into the darkness of the forest, passing the hearth as she did. The flames roared angrily as she walked by, then settled into seething quiet again.

Llauron's face grew intent. 'And I do, my dear, far more than you realize. Perhaps you would be kind enough to answer just one more question for me, before we address the concerns you brought here tonight.'

She did not turn around. 'What would that be?'

'I'd like to know what role you intend to play in my son's life when this is over. I know that you will be honest in your answer, but I would also appreciate your candor – and some specifics.'

Rhapsody looked down at the windowsill, watching the reflection of the fire and the room behind her move in the glass. She stared into the darkness again.

'Ashe will always be able to count me as a friend and as an ally.'

'And nothing more?'

She finally turned and looked directly into his eyes. 'Isn't that enough?'

'It is for me,' Llauron said seriously. 'Is it for you?'

The blood was pounding in Rhapsody's ears, and it crept into her face, already rosy from the heat of the fire. 'What do you want, Llauron? What is it you're really asking me?'

Llauron stood slowly and came across the room. He stopped directly in front of her and looked down into her face.

'I want to know that you will not interfere between my son and whomever he chooses as his Lady. Though you are of common birth, I know you understand the destiny to which he is committed. I need to know that Gwydion will live up to his responsibilities as ruler of the united Cymrian peoples, and not allow his heart to jeopardize his duty.'

Rhapsody put down her glass; the grip with which she had been holding it had tightened to the point that she was afraid it would shatter.

'You asked me to be candid; very well, here's my answer. First, I think this is none of your concern. Your son is a grown man, and a wise one, and I believe he has more than earned your confidence as far as the fulfillment of his duties is concerned.

'Second, I have never interfered in any way between a man and his wife in my life, and I never intend to. Whatever else you may think of me, Llauron, know that being of low birth does not mean one is without honor, any more than being born royal guarantees that one has it.

'Third, if your concern is that I will in any way try to attach myself to some vestige of your family's royalty, you may rest assured. I care for your son in spite of his heritage, and not because of it. Having seen the unhappiness that heritage has bequeathed to its heirs, I am glad to be considered unworthy of it.

'Last, I believe I have proven myself a friend to your cause, the goal you cherish to the exclusion of everything else. It has cost me more dearly than you will ever know, and I may never forgive myself for it. May those who love you forgive you for what it has cost them as well.' She turned and faced the window once more, trembling with rage and anguish.

Llauron watched her for a moment, then raised the glass to his lips and emptied it. He walked back to the fireplace and set the snifter on the mantel, then turned to look at her again.

'Thank you for your honesty, my dear,' he said gently, 'and for your wisdom in the choices you have made, whatever they cost you. My son is not the only one in this family who loves you, you know; in many ways you have been like a daughter to me. For what it's worth, I believe you would make some lucky man a wonderful wife and an exceptional mother.'

Rhapsody didn't look at him. 'Apparently it's not worth much.'

Llauron sighed. 'No, I suppose not, in the grand scheme of things. I'm going to go see what's keeping Gwen; she should have the disguise ready by now. Why don't you have something to eat from the tray, and then we can plan your trip to get the gladiator, hmm? I'll be right back.'

Rhapsody waited until the door had closed behind him, then leaned against the window and let out a deep, painful sigh. She rested her burning forehead against the coolness of the windowpane, missing Ashe desperately and feeling guilty for it. Her eyes sought the comfort of the dark sky, but through the cloudy pane no stars were visible.

She picked up her glass once more and drank the rest of the brandy, then walked to the fireplace and placed the snifter on the mantel next to Llauron's. The curve of the bowls caught the somber firelight, a grim toast drunk to a future she wished would never come.

25

'Please tell me this is a joke.'

Gwen smiled uncomfortably, then draped a thin, frost-colored veil over Rhapsody's head and shoulders. 'I'm afraid not, my dear. This is what they wear in Sorbold.'

'Where's the rest of it?'

'This is all, dear; it's warm there most of the year, and the proximity that the arena has to the hot springs keeps it very steamy inside. Everyone exposes the body; it's considered natural there.'

'What is the problem, Rhapsody?' asked Llauron, an undertone of annoyance in his voice. A faint glow issued forth from his hand; he was fingering a small globe of water in which a tiny flamed burned. Crynella's candle, the token of love that his grandfather, Merithyn, had once given to Elynsynos, his dragon grandmother, was the melding of two elements, fire and water, that served as his key ring. Llauron had once said that he had purchased the ancient artifact from an antiquities merchant, and worried it between his fingers whenever he was frustrated. Rhapsody swallowed nervously and turned back to the mirror.

She stared into the looking glass in dismay. 'First, it's the middle of winter; I'll catch my death of cold. Second, you want me to go into a barracks of gladiators dressed like this? Llauron, are you out of your mind?'

'Come now, Rhapsody, don't be so provincial. I would think a forward-thinking young woman such as yourself would be hesitant to sneer at the practices of other cultures.'

'I'm not sneering at anything,' Rhapsody answered, turning her back to the mirror and blushing as she saw how little was covered. 'I just don't want anyone sneering at me. I mean, for goodness' sake, Gwen, what am I supposed to hold this thing up with – determination?' She gestured uneasily at the entwined scarves that formed the bodice of her outfit.

'Oh, now, Rhapsody, you aren't that small on top,' said Llauron's servant woman.

'Bless you, Gwen; I believe you are the first person in my life ever to say that. Under different circumstances I would be moved to thank you, but at the moment I think I would like to go get dressed.'

Llauron stood up impatiently. 'You know, Rhapsody, I was under the impression you were serious about this mission; I had no idea you were only toying with the idea. Had I known it, I would not have wasted Gwen's time or mine.'

Rhapsody looked abashed. 'I am serious, Llauron; I just didn't expect this kind of costume.'

'Well, I'm very sorry, but you have to dress like the people do in the place you have to infiltrate, Rhapsody. If you are annoyed with the choice of location, you will have to take that up with your gladiator friend. But if you were to walk into some parts of Sorbold dressed as you were at supper, you would immediately be sold into slavery, and end up in something even more revealing, no doubt. Now, what will it be? Do you wish to continue with this, or are you going to back out?'

Rhapsody sighed. 'Of course I'm not going to back out,' she said, looking around for a robe. She finally went to the coat tree and pulled off her cloak, wrapping herself up in it. She sat in a wing chair near the triple mirror that Gwen had dressed her in front of. 'Now, can we discuss strategy?'

Llauron seem to relax. He returned Crynella's candle to his pocket, then unrolled the large parchment map he had brought. 'Well, you're in luck in a way,' he said. 'The gambling complex is in the city-state of Jakar, the one closest to the southern edge of the Orlandan forest; just to the southeast of it, actually. That means you won't have to travel through much of Sorbold to get there.

'This is a good thing. Sorbold is a far more martial place than Roland, and you would undoubtedly be stopped if you were to ride through much of it.' Rhapsody nodded. Llauron glanced at Gwen, who excused herself wordlessly and left the room.

'Now,' Llauron continued, returning to the parchment, 'here is a diagram of the gambling complex. This large central area is the arena, of course; it will be easy for you to lose yourself in the crowds on a day when a bout is scheduled. I doubt you will have seen more people in your life than will swell the thoroughfares.

'If I am not mistaken, they fight on the lunar cycle, with bouts every day except at the new moon and each full-phase day. Your gladiator will have the best chance of being on the bill if we can time your arrival to coincide with the day after the most recent fallow day.'

'His name is Constantin; have you ever heard of him?'

'Yes,' said Llauron. 'He's been in the game for some time. I don't know much about him, but he is undoubtedly the standard Sorboldian gladiator, all brawn, no agility.'

'Oelendra said the key was not to take him on one-to-one.'

Llauron's lip curled slightly at the mention of the Lirin fighter's name. Rhapsody had noticed this infinitesimal reaction a few times before, and never was sure if she was imagining it or not. 'That's going to be a bit difficult, don't you think? I thought this was a mission of top secrecy.'

'It is.'

'Well, then, who do you plan to have help you if you are going in alone?'

Rhapsody blinked. 'Alone? I thought you said Khaddyr was going to be my support. I assumed – well, I assumed that he would bring troops as well, or at least a few foresters.'

'And he will, but not inside the complex itself. I will send Khaddyr and one or two highly trusted others to meet you in the woods just outside the complex. They will be waiting with horses and supplies to escort you through the forest and back to Tyrian. Are you familiar with those woods?'

'No, though I walked through them once on the way to Lord Stephen's, I think.'

'Yes.'

'But that was just the northern exterior fringe; I have no idea what they look like in the south.'

'That's where Khaddyr and his men will help you.' Llauron looked at the fire on the hearth; it was burning uncertainly.

Rhapsody's facial expression was doubtful as well. 'I wonder, Llauron,' she said hesitantly, 'it seems to me that if I were planning something like this with Achmed and Grunthor, I might go inside to lure the gladiator into the place they'd be hiding, but I don't think they'd expect me to get him out of there myself.'

A reptilian glint entered the old man's eye. 'Then perhaps you'd like to go back to Ylorc and see if they want to accompany you instead, Rhapsody.'

Rhapsody stared at him coldly in return. They both knew what he had suggested was impossible. Grunthor would not be able to sneak into any place, even a complex like the one in Sorbold, and if Achmed were caught in Sorboldian territory kidnapping a valuable slave, it might mean war with Ylorc.

Seeing the ice form in her eyes, Llauron's tone became gentler. 'Buck up, Rhapsody. Surely one gladiator is no match for the Iliachenva'ar. You have been trained by the Lirin champion, you have the power of the stars and of fire at your disposal, not to mention your music. If all else fails, you have quick wits and a ready smile; they will get you anywhere you need to be. Don't underestimate your power alone. You have been working as part of a trio too long.'

She said nothing, but continued to meet his gaze. Finally Llauron threw up his hands, relenting.

'All right, I'll make certain that Khaddyr and his men are just outside the barracks of the gladiatorial complex so that once you have rendered him unconscious, they can come in and help you get him out of there. Now, look at the diagram of the complex again. Here is an alcove you can hide in on the outside if you need to. I would suggest you enter the city here; this will be the easiest entrance and egress, especially if you and the others are dragging an unconscious gladiator.'

'How am I supposed to make him unconscious?'

Llauron went to the table. 'I have that all arranged.' He lifted a small pouch up for her to see, and pulled from it a clear, stoppered bottle. 'This will render him unconscious in a matter of seconds once he inhales it. Be sure you don't do so yourself, by the way. There's enough in here to work initially and keep him in a stupor until you get to Tyrian. Don't waste it.' He slipped it back into the pouch and handed it to her.

'Thank you,' Rhapsody said.

'Try and see if you can make him gasp as he inhales it; doubtless it will work better that way.'

'And how am I supposed to do that – scare him? Tell him a joke?'

Llauron's eyes twinkled in a way Rhapsody found disturbing. 'I'm sure you'll think of something, Rhapsody.' His reaction made her draw the cloak closer about her.

'I still am not certain of this costume.'

'For goodness' sake, they'll think you're a healer. They run around in the complex dressed like that all the time. Besides, after he's fought a bout for his life, the only thing the gladiator will want from you is medical attention, and perhaps a massage.

'You needn't worry that your virtue is in jeopardy.' There was a terseness to his tone that Rhapsody didn't like. Llauron's voice became softer, as if he were reading her thoughts. 'Not only are the gladiators forbidden to engage in sexual relations before an impending bout, but after a bout they are in no condition to do so. You'll be nothing more than a pair of hands administering relief to his pain. He won't even look at you twice; or do you think you have some special appeal that will make the men notice you when they are used to all women being attired like this?'

'No,' she admitted.

'Then please, relax. It will be a good experience for you to see how people in other cultures live. Now, I think you should leave the sword here while you're gone, just in case.'

'I had thought about that already,' she said, looking out the window into the darkness. 'I left it with Oelendra.' She could feel the same tingle in the air that came about when Ashe was annoyed or angry but not willing to say so.

'Very well, then, I believe we have a plan. Just remember, if you get lost inside the complex, follow the heat; it will lead you to the hot springs near the arena. I will not be informing Khaddyr or anyone else about this until the very last moment, just to ensure that no one overhears. Speaking of Khaddyr, I have to go check in on some of his patients, victims of another senseless raid.'

Rhapsody sat up. 'Do you need some help? I brought my herbs with me; my new harp as well.'

'No, no; their injuries are minor, and they're undoubtedly sleeping by this time. Besides, we want to keep your presence here a secret. Did anyone see you come through the hidden entrance?'

'No, I'm certain not. I was careful.'

'Who knows you came to see me?'

'Only Oelendra. And Gwen.'

'Good. Now get some sleep, my dear; you'll need to leave quite early.' Llauron gave her a kiss on the cheek and left her room, closing the door gently behind him.

Rhapsody watched him go and sat in silence for a long time afterward. Something was not adding up to her, but she couldn't place it. She knew that if Llauron was wrong about any element of the plan it could be disastrous, but contemplating that was more than she could bear.

She took off the cloak and the flimsy scarves of the slave-girl costume, then rummaged for her nightgown and dressed, thinking of Ashe. He would have gone with her in a heartbeat; would have been impossible to keep away, in fact, which was why she had not told him about the mission.

She pulled back the blankets and covered herself over, thinking of home. *Ryle hira*, the Ancient Lirin saying; life is what it is. All this had come to pass from the evil of the F'dor. *Evet ra hira mir lumine*, but you can make what it is better, her own motto. If she could save the children, even this one, separate out the blood as a tracer for Achmed to find the demon, and help the children to heal, perhaps by the time she told Ashe everything the ending would be happy enough to forestall the pain. She sighed at the thought, and drifted into the nightmares that had returned with the loss of the dragon who had guarded her dreams.

26

The Northern Wastes Beyond the Hintervold

She stood at the window, listening to the north wind moan through the pale mountain crags as it always did, keening its haunting song. The fire on the immense hearth burned cold and silent in the shadows of her otherwise dark lair. Its light reflected off the tall panes of thick glass before her, causing her coppery hair to shine incandescently, waves of red-gold illumination blanketing the frosty, barren peaks beyond.

Another night of lonely vigil, no different than the others had been these last few centuries, here within the lifeless mountains.

The Seer looked down at the tarnished spyglass in her hands, gleaming dully in the reflection of the fire as well. She closed her eyes, feeling the pull, almost erotic in its intensity, of the power that lay dormant within the artifact. She opened one eye and raised the scrying instrument to it once more, scanning the waves of Time, looking for a comforting memory to keep her warm on yet another frozen, empty night, but found nothing that soothed, only a history of silent accusation. She lowered the glass.

My flame.

She whirled in shock at the sound of the rich, sweet voice, thin and crackling. Her vibrantly blue eyes darted around the vast chamber with serpentine quickness, their vertical pupils expanding with the increase in the beating of her three-chambered heart.

Here, sweet.

Slowly she set the spyglass back on its altar and walked cautiously toward the fire, burning darker now. The flames twisted and danced in anticipation at her approach.

'To the Void with you,' she whispered. 'You dare to come to me? After all this time?'

From within the cold, dark fire she could hear an unmistakable chuckle.

Now, my dear, don't be petulant. I come as I am able. You know this.

'Four hundred years?' she spat, drawing her brocade gown closer about her broad, thin shoulders. 'You come only when it benefits you. What do you want this time?'

The firelight twinkled, almost merrily, but with an undertone that was sinister.

I've missed you. She turned angrily away in a swirl of ancient silk. *And the time is coming soon. I thought perhaps you might wish to be ready.*

'Curse your riddles. What do you want?'

A firecoal spattered, then exploded with a sharp *pop*, followed by a sustained hiss.

You, my love, the silky voice whispered from deep within the flames.

Something within the depths of her loneliness began to sting painfully.

'Begone,' she murmured, keeping her back to the hearth. 'I have done as you asked. Look well on what became of it.' She gestured angrily at the immense, cavernous castle, empty and sparse. 'You promised me sole dominion, and you fulfilled your oath – here I dwell, Queen Undisputed of the frozen world, banished from all I held dear, forgotten in the sight of the world and the minds of men. A thing of the Past; how ironic. I want no more of your hollow promises, no more of you. Begone.'

Draw nearer, sweet.

'No.'

Please. Gone was the wheedling tone, replaced by something darker, more ardent. It was the husky timbre she remembered from so long ago, and the flesh between her legs began to burn again. Reluctantly she turned; the fire leapt excitedly when it met her gaze.

Gwydion lives.

The serpentine eyes opened wide, then narrowed immediately.

'Impossible,' she said defiantly. 'That pathetic Lirin traitor carried him to the Veil of Hoen, where he died. He never returned; I would have seen it.'

Sit beside me, sweet. The fire crackled invitingly. *Please.*

She continued to glare into the cold inferno, then slowly sank to the floor, her gown whispering around her as it fell in silken folds.

The fire gleamed ever brighter, casting flickering shadows and, finally, heat into the frigid chamber. Beads of perspiration moistened her hairline, the nape of her neck.

'Impossible,' she repeated.

Apparently there are things in this world that are hidden from your eyes, my flame. A roar of new heat, then the fire settled back, burning warmly. *It matters not. He is no longer the one I seek.*

'Why?' Her surprise made the word fall out of her mouth, and she swallowed hastily, as if that would help her call it back.

The firecoals glimmered. *He must be even stronger now than he was then. As I said, it matters not. I have chosen another.* A second pulsing glimmer. Then the voice again, whispering low. *Take down your hair for me. Please.*

As if it had a will of its own, her hand reached into the thick mane of tangled curls and touched the jeweled clasp at the nape of her neck. Her hand trembled as her fingers struggled to unbind it. Finally the clasp came free, and the mass of gleaming copper hair fell heavily across her shoulders. She could hear an audible intake of breath from within the hearth.

'You will spare him, then?' She hated the tremulous note that had crept into her voice.

The flames burned darkly for a moment, then resolved into bright heat again.

Do not ask questions you really don't wish answers to, sweet. It dampens the mood.

The Seer laughed sharply. 'Ah, so you don't wish to be reminded of your own failures, then? I have not seen the death of the Patriarch that you predicted so long ago. Now, why is that? Did your plan fail you, as it did me? Or is the Patriarch your host now?'

The flames blackened immediately at her words, and the fire roared angrily.

Gentle, sweet. This is not ground on which you wish to tread. The fire burned hot, then settled once more into glowing warmth. *The Three have finally come, as I assume you know.*

She laughed. 'Indeed. And they have taken Canrif, but what they are doing there defies my gift; I cannot see into the mountain.' Her tone grew darker. 'When Gwylliam banished me he sealed that realm from my eyes; it is forever beyond my sight.'

The flames crackled erotically. *Unlace your gown.*

She laughed again. 'You would pleasure me, then?'

Indeed. Unlace your gown, my flame, and I will tell you what else is beyond your sight. I will tell you of the Future.

The vertical slits in her blue eyes expanded in interest, though she fought to keep her face calm. Her fingers flew to her bodice, and quickly began to tug at the laces of her gown.

The voice in the fire chuckled. *Ah, you still crave it, do you, sweet? It must be painful, never being able to experience the Present until it has become the Past.* The flames danced as her fingers ceased untying the laces. *Don't stop, sweet. My time grows short.*

Slowly she opened the bodice and slid the filmy sleeves from her arms. The firelight licked her golden skin, scored with infinitesimal lines resembling tiny scales, making it shine like burnished metal. She dropped her eyes, naked to the waist in the reflected glow.

You are ever beautiful, sweet. The warm words inspired a ferocious blush, starting at her lonely heart and radiating outward to the tips of her long fingers. *Time has not marked even a day on you since last we coupled in passion on the floor of the Great Hall. Do you remember, my flame?*

'Yes.'

Come closer. Remove your gown.

Slowly she stood, the bodice and sleeves gathered in her arms, clutched across her waist. Then, with one fluid movement she let go, and the brocade silk nightgown rolled to the floor like an ocean wave.

'Why do you not come to me in the flesh?' she whispered. 'It is so lonely here in the cold mountain.'

Certain obligations of my current host proscribe that pleasure of the flesh from me now. But fear not, sweet. Soon I will give up this body and move on to one you are certain to enjoy more. The fire settled back into coals. *Come into me.*

She laughed, not the tinkling laugh of a young woman, but the strident sound of trumpets blaring victory. 'Words I once spoke unto you.'

I remember. The flames died back even further. *Come into me, sweet.*

Slowly she approached the hearth, then knelt down before the fire. Trembling in anticipation, she lay back and slid her long legs slowly into the maw of the vast hearth.

The firecoals gleamed gently, then more intensely. Tiny flames appeared, and began licking her legs, dancing over her body, heating her blood. She exhaled and moved closer, letting the growing heat melt the bitter sting between her legs.

Sweet.

Sweat trickled between her breasts now, as tongues of flame crawled over her thighs, seeking to explore her more intimately. The harsh loneliness that had taken root within her warmed and withered to ashes, leaving nothing but willing need, calling in silent, multitoned voices from within her wyrm blood.

The flames surged, rolling up over her waist, lighting her breasts with a glowing radiance. She closed her eyes, concentrating on the fire's blissful ministrations, then spoke again as her excitement began to mount.

'Tell me,' she whispered. 'Tell me of the Future.'

A billow of heat pushed her legs further apart, reaching up into her, and she gasped in pleasure.

Soon I will take the Patriarchy, the voice from the hearth whispered back. *The setback on the Holy Night was temporary. When I am Patriarch I will crown Tristan Steward king, and then take him as well, in the moment before the crown touches his brow, while he is still the weaker of us, discarding the old body like chaff.* The fire surged again, wrapping around her, entering her fully, and she cried out in joy. *Finally the army will be mine; Roland will join with Sorbold and Gwynwood. We will take the mountain. Then I will have the Child. And then the key. And then the Vault. And then the Earth.*

'From without? But—'

The flames crackled, sending hot shivers through her, and she gasped again.

No, sweet; I have already thought of that. Even you could not wrest the mountain from your accursed husband; the mountain fell from within, as well as without. The flame pulsed abruptly, showering her with sparkling embers. *The means are already in place.*

She began to breathe more shallowly, stretching her arms lazily above her head, feeling the fire move over her, swirling in rivers of flame around her breasts, caressing her throat. Her moan of ecstasy all but drowned out the quiet words.

I require your assistance, sweet. Say you will.

'How—'

No. The word was terse and cold; with its utterance, the fire died back, smoldering in angry coals. She shivered violently with its loss. *No, my flame. Do not ask 'how' first. Once you pledged me anything I asked to achieve your ends, and I fulfilled the bargain. You are still in my debt, sweet. You will deny me nothing. Say you will do whatever I ask.*

'Please,' she whispered, lost amid the ache of denied passion and the grip of uncertainty.

Say it.

'I will,' she snarled. The air in the room grew thin and static, a sign of her dragon blood rising, rampant. 'But then the scales are balanced; agreed?'

Agreed.

The fire roared back, swallowing her in its jaws, tongues of flame darting, serpentine, in all the places that cried out for its touch. She lay back again, her mouth open, panting, as the flames consumed her, pleasuring her ancient blood, her lonely flesh. She cried out in fury mixed with rapture; thunder rolled through the pale mountains, shaking the snowcaps loose, sending avalanches tumbling down into the distant valleys.

Later, as she lay, spent, in the shadows of the flickering hearth, she listened absently to the words whispered in the fire. She nodded slightly, trying to recover her breath.

I need your memories.

'I understand.'

Ylorc, in the Deep Tunnels

Achmed stood at the convergence of five tunnels, lost.

This was surely the place to which the Sleeping Child, through her hand-shaped map on the stone wall of her chamber, had directed him. He had stood for hours over the device in Gwylliam's hidden library that monitored the movement of the Bolg throughout the mountains, watching this place, but no one ever came. He had listened with unending patience at the apparatus that led to speaking tubes throughout all of Canrif, trying to discern what was happening beneath his nose. His efforts were not getting him far.

Now, as he waited, hidden, at this strange, handlike crossroads, he felt something he had never truly felt before, a kind of growing despair that perhaps what faced him was beyond his means to keep in check.

Getting control of this mountain was like trying to inhale all the smoke from a forest fire. No matter how hard he drew it in, tendrils escaped, wisped away to lost, unknown places, old Cymrian claims, or the hiding places of those long dead. And he couldn't inhale forever.

Only one word whispered up through the ancient tube had caught his ear in all his long hours of wait. It was a simple word, at the same time a strange one, with no explanation attached to it, spoken between a midwife and a common foot soldier in passing.

Finders.

Nonetheless, that single word was the key; he knew it deep within the parts of him that sensed the heartbeat of the Bolg kingdom, that gave him power over the land and its occupants. More and more since he had become the warlord in this abandoned ruin peopled by monsters of his own kind he was beginning to understand the concept of royalty, of kingly authority that ran in blood. Only it ran in more than blood – Achmed felt it in his nerves, in his teeth, in the hair of his head and his skin-web; these were his people, and they had a secret from him, a secret so well guarded that even Gwylliam's endless library held not a single reference to it.

Now, as he waited at the place the Earthchild had suggested, he felt them, like mice in the dark, or the first stirrings of lice, and understood what Gwylliam must have felt trying to keep the mountain from exploding at the beginning of the end of it all.

He knew that though the Bolg were a mutable race, certain features held true: they valued strength, they prized children, they craved movement, they lived spare and traveled light. Even their language was all action and function, with few objects. So in that one word – Finders – he knew there was power, something deep and intrinsic to this place, something he should know about, but did not.

He carried no weapons but the cwellan and a concealed skinning knife that only Grunthor knew about. It had a dark, rainbow-black steel blade, and was a parting gift from the old world. In most circumstances he could rely on his path lore to find the way to what he sought, but he still was uncertain what he was looking for.

Slowly Achmed paced the centerpiece of the tunnels, listening at each one of the fingers, hearing nothing. Doubtless down one or more of them were the Finders that he sought, hiding at the edge of his awareness, taunting him, however inadvertently, like children playing a game of blindman's buff. Whether they were the ones selling his weapons to Sorbold no longer mattered now. What did matter was that they had a secret from him, and he could not abide that.

But he would have to abide it a short while longer.

Perhaps, once Rhapsody returned with the blood of the demon, he himself would now be a Finder. He had often contemplated the ritual he would use once she delivered it to him; it would need to be done in a special place, a place secure from the wind, and from the eyes of the world.

He wondered, as he examined the openings in the Hand, if this were the place.

The proper site to have done it would have been beneath the great pendulum of the long-dead Dhracian colony, a place that allowed no essence to escape. He had trained with the Grandmother in the Thrall ritual there, learning the secrets of his Dhracian heritage, the primordial power granted them to hold both sides of F'dor, man and demon, in thrall, a skill bequeathed them as the jailors who once gave up life in the wind from which they originated to stand guard over the great Vault of the Underworld in which the F'dor had been imprisoned. But that place was sealed now; there was no way to get back in without risking the safety of the Sleeping Child. He spat on the sandy ground at the mere thought of it.

The five corners of the hand shared similar characteristics to the vast vertical chamber in which the pendulum swung. In a way it cycled the signals that fell to its center, like water in sea caves, washing away from the depth with the tide, but then falling back to level, unable to escape.

This was the place.

The last message she had sent with the bird had indicated she was successful in her undertaking, and would be home soon. The anticipation was painful.

Achmed listened once more, then hurried back up the corridor from which he had come.

In the distance, the Finders watched him go, wide eyes blinking in the dark.

27

Sorbold

The gambling complex of Sorbold was the largest group of buildings in the city-state of Jakar, and sprawled threateningly across the southern end of the borough of Nikkid'saar. On days when gladiatorial bouts were not scheduled it lay quiet and more or less undisturbed, except for the occasional delivery caravan and the entry and exit of the slaves and free workers whose efforts kept the complex running. On the days of the fights, however, this end of the borough writhed with humanity and animal life, as tens of thousands jammed the streets around the arena, teeming with the excitement and commerce of blood sport.

Rhapsody could see that Llauron was right about the schedule of events; this had been a day of contest, and an enormous stream of people, complete with its accompanying noise and smell, was flooding back into the roadway around the arena, filling the streets with the sounds of jostling and screaming, laughing and bickering. It was easy to get lost in the cacophony, and she happily did, blending in with the crowd until she found the entrance into the arena closest to the sprawling addition at the rear of the complex. This addition must hold the gladiators' quarters, she reasoned, and she looked for a point of exit near to the southern gate of the borough, where she had left the horse and where Khaddyr and the reinforcements would meet up with her.

Rhapsody found a sheltered area to wait in as light snow began to fall, turning the streets to mud and the mood of the masses ugly. She watched carefully as she passed the time, noting that there were, in fact, a number of women dressed in clothes similar to those she was wearing under the woolen cloak. Their attire seemed drabber and more modest by comparison, but perhaps it was just a factor of her discomfort with the revealing nature of the disguise.

In addition, the women dressed as she was were often being roughly herded in and out of the complex, occasionally with the sting of a whip. Rhapsody's blood boiled, and she could feel the fire within her rise to the surface of her skin, but she swallowed her anger at the sight and steadied her resolve. She was here to save the gladiator, not change the culture of Sorbold, however much she may have wanted to.

The streets surrounding the arena contained feeder alleys that led into small courtyards. In each of these central areas that she had passed, Rhapsody saw minor bouts of fighting taking place amid a smaller, loose crowd of observers, peasants and merchants who broke into hooting cheers as particularly bloody hits were landed.

The combatants in these street bouts often appeared to be barely out of childhood, boys and occasionally girls as young as perhaps nine summers, attacking each other with such zealous ferocity that the victor often had to be restrained from gutting his fallen opponent. Rhapsody shuddered as a great cry of delight rose, along with an arching spray of blood, from a contest between two young boys no older than her adopted grandson, Gwydion Navarne.

The closer courtyards to the arena held the semi-professionals, gladiators in training who were not yet deemed worthy to fight in the arena, but who had already garnered, in most cases, a large and devoted following among the street audience. Gambling was widely evident, with oddsmakers working the crowd furiously, trying to coax from them some of the Sorboldian goldstones they had brought to wager in the arena itself.

In the last of these courtyards immediately outside the gladiatorial arena stood a large wooden scale, bound in rickety metal and balancing two large disks, scale plates large enough to hold an ox for weighing. Rhapsody recognized this instrument as a cruder version of the ones that stood inside the various fighting pits within the complex. Llauron had explained their use to her as part of their planning.

At the decision point of each major bout, and apparently a few of the street matches as well, a fighter who had been disarmed or injured to the point of not being able to continue was deemed, by the sound of the arena master's gong, to be Tovvrik, or compromised. It was at this point that the crowd turned to an enormous set of scales to decide the warrior's fate.

The country of Sorbold was situated, for the most part, on the leeward side of the Teeth, making it a dry and arid place, a realm of almost endless sun and desert. The religion of Sorbold, while a See loyal to the Patriarch in Sepulvarta, carried with it a hint of the old pagan days, a devotion to the balance of the natural world. In a land where one overirrigation of a field might mean the permanent loss of a village's drinking-waterwells, nature's balance was a matter of life and death.

So it was in the gladiatorial arena as well. With the sound of the gong, a crowd would take up the chant: *Tovvrik, Tovvrik, Tovvrik.* The reverberation of the word would echo in the arena, increasing in momentum, gaining fury, until the seats began to tremble, or so Llauron said.

While the victor in the bout strode to the Winner's Rise to await the acclaim and adulation of the masses and the nobility, the unfortunate loser was carried, amid growing pandemonium, to the scales, which had been wheeled to the middle of the arena floor like a great god of sacrifice, where he or she was unceremoniously dumped onto one of the weighing plates. Two pairs of dray horses with wheeled carts affixed to their hitchings stood, one at either side of the mechanism, each of the scale plates resting atop a cart.

Now the bargaining began. If the fighter was a slave, and valuable to his owner, ofttimes the owner would hold up a slate with a life offering inscribed on it. At the arenamaster's signal, large, multicolored weights corresponding in poundage to the amount of the owner's offering would be carried to the opposing scale plate and set in it. Other members of the nobility and, ultimately, the crowd, were allowed to cast their life offerings into the opposing plate as well. Sometimes even other slaves, both women and men, were offered up, particularly when the fighter had established a reputation for skill and profitability.

If the fighter was a freeman, the task of making life offerings was left to the crowd or his admirers among the nobility, proving in a time-honored way the high cost of freedom. As a result, even when they had accumulated a great deal of personal wealth and more than enough bout credits to purchase their freedom, many of the best gladiators chose to remain in slavery, improving their chances that someone would bid to save them when in Tovvrik. Constantin was not one of them.

When all the life offerings had been made, the arenamaster's gong rang again, and the two horses were led, slowly, away from the scales. The arena would grow absolutely silent as the crowd waited for the enormous apparatus to weigh the results. Then, if the scales balanced, or weighed in the fighter's favor, he or she was taken from the massive scale plate by the complex physician's healers and led or carried away amid a ferocious chorus of mixed applause and hissing sneers. Half the life offerings were whisked away to fill the coffers of the regent whose city-state owned the arena, while the other half was presented, amid tumultuous cheering, to the victor.

If, however, the scales decided against the one in Tovvrik, an even greater roar went up from the crowd. While the content of the entire plate of life offerings was presented to the victor, the event that was more central to the interest of the crowd was prepared. A large, saw-bladed sword was placed in front of the scales, in the direct line of sight of the regent's box, while long straps of leather were bound rapidly to the loser's ankles. The loser was then dumped from the scale plate. The arenamaster waited long enough for the scale plates to balance, a matter of a very few seconds, before ringing the gong one last time.

If the unfortunate fighter could scramble to the sword in the intervening time, he or she could take the opportunity offered, and quickly bring life to an end in a somewhat honorable manner by falling on the weapon. Such feats of speed while compromised were almost always greeted with a chorus of furious hissing, as they denied the eager crowd the true spectacle. For if the fighter did not reach the sword before the gong rang again, the horses were loosed, tearing forth ahead of a sharp spurring and the deafening sound.

The crowd would burst forth in orgiastic screaming, thundering the stands while the unfortunate was dragged to a gruesome and ignominious death, ofttimes the horses being caught and brought to a halt only after the corpse's head had come off and rolled to a stop. Rhapsody shook off the thought and steeled her resolve, waiting for the right moment to enter the arena.

As night began to fall the streets cleared of their traffic, and Rhapsody crossed the thoroughfare carefully, slipping into the entrance she had marked as most likely to take her where she needed to be. Once inside she clung to the dark wall, moving silently down the fetid corridors until she heard noise echoing before her that she recognized as a convocation of human beings.

She quickly pulled off the woolen cloak and her boots, as she had not seen shoes on the feet of the slaves whom she had observed outside the arena. She looked around for a moment, finally coming in sight of a small alcove, where she hid her cloak and boots, hoping to recover them once she was outside again. Then she put the small bag with the bottle of liquid that Llauron had given her to render the gladiator unconscious into the waistband of her outfit.

She noted the clothes of the women slaves; some were revealing, like the ones she wore, but more were simple sets of tunics and knee pants. The women who wore clothes such as those seemed to be of a higher level of training, and often carried bandages or shrouds. Rhapsody wished that she had known about the option, but Llauron knew this culture well, and she trusted his judgment.

She pulled the frosty veil up over her face and followed the corridor into the belly of the arena, stepping past puddles of water pooling from the melting snow blowing in the cracks. The deeper she went, the more populous the corridor became, until at last she was standing outside what was obviously the main subterranean entrance to the arena, one of many hallways leading back into the fighters' complex.

As she passed the opening she could hear in the distance a deep resonating ring, followed by a surge of shouting: *Tovvrik, Tovvrik, Tovvrik.* She hurried ahead of the rolling cheers, into the back tunnel and away from the gruesome noise, the sound of celebration.

A crude list of the gladiators and their bouts was scrawled in chalk on the wall of the arch that led to the bowels of the arena. In each bout one of the two names had been struck through. It was not difficult to find Constantin's; his was the final bout of the evening on the main program, and, from what she could tell of the number system in the language of the Sorbolds, it had been the match that had supplied the most lucrative odds.

Slaves were milling around the musty hallways, carrying food and bottles of medicine, emollients and wine, the women dressed as she was, gathering in a penlike area to the left of the archway. Rhapsody pulled her veiled hood closer and slid into the stream of human traffic, letting it carry her into the pen, hoping she was in the right place.

In a moment her hunch was confirmed. A short, muscular man with thinning gray hair and robes far richer than any the slaves wore appeared at the other end of the tunnel, and as he approached the women fell silent, looking at each other and watching with anticipation. He strode through the tunnel, came out through the archway, and then climbed an area of steps at the forefront of the pen, his eyes alternately scanning the crowd of slave women and the chalk writing behind him.

He turned behind him and shouted to one of the manservants down past the archway, and after a moment another man came from down the corridor and handed him a parchment page. The slave bowed respectfully and referred to him as Treilus; Rhapsody made note and tried to shrink behind some of the taller, more eager women until Constantin's name was called.

'Assignments for this evening's healers,' Treilus announced.

Her stomach turned as she watched the process of selection. Most of the women slaves were vying for the opportunity to be chosen, displaying their bodies to their best advantage, and Rhapsody had to remind herself that some duties they faced must be even worse than this one.

Memories of her own past threatened to flood her with the mental equivalent of bile; she struggled to keep those thoughts at bay. Her stomach turned at Llauron's naïveté. Treilus might say he was looking for healers, but she knew a whoremaster when she saw one. Her plan dissipated in a puff of desperation. Rescuing Constantin had just become a secondary concern. Now it was a matter of trying to survive what might be coming.

The first two fighters for whom women were chosen clearly had a connection to powerful people, and the slave women jostled and scratched each other, trying to position themselves appropriately. Then Constantin's name was called, and the pushing and preening stopped. The crowd of slaves became eerily silent, a sign that Rhapsody felt did not bode well for her.

Swallowing her dread, she dropped the veil that covered her face and hair and moved subtly into better view as Treilus was scanning down his list. When his eyes rose from the document they went immediately to her, and she shuddered as his mouth dropped open and he moved the parchment list in front of his lower abdomen to cover a sudden obvious change in the area. She hoped that his task was foremost in his mind; it hadn't occurred to her that he might be shopping for his own evening's entertainment as well as medical care for his gladiators.

Treilus came down off the step and pushed his way through the crowd of slave women until he stood directly before her. His eyes roamed unabashedly over her body as he walked around her, examining her from different angles. When he stood before her again he took hold of the scarf that served as a bodice for her costume and pulled it roughly toward him, looking down at her breasts inside the flimsy cloth. He released the scarf with a coldly professional air, and reached out absently to inspect a lock of her hair. His fingers caressed the golden strands, drawing them across his lips as though he was tasting them or investigating their softness.

He must have found them satisfactory, because he coughed and looked down at her, approval spreading over his face. 'I don't recognize you,' he said in a gratingly high voice. 'Who are you? To whom do you belong?'

Rhapsody stared at him, trying to look as though she didn't understand him. 'Can you speak Ancient Lirin?' she asked, in her native tongue. Clearly he couldn't; the blank look that crossed his face at her response was replaced almost immediately by a delighted smile.

'A captive!' he said, rubbing his hands together in glee. 'Constantin will be very pleased.' The slave women looked at each other, some wearing grim expressions, others seeming relieved. Treilus motioned to one of the manservants, who brought forth a bottle of emollient and handed it to him.

'Can you understand me?' he asked in an exaggerated tone. She nodded slightly, trying to maintain her look of mild confusion. 'Good, listen well,' he continued, handing her the bottle. Rhapsody stuck it into the scarf between her breasts and gave him a foolish grin; Treilus burst into laughter and rubbed his hands together again. 'Oh, you will be perfect,' he said, patting her cheek. 'You will be delivered to Constantin's room, where you will service all his needs. Are you skilled in massage?'

Rhapsody nodded eagerly. 'You are a toad,' she said meekly in her best Ancient Lirin.

'Excellent!' Treilus exclaimed, growing more excited. 'Remember this, though: whatever else you do, you must be sure to massage the muscles of his back and shoulders before morning. He needs to be returned to fighting condition by tomorrow afternoon. If he is not, I will have you beaten mercilessly. Can you remember that?'

'Of course. May you be blessed with unstoppable diarrhea,' she answered, lowering her eyes respectfully.

'You'd best attend to that part first,' he said, a wicked look coming into his eye. 'You might not be in any condition to do so afterward. Go, then, and service him well.'

'I hope you die in pain for what you are doing,' she said in her unique language. 'And I hope that I am able to help bring it about.' She bowed and followed the manservant into the corridors that led to the gladiators' sleeping quarters.

'What a beautiful creature,' Treilus said to the nearest manservant. He dug his fist into his side, trying to quell the sudden wave of gas that was roiling through his intestines. 'Have her brought to my chambers in the morning when Constantin is done with her, if she is still alive.'

Invoker's Palace, the Circle, Gwynwood

A knock sounded on the antique door, stirring Llauron from his reverie.
'Enter.'

The door opened and Khaddyr came in, looking unusually breathless.
'You wanted to see me, Your Grace?'

Llauron smiled. 'Yes, Khaddyr, thank you for being so prompt.' The Invoker rose from his chair and gestured for his chief healer to enter the room, which Khaddyr did, closing the door behind him. 'There's a supper tray here; please help yourself.'

Khaddyr nodded but did not yet avail himself of food, instead hanging his heavy winter cloak on one of the pegs by the door. Then he went to the hearth and stood before the fire grate, warming himself. The wind had grown chill and bitter, and a storm was predicted. His hands had almost frozen in the time it took to journey here from the hospice.

Llauron poured himself a snifter of brandy. 'So how are the patients doing?'

'Most are recovering quite well, Your Grace.'

'Good, good. I am particularly interested to know the conditions of the survivors of the Lirin raid on Lord Stephen's border patrol this morning.'

'None of them lived, Your Grace.'

Llauron's eyes opened in surprise. 'None?'

'Yes, they were apparently far more grievously injured than we originally suspected.'

The Invoker inhaled the bouquet of the brandy, then took a sip, allowing the liquid to swirl around his mouth and over his tongue. He swallowed. 'Even what-is-her-name, Cedelia, that woman with only the leg wound?'

'Yes, Your Grace. It must have gone septic.'

Llauron's cool blue-gray eyes narrowed almost imperceptibly. 'I see. Were you able to get anything out of them before they succumbed?'

Khaddyr went to the tray and picked up a plate. He began to fill it, glancing back at the Invoker, who was staring out the window. 'The usual, Your Grace. They denied knowing why they were in Navarne, or traveling through Avonderre, or participating in any way. All they remembered was being in Tyrian, and then waking up, wounded, on the forest floor in Navarne. I wish they could have been more enlightening.'

'Indeed.' Llauron sat heavily back down in his chair.

Khaddyr took the seat opposite him. 'On another topic, when do you expect to begin your journey?'

Llauron drained the brandy snifter. 'In a month or so; the date hinges on a few things that haven't been sorted out yet. I'll be sure to give you as much notice as possible to make sure things are in order for you while I'm away.'

Khaddyr smiled. 'Thank you, sire. I'm sure everything will run smoothly in your absence. I will see to it.'

Llauron met his smile in return. 'I'm sure you will.'

'Did I hear the guards say that Rhapsody was here earlier?' Khaddyr rubbed his hands together, massaging the chill from his knuckles.

Llauron folded his hands. She had come through the secret entrance; this was most interesting. The breach in his security was more widespread than he had realized.

'Yes,' he said. 'She was here to procure medicinal herbs and salves for Ylorc's infirmaries. She's gone back there now. I'm sorry you missed her, but she didn't want to be away from the Bolg for a moment longer than necessary. Seems they are in the throes of some sort of horrific endemic influenza.'

'What a shame,' Khaddyr said sympathetically. 'Can we offer any assistance? I have some acolytes who have completed their medical training; you could send them to Ylorc with the next mail caravan to help in the hospitals.'

The Invoker rose and went to the supper tray. He took a plate and began to fill it, trying to keep up the appearance of an appetite that had utterly vanished.

'What a very kind thought. I'm afraid it's too late, however. She was terribly upset. When she left Ylorc the bulk of their army had already succumbed; I fear by the time she returns there will be nothing left but a few surviving fragments of the population. Epidemic disease is a terrible thing, but it is even more devastating for primitive cultures.'

'I see. I'm certainly sorry to hear it. Well, is there anything else you wished to discuss with me, Your Grace?'

Llauron turned back to the fire. 'No, not specifically. I just thought I'd invite you to supper; it's been a long time since we've had a good chat. I suppose I just wanted to see what my old protégé is up to.'

28

Sorbold

As Rhapsody followed the young manservant away from the arena and into the part of the complex that housed the gladiatorial barracks, a shout went up behind them. A few seconds later a man in loose, rich robes of the same color that Treilus had been wearing dashed into the corridor, pushing past them hurriedly, a look of panic contorting his face. He shouted again. The servant pulled her to the wall as the man came to a halt a few feet in front of them.

He shouted once more, and the sound was answered by the noise of running footsteps. Two women and a man, dressed in various forms of the healers' uniforms Rhapsody had seen since entering the complex, ran forward to meet him, stopping as he had, looking grave. They conferred quietly in the Sorbold tongue; Rhapsody caught a few words – *Treilus* – *fundament exploded* – *excrement, blood* – before the group wheeled and hurried back past her and the manservant. She pressed even closer to the wall to stay out of their way until they disappeared around the corner again.

A hollow numbness began to spread through her as she realized what was happening. *May you be blessed with unstoppable diarrhea,* she had said to Treilus. It appeared that she had inadvertently called upon her abilities as a Namer; though she had not intended the insult literally, her unbreakable vow to the truth was being kept, intentionally or otherwise. Rhapsody shuddered, remembering her last words to him.

I hope you die in pain for what you are doing. And I hope that I am able to help bring it about.

Ever since she had accidentally renamed Achmed and freed him from his demonic bondage she had been painfully aware of the power of her words.

She had slipped this time, had given in to her anger. And now because of her petty insult a man was dying hideously. Even if he was a reprehensible man, the thought still made her stomach writhe.

The manservant waited until the noise of the group had been swallowed up by the vast corridors of the complex, then gestured toward the entryway into the barracks. Rhapsody nodded, turning away to avoid the look of pity in his eyes, and followed him into the fighters' wing.

She kept her head low and her eyes down as she obediently walked down the hallway. This area of the complex was far more elegantly appointed than the caverns beneath the arena, with polished floors and doors bound in brass fittings. The wood of the doors was thick and solid, but even so she could hear the occasional moan or scream of passion as she passed; it was a sound that made her gorge rise.

The manservant stopped before the door at the very end of the hallway, pointing to it to indicate this was where she was to go. She saw the look of sympathy in his eye change to dread, and gave him an appreciative smile. Then she shooed him away with her hand, nodding to signal she understood what she was to do.

She waited until he had left the corridor and was gone from sight. Then she pulled from her waistband the small bag that held the bottle Llauron had given her. She removed the vial of emollient from her bodice and slipped it into the bag, straightened her costume, and touched the upswept knot that held her hair off her face and neck. She held her breath, cast one more look around to be sure that no one was watching, and knocked on the heavy wooden door.

'Come,' said a voice within the room. The depth and power in it gave her a chill.

Rhapsody opened the door quietly and peered inside the room. It was large and spare, with an abundance of candles burning in multiple taper holders. In the center of the room was an enormous wooden bed, and even from the doorway she could see that its sheets were of the finest satin. The walls were hung with weapons and martial trophies, and discarded clothes lay in a heap by the foot of the bed.

The gladiator rose into a sitting position. Rhapsody had expected him to be powerful and large, but she was not prepared for the reality of his size. He was almost as tall as Grunthor, with immense shoulders and a titanic chest that rippled as he moved. He was surprisingly handsome, with white-blond hair that stood in waves and eyes that even in the darkness glowed dark blue as the sky at sunset. He exuded a power that made Rhapsody's palms sweat, but she was not afraid, at least not yet. She couldn't tell if it was the presence of the demon blood within him, or just a factor of his strength. The vulnerability she felt in the skimpy costume caused her skin to rise into goosebumps, but it was too late to turn back.

'Constantin?'

His eyes narrowed. 'Yes?'

Rhapsody swallowed, wishing she had thought of a different plan. 'I am sent from Treilus,' she said, hoping her use of the language was right. 'He directs me to massage your back, if you wish.'

'Come in,' he answered tersely. Rhapsody came inside the room. She could feel his eyes wander over her and even from the doorway she could sense arousal. She glanced about the room, looking for a window or another exit, but saw none.

'Close the door.'

She obeyed, leaving it unlatched by a hairsbreadth.

'Come here.'

Rhapsody took a deep breath and crossed the room, stopping a few feet from the bed. Sickening memories were beginning to churn inside her, but she pushed them down and tried to stay calm.

'Sit here,' Constantin directed, indicating the bed beside him. The depth of his voice and the keenness of his gaze was having a commanding effect on her. Rhapsody came closer, opening the small sack she had brought with her.

'I have emollients to soothe your muscles,' she said, hoping to remind him of the task she had supposedly been sent for.

'You may begin with this one,' he said, and threw back the blankets. He was naked, and fully erect; the size was proportional to the rest of him.

Rhapsody felt calm settle over her as it did whenever she became aware of imminent danger. It was now obvious that Llauron had misled her; she was willing to believe it was unintentional, but it didn't matter. She cursed herself for being so stupid as to believe that she would be safe attired as she was. She shook her head, adopting a look of confusion.

'No, your back. I am to massage your back,' she said. 'You did fight today, yes?'

'Yes,' said Constantin, his tone deepening. 'Sit down.'

She moved closer, unwilling to anger him. 'Did you win?'

He looked at her with disdain. 'Of course.'

She nodded, coming to a stop a few feet from the bed. 'Was a Tovvrik decided?' she asked nervously.

Constantin smiled coldly. 'I never leave an opponent uncompromised,' he said. Then, with speed that rivaled that of Achmed's, his hands shot out and seized her, dragging her onto the bed next to him. He tore off the twisted scarf that covered her breasts and stared at her, his glare relaxing into something more frightening.

'Tomorrow you will tell Treilus that he has chosen well,' he said with a note of admiration in his thunderous voice. 'Your breasts are like the rest of your body; on the small side, but perfect and desirable. You will do.' And then he pulled her roughly into a deep kiss, one arm surrounding her shoulders while with his other hand he began to coarsely fondle her breasts. She could feel the arousal she had seen becoming even more intense.

Rhapsody began to calculate as his hands moved to her abdomen. She could kill him if worse came to worst, but she was not sure if she could escape his grasp while he lived. His hands were large enough to span her waist, as he was doing now; the tips of his fingers touched behind her back, the thumbs in front of her sternum. She was aware that he could conceivably crush her rib cage if she made him angry. Detachment was setting in; she tuned out what was happening to her in order to better concentrate. Singing was not an option, at least for the moment, because his tongue was forcefully probing her mouth and stealing her breath.

His grip relaxed a little as his hands moved up her torso, cupping both breasts and caressing them brutally with callused palms and fingertips, obviously the results of many years of training and use of the weapons of his trade. She was weaponless, and it was clear to her that he would be immune to any pain that she might ordinarily be able to inflict through an attack; to do anything of the like would be foolhardy. She could unleash her fire lore against him, but it would likely kill him, and her purpose here was to save, not destroy him. Her calculations were pointing to a conclusion that she was dreading; it was possible that she would be unable to avoid being violated unless she was willing to kill him – or perhaps die in the attempt. And she had brought it on herself.

One of his hands crept into the waistband of her skirt and forced its way between her legs. At his touch she felt a strange sensation, which, much to her horror, caused her to tremble inside where his fingers came to rest.

She felt him smile as he continued to force kisses on her; he was aware of the false physical reaction he had brought in her and was pleased by it. She was familiar enough now with elemental power to recognize it, but she was not acquainted with what he was wielding against her. It seemed to be able to summon a reaction from her very blood, and as the thought occurred to her she realized it must be right. His success as a gladiator could be explained easily if he was tied to blood, as Achmed had been. Perhaps he had the ability to let, and control, it at will.

Rhapsody gasped as his fingers probed more deeply, stroking her until they located the unnatural moisture brought about by his initial touch. He caressed her there, seeking to force her excitement as his own grew, and he shifted his weight in the bed, preparing to move her into a more accessible position. She knew that if this happened her chance to escape would be lost, so with all her might she jerked away and threw herself blindly off the bed and onto the floor, rolling to a stand before he could grab her.

She stood looking at him wildly, naked from the waist up, her hair coming down. She thought about pulling her hair around to cover her breasts but rejected the idea immediately; it might excite him even more. His face contained a look of shock that was metamorphosing into rage.

'Please,' she said, doing her best to look frightened, and not having to work too hard at it. 'This is not what Treilus sent me for. I am here to massage the muscles of your back. If you are not returned to fighting condition tonight, he says I will be beaten. Please, let me do what I was sent here to do.' Her eyes glistened beneath strands of shining hair, and with all her skill she made her voice as appealing as she could.

The gladiator stared at her, his rage disappearing and leaving his face blank. He looked her up and down, and then slowly a more pleasant expression took up residence on his face. 'Very well,' he said, rolling to one side. 'Get on with it.'

Rhapsody sighed with relief and picked up the bag again. She pulled out the bottle with the liquid that would make him unconscious and came over to the side of the bed again. 'If you will turn onto your stomach I can sit on your back as I rub your muscles,' she said, shielding her breasts with her arm.

'That would be difficult; there's a major obstacle in the way,' he said, but he still managed to comply. He seemed far less frightening on his stomach. Rhapsody climbed onto his back, preparing to uncork the bottle.

Like lightning he rolled onto his back again, grabbing her around the middle and pulling her so she was straddling him, her knees astride his waist. Rhapsody was now without purchase, one hand holding the bottle, and she was helpless as he ripped off the rest of her costume and pushed her down along his abdomen until she came in contact with ominous throbbing heat.

One of his arms wrapped around her waist in a stranglehold; she was small enough that it was sufficient to completely surround her, pinning her to his chest. His other hand returned to its exploration between her legs, pulsing insistently. His mouth sought her neck and she felt his tongue circle slowly up her throat, coming to a stop as it began delving feverishly into her ear. Then he spoke.

'Listen to me,' Constantin said harshly, his voice deep with power and arousal. 'You will massage me now, though I have already returned to fighting condition.'

He could sense her fear, no longer feigned, and it seemed to excite him even more. 'Your hands could not possibly stroke me the way the muscles that I have in mind will.' His voice became softer, almost silky, as he spoke into her ear. 'I will have you. I intend to take you in every way I can think of, and I am very inventive. I don't have another bout until the afternoon tomorrow, so we will be engaged for the rest of the night and into the morning.

'Now, you have a choice. You can relax and accept that this is going to happen, and I promise you that it will be like nothing you have ever experienced. You may even come to like it. Or you can continue to fight it; I hope you do, because I will enjoy it that much more. Your muscles struggling against mine – which do you think will win? It will be a rubdown that I will insist on having after every victory.' He took his hand from between her trembling legs and positioned her closer, until his pounding heat was just barely outside her body.

Rhapsody struggled to keep the fear she now felt washing over her from taking control. 'I don't want to fight it,' she said, her voice shaking in earnest. 'But you're too large for me to handle.' Her meaning was different than his interpretation, but her words pleased him. He pushed her hips down again, making her gasp as he probed her once more, teasingly.

'Please,' she whispered. 'Let me at least use this. It will make things easier. Please.' She held up the bottle. *Please let me do this,* she thought. She could feel her fire lore bristling beneath the surface of her consciousness, waiting to be unleashed. *Please don't make me kill you.*

She looked into his face with real tears brimming in her emerald eyes, and saw the look of cruel excitement temper a little. He seemed to consider for a moment; then he pushed her up into a sitting position on his thighs. 'Very well,' he said, his hands moving to her breasts once more. 'Anoint me.' His mouth closed around one breast as she uncorked the bottle, her hands shaking violently. His tongue circled the nipple while his hand groped her other breast, pulling it closer to receive the attention of his lips as well. As his head bent to take her second breast into his mouth he stopped and looked up, an unpleasant look on his face.

Rhapsody knew immediately what was giving him pause; the liquid in the now-open bottle had a harsh, astringent odor. Llauron's voice rang in her ear.

Try and see if you can make him gasp as he inhales it; doubtless it will work better that way. I'm sure you'll think of something, Rhapsody.

Pragmatism took over. She quickly put her thumb over the opening and took him in hand, his look of concern changing to one of surprise, and then pleasure.

Choking back disgust, Rhapsody leaned forward quickly and kissed Constantin, causing his eyes to close and his hands to move to cradle her head, while her free hand stroked him with a sensuous technique she had learned a lifetime ago.

Rhythmically she worked, using her charms with great success; his mouth broke with hers and he began to breathe hard, spanning her upper body with his hands and running his thumbs over her nipples. As she felt the pressure from his hands growing, she intensified her motions and rested her hand that held the bottle on top of his head, trying to avoid the stabbing movements he was now making with his lower body.

Constantin began to gasp with delight, and he grabbed her hips, trying to delve into her. As he did, Rhapsody doused his head with most of the liquid from the bottle.

His gasping sounds became rasping, then choking as he bucked backward, landing on his back. She grabbed a pillow and held it over his face as he struggled, lunging with his abdomen into the air with her atop him.

His fingers dug into her sides with a strength that made her cry out in pain, bruising the areas that had only recently healed from the thorns of the demonic vine that had tried to bind Jo in life and death. Nauseating sounds gurgled from underneath the pillow, and then his body went limp, his climax grinding to a halt.

Rhapsody stayed astride him for a moment longer, waiting to be sure the liquid had worked, then slowly climbed down, her body trembling violently. She left the pillow in place for a moment longer, then removed it to allow him air. His eyes were closed, and he did not move.

Carefully she leaned down next to his ear. 'Tovvrik,' she whispered. 'But you are valuable in more than the arena, Constantin, so now I am making a life offering for you.'

She moved, still trembling, to the floor by the bed and found the remnants of her costume. She donned it quickly, her hands shaking so violently that she was almost unable to tie the bodice scarf. Casting a glance back at Constantin to make sure he was still unconscious, she went to the door and listened to see if anyone had been alerted by the sounds of their encounter. Hearing nothing, she opened the door onto the deserted corridor, looked around, and then silently closed it again.

29

The Invoker's Palace, The Circle, Gwynwood

Llauron waited until his house servants had retired for the evening before climbing to the northern tower of the tree palace where the aviary was housed.

Traversing the palace's twisting wooden hallways, Llauron stopped for a moment and stared out a diamond-shaped window. He watched the darkening sky as the storm worsened, blowing translucent sheets of snow in twisting patterns across his dormant gardens.

Farther out in the darkness the low limbs of the Great White Tree undulated in the wind, its bare arms writhing in an ominous dance. Llauron sighed; as always, there was wisdom in its warning.

Quietly he opened the door to the tower stairway and climbed the ancient steps, still as smooth and shiny as they had been when he was a boy. Those had been happy times; it was hard to believe now, in the wake of history, that there had been love, or something like it, here once.

The stairs spiraled upward in three tiers to the circular aviary, the place Gwylliam had built to house his lovebirds when the family was on holiday at the tree palace. When her children were young Anwyn had been insistent on leaving the darkly beautiful mountains of Canrif at least once a year, in rotating seasons, so that her sons could spend time at the foot of the Great White Tree, caring for it and learning its history, developing respect for the lands their grandmother, Elynsynos the dragon, had so long held as her own.

Llauron had loved the Tree from the first moment he beheld it; it was a soul-deep devotion that defied all others over the years of his life save one. He alone understood its significance, and what its loss would mean. The time was coming when he would no longer be able to protect it.

As he ascended the stairs he could see its branches above him through the aviary's open ceiling. Though the trunk of the tree stood in a wide clearing several hundred yards away, its canopy was so vast that its most distant branches reached above the palace's roof, intermingling with the boughs of the forest trees in and around which it was built. Even in winter's bare the white branches stood out from the others, gleaming silver in the dark.

A blast of wintry air swirled around him; Llauron drew the cowl of his gray robe closer around his neck and stepped out onto the aviary floor, which was covered with a thin, frosty carpet of ice crystals.

The cages encircled the center of the room, with the rookery forming a ring behind them. At his arrival a few of the birds began to twitter and trill; they were not accustomed to his presence at night.

Llauron brushed the snow from his shoulders and began to coo a response. At the sound of his voice the birds settled down again. He walked past the open cages, each a marvel of wooden artistry built to resemble one of the great pieces of Cymrian architecture, to the sheltered area where his desk and inkwell sat.

He sat down in the wooden chair and opened the lowest drawer, withdrawing some tiny oilskin sheets, then felt around inside for his tinderbox.

A warm glow appeared as he struck the flint and lighted the oilpot below the frozen inkwell. His quill was gone, probably a casualty of the wind that blasted down through the open eaves. Llauron rose testily and went to the rookery, searching for a replacement.

'By your leave, madam,' he said to the nesting raven who was eyeing him suspiciously. He withdrew the loose feather from the nest quickly to avoid disturbing her and returned to the desk, where he took out his quill knife. After a few whittled cuts the quill was ready; he dipped the end in the thawing ink, shook loose the icy overage, and began to write in a tiny script.

King Achmed of Ylorc
  Your Majesty:
In great sorrow I have heard R's tale of the terrible illness that has befallen your people and the tragic loss of your army. I extend my condolences and offer whatever assistance you may need in medicines or burial herbs.
  Llauron, Invoker – Gwynwood

Satisfied, he copied the message seven times over, then blotted the oilskins dry.

When the ink had set he extinguished the oilpot and rolled the messages into tiny scrolls, transferring them to his pocket. He returned to the circle of cages and stood for a moment, considering.

Each cage held both nesters and messenger birds, trained to fly to the building or structure that their cage had been designed to represent. The messengers homed to specific perches where they were fed and rested and ofttimes refitted with a return message, while the nesters only sought to roost within the eaves of the buildings.

The use of nesters had an ignominious history. Anwyn had employed them to great effect in the war against Gwylliam to carry disease or vials of poison, and in one hideous battle, burning embers that had engulfed the thatched roofs of the outer villages of Bethe Corbair, burning it to the ground. The weapon was doubly effective because Gwylliam had loved the birds, and knew that she was employing them to destroy his holdings. It was a shameful episode in a shameful era, and Llauron was well glad to be rid of that use, though what he contemplated now had some of its hallmarks.

The avian system worked well to carry messages of importance to other heads of state or religious leaders, though in winter it was less reliable than in the warmer seasons. With the advent of the guarded mail caravan that Achmed had instituted sometime back, the avian messenger system had fallen into disuse, if not obsolescence.

Llauron peered thoughtfully into the cages that meticulously resembled each of the duchy palaces of the provincial states – the Great Hall of Avonderre; Haguefort, Lord Stephen's keep, in Navarne; High Tower, where Cedric Canderre held court, in the province that bore his name; the Judiciary of Yarim, home of Ihrman Karsric, its duke; Greenhall, the provincial seat of Bethe Corbair; and the Regent's Palace of Bethany, where Tristan Steward lived. One cage was also a representative model of Sorbold's Jierna Tal, the Place of Weight, where the great scales of justice stood and the crotchety Dowager Empress lived with her pantywaist son, the Crown Prince.

He had long suspected that the F'dor's host was one of these men, or someone high up in their ranks, though after all his years of searching he had not been able to discern which one. The writer's cramp he had just earned would be worth the pain and effort if the false message found its target, though these first seven birds were not the crucial ones. Llauron grasped a handful of leg containers from the shelf below the cages.

Quietly he reached into each house, selecting roosting nesters, who squawked and chirruped in protest at the disturbance of their slumber. Llauron gently billed their necks with his finger, clucking softly to settle them down.

'I do most sincerely apologize, dear lady, for disturbing your sleep and warmth,' he said to the first, a snow dove, as he affixed the leg container. ' 'Tis unavoidable, I fear.'

He carried her carefully to the window that faced the Great White Tree and stood for a moment, watching the snowflakes writhe on the dark wind. Then he opened the window, bracing himself against the cold blast, and tossed her out into the night, closing the window quickly behind her.

He repeated the process until each of the buildings of state had a roosting bird winging its way toward it. Then he went to the vast cage that had been rendered to look like the mountainous realm of Canrif.

The messengers in this cage were black martins, tough little winterbirds with a remarkable range, plain of plumage and unremarkable to the eye. They were tried and reliable, having been used frequently for correspondence with Rhapsody while she was still in Ylorc.

Llauron choose Oberlan, a cock, his favorite of this nest, and took him to the window. He looked the bird squarely in the eye.

'You alone must find your way without fail, old boy. Can I rely on you?' The bird's eyes glittered in the dark. Llauron smiled.

'I thought so. Now, go to Rhapsody's aviary – I doubt whoever receives you will spoil you as she did, but you will be welcomed; I have no doubt about that. Firbolg hospitality! Oh, my. Aren't *you* the lucky bird.' He released the messenger and watched it catch a warm updraft, then bank east into the night, where it disappeared from sight. He waited, nonetheless, until he could no longer feel the bird within his lands, then went back to the wooden chair, where he sat down brokenly.

The Invoker reached into the folds of his robe, and slowly pulled forth the key ring on which hung Crynella's candle. The tiny globe of melded fire and water gleamed gently in the snowy darkness.

'I am so sorry, Rhapsody,' he whispered.

Sorbold

It seemed to take an inordinate amount of time to find clothing to dress the gladiator in; there didn't seem to be much in the room besides a silky shirt and a few long muslin scarves Rhapsody ultimately realized were to be tied into loincloths.

Finally under the bed she discovered some discarded trousers and a heavy wool shirt, as well as a carefully folded handkerchief tucked beneath the edge of a braided rag rug. She was terrified he would come around while she was prone on the floor, looking under the bed, and she kept darting furtive glances up at the silent figure in the crumpled sheets. Despite her worry he remained unconscious, even as she dressed him, bound his hands and feet, and wrapped him in the heaviest of the blankets from the bed.

Rhapsody pulled his silk shirt on herself and finally worked up the courage to look into his face, hoping she had not injured him with the pillow. A small trail of saliva had escaped his mouth, and in his stupor he seemed much less frightening than he had been moments before. Her stomach was still heaving, and she took shallow breaths to try and maintain her calm. Now was not the time to lose control.

Despite everything that had happened, she felt pity for him. None of the people she had seen in this place, with the possible exception of Treilus, were here of their own volition, and knowing where he had come from made her wish his circumstances were different. Still, she had no doubt that if she didn't get him out of here, and into the care of her reinforcements waiting just beyond the borderlands, he would be willing to show her none of the mercy she extended to him.

She dabbed the saliva off his face with the handkerchief she had found under the bed and rose to go. As she did a silvery flash fell from the folded linen, and she stooped to retrieve it. It was a woman's necklace, crudely wrought of silver, without a charm. A love token, perhaps, from a slave girl? Rhapsody remembered the way the women had become silent when Treilus had called his name, and decided her thought was unlikely. Whatever it was, it would have to wait. She slipped the necklace into her bag, along with the remains of the liquid, and crept to the door again.

The hallway of the gladiators' quarters was empty and silent except for the muffled cries that issued forth sporadically from behind the heavy doors. The occupants that lived on the hallway were clearly otherwise engaged, unlikely to see her leave. Their trysting partners for the evening were earning their keep, filling the night air with occasional exaggerated sounds of ecstasy, undoubtedly hoping to avoid being considered uncooperative.

Rhapsody shuddered. She hurried down to the windowed doors on the courtyard where Khaddyr and his soldiers would be waiting.

When she reached the courtyard she peered out into the snowy night.

No one was there.

The window opening spanned the wall from floor to ceiling and looked out into the empty courtyard, obviously reserved for the fighters as an exercise yard. Snow was falling lightly as she opened the window and stepped out onto the icy ground. The cobblestones stung her bare feet and she cringed, thinking of the long walk to her meeting point if her reinforcements did not come soon.

After a few minutes her feet began to feel numb. Rhapsody climbed back in the window, shutting it carefully, and hastened back to the gladiators' quarters.

She checked Constantin's breathing again; he was still unconscious but alive. With one more careful look around the hallway she took hold of the blanket and dragged it out the door of the room.

When she finally made it to the courtyard again, there was still no sign of Khaddyr. A deep groan escaped the blanket, but the gladiator did not move. Rhapsody opened the door. Snow swept over her almost naked body, making her shiver with cold as she had earlier from fear.

'Oh, be quiet,' she muttered. 'At least you're dressed and have a blanket. I could have put you in a loincloth, and then you'd know how I feel.'

Only the wind howling in the night answered her.

By the time Rhapsody reached the rendezvous point, her feet were stinging and striped with blood. She cursed her lack of footwear, wishing she had been able to stow her shoes in a place they could have been retrieved, but her exit from the complex was at least a half-league from the arena; there was no way she could have gone back for them.

Khaddyr and the reinforcements had not yet arrived when she got there, but her mare was still where Rhapsody had left her, hidden in the same thicket that she had been tethered in. No sign of footprints disturbed the covering of snow that had fallen while she was away save for the horse's own hoof marks. The animal seemed glad to see her, and Rhapsody rifled through her saddlebag, bringing forth a ration of oats to appease her for her long wait. Then she took out the few clothes she had brought with her – a pair of leggings and gloves, which she donned hastily.

The snow had begun to fall heavily now. Rhapsody shielded her eyes and looked up at the darkening sky. A storm was coming, and in the distance from where she had been she could see the wind picking up, laying the fields between Sorbold and the forest low as it streaked through. The lights of the city-state of Jakar twinkled at the far edge of her vision, slowly disappearing as the snow came down harder.

Rhapsody rubbed her hands up and down her arms, trying to stay warm. The silk shirt she had taken from Constantin's chambers did little to keep out the wind, let alone the cold. *Khaddyr and the reinforcements certainly should be here by now,* she thought ruefully as the gladiator groaned under the blanket. He needed to be off the ground or he would freeze, she realized.

She found a strong tree in the thicket and secured her horse to it, using her rope in a pulley system wrapped around herself and the animal to hoist Constantin's inert form onto the mare's back. The gladiator outweighed her easily by three times. She narrowly avoided disaster when the rope slipped from her numb hands. The heavy body might have injured the horse if she hadn't grabbed it in time, resulting in being dragged on her stomach through the snow a short distance.

Finally she secured him, wrapping him in the blanket and the last remaining rags she had with her. She fed him some of the contents of her wineskin and her day rations when he regained a little consciousness, returning him to his stupor with the remnants in the bottle of sleeping tonic afterward.

Daylight had come, and the snow was beginning to mix with rain and freeze, burning the naked areas of Rhapsody's body as it fell. She scanned the horizon but could see nothing coming for as far as her vision reached. The awful thought she had been beating back all night was beginning to take new ground in her heart. Maybe Khaddyr wasn't coming.

There wasn't much she could do but wait. She had no food or water to speak of, and neither of them would survive the cold exposed as they were to the elements. Rhapsody used her fire lore to warm herself and her captive, but after the sun began to set, the freezing wind started to take its toll, and her ability began to ebb. Finally, when an entire day had passed, she decided that she was alone and would remain that way. She had no idea if her reinforcements had been waylaid, or had gotten lost, or even had been killed, but she couldn't wait anymore regardless. She knew Llauron would have been careful to see that they arrived on time, and so they were probably in no position to help her anyway.

Rhapsody took stock of her minimal supplies, checked her remaining gear, and adjusted the bindings that held the gladiator to the horse. She thought about how her mother had always been insistent that she bring an extra shawl wherever she went; it was another piece of advice that was proving true too late. This forest was unknown to her; she had expected to rely on Llauron's men to guide her through and back to Tyrian. She thought perhaps she and Ashe might have traveled through here long ago on their way to Tyrian; if so, maybe she would get her bearings somewhere along the way. In any case, she could stay here no longer.

She clicked to the mare, and set out into the wind and the thickening snow, her feet growing numb, her heart focusing on Oelendra's roaring hearth and the warmth she knew she would find there.

30

Haguefort, Province of Navarne

It had been a long, difficult day. A bitter wind had blasted around and through Haguefort's rosy brown stone walls and windows for the better part of the week, trapping Lord Stephen's children within the keep and requiring the heavy winter fires to be fed constantly. The air in the castle hung heavy with smoke, making it difficult to breathe.

That by coincidence it was also the birthday of Gwydion of Manosse, dead twenty years now, did little to make breathing easier. Sorrow at the memory of finding his childhood friend so long ago, broken and bloody on the grass beneath the firstsummer moon, squeezed Stephen's heart, opening the doors for that sense of loss, and the loss of Lydia, to weigh upon his chest like bricks. He tucked Melisande into bed without her customary lullaby, kissed Gwydion good night without their accustomed talk, truthfully pleading a pounding headache.

Around midnight the gale died down, and Stephen decided to risk the cold for a moment. He opened the balcony doors and stepped outside, bracing himself against the outer wall as the shattering breeze blew through again, freezing his face and hands. Despite the cold, the air felt sweet and clean as he drew it into his lungs, though he could still taste remnants of the smoke that was venting from the castle's many chimneys.

The lightposts were dark; the lamplighters had given up attempting to ignite the lamp wicks in the wind, and so the courtyard below him was darker than usual. Stephen's eyes could make out the buildings below: the newly rebuilt stable and barracks, which had burned, casualties of an unexplained peasant revolt last spring, and the Cymrian museum that edged the courtyard on the northern side, its solid stone walls marred with soot but otherwise undamaged in the raid. All seemed quiet, as if frozen in time by the wind.

Then he saw it. At first he thought he'd imagined it, a bluish glow that gleamed for a moment in the museum's solitary window, and then was gone. Stephen blinked back the water the stinging wind had brought to his eyes. It was there, he was certain of it.

And then again.

Stephen crossed the icy balcony, pulling his tunic closer around him, skidding momentarily on the snow that had frozen in between the stones of the elevated floor. He stood at the rail and watched again. He was certain he had seen it.

There it was.

It would take a great deal of time to get to the museum by going back through the keep. Stephen discarded the thought and climbed gingerly over the railing at the top of the curving exterior staircase that led from the semicircular balcony down to the courtyard below, hurrying down the stairs through the heavy drifts of snow that had accumulated on the steps.

By the time he had crossed the courtyard his legs were stinging from wading through the knee-high snowbanks encrusted with ice. His ears and hands screamed in mute objection as the wind blasted through again.

The museum's door was locked, and there was no sign of light, bluish or otherwise, in the building's one window, a small arched pane over the doorway on the second floor. Stephen fumbled for his key with hands that were beginning to tremble with cold.

When he located the large brass key on his ever-present ring, he inserted it quickly into the rusty lock and turned it. The door moaned in protest as he pulled it open, its wail swallowed in the howl of the wind. Stephen hurried inside and pulled the door closed behind him.

The windowless ground floor was more akin to a mausoleum than an artifact depository. It had been built at a time when, as now, Cymrian lineage was something to be ashamed of, or at least not boasted about. The population of the continent had suffered greatly as a result of the war between Anwyn and Gwylliam, and thus had little tolerance for the descendants of those who had been loyal to the Lord and Lady, and had wreaked so much devastation, not only on themselves but on those around them as well. The museum had been designed without windows for two practicalities. The first was to protect the historical treasures inside from the damages of direct sunlight. The other was to protect them from potential damage caused by resentful vandals.

Casting a glance around at the artifacts now, Stephen could understand the impulse the non-Cymrian population might have to destroy, the impulse the Cymrian descendants might have to hide their lineage. The frowning statues and pieces of Cymrian history had fascinated him since youth, but to another they might seem relics of an era of braggarts, people who had been endowed with powers they didn't understand and therefore assumed themselves to be divine, godlike. Certainly in the wake of the destruction their once-great civilization had wreaked, resentment was understandable.

Understandable, but sad. Stephen looked at his historical handiwork, the carefully preserved artifacts, the meticulous reproductions of ancient manuscripts, the polished statuary, exhibits that had been lovingly displayed for no one to see. There had been a greatness to the Cymrian Age that none but a historian could appreciate, a spark of genius and excitement, a deep interest in life itself and its possibilities that Stephen had been endowed with since birth, could still feel in his blood, even in the face of all the sadness, and madness, of his existence.

Above his head the stone ceiling thumped, and Stephen started. 'Who's there?' he shouted.

A blue light answered him, filling the stairway at the far end of the tiny building. Stephen turned quickly to one of the weapons displays and snatched up a broadsword, the blade carried by Faedryth, King of the Nain, and left in the Great Moot at the final Cymrian Council. It was said that Faedryth had tossed it into the Bowl of the Moot in disgust, severing his ties and those of his people to the Cymrian dynasty forever, then left with his subjects to lands beyond the Hintervold.

Slowly he approached the stairs, where the light was now billowing in waves from above.

'Who's there?' he demanded again.

In response the light grew brighter, more hypnotic. Stephen was put in mind of the immense blocks of glass embedded in the walls of the great seaside basilica Abbat Mythlinis in which he worshipped. The glass blocks had been positioned beneath the sea line to allow the water to be seen through the vast temple's walls. It filled the basilica with diffuse blue light that rolled in waves over the worshippers. He shook his head to clear it and climbed the stairs slowly, silently.

At the top of stairway the copper statue of the dragon Elynsynos glittered in the azure light, its jewels and giltwork sparkling ferociously. Stephen crouched low to the stairs, keeping his cover. Then the light disappeared.

'Hello, Stephen.' The voice, soft and vaguely familiar, came from the far left corner of the room.

Stephen stood straight at the sound of his name, and stepped onto the second floor, the Nain king's sword in his grip. A figure, cloaked and hooded, was standing in the darkness of the room, looking at the small exhibit on which Stephen had displayed the belongings of Gwydion of Manosse: the man was running his hand gently over the embroidered cloth that dressed the table. His fingers came to rest on the rack of unlit votive candles that stood in front of the display.

'Birthday candles?' The figure's voice was warm, and held a hint of teasing.

Stephen gripped the sword tighter and raised it slightly. 'Memorial votives. Who are you? How did you get in here?'

The man turned to face him. 'The second answer first. I got in with the key you gave me.'

Stephen moved closer. 'A lie. No one has a key except me. Who are you?'

The cloaked man sighed. 'No one living, perhaps.' He reached up and took down his hood. 'It's me, Stephen; Gwydion.'

'Get out, or I'll summon the guards.' Stephen backed up a step and reached for the banister.

Ashe took hold of the sword's hilt and pulled it free from its scabbard. Kirsdarke's blue light roared silently forth, glistening in waves like moving water, illuminating his hair and features, adding a blush of copper to the blue light.

'It really is me, Stephen,' he said softly, adopting a passive stance. 'And I do live, thanks in part to your ministrations to me the day you found me on the forest floor.'

'It's not possible,' Stephen murmured, shock making him go numb. 'Khaddyr – Khaddyr couldn't save you. You died before I returned with him.'

Ashe sighed uncomfortably and ran a hand through his copper curls. 'I'm sorry you were lied to, Stephen. There's no way to explain adequately.'

'You're damned right!' Stephen shouted, tossing the Nain sword to the floor and wincing as it clattered on the stone. 'You're *alive?* All these years? What kind of obscene *joke* is this?'

'A necessity, I fear,' Ashe said gently, though the contortions of pain on the face of his friend twisted his heart and his stomach. 'But not a joke, Stephen. I've been in hiding.' *And you know it, if you are the F'dor's host yourself, his dragon nature whispered suspiciously.*

'From me? You couldn't trust *me?* You've allowed me to believe all these years that you were *dead?* Void take you!' Stephen spun angrily and started down the stairs.

'It almost did, Stephen. Sometimes I'm not certain that it didn't.'

The Duke of Navarne stopped where he stood. He looked back at the shade of his friend, standing in the blue shadows. His eyes ran up the watery blade.

'Kirsdarke,' he said brokenly. 'I gave it to Llauron after your – after he told me—'

'I know. Thank you.'

Stephen stepped back onto the second floor, rubbing his hands together awkwardly. 'I was afraid to take it, and more afraid to leave it there, with you so grievously injured,' he said slowly, his mind wincing at the image in his memory. 'I – we – had always joked about me stealing it from you, after you gained it—'

Ashe dropped the sword and ran to his friend, meeting him halfway across the museum floor in a desperate embrace. Stephen was trembling with shock, and Ashe cursed himself, and his father, again.

'I'm sorry,' he whispered, squeezing the duke's broad shoulder. 'I would have told you if I could.'

'May the All-God forgive me for spurning His blessing,' Stephen answered, returning the embrace. He loosed his grip on his friend and walked through the billowing blue light to where the sword lay, bent, and picked it up, handing it to Ashe again. Ashe took it and sheathed it, dousing the light once more.

'Come back with me to the keep,' Stephen said, turning toward the dark stairs. 'It's cold as a witch's tit in here; we'll sit before the fire and—'

'I can't, Stephen.'

'You're in hiding still?'

'Mostly.' Ashe went back to the corner and looked down at the table again; Rhapsody had once referred to it as a shrine, and he could see why. Aside from the altar cloth and candles it held the last of the possessions that he had been carrying the day he went after the demon: his gold signet ring, a battered dagger, and the bracelet Stephen had given him in their youth, fashioned of interwoven leather braids, torn open on one side. Attached to the wall behind the display was a brass plate, intricately carved and inscribed with his name. His dragon sense noted a lack of tarnish on it compared with the brass plates of the museum's other displays.

'Why, then? Why do you reveal yourself to me now?'

'Because it's my birthday?' Ashe said jokingly. His smile resolved into something darker. 'I'm no longer hiding as I was these past twenty years; I didn't show my face to anyone, Stephen, even to Llauron, in all that time. Now I'm being very careful about when and to whom to reveal myself. The demon is still looking for me, no doubt. I want to be the one to choose the time when it finds me.'

'I remember hearing sightings of you, years back, and fairly recently, but it was laughed off as rumor and myth.'

Ashe shuddered. 'It was neither, I'm afraid. Nor was it me.'

'Can you tell me what happened?'

'That's why I came tonight. Yes.'

Stephen smiled for the first time. 'I don't believe that,' he said humorously. 'You were undoubtedly just hoping to scrounge a piece of birthday cake and a drink. Come; I can get you into the keep unnoticed. We can go through the stables to the wine-cellar tunnels. Perhaps we'll pick up something to celebrate your birthday with on the way.'

31

Rhapsody could no longer feel her feet; the stinging snow had numbed them into oblivion. How many days and nights she had been out here she no longer knew, only that her strength was ebbing and her goal was nowhere in sight. She no longer had any idea where she was.

All around her the wind shrieked, and the forest spread forth in a vast, unending pattern; copses of trees and brush melded into identical copses of more trees and brush, until the landscape around her blurred into a white whirl of sickening confusion. Rhapsody was exhausted, and she was lost.

She tried to navigate by the stars, as her grandfather had taught her, but the stars here were foreign to her, even if she could have seen them through the building storm, which blotted out all visibility. The gladiator no longer even tried to awaken; she expended all of her diminishing fire lore keeping him from freezing across the back of the horse.

Finally she could go no farther. She sank onto her knees in the snow, the sharp ice crust jabbing her legs as she fell. Her hair whipped around in the wind, and she watched it dance before her eyes, like branches of a golden tree bowing before the same gale that commanded the flailing arms of the forest. The wind bit at her ears, its howl a fluctuating musical note that spoke of sleep and dark dreams. And something more – there was power in the wind, power she should remember.

Then it came back to her – the Kinsman call Oelendra had taught her. Rhapsody curled up, resting her head on her thighs, and tried to block out the insistent shrieking all around her. Her breath no longer provided her any warmth, and she tucked her hands under her arms so that she could concentrate, searching in the howling roar for the single note that would carry her cry of help to the brethren of the wind. Finally she found it; the clear, quiet tone ringing under the tumult, humming steadily as the wind raged and ebbed.

'By the Star,' she whispered, her voice cracking from the cold, 'I will wait, I will watch, I will call and will be heard.' Around her the storm diminished, almost imperceptibly, and the quiet tone rang truer. Rhapsody summoned her strength.

'By the Star,' she sang again, in the words of her birthplace, the language of her childhood, her volume increasing steadily, 'I will wait, I will watch, I will call and be heard.' The tone sounded, clear and bright, then whistled down into a humming breath and wrapped itself in the wind, disappearing into the night.

Rhapsody listened as it left, praying that help would come, but her heart reminded her that the star she swore by now lighted the sky over the sea a world away; the place where lived the wind that had answered the call of Kinsmen was long gone beneath the waves. Still, perhaps Oelendra would hear. Just to be sure, she sang her mentor's name, sending messages of love to her, to the children, to her friends. She did not mention Ashe, for fear he might come.

Time passed, unhurried and unmarkable. The horse shivered and began to walk, trying to stay warm. She made a grab for the bridle and missed, toppling chest-first onto the icy ground. As she pushed herself upright again on her hands she thought she saw the figure of another horse at the edge of her vision, slipping in and out of the black trees at the horizon; then it was gone.

The snow began to harden as the temperature dropped even more, the soft flakes changing to crystals of ice, spraying as gusts of wind kicked up. They stung her face and blinded her; now she could not even see where she was. Rhapsody tried to press forward, walking on her knees, coming alongside the horse. Her father's face danced before her, calling her name, and warmth began to descend; she knew she was freezing to death.

In the distance she could make out the silhouette of a dark figure standing erect in the changing patterns of swirling iceflakes and, even further at the edge of her disappearing vision, what was probably the horse she had imagined she'd seen. With great effort she raised up onto her knees on the hard crust of the snow, and strained to see better.

The figure seemed to move toward her. It appeared to be a large man and wide, with billowing edges that flapped in the screaming wind. It pressed forward with none of the difficulty she was having. The figure seemed to undulate as it moved; Rhapsody realized this was a result of the violent shivers that had taken over her body. She fought to stay alert, but her mind had already progressed to a stage of fogginess that she could not overcome.

She reached a trembling arm up to touch the horse beside her and felt for the leg of the gladiator; it was still warm beneath its shroud of blanket and cloaks. She blinked repeatedly to stay focused. If the approaching man threatened them, with her last ounce of fire and Naming lore she would spur the horse with heat and order it home. Rhapsody patted the muscular leg in apology, knowing she had failed in her attempt to rescue him, and praying as the darkness began to set in that she had not put him in even a worse place than he had been.

'Rhapsody?' The darkness deepened and ebbed as she struggled for consciousness. She thought she could hear the wind calling her name. Then the snow began to crunch loudly as the figure sped its approach, and she heard her name again as the biting breeze whipped around her ears and echoed throughout her head.

'Rhapsody? Gods, is that you?' The voice was clearer now, and deep; in her diminishing awareness she felt she recognized it, but was unsure from where. It reverberated and expanded, making her head spin. She tried to rise but found she had no dominion over her legs anymore, and, in fact, no feeling in them. She grabbed the horse's girth and held on, her hip scraping the ground as the animal danced in place at the change in weight.

Then he was upon her, dragging her to her feet and out of the snow. Through the haze of her vision that remained she saw that she was facing a mail shirt of black rings interwoven with silver beneath a flowing black cloak that again seemed familiar, though she was still unable to place it, or even to determine if she was in danger or not. Her perspective swayed again as one of his hands released her upper arm and in a gyration of white snow and black wool she felt his cloak encircle her, touching her numb body with the warmth that a moment before was his own.

'Criton! By the Kin, it *is* you. What in the name of all that is good are you doing out here? And all but naked? I knew you were dim-witted, but I hadn't realized you were insane. Or are you suicidal?'

Rhapsody tried to see through her ice-caked lashes, but she couldn't get a fix on his face. There were patches of light and dark alternating, as if he wore a beard, and his eyes were the same shade of blue as Ashe's, but without the vertical pupils. He was holding her off the ground in front of him, with arms strong enough to keep her suspended thus without a hint of effort.

She concentrated as best she could on the vibration emanating from him, until a hazy picture formed in her mind of the last time she had seen him. It was in this same place, or very near it; at least, in the place she thought this was. Finally, as the image took shape: Llauron's brother. Anwyn and Gwylliam's youngest son. Ashe's uncle. The soldier who had almost run her down on a forest road the year before. She thought she recalled his name.

'Anborn? Anborn ap Gwylliam?' In her daze she didn't recognize her own voice, cracked and raspy as a crone's and shaking audibly.

'Yes,' he said, putting his arm under her knees and drawing her frozen feet under the cloak. 'It was you that called on the wind? Gods, if I had known you were like this I would have summoned others – healers.'

'No,' she gasped, her voice resisting being discharged from her throat. 'Can't. No one – must know. Please.'

'What's that?' Anborn asked tersely, nodding toward her horse.

Rhapsody's teeth were chattering so violently she could barely get the word out. 'Gladiator.'

Anborn wrapped the edge of his cloak tighter around her feet and pulled her against his chest, trying to warm her with the heat from his upper body. 'You stole a gladiator? From where – Sorbold?' She nodded. 'I hope you had a good reason – he's not for your private entertainment, is he?'

Rhapsody started to shiver uncontrollably as her frozen limbs began to absorb the heat, and her head shook with the rest of her.

'You went into Sorbold, alone, to kidnap a gladiator, dressed like that? Whose brilliant idea was this?' He made a whistling click, and his horse immediately began to canter toward them.

She tucked her hands under her arms again, trying to warm them and keep from jerking with the convulsive spasms that were beginning to take over her body. 'Llauron.'

As the horse came up alongside him, Anborn pulled a small saddle blanket that had protected its neck from in front of the saddle. He lifted her onto the horse sidesaddle, and set about wrapping her legs in the saddle blanket. 'When you lose both feet to this little venture, please remind me and I'll go thrash him for you, the fool. What happened? Why are you here?'

Rhapsody's ears began to ache in the stinging wind as feeling returned to the rims of her lobes. 'Reinforcements – never came.'

Anborn looked up at her, regarding her with a thunderous frown on his broad face. From his saddlebag he brought forth a metal flask and held it out to her. 'Drink this.' She tried to reach out for it, but her arm trembled so furiously that Anborn reconsidered and held the flask to her lips, bracing her back with his hand. The burning liquid made her choke, and as she coughed some of it spilled over her lips, leaving them even more vulnerable to the bite of the air.

Anborn wiped the spillage off with the edge of his cloak. 'Are you awake?' he demanded, grabbing her chin in a firm grip. 'If you're not, wake up now, or you will die. Do you hear me? You are closer than you may know. How long have you been out here, exposed like this?'

Rhapsody struggled to remember, fighting off the fuzzy edges of unconsciousness that were trying to close in. 'Seven days, eight? Maybe more,' she whispered, the effort to speak threatening to shut her down.

Anborn said nothing, but the grim look on his face turned even more forbidding. He took a rope from the saddlebag and lashed her to the saddle, knowing she did not have the strength to hold herself up on the horse, and led the animal back to her mount. Rhapsody huddled under his cloak, motionless, as he examined the unconscious form of the gladiator.

She watched as he made a few adjustments and poured some of the liquid from the flask down the fighter's throat, belting Constantin into senselessness again as he stirred with a single blow. Then he returned and mounted behind her, tying her horse's bridle to the reins.

'You really are an idiot,' he said, scowling down at her. 'The brute is warm, and wrapped, and you have been feeding him at your own expense. You are lucky you are not under my command – I would have you whipped for jeopardizing a valuable life in favor of rubbish.' He looked into her eyes and saw they were not responding, a glazed look within them, and took her face in his hands.

Anborn touched her lips with his own and began to breathe heat into her mouth. Passionlessly he exhaled, filling her lungs with warmth that spilled over onto her face. After a few breaths he waited, watching for signs of response. When he saw none he returned to the technique, trying to warm her internally.

After a moment Rhapsody's eyes fluttered open, and Anborn watched in amusement as a look of surprise weakly crossed her face at finding herself lip to lip with him. 'Now, stay awake or I shall have to do that again,' he said, pulling the cloak up over her head and holding her against his chest as he set out with both horses for shelter from the storm.

32

Many miserable hours' riding later, the horses finally came to a stop, walking directionlessly in place as they came to rest. The night had come long ago, and each time Rhapsody had begun to feel sleep taking her she had been jolted painfully awake by Anborn's fingers digging sharply into her ribs, ugly epithets snarled into her ringing ears. She settled into a semiconscious state, remaining able to respond most times to his inquiries about being awake.

At last they arrived at a dark cottage. Rhapsody could barely see its outline among the trees and still-falling snow, hidden in a forest glade as well as the houses of the Lirin border watchers.

The door and shutters of the cottage were thick and solid, with deep scars scoring their surfaces. Anborn dismounted and swung her down from the horse, throwing her like a sack of meal over one shoulder as he unpacked his saddlebag. Then he carried her into the cottage, depositing her in a large, musty chair as he moved about the room, opening the fireplace flue and building a fire.

Rhapsody lay still, unwilling to open even a little the cloak that had warmed her through the journey. Her bleary eyes scanned the room; its walls were bare and the freezing air within it was old and stale. In the darkness she could make out a single bed and a table, in addition to the chair she sat in, as well as doorways to the outside and to what was probably a closet.

A moment later the cottage filled with dim light as Anborn lit a lantern and the fire began to crackle. He left the cottage and was gone quite some time; Rhapsody took advantage of his absence to fall into a light slumber. She was jostled rudely awake when the door slammed; Anborn strode back into the room, carrying a large tub that looked as if it was used as a trough.

He set the tub in front of the fireplace after dumping some debris out of it onto the dirt floor, then left the room again, returning with a large black pot, which he hung over the fire. Once more he left the cottage, and as the strength of the fire began to grow Rhapsody felt pain in her limbs as they started to thaw. She tried to rub her arms and legs under the cloak but found her hands unresponsive. Panic was starting to set in when Anborn came back.

This time he had two enormous buckets, and he filled the tub in front of the fire. Then he went to the pot over the flames, removed it carefully with a piece of leather shielding his hand from the red-hot handle, and poured the water from it into the tub as well. Steam rose to the thatched roof, and Anborn came to her, stripped the cloak from her, lifted her out of the chair, and dumped her unceremoniously into the tub.

A choked gasp escaped her and she began to weep tearlessly as the hot water blasted her still-frozen body, returning feeling to her extremities and agony to her torso. She trembled uncontrollably as skin from her toes and fingers peeled off and rose to the surface, floating among the flimsy scarves that she still wore.

Anborn left the cottage again without a word or a backward glance. He returned again shortly with more water, with which he refilled the pot over the fire. Then he came to the tub and stood over her, watching her cry. He crouched down to her level and regarded her coolly, then reached out and pulled off the scarf that barely covered her breasts.

'Get that thing off,' he said, indicating the lower part of her costume, which was skimming the surface of the water along with leaves, twigs, and other forest debris. Rhapsody tried to slide out of it, but she couldn't raise her hips high enough; Anborn reached into the tub impatiently and tore it loose, tossing it onto the floor behind him. His eyes ran over her body, the look on his face professional, as though he were sizing up an animal at a farm auction. Then he went back to the fire and stirred the water in the pot.

'Is the feeling coming back yet?' he asked, his back to her.

'Yes,' Rhapsody sobbed, trying to regain control of herself. She watched as black skin from her knees cracked and rubbed off into the water, leaving raw pink patches beneath. 'Where is the gladiator?'

Anborn turned, a look of disgust on his face. 'You certainly have your priorities backward,' he said, annoyance riddling his voice. 'You should be wondering whether we can save the use of your hands and feet, not your toy.' He pulled the pot from the fireplace and poured more of the steaming water into the tub, watching with grim satisfaction as Rhapsody cried out in pain again.

'Well, that seems promising, at least,' he said, returning the pot to the fire again. 'Now, what did you want to ask me?'

Rhapsody took shallow breaths, trying to control the agony that was coursing through her, making her arms and legs ache to the bone. 'Please, Anborn,' she stammered, 'where is he?'

Anborn looked at her again, his eyes dark and piercing. Finally he spoke. 'He's in the root cellar,' he said sharply, crossing his arms in front of his chest. 'Is he your lover?'

The scene in Sorbold came flooding back to her, and the sheer irony of his question caught her off guard. Revulsion that she had suppressed for survival purposes flooded her, and she began to convulse in pain and the memory of what had happened.

She had tried to hold it in, hoping that she could wait until she was in Oelendra's strong arms to lay it down, but the trauma was too strong and her defenses were gone. She wept aloud, the terror she had felt in the gladiator's grasp mixing with her agony. Anborn turned rapidly back to the fire. He brought the kettle forth again, this time pouring it slowly in the far end of the tub, disturbing the water as little as possible.

When he was finished he rested his hand on her shoulder. 'All right,' he said, his voice gruff but not unkind, 'that's enough. You can cry later; it offends my ears. I'll take that as a no. So why did you undertake this asinine kidnapping?' He reached into the water and began to cup it into his hand, pouring it over her shoulders and parts of her upper body that were above its surface.

Rhapsody's eyes cleared a little, and went from the room around her to the man bathing her. They were both very rough, a wilderness cabin with mud-caulked walls and no ornamentation, much like Anborn himself. She watched, hiccoughing, as he skimmed the pieces of dead skin that floated on the muddy water's surface, tossing them onto the dirt floor behind him. Then he took hold of her shoulders and raised her upper body farther out of the water to keep her head above it, much in the same way she had when bathing the children of the F'dor before Oelendra's roaring hearth.

Rhapsody shivered, and when she calmed down she tried to explain the plan and what had happened. As she spoke her voice grew smoother, and soon the hiccoughing that had interrupted almost every word eased to an occasional vocal cough. When the feeling returned to her hands she ran them along her arms and legs, bathing them in the steaming water as

Anborn was bathing her upper body, a look of dismay on her face as still more pieces of skin flaked off, leaving painful sores exposed to the heat of the dirty tub.

Finally, when she had finished, Anborn shook the water from his hands and regarded her seriously. 'Are you sworn in allegiance to Llauron?' he asked.

'No,' Rhapsody said. 'But he taught me a great many things about healing and horticulture. I try to follow the goal he outlined for me.'

Anborn snorted in contempt. 'Listen to me. Here is the first rule: when your allegiance is sworn, you will follow that person's instructions, unquestioningly, until death or later. Do you understand?'

'Yes,' said Rhapsody testily. 'What's your point?'

'The second rule,' Anborn continued, 'is that when you are *not* sworn, you owe nothing to anyone, and you never put yourself into situations that can harm or kill you unless it benefits you personally. You have faced, and may still suffer, rape, injury, the loss of limbs, and death, for someone to whom you have no oath of loyalty. That is stupid, miss. You owe Llauron nothing.'

'You don't understand,' she answered, shivering under his glower, either from the disdain in his eyes or the dropping temperature of the water. 'Llauron did not direct me to get the gladiator. It is I that have been gathering the children of the F'dor.'

'And a good thing for them, too – had I known that was what they were I would have put them to the sword myself and been done with it. In fact, I think I still will.' He stood up and went to the corner where he had left his gear and brought forth from its scabbard an enormous bastard sword that glinted in the dim light. Rhapsody watched in horror as he strode to the door, murder on his face.

She tried to get out of the tub to stop him, but her legs betrayed her and refused to budge. In desperation she called his name, using her deepest powers of Naming.

'Anborn ap Gwylliam, stop,' she commanded. The air in the room became instantly warm and still, and Anborn froze in midstep, his back to her. She could see rage swim through the muscles of his shoulders and could hear him breathe in angrily. 'You will not harm him, Anborn. He is under my protection.'

'Really?' Anborn sneered, still not able to turn to face her. 'And who will protect *you* now, Rhapsody? You can't even protect yourself; that's a bad position to be in alone with someone like me.' His voice pulsed with the unspoken threat.

'*You* will protect me, Anborn,' Rhapsody answered, her voice filled with humility and respect. 'You will because you have, and you are noble of spirit. You had no reason to answer the Kinsman call in the freezing night, either, but you came.'

His shoulders became less tense, but still he could not move. 'That's different,' he said tersely. 'I am sworn as a Kinsman; I have no allegiance to this abomination. Or to you.'

'Kinsmen come in all shapes and sizes, Anborn,' she said gently. 'They come in all walks of life – some of them even are Singers. And some of them aren't very tall; slight, even, you might say.' With that, she released him. 'You have honored MacQuieth and the ancient warriors, as well as those who serve now. Sometimes the greatest feat of a soldier is to aid the helpless, and you have; I give you respect, and I thank you.'

General, first you must heal the rift within yourself. With Gwylliam's death you now are the king of soldiers, but until you find the slightest of your kinsmen and protect that helpless one, you are unworthy of forgiveness. And so it shall be until you either are redeemed, or die unabsolved.

Anborn turned slowly and regarded her with a look she had not seen before. He dropped his eyes as if aware of her nakedness for the first time, then slowly returned to the corner and resheathed his sword. 'You are one of the Three,' he said, the question unasked but present nonetheless.

'Yes,' Rhapsody answered, 'and you have fulfilled the prophecy. May grace come upon you for it.'

If you seek to mend the rift, General, guard the Sky, lest it fall.

Anborn looked at her once more, his eyes free of the anger she had heard in his voice a moment before. He walked behind her and went to the closet, returning with a rough blanket and a garment slung over his arm. Without a word he handed her the blanket and helped her to stand. She wrapped it around herself; he lifted her from the tepid water and shook her to dry her off. Then he gave her the garment; it was a soft wool tunic of fern green, long of sleeve, pointed at the wrist and clearly cut to fit a woman, though one considerably bigger than Rhapsody. As she dried herself with the blanket and prepared to don the garment, Anborn left the cottage.

When he returned Rhapsody was dressed and drying her hair before the fire, which was burning steadily, though quietly. He was carrying a lumpy burlap sack from which he drew forth a winter apple and offered it to her. She smiled and accepted with hands that only trembled slightly.

'I want to apologize,' he said, looking down at her seriously. 'I hope you'll forgive me for any offense I've committed.'

'Well, the only one I can think of was saving my life, which is offensive only to some people who know me,' Rhapsody said, smiling again. 'Anborn, just because my arrival here was foretold doesn't mean I'm some kind of mythic person. I'm just a commoner with an extremely checkered past, and I prefer that you be yourself with me rather than treating me like some legendary thing I'm not. If you recall, at our first meeting you referred to me as a "freak of nature," and I didn't hold that against you. So insult me if you want to – I'll get past it.'

Anborn smiled; it was the first time Rhapsody had seen him do so without a sarcastic smirk, and she liked the way it looked on his face. 'There is nothing common about you, Rhapsody. It's my honor to have been able to help you. I think you're warm enough now; why don't you lie down and get some sleep?' He gestured toward the bed.

'Only if you promise to keep your knuckles out of my ribs if I do,' she said, grinning. The fire sparked more now, the flames burning certainly and surely. She went over to the bed, which was a hay mattress covered in burlap with a woolen coverlet, and slowly eased herself down onto it. 'And if you promise to waken me for my watch. After all, you should have a turn to sleep on the bed as well.'

'We'll see,' said Anborn noncommittally as he pulled the flask out of his pack. He passed it to her and she took a deep draught, coughing as the liquid scorched down her throat.

'What the blazes is this *hrekin*?' She handed it back to him and dabbed the beads of perspiration that burst onto her forehead with the sleeve of the green tunic.

Anborn laughed. 'Trust me, you don't want to know.'

Rhapsody looked at the green sleeve with interest. 'This doesn't look like it would fit you too well, Anborn. To whom does it belong?'

'It belonged to my wife,' Anborn said, settling into the musty chair. 'She won't mind you wearing it – she's been dead eleven years now.' His voice held no trace of regret. 'It looks far better on you, by the way.'

Rhapsody blinked at the callousness of his statement. 'I'm very sorry,' she said, searching his eyes in the dark for hints of deeper sorrow. There were none.

'No need to be,' he answered directly. 'We didn't like each other very much. We didn't live together, and I rarely saw her.'

Rhapsody took a bite of the apple; it was dry and withered, mealy with a heavy sweetness that hinted of riper, fairer days. The irony saddened her.

'But you must have loved her once,' she said, feeling like she was treading on sensitive ground but needing to nonetheless.

Anborn smiled at her, shaking his head. 'No,' he said simply. 'For such an intellectually gifted woman, Rhapsody, you can be charmingly naïve.'

The shivers that had racked Rhapsody's body had subsided to a mild occasional tremor, and she could feel her strength and heat begin to return. 'Then why did you marry?'

Anborn took a deep sip from the flask. 'She wasn't an unattractive woman. Her family was an old one, and she was principled; if she ever cuckolded me, I never knew it, and I believe I would have. I was loyal to her as well, until she died.'

Rhapsody waited, but no more commentary was forthcoming. 'That's all?' she asked, amazed. 'Why bother?'

'A fair question, to be sure,' Anborn answered, beginning to remove his boots. 'I'm afraid I don't have an answer for you.'

'Did you have children?'

'No,' he said; his expression and tone did not change. 'I'm sorry to disillusion you, Rhapsody. You obviously know what my family is, and so know that we don't have the most romantic history.

'All that fanciful hogwash about my grandparents is claptrap as well.

Merithyn was seduced by Elynsynos because the human form she assumed was what she perceived in his heart was attractive, and the old boy had been at sea for years, anyway. She could have been a sheep, and he would still would have knobbed her.'

He looked over at Rhapsody, and the look on her face caused him to laugh out loud. 'I'm sorry, dear, if I'm despoiling your fantasy. And if that's not enough, I can assure you there was no love lost on Elynsynos's part, either. He was the first Seren she had ever seen, and she wanted control over him.

'So, from the very beginning, sex and mating in our family has been about power and control, and it has remained thus. And I can't foresee a time when that will change – dragon blood is pervasive, you know.' Rhapsody sighed deeply, knowing from personal experience how true his words were. 'Sorry to disappoint you. I hope you're not offended by what I said about Merithyn.'

She lay back on the bed slowly, suddenly aware that she was exhausted. 'Why would I be offended? He was *your* grandfather. Besides, if you were Achmed, the analogy would have been far worse. But since I don't think I can bear the prospect of hearing a mythic character's sexual discrimination be limited to trees with knotholes of appropriate height, I think I will go to sleep now, if you don't mind.'

Anborn roared with laughter. 'Actually, I think that is a very wise idea. I don't want to be responsible for disillusioning you utterly. Besides, I think it's fair to say that you've had a rough few days, eh? Rest up, and we will bandage you to travel in the morning. I will look in on your gladiator through the night, and tomorrow we shall get you started on the way back to Oelendra.'

Rhapsody was already asleep. The fire grew throughout the night, gaining strength in the darkness and quiet of the safe, sheltered place.

33

Haguefort

Lord Stephen reached behind the bottles in the first row of the rack and felt around until he located the reserve brandy.

'Here,' he said, and handed the bottle to Ashe in the dark. 'You used to like this one.'

Ashe smiled. 'I'll take your word for it, since I can't see it.' His dragon sense had already assessed the vintage, as well as all the others in Stephen's cellar; Stephen had chosen wisely and generously.

'It's Canderian, of course,' Stephen said, taking the bottle back. 'Has a lovely color and a superior bouquet. You'll appreciate it more in the light by the fire.'

'No,' Ashe said brusquely. His voice was harsher than he meant it to be, and he felt Stephen flinch at the sound of it. 'I'm sorry. Let's just talk here.'

Stephen shrugged. 'It's your birthday. If you want to spend it among the rats of my wine cellar, who am I to object?'

'I'll feel right at home,' Ashe chuckled. 'You know my family.'

Stephen laughed and sat down on a large barrel against the dank wall. He pulled a bottle of lesser-vintage brandy from the forward rack and uncorked it, taking a deep swig.

'I'm afraid I don't keep the snifters down here. You shall have to drink your celebratory libations straight from the bottle like the barbarian that you are.'

'And I would do so even if you *did* keep the snifters down here.' Ashe pulled the cork carefully from the bottle, surprised at how the connoisseur's technique had come back naturally to him after two decades of finding refreshment in forest streams and the rain gutters of backstreets. He passed it under his nose, inhaling the rich bouquet. 'Ah, Stephen, you are far too good to me.'

'Truer words were never spake. So, have a drink, and tell me what happened.'

Ashe sat down on the barrel next to Stephen's. He closed his eyes and rested his head against the wall, reluctantly recalling the gruesome memories that Rhapsody had cast out of his mind. He tried to determine with his inner sense if there was any reason not to trust Stephen with the information; at the back of his mind the dragon's paranoia whispered repeated cautions. Defiantly he crushed it into silence.

'It was the first night of summer.' Ashe's voice choked off suddenly as the memories came flooding back. Stephen sat quietly as the silence consumed his friend. When finally the duke spoke there was a joking tone in his voice.

'I remember. I was sitting vigil for the Patriarch, as those of us of the *true* faith do on firstsummer night. Perhaps now you'll *finally* see the error of your ways and convert.'

The joke broke the hold the memories had on Ashe, and he laughed. 'All right. I had gone to the House of Remembrance because I overheard my father talking with Oelendra about the F'dor. Somehow they had determined it would be there, and vulnerable, so she was going to destroy it. When she had left the tree palace I confronted Llauron and demanded to go to help her.

'At first he wouldn't hear of it, but I suppose he finally saw the wisdom in the idea. There was no one else in whom he was willing to confide. He – *we* have been chasing this thing for as long as I can recall. It has been the consuming goal of his life, and, as a result, mine.'

'I remember,' Stephen said again softly, staring at the wine cellar ceiling. 'When I went off to train with Oelendra, Llauron warned me not to agree to become a champion in her cause, because he wanted to direct me himself.'

'My father believes that everyone on Earth's sole purpose for existence is to serve his needs,' Ashe muttered. 'Even when his causes are good ones, it can get tiresome being treated as his tool. The truth is, Stephen, even if he had forbade me I would have gone anyway. You knew me then; I was reckless and stubborn, and had nothing to live for.'

Stephen cast a glance at Ashe. 'And do you now?'

Ashe sighed. 'I don't know. I thought I did.' His thoughts went immediately to Rhapsody, and the devastation in her eyes, hidden by a brave front, when he said goodbye to her for the last time.

I am holding the memory for you, Aria. One day it will be ours to share again.

No. It may be mine to keep someday, but it's time for you to begin making memories with someone else.

Tomorrow. Today I am still here with you.

He closed his eyes and shook the thoughts from his mind. 'I don't remember much after that. I followed Oelendra's route to the House of Remembrance – she's virtually impossible to track.' Stephen nodded. 'I never found her. When I got to the exterior gate of the House there was no one there; everything was silent as death. It was past midnight, so the solstice had passed. I didn't realize it at the time, but it meant that the period of the demon's vulnerability had passed as well.

'I don't remember meeting the F'dor, or who it was. Everything was dark. I just remember an explosion of dark fire, and the most searing pain I have ever felt, a pain that only death could quench. And then it took a piece of my soul. It reached inside me and spread through me like a vine growing up my spine, until it had clawed through my entire chest cavity, grabbing hold of my very essence.' Even with his eyes closed he could feel Stephen shudder.

'In that moment I remember knowing that death would be preferable to what was about to happen. I could feel its will, and it wanted me, was going to take me as its host. It would devour my soul and become what was left of me. I saw the Void, Stephen, *saw it.* And somehow I was able to use Kirsdarke to sever the vine, knowing that it would mean leaving a piece of my soul behind in its possession. It was the only thing I could do.'

'Sweet All-God.'

'And that's all. I don't remember the rest except for flashes and fragments that come to me in dreams. I vaguely recall crawling through the forest toward Haguefort; it was a conscious choice to seek your aid. I've dreamed many times of your face as you bound me with your cloak, though I'm not certain if that's memory or imagination. So much of that time is just cloudy dreams accentuated by excruciating pain.'

'What happened after I left you to find your father?'

Ashe hesitated. Though his heart told him that Stephen was trustworthy, the dragon began to whisper its doubts to him again, just as it had with Anborn.

'I'm not certain. I was healed enough to go into hiding, though the pain was barely diminished. Pain of the soul surpasses any you can imagine.'

'And are you still in pain?'

Ashe took another swig of the excellent brandy, then rested his arms on his knees. 'It's better now,' he said finally. 'But the pain was hardly the worst of it.

'The F'dor took the piece of my soul that was left behind and formed it into a Rakshas, a demonic construct built of its own blood and that of feral animals – wolves, mostly – and ice. It was endowed with my soul fragment, my spirit, and looked almost exactly like me. It was mindless but intelligent, and was a powerful tool for the demon for a long time, wreaking murder and mayhem across Roland and Tyrian. I know this because I spent whatever time I could tracking it, trying to right some of the wrongs it had undertaken, spying on its movements for Llauron. It was this creature that kidnapped the children of your province, that drained them of their blood for the F'dor's purposes.'

Stephen stood up, wiping his forehead with the back of his hand, still holding the bottle. 'I will kill it, I vow it,' he said, beginning to pace.

Ashe smiled. 'No need. It's been done.'

'And your soul?'

'Whole again.'

'Thank the All-God.' Stephen pacing grew in intensity, frenetic energy seeking release. 'What can I do to help you?'

Ashe stood as well and clasped his shoulder. 'Keep my secret, for now.' He smiled at his best friend. 'And show me my namesake and his sister.'

'Done.' Stephen tossed the bottle aside and led him up the dark passageway to the keep.

'Are you certain she's asleep? I don't want to frighten her. With my hood up I look like the stuff of nightmares.'

'She's deeper than the sea,' Stephen said fondly, running his fingers affectionately through Melisande's golden curls. 'And you look like that with it down as well. Always have.' He kissed the child's forehead and pulled the blankets up around her neck; Melisande smiled but didn't move.

'She's beautiful, Stephen.'

'Indeed she is. She has her mother's black eyes. I'm sorry you couldn't see her awake.'

'Who was her mother?'

'Lydia of Yarim.'

Ashe chuckled. 'Ah, yes. Good choice.' He voice grew soft. 'I'm sorry, Stephen.'

'And well you should be. She would have liked you, Gwydion.'

'A rare woman – extremely rare, if that be true.' The warmth in Ashe's voice held a tinge of melancholy. 'Your son is so big. So many years I've missed; he's almost a man.'

Stephen sighed in agreement, then passed his hand through a cloud of mist that hovered in the air of the dark room. 'Where does this come from?'

Don't tell, the dragon hissed. 'From Kirsdarke,' Ashe said quickly, beating the wyrm voice back again. 'It embues my cloak with its power over the element of water. It protects me from those that can find me vibrationally, or otherwise.'

'So that's how you've been able to remain in hiding.' Lord Stephen rose and gestured toward the door that adjoined his chambers.

Ashe followed him. 'Yes.' As they passed the door from Melisande's room into the common hallway he stopped. 'Who sleeps across the hall from Melly?'

Stephen stopped as well. 'The children's governess, Rosella. Why?'

'She has a substantial amount of extract of adder-flower in her possession. It's a deadly poison.'

Stephen's face went slack. 'How do you know this?' he whispered, casting a glance at his sleeping daughter.

Don't tell, the dragon insisted violently. *Don't tell!* Ashe swallowed. 'My senses are heightened,' he said softly. 'I can smell it.' It was a small enough lie; Stephen must have forgotten some of his training in herbalism with Lark. Adder-flower had no scent or taste.

'Has it any other use?'

Ashe shrugged. 'It's a fixative for dyes in small concentrations. Weavers add it to coloring compounds like lavender and butternut hulls to make cloth hold color.'

Stephen's worried face relaxed and he exhaled with relief. 'That's undoubtedly the reason, then,' he said. 'Rosella is also a talented seamstress; she makes many of the children's clothes. You had me worried for a moment there, old boy. But Rosella would never think of harming the children. I'm certain of it.'

Ashe smiled at his best friend. 'I'm sorry. Extreme suspicion of everyone and everything around me is the only thing that has kept me alive all these years. I suppose if I'm going to become a real person again I'm going to have to put that behind me.'

'Indeed. Come; my chambers are through here.'

When they reached Stephen's bedroom Ashe went to the balcony door and peered out the window.

'Your wall looks as if it has taken some damage,' he said wryly. 'Harsh winter?'

The Duke of Navarne leaned against his writing desk. 'You've heard about the solstice festival?'

Ashe nodded, still staring into the darkness. 'Yes. I'm sorry, Stephen.'

Stephen nodded. 'Then you know about Tristan taking control of the armies?'

'Yes.'

The duke rubbed his chin with his thumb and forefinger. 'Do you plan to do anything to oppose him? Now that you're back?'

Ashe chuckled. 'Why would I?'

'Because – well, because it was always assumed that *you* would be the one to unite Roland. You're the one born to it.'

Ashe laughed and turned back to face his friend.

'Now, that would make for some interesting name possibilities,' he said. 'How do you like "King Gwydion the Dead"? No? How about "The Once-Dead"? "The No-Longer Dead"? "The Undead"? I don't think so.' He pulled his gloves from the pockets of his cloak and put them on. 'Thank you for the birthday drink.'

'You're going then?' Stephen asked, disappointment heavy in his voice.

Ashe nodded, resting his hand on his friend's shoulder one last time. 'I have to. Just as I had to come here tonight and tell you what happened.'

'There are still so many things I want to know,' Stephen said. Desperation clouded his blue-green eyes. 'When are you coming back?'

'When I can. I wish I could be certain. But know that in all these years, Stephen, you have never left my thoughts. Seeing you are safe and well has been a great comfort to me. The day will come when we can walk in the open in peace again.'

The duke smiled. 'I hope it comes soon. Your namesake is growing to manhood too fast for me to keep up. His godfather should be lending a hand in some of his training, and that of his sister as well. He needs you, Gwydion. I need you, too; between the two of them I'm growing more elderly and infirm every day.'

Ashe laughed, then embraced his friend, letting go reluctantly. 'When this is over there will be time to live life as it should be lived. We'll pick up where we left off, do great deeds, live heroically, love extraordinary women and—'

'—have statuary erected to us all over Roland,' Stephen finished, completing their boyhood motto, laughing. His grin resolved into a slight smile as their eyes met. It seemed strange that many of those childhood goals had already been accomplished and lost; it was a painfully hollow feeling. 'I'd settle for having you sit in my buttery after the cooks have gone to bed, eat the heels of brown bread, and talk into the morning hours the way we used to.'

'I look forward to it,' Ashe said. 'We can celebrate the joy of the ordinary for the rest of our lives. We'll both be in our dotage soon, anyway; we can hide in your wine cellar, drink ourselves into a fine stupor, and tell each other the stories that would bore anyone else to death.'

'Done.' Stephen's face grew serious. 'Know that I stand ready to help you in whatever you need, Gwydion. The land is balancing on the brink of war. Perhaps your return from death may spare the continent from its own.'

'Goodbye, Stephen,' Ashe said. 'Take care of yourself and your children first. We'll meet again soon.' He opened the door to the balcony and was gone, leaving Stephen staring out into the darkness and flying snow as the bitter wind howled around and through the windows and doorways of Haguefort.

211

34

Ylorc

The torches were just beginning to be lit in the darkening hallways of the Cauldron when Greevus knocked on the door of the council room behind the Great Hall. Achmed did not look up from the field map he had been examining; Grunthor waved him into the room, then turned back to the map as well.

Greevus waited in silence as the Sergeant-Major continued to confer with the king. Finally Achmed rolled the map into a tight scroll, irritation apparent in his sharp movements.

'Yes?'

Greevus cleared his throat. 'M'lord, bird came in to Grivven Tower with message for you. Seemed strange.'

For the first time since the general had entered the room the king looked up; he fixed his disturbing gaze on Greevus for a moment, then extended a gloved hand. The soldier placed the small scrap of oilskin tied with string in the king's palm, then bowed quickly and retreated to the dancing shadows near the wide hearth.

Achmed and Grunthor exchanged a glance; then the Sergeant-Major strode to the hearth, took a long twig of kindling from the woodpile, and caught a spark from the fireplace. He returned to the table and kindled the lamp on it while the king unrolled the tiny scrap of oilskin beneath it and bent over to read it. A moment later he did so aloud.

> King Achmed of Ylorc
>> Your Majesty:
> In great sorrow I have heard R's tale of the terrible illness that has befallen your people and the tragic loss of your army. I extend my condolences and offer whatever assistance you may need in medicines or burial herbs.
>> Llauron, Invoker – Gwynwood

The king and the Sergeant exchanged another glance; then Grunthor dismissed Greevus with a nod. The general bowed, then closed the door behind him.

After a moment Grunthor took off his helm and scratched his head, running his neatly manicured claws through his heavy hair.

'Well, what do you make of that? What is it you're thinking?'

Achmed held up the oilcloth before the fire and read the words again, watching the flames twist behind the paper, their colors and intensity muted. Finally he spoke.

'That I have been wrong about Llauron.' He tossed the string from the oilcloth into the fire where it blazed brightly and vanished in a cloud of acrid smoke.

Grunthor waited patiently as Achmed dropped into a chair before the hearth, brought his fingertips together, and rested them on his lips. The king stared into the fire as if trying to discern its secrets.

'Llauron is not the F'dor,' he said.

'How do you know?'

'Rhapsody would never have said such a thing to Llauron – I doubt she even knows about this missive. The story of the illness, the decimation of the army is a lie, of course – and Rhapsody doesn't lie. This is a message to her as much as to me; there is a coded subtext to it.'

The Sergeant nodded. 'Can you tell what it is?'

Achmed's brow wrinkled above his veils. 'I believe so. For some reason of his own, Llauron has intentionally spread this lie; he doesn't believe it himself. This is his way of making me aware of what he has done. If he were the F'dor, he would never have given me such notice.' Grunthor nodded as Achmed curled forward, staring even deeper into the fire. 'Perhaps he is trying to flush the F'dor from its hiding place by disseminating the information that the Bolglands are vulnerable. That would explain the part about the destruction of the army.'

Grunthor's face grew solemn in the flickering shadows.

'And you know what that means, then.'

Dark rage burned in the king's eyes. 'Yes. He thinks the F'dor's host is in a position to take advantage of the situation. I will have to think of a special way to thank him for using my kingdom as demon-bait – if we survive the attack that is no doubt massing at this moment.'

Regent's Palace, Bethany

Come in, Evans; it's rude to lurk in doorways.'

Evans, Tristan Steward's elderly councilor and court ambassador, had been standing at the entranceway to the dining room of the Regent's Palace for some time. He exhaled and crossed the vast hall, his footfalls on the polished marble floor echoing loudly against the tall panes of the floor-to-ceiling glass windows, an architectural hallmark of the palace that was Bethany's capital seat. The light from the hearth fire cast long shadows through which he passed briskly, musing.

He had swallowed his ire at the sound of the Lord Roland's voice, thick with drink and self-pity; it was a timbre he had heard much too often over the last few weeks. Whether the regent was mourning the tragic turn of events at the winter festival, or feeling extreme pressure from his recent assumption of command of the Orlandan armies, or merely in a state of panic at his upcoming nuptials, Evans was not certain, but any of those cases seemed to warrant excusing.

The man was, after all, betrothed to Madeleine, the Beast of Canderre. The joke in ambassadorial circles was that Cedric Canderre produced fine, strong libations out of necessity to ensure that someone might one day be drunk enough to seek his daughter's hand. *Tristan must have consumed an entire full-cask by himself, and then some,* Bois de Berne, the Avonderrian ambassador, had suggested mirthfully at the time the betrothal was announced. Evans remembered chuckling then; now the sound of the prince's voice, and all that had happened since those days, only made him want to weep.

'I thought you might want to see this, m'lord,' he said as he approached the regent's table, noting that Tristan's supper was largely untouched, but the decanter next to his brandy snifter was empty. 'It was discovered at sunset by one of the archers on the western inner tower in the leg-sleeve of a bird, an avian messenger that most likely got caught in one of the recent storms and misdirected.'

Tristan stared into the snifter, swirling the last of the brandy around, watching the light from the fire dance in rings on the heavily carved dining table. He sighed as Evans held out the oilcloth scrap, lifted his snifter and tossed back the brandy, then held his hand out for the paper.

Evans watched the Lord Roland's expression metamorphosing each time the shadows shifted on his face as he read the note. First confusion, then shock took hold, changing to wonder, then an almost manic glee. Evans ran his hands up and down his elderly arms to stave off the sudden cold chill that came over him as the prince put down the scrap of oilcloth, threw back his head, and laughed uproariously.

In the darkness of his study the holy man could hear the Lord Roland laughing; whether the sound was carried on the wind, or through the hearth fire, or just in the depths of his mind where he and Tristan were bound he did not know, but he could hear it cleanly, as surely as he could hear the crackle of the flames.

He had no idea why the prince was laughing, but the bloodlust he could hear below the surface of the merriment cheered him immensely.

35

Gwynwood, North of the Tar'afel River

The stream that flowed from the waterfall was crusted with ice, broken in patches by snowfall. Ashe knelt beside it beneath the boughs of the bare crabapple trees, lost in thought. He had come to cleanse the blood from his sword in the clear water of this place that he thought of as his own, as his safe haven, but was regretting the decision now. It seemed wrong, selfish even, to befoul the icy water, the pristine snow, with the gore he had carried since his last fray in the gently rolling forest of northern Navarne.

After leaving Stephen's keep he had come upon a Lirin raiding party, small in number but keen in murderous intent. The villagers of the forest settlement, scarred still from the slaughter of the winter solstice festival, were making a good rally of it, fighting for their homes with pitchforks, harrows, and scythes. Ashe could smell the burning cinders from the thatched huts that the Lirin had set aflame from several leagues' distance, and so turned his sword and his attention first to melting the snow that burdened the heavy boughs of the forest evergreens which sheltered the village. Kirsdarke's blade had run in intense blue-white rivers as he held it above his head, commanding the element of frozen water to thaw and pour down from the trees, quenching the fire.

For a moment both villagers and attackers had stood in silent amazement at the sight of him, staring as if entranced by the waves of light from the gleaming water sword. But a moment later a deeper enchantment took over, and the Lirin thralls resumed their mayhem. Ashe was left with no choice but to join the villagers until the last Lirin was dead. He had broken through the clutching gratitude and stumbled away through the smoke of the forest, heading here, to this place, where he could cleanse the horror from his blade and his soul.

But even now, as he knelt beside the stream, he felt uneasy.

We are not alone, the dragon in his blood whispered.

He took a deep breath in agreement. At the edge of his senses someone was approaching. The dragon itched beneath his skin in excitement.

Let me sense, his wyrm nature insisted.

Seeing no alternative, Ashe sighed and surrendered to his nether side.

A moment later he had his answer. The dragon in his blood recognized its own kind.

Anborn was approaching the stream.

Ashe slid Kirsdarke back into its sheath. His hood was down, so no doubt Anborn had an inkling that he was there as well. He took off his gloves and broke through the ice, scooped some of the frigid water into his hands, and slapped it on his face, bracing himself against the sting. He cupped his hands again, drank deeply, then turned to face his uncle.

Anborn had dismounted and approached the stream on foot. When he came within a few yards he stopped and nodded.

'Nephew.'

Ashe smiled. *'Uncle.'*

Anborn snorted. 'We can revert to our old nomenclature if you prefer – I can call you "Useless" and you can refer to me as "That Pompous Bastard."'

'I only did that once, Uncle, and I apologized, I believe. I can feel my father's grip on the back of my neck to this day; it made a lasting impression.'

The Cymrian general nodded. 'I just came from your father's palace. He was alive when I left him.'

'I had no doubt he would be, Uncle,' Ashe replied pleasantly. 'What I don't know is why you are here, so deep in Gwynwood.'

Anborn chuckled. 'I knew this glade nine centuries before you were born, lad. I am the one that showed it to you, if you recall.'

Ashe nodded. Anborn had, in fact, once discovered him in the woods at play as a youth, and had shown him the crabapple glen, had taught him to hurl the small, hard projectiles side-armed, much to the eventual consternation of his father, who later had to ameliorate the complaints from the Filidic priests whose window shutters were his prime targets. He felt a strange sense of awkward warmth; he *did* have one pleasant memory, however brief, of his uncle.

That warmth was coupled with trepidation. The crabapple glen was the doorstep of the waterfall, and the waterfall hid his secret sanctuary – a one-room turf hut secreted behind the shale wall of the vertical stream. To his knowledge only one other person in the world knew the location of the hut – Rhapsody.

Beneath the surface his dragon nature stirred again, bristling with nervousness. The security of the tiny cottage was paramount to him, one of the few places in the world he knew he was safe from detection. More than that, he had encouraged Rhapsody to meet him here should she ever be in need of him, or to come here to hide. Anborn's presence seemed to indicate the folly of that offer.

Mine, the dragon whispered furiously. His uncle, and his presence, was now a threat.

Just as the jealous rapacity of his wyrm side began to rise, his pragmatic human outlook descended. Between a single pair of heartbeats he reached down inside himself to the place where he was tied to the element of water, the pure, elemental liquid core of his soul. That water bond, dormant within him, rose to glistening life and sang to the waters of the frozen cascade, banished now to a mere trickle beneath the hoary frost of winter.

At first the stream was silent; then, quietly, from beneath the frozen strata of ice shards, the voice of the slumbering waterfall answered.

No one has come, the waterfall whispered. *He does not know. The place I guard is still yours alone. I have protected it well.*

My thanks, Ashe replied silently through the elemental bond. *If the woman should come, let her in – guard her well. Protect her for me.*

A crackle of breaking ice answered him; only a heartbeat's time had passed.

'Indeed,' he said to his uncle. 'Yes, you did. So why have you come here now? Surely not out of concern for my technique of throwing crabapples.'

'Surely not,' Anborn agreed testily. 'I have come to tell you that I have granted you a boon.'

'I don't remember asking one of you.'

'No, but I assume you will appreciate it nonetheless.'

'Oh. Well, thank you, then,' Ashe said mildly. 'Do you mind if I ask what it is?'

'Not at all. I have spared your father from the thrashing of his life, one that is long overdue, and well deserved. He lives, untouched, because of your kindness to my man-at-arms, and *only* because of it. My debt to you is repaid now, nephew. The scales are balanced between us.'

Ashe smiled slightly at the strange Sorboldian expression, trying to sort out the confusion he felt.

'I certainly appreciate your forbearance. What was it that you felt the need to thrash Llauron over? I might have been willing to help you if it had been well enough deserved.'

The Cymrian general regarded him thoughtfully, then flexed his hands within their leather sheaths. 'You might have at that,' he said after a moment. 'Any man with a beating heart would have, had he seen the woman your accursed father left to die in the snow of the southern forest.'

Ashe shook his head. 'Llauron? Left a woman to die?'

'Do not deny his capability to do such a thing. Your father has committed more atrocities than you have hairs on your head – as have I,' said Anborn sullenly.

'I do not doubt the depth of my father's capacity to do anything, good or ill, that benefits his plans,' Ashe replied. 'Still, it seems out of character that he would have left a woman so compromised, especially were she one of his followers.'

'I doubt that she is.'

'Was she Lirin?'

'Partly.'

Ashe's stomach constricted suddenly. 'Who was she?'

Anborn looked away and whistled. The dragon in Ashe's blood followed innately the vibrations from the sound to the ears of the horse a thousand paces away, hidden in a copse of winter birch; the noise reverberated against the animal's auditory bones and sent a signal to its brain to come, which, seconds later, it obeyed. He could feel the thudding of the animal's hoofbeats long before they reached his ears, instinctually measured its tides of breath, the blinking of its eyes, the compensation in stride that it made to favor the sore knee of its right foreleg. Ashe shook his head; the dragon was lurking much too near the surface, much too acutely aware for comfort.

The general turned back to his nephew. 'It matters not – she was someone who came to him for aid, for advice in an important matter, and he steered her into harm's way. The disguise in which he clothed her would not have kept her safe from frostbite if she were inside in the warmth near a hearth, let alone outside in the frozen wastes of the southern forests, and in a black storm to boot. No food, no water, no reinforcements, no aid of any kind. Despicable, and stupid, and above all else, proof that Llauron is as blind as he is heartless.'

Ashe breathed shallowly, trying to control his pounding heart, feeling the flush that had started with his face move through the rest of his body, enflaming his wyrm nature even more.

'She was comely, then, this woman?'

The horse trotted into the clearing, a beautiful black stallion with a plaited mane. It stopped beside Anborn and nickered softly; the general patted its cheek, then in a fluid motion pulled himself into the saddle. He took up the reins, looking down at Ashe, and smirked.

217

'One might think so.' He clicked to the stallion, and it followed the nod of his head to the icy stream, where it drank deeply at a thawed spot in the shallows. When its thirst was slaked it raised its head, and Anborn tossed his cloak back over his shoulder, preparing to depart.

Ashe leaned casually against a tree in an attempt to quell the trembling of his body, struggling not to succumb to the rising ire of the dragon. His head ached with the intensity of the hum that vibrated in his blood as the beast within him searched the minutiae of Anborn's cloak. It was stained with specks of blood from more than one person – Shrike's was there, without question, because it matched similar smears on his own saddle blanket. And then, tucked away in a fold of the hood, his dragon sense found what he feared it would.

A strand of golden hair, pure as sunlight.

'Was she all right, this woman?' he asked, his voice betraying his worry with a slight tremor. 'Did any harm befall her?'

Anborn chuckled and pulled up his hood. 'That depends.'

'On what?' Ashe gripped the tree more tightly as waves of alien power flooded through him, making him nauseous.

'On whether or not you believe I could rein in my base nature when left alone with a ravishingly beautiful woman – a *grateful* woman – compromised, naked, alone within my domain. A gambling man with any sense would wager against it. Goodbye, nephew.' He patted the horse's neck and trotted off into the forest.

As soon as Anborn was gone from his sensibilities, Ashe released the tree he was clutching. He grasped the hilt of the sword and drew it angrily from its sheath, then turned and plunged it into the clear-running stream, staining the sparkling water, sweeping it around in the currents until they ran red.

36

The Tree Palace at The Circle, Gwynwood

Llauron sighed as the heavily carved door of his house swung open and slammed with the force of a thunderclap. He had been expecting that Ashe would show up sooner or later ever since Anborn had practically torn the thing off its hinges two weeks before. He raised a hand as the guards forced it open again and spilled into the front hallway.

'It's all right, gentlemen. You may go about your business.' He rose and walked past his glowering son, then closed the door gently himself. 'Well, good day to you, too, Gwydion. Was the back entrance blocked, or has destroying the antique door of the Crossroads Inn become a hobby for you and your uncle? I see you have chosen to reveal yourself to him; do you really think that was wise?'

'Give me a good reason I shouldn't burn this place down around your head right now.' The fire in Ashe's voice could have ignited the tree palace by itself.

'Hmmm, let's see: how about the sheer waste of it? What did my home do to deserve your ire? Really, you must learn to control your temper. Your outburst makes you look ridiculous; as Lord Cymrian it would make you seem asinine.'

'You presume there will be a time when that will matter. At this point, I expect you will be looking at a Lord Cymrian outside of our line, as both Anborn and I are considering renouncing our claims and dissolving any tie with this family.'

For the first time since his arrival Ashe saw his father's dark brows furrow together and black anger spread across his face. 'Careful, Gwydion; that sounded like a threat. I don't need to remind you how I respond to threats.'

Ashe was far past the point of caring. 'How? How could you do that to Rhapsody? Why are you trying to kill her?'

Llauron's face returned to its previously placid state. Obviously Anborn had told his son of Rhapsody's rescue, but not of the plan. 'What rot. I won't even dignify that statement with a response.'

'What in the name of your sacred One-God was she doing for you in the southern forest anyway? You have any number of foresters and scouts who know that area; she doesn't.'

'I am not going to discuss this with you. Besides, would you have preferred I went ahead with the plan as she understood it? I had intended to send Khaddyr as her reinforcement. Unfortunately, while you were otherwise engaged, distracted by whatever it is that keeps you from making your meetings at the assigned times, it was revealed that he, in fact, is the traitor in our midst.'

Ashe's words came out in a choked gasp. 'Khaddyr? It's Khaddyr? Not Lark?'

'Apparently my original information was wrong. Lark may be involved in the assassination plot as well; I am no longer certain. But I discovered, on the verge of telling Khaddyr where Rhapsody was, that he knew things only the renegades would know, specifically that the Lirin raiders had traveled through Avonderre. In addition, a number of patients in his care who could possibly identify the F'dor's host have died mysteriously. Under the circumstances, it seemed better not to send anyone.'

'You didn't send *anyone*? Are you insane? She was expecting to meet Khaddyr, and you sent *no one*?'

'I had no one else available I considered trustworthy.'

The cords in Ashe's neck stood out like iron bands. 'No one else? What about me? You know I have been nearby for weeks now.'

'You were not an appropriate choice either.'

The blue dragon eyes narrowed to slits. 'Would you care to explain that?'

Llauron returned the piercing glare without blinking. 'No.'

Ashe paced the room angrily. 'So you decided it was appropriate to abandon Rhapsody to the elements, alone? Anborn said you left her to die in the snow, with no food, no reinforcements. He said what she was wearing wouldn't prevent frostbite inside by a fire, let alone in the forest.'

'Well, she's your inamorata. Perhaps you should speak to her about her inappropriate choice of attire.'

'It was your plan!' Ashe exploded. Llauron said nothing. Ashe walked to the window and stared out into the windy meadow, running his hands angrily through his hair.

He turned back to Llauron, his eyes smoldering with blue fire. 'This is the end of it, Father – the *end*, do you understand? I'm calling a halt to your idiotic plot once and for all. Rhapsody is no longer your pawn; you will have to find some other way to achieve your ends. Leave her out of it.'

The Invoker's look of amusement flattened to a cold stare. 'You're going to intervene?'

'Yes.'

'How?'

'I'll tell her your plan, Father – I'll warn her – *forbid* her – from going anywhere with you.'

Llauron chuckled. 'Now, if I recall correctly, you once accused me, in very ugly terms, of using her shamelessly, of making her decisions for her. What do you suppose you are doing now yourself, my boy? "There are somethings you cannot manipulate, and somethings you cannot repair once they are betrayed," you said. How do you suppose she will feel when she discovers your part in all this?'

Ashe rubbed his clenched fist with his open hand. 'She'll forgive me. She will understand.'

'Will she?' The Invoker decanted a splash of brandy into a crystal snifter and held it up to the firelight. 'What was it you said to me last spring? Hmmm – now, let me think; it really was rather pithy, if I recall. Oh, yes: "You can't expect someone to stand by you when you've used them as a pawn to accomplish your own ends to their detriment." Yes, that was it.' He took a sip, then regarded Ashe solemnly. 'If you intervene, if you depart from the course of events now, you will not only ensure my death – my actual one – but you will be handing Khaddyr the staff of the Invoker in reality. Is that an end you wish to see achieved?'

'No. Of course not.'

'And Rhapsody – once Khaddyr no longer sees her as useful to him, once she is no longer valuable as a herald, what do you suppose he will seek to do with her?'

Llauron could feel the cold of Ashe's shudder from across the room. When he spoke his voice was kind. 'You have to let it unfold as it will now, Gwydion. Rhapsody needs to play her part, just as we all must. She will survive it – we will all survive it. With any luck, we will all get what we want in the end.'

'Why should I trust your judgment of what the impact will be on Rhapsody – you, who promised her reinforcements, but left her alone in the storm? How could you do that to anyone, and especially to Rhapsody? How could you expect the unswerving loyalty she had given you, and then abandon her to her death?'

'Aren't you being a little histrionic? She didn't die, did she?'

'No thanks to you. You should be mortally ashamed, though I doubt you have the honor to be.'

'Spare me your righteous indignation. I have already had enough of that from your uncle.'

'Would you prefer murderous rage? That's much closer to what I am feeling.'

'Feel whatever you like, but spare me from it. I have no patience for this disrespect and will not tolerate it.'

'Do you have any idea what could have happened to her in Sorbold, dressed as she was?'

'Nothing that hasn't happened to her before.'

Ashe's eyes narrowed even further in anger. 'What is that supposed to mean?'

'Oh, come now, Gwydion, it's not like she's a blushing maiden, as she was when she first came here. Surely you must know that as well as anyone, I expect.' A vase of flowers exploded behind him, spattering shards of porcelain and water over Llauron's desk. 'Well, that was mature. Are you taking offense at me pointing out that there is no honor there to defend anymore?'

'Rhapsody has more honor in one strand of her hair than you have known in your entire selfish life. I hope you are not saying that she deserved to have something of that nature happen to her. I would hate to have to add patricide to my list of crimes.'

'Not at all. I'm merely saying that I felt Rhapsody was capable of handling whatever befell her alone. She is the Iliachenva'ar, after all.'

'What did she ever do but help you, when was she ever anything but kind to you? Why do you hate her so?'

Llauron stared at his son incredulously. 'Have you lost your mind? What are you talking about? I love that girl like my own daughter; I have nothing but the greatest respect for her.'

'Oh, of course, a daughter. No wonder you thought you could abuse and manipulate her with impunity; you mistook her for family.' The anger in both sets of eyes now matched. 'What is it that makes you want to hurt her? Are you jealous, afraid she will capture the hearts and minds of the Cymrians in a way our line never could? Do you doubt her wisdom, if they should choose her as their leader?'

'Of course not. Rhapsody would be a magnificent leader. She has a noble heart and a beautiful countenance. I have no reservations about her at all.'

'So why? If you love her, you respect her, you think she would be a magnificent leader, why are you trying to *kill* her? Or is it that you feel perhaps it is I that don't deserve her? Is that it? Are you trying to keep her for yourself?'

221

'Don't be absurd.'

'Then why? Tell me, Father. Why? Why are you trying to destroy the only happiness I may ever have? Do you hate me so that you want to see me miserable again?'

Fury filled Llauron's face and he turned away. 'What a stupid thing to say.'

'Then explain it to me, Father. Tell me why you have interfered in my happiness, jeopardized my potential marriage to the one person who can make me whole? Who *has* made me whole?'

The Invoker said nothing for a moment. He walked to the window and stared into the darkness, his mind wandering down old roads. After a long moment he spoke, and his voice was toneless.

'Tell me, Gwydion, do you judge your dragon side to be more a part of you than mine is of me, or less?'

'More, obviously; otherwise we wouldn't be undertaking this idiotic plan of yours.'

'Very well, then. I assume you are aware of what happened to your own mother upon giving birth to the child of a partial dragon?' Llauron could feel the blood drain from Ashe's face even beneath the hood. 'I have spared you the details up until now – shall I give them to you? Do you crave to know what it is like to watch a woman, not to mention one that you happen to love, die in agony trying to bring forth your child, hmmm? Let me describe it for you. Since the dragonling instinctually needs to break the eggshell, clawing through, to emerge, the infant—'

'Stop,' Ashe commanded, his voice harsh as acid. 'Why are you doing this?'

'To answer your question, ingrate son. I know that you love her. I knew you would before you even met her – who wouldn't? How could you possibly resist her? And I also knew that somehow the training, and the natural stoicism of our family, has managed not to make an impression on you. You have always been moonstruck, babbling about your dead soul-mate, pestering Anwyn for information about something that was only a dream.

'So when it became obvious that you had lost your heart to this one, I needed to step in to remind you that you have a responsibility that supersedes the heat of your loins, one that involves not only responsibly choosing a marriage partner, but also producing an heir. And that will, in all likelihood, mean that your mate will die, like mine did. Your child will be even more of a dragon than you were, so the chances of the mother's survival are not good. If your own mother could not give birth to you and live, what will happen, do you think, to your mate?

'You accuse me of hating you – how stupid you are being. It is, in fact, my love for you that has informed my actions. I don't wish you to suffer as I did. If the Lirin queen had accepted my proposal, I would have never suffered the pain I did when Cynron died; but life works out as it does. So instead I watched with horror the greatest sadness of my life in the face of what should have been my greatest joy. And I don't wish for you to repeat my mistake, nor do I want to lose Rhapsody to our world. You would become ineffectual, and this place would be a darker one. So strike out at me in your frustration all you like – the truth is, I am trying to spare you pain from which you may never recover.'

Llauron heard no sound when he stopped speaking; it was as if all the air had gone out of the room. He turned slowly to face his son, who was standing rigid across the dark study. He took a step toward him, and watched as Ashe's body relaxed, a sure sign he had rationalized things in his mind.

'We will just forgo having children,' he said, his voice tinged with sadness but weak with relief. 'Rhapsody adopts every child she comes upon who needs her. We won't be childless. There will be more than enough love in our lives, with or without them.'

'Not an option,' said Llauron coldly. 'You know better by now. You have a responsibility to produce an heir, and it must be of the blood. How would a child without Cymrian lore rule a people so innately powerful? You were gifted with the line of MacQuieth, the blood of the Seren kings and the elemental ties of the Dragon; who else could assure that they will live in peace? Who else could undo the damage caused by both your grand-parents?'

Ashe felt relief break, like an egg, over him. 'Manwyn.'

'What?'

'Manwyn. She has already foretold this. She told me clearly that, though my mother had died giving birth to me, that my children's mother would not die giving birth to them. She's safe, Father. Rhapsody is safe. The Seer has said so.'

Llauron considered. 'How do you know she was referring to Rhapsody?'

Anger sparked in Ashe's eyes. 'Because, as I have told you, I will have no other than she. No other woman will bear my children; therefore, she is safe.'

Llauron sighed. 'I have only a short time left with you, Gwydion, so I will choose my last bits of advice to impart to you carefully, in the hope you will actually pay them some heed for once. Beware of prophecies; they are not always as they seem to be. The value of seeing the Future is often not worth the price of the misdirection.'

'Thank you for the advice. In the meantime, I plan to stop living in the shadows of fear and take what is rightfully mine.'

'Good, good.' Llauron rubbed his hands as if to warm them. 'Now, that's more like it. I am glad to see you are finally coming into your own, at peace with your destiny.'

Beneath his hood, Ashe smiled. 'That's not at all what I meant. What is rightfully mine is my own life, Father; I have been living it without any say in it for long enough. I will honor my destiny and my duty in the best way I know how – by doing whatever I can to make Rhapsody my wife and the Lady Cymrian. I cannot imagine there is another who would be better – you said so yourself.'

Llauron sighed. 'You're right, I did, didn't I? All right, then, a word of warning: remember your grandparents. Never raise your hand to her, and never let your personal quarrels harm your subjects.'

'Of course not.' Even without being visible, the insult Ashe felt was clear.

'Very well, then, since you seem to be set on it, and time is growing short, let me give you my blessing.'

Ashe's mouth dropped open. 'Excuse me?'

Llauron smiled, but there was a tinge of annoyance in his voice. 'Now, Gwydion, don't spoil this tender fatherly moment. Kneel.'

Ashe bent before him, and Llauron laid a hand on the coppery curls, a wistful look in his eyes. 'First, be happy. Treasure her.'

Ashe waited, but nothing more was forthcoming. 'That's all?' he asked after a moment. 'No lecture?'

Llauron laughed. 'No, no lecture. I told you, time is growing short. Too many words dissipate the meaning. I do want you to be happy, and if you do as I suggest, I know you will be. Now, how's for a brandy? That's one aspect of humanity I shall miss; a good snifter of the golden elixir now and then.'

Ashe walked with him to the cabinet as the warm light from the sunset began to shine on the floor in windowpane patterns of pink and gold.

'Now, Father, you don't need to live without that just because you're a dragon. I know a place where I can get you a large trough. You should be able to have a good slurp from time to time.'

'Barbarian.' The guards outside heard the sound of laughter emerge from behind the door, and sighed.

37

Haguefort

Gerald Owen, the chamberlain of Haguefort, was on his way to his bedchamber to retire for the evening when he passed the library doors.

Though the double doors were closed, an icy gust of wind blasted from beneath them. Gerald stopped, surprised, and rested his hand against a mahogany panel; it was cold to the touch.

Perhaps the duke is up late, he mused, but discarded the thought as soon as it occurred. Lord Stephen had turned in for the night a few hours before, citing a need for rest in order to be ready to review the rebuilt barracks and the wall guard posts in the early morning hours with the master of his regiment. Gerald opened the door.

The shock of the cold air stung against his face and exposed skin. While not an elderly man, Gerald was long past youth's prime, and was more vulnerable to the aches and pains he had remembered plaguing his father in his later years. Like his father, Gerald never complained, seeing each twinge and spasm as something to be endured silently, with grace, so as not to distract the duke or the household staff who served under him in any way. He expected as much from the staff as well.

The vast, dark room was filled with shadows and slashes of white light reflecting through the towering windows from the sheets of snow that were writhing outside them. Those billowing shadows danced across the furniture in time to the music of the breeze. A discordant wail rose and fell as the wind whipped around the keep, fluttering the drapes of the open balcony door wildly. The fireplace was cold and dark; the ashes were lifeless.

Gerald entered the library and quietly closed the doors. The howl of the wind diminished somewhat, and the drapes settled back, rustling now instead of flapping. His footsteps were swallowed by the moaning wind as he crossed the enormous room to the balcony doors, passing through wide fields of snow shadows flickering on the polished marble floors and thick silk rugs.

When he reached the doorway he looked out onto the balcony. The stone benches were crowned with several inches of pristine snow, as was the wide stone railing, ornately sculpted, that ringed the semicircular balcony. The carpet of snow on the balcony floor, however, had been marred by numerous small footprints, not much larger than those of a child, dimpled impressions of toes that put him in mind of a distracted kitten's, leading to the edge and back again several times. There was no one on the balcony.

Gerald hurried out into the bitter night, covering his ears with his hands, and looked down at the ground below the balcony. The snow of the evergreen trees and the courtyard below was unmarred; an ice crust had formed, smooth and serene, dusted by crystals scattering before the insistent gale. Satisfied that no one had fallen, the chamberlain hastened back into the library, pushed the doors shut, and locked them. The cries of the wind softened to a distant keen.

Gerald Owen took out his handkerchief. He bent slowly and wiped up the crystals of snow that had accumulated on the library floor while the door was open.

He was rubbing his hands and halfway across the room again on his way back to the hallway when a white shadow, slightly more solid and stationary than the others, caught his eye. It was huddled amid the dancing shades on the floor next to the sideboard, trembling.

Gerald walked slowly over toward the figure. In the darkness her enormous eyes were even larger, her light brown hair hung in loose waves over her thin shoulders. Her hands were clutching a small cloth sack; the duke's decanter of after-dinner brandy was sitting on the floor beside her, the glass stopper in her lap.

'Rosella?'

Upon hearing her name the woman in the white dressing gown looked up sharply. Her eyes darted around the room madly, resting momentarily on

Gerald's face, then dashed off again, as if pursuing flying objects only she could see. Gerald slowed his steps even more.

When he was within an armspan of her, the governess began whispering wildly.

'I do, I love the children, sir, I love them, and the duke, of course, the duke has my undying devotion as well. He does. I do, I love them all, would die for any one of them, you have to believe me, sir, I would, I would die for any of them. I love them.'

Gerald crouched down before her and reached out his hand, but the girl shrank away. He withdrew it and spoke as gently as he could.

'Of course you do, Rosella, as do we all. No one would ever doubt your loyalty to Lord Stephen or the children.'

Rosella's gaze came to rest on his face and remained there; within her eyes Gerald could see madness burning.

'I do, sir, I love them all.'

'Yes, yes, of course you do.'

'I love them.'

'I know.'

Outside the windows the wind picked up, howling furiously. Rosella's dark eyes darted away again, and she began to whimper like a frightened child.

Gerald reached out to her once more, and once again she reared away. 'It's all right, Rosella,' the chamberlain said soothingly. 'It's all right.' The governess began to mutter to herself, incoherently now. When Gerald caught her eye again, it had clouded over, reflecting the light of the snow.

'The duke,' she whispered repeatedly. 'The duke.'

Gerald Owen remained crouched for a long time, ignoring the screaming protest of his knees and back, not moving, until her muttering finally ceased. Afraid what she might do if he were to frighten her, he stood slowly and backed away. He put out his hand again.

'Rosella?'

'The duke,' she whispered. The terror on her face resonated in Gerald's soul.

'I'll get him,' he said. 'Don't move, Rosella.'

As the door closed behind the chamberlain, the voice in the wind grew louder.

Now, Rosella.

It had been howling at her for hours, directing her to its will, berating her incompetence, her stupidity. It no longer threatened, no longer growled, only whispered softly in the darkness past the closed windows.

Now, Rosella.

The governess's face hardened, and her trembling stopped. The pain in her frozen feet from when she had stood at the balcony edge in the snow ebbed until it vanished.

Slowly she rose and went to the sideboard. The heavy stopper of the decanter tumbled smoothly down the skirt of her dressing gown and onto the floor, where it spun in rolling circles under the table. The small shard of glass from where the fall chipped it twinkled in the reflected light.

She took a crystal snifter and righted it, then held it up in the dancing light of the snow. The curved bowl caught the illumination and held it in the glass like liquid moonlight.

Now, Rosella.

Rosella set the snifter on the sideboard, then opened the tiny drawstring of the cloth sack, damp and deeply wrinkled from the clutching of her hands. She upended the sack into the snifter, then took the decanter of brandy from the floor and splashed a finger of the liquid into the glass. She swirled the snifter slowly, watching the fine powder catch the currents in the brandy and vanish into them, then held the glass up to the snowy light again.

Now, Rosella.

She put the glass to her lips.

'If you love me, or my children, you won't drink it.'

Rosella spun around. Lord Stephen stood before her in his nightshirt; in the light spilling from the hallway she could see Gerald Owen as well at the door.

'Give me the glass.'

'M'lord—'

'*Now*, Rosella.'

The words of her beloved master shattered the grasp of the voice in the wind that had wound around her mind. She reached out her hand with the glass; it was shaking violently.

Stephen took the snifter, gently prying her fingers from around the bowl. He walked to the cold fireplace and hurled it into the dark stones at the back, then returned to the sideboard.

'Who gave you the adder-flower extract?'

Rosella's lip was trembling, but her gaze was clear.

'I don't know, m'lord.'

'You don't *know?*'

'Forgive me, m'lord,' she whispered. 'I can't remember.'

Stephen felt his heart lurch. The words were the same; he had heard them spoken before. They came from the lips of a Lirin soldier, just before the hangman slipped the noose around his neck. The man had been caught, along with the rest of his party, slitting the throat of Stephen's wife. He had continued to saw at Lydia's neck, decapitating her, even as Stephen's soldiers dragged at him, choosing to remain focused on his grisly task rather than to fight or escape.

Why? Stephen had demanded, his voice breaking along with his heart, as he stood face-to-face with the man on the gallows. *At least tell me why.*

I don't know, m'lord.

Who gave you the order?

I – I can't remember.

It had been the same with each of the soldiers executed that day, even to the last, whose sentence he had offered to commute in exchange for the information.

I can't remember. I am sorry, m'lord.

The soldiers of the Sorbold column that had attacked the winter carnival had stood, staring blankly at the smoking ruins of the holiday festival.

Why?

I – I don't know, m'lord.

Who gave the order?

I can't remember.

The woman standing before him was trembling violently. Stephen stared into her eyes, which were filled with dark terror and uncertainty, and felt for a moment he could see straight into her heart. He took her into his arms.

'All right, Rosella,' he said finally. 'All right.' He gestured at Gerald Owen, who in turn opened the door and allowed the two guards who had been waiting outside in the hall at Stephen's command to enter the library.

'Take her to the tower,' he said quietly to the chamberlain as the guards led her away. 'Make her comfortable; do not treat her like a prisoner. She's ill.'

'Shall I send word to Llauron, m'lord? Perhaps Khaddyr could do something for her.'

Stephen shook his head. 'No. I have to think about this, Owen. Until I decide what to do, I'm not going to involve anyone else, not even Llauron.'

'I understand, m'lord.' Gerald Owen picked up the decanter and the small empty bag, bowed, and left the library.

Stephen sighed as the door closed.

'I wish I did.'

38

Deep in the Forest of Tyrian, at the Veil of Hoen

The morning light broke over the forest, shining through the flakes of quietly falling snow. All around them the woods were silent, and the absence of sound seemed to grow deeper with each step. Occasionally one of the children would whimper, or giggle nervously, but by and large even they felt the heavy stillness in the air and succumbed to it.

Oelendra stopped, and Rhapsody followed her lead, clicking softly to the mare. They were in a forest clearing, unremarkable in its appearance, with heavy woods around them on all sides, impenetrable to the eye. There was a solemnity to the place, a deep and ancient song of power that Rhapsody could feel in her bones. She looked at her friend.

Oelendra was casting her gaze around the forest, as if trying to discern a direction. Finally her eyes opened wider, and she pointed off into the distance.

'There 'tis, the alder with the split trunk. That was my landmark.'

Rhapsody followed Oelendra's direction with her eyes until she, too, saw the tree, and she nodded. 'How far is it from there?'

Oelendra shook her head. 'I don't know,' she answered quietly, her voice barely audible in the stillness of the clearing. 'You'll see what I mean in a moment. There's a bend in Time around here somewhere; 'tis the best I can describe it. I had passed this way a thousand times before that night and I had never seen the Veil of Hoen.'

Rhapsody nodded and looked off into the distance again. The Veil of Hoen, the Cymrian word for Joy, was the doorway to the realm of the Lord and Lady Rowan, the entities Oelendra had told her about the first night they met. There was something mystical about these legendary people, the Keeper of Dreams and her mate, the Peaceful Death, something beyond Rhapsody's comprehension. Had anyone but Oelendra related the tale of Ashe's rescue to her, she would have suspected an unhinged mind or an excessive amount of ale, but Oelendra's words were always carefully considered, and carried the ring of knowledge when she used them. The Lord and Lady, she had said, only intervened, only allowed guests, in cases of life and death. She swallowed, hoping they would consider this situation worthy.

'Perhaps it only is visible when you need it to be,' she suggested, patting the mare on the flank.

Oelendra shrugged. 'Perhaps,' she said, and she squinted, looking into the forest again. Then she turned and took Rhapsody by the shoulders. 'There is something you need to remember. Time does not pass there the way it does here. I was within their realm for hours, perhaps days, when they were working on Gwydion.' The reflection of a cloud passed in her silver eyes, or perhaps it was just the irony of the memory. Oelendra had taken the news of Ashe being alive with a solemn silence, back when Rhapsody had first returned to Tyrian, seeking her help with the children of the F'dor. She had often wondered what the Lirin warrior was thinking, but Oelendra never shared her thoughts about it. 'When he – after there was nothing more I could do, and the Lord Rowan sent me back, nothing had changed from the moment I had entered, Rhapsody; my saddle was still warm. You may find yourself staying for a very long time, months, years perhaps, but when you come back it may only be a moment later than when you went in. It may be hard for you to find your place in Time again.'

Rhapsody patted her hand. 'Thank you,' she said. 'I know where I will come first for help if I lose my way.'

For the first time since they had entered the wood Oelendra smiled. 'Well, that's a lesson you have learned well. My door is always open to you, dearest. My home is yours. Now, I will wait here with the children, and him.' She gestured toward the gladiator, propped up in the saddle of the roan Oelendra had led, his eyes bleary in the herb-induced stupor. 'I hope you find them.'

Rhapsody swallowed hard. She tried not to think about what she would do if she couldn't. Slowly she drew Daystar Clarion and held it before her, watching the twisting flames whisper up the shining blade, gleaming with the light of the stars. She ran the tips of her fingers through the fire, feeling the humming pulse in her skin; at her touch the flames leapt and roared, quieting into a windy billow a moment later. Then with a decisive jab she plunged sword, tip first, into the snow to serve as a marker and walked away without looking back.

She had walked for what seemed like a very long time, stepping in the ankle-deep snow, leaving almost no trail. The wind blew gently here, and the breeze was warm, even in the depths of winter. Though she had no idea where she was going, and barely knew from where she had come, Rhapsody did not have the sense of being lost. She closed her eyes and drank in the song of the forest, deeper, more solemn, than the song of Tyrian she had come to know so well.

The song resonated louder to the west, and she followed it blindly, her hands outstretched before her. It was a deep, warm melody, like the song of miners in the depths of the hills, what the Earth itself sounded like when she heard it singing while traveling along the Root. It undulated on the wind, growing stronger in one direction; Rhapsody turned toward it and opened her eyes.

The air before her and all around her was shrouded in mist, thick with silver vapor. The droplets sparkled in the air, reflecting the light of the rising sun. It was like standing within a cloud, with the sky and forest no longer visible. She put out a hand to brush the mist away; it did not move, but rather hung heavy in the air, like rain that had frozen in time.

Rhapsody wandered for a while, trying to find the other side of the misty Veil, but the fog was ever-present, inviolable. She called out every few minutes, but heard nothing; no voice or birdcall answered her. Directions became difficult, then impossible, to discern. She began to fear losing her way. Finally she sighed, the sound swallowed by the thick layers of vapor, and turned back to Oelendra and the children again.

She could see them at the very edge of her vision after a few minutes, clustered around and on the horses in the distant part of the fog. Rhapsody quickened her step, trotting through the snow, until she came within clear sight of them. She stopped in her tracks.

The children of the demon were as they had been when she had left them. The person holding the reins of the roan was not Oelendra, however, but rather a slim, pale woman with hair as white and silver as the mist, dressed in a plain white robe. She smiled and held out the reins of the mare to Rhapsody, who took them as if entranced, then turned and walked off into the thickening fog. A moment later Rhapsody shook her head as if shaking off sleep, and followed the woman, leading the horse and the children into the mist.

After a long time the fog began to dissipate. At first Rhapsody didn't notice it, she was too focused on following the woman in white and the children, but eventually she became aware of a few trees here and there, then some denser patches of woods, until at last the mist evaporated like smoke in the heat of the sun rising in the sky above them. Rhapsody found herself in a forest not unlike Tyrian, except that it was spring or early summer. The ground was green, as were the leaves and new shoots of the trees, many of which were white birches, ashes, silver maples, and pale beech trees, their ivory bark giving the woods an otherworldly appearance.

The children, who until then had been solemnly silent, began to talk softly to each other, then laugh, and finally to run about, enjoying the sun. It was as if an enormous weight had been lifted from them; now they felt as if they could fly, and so they tried, extending their arms wide and dashing in between the trees and up small rises, leaping and giggling.

Rhapsody smiled as she turned to survey them all and caught the eye of the Lady, who had been watching her intently. She colored under the stare, and the woman smiled. Then she turned toward the deeper part of the wood and two young men appeared, dressed as the woman was, in white robes. They took the semiconscious gladiator down from the roan and led him and the horse away toward a settlement of small huts, visible to Rhapsody for the first time only in that moment.

Rhapsody turned back to the children and her heart leapt to her throat; they were gone. Only the woman in white remained, and she approached the Singer slowly, her hands extended. Rhapsody took them in her own; they were warm, as her mother's had been as she brushed Rhapsody's hair before the fire in childhood. Aches and pains she did not even know she had been carrying vanished, along with the raw, black patches of frostbite, leaving her feeling whole and rested, though not entirely awake. The pale woman spoke. Her voice was like the soft sigh of the warm wind.

'You need not fear, they are well attended. Come; I will show you your place here.' She led Rhapsody by the hand over the rise of a hill to a small thatched hut, the same as she had seen in the settlement. She nodded to it. Rhapsody blinked in her inner fog.

'But what if they wake in the night, crying?' she asked. She had not even thought of the question; it was as if it had been placed directly into her mouth, bypassing her mind.

'They never will,' a voice answered behind her. Rhapsody turned to see a pale man, attired in the same type of robe, but the color of night. His eyes were black as pitch, and deep; Rhapsody felt she easily could fall into those eyes. They were crowned with black thundercloud brows that gave way to snowy white hair. Suddenly she realized that the question had been put into her mouth so that she would hear the answer. She felt the heavy sleep fall off her shoulders like a woolen cloak, clearing her mind at last.

'Thank you for taking them in, m'lady, m'lord,' she said. 'I will do whatever I can to help in any way.'

'Good,' said the man. His face was solemn. 'They will need your help more than you can imagine.'

'Come, child,' said the woman, smiling. She held out her hand again. Rhapsody took it once more, and followed the Lady Rowan deeper into the peaceful forest.

The realm of the Rowans was a serene one by all appearances. The children ran about, playing in the sunshine, their joyful voices shrieking and laughing through the forest, breaking the stillness. Rhapsody did not see the gladiator, but all the other children were there, frolicking in between the trees, even Quan Li, the oldest girl, who up until that point had been serious and reserved. The sight gladdened her heart. She felt a hand touch her elbow, and she turned. The Lady was beckoning to her.

They walked over the rise of a hill and came to a stop under a stand of white birch trees. In the valley at the foot of the hill was a large wood building without ornament except for a thin wooden steeple crowned with a silver star. She followed the Lady down the hill and into the building.

Inside it was dark and cool, with a rotunda off which were a number of doors. The Lady opened one across the rotunda from the door they had entered by and stepped back, allowing Rhapsody to go in.

The room was dark as well, with a wealth of beeswax candles in boxes and the minty smell of pipsissewa, a herb used for easing the pain of the dying. Open bags of other medicinal herbs, juniper puffballs and shepherd's purse, lay on the table, their contents scattered across its top. In the center of the room was a plain cot with short legs, close to the floor, and several tables with strange-looking implements and containers. The Lady offered her a candle, and she took it. The beeswax was soft and fragrant; there was something hypnotic about holding it. She extended a finger to light it, but the Lady shook her head.

'Not yet.' Rhapsody curled her finger back into her fist quickly. The Lady smiled reassuringly. 'Before you light the candle, you must understand that it is a promise.'

'A promise?'

'Yes, and one you may not be willing to make.'

Rhapsody blinked. 'What is the promise?'

'Come, and I will show you.' The Lady walked through the door of the room and went to the next door, which she opened as before. Rhapsody looked in to see an identical room, except that on the cot was the gladiator, asleep. She turned and looked questioningly at the Lady, who nodded at the demon's oldest child. Rhapsody looked back at him again.

'Stay here.' The Lady Rowan entered the room and bent next to the cot, touching the gladiator's forehead gently. Behind her Rhapsody could hear the door of the building open. The two young men entered and joined the Lady by Constantin's bedside. They were carrying a crystal beaker and several sharp metal implements and glass tubes that Rhapsody did not like the look of. She opened her mouth to speak but her question was choked off before she could utter it by a sharp look from the Lady Rowan.

A moment later, the Lady took the instruments from the men and arranged them on the table next to the cot. The men took hold of the gladiator's feet and wrists. The Lady Rowan nodded to her assistants and turned back to him, a long awl-like needle in her hand. As Rhapsody watched in horror she plunged the needle into Constantin's chest. He awoke in agony, screaming.

Rhapsody tried to run into the room but found her way barred by an unseen force. She struggled against it futilely and banged on the doorframe, producing no sound; she cried out, but her voice was silent as well. She could only stare in dismay as Constantin writhed in pain, pleading with his tormentors to stop. The tears that ran down his face were mirrored on Rhapsody's own.

The procedure seemed to last forever. Finally the Lady held up a thin glass tube filled with red liquid, a slash of black in the middle. She nodded to the assistants and removed the implement from the gladiator's chest, causing him to shudder in anguish once more. Then she handed the tube to one of the men and carefully bandaged the chest wound, speaking softly to Constantin as he lay on the cot, weeping. Rhapsody's heart wrung in sorrow. Pain great enough to reduce the gladiator to sobbing must truly be unbearable, given what she knew about Constantin's life and profession. The Lady Rowan bent to kiss his forehead; his shuddering stopped and he fell back asleep immediately. The Lady came out of the room and took Rhapsody's elbow, leading her back to the empty room. The Singer was shaking.

'This is the procedure that we will have to perform every day, on each child, to separate them from their father's blood,' the Lady Rowan said simply, ignoring the Singer's tears. 'It must be removed directly from the heart. As you can see, it's extremely painful.'

Rhapsody choked. 'Even the baby?'

'Yes.'

'No,' Rhapsody stammered, fighting nausea. 'Please.'

'The alternative is far worse, isn't it?'

Rhapsody stared at the Lady in silence, then bowed her head. 'Yes.' The Lady Rowan watched her intently; Rhapsody could feel the woman's eyes on her. 'For how long?'

'Years. At least five; probably seven. To do it faster would mean to take more heart's blood, and that might prove fatal. If they die before the separation procedure is complete, they will join their father in the Vault of the Underworld, for eternity.'

'Gods,' Rhapsody whispered. She looked over at the table, at the instruments identical to those that had been used on Constantin. 'Please, tell me there is another way.'

'There is no other way to separate out the blood,' said the Lady Rowan directly. 'There is, however, something you can do, if you choose to.'

'Whatever it is, I will do it,' said Rhapsody quickly. 'Please tell me how I can help.'

The Lady Rowan's eyes narrowed. 'You are rash, child; that is not good. The children will need you to tend to their daily needs for love and comfort; you should not be agreeing to something you have not heard yet.'

'I'm sorry,' said Rhapsody humbly. 'Please tell me what I can do.'

The Lady looked at her evenly. 'You can take the pain for one or two of them, if you should so choose.'

'Take the pain?'

'Yes. You are a Singer, a Namer; you can make their namesong your own, and keep the pain for yourself. It is much to ask, and much more to give. If you should choose not to do so, no one would blame you. I know you seek to be a healer; it will teach you much. It will make you empathetic, make you able to heal others by taking their injuries yourself. But you will feel the pain in its fullness, sparing one or two of the children the daily suffering you have just witnessed. It will be agony for you.'

Rhapsody stared at the floor. 'One or two? How on earth could I ever choose?'

A sympathetic smile crossed the Lady's face. 'That will not be easy, either. It may seem to make sense to choose the smallest ones, but suffering is suffering, no matter who experiences it, as you have just seen.'

Rhapsody considered her words. 'And will it do me damage physically?'

'No. It is only the pain you may take, not the procedure; you will not have a wound or a scar.'

Rhapsody's eyes cleared. 'I'm not concerned about any scarring except that which the pain will inflict on those children's souls,' she said. 'And if I light the candle, is that the promise to sit vigil for a child, to take his or her pain?'

'Yes.' The Lady smiled at her. 'Are you going to do so?'

'Yes.'

'I thought so. Shall I set aside one candle, or two?'

Rhapsody smiled back at her, and took two candles out of the nearest box. She set them on the table. 'Here?'

'Yes. You are very brave.'

'Do I light them now?'

'Yes, but then you must name the children for whom you are going to sit.'

Rhapsody extended her finger and touched the first candle. 'Aria,' she said softly. The flame sparked to life between her thumb and forefinger, snapping for a moment, then glowed on the wick. She moved to the next candle. 'Mikita,' she said, lighting the second taper. She turned back around to face the Lady, who nodded approvingly.

'You should lie down here now, child. I will give you such herbs as I can to ease your pain, but I should warn you: I gave them to the gladiator before the procedure as well. I must tell my assistants to retrieve those two children.'

Rhapsody reached into the box and pulled two more tapers forth, setting next to the lighted ones. She touched the first one. 'Jecen,' she said as the candle began to glow. 'Aric.'

The Lady Rowan reached out and seized her wrist. 'What are you doing, child?'

'You said it would not harm me physically, that I am just agreeing to take their pain.'

'Yes, but—'

Rhapsody pulled her hand away and lit two more tapers. 'Ellis. Anya.' She looked back at the Lady. 'How can I possibly choose? Having to let even one of them go through agony like that would be the same as experiencing it myself anyway.'

'Don't underestimate the combined effects, child. Your heart may be willing, but your body will be racked. You are still healing from the effects of the exposure on your journey here; I don't think you understand what you're doing.'

Two more flames appeared. 'Marl. Vincane.' She smiled at the Lady Rowan. 'No doubt, but I have nothing better to do while I'm here. Besides, which of their mothers wouldn't have agreed to do so? They aren't here, so someone has to.'

'But you are not any of these children's mother.'

Rhapsody's eyes glowed in the light of the brightening room. 'Quan Li.' She looked up. 'No,' she said, smiling. 'I'm their grandmother. I have much to atone for in my life. Perhaps this will serve as a beginning.' The last candle sparked to life.

'Constantin,' she said.

39

The sound of merry shrieking filled the sleepy glen. Rhapsody smiled as the children charged her, swarming like excited bees, clamoring for her attention and talking excitedly all at once. She put her hands over her ears.

'Goodness, calm yourselves,' she said, laughing. 'I'll go deaf.' She closed the door of her hut behind her and walked out into the light of late morning, dressed in her clothes for playing with them and carrying a burlap sack. Eight of the children were there, with the eldest and youngest absent. Her goal today was to learn more about their individual needs for education, both physical and intellectual. To that end she had been up most of the night making toys to test their agility. They were playthings of Lirin design, known to the Liringlas as anklesingers. She took one out of the pack now.

'Here, I have something for you.' Rhapsody held out the anklesinger and the children crowded around, eager to examine it. It was crudely made, but smooth, and delighted voices rang through the forest as it was passed from child to child.

'How does it work, Rhapsody?'

'Give it to me and I'll show you.' She took it back and held it up for them to see. It consisted of two wooden rings joined by a length of twine, one of which was hollow and pierced by small holes. Rhapsody sat on the grass and extended a leg, slipping her ankle through the solid ring. Then she stood.

'All right, move back, lads and lasses, and I'll give it a try. I haven't done this since I was little.'

'You still are little,' said Vincane. Now that he was within the realm of the Rowans he had lost much of the sharp look and streetwise nature that had made him such an adversary in the world beyond the Veil of Hoen. Now he just appeared to be a boy on the threshold of adolescence, taller than she and full-bodied; Rhapsody laughed at the look of insolent mischief on his face.

'Very well, I haven't done this since I was *young*. And Vincane, don't confuse "big" with "tough." If you want, I'll show you what I mean later. We can go another round as we did in the tile foundry, if you'd like.'

'No, thank you,' said the boy hastily. Rhapsody smiled; she knew he had hidden and watched her training that morning.

'This is how it works,' she said. She hopped over the string and swung the ring around her ankle in a circular motion, jumping over the twine each time it came around. After a few rotations it was humming smoothly around her foot, and she was leaping over the cord with each pass. The second ring began to vibrate, then whistle, finally producing a clear, sweet tone. The children laughed and clapped, clamoring for a turn.

'Here, don't grab, I have one for each of you.' Rhapsody let the anklesinger come to a halt. She pulled it from her foot and handed it to Jecen, who squealed in glee. Rhapsody turned and went back to the burlap sack, bringing out a handful of the toys. She dispensed them to the clutching hands and stepped back, watching in interest as the children put them on and tried to make them work. Some were more nimble than others, and it was a good measure of their agility; Rhapsody made note of each child's ability, devising a mental plan to train the competent children and work with the more clumsy ones specially.

'You'll find your names carved on them,' she told them when they grew tired and came to a stop. 'Each one makes a different musical note, and once you get used to them you can play songs if you work together. Now, I can hear Cyndra calling you; it must be time for noonmeal.' Happy shrieking echoed through the drowsy glade again, and in a flurry of kisses and hugs the children were off, leaving Rhapsody alone, smiling and breathless.

She rose and, brushing the leaves and dirt from her trousers, walked back toward the white buildings where the children were cared for, listening for birdsong as she went. Behind some trees not far away she felt an alien vibration and concentrated on it; she recognized the signature – it was Constantin. He had been watching her with the children, and now was following close behind her.

Rhapsody did not change her pace, but continued toward the compound. She felt him adjust his path to intersect with hers, and kept walking, a strange sense of security washing over her. As she reached the edge of the woods he stepped in front of her, cutting her off from her destination.

He had recovered from the ordeal, and appeared in fit condition and good health, though somewhat thinner. The gladiator was clothed in a white cambric shirt and pants, and as he interposed his body into her path, Rhapsody stopped reluctantly.

Constantin's arm came to rest pointedly on the tree before her, blocking her egress, and he stared down at her with a piercing look that made the small hairs on the back of her neck tingle. She returned his stare placidly, without any aggression or fear, and waited to hear what he had to say.

Moments passed, and still he did not speak, but watched her with an intense stare. At the edge of her vision Rhapsody saw a slight movement, and, turning her head, she noticed the Lord Rowan leaning against a tree, observing their interaction. She exhaled, relief filling her lungs. Unlike the night before, the robes he wore seemed to be of forest green, as if he had more substance than when she had first seen him. Finally she spoke.

'What is it, Constantin? What do you want?'

He glared at her a moment more, then finally spoke. 'You.'

'Excuse me?'

'I should have you,' he said, his voice low but unpleasant. 'You tricked me; and you owe me. I should have you.'

Rhapsody felt color rising from her neck to her face. 'I'm sorry about tricking you,' she said, checking to make sure the Lord was still there. 'There really was no other way; it was not my intention to lead you on.' He laughed, a sharp, ugly sound. 'I needed to bring you to this place, and I'm sorry if I've hurt your feelings.'

His head moved closer to hers, and she could feel his breath on her neck. 'Oh, you have. I am very hurt. But you can fix that, you know. You have just the right medicine for me, Rhapsody – that's your name, isn't it? Pretty; it suits you. You really are amazing, you know. I'm glad I never had to fight you in the arena. You come off as fragile, helpless, but you're not, are you? You play on a man's sympathy, but you are stronger than most, and that's when you take advantage.'

'Stop it,' Rhapsody said, becoming annoyed.

'What's the matter – you can swear to speak the truth but are unwilling to hear it? You lied to me, in a way. You came to my bed and made yourself available to me, dressed for seduction. You said you had been sent by Treilus, the whoremaster. What was I supposed to think?'

She looked away. 'Probably just what you did.'

Even without looking at him she could feel him smile. 'Good; then you agree that I came to the right conclusion.'

Rhapsody's gaze returned to him. She thought about arguing the facts, reminding him what she had actually said, how she had only indicated she was there to massage him, but the words were too heavy to utter. Llauron had known all along what Constantin would think she was there for, and she had been foolish beyond measure to believe otherwise. She hung her head.

The gladiator bent forward until his lips were just outside her ear. 'You owe me,' he said quietly. 'Perhaps just once, but you owe me, and you know it. Without speaking, you promised me a night with you in my bed. Surely you will not go back on your word – a Namer? I know you are one, by the way; last night I heard you whisper my name deep in my soul, and the most wonderful feeling came over me. Would you like to guess where it was most outwardly obvious?'

She blinked but said nothing. He had undoubtedly felt her light the candle and pledge to sit vigil for him, to guard him from pain at her own expense.

The gladiator's smile grew more confident. He reached out an enormous hand and carefully slid his index finger into her hair, drawing it down along the lock nearest her face. When he reached her cheek he caressed it with his rough fingertip.

'Come with me,' he said soothingly. 'I am no longer angry; I will be gentle with you. You have nothing to fear; I won't put it in all the way. Pay your debt, Rhapsody.' He leaned forward on the tree, his breath warming the side of her neck. 'I must have you,' he said.

The Lord Rowan appeared, to her left and nearby. Both Rhapsody and Constantin looked and noted his presence, then Constantin dropped his arm and turned to leave. As he did, his lips brushed the top of her hair.

'I will have you,' he whispered. 'I promise.'

As he walked away, Rhapsody felt her voice return. 'Constantin?'

He looked back at her; there was no fear in her eyes, and her face was placid again.

'You may be right,' she said directly. 'But if you do, it will be only because we both want it to happen. Do you understand?'

He stared at her for a moment, then he was gone.

Rhapsody felt a warm hand touch her shoulder, and in that moment, peace such as she had never felt coursed through her, filling her with a longing to sleep.

'Are you all right, child?' the Lord Rowan asked, his voice silky as warm wine.

'Yes, m'lord,' she replied, turning to face him.

'I will speak to him.'

Rhapsody opened her mouth to explain. As she did, she felt the despair of the Future return, the hideous knowledge that she might be doomed to repeat her same mistakes eternally, watching the consequences of her actions for all Time. Exhaustion flooded her as Ashe's words of long ago came back to her: *You will never die. Imagine losing people over and over, your lovers, your spouse, your children.* Rhapsody felt more tired than she ever remembered being. She looked into the stern face of the Lord Rowan, and from deep within her tears came, unbidden.

'Why do you weep?'

'It's not important,' Rhapsody answered, looking into the black eyes. 'M'lord Rowan, will you grant me a favor? Please?'

'What is it you wish?'

'Will you come for me one day? Please?'

The solemn face flickered with the hint of a smile. 'Fascinating,' he murmured. 'Usually I only hear prayers asking me to stay away, though you are not the first Cymrian by any means who has prayed for my assistance. You are the first one in the bloom of youth, however.'

'Please, m'lord,' Rhapsody implored. 'Please say you will come for me one day.'

The Lord Rowan watched her for a moment. 'I will if I can, my child. That is the only promise I can make you.'

Rhapsody smiled through her tears. 'It's enough,' she said simply. 'Thank you.'

40

Evening shadows were starting to lengthen in the peaceful forest. Rhapsody stopped before the door of the small hut and breathed deeply for a moment, trying to remain calm. Then she knocked.

'Come.'

She shuddered at the memory the word and the deep timbre of Constantin's voice evoked. Slowly she opened the door of his chambers.

The former gladiator was sitting on the bed. When he saw her he rose immediately and crossed the room to the doorway. Rhapsody swallowed nervously, observing the speed with which he moved; it was small wonder he had been lethal in the arena. He interposed himself between her and the rest of the room, filling the doorway and staring piercingly at her.

'What do you want?' he asked harshly.

Rhapsody smiled, hoping to defuse the suspicious, hostile tone. 'I have something that I believe is yours.'

His eyes narrowed. 'I don't think so.' Rhapsody could tell by the look on his face that he had had his conversation with the Lord Rowan.

'Well, I won't bother you for long, then,' she said breezily. 'May I come in?'

Constantin stared down at her for a moment, then held the door open, standing out of the way. Rhapsody walked under his arm and came into the room. It was similar to the rooms of the other children, but without any decoration or colorful appointments; in fact, it looked much like her own, only the bed and furniture were much bigger.

She sat down on the room's only chair. Constantin looked hard at her, and then dropped his eyes, smiling to himself. He watched under his eyelids as she reached into the small bag she was holding. Rhapsody pulled out the silver chain she had found in his chambers, and held it out to him.

'Does this belong to you?'

Constantin's eyes widened in shock, and a look of panic crossed his face. Then, as quickly as it had come, the look was gone, replaced by the familiar stare.

'Where did you get it?'

'I found it in your room that night.'

His face began to blacken with anger. 'And now you have come to ransom it back.'

Rhapsody's mouth opened in surprise. 'No, I thought—'

'Of course, I am without anything of value to pay for it here,' he said, his muscles coiling under the tension of self-control. He backed away from her. Rhapsody regarded him with sympathy. She knew what he felt was violent, and she could see him struggling to keep it in check.

'You don't understand,' she said quickly. 'I brought this to give it back to you.'

Constantin regarded her suspiciously. 'What is the value in that to you?'

Rhapsody's brow furrowed. 'None; why should there be any? If this belongs to you, Constantin, you're entitled to it. You don't have to fight for what is yours here, this is not Sorbold.'

'Then why did you steal it in the first place?'

Rhapsody swallowed the insult. 'I didn't steal it,' she said as gently as she could. 'I brought it because I thought it might be special to you. I had no intention of ever returning you to that gladiatorial complex, so I thought it best to get what you might need or want to have while I could.' She rose and crossed to where he stood, took his hand and placed the chain in it, then closed his fingers around it.

Constantin looked down at the trinket in his hand. His eyes lost some of the intensity of the moment before, which was replaced by a deeper, more complex expression. He stared at the necklace for several moments, then looked back up at Rhapsody.

'Thank you,' he said. His voice was uncharacteristically quiet.

She nodded. 'You're welcome. I'll get out of your way now.' She turned and opened the door.

'You're right,' he said quickly; she turned to face him in surprise, having thought the conversation finished.

'About what?'

He looked down for a moment. 'This is something I need and want to have.' It was the closest he had ever come to initiating a conversation; Rhapsody could tell instinctively that he wanted it to continue. She closed the door, folded her arms and leaned back against it.

'Was it a gift from someone special?'

Constantin stared at her; she was becoming more used to the unsettling look. Then he went to the bed and sat down.

'Yes,' he said. 'My mother.'

It took a moment before Rhapsody realized her mouth was open; she closed it abruptly. 'You knew your mother?'

The gladiator shook his head; the sunlight that filtered through the window caught his white-blond hair and made it burn golden for an instant. 'No. All I have is a fragment of a memory, one that I'm not even certain is real.'

She came to the bed and sat down beside him; he did not move or tense as she thought he might if her closeness was unwelcome. 'What is it, if you don't mind my asking?'

Constantin ran the necklace through his fingers; it gleamed in the sunlight as well. 'Just the image of a woman with love in her eyes and a gift.'

Rhapsody own eyes stung at his words. She patted his shoulder. It was meant to be a gesture of sympathy, but it made the gladiator jump away, cringing. Rhapsody's face froze in alarm.

'I'm very sorry,' she stammered. 'I didn't mean to upset you.' She rose hastily and hurried to the door again.

'Rhapsody, wait.' Constantin stood and came to her, stopping a few feet away. She looked down at the floor; the last thing she wanted was to agitate him further. 'You didn't upset me. I'm trying not to hurt or frighten you again.'

Rhapsody met his glance; his eyes were gleaming with blue intensity, but with none of the ferocity they had held the night she had stolen him from Sorbold. Perhaps even just the slight amount of demonic blood that had been removed from him had made him more human.

'Constantin, whatever happened in Sorbold was my fault alone. The plan was stupid and ill considered, and any reaction you had was due to my miscalculation. I ask your forgiveness, and I hope you understand that no matter how callous or manipulative it seemed, I really was trying to help you.'

Constantin nodded. 'I've noticed that you often seem to feel compelled to do that.' The depth of his voice made him seem much older than his years. 'I think that's why it's so hard for me to be in the same room with you.'

'If my presence is disturbing, I'll try to avoid—'

'It's not,' he interrupted. 'It's more, well, distracting.' He looked out the window; as the sunset grew rosier, his voice became softer. 'I guess I have just never known a truly gentle person before. I don't know how to behave around you.'

Rhapsody laughed. 'There are quite a few people in this world who would find your description of me amusing. And you're doing fine, really.'

'It's a struggle,' he said. The words seemed to surprise him a moment later, having slipped out easily. 'The necklace is not the only thing I need and want to have.' He averted his eyes as the color of the sunset came over his face.

Rhapsody's throat tightened, and heat coursed through her. Unconsciously her hand went to her throat. It came to rest on the locket she always wore. A thought came to her, and she carefully opened the clasp and removed the necklace. When Constantin worked up the courage to look back at her she held it up for him to see.

'I guess we have something in common,' she said. 'This is all I have left of my mother, too.' The tears that had crept into her eyes welled again.

'Do you dream of her?'

Rhapsody turned away. 'Not anymore,' she said sadly. 'I used to, but now she never comes to me in my dreams. I cannot see her face.'

'I dream of my mother every night,' said Constantin. 'I have no idea if she was anything like what she seems in my dreams.'

'How does she seem?'

'Kind. I suppose that proves it's just a dream and not a memory.' He sat back down on the bed.

'Why?'

The gladiator looked up at her and smiled ironically. 'Obviously you don't believe in family traits.'

Rhapsody moved back a little to get a better look at him. 'Are you saying you are unkind?' The gladiator's laughter caught her off-guard and she jumped. She waited until he stopped, then looked at him seriously. 'I wasn't joking.'

Constantin's face lost its smile. 'Yes; it should be obvious even to you that kindness and I haven't been formally introduced.' He looked away. 'I have seen it from afar, however, though perhaps only once.'

Rhapsody looked down at her hands. 'Perhaps you and kindness are better friends than you think.' She could feel his eyes stare at her questioningly, and she struggled to keep from turning warm under his gaze, but she was unsuccessful; the blood rushed to her face, stinging her cheeks as they reddened. Awkwardly she sat down in the chair again.

'Would you care to explain what you are talking about?'

'You could have hurt me that night if you had wanted to,' she said, staring at the calluses on her fingers. 'I know you were moved by my fear; I saw the cruelty dim in your eyes. Despite what your world has been, you have maintained some compassion, even if it is just a seed.' Her words sounded vaguely familiar to her; she thought back to the night Ashe had first come to her in Elysian.

I love that you have survived the cataclysm of your whole world, and have lived among monsters, and still always attribute honorable intentions to people.

Constantin smiled ruefully. 'You're wrong, Rhapsody. I had no intention of letting you go that night. I would have hurt you, and enjoyed doing so. You don't know me very well.'

Rhapsody finally found the courage to look into his eyes. 'Perhaps. And perhaps I know you better than you think. Do you still want to hurt me?'

The gladiator stood suddenly and crossed to the farthest corner of the room. 'Perhaps it is best if you go now.'

'As you wish.' Rhapsody rose as well, and went to the door. She turned and looked at his back, the muscles coiled like a spring. 'I'm not afraid of you, Constantin.'

'You're also not very bright, I'm sorry to say.'

She laughed. 'Well, there's no denying the truth in that, but in fact I have seen far crueler men than you; I've suffered much worse atrocities at their hands than anything you could ever have inflicted on me. I can tell the difference between a warped spirit and an evil one. Your soul is twisted, Constantin, not rotten. It just needs some time to stretch and some sunlight to purify it again. You'll be good as new in no time.'

Constantin stared out the window. 'If I live through the torture.'

Rhapsody let go of the door handle. 'Torture?'

He looked at her again with the same intense stare. 'Don't play the fool. You brought me here; you must know what they do.'

She came to him then, and turned him to face her, leaving her hands resting on his arms. 'Do you mean what happened last night?'

He tried to pull away. 'Of course.'

Rhapsody sighed. 'I'm very sorry about that. And though I wish you never had to endure the procedure again, I can promise you that you will never again feel the pain. From now on it will be painless.'

'Why are they doing this? I have been bled before, but never from the heart.'

She took his hand and led him back to the bed, then sat in the chair facing him. Slowly and meticulously she explained about his origins, about the F'dor and the Rakshas, and the program of systematic rape they had undertaken. Constantin's stoic face turned stony as she spoke, but his eyes began to gleam in a way that made Rhapsody wish she had left the tale to the Lord Rowan.

Finally she told him of the rescue of the children of the demon, and the plan to spare them damnation by separating out the blood of their father and using it to find the F'dor. When she was finished he regarded her seriously again.

'And you have no idea who my mother was?'

'No.' She detected a slight falling of his face. 'I wish I did, Constantin; but you see, she was an innocent victim. It's entirely possible that she was the woman you dream of, someone who loved you very much, despite everything she – everything she endured in having you.'

Constantin looked back out the window into the darkness; night had come into its fullness while they had talked, and now the quiet glen was blanketed in darkness. 'Somehow, as unlikely as all that seems, I believe you.'

She patted his hand. 'I wish I could make it better for you. I once believed I had the power to do that.'

'And what made you decide that you didn't?'

Rhapsody let her breath out slowly. 'The death of my sister. She was a friend, actually. She was the first person in this land I tried to help, and it killed her. If I had left her on her own, in her life as it was, on the street, she'd be alive now.'

The gladiator turned to look at her. 'How do you know that?' Rhapsody blinked. 'Street rats die every day; in Sorbold I put a number of them to the sword myself, just for getting in my way. Stop punishing yourself for trying,

243

Rhapsody; at least you made the effort. In the end, that's more than most people bother to do.'

'What about you? Do you forgive me for the pain I've caused you by trying to save you? Are you willing to clean up the mess my good intentions have made?'

Constantin sighed. 'Rhapsody, no one has ever tried to help me in my entire life. I don't have the ability to comprehend why you did, let alone express how I feel about it. If you're referring to the fact that my hands can't stop trembling around you, that you are growing less safe each second you remain here, that's my problem to solve.

'It's far more important to me, now that the Lord Rowan and I have discussed my future, that I keep from causing *you* any pain. It's a terrible dilemma; I feel as if I would be better off to never see you again, because that is the only way I can keep from wanting you. But at the same time I need you, if only just to talk to; there really is no one else here. Perhaps you had best forget me and let me sort it out alone. But one thing I can assure you of: I am far better off than I would have been if you had not tried to help. Eternal damnation may be a fate I deserve, but I'd like to avoid it just the same.'

'Whatever else should happen, I can promise you that I will never forget you, Constantin.' Rhapsody wished she could embrace him; it was what she felt moved to do, but she couldn't allow herself to frustrate him any further. The genesis of their relationship had been sex; despite her better judgment she had incited him into wanting her, and the impulse had not faded. It stood between them like a locked door, and would until it was resolved.

She thought about giving in to it. She had done it before, had slept with men she didn't know or even hated, with far less reason to. She could give herself to Constantin; it would facilitate the healing that was needed to right things between them.

The thought squeezed her heart like a vise, making her choke up. Ashe's face appeared before her in her memory, smiling at her in a way she did not remember ever seeing. But Ashe was no longer her lover; he would belong to another soon. It was time to drive him out of her heart forever.

A sudden thought occurred to her. 'Constantin, I have to go get something. I'll be right back.' He watched in surprise as she leapt from the chair and ran to the door, disappearing into the moonlit shadows of the forest.

41

She returned a short while later, her arms filled with scented candles, her lute slung across her back. Constantin opened the door and caught some of the tapers as they fell from her overfull grasp. They had been a gift from the Lady Rowan the night before. *Something to improve your dreams*, she had said. Rhapsody had lit a few of the pastel-hued candles before falling asleep, and found that her dreams were sweet and free of nightmares, much as they had been when she slept in Ashe's arms, or with Elynsynos in her cave. In addition, the dreams she had of home were intense in their clarity, and left her, upon waking, with the sensation of having actually visited with the family members of whom she had been dreaming. She had seen and embraced her father, all of her brothers, and many of her friends, but her mother had eluded her; she had wandered the fields of her homeland, searching for her in vain.

'There is already sufficient light in here from the moon,' Constantin said as she began setting the candles on the nightstand.

'These are not for light; they're for your dreams,' Rhapsody said. She touched the tallest of the tapers and watched as it sparked to life. When she had lit them all she turned to see the gladiator staring at her in the soft glow of the candlelight. 'The Lady Rowan is called Yl Breudiwyr, the Keeper of Dreams, the Guardian of Sleep. Under her eye, the dreams you have in this realm can seem more real than they normally do. Back in the other world, they are only fragmented visions of what happens in this realm. Here it's as if you are actually experiencing what you're dreaming about.'

'So what are the candles for?'

Rhapsody smiled. 'I don't know what she makes them of, but they should help make the reunion an almost-tangible one.'

'Reunion?'

'Yes, didn't you say you dream every night of your mother?'

Concern, and deeper emotions, filled Constantin's face. 'Among other things.'

'Well, these candles seem to hold the unpleasant dreams at bay, while bringing out the ones in which your heart speaks. If you will allow me, I'll play my lute to lull you to sleep, and keep playing to help encourage the dream to stay for a while. I can make the candles burn longer than they normally would, and that would give you more time with her.

'My mentor used to say that memories were your first lore, the strongest you would ever know, because you wrote them yourself. Only you have this memory, the memory of your mother. Working together, we may be able to bring her here, if only for a few moments.'

The piercing glance was back. 'You would do that for me?'

'Only if you want me to. I don't want to make you uncomfortable in any way.'

Constantin smiled. 'I'm honored,' he said in his deep voice. 'And it isn't me that is likely to be uncomfortable.'

The gladiator had been asleep for more than an hour; the candles were burning brightly, but still Rhapsody saw no sign that he was dreaming. He lay in the massive bed curled on his side, snoring intermittently.

Rhapsody's fingers were beginning to cramp slightly; it had taken him a while to fall asleep. The smell of the dream-inducing herbs she had brought in, cinquefoil, agrimony, angelica, and star anise, was beginning to make her head swim. All in all she had been playing for more than two hours, and was beginning to wonder if this was a good time to stop.

She had her answer within a moment. Through the haze of the candle-light and the soft smoke in the room she thought she saw the door open. Standing in the doorway was a tall, broad-shouldered woman with gray-blond hair touched with white. Her face was handsome, and she had the same intense blue eyes as her son, who sat up in his sleep as she entered.

Rhapsody watched, entranced, as the dream-woman embraced Con-stantin, sitting beside him on the bed, and cradling him in her arms like a lost treasure. The gladiator wept in his sleep. Rhapsody continued the lutesong, playing softly. As the aroma from the candles reached her she struggled to keep from falling under its spell herself.

For a long time the two sat, speaking in a language she recognized as the tongue of Sorbold, though she could not make out what they said over the sound of the lute. She didn't want to intrude in any way on their conversation, but was having trouble keeping her eyes open and her hands moving over the strings.

Finally the woman rose, kissed her smiling son on the cheek, and whispered final words in his ear. Then she left the room and Constantin lay down, falling back into his sleep, still smiling.

Rhapsody was bringing the song to an end when Constantin turned over, still in the throes of slumber. The door opened again; this time she saw a dream image of herself enter the room, closing it softly behind it. Rhapsody's heart skipped a beat; it was all she could do to keep the song going.

In the darkness of his dream she was dressed in the same white robe they all wore in the realm of the Rowans, which the dream-image dropped to the floor as she stood beside his bed. Rhapsody saw the look in his eyes as he stared at the image, more real than it must usually have appeared to him owing to the candles, now short in their remaining life, and the song she had played to extend them.

Her stomach twisted as he drew the image of herself closer, resting his hands on her waist. She knew what was about to happen, and did not want to watch it; her skin burned as Constantin set about enacting his fantasy. Rhapsody would have closed her eyes, but felt compelled to observe one interesting thing about his actions: they were tender, gentle, without the brutal fervor she remembered from Sorbold. He was making love to what he thought was her, not ravaging her as he said he would have in the bedchamber of the gladiatorial arena. The knowledge that what she had viewed as a dangerous predator was capable of such mild and affectionate actions brought a lump to her throat; she had been right about his familiarity with kindness. She closed her eyes, leaving him to his privacy, and plucked the strings of her lute a little more firmly to cover any sounds that might issue forth.

When she was sure the dream was truly over, she went to the bed and stood over him, looking down at him tenderly in the shadowlight of the two remaining candles that burned low in their stands now. His immense size and the scars he bore belied his age; he was like her, seemingly young, but bent under the weight of the experience he carried. With his eyes closed and a content look on his face he seemed vulnerable.

You promised me a night with you in my bed. Surely you will not go back on your word.

Rhapsody extinguished the candles and pulled back the covers slowly, as if in a trance. She crept into the bed and between the sheets, careful not to waken him, then slid through the rough fabric until she felt him beside her. She lowered her head gently onto his shoulder, and wrapped her arm around his waist, settling in next to him as she had with Grunthor when they traveled along the Root.

In his sleep Constantin pulled her closer and sighed; the sound went to Rhapsody's heart. *Ryle hira,* she thought. Life is what it is. She just wished it weren't so damned sad sometimes.

She rose just before the sun did, timing her exit to coincide with its first rays touching the floor of his room. As the first shaft of light fell across the blankets on the bed, she rested her hands on his shoulders and leaned over him, as she had seen the image of herself do in his dream. She gave him a long, warm kiss on the forehead, allowing her hair to brush against his chest, as he inhaled the scent of her skin with his first waking breath.

His eyes were just beginning to open when she took both his hands in hers and kissed them, too.

'Now the scales are balanced between us,' she said softly.

She walked to the chair where her white robe lay. She slipped it on, smiling at him as he watched in amazement; then she opened the door and left, closing it behind her softly.

Rhapsody slept beneath the warm glow of one of the Lady's candles herself that night, a sweet pillar of rose-colored beeswax perfumed with lilabelle, a flower known for its calmative properties and ability to promote clarity. The spicy smoke seeped into her mind, clearing away much of the confusion, leaving her head aching from its effect. Pooling tufts of misty vapor gathered, then dispersed in her dreams as if blown away by a cold, cleansing wind.

In the haze of painful sleep Rhapsody opened her eyes. Standing before her was the Lord Rowan, garbed in forest green, leaning upon a staff of winter wood.

Do you understand now what you are fighting for? The words filled her mind, though they did not fall from his lips.

Her answer came like a song she didn't remember but had known once, long ago.

Life itself, she replied. *The F'dor hate life, seek to snuff it out. We are fighting for Life itself.*

Yes, and more. The Lord Rowan began to walk away into the misty forest of her dream, then turned for a moment and looked back at her. *You are fighting for the Afterlife as well.*

I don't understand.

The battle that is being waged is not just for this life, but for the Afterlife. There is Life and there is Void. Void is the enemy of Life, and will swallow it into oblivion if it can. Life is strong, but Void grows stronger.

The Lord Rowan faded into the mist, leaving only his words hanging in the foggy air of her dream.

In this you must not fail.

42

The pace of the time that was passing refused to be hurried. Fresh mornings melded into warm afternoons of slanted sunlight that wended their way toward sweet, lazy evenings and into the deep darkness of night, only to begin anew again with the rising sun. It was the same cycle as everywhere, but for some reason the days seemed longer to Rhapsody, though she had no need for them to be shortened. The realm of the Rowans was a peaceful, drowsy place, even though the children seemed largely invulnerable to its sleepy call. The children were happy here, growing stronger and healthier beneath the watchful eyes of the Lord and Lady, and the comforting love of their beautiful young grandmother.

The seasons in the glade did not change; it was always spring-approaching-summer; though autumn was Rhapsody's favorite time of year, she barely missed it. That was part of the enchantment of the place as well; beloved friends and familiar things faded into memory, unaccompanied by a notice of their absence. Time just moved on, oblivious of it all.

The only difficulty was the night. As the sun was setting Rhapsody would look over her shoulder to see the Lord or Lady nodding, indicating it was time. She had chosen the schedule herself; it allowed her the chance to sing her evening vespers, and she knew that the Lady, hovering in robes of sky-blue, kissed each child to sleep at the ending of the procedure, so it made sense to her to do it then. Her nights had long been haunted by disturbing dreams, anyway; they could hardly be made worse by this, she had reasoned.

She was wrong.

There was no becoming accustomed to it. The pain was excruciating, causing her to scream in agony, crying out freely in the knowledge that she could not be heard in the round building that swallowed all sound.

In the beginning she had clung to the edges of the cot, grasping until her fingers bled, desperately seeking some way to lessen the suffering. It was no use. Each jab of the needle felt as if it tore a piece of the flesh from her chest, searing her heart and sending it into spasms of pain the likes of which she had never imagined, let alone felt. It was a final communion with Ashe, in a way; at last she understood fully the agony he had carried.

She tried to concentrate on the children, on the knowledge that, because of her agony, they felt nothing, but that only worked for a moment once the procedure had begun. Finally she gave in to the futility of it all and accepted that she could not be stoic or brave; she was meant to suffer this in their stead. She had agreed to willingly. As she lay on the floor between each procedure, having convulsed off the cot in her misery, she comforted herself with the awareness that each child was sleeping in peace because of this. It gave her what little will she could muster to go on.

After one particularly brutal session, when she lay sobbing on the floor, trying to catch her breath, the Lady Rowan entered the room and drew Rhapsody into her arms. She ran her warm hands over the golden hair and as she did, the pain subsided along with the sobs. She turned the Singer's tearstained face up to her own and looked deeply into her eyes.

'They are stronger now, and older. Aria is no longer a baby, and Quan Li is almost a woman. Some of them can bear this on their own. Why don't you let them?'

Rhapsody shook her head. 'No,' she said, her voice catching in the back of her throat. 'I'm all right.'

The Lady regarded her seriously. 'You are holding something back from me. What is it?'

Rhapsody looked away, only to have the warm fingers turn her face back again.

'Tell me,' the Lady said. Rhapsody knew the Lady already had the answer, and was waiting for her to admit it to herself. She met the Lady's eyes.

'My mother,' she said quietly.

'What of her?'

'I know now what she felt, how she suffered when I left. It was like a piece of her heart had been taken; in a way I believe I am atoning for it.'

The Lady touched her face tenderly. 'You are carrying great pain about your mother in your heart, are you not?'

Rhapsody looked down. 'Yes.' She could feel the warmth of the smile above her.

'For the equivalent of three years now you have borne the physical pain for these children as a mother would because the thought of them in pain was worse for you. How do you think your own mother feels, knowing her child carries so much unnecessary pain on her behalf?'

Rhapsody's eyes met the sky-blue ones instantly; realization came more slowly. When it did, the Lady Rowan took her hand.

'My guilt about her is hurting her more.'

The Lady smiled. 'Let yourself heal, child; otherwise your mother never will.'

*

249

That night, as she slept in the solid darkness of her room, the Lady opened her door and came in, carrying a small scented candle wound with fragrant wood. Rhapsody opened her eyes, but the Lady merely shook her head and placed the candle holder on the table beside her bed. She bent over the sleeping Singer and kissed her forehead gently, then left as quietly as she came.

After a moment the door opened again. Rhapsody sat up in surprise as the young woman came in, smiling, and sat down in the chair, putting her feet up on the bed. She pulled out a long, thin knife and began a game of mumblety-peg, stabbing agilely between her fingers with it as they rested on her knee.

'Hi, Rhaps,' Jo said.

For a moment Rhapsody could only clutch at the bedclothes, struggling to awaken but finding that the sweet, fragrant smoke of the candle weighed heavily on her eyelids. Finally she mustered enough strength to rise and reach out toward her sister's knee.

'Don't,' Jo said pleasantly, not looking up from her game of mumblety-peg. Rhapsody sat quickly back on the bed, her head suddenly light and a queasy sensation of mixed joy and shock filling her stomach.

'Is it really you, Jo?' she asked. Her voice trembled; she didn't recognize the sound of it through the thickness of the haze.

'Of course not,' Jo replied, still intent on her game. 'What you see is only what your memory tells you.' She looked up and met Rhapsody's eyes for the first time. 'But my love is with you. You needed to see me, so I came, at least a little.'

Rhapsody nodded as if she understood, but she didn't. 'You're here, then? In the realm of the Rowans? Between the worlds?'

Jo shook her head. 'No. I'm in the Afterlife. But I'll be here when you need me to be, Rhaps. It's the least I can do, after all you did for me.'

Rhapsody rubbed her head foggily. 'I don't understand.'

'Of course you don't.' Jo slid the dirk back into her boot, leaned back in the chair, and crossed her arms over her chest. 'You won't. And I can't explain it to you, either. It's beyond your comprehension now.' A wry smile played on her lips. 'Funny, isn't that? In life it was always you that tried to explain things I didn't understand to me.'

'Tell me of the Afterlife, Jo,' Rhapsody said, choking on the words.

'I can't. Well, I can, but you won't understand. You can't. You have to have passed through the Gate of Life to know. Here, in this place, you can only see a little of what has passed through, because this is a place of transition. Now you can only know the things you knew on your side of the Veil of Joy. Once you pass through the Gate, you'll know everything. I'm sorry, Rhaps. I wish I could make you understand.'

'Are you happy, Jo?'

Her sister smiled. 'I'm content.'

'But not happy?'

' "Happy" is a word from your side of the gate. It is only part of contentment. You can't understand, so if it makes you feel better, believe that I am happy. It's as true as anything else.'

'I want you to be happy, Jo. I'm so sorry for what I did to you.'

The image of her sister laid the dirk aside and regarded her thoughtfully.

'Now, if you want me to be happy, you can't feel guilty; that is something I can feel as well. What you did to me, Rhaps, was give me a chance to live forever.

'You are the first person that I ever knew that loved me. That's the key, you know – it's the connections that we make in life that allow us to know love in the Afterlife. You told me my mother loved me, and you were right; she does. You helped me to find her beyond the Gate because of it.'

Jo slid the knife back into her boot and stood.

'I have to go. Don't,' she said as Rhapsody struggled to sit up again. 'Keep working with those kids, Rhaps. You joke about being their grand-mother, but the ties on them in the Afterlife go both ways, if you know what I mean. What you're doing is cutting the chains that could drag them in death to the Vault of the Underworld. You know I have no great fondness for kids, but nobody deserves that. Bye.'

The door closed behind her, leaving Rhapsody both blissful and bereft.

For the next few nights her sister came to visit. The dream only lasted for a few moments, so Rhapsody became adept at saying whatever was most in need in her heart as soon as her sister came in the door; she was still trying to learn to say goodbye as easily when Jo told her she could not be coming again.

'You know the answers you needed most,' she said as Rhapsody fought back the tears. 'I love you; there is nothing to forgive. And, by your definition, I am happy; may you be, too, Rhaps.' She rose, ignoring the Singer's pleas to stay, and left by the door she had come in.

In spite of the comforting scents from the candles, Rhapsody bowed her head and gave in to grief. It was then that she felt the soft hand on her forehead. Rhapsody looked up in her sleep to see the face so like her own smiling down at her.

'Don't cry, Emmy.' Her mother's hands were gentle, caressing the tears from her face.

Finally it was done. One clear day, no different seemingly than any of the others, the Lady met Rhapsody in the forest and extended her hand. In it was a vial of liquid, black as pitch, slender as an arrow shaft, no longer than her palm. When Rhapsody looked at her in confusion the Lady smiled.

'After all you have suffered for it, I would think you would recognize it.'

Rhapsody's eyes opened wide. 'This is it? This is seven years' worth, from all ten of them?'

'This is all that remains. It has been clarified down to the essence of its demonic nature, evil in pure form.'

A shudder rumbled through the Singer. 'Is it safe to carry?'

'For a while. Not for long. I suggest you put it in the hands of the Dhracian as soon as you can.' She opened her palm; in it was another vial, this one made of silvery hematite, a mineral the Lirin called bloodstone. It was shaped like a chevron, an angled rafter of a roof, and the bottom was lined with cork. The Lady Rowan uncorked the hematite vial and gently slid the glass one inside it, then sealed it shut. She extended her hand to Rhapsody.

'This should fit within Daystar Clarion's sheath at the tip where the sword does not reach. The elemental power of fire and the stars will hold it in stasis until you can give it to the one who will seek the F'dor.'

Rhapsody nodded, still afraid to touch the vial. 'I'm to go now, then?'

'Yes.'

'And the children?'

'Any that wish to return with you may go. Those who do not may remain here, if they wish; they have earned the right to eternal peace if they so choose.'

Rhapsody nodded and mustered a smile. 'I am forever grateful for your kindness, and that of the Lord.' She reluctantly took the vial.

The Lady looked at her seriously. 'Don't be, Rhapsody. Favors generally come with sacrifice; I don't think I need to remind you of that.'

She was about to ask if any more was owed on this one when the children spilled out of one of the huts, laughing and calling as they ran to her. The Lady smiled at her once more, growing fainter as the air grew cloudier around her. Rhapsody looked around her anxiously and saw Constantin standing some distance away. She put out her hand to him and he came to her.

'Come with us,' she said, taking his hand in hers.

The gladiator shook his head. 'No, I'm going to remain here.'

Tears sprang to her eyes. 'Why?'

'It's not time.' His voice was gentle, deep as the sea.

Desperation crept into her voice, the Veil of fog was growing thicker. 'Please come, Constantin; I'll never see you again.'

All that remained visible were the clear blue eyes, piercing the fog like sapphire beacons.

'You will, one day.' He closed his eyes, and was lost to her in the mist.

She called his name, but the only sound was the wind in the trees of the forest. Rhapsody buried her face in her hands, feeling the icy sting of her own tears.

'Rhapsody, look! The sword!'

She looked up at the word; a few feet away she could see the blade of Daystar Clarion, the flames billowing up it in the wind. It was still embedded in the snow, point down. The falling iceflakes had dusted the hilt, covering it up to the pommel with a thin crust of white. Seven years had passed in the realm of the Rowans; it was as if she had been gone only for less than a day.

She thought of Constantin, of the look in his eyes that night as he held the image of her, of the same eyes disappearing into the fog behind the Veil of Hoen. *The Veil of Joy*, she mused sadly, remembering the dreamy days there, and the horrific nights. *Above all else, may you know joy*, the Patriarch had said. Perhaps now that she was gone Constantin would begin to find some of it.

A blast of wintry wind snapped her out of her reverie. She looked down at the small faces, looking up at her expectantly.

'Where are we going now, Rhapsody?'

She smiled at them. 'Home. We're going home.'

43

The House of Remembrance, Navarne

Even in the depth of winter, there were birds here now, Achmed noted.

He had left his horse in a clearing outside the area that was tainted the last time he had been in this place. It had not been difficult to find the boundaries of the corruption. This ancient forest grove, dark green stands of old wood stretching for miles across the rolling hills of Navarne, had a central sector newly grown over with white birches, poplars, and pale-barked pines, youngling trees whose sallow trunks made the area appear pasty, blanched, as if it were ill. More than a year had passed since the Rakshas had been routed here, since Achmed and his companions had put an end to the blood sacrifices of children it had been making on behalf of its master, the F'dor, but still there remained a heavy silence in the air, a palpable lack of life.

But at least there were birds, resilient little winterbirds who hopped about on the snow or issued a rare chirp from a tree branch, scavenging for food. If the birds were willing to eat the dried berries and frozen seeds of this place, the corruption, the evil taint that had seeped into the very soil of the forest, must truly be gone. The wildlife had been utterly absent before.

To the west he heard the crackle of the snowcrust breaking, a rustle of twigs, a disturbance caused by something the weight of a man, not a bird.

Rhapsody knew to wait in the courtyard of the House, he thought as the noises continued; the intruder came closer. He could sense her heartbeat farther up ahead; she was where she should be. Achmed sighted his cwellan.

He willed his breathing to slow, standing as silent and motionless as a shadow cast by the setting sun. Inwardly he cursed; in the old world, when he still had his blood lore, he would have been able to sense the heartbeat of this stranger, too, to know within a hairsbreadth where it was, and where it was vulnerable. Now, as he had been since coming to this new land, he was blind, relying only on his fighting skills for his survival.

And Rhapsody's.

In the distance to his left he caught sight of something moving slowly through the pale trees, taking its time. The pulse in his gloved finger throbbed against the weight of the cwellan's trigger.

Suddenly, a stone's throw to his right, the brush of the forest floor parted.

Achmed wheeled, resighting the cwellan with speed born of centuries of experience.

The stag in the brambles ahead of him froze.

For an instant Achmed froze as well. Then, slowly, he lowered the weapon to his side, inhaling deeply.

The animal stared at him for a moment longer, then turned and bounded off into the depths of the forest, snorting furiously. To the west he heard the sounds of its mate crashing through the snowcrust, snapping branches as she fled with him.

Achmed inhaled again, blowing his breath out slowly, then hurried on to the House, up in the distance ahead of him.

A hundred yards before he reached the place where the House had stood Achmed could see the damage caused by the ball of fire that had ripped through this place. Snow had covered the piles of ash and cinders, so that with each step his footprints turned black against the white ground. The trees in the area were scarred, their bark burned away or striped with soot, degrading in layers the closer they had been to the House, from blackened hulls that had once been the outer ring of maples to the fine, sooty rubble that had been the birches nearest the outer courtyard. The House itself was gone, nothing more than a fragile, skeletal tower and mounds of scorched wreckage.

The white oak in the center of the courtyard had survived, however, a sapling of the World Tree, Sagia, protected by the endlessly playing music of the harp Rhapsody had left in its branches when they departed from this place. Even the inferno of elemental fire half a year later that had purged the tree of its polluted root, and ignited the House as well, had not burned a single leaf. It remained as if in perpetual summer, blossoms of white waving raggedly on the wind that whistled through its branches.

Rhapsody crouched beneath the tree, tossing something on the snowy bricks of the courtyard floor to a small flock of winterbirds that scattered when he came through the trees. She looked up, then stood, brushing her hands off on her trousers as she did.

Achmed's skin began to sting fiercely as he looked her over. It had been humming intensely since he had received her note a week before, the message he had been awaiting from the moment they had parted on the Krevensfield Plain. The Bolg soldier who had brought the scrap of oilcloth to him had shuddered at his reaction, even though the king had not moved a hairsbreadth upon reading it. Apparently the look in his eyes had been sufficient to send the guard scurrying back to the aviary at double march time.

Achmed had stared at the scrap for hours; it was a simple piece of tattered oilcloth containing but one word: *Yes*. That one word was the key that the end was beginning.

It had been a battle of will from that time. The deep racial urge of destruction whispered relentlessly in his ear, demanding the hunt. It was all Achmed could do not to succumb to the blood rage, the compulsion anyone of Dhracian heritage felt innately: the all-consuming need to destroy F'dor. He had learned in his time that the primal instincts of his Dhracian blood worked as much against him as they aided him in his hunts. He measured his breathing, trying to maintain calm.

Rhapsody was watching him just as intently, hands on her hips. It had only been a few weeks since he had last seen her, but she seemed worlds changed. Her face was calm, but her eyes burned with a quiet intensity. Her hair, bound back as it always was in a black velvet ribbon, reached to her knees; when they had parted it had been merely down to the middle of her back. She was studying his face; finally she waved him over to where she stood, in the courtyard's center, beneath the slender boughs of the young tree that had been brought from their homeland on the other side of the world.

He felt the heartbeat of the world thrum in his ears as he came to her, knowing what she had brought him.

'Blackberries,' she said as he stopped beneath the branches of the tree.

'What?'

She pointed at the ground where some of the birds had returned and were pecking guardedly.

'Blackberries. From the bushes in the clearing. When last we were here they were tainted brambles, mostly thorn. I didn't think they would ever see fruit. Perhaps it's a good sign.'

Achmed nodded. 'We can use all of those we can get. Where is it?' His voice came out harsher than he intended it to.

In response she unbelted Daystar Clarion and held it aloft, point up, perpendicular to the ground. Slowly she slid the weapon from its black ivory sheath; a quiet, silver sound like a restrained trumpet call whispered through the empty courtyard. Resting on the sword's tip, the cork layer burned and blackened from the flames, was the strangely shaped hematite vial. Rhapsody reached into the fire and plucked it deftly from the weapon's tip.

'Here,' she said, holding it out to Achmed. 'Put it to good use.'

He held it up before his eyes. 'This is all there is? From ten demon-spawn?'

'Yes. It's been clarified down to its essence. There is nothing else in there, none of the mother's blood, or even of the Rakshas. This is it – pure. There will be no mistake when you find the host.' Her emerald eyes sparkled with something that looked like excitement, but Achmed suspected it was closer to fear. 'What are you going to do with it now?'

Achmed continued to examine the hematite vial. The stone was warm to the touch, perhaps a residual from the sword's fire, but more likely generated from within. Sealed as it was, there was still something deeply resonant about it, soft voices chanting dark lauds in the crackling fires of the Underworld. He could feel its power, its evil, through the stone, calling to him, wheedling, commanding, taunting his Dhracian soul. The blood behind his eyes burned.

Open it. Let us out. Let us out of the Vault.

Achmed slid the hematite vial inside his shirt. 'Nothing.'

The green eyes across from him widened dramatically.

'Nothing? After all this? What do you mean?'

'You asked what I am going to do with it now – and I said nothing – Grunthor is not here, and we are not ready to go after the demon yet. We have to be together, I suspect; otherwise that dim-witted Seer has been babbling about the Three of us for nothing.' He cast a glance around the courtyard as the wind raced through, spinning the recently fallen snow into spiraling sheets of icy white. 'I'll wait until you get back to Ylorc before I undertake this; I need to be prepared for it.'

'Until I get back to Ylorc?' Rhapsody glanced around the courtyard as well. 'Aren't I going with you now?'

'Perhaps – but I thought you might need a few days' delay.' Achmed reached into another fold in his robes, produced a cream-colored linen card with a broken golden seal, and handed it to her.

'What's this?' Rhapsody asked, turning it over in her hand.

'Tristan Steward's wedding has apparently been moved up. The ceremony is now three days hence, in Bethany.'

Rhapsody studied the invitation. 'Yes; Oelendra told me when I returned from the Veil of Hoen. Rial is planning to attend. What does this have to do with anything? The wedding is trivial next to what we have on our plates. Surely there is nothing more important, nothing we have waited for longer, than going after the demon?'

'That's true,' Achmed agreed, 'there isn't. But I have never done this before. It will take preparation, focus. It's best done in the quiet, secrecy, and safety of the mountain. I have no idea how long it will take or what it will cost. It may be like fighting the beast ahead of time. I don't know.

'What I do know is that Tristan will use any excuse to speak against the Bolg. We must be represented at the wedding; it's an occasion of state.'

'You want me to go to the wedding.'

'Yes.'

'After all this?'

'Yes.'

'You want me to go to the *wedding?*'

'You think it's better that *I* go?' Achmed snarled.

Rhapsody didn't blink. 'Of course not. I just thought we would send our regrets. I all but did that already, when the messenger came to deliver the invitation the first time.'

Achmed exhaled. 'Much has changed since you've been gone, Rhapsody. War is looming, and the enemies are both without and within. The attack could come from anywhere; I'm beginning to understand that vision where you saw it coming from everywhere. The only thing that could have dragged me away from the mountain at this point was this meeting, though Grunthor certainly plans to make use of the opportunity.' Rhapsody said nothing, but looked at him quizzically. The Firbolg king scowled. 'We've had a few problems with disloyalty and illegal commerce of Bolg weapons to Sorbold. It apparently first occurred when I was off hunting spawn with you.'

'Gods!'

'Yes, gods. May they help any Bolg foolish enough to try it again while I'm away; Grunthor's lying in wait. If you see any body parts decorating the crags of Grivven when you return, you'll know why.

'In the meantime, put in an appearance on behalf of Ylorc at Tristan's wedding. You'll buy us some time, at the very least. You may hear something about their preparations for war as well. Continue to behave as if nothing out of the ordinary is happening. I will send word to you when I am ready if you haven't already returned.'

Rhapsody said nothing. Though the jangling thrum of the harp music in the branches of the young tree masked their words, she was not prepared to give voice to her feelings, knowing that there were ears listening to the winter wind. More than anything, she wanted to tell her friend of the Veil of Hoen, what she had seen, how long she had been away, what she had learned, about the threat to Life and the Afterlife, but she did not dare, not here, not in the open, beneath the sky. Better, as he had said, to wait until they were in the dark of the mountain, hidden away from prying eyes, their voices shielded from the wind.

She looked around at the ruins of the House of Remembrance, the place where their path had first become known to them. This repository of history, this outpost of the First Cymrian wave, had been built fourteen centuries before, with so much hope; it had been desecrated so brutally. The Rakshas had even sought to use the roots of Sagia's sapling to reach within the Firbolg mountain and snatch the Sleeping Child. Such a horrific turn to what had started out as a story of great promise.

They had chosen this place to meet today, to forge a new beginning, for good or ill. The irony that here, in this place, where the demon had used the blood of children to its ends, she was giving the Dhracian the demon's own blood, from the veins of its children, to find it, was almost too much for her to bear.

Rhapsody looked back at Achmed. He stood before her now, the reluctant savior, the key to their finding the demon, to its ultimate destruction, returning her gaze unblinkingly. Her stomach turned suddenly, and she felt the world begin to spin; he must have seen it, because he reached out and grasped her arm, bringing solidity again.

'I don't know if I can do this,' she whispered, unwilling to leave him now, now that the blood was in hand, and that the die was about to be cast. 'I want to get it over with. I want to go home.'

The Firbolg king shrugged. 'Can't. You have to attend to this first. It's all part of the design.' He leaned forward and spoke into her ear.

'It's your destiny.'

The windy silence of the courtyard grew even stiller. Destiny – just the sound of the word made her weary. *How many times have I heard that since coming to this place, this new land of demons and nightmares?* she thought bitterly, biting back her anger. The words of the Grandmother, the Earthchild's late guardian, came into her mind.

It is your destiny. Deny it, and it would be better to hurl yourselves into the abyss now.

It was a word employed to threaten; Oelendra had made use of it, too.

Your destiny is foretold, and you can shrug at it all you like, but you will kill the F'dor, or die trying. You have no choice.

Ryle hira, the Liringlas said. Life is what it is.

'Balls,' Rhapsody snorted. 'Hogwash. We make our own destiny.'

Achmed smiled. Rhapsody laughed.

'You said that just to infuriate me, didn't you?'

'Yes.'

'It worked.'

'I know. So will you go to the wedding?'

Rhapsody threw up her hands in mock disgust. 'I have nothing to wear to this event, Achmed. Last I heard it was a formal occasion.'

'You depleted my coffers by an obscene amount to buy the thousands of useless frocks you have stored down in Elysian, and you have nothing to wear? Spare me.'

'If the wedding is in three days I will have to ride directly from here. I didn't bring any of those useless frocks with me.'

The Bolg king sighed. He reached into his robes again and pulled out a piece of folded leather, which he handed to her.

'Here's some Orlandan coinage, and a few notes of tender. You can buy something to wear with this. Keep your ears open for anything you might hear about the Bolg or Bolg weapons at the wedding.'

'Somehow I doubt either of those topics will come up.'

'Perhaps not. Just your presence there may distract Tristan enough to delay him, if he's the one plotting to attack. Try to find the ambassador from Sorbold; I worry much more about it coming from there. Do whatever you need to do, and then come home.'

'I will.'

'Good.' He turned to leave, then looked back over his shoulder. 'It won't be long now. All in good time.'

She smiled, her eyes gleaming in the fading light. 'I know.'

'Travel well,' he said. He watched as she nodded and disappeared into the forest.

Then, with the loss of her innate musical vibration, the whispering voices returned, scratching at his ears, screaming in his veins.

Achmed pulled the hematite vial from its pocket within the shirt beneath his robes. He held the smooth silver bottle up to his eyes, absently running a finger over the slippery stone.

'All in good time,' he said.

44

Capital of Bethany, at the City's Western Gate

Rhapsody had been to Bethany only once before. Her initial impression was that it was a city under a silent siege. It was a round city, vast in size and in aspiration of design; as far as she had seen, no other of the Cymrian cities still standing had been outfitted with the riches of paving stones, street lanterns, roadways, public baths, marvels of architecture, horse hitchings, and all the other luxuries she had come to associate with wealth. Wealth in Roland seemed to be a sign not so much of successful trade but of the collection of taxes, and the collection of taxes was a sure sign of where power lay. Bethany had all the makings of a royal city, despite the fact that there was still no king on the throne.

The siege aspect came from the plethora of soldiers, both at the city's outskirts and on its well-manicured streets, constantly patrolling the eight gates and four main thoroughfares, consigning the cattle and animal trade to certain districts, while keeping other streets, notably those around the central palace and its extensive private garden, pristinely clear for genteel foot travel. Markets and mercantile areas were found in the eastern and western sections, while museums and public gardens were located in the northern and southern parts of the city. The prince's palace and the great circular fire basilica made up the central section. Only the barracks of Bethany's enormous army were found in every quarter.

By the time she had made it through the western villages that had once been part of the outer ring of the city, it was clear to her that Bethany had changed dramatically in a relatively short time.

When she had first come here, more than a year ago with Achmed, Grunthor, and Jo, the city's outer ring had been a lively place, an endlessly sprawling ragtag village of peasants and paupers, workmen, tradesmen, and street urchins, people far too poor to live within the confines of the pristine inner city walls, but happy nonetheless to prosper from those who went in and out of its gates to trade. She had once unintentionally caused a riot in these outer villages, intervening with a man who was beating his son. It was only thanks to a speedy rescue by Grunthor and Achmed that she had managed to survive the melee that ensued.

Now, the population of that massive peasant town was gone. In its place were new barracks, most still being built, with additional ramparts being erected around the city wall. It didn't seem as if the preparations were for a temporary event, but rather were darker and permanent in nature.

Rhapsody was in awe at the sight, her heart wrenched in sudden fear. *Could all of this be for the wedding?* she wondered as she looked out the carriage window, waiting in line at the newly erected guard post at the western city gate. She pulled the hood of her woolen cloak tightly about her face.

Past the gate she could see that the city itself was glittering in the light of the winter morning, with silver flags flying from every streetlamp, and great garlands strung from rooftop to rooftop. The mosaics on the walls and in the streets had been polished to a bright sheen, and from every tree hung a silver star, the symbol of the Patriarchy. Rhapsody was amazed that so many extensive preparations had been possible in such a short time.

The wedding of the prince and his bride, Lady Madeleine of Canderre, had been originally scheduled for the first day of spring; Rhapsody had reread the invitation over many times since she had returned to Tyrian from the Veil of Hoen. Oelendra had told her by chance that the date had been moved up owing to a horrendous slaughter at the winter festival; the tale had made Rhapsody's blood run cold.

Rial, Tyrian's loyal Lord Protector, had also been invited to the wedding, and so she had met up with him on the forest road and traveled with him and his guards, grateful for the chance to be able to ride in a coach in winter rather than on horseback. Originally her invited escort was Achmed, but he had snorted in a way that made it very clear to her that he would not be coming. The tossing of his invitation into the fires of the Great Hall of Canrif, followed by a giant projectile of spit, had sealed her impression the previous summer. Events at the House of Remembrance notwithstanding, it was not really surprising that if Ylorc was to be represented at this state occasion, she would have to be the one to go, and go alone.

Secretly she was looking forward to the event. Weddings had always been a time of great celebration in the Seren farming village of Merryfield, where she was raised, and she had always loved to dance. In addition, since Achmed had grudgingly given her several notes of tender to purchase clothing and appropriate jewelry, her excitement had grown over each league of the journey. And finally, deep in her heart she hoped Ashe might be there, as they had tentatively planned. For all of Llauron's ugly warnings, she hoped to see him one last time before he was wed himself.

Now, however, sitting in Rial's coach at the western gate in a line of other guests waiting to enter the city, she was nervous. There were soldiers everywhere, at least four times as many as there had been when she was last here, and the attitude was much more threatening than it had been. She laid a hand on Rial's arm as they waited.

The Lord Protector, wrapped in a deerskin cloak over his standard dark red cape, turned to her and smiled. The smile faded when he saw the look in the eyes within her hood.

'Rhapsody? Is something wrong?'

She gestured out the window. 'Doesn't it seem more – more martial than it has been here before?'

Rial chuckled. ' 'Tis not an answer I can give, dear one. This is my first time in Bethany. But I have heard from the mail caravan that Tristan Steward has taken control of the armies of Roland. Most probably the first step in seizing the crown.' Rhapsody shuddered.

'Who seeks to enter?'

The voice was harsh and deep, and seemed to come from right beside her. Rhapsody turned and looked into the eyes of the brown-bearded soldier who had thrust his face through the carriage window; they were now at the gate. Eleven other soldiers were deployed around the area, standing guard and checking tradesmen who were bringing in goods for the wedding, and turning away others who wanted to enter the city.

She averted her eyes as Rial spoke up.

'Rial, Lord Protector of Tyrian, here for the wedding by invitation,' he said in his smooth, warm voice. He took Rhapsody's invitation from her hand, added his own to it, and handed it out the window to the guard. 'With me is the Lady Rhapsody, the, er, Duchess of Elysian,' he continued, a twinkle in his eye. Rhapsody hid a smile at the joking title Achmed had given her when he had made the hidden island cottage her own.

The soldier had looked at both invitations, passing Rial's back without comment. He turned Rhapsody's over several times, then stared at her.

'Show your face, lady,' he commanded.

Before she could move, Rial leaned forward, his body tensing.

'Why?' he demanded. 'How dare you speak this way to an invited guest of the prince? Nay; the invitation is in order. Move aside, soldier. The weather is bitter. Let us pass.'

The guard drew his bastard sword menacingly, and the others at the gate turned their attentions to the carriage. Rhapsody turned hurriedly to Rial.

'It's all right, Rial,' she said quickly. 'They are just being careful.' She looked back at the guard, then took her hood down.

The soldier's eyes widened. He blinked rapidly, then averted his gaze and passed a hand over his face to regain his composure. He returned the invitations to Rial and gestured for the coach to move inside the city gates.

Rhapsody pulled her hood back up. 'Are you going to the guest housing directly, Rial?'

The Lord Protector smiled. 'Aye, as I know no other place in the city. Did you have somewhere you prefer to go first, Rhapsody?'

She nodded, staring absently out the window at the throngs of tradesmen and soldiers streaming through the streets. 'I need to get to a dressmaker. I did not bring appropriate attire with me; I've been journeying for a long time now.' *More than seven years, though no time has passed on this side of the Veil of Hoen,* she mused silently. She turned to Rial, who was watching her intently, and smiled.

'Besides, I'm looking forward to the chance to spend a good deal of Achmed's money.'

The holy man sighed silently. Logjammed in a line of carriages yet again. He shook his head, urging the harsh, wheedling voice within to be patient.

There was no true sport to be had at the wedding, sadly. Tristan's forces, now loyal to him as regent and supreme commander, were already sworn, and therefore all but impossible to turn in any way that would bring harm directly to him or his interests. The ranks had swelled prodigiously; the army of Roland, quartered still in their home provinces but relocating to Bethany more by the day, would soon surpass one hundred thousand soldiers. His eyes burned with excitement at the thought.

Still, it was hard to pass up such a plum opportunity to make mischief, to wreak havoc on such a grand scale. A royal wedding, the first in many years, was a prime hunting ground, an almost irresistible chance to cause an eruption of violence. He had already arranged for a small surprise of that sort, though he doubted it would do much to disrupt the actual festivities. He sighed again humorously. Such a loss.

He pushed back the curtain of his carriage window and leaned slightly into the wind.

Now, my good folk, he whispered. *You may come.*

Outside the city proper, on the western bank of the Phon River, the central waterway of the province, far beyond the view of the soldiers, hidden in the dark wastes of makeshift huts and ramshackle stalls that had been erected to house the displaced residents of Bethany's outer villages, the eyes of the blacksmiths who had, a few days before, shoed the horses that pulled the holy man's carriage began to burn at the edges. Deeper within, a darker fire began to kindle.

Silently they ceased their chores, left their hovels, and gathered their tools in the bitter wind.

45

Four street corners east from the northern district's secondary well, then eleven streets south. Rhapsody counted silently as she followed the pattern of foot and cart traffic, keeping her head down and the large cloth bag tucked carefully over her arm, taking care not to drag it in the icy filth of the city's cobbled streets. Her breath, warm from her pace and the anxiety that swirled in the air around her, formed thin clouds of white mist that caught the wind and vanished with each inhalation, each hurried step.

In the height of summer, during their days as lovers, Ashe had given her specific directions to a number of safe places hidden within various cities and towns across the land, garrets and cellars and storerooms he employed in need. Each direction had come with the warning that these places were inconsistent in their status; most of his time was spent traveling overland, and it was very rare that he ventured into a city or town, so much time elapsed between his visits. The rooms, he told her, might not be safe the next time they were visited; there was but one, the turf hut hidden behind a waterfall in northern Gwynwood, that he felt certain would be secure at all times. He had urged her to make use of these safe havens nonetheless. There was one somewhere here in Bethany where they had agreed to meet before, and perhaps after the wedding, if she could only find it.

At the eighth street heading south she noticed a decrease in the traffic around her, and stopped to take a better look. Rising above her in the near distance were three enormous towers, each topped by a vast cistern that collected rainwater for the town's use. The rainwater from the cisterns irrigated the public gardens, fed the ancient Cymrian aqueduct and sewer system, and supplied water to the palace and basilica. The streets that surrounded the towers were lined with smaller stone cisterns and tanks for storing the rainwater, as well as barracks for the workers who maintained the water system and the soldiers that defended it. Each tower had a guard post for the soldiers who stood watch at the cisterns night and day to prevent the royal water supply from being poisoned.

Rhapsody followed the seemingly endless wall of curving stone for three more streets until she came to the spot where the door should be, if she remembered Ashe's directions correctly. She looked around furtively, and, seeing no one near, darted quickly down a side alley that ended in a stone wall covered with thick thorny growth, as were all the outer walls of the water system.

The evergreen vegetation, known to the Filids of Gwynwood as underthorn, was a popular defense employed across the western part of the continent, a natural barrier with serrated spines that grew in double rows and delivered tremendously painful wounds that continued to bleed long after they should have healed. Rhapsody had studied underthorn with both Llauron and Lark, the Invoker's shy Lirin herbalist, during her time with him in Gwynwood, and therefore knew its dangers. She also knew how to circumvent them, both with the techniques she had learned in Gwynwood and her own Namer abilities.

She cast another glance around as the sound of a horse-drawn coach clattered up the alleyway and passed by. *Good*, she noted. The carriage routes were not far; it would be easy to hire a coach to get to the wedding. Once the sound had died away she turned back to the thorny wall and slid her hand under the first shaggy layer from the bottom, away from the direction in which the thorns grew.

Verlyss, she sang softly, speaking the plant's true name. She could feel the musical vibration of the rough bark, the spiked thorns, in the air around her as the vegetation attuned itself to the call.

Evenee, she said. Velvet moss.

The savage thorns that rested against the skin on the back of her hand softened, became slippery and harmless, tender as the green lichen that covered fallen trees in springtime. Gently she pulled the tapestry of vegetation aside. Behind it was a stone door without a handle, as Ashe had said there would be.

She felt around the edges of the door until she found an indentation to use as a handhold, and pulled. The door opened silently and she stepped quickly inside, closing it behind her again.

She was in a small, dark room that had once been part of a street-level cistern in Cymrian times, perhaps a caretaker's dwelling, long since forgotten behind the wall of swordlike thorns. A tiny recessed grate served as a window, letting light but no sound into the room.

Rhapsody fumbled in her pack for a candle. Upon finding one she willed it to light; as the flame sparked she felt a pleasant surge from her inner fire, connecting momentarily to the elemental bond within her. She held up the candle and looked around.

The room contained a bed, a chest of drawers, and a doorless closet. A threadbare armchair, much like the one in Ashe's room behind the waterfall, stood by the window next to a small table on which a lantern sat. The room was remarkably free from mildew and comfortably dry, though cold. All around, on the floor and the chest of drawers, were large beeswax candles.

Rhapsody went to the doorless alcove and hung up the cloth bag that contained her dress for the wedding, put her pack atop the chest of drawers, then set about lighting the beeswax candles from the taper in her hand. She sat down on the bed, watching the wicks catch more thoroughly, and the light grow brighter. As she settled back to wait for Ashe, she smiled as she heard her mother's voice.

Even the simplest house is a palace in candlelight.

Rhapsody closed her eyes and sought her mother's face in her mind. It appeared, smiling in return.

'Thank you, m'Lord and Lady Rowan,' she whispered. 'Thank you for giving her back to me.'

On the balcony of the upstairs ballroom at Tannen Hall, the royal residence where the wedding guests were being housed, Llauron crossed his arms and inhaled the frosty wind that was turning even colder with the coming of night. He scanned the sky in the west, watching the clouds winding in hazy gold spirals as they chased the sun beyond the rim of the horizon. *How beautiful,* the Invoker thought, running his hands absently over his arms for warmth. *Soon I will know firsthand what it is like to be part of that beauty.*

The evenstar appeared in the sky, glittering brightly in the darkening firmament. As if waiting for the lead to be taken, one by one the rest of the stars began to shine, winking with cold, burning brightly, eternally. Tears stung the edges of Llauron's aged blue eyes.

I come, my brothers, he whispered into the wind. *I come.*

The balcony door opened; Llauron turned away from the dark beauty of the night, back toward the light and merriment within the royal hall. A servant stood, silhouetted against the bright backdrop of moving shapes and laughter.

'Is everything all right, Your Grace? Can I assist you in anything?'

The Invoker smiled.

'No, thank you, my son,' he said, walking slowly back toward the door. 'I was just making a wish on the evenstar that all goes well tomorrow.'

46

The white linen blouse beneath Tristan Steward's sky-blue velvet wedding doublet clung uncomfortably to the muscles of his chest and beneath his arms, wet with nervous perspiration.

He had been pacing back and forth since sunrise, striding the long corridor outside the Great Hall of his palace with an aspect that at sometimes resembled that of a condemned man, and at others that of a caged beast. Now he was wearing a path in the woven silk carpet of his office, which had been outfitted as a dressing chamber, running his hands through his hair, displacing the ceremonial ribbon of state that had been plaited neatly through his forelock.

For the third time in the last hour he summoned James Edactor, the chamberlain, scowling as the door opened and quickly closed behind the man.

'Yes, m'lord?'

'Is she here yet?' the Lord Roland blurted, turning from his desk and knocking a sheaf of maps and papers over in the process.

'Lady Madeleine?'

'No, you thickheaded lout.' Tristan Steward scowled. 'Did I not thrice ask you to have the representative from the Bolglands sent to me?'

The chamberlain cleared his throat uncomfortably. 'Yes, m'lord, but we have been unable to locate her.'

The Lord Roland's face went pale. 'What? What did you say?'

'We cannot find her, m'lord, I am sorry. She presented her invitation at the western gate yesterday, but she did not arrive at Tannen Hall to secure her guest quarters. She is undoubtedly elsewhere in the city, perhaps visiting friends.'

The Lord Roland whirled, sweeping his arm angrily across the newly erected dressing table. A silvered glass tray with a toilette set went flying off the table, shattering on the marble floor in a great hail of bottles of cologne, combs, and razors. The chamberlain leapt out of the way to avoid the flying glass shards.

'Oh, you know that, do you?' he snarled, storming through the debris toward the office door. 'For all you know, she has been abducted or ravaged or worse.' *Or is trysting with one of the other dukes or nobles in the comfort of their private halls in the inner circle of Bethany,* he thought. *For all you know, Edactor, they have draped her in jewels, promising her wealth and a safe exit from the Bolglands in return for her favors. At this moment she could be wrapped, naked, her skin gleaming, in their finest silk sheets, entwining her glorious legs around their pasty chests, giving herself to Ivenstrand or Baldasarre or MacAlwaen, when it could be me.*

New beads of sweat sprang out in his already-perspiring forehead at the thought. Perhaps it had even been arranged before her arrival; perhaps she had been wooed by one of the ambassadors who had come to the court of Ylorc to pay tribute to the despised Bolg king on behalf of one of Tristan's rivals. Perhaps they were even now lying in bed, laughing at him, indulging in splendid lovemaking between bouts of merriment at his expense, chuckling at his looming marriage to the Beast of Canderre amid bouts of torrid debauchery.

The shock on the face of the chamberlain as he strode past the man did little to clear his head. The blood of rage, and something darker, was pounding behind his eyes, filling him with painful arousal, making his hands shake in fury.

'Now, go to the captain of the palace regiment and have them comb the streets. Find her. I want to see her before the wedding, here, in my office. I have important diplomatic issues I need to discuss with her before I can concentrate on throwing my life away and binding myself for all time to that hag from Canderre. Is that clear, Edactor?' He seized the door handle and dragged the heavy door open with an emphatic scream of iron hinges. 'Find that woman and—'

He stopped, his voice cracking like a youth's as he skidded over the last word. Standing outside the doorway was a trembling little girl bedecked in a frilly white gown, flowers entwined in her hair. It was one of Madeleine's handmaidens, bearing the traditional bridemeal for him, a tray laden with pastries and steaming tea, fresh porridge and aromatic sausages. The bridemeal was customarily cooked by the bride herself on the morning of the wedding as a promise of future repasts she would provide as a wife, though undoubtedly Madeleine had merely ordered that it be prepared by the palace servants. Tristan could not fault her at that. He had done the same with the flowers he was supposed to handpick and present to her as the bridegroom. He stared down at the girl in dismay, then coughed.

'Find that woman, Edactor, and when you have, thank her for this splendid breakfast. Tell my Lady Madeleine that her devoted bridegroom awaits his ladylove at the Altar of Fire in the basilica.'

Ashe was almost to Bethany's northwestern gate when he felt a strange tremor on the surface of his skin.

The sun was just cresting the horizon, shining on his face, lighting the path before him and casting his shadow, grotesquely elongated, behind him. Ahead in the near distance the towers of Bethany reached skyward to meet the rising sun, gleaming with promise. Deep within those streets, beyond the city walls, Rhapsody was waiting for him, a clandestine meeting planned in autumn. It was all he could do to contain his exhilaration. The pain that had once radiated constantly through his chest and body was gone; there was joy to be had in inhaling the fresh, cold air, joy in being alive, for the first time since boyhood.

But now, no more than a league from the northwestern gate, something bristled in the air behind him, causing the dragon within him to stir.

Ashe reined the gelding he had taken from the battlefield at the edge of the Krevensfield Plain to a halt and turned around to taste the wind, allowing his dragon nature to sense more fully. At the outer edges of his consciousness he felt stealthy movement, dark shadows, elongated like his own in the morning sun, creeping eastward from beyond the Phon's western bank. Though the dragon was powerful in its awareness of the minutiae of the world around him, Ashe could not look into men's hearts. There was no doubt in his own, however, that his sense of foreboding was well placed.

Black anger flashed through his mind, resonating throughout his body. Another incursion, another manipulation of the F'dor. Another attack that would doubtless allow the demon to prey upon the unsuspecting, spilling more innocent blood. He was accustomed to intervening in such incursions.

Not, however, when the woman he loved, and had been separated from for what seemed like an eternity, was finally within his reach. His anticipation of seeing Rhapsody, gowned in her wedding finery, had been the only thing that had kept him from madness over the last months.

Ashe looked back at the wakening city coming to light with the dawn. Growling a string of ugly profanities, he tugged the reins and turned west again, leaving the shining light of daybreak in Bethany to cast longer, angrier shadows ahead of him now.

Rhapsody was growing desperate. The great clock in the bell tower of the Regent's Palace had struck the quarter hour twice in the time she had been standing at the street corner's edge, waiting to flag down a passing coach. She had watched carefully from the grated window in the abandoned cistern the afternoon before, and had noted carriages passing every few minutes, their drivers calling their availability for hire. Now, however, the streets of northern Bethany were deserted; all the townspeople were either at the palace hall preparing the wedding feast, or standing outside the fire basilica, hoping to catch a glimpse of the royal couple. Undoubtedly every available carriage was currently employed delivering the invited guests from Tannen Hall to the basilica, even though it was only a few streets away.

She stamped her foot in frustration. How foolish it had been to forsake the comfort and proximity of the guest lodging for a night alone in an empty stone cistern. Ashe had never come; she had passed the time waiting writing sonnets in her worn journal by candlelight, trying to keep her heart from betraying her. By sunrise she had given up trying to fall asleep and had gone to the northern well, drawing water to cleanse herself with before dressing for the wedding. The square in which the well stood was crowded with squabbling men and women, shrieking babies, and children running madly about in the excitement of the wedding; it had been a simple task to slip in and out without notice.

Now she was dressed and ready, but had no way to get to the wedding.

The gown of stiff amethyst silk was glorious; she had reveled in the crisp touch of it the night before, running her hands down the skirt to smooth any wrinkles that had occurred in its transport to her hiding place. In the morning light the color was even more stunning, dusky and rich, matching exactly the sparkling jewels she had purchased to accentuate it. Her slippers, formed of satin dyed to match the dress, would never survive the long walk to the basilica in the filthy snow of the cobbled roadways. Her gown would fare no better.

She looked anxiously up and down the empty street, wondering if her purchases, her preparations, in fact, her visit to Bethany had been in vain. In that moment in the distance she heard the clip-clop of horses' hooves.

A moment later a tinker's cart rounded the corner a few streets away. An ancient mule, mottled skin visible beneath her tattered blanket and wearing blinders over her eyes, plodded slowly through the cobbled streets, pulling the rickety wagon hung with chamber pots, cooking pans, tarnished oil lamps, and scores of other metal objects, all clattering into each other in quiet cacophony. Rhapsody chuckled.

'Excuse me,' she called to the grizzled tinker as the cart approached. 'By your leave, sir, might I beg a ride of you? I must get to the royal wedding.'

The man, wearing an eyepatch over one eye, turned and stared at her. Obviously the sight of a wedding guest in a gown and velvet cloak was confounding, Rhapsody thought, because for a moment the shock on his face was so great that she feared he might fall from his seat. The reins dropped from his hands and the mule, sensing the slack, ambled to a stop.

Gathering her skirts, Rhapsody hurried across the roadway and climbed nimbly into the cart beside the tinker.

'Thank you,' she said in relief. 'I was afraid I was going to miss it.'

The man nodded dumbly, still staring at her with his solitary eye. Rhapsody waited for a moment, then picked up the reins and gently put them into the tinker's hands.

'Shall we?' she asked politely.

The man cleared his throat nervously and the mule, noting the change in tension on the reins, began to plod forward, wares crashing, on the way to the Regent's Palace and the basilica of fire.

47

The ceremonial procession of nobles had just begun as Rhapsody hurried to her seat next to Rial in the secondmost inner Ring of the circular basilica. The crowd, which now filled the entire central square of Bethany and had swelled through the streets all the way to Tannen Hall, were murmuring with excitement, pushing and pressing to get a closer look at the wedding party.

One by one the dukes of each of the Orlandan provinces, and the lesser nobles whose lineage had a historic significance in Roland, were coming down a shining carpet of royal purple that blanketed the long southern aisle leading into the temple; a similar carpet adorned the northern aisle, ending in the center at the round basilica. Each stone in the mosaics of flames that decorated the outskirts of the circular building, giving it the appearance of the sun when viewed from above, had been polished to a glittering sheen. As each nobleman passed, the crowd erupted in cheers.

Quentin Baldasarre, the Duke of Bethe Corbair, was entering the basilica just as she sat down. The duke's face was haggard and wan, his burning eyes the only betrayal of an otherwise stolid expression.

'Where have you been, my dear?' Rial asked worriedly. 'I was beginning to think you had changed your mind and returned to Ylorc.' He took her hand and slipped it through the crook of his arm. 'You look lovely.'

'Thank you. I apologize for my lateness; it was a miscalculation of several factors.' Rhapsody shuddered as Ihrman Karsrick, the Duke of Yarim, entered next. He was dressed in black silk breeches, with a white shirt, gleaming silver doublet, and cape, and wore upon his head a great horned helm, much like the figure who had aided the Rakshas when she fought him in the basilica of the Star the previous summer. A moment later she saw that the benison at the altar wore a similarly horned helm, though his robes, like his helm, were red. *That would be Ian Steward, the Blesser of Canderre-Yarim, Tristan's brother,* she thought, staring at the young man's sober face through the flames of the fire from the Earth's core that burned in the center of the basilica.

A fanfare of trumpets blasted, sending a rumble of excitement through the crowd and prompting the invited guests to rise. A great shout went up as Tristan, in his sky-blue and white wedding garb and a long white cape trimmed in ermine, appeared at the edge of the northern aisle. His eyes scanned the Rings of the basilica, coming to rest after a moment on the section in which Rhapsody and Rial stood. Then, with two young male pages in tow, he strode defiantly down the aisle to the Altar of Fire in the center of the basilica and bowed perfunctorily to his brother.

Another cheer, this one louder than all the others, went up. Rhapsody and Rial looked south. Madeleine of Canderre stood, bedecked in a beautiful white silk gown glowing with the sheen from the thousands of pearls that encrusted it, her hand on the outstretched arm of her father, Cedric Canderre. She was fashionably pale, her face and neck powdered white, her long hair swept severely back and woven with ribbons of state and flowers native to Canderre. The duke's expression was mild, but Rhapsody thought she read great sadness in his eyes, even as distant as she was from him.

As the bride and her father proceeded down the aisle, followed by two tiny handmaidens bearing chests similar to the ones that followed Tristan to the altar and the ridiculously long train of the wedding gown, Rhapsody felt a gentle touch on her elbow.

'Well, there you are, my dear,' came Llauron's warm, cultured voice. 'I am so happy to see that you are well, and able to attend the wedding.' He leaned forward conspiratorially with a twinkle in his eye. 'Was that a tinker's cart I saw you alight from a few streets away? An interesting choice of transportation for a guest of the regent.'

'Hello, Llauron,' she replied, kissing the Invoker politely on the cheek, then eyeing him suspiciously. The seven years she had spent with the Rowans had not removed the sting of his failure to send reinforcements to help her in Sorbold. 'We peasants travel in such carts all the time, and are rarely invited to royal occasions.' She turned back to watch, fascinated, as Madeleine arrived at the Altar of Fire. 'I've never seen a wedding ceremony in Roland before.'

' 'Tis a barbarous thing,' said Rial humorously, bowing to the Invoker. 'Well met, Your Grace. I imagine you agree?'

Llauron chuckled. 'Indeed; we of the *true* faith favor simplicity and none of their crude rituals. Strange, given that we worship nature in all its untamed glory, while they are the supposedly more civilized sect. Ah, well.'

'It doesn't seem that barbarous to me,' Rhapsody protested as Tristan sank to one knee and bowed before his bride.

'Wait, my dear,' said Llauron, smiling. 'We haven't begun the Unification ritual yet.'

'What brideprice do you offer?' the benison asked Cedric Canderre.

'Forty thousand pieces of gold, one hundred Orlandan bars of platinum, fifty ingots of ancient rysin,' replied Cedric Canderre stoutly. 'This is the bargain we have struck in accordance to the custom of the church and the laws of Roland.'

'I'd wager he'd have paid a lot more than that to be rid of her if Tristan had held out,' a guest in front of Rhapsody whispered to the elegantly gowned woman next to him, who nodded seriously.

'What is a brideprice?' Rhapsody asked Llauron.

'The amount her father is willing to pay Tristan Steward to take her off of his hands,' the Invoker replied with a chuckle. 'It is the custom in all such weddings, but in this case, the vast amount is particularly resonant.'

Rhapsody watched doubtfully as Cedric Canderre produced a parchment scroll and a quill. 'I suppose it's not much different than the dowries paid in the farming community I was raised in,' she said uncertainly as Tristan examined the paper, nodded, then took the quill and signed the scroll on a wax tablet the benison held out for him to bear on. 'Though usually it was seen as a gift from the bride's family to help the couple start out.'

'Perhaps that was your experience. But here, should the bridegroom decide within one year's time that his wife was not worth the brideprice, he may return her to her father, and must repay him half of it.'

'Half?' Rhapsody asked incredulously as Cedric Canderre kissed Madeleine on the cheek and withdrew to his seat within the Inner Ring. 'Only half? Why?'

'Because, as she is no longer, er, untouched, she has been devalued.'

'But—'

'Now, Rhapsody, don't sputter; it's a fine system,' said Llauron jokingly. 'The first anniversary is an extremely festive occasion in the Patriarch's faith, as it means that the husband has chosen to keep his wife permanently. The parties are really quite splendid, I'm told. Ah, ah – now, don't be flabbergasted, my dear; your face is red as a beet, not at all a complementary color to your lovely gown. I thought you had learned by now not to sneer at the customs of others.' He leaned closer and whispered in her ear. 'I cannot tell you how relieved I am to see that you survived your ordeal and Khaddyr's failure to meet up with you, and still met with success in your mission. I am very proud of you.'

'What—'

'Shh, my dear. The ceremony continues.' Llauron quickly turned his attention back to the altar. Rhapsody's eyes narrowed, then she relented in her annoyance, amused in spite of herself. Llauron's personable nature was always disarming. She made note to not let him wriggle out of providing an explanation for the mishaps in the forest, and looked back to the wedding ceremony.

Ian Steward was addressing his brother. 'Tristan Steward, son of Malcolm Steward, Lord Regent of Roland and Prince of Bethany, what do you pledge to this woman?'

Tristan stood straighter, his auburn hair dark and plastered flat with sweat in the light of the altar fire.

'Field and fortune, family and fealty, by faith and the Fire, this is my pledge,' Tristan intoned.

As the benison asked for and received the same pledge from Madeleine, Rhapsody looked around, hoping to catch sight of Ashe. Though he hadn't been able to meet her in the cistern, she hoped he would eventually catch up to her at the wedding. Whether he was here now, in the crowd somewhere, was impossible to discern, especially since his mist cloak shielded him from the normal means of detection. She sighed and settled back again to watch the ceremony.

The call of the pure element of fire from the wellspring caught her ear; there was music in the flames, music sweeter than the strains of the orchestra that was playing in the basilica.

How long she drowsed she did not know, but her attention snapped back at the benison's next words.

'The pledge of field,' he said, his voice a drier, clearer version of Tristan's. Tristan turned and nodded to his pages, as did Madeleine. One of each of the chests were quickly opened, and two pieces of parchment brought forward to the bride and bridegroom. Each piece was a map of the lands under their dominion, and together they laid the pieces on the altar, fitting them together to symbolize the union of their respective holdings.

271

'The pledge of fortune,' said the benison.

The chests opened again, and two great necklaces of state were lifted out, heavy with jewels. The gems in the state necklace of Bethany were rubies and diamonds, while the royal necklace of Canderre was set in emeralds as green as the province's fields.

The benison took the necklace of Canderre and placed it carefully around the neck of Tristan Steward, who bowed. He then placed the necklace of Bethany around Madeleine's neck and she bowed as well.

'Well, there you have it. With a simple exchange of jewelry and maps the destinies of two lands are decided,' Rial said quietly. 'The people of the province, through the various nobles who own their lands, swear fealty not to a person, but to a necklace, a chain of jewels that passes from generation to generation without regard to the wisdom of the person wearing it. Tristan has just received the pledge not only of his wife, but of all the people of her land, just because she has given him a necklace. It seems odd to me.'

Llauron nodded. 'In the days of their ancestors, the Lord and Lady were always confirmed by the people themselves through the Great Moot in which they met. The land on which the Moot was built was magical; it had the power to count the affirmations of the people, and confirm or deny a claim to the throne. But, like almost everything else about those days, the meaning has been lost. Much like the Patrician religion itself, where the individual prays to intermediaries, who pray to highter intermediaries, who pray to benisons, who pray to the Patriarch, who alone has the right to pray to their God.'

Rhapsody said nothing. Raised as a peasant in a human farming village, she had never seen the political process of a land at work, so none of the rituals of the passing of power surprised her; it had always been outside of her understanding. She remembered her mother, as a Lirin among humans, having the same befuddlement as Rial now expressed.

'The pledge of family,' said the benison.

A murmur rippled of excitement through the crowd. At each edge of the carpeted aisle a soldier appeared; they were dressed in the uniforms of Canderre and Bethany. The two men drew their swords simultaneously and came down the aisle, where they saluted the couple.

'What's happening?' Rhapsody whispered to Rial. The Lord Protector inclined his head in the direction of the altar.

'The sealing of the blood,' he said.

The little pages reached into their wooden chests again, and drew forth sheets of white cloth the size of large handkerchiefs.

'I don't think I want to watch this,' Rhapsody said.

'As you can see, the crowd considers this the best part,' Llauron said as the couple bared the backs of their wrists. 'It is considered highly fashionable for the bride to faint.'

Rial's face bore a look of concern. 'If this is truly upsetting to you I can escort you out,' he said.

Rhapsody grimaced as the wedding couple drew the backs of their wrists across the blades of the soldiers' weapons as the men held them stationary, then joined them. 'I am certainly not disturbed by the sight of blood – but at a *wedding?*' She watched in bewilderment as Madeleine calmly wiped the back of her hand off on the linen handkerchief held by her page, and then sank dramatically to the floor.

' 'Tis a symbol of the joining of the royal bloodlines, of the pledge to favor the future by producing children,' said Rial. 'I witnessed the wedding of Lord Stephen in Navarne fifteen years ago, and he and his wife chose to kiss at this part instead, as do most couples of the Patrician faith, I would wager. Perhaps the Lord Roland wishes to ensure that he has a large brood.'

'Madeleine and Tristan's children, hmmm, now *there's* a cheerful thought,' Llauron murmured as the Lord Roland lifted his bride from the floor of the basilica. Rial chuckled.

Rhapsody shook her head. 'You two are worse than a pair of fishwives. Honestly.'

'By the Fire, it is done,' declared the benison. The newly married couple were handed a brass pole that held a long wick. Together they dipped it in the fire of the altar, then kindled a bowl of oil at the end of a channel that ran to the roof of the basilica. A flash of flame ignited, then quickly spread along the channel and up to the circular ceiling of the temple, erupting into an enormous brazier, blazing in fire taller than a man's height. As the crowd roared, the royal couple waved, joining hands beneath the burning image of the sun.

'There will now be a good deal of merriment, dampened by long and ponderous speeches,' Llauron said, turning toward the palace, where the colors of both Bethany and Canderre were flying in the stiff winter breeze. He turned to Rhapsody and smiled warmly.

'I hope, my dear, that you will favor your old mentor with a dance or two.'

It was hard to resist the warmth of his voice, their past history notwithstanding. 'Of course.' She leaned forward and spoke into his ear. 'After I eviscerate you for leaving me to die of exposure.'

The Invoker laughed, ignoring the subtext of truth in her statement. 'Not I, my dear – Khaddyr. Please don't blame him; his patrol met with misfortune on the way to help you.'

Rhapsody's look of suspicion tempered to one of concern. 'Oh no – was he killed?'

Llauron's eyes glittered, but his expression did not change. 'No, no, thankfully he survived. Now, though I know you are in a hurry to return to Ylorc, I have a boon to ask of you.'

'Yes?'

'Would you accompany me on a short journey on the morrow? I thought since we were here in Bethany, near the end of the Cymrian Trail, that you might like to see some of the historic landmarks that commemorate the founding of this land after the refugees from Serendair landed here. I believe I told you about them when first you came to study with me. They have fallen, sadly, into disrepair, and it is my responsibility to see that they are maintained. Would you grant me this favor, my dear? It would only require a few days' delay of your return, and would mean a great deal to me. At my age, it is not wise to travel alone. Please?'

Rhapsody turned as a Bethanian page appeared in the Ring to shepherd the guests from the basilica to the palace where the wedding feast would take place.

'I have been gone a very long time,' she said uncertainly. 'I promised Achmed I would return as soon as possible.'

'We can send him a missive by avian messenger from the palace. If you are reluctant, however, I will certainly understand. I am old enough, certainly, to look after myself.'

Rhapsody studied his face. There was none of the glint that she had seen before in the gray-blue eyes that signaled his hidden annoyance, just a mild, fond expression.

'All right,' she said, pulling the hood of the velvet cloak up in preparation for the exodus from the basilica to the palace hall. 'I can certainly spare a few days to keep you company. Perhaps on the journey you can tell me what happened to the reinforcements that were supposed to meet me in the southern forest.'

'Indeed,' Llauron agreed, taking hold of her elbow as they followed the crowd of guests. 'I will be certain to tell you the whole story.'

48

Ashe struggled to breathe steadily, his wounds stinging his skin and lungs. It was not too much farther to the room in the abandoned cistern, and he prayed Rhapsody would remember this place as a meeting spot. He had sought her at the wedding hall and at the basilica in Bethany, but she was not there. Perhaps she had forgotten their arrangement to meet clandestinely at the wedding; it would be more than he could stand if she had.

The demon's minions had been townspeople, blacksmiths and carters, not soldiers, an especially difficult group to fight, as he did not want to kill innocent civilians. Despite this, they had fought fiercely at the bridge over the Phon, as intent on crossing as he had been on holding it. He had prevailed, but at great cost.

He opened the door wearily and smiled. She was there, nestled in the old chair with the threadbare arms, still in her wedding finery. Her dress was the color of smoky amethysts, and it was bunched around her as she slept, her golden hair swept up in a swirl atop her head, just beginning to come down.

One of her slippers had fallen off and lay on the floor below her tiny bare foot. At her throat was a jeweled choker; a large amethyst, the same color as her dress, surrounded by tiny pearls, was held in place by three strings of the same milky-white jewels. In her lap rested a pair of earrings and two crumpled gloves.

He stood and stared at her for a moment, drinking in the sight of her, and was overwhelmed with longing and emptiness as he had not been since before she had come into his life.

And then the pain was gone as the realization finally caught up with him that she was really here, waiting for him. He hurried to her and lifted her carefully out of the chair, holding her tightly to his chest as his lips brushed her hair and face. He breathed in her scent, reveling in her sweetness, her softness, as she stirred in his arms and awoke, smiling.

'I missed you,' she said, her eyes beaming at him in the way that always touched his soul. 'Did you get waylaid?'

He carried her to the bed and set her down. She could see that it cost him some effort where normally it did not.

'Ashe?' she said, concern sweeping over her face. 'What's the matter – are you hurt?'

'It's nothing,' he said, sitting down beside her and taking her back into his arms. But her eyes darkened with worry and she ran her hands over his chest, looking for signs of injury. She gently pulled his shirt open and gasped in horror at the slash-wounds and bruises, now beginning to heal.

'What happened?' she asked in alarm, removing his shirt completely and pulling out of his embrace to examine him more closely.

'Rhapsody, please, don't pull away,' he said, trying not to grimace. 'I need to hold you – I'm all right. Just hold me in return – please.'

Carefully she wrapped her arms around him, trying not to touch the wounded places. 'I hope you're not going to make a habit of this,' she said, a humorous note in her voice. 'I really do have better things to do than to be constantly fixing your sore chest.'

His answer was a long, deep sigh, and he rested his head on her shoulder, overwhelmingly glad to be back in her arms. She stroked his hair and began to hum a wordless tune that chased his headache away and made the throbbing irritation of his wounds recede. Her hands gently rubbed the muscles at the base of his neck and the top of his shoulders, bringing comfort and ease to his body and soul.

How much time passed he was not sure, but when he woke he was lying on the bed with his head in her lap and she was still singing softly to him, in words he understood only intermittently. He made a half-turn onto his back and looked up at her, smiling down at him, inverted above him, and noted that she was every bit as beautiful upside down as she was straight on. Her hair was now straining against its bonds and threatening to fall about her shoulders at any moment.

Never one to take a threat lightly, Ashe reached up and carefully pulled the jeweled clip from the back of her head, smiling as the long waves of golden silk tumbled from above her neck and down her front to below her waist. He blinked in astonishment; the move to unbind her hair had been both pain-free and effortless, as though his injuries had never happened. In addition, the exquisite locks he was so fond of and had been so intimately acquainted with were vastly longer than they had been only a few months before, when last he had seen her. Had she been standing, they would have brushed the back of her knees.

'What's this?' he asked, holding a long strand in his hand, puzzled.

'I believe in your language it is generally called "hair,"' Rhapsody replied, mischief in her eyes. 'Do you need any additional information, like where you are, what year this is; your true name perhaps? I can answer the first two questions, but I don't have enough time to get into the third; it's longer by itself than most twelve-verse folktales.'

Ashe sat up and faced her, his dragon senses wandering over her. He could feel the remnant of pain in her torso, like a series of wounds that were almost healed. He took hold of her bodice in a panic and pulled it down, shock crossing his face as he saw his own injuries mirrored on her body, faded to a pale pink as though they were just about to disappear.

'Gods, Rhapsody! What have you done?' he demanded, his voice choked with panic. Rhapsody glared at him and pushed his hands away, pulling the stiff taffeta back over her camisole.

'*Excuse* me,' she said, annoyance in her tone. 'You could at least send flowers first. What kind of girl do you think I am?'

'A reckless one, at least,' he answered, touching the rim of the wound that peeked over her low neckline. 'How did you do this?'

'It's a new little trick I learned a while back,' she replied, slapping his fingers away again. 'Keep your hands to yourself.'

'A new little trick? Empathetic healing?'

'Useful, isn't it?'

'You're insane,' he said, calming a little as he determined she was not seriously compromised by the technique. 'You had no idea how those wounds were inflicted, or how serious they were.'

'No,' she admitted, rising from the bed and brushing out her skirt, her hair cascading down behind her. 'But it didn't matter. Do you feel better?'

Ashe stood and followed her, taking her by the shoulders and turning her to face him. He looked down at his wife, a wife who thought of him only as a past lover, and a wave of tenderness crested inside him. She was putting him first, as she always did, unselfishly and at her own expense. He bent to kiss her but she backed away and turned from him again, crossing to his chair and picking up her scattered belongings.

'I do now,' he said encouragingly, hoping to bring her back. 'Gods, Rhapsody, the memory of you is marvelous, but it doesn't do justice to the reality. What happened to your hair?'

'It grew,' she said simply, folding the gloves and putting the earrings on his bureau. 'I'll tell you about it later. How did you get hurt?'

'I ran into a group of Bethanian villagers, demonic thralls, on their way to the wedding, planning to ambush some of the guests, and thought it might be a good idea if they had a last-minute change of plans,' he answered, unconsciously rubbing his shoulder. 'By sheer coincidence, the Phon River spilled over its banks, sinking them up to their waists in mud. I wish I had thought to use the power of Kirsdarke before they beat the stuffing out of me. I assume if their command was to disrupt the wedding that they will be released from the thrall of the F'dor now that it is over. By the way, how was the wedding?'

She was putting on her shoes, and his question made her excited; she swayed in the heels and almost toppled over, like a baby learning to walk.

'Oh, it was beautiful,' she said, her face glowing. 'So many candles and such lovely music; and they looked so handsome, the bridal party. And the ballroom was filled with the most exquisite clothing I've ever seen in one place before. It was very different from any wedding I've been to. I'm sad that you weren't there; I think you would have enjoyed it.'

'I'm certain I would have,' he said, watching the memory dance through her eyes and make them sparkle like sunlight on water.

'The wedding gown must have weighed an earthsweight; it had a train that was a league long, long enough to still be following her down the aisle of the basilica when she was already at the Altar of Fire. I have to admit, I would never want anything like that. I'll bet her back hurts tomorrow.' She chuckled wickedly at her naughty subtext. 'Anyway, I'm sorry you missed it. She really was the most beautiful bride you ever would have seen.'

Ashe smiled with her, feeling her joy innately. 'No, I don't think so,' he said tenderly, recalling her in another moment of which she had no memory.

She went to the closet and pulled out a covered wicker basket. 'Are you hungry? I thought you might like some supper.'

Ashe considered her question. 'Yes,' he said, 'I suppose I am.'

'Well, by all means, help yourself,' she said, pulling the cover off the basket and offering it to him. 'There's some cold ham and fruit, and a bottle of Achmed's best vintage – no nasty comments, please; it's actually not bad.'

'I would never be so ungrateful as to insult anything you brought me,' he answered, taking the basket from her and setting it on the small table in the corner. 'How about you? What would you like?'

'Just wine and a little bread, please,' Rhapsody answered, settling in his worn chair again. 'I ate an embarrassing amount at the wedding.'

'Now, that is something I would like to have seen.' He set about arranging their meal, handing her a glass of wine with a proper military bow. 'How are you feeling? Are the wounds gone yet?'

Rhapsody peeked inside her bodice. 'All gone.'

'Prove it,' Ashe said playfully.

She smiled at him but did not comply; instead, she took a deep draught of wine. He returned his attention to the basket, knowing the distance she was keeping was due to her belief that they had put an end to their relationship as lovers, and he silently cursed his father and grandmother once more for it.

'So, what made your hair grow so fast?' he asked, sitting on the bed with his plate of food.

Rhapsody took another sip, then lowered the goblet. 'It didn't grow fast, actually,' she said, her eyes darkening. 'I'll tell you about it, but it has to do with another matter I need to discuss with you. I don't know if that will be a conversation that you will like, so if you want to have a few more moments' peace, perhaps we should wait to talk about it. After we're done, I have to be going. I am going for a walk with your father in the morning.'

Ashe's stomach turned. 'Tomorrow? You're going with him tomorrow?'

'Yes,' she replied. 'Llauron and I met up at the wedding. We're taking a walk along the Cymrian Trail, the places that the First Fleet Cymrians stopped after they first landed. It should be interesting.'

Ashe's appetite disappeared. 'It's too soon,' he said, putting his half-full plate back on the table. 'You really are in no condition to go overland with Llauron now, Rhapsody. You just lost Jo a little while ago. You're grieving, and you were seriously injured. You should spend sometime in Elysian, healing.'

Rhapsody smiled as she ran her finger around the rim of her wineglass. A soft, ringing musical note sounded, and she sang along, matching it wordlessly, sending it around the room like a servant doing her bidding. It dissipated after a moment, and she swallowed the rest of the wine, depositing the glass next to his.

'I have healed from that, Ashe,' she said gently, looking him in the eyes. 'It's been about seven years for me now since that time.'

'What are you saying?' Ashe asked, his face losing color. 'Where have you been, Rhapsody?'

She rose and came to the bed, sitting down beside him. 'I went to see the Lord and Lady Rowan,' she said, keeping contact with his gaze. 'As you know, time passes there much differently from here; that's why my hair is so long. While I was there I saw Jo – a few times, actually, and mostly when sleeping under the eye of the Lady. She's happy now, Ashe, and she forgives me. I don't feel pain about her anymore, though I do still miss her. I believe I'll be with her again one day; the Lord Rowan promised me he would take me if he could.'

Ashe fought the urge to vomit. 'You went to the Rowans, and you could find them? Gods, Aria, I had no idea you were so ill and in such pain about Jo. The Rowans don't generally accept guests unless it's a matter of life and death.'

'I know,' she said, breaking their locked gaze and looking away. 'But I didn't go there because of Jo, or for an illness of my own. I went for another reason. Before I tell you about it, though, do you still believe in me? I mean, do you trust that I would not lie to you?'

'Absolutely.'

'I'm glad,' she said, looking at him again. 'Then please believe me when I tell you this situation is resolved, and everything is going to be fine.'

Ashe was beginning to tremble. 'Rhapsody, you're frightening me. What are you talking about? Just tell me, before my heart stops.'

Rhapsody took his hands, and a breath, and then began. 'I have ten new grandchildren,' she said, her eyes glistening. 'They are of all different races, and ages, including a Lirin child I delivered myself. Her mother died in childbirth.' She waited for him to absorb what she had said.

The look on Ashe's face went from one of dread to one of relief. 'Childbirth? The mother died, but the child lived? Like Manwyn's prophecy?'

'Yes.'

Ashe felt himself begin to breathe regularly again. 'I am very sorry to hear that,' he said, caressing her cheek absently.

'Don't get comfortable, Ashe. This is not the bad part.'

'What, then?'

Rhapsody lowered her eyes. 'These children all have the same father. They are all the children of the F'dor.'

Ashe listened, not comprehending. After a moment his understanding was no clearer. 'That's impossible. The prophecy said that the demon could not inhabit the body of someone who had borne or sired children, nor could it do so itself.'

Rhapsody sighed, then plunged ahead. 'These are the children of rape, Ashe. The F'dor impregnated their mothers by proxy through the Rakshas. The Rakshas's blood was his, and so its issue is his as well. It found a way to get around the prophecy.'

Ashe stared at her for a moment more. Rhapsody could feel a humming beginning; it was a vibration that frightened her, lodged within the fabric of the room and air around them, and she knew the dragon was coming forth. She put her hands on his shoulders and tried to make him look into her eyes.

'Listen to me, Gwydion ap Llauron,' she commanded, using her powers as a Namer. The humming stopped increasing but remained, hovering in the air as the color roared back into his face and his eyes began to glow. 'This may seem awful now, but it is actually a very positive thing. The children have immortal souls, every one of them, because the Rakshas carried a bit of yours. If not for you they would have been demonic. But because of you, they have contributed to the destruction of the F'dor by having what is demonic separated from their blood, giving Achmed a tool to find the demon.'

Her words rang in his soul, at the very deepest, darkest part, that had one time been the power source that the icy form of the Rakshas had taken shape around. The memories of the incidents that generated this abomination flooded back, a series of assaults so brutal that at first they seemed as if they could only also be murders. Each atrocity flooded into his mind simultaneously, filling his head with screaming and the sound of his own insane laughter. Ashe felt the horror of it as if he were witnessing each of the acts again. He broke loose her grip on his hands and screamed himself, a roar like an earthquake issuing forth. Small items blew off the dresser and nightstand, and the basket flew off the table, spilling its contents across the room.

As the room began to shake beneath and around them, Rhapsody threw her arms around his neck and held on to him as tightly as she could. Waves of power and pain were visible now, swirling red and angry about them. She clung to him, fearing she would lose him in the vortex that was opening above them. He clawed at her, trying to shake her loose, but in his grief and fury he only succeeded in scratching her face.

Rhapsody looked over their heads into the spinning darkness and shivered. It was coming closer, threatening to swallow them together into oblivion. She tried to make contact with his eyes again.

'Gwydion! Gwydion ap Llauron, listen to me.' Her voice was calm and strong, made ringing by the ancient power of the music in her soul. 'Let it go. Let it go.'

He looked into her eyes, the vertical slits of his pupils thin as a whisper. There was a moment that he would be held in thrall by his name, and then she would lose him to his anguish again. Rhapsody concentrated on maintaining the vibration, forcing him to listen a moment more.

'I love you,' she said, using the powers of true speaking. 'I love you from my soul, Gwydion ap Llauron. I would not lie to you, and I tell you truly that, as much as this causes you pain, it is as it should be; good will come from this. Please, please believe me.'

Ashe did not break her gaze, but his face grew reptilian, and he began to shake from the core of his being. Rhapsody knew that the dragon was rampant, and furious, but what motivated it was beyond her understanding. She could feel him slipping from her, and she tightened her grip on him to try and stop it from happening.

It was a mistake. A bellowing shriek came forth from his mouth, open in fury, and with a strength she had never witnessed he pried her off him. He twisted away from her, turning violently, trying to pull away. The force of his attempted escape sent Rhapsody spinning across the room into the wall. She sailed through the air with a tremendous force and hit the wall hard with a sickening thud, crumpling to the floor. As she lost consciousness she cursed her stupidity, praying that he would not rampage and lay waste to the land.

The shock of her impact caused Ashe to stop for a moment, and as he witnessed what he had done, the uproar stopped. The dragon, now in control, grew alarmed to see its treasure lying limp on the floor, not responding. The human soul within him panicked and fought its way back to dominance, running to her and gathering her in his arms, shaking with fear.

The swirling power that had been rending the room a moment before shattered like a snowflake and shimmered to the ground around them as he laid her on the bed, his hands trembling in worry. He went to the pitcher on the bedside table and drew forth water which he splashed her face with, but there was no response.

He stayed beside her, growing more and more anxious, stroking her face and pleading with her to wake. Finally, after what seemed like hours, she groaned and winced.

'Rhapsody? Rhapsody, please say something. Please.'

One eye opened slightly and regarded him woozily.

'Is your temper tantrum over?' she asked, her face contorted with pain.

Ashe burst into tears that until now he had been too frightened to shed. He bent his head over her and wept, burying his face in her abdomen.

Rhapsody patted his head with a disoriented hand. 'Ashe,' she said gently, but with effort. 'Please stop it. I'm all right, and I understand – it's not your fault. Besides, you're making my headache worse and spotting my gown.'

'I'm sorry; gods, I'm so sorry—'

'Don't,' she answered, her voice a little stronger. 'Please don't. It isn't necessary. I knew it could happen – it was too much for you to take. I was prepared for it. But I expected you to lash out; I didn't think you would knock me into the wall trying to keep from hurting me. A tactical error. It was my mistake for grabbing on just then.'

'Your mistake?' he asked incredulously. 'How in the name of all—'

'Ashe,' Rhapsody said, sounding annoyed. 'Please, can we not have this conversation? For my sake. Please. I'm going to be fine in a moment. That's why I had the wine. I expected this reaction. I know you didn't mean to hurt me. Can we please drop it now? I don't want our last few moments together to be spent like this. Here, help me up.'

Carefully he slid his hands around her waist, assisting her to stand and sensing the damage he had caused her. She was bruised but nothing was broken, and she had pain in her shoulder but no bleeding.

She limped to the chair and reached for the pitcher next to the bed, which he quickly got and gave to her. After splashing water on her face and drying it with the cloth he handed her, she sat down, reached out her hand to him, and pulled him over to her. He knelt on the floor in front of her to be on eye level with her, his face still twisted with anxiety.

'I'm really fine,' she assured him, patting the side of his face. 'What I am trying to tell you is that the children are all fine, too. They are with Oelendra, and when the F'dor is dead I will go and retrieve them. They will be loved and cared for, a far better future than the one they faced before.'

'And their mothers? What happened to the women?'

Rhapsody took his head in her hands and kissed the top of it. 'Their mothers are all at peace,' she said, trying not to upset him again but unwilling to lie to him. 'Aria – that's the baby – her mother got to hold her before she passed, and I know she left for the light happy.'

'You named her Aria?' His face softened, and she could see he was touched.

'Well, it's such a beautiful thing to be called,' she said, smiling slightly. 'It's a wonderful old name that is lost to this world if no one uses it, and that would be a shame, don't you think?'

281

Ashe's eyes filled with tears again. 'Yes. Yes, I do.'

'And if you're wondering why I can forgive you for hurting me, you can find the answer in what you said a moment ago. You know I'm no willing victim, Ashe. You've tasted my anger and my fist before. But the reason you went raging on me was that you were overcome with the thought of the pain you witnessed, and you feel that you participated in, maybe even caused. I felt that pain too, even though, unlike you, I wasn't there to see it. It was horrific to a level that could not be borne and remain sane.

'You are a good man, Ashe. You have nothing to make up for, because you didn't do anything wrong. You were a victim too, in case you've forgotten. Yet you still feel responsible, even though you're not. You will make a wonderful Lord Cymrian because you will be the first one with a conscience, and certainly the first one who is willing to listen to his heart. Remember that old Lirin saying? *Ryle hira*. Life is what it is. We can only do the best we can to make it better; these children are part of the way to do that. So please, trust me. The situation is well in hand. Now, go. Be happy. Do what you need to do.'

He looked at her with an expression that broke her heart. 'I don't deserve you; I really don't.'

She laughed. 'I know, but you are stuck with me, my friend.' She rose slowly and walked to the dresser, gathered her belongings, and took her cloak from the peg by the door. From the closet she pulled a pair of boots and she put them on, tucking the satiny shoes into her pockets. She went to the door and began to open it, when he spoke.

'Rhapsody?'

She turned to see him one last time. 'Yes?'

His voice was so low she could barely hear him. 'Do you love me still? Even after all that time with the Rowans?'

She met his gaze, her eyes glimmering, shining like the depths of the sea. 'Always.'

He sighed, and a smile crept over his face again. 'Then everything else will resolve itself.'

'It always does,' she answered simply. 'Can you tell if it's snowing? Maybe I should put on something warmer.'

He turned and went to the window, looking into the clear night sky studded with stars. 'No, I don't think it—'

When he turned to her again, she was gone. She had tried to spare him the pain of watching her go; in her last gesture, she was still thinking of him.

He closed his eyes and waited until the last subtle vibration of the closed door had died away. Then he looked out the window at the night sky again.

'Goodbye, Emily,' he said.

49

Seeing the landmarks on the Cymrian Trail with Llauron was like seeing them for the first time. That they were on horseback this time was part of the difference; Llauron had loaned her a dappled gray gelding, keeping his prized white Madarian for himself. Rhapsody had smiled when she saw the elderly man mount; Anwyn's sons appreciated fine horseflesh. Anborn's black charger was among the most beautiful she had ever seen. Llauron's steed was almost as impressive.

They had gone first to check on the House of Remembrance, finding it in ruins, nothing but the shell of the frame remaining. Rhapsody's heart had constricted when she saw it. She thought of the marvelous library, and the significance of the outpost historically, that had caused her to take the time to extinguish the fire that had ignited in battle when they first visited the House. The raging fireball that had destroyed the demon-vine which had invaded Ylorc in search of the Earthchild had destroyed the House of Remembrance as well. At least the grisly scene of sacrificial horror had been purged, leaving nothing but blackened timber and ash.

She looked with concern at Llauron, whose family heritage had been so much a part of the outpost, but the old gentleman seemed quite calm. He crouched down and ran a hand through a nearby pile of gray cinders and black ash which contained the scorched remnants of what had once been leather book bindings, sifting the debris through his fingers. After a moment's reflection he looked up at her and smiled slightly.

'Pity, isn't it? It was once such a marvelous museum.' Llauron tossed the ashes back to the ground and stood, wiping his hands on his gray robes. 'Ah, well, now that the next Cymrian Age is in the offing, we will need to build new outposts, new museums, won't we, my dear?'

Rhapsody smiled at him. 'I suppose.'

Llauron's face grew serious as they traversed the charred cobblestones lining the remains of the courtyard to its center, where the tall sapling of Sagia, the Oak of Deep Roots on Serendair, still grew, healthy and vibrant among the destruction. 'You know, Rhapsody, it is within your grasp to leave this land as great a bequest as ever has been given it. That's a tremendous opportunity for a peasant of common birth; it is the chance to affect history as none but the Lords of the Cymrians themselves did.'

Rhapsody swallowed the sarcastic comment that rose to her lips. 'And what opportunity would that be, Llauron?'

The ever-present twinkle in Llauron's blue eyes disappeared. 'Protect the tree.'

Rhapsody glanced at the young Sagian oak, remembering how diseased and dead it looked when she had first beheld it so long ago. Llauron himself had given her the salve which she had used to bring about its healing, anointing its polluted roots and protecting it with a song of healing. Its gleaming branches now towered above her head, white wooden arms outstretched to the clear winter sky, laden with bright blossoms. She smiled and pointed to the small shepherd's harp that was nestled in the lowest crotch of the trunk, playing its repetitive roundelay. 'I believe I already have,' she said.

The Invoker's smile returned. 'I'm sorry, my dear, I misspoke. Of course you have cast your mantle of protection on this tree. It was the Great White Tree to which I referred.'

She shook her head in surprise. 'The Great White Tree?'

'Yes.'

A sudden blast of winter wind blew through, rippling her cloak and making her arms shudder with the chill. 'I don't understand, Llauron. Do you not protect the Tree yourself, as Invoker?'

'I do.' The old gentleman's voice grew soft and deepened, as it had back in the days when he was instructing her in history or woods lore. 'And I will continue to do so until the end of my days. But it seems to me, my dear, that your ministrations have been able to impart a special protection to this young sapling that even the Great White Tree does not enjoy – a protection from the ravages of fire.'

He smiled as he stretched out an arm in a panoramic sweep. 'Look about you. Centuries of history, both building and contents, reduced to nothing more than soot and embers in a matter of moments – and yet the tree still stands, unblemished, not even a scorch mark or stain. Quite remarkable, really, and quite unprecedented. In the various conflicts of the Cymrian War, and in many terrible thunderstorms over the years, the Great White Tree has been greatly damaged, once almost burned to its destruction in the Battle of the Outer Circle. Even I, as its sworn guardian, cannot protect it thus.' His eyes glittered.

'But you, my dear, you seem to be able to rebuke fire itself, to deny it claim on those things which you protect – that you love. I have watched you for a long time, Rhapsody, watched as fire responded to your every move. I've seen how it leaps to greet you when you pass, settles into a low, steady burn at your command. It is a great gift, and doubtless it rests in the best of hands. Now, I ask only for one boon, as your old mentor – that you grant this protection to the holiest entity on the continent: the Tree itself. It is the marker of the last of the five places where Time began – what could be more important?'

'Llauron—'

'Rhapsody, you do remember the legends of the Island of Serendair that I told you when you studied with me, do you not?'

Her throat went dry. 'Yes.'

'That was once a place of deep magic, Rhapsody, the homeland of many enchanted beings, a place where ancient power was heavy in the air. The world now is a much more ordinary place since the Island's death – do you know why?'

Rhapsody had her own reasons, but merely shook her head.

'It was the loss of the Tree, my dear, the great Oak of Deep Roots, Sagia.

284

Sagia's death took with it much of the magic of the world. Each of the great trees – there were five of them, legend has it – grew at one of the five birthplaces of Time, where one of the five elements had its beginning. Sagia grew at the place where ether was born, where starlight first touched the Earth. Ether was the first of all the elements to be born, and its magic was the strongest. Sagia sank beneath the waves when Serendair was destroyed. The loss the world suffered when the Island was consumed in the fire of the Sleeping Child is incalculable.' Llauron began to wheeze suddenly, then erupted into a fit of hacking coughs. Rhapsody put her hand out to him, but he waved her away, intent on his tale.

'The Great White Oak grows at the last of the birthplaces of Time, where the element of earth was born; it protects the Earth, keeping *its* magic alive. Imagine what kind of place the world would be if we were to lose it, too? Surely life would become so colorless, so meaningless, that it would scarcely be worth living. You, of all people, a Canwr, a *Namer*, would hardly wish to see anything so disastrous come about, would you?'

Rhapsody hid a smile at the dramatic ending of Llauron's discourse. 'No, of course not.'

'Excellent. Now, my dear, favor me thus, please. Promise me that upon our return to my keep in Gwynwood you will work whatever charm you did upon this young sapling on the Great White Tree as well. As a gift to your humble admirer.'

Rhapsody swallowed but said nothing. The fire that had destroyed the House of Remembrance had been, in a way, her doing; it was the means she and the Bolg had utilized to destroy the demon-vine that once grew from the sapling's roots. It could have destroyed the tree as well; she was not certain what had prevented it. Still, Llauron seemed so intent, desperate even, to obtain similar protection for the holy oak he guarded that it seemed little enough to promise.

'All right, I will try,' she said, smiling and adjusting the Invoker's cloak where it had fallen from his shoulder. 'You, in return, must endeavor to be more careful with your health, Llauron. Leaving your neck exposed to the elements like this is tempting frostbite, and you could take cold.'

'Let us strike a bargain, then,' Llauron said merrily. 'I shall put on my hat and gloves, and keep my neck well swathed, if you agree to work whatever rite of protection on the Great White Tree that you did on this young sapling to spare it from the destruction of fire. Then the scales will be balanced. Agreed?' He put out his hand.

Rhapsody looked at him strangely. The expression of scales balancing was one she had primarily heard used in Sorbold; perhaps it had farther-reaching influence that she had realized. In the back of her mind she heard the terrifying chant begin again, low and thunderous: *Tovvrik, Tovvrik, Tovvrik*. She shuddered involuntarily and looked up into Llauron's expectant face; there was something about the way his eyes glinted in the winter light that unsettled her, but his request seemed reasonable enough. She pondered a moment longer, then took his hand and shook it.

'Agreed. However, I had not planned to return to the Circle with you, Llauron,' she said. 'I really need to be heading back to Ylorc soon. But I believe I might be able to do it from here, through the roots of the sapling. They intertwine with those of the Great White Tree, or so Grunthor said.'

'How wonderful,' Llauron said. He walked briskly to the horse and opened the left-flank saddlebag, removing from its depths a pair of gloves, a hat, and a scarf, all made of soft, undyed wool.

Rhapsody glanced around at the ruin of the House of Remembrance, trying to dispel the deep chill that had settled on her like snowfall. She waited until Llauron returned, more warmly dressed, then went to the foot of the sapling.

'Do you know the Great White Tree's true name?' she asked.

Llauron looked down into her face. He watched her seriously for a moment, then shook his head.

'I'm afraid not,' he said reluctantly. 'Will that prevent you from working your magic on the Tree?'

Rhapsody exhaled. 'I don't know. I don't think so – I know a few of the names that the Filids and the Lirin call it – but it would be better to know its true name.'

'Alas,' Llauron said. 'I suppose we will just have to make do, then. Go ahead, my dear. I'll try to be as quiet as possible.'

She stared up into its smooth white branches, dancing in the winter breeze, the bright blossoms rustling under the clear sky, then closed her eyes and listened to the song of the wind singing harmony with the tree's own melody. It was the same sound she had heard within the Earth as she and the two Bolg traveled along the roots of Sagia, this tree's mother, a rich sound, full of wisdom and power, a melody that moved slowly, changing tones infinitesimally, unhurried by the need to keep pace with anything, though younger, brighter, than it had been below ground, blending with the music of the sky that surrounded it.

Gently she rested her hand on the sapling's trunk, then attuned herself to the pitch and began to sing, calling to each of the primordial elements save for the one from which she wished to protect the tree, knowing that those elements held the power of all magic within them.

> Green Earth below thy roots, guard thee
> Wide Sky above thy branches, shelter thee
> Cool wind buffer thee, Rain fall down upon thee,
> Fire shall not harm thee.

After a few moments Rhapsody could feel the song moving through the young tree's trunk and out through its branches, down to the very blossoms that graced its twigs. Like sap she sensed it traveling through the tree and into the ground along its roots. Slowly she chanted some of the names she had heard the Filids call the Great White Tree, hoping to direct the song to it.

> Signpost of the Beginning, live
> Mother of the Forest, flourish
> Temple of Songbirds, sustain,
> Fire shall not harm thee.

An infinitesimal harmony began to emanate from the sapling, joined a moment later by a deep, rich counterpunto that could only be the voice of the Great White Tree singing in response. It was a silver sound that sent a thrill through her blood, bringing with it memories of long ago, in a land long lost to Time, when she had first heard the voice of the great tree's Root Twin, Sagia, the tree that had sheltered her and her two companions from danger, had given them passage here, to safety and life in this new land. She moved into the last verse, calling forth characteristics of fire that would touch but not bring harm to the tree.

> Light of early spring, illuminate thee,
> Heat of summer sun, warm thee,
> Leaves of flaming color, bejewel thee,
> But fire shall not harm thee.

The harmonic surged, blending into the song of healing she had left playing on the harp a year before. Rhapsody smiled, satisfied, and turned to Llauron, who was watching her with great interest.

'That's the best I can do, I'm afraid. I don't know if it will work.'

Llauron smiled warmly in return. 'I'm sure it will. And I do appreciate your efforts, my dear. Thank you.'

Rhapsody nodded and pulled up her hood. 'You're welcome. Now, let's be on our way. We still have a long ride and much work ahead of us.'

They walked along the original trail, leading their horses through the wood, stopping to observe markers that had been overgrown with weeds, buried in snow and all but forgotten by time. Rhapsody had brought the dragon-claw dagger with her; she only employed it now to till the earth, trying to make positive use of it. The memory of its part in Jo's last moments was too strong to carry it as a weapon ever again.

Carefully she stripped away the frozen weeds and thorns that obscured the various commemorative plaques and stones, noting the growing warmth of Llauron's smile as she did so. She sang a song of tending at each place, calling to the windflowers that still slept, dormant beneath the snow, in the hope that the spring would bring a new beauty to the place. The trail held little significance to her; she had not known the Cymrians, and felt them to be a strange and troubled people, from what little she did know, but it meant a great deal to Llauron to see her honoring their history, so she refrained from making the suggestion that nagged in the back of her mind that they turn back.

They crossed over the unmarked border back into Navarne, where many of the landmarks were hidden by excessive growth and neglect. 'You know, I'm somewhat surprised that Lord Stephen isn't tending to these markers better,' Rhapsody said, rising and repacking her dagger after tending to the third site in Navarne. 'He's the Cymrian historian, after all.'

'This is a difficult era to be an Orlandan lord of Cymrian heritage,' Llauron replied, bending over and peering at the marker. 'The royalty of the lineage is recognized, but there is still the taint left over from the war and the crimes of Anwyn and Gwylliam. Stephen's actions represent in a way the attitude of many later-generation Cymrians: it's acceptable to keep a small museum in your own castle, but the outer signs of the Cymrian ancestry fall by the wayside. Ah, well, that will all change soon, won't it, my dear? Gwydion will give us all reason to be proud of our heritage again.'

Rhapsody smiled as they mounted the horses. 'Yes, I'm sure he will.'

Within their hiding place in the copse of trees to the south, Lark gestured the others into silence, then listened to the sound of the hoofbeats as they waned.

When she could no longer hear the sound of Llauron's Madarian, she turned to the others, renegade Filids all, and nodded.

'Are you ready, Mother?'

Lark nodded again.

'All right, then,' said Khaddyr, nervously fingering the belt of his robe. 'Don't follow too closely – we need him to be exhausted from his travels; understood?' The nods of silent assent brought a smile to his face. 'Good. Let's be off.'

50

The section of the trail in the northwestern region of Navarne outside of Gwynwood took three days to complete, much of it through rough terrain. Rhapsody could see that the journey had been difficult on Llauron; he had not slept well by the fire at night, and seemed especially susceptible to the cold. A slight cough had settled into his chest, and though she had given him such herbs and tonics as she had with her, it seemed to do little to help. Each of the nights on the trail she had sung him a song of healing, and he seemed to improve a little, only to slip back into consumptive coughing again when the sun rose. Finally she put her foot down.

'Llauron, this is insane. This is making you ill. We have to go back now. I will come back in the spring and tend to the entire set of markers on the trail; it will have to be redone then anyway.'

'There are only three more in this part of Navarne, my dear, and they are really quite close. Why don't we see if we can get them finished by noon, and then we can drop in on Stephen. His keep is an easy ride from here, and I'm sure he would love to see you.'

Rhapsody considered, and decided that was probably wisest. Llauron was too exhausted to make it back to Gwynwood at a reasonable speed anyway, and Lord Stephen would no doubt see to his health and make him comfortable within Haguefort, his castle of rosy-brown stone.

'All right,' she agreed, kissing his cheek. 'But don't try and talk me into any more on the way. Three, and that's all. I don't want to risk getting caught in another storm, like the poor rangers you sent to help me in Sorbold. I don't want you adding to theirs on my conscience.'

'Agreed,' said the elderly gentleman, his eyes twinkling in the morning light.

They were in the process of restoring a stone marker listing the names of the first settlers of western Navarne when Rhapsody felt a chill come to the clearing. Llauron had been standing behind her, watching above her as she dug around the stone, clearing the brambles from its base. When she turned she saw Khaddyr come into view behind him. Rhapsody rose, standing with the Invoker, as four men and a woman came into the clearing behind Llauron's chief advisor. She glanced quickly at Llauron. The woman was Lark, Llauron's own herbalist and one of his chief priests, with whom Rhapsody had studied.

The old man's brows drew together.

'Khaddyr. I thought you were attending to the preparations for the vernal equinox.'

Khaddyr nodded as the priests closed ranks around him. 'I am, Your Grace. I mean to see that it is celebrated under the leadership of a new Invoker.'

Rhapsody's stomach froze like the ground beneath her boots. 'What is that supposed to mean?'

'It means he is enacting an ancient ritual of passage, my dear,' said Llauron calmly. 'He is challenging me under the law of Buda Kai.'

Rhapsody's hand moved unconsciously to the hilt of Daystar Clarion. Buda Kai was the Filidic fight for dominance, a rite not practiced in the time since the Cymrian War. Llauron himself had not ascended by means of it, nor had his predecessor. Khaddyr himself had told her as much when he was her tutor. The victor would be recognized as the Invoker. It was a fight to the death.

'Don't be ridiculous,' she said to Khaddyr. 'You yourself said it was a barbaric and outdated ritual that no one practiced anymore.'

Khaddyr smiled, and Rhapsody shivered involuntarily. There was a cruelty in his eyes behind his cultured voice, a hard and unyielding glint.

'Then I see we are both of the same mind. You are restoring monuments to the faded glory of a dishonored people, while I am invoking an ancient rite for purposes of returning honor to a religious sect led by a crumbling bastion of the same line. How ironic. Lark will stand as my second. It appears Llauron has no alternative but you. I am sorry you have to witness this, my dear. I would have spared you if I could.'

'Oh, no, Khaddyr, I wouldn't have it any other way,' Rhapsody said, fury seething in her voice. 'This way I can stand in for him. You'll have to fight me first.'

'Excuse us for a moment, please,' Llauron said to Khaddyr, who nodded. He took Rhapsody by the arm and led her twenty feet away behind a stand of birch trees.

'Rhapsody, I'm sorry this is happening now, when we were just getting to spend sometime together again. I'm afraid I must tend to this. The challenge must be met.'

'This is absurd,' Rhapsody said, glaring over her shoulder at Khaddyr and his second. 'Imbeciles. Well, name me your champion and I'll wipe that smug smile off his face. It will give me the opportunity to repay him for groping me when he first brought me to you.'

Llauron's hands were gentle as he took her shoulders and smiled down into her face. 'No, my dear, I'm not going to do that. I appreciate the offer, of course.'

Rhapsody was astonished. 'What do you mean? Is someone else coming? Is Ashe nearby? Anborn?'

'No, I'm afraid not. This is a battle I will have to fight alone. Part of the office, you know.'

Rhapsody's voice was gentle, but the overlay of concern was obvious. 'Llauron, that's ridiculous. Your strength is in your mind, in your wisdom, not your body. Besides, it's my job to champion just such causes as these; that's why I have the sword, remember? Please, just go tell Khaddyr that I will fight him, or Lark. I hope it's the bastard himself, I have a debt to him I am looking forward to repaying with interest.'

'Rhapsody, listen to me,' Llauron said, his voice a little more commanding. 'You will not be named champion. You don't understand the intricacies of my office. This is a battle I have to fight alone. I need you to do something for me, though.'

'Name it, Llauron.'

'I need you to be my witness; to act as herald when this is over. Whatever you see you must report accurately. The fate of the Filidic order depends on it. As a Namer, you guarantee the truth will be told.'

'Of course, but—'

'And I want you to swear a holy oath on your sword that you will not intervene here; that, no matter what happens, you remain out of the fight.'

'Are you out of your mind?' Rhapsody snapped before she had time to temper her words or her anger. 'Llauron, this is what I've trained for, what you wanted me to do. This whole idea is insane; you're exhausted and ill. Please, either walk away from this, or let me handle it.'

'Rhapsody, time grows short. Listen to me; either you will forswear intervention, and act as my witness, or I shall be forced to ban you from the fight. My lore here is stronger than yours, my dear. I can exile you to outside this forest, and then you condemn me to face this alone, without a herald, without a friend. I hardly think that is something you would abandon me to, is it, Rhapsody? Would you, a Namer, a Lirin Singer, deny me a friend in the face of death?'

Rhapsody began to tremble. 'No.'

'I thought not.' Llauron's face and voice grew gentle again. 'I appreciate your selfless intentions, my dear. But this is an act that is foreordained; you can't be part of it. You would dishonor everything I hold holy if you break your oath and participate in any way. Do you understand?'

She lowered her eyes as they filled with tears. 'Yes.'

'Good, good. All right then; we will accept the challenge.'

Rhapsody tried one last time. 'At least tarry a little while,' she said, her voice coming out in a choked whisper. 'Please, Llauron; demand a delay. Do this when you are fresh and rested, with your powers at their height.'

Llauron laughed. He reached out a wrinkled hand and caressed her soft cheek. 'You are so lovely, my dear,' he said as the tears began to fall.

'Please; please, Llauron.' The pain in her eyes coupled with the tears made Llauron think of looking up into the forest canopy during a rain-shower. He smiled at her again.

'My son is a lucky man,' he said gently. His tone had the ring of sincerity to it.

Her face twisted in agony. 'I'm not seeing your son anymore, Llauron,' she said sadly. 'I've done as you asked; we've parted company.'

Llauron looked surprised. 'What a shame,' he said, as if to himself. 'And after I specifically gave him my blessing. A shame; I am sorry, my dear.'

Rhapsody felt her stomach turn to ice. Llauron's words, however well intentioned, had caused a new wound in her soul. If he had removed his objections, then it meant that Ashe himself had been the one to decide her unworthy. She choked back the bile that rose to her throat, and drew her sword.

'Please change your mind,' she asked again. 'I fear I am about to witness your death, and I have sworn to prevent that with my life. I will be responsible.'

'I absolve you of any duty,' Llauron said solemnly. 'I ask only one thing of you, Rhapsody.' She nodded. 'If I should die here, I would like you to immediately commit my body to the stars and the fire. Make me a pyre here; it serves no purpose to return me to the Tree. Use Daystar Clarion to free my soul with a strike of fire from the stars. Oh, and if you would favor me with the Song of Passage, I will smile on you from wherever I go.' He ran his hand down the lock of golden hair that had fallen free of the black ribbon.

Rhapsody dissolved into tears. 'Please don't do this.'

'Rhapsody, that's enough; now buck up, lass.' Llauron shifted his weight on the white oaken staff, and the golden oak leaf flashed in the sun. 'Kneel and present your weapon.'

She swallowed her tears, dread rising with her gorge, and dropped to one knee, her sword point-down before her.

'Now, I want you to swear on all that you hold holy, on your life, and on your sword, that you will abide by my order not to intervene,' he said. His eyes glittered faintly in the light that passed overhead as the wind brushed aside the tallest of the tree branches. He waited for her answer.

After a moment she spoke. 'I swear it.'

A victorious smile crept over his face, but Rhapsody, eyes on the earth below her, did not see it. 'Good, good. And you will light the pyre with the sword?'

She lifted her eyes. 'You don't have any expectation of winning, do you, Llauron?' The sadness in her voice made his eyes sting.

'On the contrary, my dear,' he said in his most reassuring tone, 'it is the only thing I expect to do.'

In the distance Ashe watched, his mouth growing drier, his hands shaking in fury. It was all he could do to refrain from rushing in, sword swinging, and dispatching the whole lot of them. He could feel the pain his wife experienced even this far away, and it made him want to vomit. He reached deep within himself to where he could feel that part of his soul which was bound to hers, and he tried with all his focus to reassure her, but he knew he did not reach her.

The dragon in his blood muttered; it had been doing so since he had arrived. Its words whispered in his brain, making the place behind his eyes burn with a smoldering rage. *She hurts*, it whispered angrily. *Our treasure is in pain; it cries.* When his anger ignited he might not be able to contain it.

Ashe willed himself to stop thinking about it, but he couldn't. Then, as his wrath was beginning to catch fire, he felt a new dread, a new panic, rumble through him. He ran to the edge of the forest clearing, and horror choked him.

In the distance he could see a column of white smoke ascending from the top of the forest canopy toward an irate sky, a sky that churned, black with protest.

The Tree was under siege.

Now his seething anger combusted into an inferno of hideous rage; he knew unquestionably that this diversion was meant to draw him, to prevent him from interceding for Llauron. The stupidity of the assumption only served to fan the flames of his fury; it didn't matter that the attempt was ill conceived and foolish.

Knowing that if he gave vent to the vocal aspects of his frenzy the gathering in the forest glade would instantly be aware of him, he swallowed his roar, but the earth heard it anyway, and transmitted it, by means of a violent tremor, through the woods. He knew Rhapsody could feel it, and in the back of his mind he regretted adding in any way to her distress.

He ran, slashing through the underbrush, like an avalanche, like the wind, pulling power from the air and earth around him, gathering it to him, growing stronger, ran with the speed of a hurricane-force gale but the unrelenting power of a tidal wave. When he crashed on the shore of the diversion conflict, there would be Perdition to pay. Khaddyr's co-conspirators would never receive whatever reward he had promised for their assistance.

*

Llauron gave Rhapsody a moment to compose herself, and then they returned to the clearing where Khaddyr waited. She eyed him with an ill-disguised contempt, but had come to the understanding that, no matter what happened, she would have to present a stoic face.

'All right, Khaddyr, Rhapsody has agreed to stay out of it.'

'I'm pleased to hear that. I have no quarrel with you, Rhapsody.'

'Not today,' she answered, her voice calm but seething with dangerous undertones. 'Our day will come.'

'Do you wish to take this time to say your preparation rites?' Khaddyr asked Llauron. 'I performed mine while you kept me waiting.'

'Yes,' Llauron answered without a trace of enmity. 'If you will excuse me, I will return presently.'

As the elderly cleric walked away from the clearing, Khaddyr's eyes looked Rhapsody up and down; then, satisfied her wrath was under control, he came to her. As he approached he saw her avert her eyes; the gesture charmed him. It was a sign of deference, and after this day, he expected he would see it from her on a regular basis.

The flash of the blade was the only warning he had to stop; the point of her sword pierced the ground within a hairsbreadth of his toes. Khaddyr stood in shock; waves of nauseating cold vibrated through him, beginning at the back of his neck, and radiating through the rest of him. As he waited for his body to recover he realized he had not seen even the slightest motion that put it there.

Rhapsody's eyes remained focused at the ground. 'I have nothing to say to you.'

Khaddyr swallowed. He struggled to maintain a calm voice; it would not do to have a future subordinate hear him choke.

'Such hostility,' he said, trying for a mild, reprimanding tone. 'Why are you so rancorous, my dear? This quarrel has nothing to do with you; it is an ancient rite of passage. Surely Llauron must have explained that to you. It really is not even a sign of enmity between Llauron and me. It is how our sect selects new leadership, new blood.'

'How ironic,' she replied, still looking at the ground. 'What rite would you perform if you were trying to prove your loyalty to him, Khaddyr – a ceremonial burning of his house while he slept?'

The look in Khaddyr's eyes turned cold. 'That's an insulting comparison.'

Finally Rhapsody's eyes lifted to meet his, and Khaddyr took an involuntary step backward. They were burning, green like the new shoots of spring but with a fire that was hot and white.

'That was complimentary, compared to what I would really like to say to you, but I refuse to dishonor Llauron any further than you already have. And you are a fine one to complain of insult. You belittle my intelligence with your smarmy lies about rites of passage. Do you think I don't know what the standard rites of passage are? Llauron was elected Invoker by the rites of Tanistry, as you yourself were named his Tanist. There is none within your sect with an ounce of self-respect that would believe a challenge issued to an elderly man at the end of a long journey constitutes an appropriate means of succession. I thought the Filids valued wisdom and honor over physical superiority. How disgusting.'

Khaddyr swallowed his anger. 'I am sorry you feel that way, Rhapsody. I believe in our brief acquaintance I have given you no reason to be so hostile. I took you in when you were in a subhuman state; I taught you lessons of medicine. What have I ever done to you that could possibly have engendered such a vicious attitude?'

Her gleaming eyes narrowed. 'What about deserting me in Sorbold? You left me to die in the snow. Had you forgotten that? It wasn't all that long ago.'

Khaddyr's face went slack, the anger draining away. 'I have no idea what you're talking about.' Rhapsody listened to the rhythms and tones in his voice; it was clear that he was speaking the truth, or what he believed to be such. The fury in her gaze abated as she saw Llauron approaching. She looked at Khaddyr again.

'Don't do this,' she said quickly. 'Please.'

Khaddyr stared at her as if transfixed. She could sense arousal rising in him as his eyes roamed over her body. Perhaps he would suggest a carnal compromise; Rhapsody hoped he would, as it would give her ample excuse to kill him where he stood. But as if snapped back by an invisible chain his eyes suddenly cleared and his face hardened. He turned to the Invoker as he reentered the clearing.

'Are you ready, Your Grace?'

Llauron leaned on his staff; the gold oak leaf at the top cast a glimmering afternoon light on the snow.

'Yes, Khaddyr, I am ready.'

51

'Kneel.'

The five Filidic priests who had accompanied Khaddyr knelt before him. Llauron, who stood beside Khaddyr, nodded at Rhapsody, and she knelt as well, averting her eyes to avoid burning holes through Llauron's opponent with her stare. Khaddyr looked to Llauron; the Invoker began to chant the Second's Pledge softly.

The beauty in the well-modulated voice caused Rhapsody's throat to tighten, but she had determined that her last tear had already been shed. The vow with which Llauron bound them required her to guarantee no harm to anyone within the Filidic circle there present before the rising of the next sun. Lark swore first, followed by each of the priests. Finally Rhapsody gave her word as well, wishing she had taken Llauron directly to Stephen

Navarne. It was all she could do to keep the horror she felt from taking her over completely.

The two sides retreated to the opposite edges of the clearing. As Khaddyr walked by her he gave her a final smile; Rhapsody took the opportunity to scan his body for signs of weakness. She closed her eyes and sensed the slight imbalance in his step; he favored the left knee somewhat. In addition, his breath intensified when he was agitated, and she could see his heart was not as strong as it might have been. She passed the information on to Llauron as he handed her his outer vestments, stripping down to the plain undyed woolen robe that Khaddyr wore as well.

'Try to aim for the front of his left knee,' she advised her mentor, attempting to look confident.

'Thank you,' said Llauron. His voice was serious, but his eyes twinkled. 'Don't worry, my dear; everything will work out just fine. If anything unfortunate does happen, though, don't forget your promise to light the pyre.'

Rhapsody nodded. She could feel Khaddyr and the others moving into position behind her. 'Good luck, Llauron,' she said, squeezing his hand. 'If you kill him quickly enough we may still make it to Lord Stephen's in time for supper.'

Llauron laughed aloud; Rhapsody saw the startled looks on the faces of Khaddyr and his followers and took a secret delight in them. The Invoker kissed her cheek.

'Buck up, now; don't show them you're worried.' Rhapsody watched as he took his place opposite Khaddyr, the white oaken staff in his hands. He had said nothing about Ashe.

Lark handed Khaddyr a staff as well. Unlike the smooth, finely honed wood of the staff Llauron carried, the gift of Elynsynos to a predecessor long ago, Khaddyr's weapon was a thin, shaggy-barked branch from a tree Rhapsody didn't recognize. There was an unsettling familiarity about it, however, something that nagged at the back of her mind.

Having delivered her leader's weapon, Lark returned to the edge of the glade where the seconds had taken their positions of watchfulness. Rhapsody was accorded the space in front; as a Namer she was expected to deliver the unvarnished account to the members of the church and head of state, in this case Stephen Navarne. She felt uneasy as Khaddyr's followers spaced themselves in a semicircle around her, but decided that if anything untoward happened she could take all of them easily, even surrounded as she was.

At Llauron's spoken signal the two Filidic priests commenced their battle. Despite Llauron's advanced age he was spry, and moved with as much seeming ease as Khaddyr. The rival Filid himself was not a young man, and Rhapsody could see that each move cost him almost as dearly as Llauron's actions did. They circled around each other, their staves ready, looking for openings. Rhapsody saw many that they did not take, and decided that they were each conserving their strength for a large attack or an obvious opportunity.

A moment later, Khaddyr proved her wrong. With an impressive triple strike he assaulted Llauron's weapon, alternating the sides of his staff, then aimed the third blow at the Invoker's chest. Llauron caught the blow full force and staggered back as Rhapsody gasped. The Filids about her closed ranks, moving nearer to her in the obvious belief she would break her oath. She glared at Lark, and the Filid second stepped back involuntarily.

Llauron's hand went to his chest and he took several shuddering breaths, followed by a hacking cough. As Khaddyr moved in, Llauron's hand returned to the white staff, and with surprising speed he parried the would-be usurper's second attack. He drove Khaddyr back and swung the staff like a sword, knocking his opponent's feet out from beneath him. Khaddyr fell heavily on his back to the frozen ground. A thin stream of blood broke forth from his lip, spattering the cowl of Llauron's robe and staining it red.

It was now the Filids' opportunity to gasp on behalf of their mentor. The sound caused an unexpected thrill to shoot through Rhapsody, who was watching the battle intently. Her heart jumped into her throat as Llauron landed a solid strike to the same place on Khaddyr. The younger man rolled to one side, clutching his staff, and planted it upright in the ground beside him. Llauron moved in for the kill.

Suddenly a hideous stench filled the glade. It was an odor Rhapsody had experienced before, once in Sepulvarta, once in the cavern of the Sleeping Child, and once, not long ago, on a frost-whitened Orlandan plain. The malodor was unmistakable, and it caused the Singer's eyes, burning with its acid, to open in panic.

The staff Khaddyr had planted began to writhe. Thin and scraggly before, it now began to flex with muscular strength and uncoil, extending tendrils rapidly in Llauron's direction. Snakelike vines shot out from the shaggy branch and seized the Invoker, wrapping around him with astonishing speed. They spun about his neck like whipcords and tightened immediately, drawing a deep, ugly gasp from the elderly man in their death grip. Thorns sprang from the vines and began to strike, slashing his face and arms.

'No!' Rhapsody screamed, lunging forward. The Filids caught her immediately. They had been ready for this moment and were waiting for her to move. They wrestled her to the ground, dragging her back from the clearing as she clawed her way toward Llauron in vain.

Her fire lore roared to the surface, her skin burning the hands of her captors. Lark and the men pulled back, wringing their hands in pain. Their hesitation gave Rhapsody the chance to scramble to her feet again. Her hand came to rest on Daystar Clarion, but when she touched it a violent shock shot through her. The sword had been pledged not to participate, and it was keeping her word for her.

All the horror of her first fight with the servant-vine of the F'dor flooded back, Jo's sightless eyes swimming in her memory. Rhapsody's eyes met Llauron's as the Filids grasped her again, dragging her to her knees. His face was purple, his features contorted into a look of deathly surprise. The old man's mouth opened as if to protest, then closed abruptly. He loosed one final sigh and went limp in the clutches of the demon-vine.

'No,' Rhapsody choked, her voice a raw whisper.

The Filids released her roughly and she fell forward on the frozen ground, her hands buried up to the wrists in the snow. She struggled to her feet and ran to the center of the clearing where Llauron lay, staring blindly up at the apex of the clear winter sky. The vine had grown misty, and now began to dissipate on the fresh breeze that blew through the glade with an icy sting.

Rhapsody sank to the ground and drew the Invoker into her arms. Her trembling hand slipped beneath the woolen robe to his chest, then to his neck, but she could find no heartbeat. His pupils were dilated, and deep within them she could see a vertical slit, the same as his son's, only dormant and distant. She had never noticed it before. Gently she closed the sightless eyes and bent her head over his body in grief.

Nothing but the whistle of the wind was audible in the glade, the winter breeze billowing her hair around her. No bright soul came forth to ascend to the light; Rhapsody's throat closed in horror. *He's damned,* she thought ruefully, the realization twisting her stomach. *The vine took his soul as it would have taken Jo's.* She looked back to see Khaddyr standing behind her, his face emotionless, stanching his bleeding lip with the back of his hand. Finally he spoke.

'I'm sorry, Rhapsody.'

Her eyes narrowed. 'Get away from him.'

Khaddyr's expression grew cold. 'It is my right as victor to examine the body, and to take the staff of his office.'

'You will not touch him.' The words spewed forth from her mouth with a venom that made Khaddyr cringe. She lifted one of Llauron's arms and dropped it; it fell limply in her lap. 'What additional examination do you need?'

Khaddyr nodded, still trying to regain his breath. 'None. Give me the staff.'

Rhapsody looked beneath Llauron's stiffening hand. On the ground lay the white oaken scepter, the golden leaf tip buried in the snow. She gave a blistering look to Khaddyr, then carefully slid the staff out from beneath the fallen Invoker's arm. She tossed it at the victor. As he caught it his face broke into a beaming smile. From behind him a cheer went up from the five Filidic priests. Khaddyr watched Rhapsody stand, then spoke in a gentle voice.

'I really am sorry you had to witness this, Rhapsody. I hope someday you will understand why I had to do it.'

'I understand completely why you had to do it,' Rhapsody replied in a calm, deadly tone. 'You are the whore of the demon.'

Khaddyr's eyes snapped open in shock, then narrowed in rage. After a moment he just smiled. He pointed the staff of his new station at her abdomen.

'How ironic,' he said softly, grinning hideously. 'Well, time will tell. We will see who is the whore of the demon.' He signaled to his compatriots and they gathered around him, preparing to leave the glen. 'Now, don't forget, Rhapsody, it is incumbent upon you to spread the word of my victory. See if you can do a better job as a Namer than you did as the Iliachenva'ar.' He smiled at her once more, then turned and left, his followers hurrying behind him, struggling to keep up with the exuberant step of a man who has just seen his investment rewarded.

Rhapsody waited until she could no longer smell the hideous odor of Khaddyr's contingent before she returned to the body again. She bent down slowly, tenderly touching the aged hands that were cooling in the grip of death and the winter snow. As if in a trance she cradled his head in her arms, rocking him as if he were a child, much as she had with Jo. Only this time she was grieving not only for herself but for Ashe as well. She felt the crack of her heart as it shattered yet again.

'Llauron,' she whispered brokenly.

The wind blew across her face, dry in the absence of tears. She heard Oelendra's voice wafting toward her on the wind, sounding much as her Kinsman call must have sounded to Anborn. A voice of memory.

The Iliachenva'ar acts as a consecrated champion; an escort or guardian to pilgrims, clergy, and other holy men and women. You are to protect anyone who needs you in the pursuit of the worship of God, or what someone thinks of as God.

She had failed.

Darkness came early in the dead of winter. Rhapsody stood at the top of the open hill, waiting for the stars to dawn, unable for the first time to lift her voice to greet them. It was as if the music had left her soul completely, though she knew somewhere she would have to find it again, if only to sing Llauron's dirge. She had given her word.

The pyre she had built was wet; she could find very little dried wood beneath the snow. It wouldn't matter. Even a living tree would succumb instantly to starfire.

She remembered her dream at Oelendra's, the nightmare in which she had called starfire down on Llauron, burning him alive; though she knew that was impossible, she checked him several times anyway, just to be sure. He was cold and lifeless, his face white as the starlight, slumbering eternally, peaceful in his bed of sticks and brambles.

Her heart ached hollowly at the sight of him. He had opposed her relationship with Ashe, reminding her continually of her unworthiness, but he had been kind to her, had helped her when she needed it.

My son is not the only one in this family who loves you, you know; in many ways you have been like a daughter to me.

298

He had been the closest thing she had to a father in the new land, and she would mourn him like her own.

She tried not to think of Ashe as she awaited the coming dark. The horses seemed to sense her mood and stood quietly, watching as she absently folded and packed Llauron's garments into the saddlebags of the Madarian, saving out the piece of his cowl where Khaddyr's blood had spattered. As she slid his rope belt into the pack her hand struck something cold, and she looked at it more carefully. It was the tiny globe filled with water that contained a glowing light; Crynella's candle, Merithyn's first gift to Elynsynos.

Gently she unfastened it from the belt and put it in her pouch with Llauron's cowl. It was Ashe's now, a legacy to the third and most cursed of all the Cymrian royal generations. She hoped it would bring him comfort. She felt nothing, not even sadness at the thought that the man who had been her lover was now his father's avenger. The first person, by right, he should seek to destroy was Llauron's failed champion, the Iliachenva'ar. She hoped that act would bring him comfort as well. It would bring it to her.

When finally a star appeared on the horizon, Rhapsody drew Daystar Clarion and pointed it skyward. Then, as in her dream, she spoke the name of the star and called its fire forth. A beam of light, brighter than a strike of lightning, seared from the sky and rolled like a white and flame-colored wave over the pyre on the top of the hill. Rhapsody stood near it, hoping in the back of her heart that the fire would take her as well, but the inferno washed over her, the blinding heat illuminating her golden hair like a beacon for miles around.

The wood burial mound exploded in flames, charring Llauron's body in seconds, and lifting his ashes into the wind, where they fluttered momentarily like black leaves before vanishing into the darkness above the fire. Rhapsody opened her mouth, but no sound came out. She swallowed furiously and forced the song up in her gullet, the melody burning her throat. The Song of Passage croaked forth, barely above a whisper. She sang until the fire burned low, all traces of wood and cloth resolved in white hot ash.

'I'm so sorry, Llauron,' she whispered. Only the winter wind answered her, its reply a low moan that whipped through her hair, stinging her dry eyes.

She stood vigil until morning, silently watching the daystar fade and the eastern horizon begin to pale. Then she took a handful of ashes from the cold pyre and placed them in a sack, which she slung across the back of the gelding. She mounted and rode off into the rising sun to tell Stephen Navarne of Llauron's fate.

Ashe waited in the smoke from the battle, the desolation evident in the morning light. Rhapsody would come soon, he knew; the Tree was three days' ride from where Llauron had fallen, but she would be hurrying. The loyal Filidic priests scurried around the Circle, tending to the injured and clearing away the human debris from Ashe's one-man rescue of Gwyn-wood. The raid had come to an end with astonishing speed; by the time Ashe had arrived there was nothing that could have stopped the destruction his anger brought with him. The knowledge that many of the attackers were unwilling thralls of the demon did nothing to temper his wrath; Rhapsody's tears had driven him into a rage that was unstoppable.

He could feel his father now, moving through the earth, laughing in the wind. *Is it worth it?* he thought angrily, surveying the destruction and death around him. *Are you finally satisfied now, Llauron? How many more hearts will have to break, how many more lives end, before your lust for power is abated?*

The wind whipped around him, fluttering the edges of his cloak. Ashe sighed. Llauron's last wish was to be one with the elements. It would now be impossible to know what, if anything, the wind was trying to say.

'Are you certain there is nothing I can do for you, Rhapsody?'

Rhapsody's eyes met Lord Stephen's. She saw the concern in them, but was unable even to smile in return.

'Yes,' she said simply. 'I'm fine, m'lord, thank you. Please do as you see fit with the horses. If you are able to get in touch with Anborn, he will know what to do with them.' A strand of hair blew into her eyes, and she brushed it back, looking up at the blackened shell of the single standing carillon tower, where the bitter wind blew wildly through the bells that had saved Navarne during the Sorbold assault.

The duke reached out and gently took hold of her hand. He ran his thumb over the small, sword-callused palm, and was pained by the coldness in her usually warm skin, her normally firm grip flaccid and listless.

'Where will you go now?' he asked, his eyes heavy with concern.

'To the House of Remembrance,' she said simply. 'Llauron asked but two things of me – that I herald the results of his battle with Khaddyr, which I have now done, and that I tend to the Great White Tree. I sang a song of protection to the sapling, and that should have served to protect the Tree as well. I'll do it again to be sure; I would go to the Tree itself, but Gwynwood is so far away, and I need to be heading east, not west. It's the last thing I can do for him, and so I shall. Then I will return home, back to Ylorc, where I belong.'

Lord Stephen nodded. 'Can you stay for a few days, visit the children? They have been asking after you.'

Rhapsody shook her head. 'I don't think that's wise, m'lord,' she answered. 'Please do give them my love.'

The skin around the blue-green eyes crinkled as the Duke of Navarne took her other hand in his. 'You know, Rhapsody, we're practically family. Do you think there will ever be a time when you might address me just by my first name?'

Rhapsody considered his question as thoughtfully as she could. 'No, m'lord,' she said. She curtsied deeply and took her leave of his keep, walking into the billowing arms of the winter wind.

52

In the Grotto of Elysian, beneath Kraldurge

The lake of Elysian had not frozen completely. Ashe had run all the way from Kraldurge, and decided it was worth taking the boat, if only not to disturb Rhapsody's tie to the grotto. She would feel him if he used his water lore to speed him across to the island, and it might upset her. He knew she was probably in shock, undoubtedly in mourning, but how fragile she actually was he would not know until he saw her. He did not want to risk causing her any more trauma than she had already suffered.

The house was dark; not a single light burned in the window. It was as if Elysian was dead, the gardens brown with frostburn, the light in the gazebo gone. Ashe swallowed and rowed faster. Even the song that had filled the cavern was silent; the warmth from Rhapsody's inner fire utterly absent. Ashe began to panic.

The moment the boat touched the shore he vaulted free of it and ran to the house. He opened the front door and hurried into the parlor, where his senses had felt her. At first he didn't see her; there were no lamps lit, and the fireplace was cold. Only an infinitesimal glow existed in the room at all. As his eyes adjusted to the dark he found her, sitting on the floor in front of the hearth, staring aimlessly at the blackened bricks.

His senses rushed over her and his throat tightened as they did. She had lost weight, which she could not afford; her formerly flawless face was sunken and there were dark circles under her eyes. Her eyes disturbed him the most; they were cloudy, and, though open, seemed not to focus. She was sitting cross-legged, with her arms wrapped around her chest, her hands tucked beneath her underarms. He cursed himself for misguessing where she would go, leaving her alone for so long.

As he ran to her she looked up for a moment; then, before he could reach her, she bent her neck slightly and pushed the collar of her shirt down, moving her necklace out of the way. Ashe understood the gesture, and it broke his heart: she was making herself voluntarily vulnerable to a killing strike.

The last few paces to her he made by sliding to his knees, throwing his arms around her when he reached her. He buried his face in her neck, kissing her gently, repeatedly, trying to impart wordless consolation to her. For her part, she opened her hand; out fell Crynella's candle. She clutched herself even tighter and stiffened; he knew by her actions that she expected him to exact revenge on her, to punish her for failing Llauron. The thought turned his stomach.

She whispered something he would not have heard if his ear had not been pressed next to her face.

'Please; end it quickly.'

Ashe seized her arms and turned her to face him, his eyes taking in the ravages of sorrow on her face. He gave her a gentle shake, and as her eyes focused for a moment, he looked into them with all the depth he could muster.

'Aria; hear me. This wasn't your fault. You've done nothing wrong. Please, Rhapsody; don't let any part of you die because of this. Please.'

She looked at the ground, saying nothing. Ashe took her into his arms and cradled her, trying to make her come around. Finally she spoke softly.

'I'm sorry,' she whispered. 'Ashe, I'm so sorry. I couldn't stop it; I couldn't save him. He wouldn't let me.' The agony in her voice brought bile to his throat and tears to the corners of his eyes.

'I know; I know,' he said, caressing her tangled hair.

'I tried to talk him out of it, but I couldn't.' Her face grew pale in the memory, and she began to babble. 'It was my job to protect him; that's what the Iliachenva'ar does. I've dishonored myself, I've dishonored the sword and the office. I'm sorry.'

'No. No, that's not true, Rhapsody.'

'I should have taken Khaddyr down before they even started; I could have killed him easily, the demonic bastard. He's a thrall of the F'dor, or the demon itself, Ashe; it was my job, and I didn't do it. I've brought disgrace on myself, on Oelendra, gods, on Daystar Clarion itself. I knew I wasn't worthy but they wouldn't listen to me, she wouldn't listen.' She began to tremble in his arms. 'I couldn't save your father, Ashe; I'm so sorry.'

Ashe couldn't stand it anymore. 'You weren't meant to, Rhapsody.' She didn't seem to hear him. He took her face in his hands and looked into her eyes, green-gray and lightless. 'Did you hear me? I said you weren't meant to save him. It was a hoax; Llauron is not dead; you were used. I'm sorry, I wish I could tell you in a more gentle way, but you're frightening me. I can't let you go on believing that you were responsible for any of this. And that you could even believe that I would take your life—' His voice broke, and he stopped. 'I love you, I love you,' he said when he could speak again.

It took sometime for her eyes to focus, for the meaning of the words he had spoken to take hold. When they finally did he felt her body tense in his arms. She pushed him away and turned to look into his eyes.

'Llauron is not dead?'

'No.' He tried to think of words to console, to explain, but no sound came out of his mouth. The transformation her face was undergoing kept him from speaking.

'It was a hoax?'

'Yes.'

'That's impossible,' she said, rising to a stand. 'I lit his pyre myself. I sang his dirge.'

Ashe swallowed, tasting the bile again that had risen to his mouth. 'I know, Aria, I'm sorry. I never meant to deceive you. Your starfire was necessary to allow him to enter an elemental state he could not have achieved without you.'

'What does that mean?'

302

He tried to recall the words he had used to tell her the first time, on the night she had no memory of. 'Llauron had grown weary of the limits of his existence in human form. His blood was part dragon, but that nature was dormant. He was aging, ill and in pain, and facing his own mortality – he didn't have much longer to live in human form. He wanted to come into the fullness of his wyrm identity. The starfire you called down on him gave him the power to change form, transformed him into a dragon state, much like it did for me. It made him almost immortal, like Elynsynos, and gave him the ability, like Elynsynos, to become one with the elements.'

She considered his statement thoughtfully. After a moment her face hardened with comprehension. 'Why didn't he just tell me? Why didn't you just tell me?' Ashe looked away. 'Oh. This was it, wasn't it? This was the memory you took from me that night, wasn't it, Ashe?'

He couldn't lie to her. 'One of them, yes.'

'There were others?' She sighed dismally, her anger not yet in full force, though he could feel it boiling beneath the surface. 'What else?'

His throat closed. One of the things he had come to realize in the time they had been apart, after that last glorious night together, was the danger their marriage might bring on her. Now that their souls were united, if the F'dor knew it would try to use her to find him. Or, far worse, should he be found first and killed, the demon would know his soul was no longer complete, since a piece of it now resided within Rhapsody. It would come after her. Her own lack of knowledge of their wedding was the only thing that was keeping her safe.

He had already come to the horrific realization that he couldn't tell her they were married until the demon was dead. Now, as she stood trembling before him, unspeakable hurt and growing rage taking root in her eyes, nothing in the world would have been more desirable than to give her back the memory, to tell her he was her husband, and comfort her in all the ways he knew how. But he had to keep the secret. The danger was too great.

'I can't tell you yet. Believe me, Aria, there is nothing in this world—'

'Believe you?' Rhapsody interrupted. A choked laugh escaped her. 'Forgive me if I find that somewhat ironic.'

'You have every right to feel that way.' He took a step toward her, and she took the concurrent step back. 'Aria, please—'

'Stop calling me that,' she said sternly. 'I'm not your lover anymore, Ashe. I doubt the future Lady Cymrian would appreciate it; I know I don't.'

'Rhapsody—'

'Why, Ashe? Why couldn't he tell me?'

Ashe sighed. He looked up into her eyes, the stare blistering his soul. 'Llauron needed you to act as his herald, and to do so truthfully. He needed you to spread the word, as you did, of his death, so that it would be believed. Since he was the last powerful person standing in the F'dor's way, it was his hope that his supposed death would bring it out of hiding.'

'But it's a lie. You just said he isn't dead.'

'I know.'

'And you knew this plan?'

He hung his head. 'Yes,' he said softly.

Rhapsody wrapped her arms around her waist as if she was going to vomit. 'You let me lie, Ashe. You let me believe a patent falsehood and spread it, from my lips, across the land. Do you understand what that means?'

He did. He just nodded.

'It means I am no longer a Namer; that I've violated my oath. I have lost my ability to be believed, my credibility.' Rage took over her, intensifying her trembling into furious shaking. 'Can you understand that, besides losing my profession, I've just lost myself, too? That I am a different person now than I was, because of this?'

'No, Rhapsody, not if you don't let that happen. You had no idea; you told the truth as you knew it.'

'So because it was an unconscious lie, that makes it all right?'

Ashe couldn't think of anything to say.

Rhapsody turned away from him and clutched her forehead with her hands. She ran her fingers roughly through her hair, trying to calm down. Ashe stayed out of her way, but the words that had been choking him finally made their way out of his lips.

'I'm sorry, Rhapsody. I love you.'

She stopped trembling and turned back to him, as still as a statue. 'You know, despite the incredible irony, I believe you mean that.'

'I do mean that.' His voice had a harsh tone in it that rang of his second nature.

'Well, stop it,' she said softly, her voice barely above a whisper. 'You don't even know me anymore, Ashe; even I don't know me. Besides, what happened to being unencumbered? I thought the ancient Cymrian woman you had picked as Lady deserved total fidelity and devotion, unhindered by thoughts of anyone else. Doesn't she?'

'Yes.'

Something in his eyes, a deep pain, caught her attention, and she knew he was hiding something. 'What, Ashe? What aren't you telling me?'

It was becoming more and more a struggle to breathe. 'Please don't ask me, Rhapsody.'

Her eyes cleared, and her breath grew shallow and regular. 'You've seen her, haven't you?'

'Yes.' He turned away.

'Look at me,' she said. Ashe swallowed, and looked back at her again. 'Did you propose to her?'

'Yes.' There was nothing else he could say.

Rhapsody nodded. 'And did she accept?'

'Rhapsody—'

'Just tell me, Ashe,' she said, patiently but firmly. 'I've had all the lies I can stand for one lifetime.'

'Yes, she accepted.'

She nodded again. Ashe's dragon sense picked up the increase in her heartbeat, the flush of her face as she turned away herself this time, the increased moisture on her palms. Her voice did not betray her, however.

'So, you're engaged, then?'

'No.'

Rhapsody turned in surprise. 'No? What do you mean?'

Ashe tried to think of a way to avoid telling her, to prevent the hurt, but the look in her eyes stopped him cold. 'It didn't seem a good idea to her to just become engaged.'

It took a moment for what he was saying to sink in. When it did, the dragon could feel it, though again her face did not betray her. 'You're married.'

Ashe choked. 'Yes,' he whispered. 'Rhapsody—'

She smiled at him; it was a brave smile. Behind her eyes Ashe could feel a small explosion, much like the puff of fine crystal shattering. 'It's all right, Ashe,' she said comfortingly. 'I'm glad you told me. It's not like we didn't know this was coming.'

He found his voice finally. 'Rhapsody, there is much you don't understand. After the demon is dead, I will tell you everything.'

'That isn't necessary, or advisable, Ashe,' she said kindly. 'You don't owe me anything now. You never did, really. But you do owe her something; you owe her your full focus and attention – please don't waste it on me. I don't need it, nor do I want it.'

He stood up as straight as he could. 'After this is over—'

'After this is over, I intend to call the Cymrian Council. It probably is best if you begin serious preparations to take on the Lordship, Ashe. It will undoubtedly come to pass as a result of the Council. Your life will be different, and better.'

'When the demon is dead, and the Council is over, I will introduce you to my wife, Rhapsody, and then you'll understand.'

'We'll see,' she said noncommittally. 'I'm sure I'll meet her eventually. In the meantime, I am going back to Tyrian. I think it would be a good idea if I can help work with the different Lirin factions to bring them back together. You should stop in Tomingorllo on your way to the Council. The legend there says if the Lord Cymrian can restore life to the pieces of the Purity Diamond that now comprise the diadem of the Lirin, they will recognize him as their Lord, too, and be one people with the Cymrians. That is probably advisable if you want to quell the racial hatred and border disputes.'

He nodded. 'I will see you there, then.'

'No, by then I will be in Ylorc. Once I sound the horn I have to remain within the lands of Canrif until the entire Council convenes. I won't be there, Ashe; it won't be awkward for you and the Lady.'

Ashe sighed, and said nothing for a moment. 'Is there anything I can do for you, Rhapsody?'

A sad smile crossed her face. 'Yes, you know, I think there is something you can do for me.'

'Name it; anything.'

She turned and looked at him thoughtfully; the expression in her eyes contained no hate or anger, but Ashe shivered under the chill of it anyway. It was a look of ultimate resignation.

'You can go away,' she said simply. 'I don't want to see you right now; in fact, I don't want to see you until the Council meets. I may never want to see you again after that. I wish you every good thing, Ashe, I sincerely do, and you have my very best wishes for a long and happy marriage, but please leave.'

Ashe's face fell farther than Rhapsody thought a man's face could. 'Aria, I –'

'Stop,' she said, and her tone was firm. 'You asked what you could do to help me, and I told you. I did not make the statement lightly. Just go.'

'I can't go when you are this angry, Rhapsody.'

A smile crept over her face, but the look in her eyes didn't change. 'Why not? You are only making it worse. I am still your friend, and your ally, and if you are chosen Lord I will be your loyal subject. When you seek to unite the Cymrians I will help you in any way I can. But right now the sight of you is only serving to remind me of all the lies, and all the manipulation, that led the Cymrians to their terrible war in the first place.

'Perhaps it is your nature as a people, though I cannot fathom why. The stories of the Seren king I knew always celebrated his great love of the truth and his respect for unity. Maybe the demon has made it impossible for anyone to be honest, but somehow I think the only one that excuses is you. All I know is that I finally understand why Oelendra left the Cymrian Court in disgust and went to live forever with the Lirin; you are unable as a populace to tell the truth, especially to yourselves.' She stopped when the stricken look on his face became more than she could stand.

'I'm very sorry, Ashe,' she said, and there was sympathy in her voice. 'I'm sorry that you seem destined to live in constant self-deception, in addition to the deception in which others make you live.

'Achmed was right. Believing there was a hopeful answer to this mess was my own self-deception. I guess I really am a Cymrian, gods help me. But I wish to be away from this. You knew that I could not be a Namer if I didn't live a truthful life; even now that it is no longer my profession, I wish to live what's left of it truthfully, anyway. I have done all I can to help you and your father. Now all I desire is peace. Please don't come back.'

Ashe choked back the tears and bile that rose within him. 'Rhapsody, I hope you know that, whatever I've done, I never intended to hurt you.' He stopped at the expression on her face, a face that had borne the signs of inestimable pain and sorrow when he first arrived, only to have the appearance deepen into abject disgust and loathing. *She hates me*, he thought, and for a moment worried about the possibility that the dragon might become enraged, but even that element of his soul couldn't deny her right to feel that way.

'What do you want me to say, Ashe? That's it's all right? You *have* hurt me. I'll live. It was one of the first things Achmed ever taught me: tuck your chin, you're going to get hurt, so expect it and be ready.

'It's my fault, really; I keep forgetting that the outcome is inevitable, and I let my guard down over and over. I think you would lose all respect for me if I were to tell you that it's all right again. I know I would certainly lose respect for myself. I don't want to spend one more second of my life listening to you apologize for having to lie to me, or knocking me into a wall, or frightening me. Let it rest, Ashe, please. Go back to your wife and let me heal. I'll be over it sooner or later. Please, just leave now.'

'Rhapsody—'

'Go,' she said softly. She went to the stairs and began to ascend them. 'Goodbye, Ashe. May your life be long and happy. Please close the door behind you.' She went upstairs, turning toward the turreted study.

Ashe watched her go. He could sense her moving to the window, sitting on the window seat within the turret, waiting to see him board the boat and leave Elysian forever.

He went to the fireplace and opened the door next to it, where the wood was stored. Quickly he built and lit a fire for her, unwilling to leave her alone in the cold house, chilled more by the happenings in their lives than by the freezing winter temperatures. Then he picked up Crynella's candle from the floor, the token of remembrance she had thought to bring back for him; even in her devastation she was thinking of him.

His throat tightened as he watched the fire begin to take. She had not even understood the significance of what she had done. Despite Khaddyr's assumption that the power of the office was in Llauron's oaken staff, it actually resided within the trinket he had kept on his belt, the ancient mixing of fire and water. The office of Invoker belonged to Ashe now.

When the flames had caught he took his leave, walking to the boat without looking back. When he was finally away from shore he turned to see her, watching him from the curved window. He put his hand up in the air, holding the watercandle aloft; she waved to him as the darkness of the cavern swallowed him up. Then he began to breathe shallowly, concentrating on containing his anger, until he had reached the other side of the underground lake.

Later that night, the skies above the Sorboldian plain flashed with bloody light, like the calm before a tornado. Thunder rolled across the firmament of the heavens, and the Bolg that were watching from the outskirts of the Teeth hastily took shelter as fire began to rain down from the sky, scorching the land and turning the air to arid dust.

In a distant forest, within the silent bedchamber of his new abode, Khaddyr the Invoker woke from a dream of comforting darkness in a cold sweat. He could feel the desolation of the land beneath the dragon's breath;

307

the Tree sensed every crackling flame as it plunged earthward, burning everything around it. And in his heart Khaddyr knew the dragon was coming for him.

53

Gwylliam's Vault, Ylorc

When Rhapsody came into the ancient library Grunthor was certain for a moment that she was a ghost.

He resisted the impulse to sweep her into a wild, silly embrace, and instead let out a slow breath, pushed away the platter of ham he had been idly consuming, stood up from the table, and came gently over to her, stopping an arm's length away.

'Well, Duchess, welcome home. Was starting to think you might have forgotten the way back.'

She shook her head. Her face was thinner than it had been when she left so many months before, and there were deep circles under her eyes, but by far the most dramatic change was in the eyes themselves. They were clear, as they always had been, but with something guarded behind them. In her hand she carried a cowl of undyed wool like those the Filidic priests wore, discolored with a brown-red stain.

'I have blood from someone who might be the demon's host, though more likely he is merely a thrall,' she said directly. 'I'm sorry it has taken me so long to bring it to you.'

Achmed rose from the table next to the listening and speaking apparatus whose pipes wound throughout the mountains through which he had been announcing a round of new conscriptions. At her words his skin began to hum as it had when she first gave him the hematite vial; his heart began to pound. The deep and abiding racial anger within his blood began to burn with murderous fury, but he wasn't sure whether it was his taste for the F'dor or his disbelief at how worn and tired she looked, partly on his account, when but a few days before she had seemed so healthy and content. Silently he cursed himself for leaving her to go to Bethany alone.

'What happened at the wedding?' he demanded.

'Tristan and Madeleine were married.'

'Don't be annoying. What did you learn?'

Rhapsody handed him the cowl and turned to leave. 'Nothing about the Bolg, or any plans to invade. Sorry to have failed in that mission. But it's good to be home anyway. By the way, the dead bodies strung from the high crag of Grivven were charming decorations. Did you really have to position them so that they appeared as if they were buggering each other?'

The Sergeant and the king exchanged a glance. While Achmed was away

Grunthor had caught the two Bolg soldiers pilfering the cull pile of weapons; they had been captured on their way to Sorbold.

'Yes, actually,' Grunthor said. 'Could have been a whole lot worse. Will be, if I catch any more of them. Get a real party going up there on the crag.'

'Wonderful. Well, then, if we're finished, I'm going back to Elysian. Come and get me when it's time to go after the demon.' She started for the door.

'Wait a moment, there, missy,' Grunthor said severely. 'Where do you think you're going? You've been gone all winter – and now you're off again without so much as a howdedoo? I don't think so.'

'I'm afraid I'm not particularly good mealtime company at this moment, Grunthor,' she answered, her eyes on the floor. 'I don't want to dampen the atmosphere and ruin your supper.'

'One more step, and you're going to *be* my supper,' Grunthor said. 'And quite frankly, you've *never* been particularly good mealtime company, always insisting on prissy Lirin manners like not throwing bones on the floor and eating with utensils. Have a seat, miss. I want to sit across the table and look at you, and decide whether or not I'm having dessert.' He opened his arms.

Rhapsody turned back and came into the enormous embrace. She stayed there a long time, listening to the thudding rhythm of Grunthor's heart, a cadence she knew well from all the time she had spent sleeping on his chest in their endless journeys. The words of the saying that Gwylliam had once given to Merithyn the Explorer, and all the refugees of Serendair, to greet people they met in the new world, filled her ears suddenly.

Cyme we inne frið, fram the grip of deaþ to lif inne ðis smylte land.
Come we in peace, from the grip of death, to life in this fair land.

She shook her head at the strange timing of the thought. Like those who had left the Island, she, Grunthor, and Achmed had escaped the grip of death. Whether or not this new land held life for them, or something worse than what they had left behind, she still did not know.

Finally the Sergeant released her, and she sat down in a chair on the other side of the table from him and Achmed, pulling the platter with the ham in front of her. She shuddered momentarily; the place at the table where she sat was the place in which they had once found Gwylliam's mummified body, its empty eye sockets staring at the high ceiling overhead. She shook the thought away and turned her attention to the ham.

Achmed held up the scrap of fabric she had brought. 'Whose is this?'

'Khaddyr's.'

The Bolg king snorted. 'I doubt it's him. He's too much of a pantywaist. But one never knows.'

'No, one never does. Would you care to explain what has happened to Ylorc since I've been away?' she inquired, pulling a knife from her boot and sawing a slice off the shank of meat. 'Outside it's desolate; I thought for a moment I had arrived at the wrong mountain range when I came to the abandoned outpost at Grivven. I was starting to worry until I got past the barricades and found myself in an active muster. There must be one hundred times as many guards marching through the corridors as there were when I left; I got stopped five times. Where did all those soldiers come from? What happened to the schools, the farming programs?'

'We've gone back to being monsters.'

'Why?'

Achmed leaned back and stared up at the sprawling fresco of the dragon on the ceiling overhead.

'Monsters are more likely to survive the attack that is in the offing.'

Rhapsody stopped chewing. 'From where?'

The Bolg king shrugged. 'I don't know. But you've foreseen it yourself.' He shuffled through a pile of parchment papers and picked up an oilcloth scrap, which he tossed at her. 'I received this from Llauron by avian messenger while you were gone.'

Rhapsody put down her knife and took the scrap, holding it up to the fire. Her brow furrowed as she read the tiny script. Finally she tossed the oilcloth back at Achmed.

'He was such a liar. I never said anything like that to him.'

The Bolg exchanged a look. 'Was?' Achmed asked.

Rhapsody sat back in her chair and exhaled. 'You haven't gotten any news about Llauron from the mail caravan?'

'No. What happened?'

'It appears there was a challenge from Khaddyr under the succession laws of Buda Kai, an ancient fight to the death from which the victor emerges the Invoker. Llauron lost.'

'Interestingly phrased,' Achmed noted. 'I noticed you didn't use the words "he's dead." What are you really saying?'

Rhapsody pushed the rest of her supper away and resheathed her knife.

'I've been in Elysian for a while, trying to recover from what I witnessed. Ashe came there yesterday and told me that it was a hoax; that Llauron knew all along that there would be a challenge, and was prepared for it. It was an opportunity to get what he wanted. He made it seem as if he had been killed – though I'm surprised his trick fooled Lark, because she certainly is aware of all the herbs he must have employed to adopt a deathlike state. It was horrific – I was his witness and herald, and so went directly to Lord Stephen, as the nearest head of state, and informed him that Llauron had been killed in a challenge, and Khaddyr was now the Invoker.' She coughed as sour bile filled her mouth at the memory.

Grunthor shook his head incredulously. 'Why would he do that?'

'Because all along he has wanted to transcend his human form and move on to an elemental one, a dragon form, much like Ashe was able to do, at least partially, as a result of having a piece of a star sewn within his chest by the Lord and Lady Rowan. Just as Ashe was pulled back from the brink of death, and that innate dragon's blood within his veins awakened to prominence, so Llauron wanted to pass from the impending mortality of his failing human body into elemental form, by bringing his wyrm blood alive. He needed me to do that for him by calling starfire down onto him. He also knew that I never would have agreed to that had I known he was alive. He's been planning this all along, ever since we came to this place. He used me; I played right into his hands.'

Grunthor passed her a flagon and watched as she drank deeply. She wiped her mouth with the back of her hand, then belched loudly in true Bolg fashion, earning smiles from both men. She sat back and crossed her arms over her abdomen.

'In addition, he thought that if he were to appear to die, the F'dor might be emboldened, and perhaps show itself. So I hate to disappoint you, but any festivities you might undertake upon receiving the news that he is dead are premature at the very least. I know you never liked him.'

'You're correct on that point,' Achmed said, settling back with his own flagon. 'But this would hardly be an event that warranted celebrating. Having another wyrm like Elynsynos out there in the ether somewhere is not a source of comfort for me. But I suspect that he may prove to be more an ally now than he would ever have been in human form.'

Rhapsody blinked. 'Why?'

The Bolg king held the hematite vial up to the light of the library's glowing crystal lanterns in his gloved hands. 'With the human concerns of life stripped away now, he has only the things that matter the most to him left. What did you once tell me those two goals were?'

'Finding and killing the F'dor, and the reunification of the Cymrians, most likely establishing Ashe as their Lord.'

'Right. Finally his goals align with ours, at least partially. I could not care less who the Cymrians choose as their leader; Ashe is as good as any, I suspect.'

The shock on Rhapsody's face caused both of her friends to laugh aloud. When she recovered her composure she sat forward.

'How long have I been gone?' she asked, amazed. 'Are you saying you think the reunification of the Cymrians is a good idea?'

Achmed regarded her seriously. 'It depends on what form it takes. The lands that Gwylliam and Anwyn once ruled will never be under one sovereign again; Sorbold and Ylorc have their own rulers now, and it would be a bloodbath if anyone tried to unseat them. Roland is splintered into provincial factions; Gwynwood and Sepulvarta are both in the throes of transition to new religious leaders, or will be once your friend the Patriarch spins off this mortal coil. The continent is in chaos, and that makes it a prime hunting ground and hiding place for the F'dor. The more alliances that can be made, the better, at least from my vantage point. If the old Cymrian loyalties can be resurrected, they might be deep enough, ancient enough, to supersede any new thrall that the demon might seek to wrap around a single ruler, a single army.' He drank from the flagon, then slammed it down on the table. 'Besides, Ashe is such an impotent fool that he will be a mere figurehead, and the rest of us will be left to our own ways.'

311

'You assume the Cymrians would choose Ashe at the Council,' Rhapsody interjected. 'There are any number of royal houses, including all the dukes of Roland, that have a claim as well, not to mention Gwylliam's sons Anborn and Edwyn Griffyth, if the latter is still alive. Choosing a leader may be uglier than remaining divided.'

'For them, perhaps. As far as I'm concerned, the greatest enemy is the chaos.'

Rhapsody nodded. 'Tyrian is the same. It was never part of the Cymrian realm, but the Lirin were allied with Anwyn and the First Fleet, to their eventual ruin. They are a fragmented kingdom – the people of Tyrian are divided from the Lirin of the sea, and of the cities, and even those in Manosse across the sea with whom they once had strong ties. I don't know if you could bring them into a Cymrian alliance, but it certainly would be worthwhile to try and see if they will unite for their own sakes.' She stared off into the dark stacks, endless shelves of manuscripts, scrolls, and ivory tubes containing ancient writings.

Achmed stared at her. 'So you are on your way back there, then?'

'You've just got home,' Grunthor protested.

Rhapsody sighed. 'I don't know, now. It was my plan to go and try to facilitate the reunification – I talked to Oelendra and Rial at length about it. But now that I am no longer a Namer, I don't know that I have any skills to bring to bear, any credibility. I'm an outsider there, a half-breed. It's probably best to let them work it out among themselves.'

'Who says you're no longer a Namer?'

She smiled sadly at Grunthor. 'That's how it works. I lied, and it was a lie with significant scope. I've injected falsehood into important lore, the lore of Llauron's life and death. I've violated my oath. Anything I say from here on is only folklore, like anyone else can pass along. Without the powers I gain from Singing, from Naming, there is little help I can be to the Lirin. That was my credibility with them.'

'*Hrekin*,' Achmed spat. 'You're the Iliachenva'ar – one might think that would grant you a bit of credibility with them. Stop feeling sorry for yourself. I have a piece of lore for you; listen well: Truth is subjective. Llauron proved that to you. What exactly did you say to Stephen?'

Rhapsody thought for a moment. ' "I bring news. A challenge of Buda Kai was issued by the Filidic Tanist Khaddyr. The battle took place at the waxing moon, in accordance with the laws of the faith. Khaddyr was victorious. Llauron the Invoker is dead. Khaddyr bears the staff of the Invoker now." '

Achmed slapped the table decisively. 'There you have it. There is no falsehood in that. Llauron the Invoker certainly *is* dead. If you had instead used his full name, then perhaps it would have been a different story, but no one would dispute that what you said was accurate.' He leaned forward for emphasis. 'And even if they did, you are missing the point. Your power as a Namer comes from your study, your training, not from your oath. Had your mentor not died before you were fully trained, he would have told you this. The oath you took is the way your profession protects the lore from misuse; it doesn't give you power. You have had the power all along. It is only your sense of honor and duty that prevents you from misusing it.'

The two Bolg watched as she looked away, trying to absorb what he said, then exchanged a glance.

'You might as well test it out, miss,' Grunthor said after a moment. 'Go see what you can do to help the Lirin. You've got lots of weapons in your arsenal for that particular fight.'

Finally Rhapsody looked up and met his eye. 'So now you want me to leave? After I've finally come home?'

Achmed shrugged. 'Stay, go, it's entirely your choice. But I don't think you are going to be terribly pleased with the way things are evolving here. I've had to suspend the school, the midwifery training, the agricultural programs for export. We are in battle preparations now. The entire realm has been conscripted, men and women both. The children and the old are serving as support troops. The forges are going day and night; this is probably what is was like in this place during the War, the same kind of frenzy that led to the destruction of the Dhracian Colony. I am more than happy to participate in a peaceful alliance, but I am also going to be ready for war on any front; your own vision told me I need to be. I will give you the Cymrian horn, and then it will be your decision, whether you want to call them or not. So stay if you want to, but understand that I will tolerate no deviation from the battle preparations, not even from you. On the surface, in the eyes of the world, we appear dead. It is my intention to keep up that appearance, not to make it factual.' He rose from his chair, then held the hematite vial up before his eyes.

'Thank you for this,' he said distantly. 'Now excuse me. I am going to put it to use.' He stood slowly, still staring at the tiny stone tube of blood, and gestured toward Grunthor. 'Bring me the horn.'

The words, as soon as they were spoken, filled Rhapsody's ears, echoing softly. The words repeated, expanding, the voice deepening, changing dialect slightly to the one they spoke in the old land. Her eating knife fell from her hand, clattered against the table, falling farther to the stone floor.

Bring me the horn.

The words of one king, who stood now before her with the vial of blood in his hand, staring, dissipated like smoke on an unseen wind, replaced with the same words in a darker tone, one thick with pain and fear. The words of another king. A king who had died where she now sat.

Bring me the horn.

Rhapsody clutched the table, holding on as the voice took deeper root in her mind. Her jaw clenched, with great effort she shook her head slightly at Grunthor, who had risen from his seat in alarm, and closed her eyes, letting the words spin through her head and out through her mouth.

Bring – me the – horn! For gods' sake—

Both Bolg started at the sound; it was a voice they did not recognize, a man's voice, rasping in the throes of death. Pain contorted Rhapsody's brows, and she gripped the table tighter.

Anborn! Bareth! Someone – oh, gods—

Achmed reached out quickly and seized Grunthor's arm as the Sergeant stepped toward the Singer again. 'Leave her,' he said tersely. The Bolg giant shook his hand off fiercely, but did not intervene.

No, Rhapsody choked. *Damnation! Anwyn – damn you – oh, no—*

'I don't want to watch Gwylliam die through her,' Grunthor muttered. 'Good riddance to him, and may maggots eat his soul.'

My – people, she whispered. *My good people – please – help me. Bring me the Great Seal. I must – I must—*

Even Achmed grew alarmed as Rhapsody rolled over onto her back, lying on the table, staring at the ceiling above her with glassy eyes, and began to gasp.

The Seal, she said in Gwylliam's voice. *Please – the Great Seal – and water, please, someone – give me water.*

The Bolg looked at each other. Grunthor gripped the chair in front of him until the wooden back shattered; no matter how many times he witnessed these visions it was never something he could tolerate without becoming fiercely upset.

A glazed look of bewilderment came over Rhapsody's face. *This cannot be,* she said sadly. She squinted, staring blindly at the domed firmament above her where the copper scales of the dragon fresco glittered among the crystal stars in the cobalt-blue ceiling, its silver claws extended.

Ah, Anwyn. So at last you have vanquished me, Gwylliam's voice intoned softly, bemused. *What irony your sisters, the Fates, employ, that I die here, beneath the cruel visage of the great copper wyrm I had gilt in this place to honor your mother. Even in my last moments I am forced to see you – to leave this life with the image of you in my eyes.*

The color was leaving Rhapsody's cheeks; her skin fading from the rosy blush of health to a deathlike ivory. As the tides of her breath became ragged, panic clutched at Achmed. He put down the vial and bolted around the table, followed a moment later by Grunthor, pulling her from the chair, patting her face with his left hand.

'Enough, Rhapsody,' he said quietly. 'Enough – let the vision go.'

She looked past him, as if looking beyond the Veil of Hoen. Her lips were bloodless, pale and parched.

All for naught, she said dully, the light leaving her eyes. *All my – great works, my great dreams. For – naught. Hague, you were right. You were right.*

Achmed shook her gently, trying to break the vision's hold, but it had taken root inside her. Behind him he could hear Grunthor breathing shallowly, trying to remain calm.

'It's all right,' he said to the Sergeant. 'It just has to run its course.'

'The end of that course is his *death*,' Grunthor snarled. 'Come on, miss, snap to, now.'

I stare into the Vault of the Underworld, the cracked voice whispered. *But it*

314

is a vault of my – own – making. The Great – Seal. Anwyn – forgive me; forgive me, my – people. The Seal—

'Rhapsody—'

Come we in – peace, from the – grip of – death – to life in this – fair – land—

With a great shuddering gasp Rhapsody convulsed in Achmed's grasp, shaking violently. Then her body went slack, became still. She blinked, and her eyes focused. She looked up into the fear-contorted faces of her friends and exhaled deeply.

'I really have to find another hobby,' she said.

Achmed scowled, giving her a shake for good measure, then released her and picked up the vial. 'What do you suppose all that nonsense was about the Great Seal?'

Rhapsody shook her head. 'I don't know – he was terrified, and that's all I felt; the blood was leaving his body with every beat of his heart, and he could feel himself dying by bits. What an awful sensation. I hope I go quickly.' She thought of her request to the Lord Rowan, and his pledge to try and accommodate her; the memory calmed her. 'I now have the Last Words of the Lord Cymrian.'

Achmed nodded. 'Bound to be useful one day.'

Grunthor embraced her. 'You sure you're all right?' As she nodded, he glared at her severely. 'Well, that ought to tell you something about your status as a Namer. Kind of wish you were right and it was gone, but no, you're undoubtedly going to continue to scare the *hrekin* out of me with these damnable fits you have.'

'By "Great Seal" do you think he meant the royal crest?' Rhapsody asked Achmed. 'And which one would it be? There are two in their bedchambers – the coat of arms of the Seren royal house, the same one that was on all the coins back in the old world, or the one above Anwyn's bed, the dragon on the edge of the world?'

'I don't know,' he replied, heading for the door. 'I have more important things to attend to. If you are heading to Tyrian, travel well. Send word when you are ready to call the Council – we'll keep the horn here until you come back. If you are planning to stay, remain out of sight. I want anyone who looks on the mountain with the thought of taking it to see nothing but a carcass, a shell. If they are foolish enough to make the attempt, let them have the true pleasure of discovering what's inside.'

Deep within the mountain, the Bolg had been listening to the king's announcement carefully, noting the changes in call-ups to the army and the other orders that he now imparted daily along with other military briefings.

When the orders, uttered in the Bolgish tongue, ceased, they went back to their tasks, ignoring the distant conversation that filtered down through the mountain corridors in the language of men, a tongue they didn't understand. King Achmed had the power to make the mountain speak, but he didn't always do it in their words. The Bolg knew nothing of the speaking tubes, the listening apparatus. They assumed that the king was the voice of the mountain, and its ears; he had established dominion over the earth beneath their feet, the air around them. Over time they had become accustomed to being ruled by a god.

And so most of the Bolg ceased to even hear the conversation between the king, the Sergeant-Major, and the First Woman as the sound blended into the cacophony of marching feet and ringing anvils.

Except for the Finders.

Each member of the secret society, each Bolg possessed of an inexplicable inner desire to collect the Willum belongings that bore the Sign, stood, transfixed, as the Voice began to speak for the first time in more generations than they could count. Like the forefathers they knew only in ancient tales, they felt a resonance in their souls, a command in their blood, primal and deep to the bone, painful in its insistence, unable to be denied or understood.

Bring me the horn.

54

In the Tunnels of the Hand

The faint molder of underdwelling, the scent of spore and sex and urine, faint and carried in the wispy dust. Grunthor had finally overcome the fear of the tunnels, after the flame that had burned all the way to the House of Remembrance. He had been used to the sweep of desert and the ability to throw weight and weapon against enemy. In the tunnels he was rarely unaccompanied as he was now.

There was something fey about the earth in this place, the index finger of the hand that was a nexus of five old Cymrian tunnels. This part of the mountain was so deep, so far from where the reconstruction was occurring, that it would have been years before anyone would have come down here, had he not been hunting for whatever the Earthchild had warned Achmed about. The tunnels were, more than likely, merely water drains for the sewage system that still lay, in the majority of the deeper parts of the Cymrian labyrinth, in disrepair.

He had been stumbling, all but blind, for hours, seeking something, anything, but had come upon nothing, not even a trace that the tunnels had been traversed. Even the footprints that might have been seen in the dirt of the earthen floor had been carefully covered, if they had ever been there at all.

Finally, at the end of the tunnel that took the position of the index finger of the hand he passed a dry cistern, one of many he had passed in this place. His skin hummed slightly as he passed it; he unhooded his lantern and held it up before his amber eyes.

In the wall, amid the crumbling lichen, was the convex relief of a hand.

Grunthor grinned widely, exposing his flawlessly maintained tusks to the fetid air.

'Why, thank you, darling,' he said.

He bent closer to the dry cistern. Its drawpipe was clogged, blocked irretrievably by years of vegetation and other obstacles shoved or ham- mered up the pipe. Grunthor set down the lantern and took hold of the crumbling stone of the cistern's cover, giving it a mighty heave. The top moved aside easily, so easily in fact that he stumbled and almost dropped the heavy disk.

Beyond the cover of the cistern was another tunnel, dark and clear. The Sergeant snatched the handle of the lantern and climbed inside.

It was a tight pinch, but after his journey along the Root, he was ac- customed to such difficulties. Grunthor crawled out of the pipe, dragging the lantern ahead of him, and stepped out into a vast, cavernous room, doubtless once the cistern's main holding tank.

The lanternlight revealed a hoard of objects both priceless and banal, a trove of relics and refuse from Gwylliam's time. Mounds of coins struck in gold, silver, platinum, copper, and rysin, were swept into piles with almost the same care as fallen leaves, while displayed on makeshift stands were timepieces, hilts of broken swords, bedwarming bricks, rags of garments wrapped carefully, kept dry, the metal buttons polished; cutlery, brushes no longer bearing bristles, medals, rings, amulets of office, inkwells of black clay, golden goblets, book bindings, fragments of pottery and scores of other objects, some martial, some domestic, all with but one thing in common.

They each bore the royal crest of Serendair.

Grunthor removed his horned helm and scratched his head in amaze- ment.

'What's all this, then?' he murmured.

Placed slightly forward, as if in places of honor, were four objects, most likely newer or at least more recently found than the others – a ceramic plate, a coin like the thousands of others in the hoard, the scarred lid to a box made of blue-toned wood, and finally a chamber pot with a broken handle.

'Blimey,' the Sergeant whispered.

He looked around carefully, finally discovering, back beneath a row of rotten barrels with the royal seal affixed to their taps, a heavy wooden object shaped somewhat like an hourglass. He lifted it carefully and turned it over.

On the bottom was the crest wrought in tarnished silver, with dry fragments of wax still clinging to the gravures.

A seal. A royal seal.

Bring me the Great Seal.

Quickly Grunthor gathered all the newly displayed items but the plate and tucked them into his pack. He crawled back out of the cistern, dousing the light as he did.

The Cavern of the Sleeping Child

Silence, deep and profound, filled the ruin of the Loritorium, giving it the feel of a crypt, all but for the warmth of the flamewell that burned in the center of its broken wreckage of streets, a tiny flame of sun-bright intensity that cast weak, flickering shadows through the underground vault. The quiet was solemn, not somber; there was music of a sort, slow and sweet, even in the lack of sound.

The red winter flowers in Rhapsody's hand gleamed in the inconstant light. She had gathered the last of the blossoms from the gardens of Elysian after closing up the cottage in preparation for her long journey. Now she stood over the Earthchild, marveling at the beauty and incongruity of her. Her skin was gray and polished smooth, like that of statuary, over a deeper flesh striated like marble with twisting swirls of brown and green, vermilion and purple. The heaviness of her features was balanced with a delicacy that was strangely poignant, grassy lashes resting beneath eyelids that were translucent as eggshells.

Gently she covered the Sleeping Child with a blanket of eiderdown she had brought from Tyrian, tucking the edges around the greatcoat Grunthor had left to keep her warm. She put the winter flowers next to the child on the altar of Living Stone atop which she slept, bent and kissed her forehead carefully.

'From your mother, the Earth,' she said softly. 'Even in the coldest, darkest days, she gives us color for warmth.'

The edges of the Child's lips twitched slightly, then settled back, slack again with slumber.

Rhapsody caressed the long white hair, brittle and dry as frost-bleached grain, remembering it golden with roots as green as summer grass when she had first beheld her. Like the Earth, dormant beneath its blanket of snow, she slept deeply, peacefully.

The words of the Dhracian Grandmother came back to her as she watched the almost imperceptible tides of breath.

You must tend to the child.

How am I to tend to her?

You must be her amelystik *now.*

'You miss her, I know,' Rhapsody said aloud, absently smoothing the blanket. 'But her spirit is here with you – I can feel it around me in the cavern.'

The Child did not react, but continued her steady, hypnotic breathing. Rhapsody felt a warmth, a drowsiness come over her. Slowly, without thinking, she lay down on the altar of Living Stone next to the Child and gently laid her hand on her heart, as the Grandmother had taught her.

The sensation beneath her palm was a strange one; there was no real heartbeat, but rather a vibration, perhaps from the forges and mines, ringing now in purposeful constancy, perhaps from the fire of the Earth's heart below the flamewell, that sounded almost like breathing. As much as one might think she'd be cold to the touch or hard, the sense was much more secure; the Child was thriving in this warm place, on this slab of Living Stone. She in turn radiated warmth and history and the smell of farm earth as much as that of deep mountain stone; it was a rich, green smell, and it made Rhapsody, now asleep beside her, dream of her childhood.

For the first time in as long as she could remember old dreams came back to her, dreams of leaving the farming community of her childhood, of seeing the wonders of the world, of choosing her own way in that world. The youth, the innocence that had been hers then renewed itself in those dreams, eased the lines of worry from her brow, made her skin shine with the luminous excitement of a young girl on the threshold of life. With each moment that passed in sleep she was renewed. By the time Achmed found her, deep in slumber next to the Child, the cares of life had been all but erased from her face.

He stood over them both for a long time, musing in both melancholy and tender thought. He had known someone had come down to the Loritorium, had guessed who it had been, had watched her sleep in the unlit and still shadowy vault, and considered that in this place constructed to guard riches and had never held them, here were two great treasures of the world, two sleeping children.

As he watched he experienced a collision of memory and vision. The memory that throbbed in his mind was of her lying, near death, after their encounter with the Rakshas, where she slept, bloodless and clinging tenaciously but fragilely to life in the shadow of the friend she had slain. The vision was of the inevitable future, where, long-lived Cymrian or not, she would lie, no longer sleeping, but passed from this life as all must pass; stone, a shadow of herself. He had a rush of terror like the fireball that had consumed what had remained of the Colony, a fear that this was the only way he would ever have her to himself, in death. And he knew, even if all the world had to be sacrificed, he would do that to save her.

In all the world, he understood like no one else the compulsions of the F'dor, and knew why there was reason to fear.

When she woke Rhapsody felt him watching her, even before her eyes could discern him in the shadows of the Loritorium. She knew the feeling well; this was just another of thousands of times she had come out of sleep to awareness to find him observing her carefully, like quarry.

She sat up, careful not to disturb the Child, returned his gaze, and felt, as she often did, as if she were looking through the mirror of the world, she from the outside, at him within, not comprehending the darkness he lived in. In all their time together she still had no consistent window into his soul; his breath and sustenance were a mystery to her still.

In darkness, however, there was sometimes a keyhole, an eclipse-thin chink, a tiny crack he left open to his inner thoughts, the workings of what made him enigmatic. He felt safer in darkness; in daylight it was almost impossible to glean anything from his words, or actions, or expressions. Whenever she awoke thus, with him staring at her, she always wished for him to speak first, to illuminate something before the sun came up and made him utterly inscrutable again.

This time he did. 'I knew someone had come,' he said, almost awkwardly. 'I came to make sure it had been you.'

She looked at him, robed and armed, then nodded, stretched, and patted the Child of Earth as she used to pat the giant Bolg when he had guarded her in the tunnels. 'Where's Grunthor?'

'He had a matter of preparedness to attend to. Some missing weapons to account for.' He took out a wineskin and offered her a drink, but she declined, shaking her head.

'Have you made use of the blood?'

'Not yet. I am waiting for you to leave the mountain.'

'Why? I thought you were waiting until I returned to do it.' Her query was soft; there was something pensive about Achmed's demeanor, and she wanted to tread lightly. The last time she had seen him thus they had been sitting on a crag ledge overlooking the long-dead canyon a half a league below them, staring eastward over the Blasted Heath, contemplating his army's first great loss. What they faced now was so much greater in scope and sheer destructive power, she knew, that it could only be considered soberly.

'I don't know what will happen,' he replied simply. 'It would be preferable for you to be on your way to try and talk some sense into the Lirin when I begin the ritual. I am in a sense making it up as I go; I, like you, lost my mentor early. And he would never in his wildest dreams imagine what has come to pass in this world, and the last.'

Rhapsody sighed and wrapped her arms about her knees. 'I still am not certain I can be of any help to the Lirin. It's so far to travel if I'm not going to be of use.'

Achmed snorted contemptuously.

'Are we back to questioning your status as a Namer?'

'I'm not sure of my abilities. I don't want them to fail me in the midst of something important.'

'They won't. I would think reliving Gwylliam's sorry death might have convinced you otherwise.' He stared for a moment at the distant flame from the vent at the Loritorium's center, then fixed a steady gaze on her again. 'That first night we spent by the campfire, I asked, "What can *you* do?" You replied, "I can tell the absolute truth as I know it. And when I do that, I can change things." And that's what you've done.

'The sense that a Namer is born or invested, like an albino or a virgin, and once changed can never again speak with the same power or conviction, is like assuming a healer must save every wounded or dying person she tries to help to remain a healer; that an assassin must never miss, must never be a tool or weapon for someone else's purposes; that a Sergeant-Major can never lead again once his entire company has been slaughtered. You must know, Rhapsody, that in every profession there is at least a small bit of failure to be expected. Don't be daunted by it; losing that confidence will surely drain the power that the demon could not have taken from you otherwise.

'The F'dor is in a way an Unnamer, it lies to bring the world to its end. Treaties, lives and deaths, even the form the demon takes are all subject to the way it tries to unmake the world, hide the lore, break the prison, make the Earth not a place where life goes on, but cosmic dust, nothing more than the scattered eggshell of some unimaginable beast. We have seen every-thing, there, in our trek through the world. We have touched what can not be imagined; we speak here, now, in the presence of a race as old as your oldest lore, nevertheless we do not tell all we know. We dare not. What would the Lirin do to explain, to defend, to survive the awakening of the wyrm? There is nowhere to go, no grove of safety in which to hide. How deeply must the Nain delve to protect themselves? Can any sailor sail far enough, any soldier train hard enough? When your own race decrees "*Ryle hira,*" Life is what it is, you choose instead to speak the truth that says that our individual lives mean something. Though it was not the truth of these shadows, of this child, it was truth enough to take you through the flame at the center of the world.' He turned to go back up the tunnel. 'To see the world as it is surely leads to madness. Better to see the world you wish to see. I believe you are the one who first explained that truth to me.'

'And what world do you wish to see?'

He stopped, turned slowly to see her standing, adjusting the sword on her hip, shaking her hair straight. He chuckled soundlessly.

'I wish to see a world where F'dor are extinct, a legend in distant memory,' he said. 'You wish to see a world where the Lirin are united. Perhaps we should both apply ourselves to making those worldviews ones which can someday be accurately expressed by Namers.'

Rhapsody was suddenly struck by the music in his tone, and what the subtext of his words was.

He didn't know, once she left, if he would ever see her again.

She crossed her arms, regarding him fondly.

'Tell me something.'

'What do you want to know?'

'Grunthor told me a little bit about how and where you met.'

Achmed looked at the floor and slowly shook his head. 'Grunthor will say anything to get you to stay in the mountain. And though he is one of the cleverest men I know, he is also blessed with the gift of a certain amount of naïveté. He's had all these years to understand how he is cursed, and he will mercifully never understand.'

'Cursed?' Rhapsody asked, dumbfounded. 'How can you suggest such a thing? Grunthor has such purity of purpose. He can't be cursed.'

'Grunthor is cursed deeper than you are, with your nightmares and your purposeful blindness to things you don't want to see. Grunthor has the curse of Earth, being its child.'

'I hate it when you say cryptic things like that. Explain.'

'Grunthor has a gift for guardianship, and the need for it. Surely you must have noticed; he's been guarding your arse since the moment we met you in the back alleys of Easton. It was the same with Jo; it is the same with the Earthchild, with the Bolg soldiers that he bullies and loves. It was the same in the old land. It is and has always been the same with me. If he could hold every valuable thing inside his skin and put his blood and life around it, he'd find that guardianship easier, but here, now, everything tied to the Earth has a trace of the wyrm. Protecting you will one day kill him, with your wandering, your misplaced trust and affection. And he couldn't bear to die because of the pain it would cause you. He's damned, like the polluted Earth. She hurtles through the ether, bound even the gods don't know where, carrying inside, deep in her heart, the first and last Sleeping Child, the burden whose birth may be its mother's ending. Like the Earth, like the Grandmother, Grunthor will give his life in the guardianship of you.'

Rhapsody shook her head as she checked her gear. 'No. There is no need to guard me anymore. I can tend to myself. Grunthor knows that better than anyone – he trained me.'

'I know. But you seem to be insistent on taking dangerous risks. If you are going to do that, at least do it in a worthwhile cause, so that if you die, and Grunthor does, too, in the process, that it will have at least been for a good reason.'

She looked into his eyes, meeting their steady gaze. 'And what causes that I espouse do you consider worthwhile?'

'Helping build the Bolg into a nation of monstrous men.'

'I did that. You eradicated every contribution I made.'

The Firbolg king rubbed his eyes. 'Not every one. And that is only temporary, assuming we survive whatever attack is coming. There is also the unification of the Lirin – you should be safe among them, at least for a while. Forming a Cymrian alliance, while annoying, may prove to be useful as well.'

'So what risk have I taken that you don't think is worthwhile?'

He reached within his robes and produced the hematite vial, the smooth stone catching the light of the flamewell and gleaming dully. 'You felt the need to save those creatures, those demon-spawn, even though it may have meant the end for all of us. The blood from one of them would have been enough; we should have executed the rest. But you were insistent; you put yourself repeatedly in harm's way to rescue them, even though it may eventually be your undoing.'

Rhapsody shrugged. 'I thought it more prudent to make sure that all the blood was collected, that you would have a better chance of catching the demon's scent with more of it. If you recall it was you that said trying to trace the F'dor was like trying to catch a breath of perfume across a crowded bazaar. Sometimes you remind me of the Rakshas, Achmed; these children aren't tainted receptacles of blood and nothing more. They have souls, immortal souls. It is heinous to use them for our own purposes and

322

then discard them as if they were nothing. If we really are going to live forever, or have lives so long that it seems like forever, I don't want that on my conscience. I don't think you could abide it, either.'

The Bolg king began to pace the rubble-strewn floor of the burnt-out repository.

'You have no understanding of what "nothing" is, no idea how long "forever" can be. You were never nothing. You were a farmgirl, a harlot, a harper; at your lowest, the most demeaned moment of your life, you were worth *something*, some cattle, some coin, some moment of attention. It may have felt damnably little, but it was a place, a hole in the world to land in. You think you have been nothing, but you haven't, Rhapsody.'

She reached out her hand and stopped him in his pacing, turning him to face her. As she studied his face she saw something there she had never seen before.

'Emily,' she said softly. 'My family called me Emily. And you're right, Achmed – even in those times before I knew you, I never was nothing. Neither were you.' The light from the fire behind her leapt, and Achmed could see the green in her eyes before the shadows returned, coloring them gray again with darkness. 'When I changed your name from the Brother, it was inadvertent; it wasn't meant to devalue what you were then.'

The Bolg king's gaze grew more intense, so piercing that it almost hurt to return it. He stared at her for a long time, then looked up at the pinnacle of the cracked domed ceiling above him.

'You were the second Namer to change my appellation,' he said heavily, as if each word cost him dearly. 'It was my mentor that named me the Brother, because that's what he said I was – Brother to all, akin to none. Had I followed his teachings, the path he laid out for me, I might have used my blood lore in the same way you use your music – to heal. He, too, believed that I was not nothing.' He laughed bitterly. 'I seem to be spending my life proving that his faith was misplaced. Perhaps the name we are given at birth is the truest gauge of what we will be after all.'

'What was it?' Her voice held a reverence that made his throat tighten.

The Bolg king continued to stare at her through his mismatched eyes, both of them darkening with an old, all-but-forgotten emotion.

'Ysk – that's my given name. It means spit, or venom, a discharge or insult, a sign of infection.' He exhaled slowly. 'Imagine being born Bolg, yet like this.'

Achmed took the veil that shielded all but his eyes from sight and uncovered one side of his face and neck to reveal the blood vessels vibrating just below the surface of the dark olive skin, drawing in each sensation and word, as if he were covered all over with a sensile eardrum that quivered with even the misty, breath-soft touch of her glance.

'Every squint of resentment, every glare of fear, every silence of neglect. For a long time I believed that dark spirits watched over me, gleeful. If I had known what death was, I would have found a way to get to it, to inhale it into myself and be gone. I know what it is like to be nothing, Rhapsody –

less than nothing. I don't want your pity; I want you to understand that perhaps I understand these demonic children better than you do.'

Rhapsody shook her head. The flame in her hair highlighted the darkness around them, caught rainbow-golden sparks from the distant light in its ever-changing dance. She softened the grip on his arm and gently moved her fingers up his shoulder and rested them along the line of his jaw.

'They didn't know that you were also half-Dhracian, and wouldn't have understood the significance even if they had known. The Bolg of your kingdom do not know, either, nor anyone in this world save you, Grunthor, and me – and Oelendra, who is as purposeful in the hunt for the demon as we are. Something no one knows about you will be our salvation, and the salvation of this land. It doesn't matter what the Bolg who named you thought. You were never nothing, not even then.'

He inhaled very slowly, deeply, silently. 'I was the special project of a very holy man. He tried to teach me to be a healer. Look what came of all his good intentions – and I haven't a single drop of demon's blood in me. The war to come will be terrifying. More terrifying is that I do not think I wish to stop it. The men of Roland or Sorbold will die from hatred of the Bolg, and except for the relish of justice, I don't care. The Bolg will die as well. Add that to what Grunthor has suffered, and you, and this child, and all those demonic "children," and others. What did all that training come to? What did I ever heal? Who did I ever save?'

'You can't blame yourself for any of those.'

'Then what difference have I made?' He was silent a long time.

'Who did you expect to save?'

Even before she finished the question, she felt doors open in him that she feared to approach.

Dark in the ruins of Gwylliam's treasure vault, which would never hold any of Gwylliam's treasure, in possession of the blood that might possess him, aware of the Finders yet unable to find them, Achmed looked at Rhapsody, just awakened from slumbering near the Sleeping Child, rested but not ready for all that was to come. He admired her water-smooth hair, the very glow of which washed away anger and despair and memory, breathed again through the boiling cold sensation of her fingers on his face, softly took her hand, kissed and cradled it in both of his own.

'Just one. One of those who might not even believe they need saving,' he said. 'And the world in the process. I guess that means we have more in common than could ever be imagined by anyone looking at us. We are the opposite sides of the same coin, Rhapsody.'

'Well, if we are a coin we have value.' She picked up her cloak and pack. 'I have to leave. I will send messages as often as I can. Before I go, will you answer one question for me?' Achmed nodded. 'What have you really been trying to say since you came down here?'

'Don't die.'

She squeezed his hand, the warmth of her touch radiating through the leather of his glove. 'I don't intend to. But the guiding principle of my life can't be staying alive for Grunthor's sake – or for yours.' She released his hand and leaned over to kiss the brow of the Earthchild, hearing his words behind her as she turned away.

'Then do it for your own.'

When she turned back he was gone.

55

The Hand

All but naked in the dark, with all the sounds of the labyrinth falling around him, Achmed carefully unsealed the hematite vial and examined the blood essence with his breath and skin.

At first he had been surprised at the lack of odor. He knew the stench of the F'dor, the ghastly smell of burning flesh in fire, and had braced himself for it. Instead there was a faint trace of stone; the hematite, which Rhapsody had said was silvery-black when the Lady Rowan gave it to her, now was mottled with streaks of green and brown, polluted veins striating the stone vial. Perhaps the stone itself had absorbed the stench, the burning, caustic properties of the demonic blood. He made note to destroy the vial once he was finished with the ritual in the fires of his hottest forge.

He covered the opening of the vial with his finger, then upended it, drawing out a drop of the black blood onto the fingertip. The very touch of it made his skin sting; he recoiled, feeling the needles of racial hatred coursing through his veins.

The blood was viscous, thick and opaque; not even a hint of light could be seen through it, no surprise in this place of darkness. Achmed could feel a deep pounding in his ears. The evil within the single drop on his finger was palpable, nascent; no prediction might be made about its effect on someone whose heart had for years bent more naturally to murder than mercy.

At the far distant reaches of his mind, he thought he could hear chanting, deep and harsh in tone, amid the crackling of dark flames.

He examined the blood again. Perhaps, rather than it being a tool for him, it might transform him into one instead. Chief among the dangers would be if, before he had savored it over his heart, memorized its sticky silkiness firmly into every fingerprint, it sated him. He might become unable to distinguish its scent from his own, feel it only as part of the ambient breeze of the room, instead of the tang of demon, the nettle of skinless spirit, the swollen tongue of a choking sentience.

He swallowed the fear.

It was time.

Gently he inhaled the blood's bouquet and, taking a firm hold of the vial, gingerly splashed it into his nostrils, tasted it, kneaded drops of it into the pores of his cheeks, along the ridge of bone, to better impress it into his awareness.

His heart began to race, his skin to prickle in excitement. His own blood flowed freely through his veins, making him tumescent, causing the surface of his skin to come alive with heat. He anointed his skin-web, the network of sensitive veins and nerve endings that spanned his neck and chest, feeling a scream of ecstatic agony rise up from inside him, to escape raggedly through his hoarse throat.

As the initial pain subsided Achmed came to clarity again. He was mostly naked in the center of the Hand, a gore-covered pixie in a stone palm. Painted dusky red in deliberate swaths from his forehead and earlobes nearly to his knees, he could still taste the blood's acridity and smoke. He spit into the vial to rinse the last drops of the F'dor's essence and imbibe them into the warmest crevasse of his soft palate.

Finally, when every last drop of the demonic blood had become part of him, he closed his eyes, feeling the rhythm of his own heart, a rhythm that would one day match itself innately to the beast. In between cadences, he spoke aloud to it, his prey, his quarry; his brother in blood.

Just as I have your blood on my hands now, one day I will have it so again.

The cowl Rhapsody had given him lay on the floor beside him. Slowly he bent and picked it up; it took all the effort that he could muster. The bloodstain on it was unfamiliar, had no resonance to him; he tossed the scrap of fabric aside. As they had suspected, Khaddyr was not the demon's host. Achmed closed his eyes, and willed the blood deeper into his skin.

He had lost count of how much time had passed. An hour, perhaps five, of drying without evaporation, absorbing focus as he wrestled with the monster he had taken into himself. There were remnants of each child whose blood had contributed to the aggregate; had he been of an evil nature, this might have been a way to make another Rakshas. Distantly he retasted the sand around Entudenin, the frost-hardened clay of the Hintervold, the pitch of Tyrian pines, and saffron-laced sawdust from an arena he had never seen, all seasoned with dark flame.

When the breath he drew was finally wholly his own again, and the dried blood merely red dust, he came, exhausted, into an awareness of sounds that had been gathering for some time, sounds of multiple approach.

Outside the reach of his vision, the Finders were assembling.

Shakily Achmed crouched to the ground and reached for the skinning knife; his knees buckled beneath him and he fell forward, striping his hands with his own bright blood. He was weak, weaker than he ever remembered being, and vulnerable; should the Finders, whoever they were, be of hostile intent, he knew there was little he could do to defend himself against them.

He pushed feebly against the ground, trying to stand, but there was no strength in his muscles. It took all his stamina just to pull himself into a crouch to protect his abdomen.

Achmed raised his head. In the distance of the tunnels he could make out the glimmer of eyes, hundreds of them, or so it seemed to his fading mind.

Inwardly he cursed, knowing that he had calculated foolishly, allowing himself to be caught alone after taking the caustic blood into himself, rendering him powerless. *What difference have I made?* he thought silently. *I can now recognize the F'dor's host. A shame, then, that I am about to die at the hands of a few hundred of my own people, timid cave-crawlers who would run at the mere sight of me if I were not so compromised.*

His head dropped to his chest as he heard them approach; with great effort he tried to stand again, but to no avail. His breath emerged, ragged and shallow, as one by one the shadow-forms at the end of the tunnel emerged from the complete darkness, staring at him as the wolf pack stares when encircling an injured hind.

He knelt before them, more than half disrobed, all but weaponless, painted grisly with the sacrifice granted from the Veil of Hoen.

Out of the corner of his eye he could see the new glint of weapons, hear the ratcheting of crossbows being loaded. His head became too heavy to hold erect; he struggled to raise it high enough to stare them in the eyes, light eyes that gleamed in shades of blue within dark silhouettes; they had brought some light source with them, though he could not tell what it was. He made note of the oddity; most Bolg had eyes as black as the cave darkness from which they had come. He tried to speak, to command them to withdraw, but he could not even find his voice.

The unmistakable sound of metal coming forth from leather sheaths blended with more ratcheting. Achmed cursed again, not at his impending death but at the sheer waste of it all.

As the mass of Finders took a step forward, a horrific scream rent the air of the tunnel, a roar that chilled Achmed's blood as much as it warmed his heart. From the index finger tunnel of the hand came the earthshaking sound of pounding boots and weapons clanking loudly; it was a sound of muscle in motion, fed by alarm and anger. Another shout, this time with words.

'What's all this, then?!'

In a twinkling the Finders scattered, disappearing back down the tunnels from which they had cautiously emerged. Achmed managed to lift his head high enough to see the oncoming form of the Sergeant-Major, almost as tall as the tunnel itself, and wide as a dray horse, barreling toward him out of the darkness. Within a moment Grunthor was there, in the Palm, staring down at him in a mixture of amazement and horror.

'You all right, sir?'

Achmed nodded slightly; it took all his remaining strength to do so.

Without a word, Grunthor picked him up, slung him across his back, and carried him up into the relative light and warmth of the mountain chambers of Ylorc.

'Warm enough?' Grunthor asked.

Achmed nodded testily. 'Thank you.' He struggled to sit up amid the black silk sheets of his bed, slipping slightly. 'Show me your haul.'

Carefully the Sergeant unloaded the items he had taken from the Finders' hoard. Achmed rifled through them, stopping at the pot with the broken handle.

'A chamber pot?' he said disdainfully. 'They sold out my kingdom for a *chamber pot?*'

'Bolg don't know what a piss-pot is,' Grunthor said, running his index finger over the gravures of the seal. 'All they know is it's got the crest.' He handed the wax seal to the Bolg king. 'So why do you think old Gwylliam was calling for this in his death throes? Think he wanted to issue a proclamation before he went to sod?'

Achmed shrugged. His strength was returning slowly, along with his sense of self. Hidden deep below, in his unconsciousness, however, he could feel the blood bond, the imprimatur that tied him to the still-discovered host of the F'dor, lurking somewhere west of the foothills of the Teeth.

'He called for it in the same breath as he called for the horn,' he said, pushing up against the pillows. 'Hand me that manuscript about the horn that I pulled out for Rhapsody. Maybe there is a connection of some sort.'

Grunthor rose and collected the scroll from the king's desk, and brought it to his bedside.

'Perhaps you should get some rest now, sir,' he admonished. 'I'm sure you need it; I know *I* do, after beholding you in all your splendor. In fact, I don't expect to recover any time soon.'

For the first time since they had returned from the tunnels Achmed smiled.

'Just a quick scan, Sergeant,' he said, unrolling the scroll. Grunthor sighed and settled into the chair next to him; in his experience a quick scan lasted a minimum of two hours.

He had long since nodded off to sleep when he felt a change in the air of the room. He sat up immediately and turned to Achmed, who was sitting now at his writing desk, poring over the ancient parchment.

Grunthor stretched deeply. 'Well?' he said in mid-yawn.

The Firbolg king's eyes were bright with excitement as he turned around. 'I found it,' he said.

'And?'

'The horn – it *is* the Great Seal. It is the testament, the witnessing certification, of the covenant he forced all of them to enter in exchange for their new lives in this land.

'When the Three Fleets set sail, they did so with the understanding that they were traveling across the world for the purpose of keeping their Seren culture alive. This, presumably, in Gwylliam's mind, was a culture that would maintain his birthrights. He didn't want to just save his subjects, he wanted to save his own royalty in the process.'

He held the scroll up in the candlelight for Grunthor to see. The Sergeant peered over his shoulder at the illustrations of the horn and the docks of three port cities of Serendair.

'Apparently the price of gaining passage on the ships that left the old world ahead of the cataclysm was an oath, a promise to come in response to the call of this horn. Each refugee placed his hand on it as he boarded the ship, swearing fealty to Gwylliam, for himself and his heirs, throughout Time. The horn is the Seal of that promise. It must have been similar to Rhapsody's Naming powers – the most solemn of oaths in the presence of unimaginable power, the rising of the Sleeping Child in the waters off the coast of the land where Time began, spoken by the high king of that land. That's why the Cymrians, all generations of them, feel compelled to assemble in response to its call. All those ancient, powerful people, who have either sworn fealty on the horn, or whose ancestors did, will be tied, blood-deep, to the Summoner, with the most profound of loyalty oaths.' Grunthor nodded.

Achmed sat back in his chair and chuckled.

'And what's so funny now, sir?'

The king rolled the manuscript up sharply and slapped it on the table.

'Rhapsody is going to sound it.'

56

The Circle, Gwynwood

From the earliest days of memory the legends told of the of the rampage of the wyrm Elynsynos, the tale of her laying waste to the western continent in her wrath upon the landing of the First Fleet.

When the Fleet disembarked, and Merithyn, the dragon's explorer lover, was not among them, the stories said, Elynsynos gave vent to a great fireball of rage, roaring from inside her coppery belly, full of anger and destructive fury. The flames of that angry breath torched the primeval forest that surrounded the Great White Tree, igniting Gwynwood into walls of endless fire, destroying everything to the seacoast save for the Great White Tree itself, the upper branches of which were rumored to still contain the signs of soot and blackening fire.

The fire spread rapidly eastward, the legends recounted, until it reached the central province of Bethany, where it came in contact with the open vent to the center of the Earth, which ignited in a fiery geyser that roared into the night sky, visible for miles around. Blessedly, the elemental fountain also served as a firebreak, sparing the rest of the continent from the effects of the dragon's wrath.

Khaddyr had always known the legends were lies. All of the Filids knew it as well; the forest of Gwynwood was a virgin wood, free of firestarters and other trees that would have sprung up from the ashes of so great a conflagration. There had never been a fire of any magnitude here, nothing that had even threatened a village or an outpost, just the occasional burning aftermath of lightning strikes and mishandled campfires and the destructive wake of attacks from Gwylliam's forces in the Cymrian War. Only someone completely ignorant of woodcraft or forest lore would have believed the stories of the wyrm's rampage.

He dreamt of the dragon's fury nonetheless.

The keep of the Invoker was a strangely beautiful wooden palace that stood beneath, within, and above the trees at the edge of the forest that bordered the Circle. It was a living building, a place composed of both harvested wood and growing flora, an instrinsic part of the forest. The odd palace was one of the prizes of his new office, and Khaddyr had claimed it with relish.

The first time he had entered the ancient building as its master he had been filled with conflicting emotions – a heady excitement dampened intermittently by guilty dread. Like his father before him, he had grown up knowing this marvelous dwelling as Llauron's home; his own visits to the keep were always at Llauron's indulgence. There was something perversely satisfying about walking the twisting, polished hallways as its new lord.

Llauron's longtime household servants, Gwen and Vera, had greeted him politely but coldly, refusing to meet his gaze but obeying his commands without question. On the first night, after he had ordered his supper, Khaddyr directed that the exquisitely carved bed in Llauron's bedchamber be made up with fresh sheets of Sorbold linen, swallowing a chuckle at the undisguised expressions of horror that had beset the elderly women's faces.

'Make certain the warming stones are between the sheets before I finish my after-supper cordial,' he had directed Vera. 'The night wind is bitter. I want the bed to be cozy.'

To aid in achieving that end he had already selected a young acolyte, an especially comely woman he had instructed in the medical arts several seasons before, to help him celebrate his new freedom from the celibacy prescribed to him when he was still the Invoker's Tanist. He had seen her ushered up the stairs before the meal began that first night, and was displeased by the resistance she had displayed. It appeared he would need to go over her lessons of obedience and servitude again.

Now each night when the weeping young woman was unbound from the bedropes and led away to her own chamber for the night, Khaddyr had settled back into deep, sated rest in the Invoker's bed, silent and comforting. The voice of his master that had long haunted his mind was finally silent, no longer demanding the fulfillment of his instructions.

Everything had gone according to plan. Llauron was dead. The office of Invoker was his. The fornication was everything he had always dreamed it would be and more, coupled with the unexpected pleasure of power and victory over resistance. Khaddyr had discovered that pleading and cries for help only heightened the experience for him, and now slipped off into dark unconsciousness contemplating new methods to bring them about.

It was always after a particularly good climax that his visions of the dragon were especially intense.

In the darkness of his dreams the skies would turn bloody. He was at first convinced that this had been suggested to his unconscious mind by the stained sheets he had summoned Vera in the middle of the first night to change. But after that first delicious experience the image of the bloody sky remained in his nightmares, broken now with walls of flame reaching to the firmament of clouds that roiled with ash and smoke. His mind's eye rose above the fire into the sky, fixing its gaze on a forest beyond the horizon.

In the vast distance he could see a great winged beast, serpentine, with copper scales glinting in the light of the growing fire, coiled around the base of a tall, thin white oak, a tree in bright blossom, even in winter's depth. *The Great White Tree in the days of the Earth's childhood,* Khaddyr thought to himself. *And Elynsynos herself.* The wyrm stretched in the firelight, dwarfing the small tree as it rose, wings outspread, above the smoke, disappearing into the swirling ash.

His inner sight returned again to the forest in which he stood. In the distance he could hear the panicked screaming of the Filids as they dashed about, fire ripping through their robes, falling to the forest floor and igniting the dried leaves beneath the snow. The words of calm direction he had spoken in the dream had come forth not in his own tones, but in the sonorous voice of Llauron. It didn't matter; the terrified victims paid him no heed, dashing to burning deaths so vividly gruesome that he could smell the reek of it even upon awakening.

The dragon, Khaddyr could hear a woman's voice screaming as the dream faded into obscurity. *The dragon comes.*

It had taken a few hours to shake the feeling of dread the first time the dream had plagued him, but as it settled into a random occurrence Khaddyr became accustomed to the shaking aftermath, the cold sweat. Ever since he had become a thrall, a servant of the demon, he had lost the fear of fire, the weakness of compassion. Very little worried him anymore; he was in the servitude of ultimate power, with a great deal of his own. He had waited his entire life to assume the position of Invoker. He had no intention of being robbed of the pleasure by the pangs of a conscience he no longer possessed.

'You're a *myth!*' he found himself shouting at the wooden ceiling of the bedchamber one night after awakening from the vision. 'I'll not be intimidated by a lie, even one as old as the ages! Burn yourself to cinders!'

The silence of his keep reverberated around him.

Navarne

Cold cinders lay in sodden mounds amid the scorched ruin of the House of Remembrance. They blackened the crystalline snow as it fell, leaving a desolate pit of mire where the great outpost had stood, once a monument to perseverance and bravery, now a testimony to cowardice and evil. The first outpost of the Cymrian Age, a proud and glistening fortress that withstood the perils of the land and war and countless years, had been reduced months ago to nothing more than meaningless rubble.

All except for the palm-sized harp. Nestled firmly above the first hollow of the trunk of the sapling of Sagia that stood in what had once been the central courtyard, the tiny instrument played softly, resolutely in the darkness, weaving a song of protection and healing that surrounded the young tree and the ground beneath it. There, within the silver arms of that child of the ancient tree, born at the place where starlight first touched the Earth, hope burned, a tiny candle of belief refusing to be swallowed, not by fire or storm or the darkness of coming night. In that singular place, within the icy ruin, there was eternal spring, a warmth of love so deep that it had caused the oak sapling to blossom in flowers of purest white that rivaled the falling snow.

Ashe rose wearily from an unsettling repose beneath the sapling where he had come to rest. It was easy to feel close to Rhapsody here, on the warm ground she had blessed with her song. Surely the place had absorbed some of the pure elemental fire that burned in her soul. His dreams as he slept here had been happy ones, at least at the onset, but had twisted into nightmares of dark regret and isolation. Her words came back to him now on the cold wind.

I don't want to see you until the Council meets. I may never want to see you again after that.

The world reverberated around him, as it had in flight coming here. Gently he touched the bark of the young tree. It was deliciously warm beneath his frozen hands.

'I love you, Aria,' he said softly. His fingers trembled and stung with the rise of his other nature, creeping below the surface of his skin.

Goodbye, Ashe. May your life be long and happy. Please close the door behind you.

The rage began to burn behind his eyes again. He recalled other words she had spoken long before, in a happier time, when they were just discovering each other as lovers, traveling together, hidden away in his room behind the waterfall. They were words of melancholy, spoken in a shared confidence, before a crackling fire.

My past is a corridor of doors I left open, never meaning to close them. I never closed a door if I didn't have to, in the hope that things would be right again one day if I only left the chance open.

The note of finality in her voice squeezed his chest, making it hard to breathe, enflaming the dragon in his blood.

Please close the door behind you.

Ashe could feel the snap, the dam of his human resolve breaking. Over the slippery hold he had tentatively maintained, the dragon roared forth. As if drowning in a dark flood, his consciousness gave way to that of the beast, and he was swallowed within the void of himself, disappearing into a place darker than death as the wyrm rose, rampant.

At the onset of the attack, when the first trees at the outer forest rim succumbed to the flaming bolts raining down from the sky, Khaddyr sat up in bed, wide awake and trembling. For all that he had known that the nightmares had been nothing more than the hauntings of anxiety, sublimated with ancient lies, he knew as certainly that this was different. He could feel it through the Earth.

He knew the dragon had come for him.

At first he was so choked with terror he feared he might lose his water in the bed. Then, after a moment's contemplation, calm returned.

There was far more power nascent in the forest of Gwynwood than inherent in any dragon, even Elynsynos herself. The strength of Gwynwood was the Great White Tree, the living vessel of the energy of the Earth, the last place where Time itself began. It was the reason the Filids lived at the Circle, and made their lives' work its tending and nurture. The Tree was the Signpost of the beginning of the world; the Invoker of the order that sustained it could draw upon its power to shield the holy forest. He had seen Llauron do it a number of times.

Llauron was dead. He was the Invoker now. And while he had only begun the ritual of staining the earth around the mighty Tree's roots with his blood to bend it to his master's will, he knew that in the banishment of the wyrm from the holy forest he would be able to draw on the Tree's power easily. He had been Llauron's Tanist for three decades. He was the Invoker, heralded by a Namer, undisputed.

Slowly Khaddyr rose from the beautiful bed and donned his simple gray robe. He shuffled to use the privy, then washed his face and hands in the ceramic basin. The face that stared back at him in the looking glass was a noble one, he decided, freed from the lines of care and weary duty that had long beset his features when he was still a mere healer. Becoming Invoker had imbued him with a strength of countenance as well as the power of the land. He reached for the staff of his office and ran his hand along the smooth white oak of the shaft, enjoying the way the golden oak leaf atop it glistened in the firelight.

'Let her come,' he said, smiling. The face in the glass smiled back with confident strength. 'Let the dragon come.'

By the time the fire reached the inner forest edge, it was clear that the beast was being selective about what it destroyed.

Contrary to the descriptions in the old manuscripts, no vast serpentine shadow darkened the land from the skies overhead. No earthquake rumbled through, no towering wall of water appeared on the horizon at the edge of the sea. It would have been easy to mistake the initial stages of the dragon's rampage as nothing more than a winter brushfire, sweeping through the holy forest with a brutal vengeance, heightened by the bitter wind.

The villagers from the outlying settlements, fearing just that, had swarmed in waves to the protection of the Circle, seeking shelter beneath the arms of the Great White Tree. Almost as quickly they left and returned to their homes when the flames broke along the forest roads, sparing the villages, hospices, and training settlements of the foresters who plied the Cymrian Trails as pilgrimage guides. At least one peasant was heard to remark at the power of the new Invoker, a dominion so ever-present that even the element of wildfire did not touch his faithful.

Blessed be ye, Your Grace.

Khaddyr stood beneath the Tree and watched them go.

57

Lark stepped out of the fireshadows, trembling.

The wood was burning, though the flames had passed the villages and hostels; it was as if the fire was sparing the faithful, withholding its wrath from the exterior settlements.

It was coming instead to the Circle with a vengeance.

The herbery and Lark's lands, several leagues away, had been consumed in a rolling wave of fire that crept from the forest edge, turning the white snow and the brown earth orange with its light. Branches in the trees above her burst into flame, even though the fire had not reached that area yet, rained down and fell to the ground around her, seemed to follow her as she ran.

Khaddyr, she thought desperately. *I have to get to the Invoker.*

As she hurried along the forest road ahead of the conflagration, she could see hundreds, perhaps thousands of the faithful milling through the wood, could hear their nervous talk. Tales had caught the wind, fragments of stories of a dark man walking, unscathed, through the inferno, little more than a shadow wrapped in mist.

Lark had little use for such rumors, discounted the words shouted by fleeing people above the wind of the fire, until she caught a single one.

Dragon.

She had to stop for a moment to restart her breath; her heart had constricted in fear at the word, squeezing the air from her lungs.

When her breath returned she covered her stinging eyes with her arm and hurried to the Circle.

The Invoker stood in the shadow of the Great White Tree, leaning on a white wood staff, its golden oak leaf tip gleaming in the oncoming light.

Khaddyr breathed deeply, inhaling the scent of burning leaves and smoke. All about him the Filids were panicking, hurrying westward where the fire still had not ringed the inner forest. He had tried to keep them calm, had tried to assure them that they were safe beneath the boughs of the Great

White Tree, but the fear had taken hold. He could not command them, could only stand and watch them run into the arms of death.

'Your Grace.' The words were whispered, barely audible above the distant fire's roar.

Khaddyr turned around to see Lark standing behind him, her face a mask of smoke. He smiled slightly.

'Ah, Lark, I should have known you alone were stalwart enough to stay.'

'I'm leaving, Your Grace, and so must you. Come with me; there is still time to flee west. The dragon comes.'

'Flee? To where? To the sea? To the lair of the beast herself? Don't be ridiculous.' Khaddyr smiled beneficently and held out his hand to her. 'Do not fear, Mother. Elynsynos would not burn the Tree.'

Lark stared into the reddening sky above her, the normally placid features of her Lirindarc heritage taut with panic.

'The dragon comes,' she repeated. 'You must make haste and leave at once, Your Grace.'

Khaddyr patted her shoulder, struggling to keep his hand steady.

'She cannot broach the Circle, Mother,' he said as comfortingly as he could manage. 'Wyrmkin or no, the family of Anwyn no longer has dominion over Gwynwood; that rests solely in the hands of the living Invoker.' He squeezed the white oak staff, the rising light of the fire in the distance glimmering off the golden leaf at its tip.

Lark glanced quickly over her shoulder at the darkening clouds, rolling with bloody light.

'Llauron in his time could hold the whole of the forest,' she said in a low voice. 'Recall the plague of yellow locusts, or the great midsummer storm ten years ago? He commanded the insects to be gone from Gwynwood; he told the winds to be still, and they obeyed. Something is wrong, Khaddyr. You should have been able to banish this menace from the outer rim of the wood. Yet still it comes; the forest is burning with its wrath! I beseech you, leave now and save yourself.'

Khaddyr pointed angrily toward the west, where the fire was beginning to spread through the trees.

'Go now, then,' he said tersely. 'Quit this place, Lark, if you're afraid. I do not fear the dragon. My power here is absolute – *absolute!* You saw me wrest it from Llauron, saw me take the staff from his lifeless hand. You are my Tanist; if you doubt me, then go. You no longer serve a purpose here.'

Lark's face hardened in the light of the approaching flames. 'All right, then. Deceive yourself. Stay here and burn with your absolute power – it will make a pretty pyre.' She whirled and ran through the hail of flaming leaves that were wafting about in ashes on the coming wind.

The inferno's rage burned ever closer, but still Khaddyr did not fear.

Faith, he intoned to himself. *Stay the course.*

His master's words came back to him now, spoken softly in the shadows of the winter festival bonfires.

Unquestioned authority. Invulnerability. And Life unending.

Khaddyr gripped the staff even harder, trying to contain his excitement.

I will kill her, as I did Llauron, he thought, feeling the sweat from the heat and the arousal of power course through him. *I will be the one to vanquish the mighty Elynsynos, to drive her back into the ether. I have the power now.*

He laughed aloud.

'Let the dragon come!' he shouted to the burning sky. 'Let her come!'

In reply the ground beneath him trembled. Khaddyr's eyes flew open. The walls of fire that had now reached the Circle seemed to part, opening a dark corridor in the pulsing sheets of light.

Even surrounded as he was by searing heat, Khaddyr felt suddenly cold.

In the midst of the roaring flames and billowing smoke stood the shadow of a man. The hood of his cloak was thrown back, revealing hair that gleamed in the reflected waves of light like bright copper on a hearth. Other than the shining hair, all his physical features were wreathed in darkness. The fire seemed to dance around him as if he were no more than a shadow himself.

'It can't be,' Khaddyr whispered. 'Gwydion?' *He has come back from the dead?* he thought, his mind refusing the possibility.

The Invoker trembled as he rose, shaking with age and fear. He pointed the oaken staff of the Filids, Llauron's staff, at the man in the center of the conflagration. *'Slypka,'* he whispered, willing the flames to extinguish.

The intensity of the fire dimmed a little, making the outline of the man somewhat more distinct. Khaddyr took a deep breath, then planted the staff in the parched grass next to him, leaning on it for support. When he could finally speak, his voice was calm.

'I command you by the power of the Circle, Gwydion ap Llauron, be gone from this hallowed wood,' he said. He inhaled again, the caustic smoke burning his nostrils and lungs. The lore of the forest, the power of Gwynwood, would banish the beast, he knew. His power now. He was the Invoker.

The dark figure did not move.

Khaddyr gripped the staff more tightly; the golden oak leaf at its tip glinted in the light of the inferno around them. 'I am the true Invoker, Gwydion,' he said above the noise of the fire to the dark shadow with the gleaming crown of hair. 'The ascension was justified under the laws of Buda Kai, in the presence of a Canwr as witness and herald. You cannot challenge me here; the moon is on the wane. It must be waxing to bless the results of a challenge. In addition, you would dishonor Llauron's memory if you were to—'

The staff in Khaddyr's hands burst into flame.

With a shriek the Invoker dropped the burning staff to the ground. In horror he watched it incinerate, the symbol of the office he had sold his soul to gain. It withered to ashes within seconds; they caught the smoky wind and disappeared, leaving only the gold leaf tip on the ground. After a moment it melted in the heat into a shining puddle that reflected the fire's light.

The shadow-figure opened its eyes, and involuntarily Khaddyr gasped. Burning blue, as brilliant as the flames from the center of the Earth, two points of ferocious light appeared in the otherwise solid darkness of his face, beneath the blazing hair that blended with the leaping sheets of fire behind and above him. Khaddyr took a step back, trying to keep his terror from coloring his voice; he knew his face already showed it.

'Gwydion—'

'Who is the host of the demon?' The voice that issued forth from the shadow shook the earth beneath Khaddyr's feet, causing him to stumble and fall to one knee. It was more a roar than spoken words, sounding in multiple tones of soprano, alto, tenor, and bass, crackling with the ferocity of high wind in fire.

A gagging sound came from Khaddyr's throat, and nothing more.

'Tell me,' demanded the dark figure. The fire grew more intense, matching the heat in his voice.

'I – I don't know,' Khaddyr choked.

The tree palace ignited, ripping into flame. The glass panes in the windows reflected the pounding light at the sky as the roof of each oddly angled wing burst open, showering sparks through the dormant gardens that surrounded Llauron's keep. Flames climbed the tower that reached above the tree canopy, turning it to a blazing column of fire.

'Dear One-God,' Khaddyr whispered.

From the backdrop of rolling fire behind the man another figure ascended, hazy and ephemeral. Its serpentine head reached skyward, cresting above the burning treetops. Its eyes gleamed with the same ferocious blue light that stared from the shadow-man's face, its enormous pupils razor-thin vertical slits that shrank even more as the inferno grew in strength. Great wings of shimmering copper scales, translucent in the light, stretched out over the Circle lands, casting dark blankets of mist as they unfolded. Its great hissing voice spoke in precise synchronicity with that of the man it hovered above.

'*Who is the host?*' The thunderous demand shook the very earth.

Khaddyr swallowed, tasting blood in the back of his throat. 'Forgive me, Gwydion, I can't. I fear you in life, but I fear him more in death. Have mercy.'

The shadow-dragon let out a furious roar. Over the cacophony of the burning forest and the screams of the evacuating Filids, it shattered the remaining panes of glass and shook the branches of the Great White Tree which stood alone, unscathed, in the midst of the fiery nightmare. The searing blue eyes in the human figure closed, disappearing back into the dark face again.

'I did not give you leave to die yet,' Ashe said, his words ringing in the multiple tones of the wyrm. He raised his arm and pointed at the Filid priest, the great healer, now prostrate on the forest floor.

'*Luhtgrin*,' he said in the language of the Filids. *Invert*. '*Cartung*.' *Sustain*.
Khaddyr felt his feet go numb. Then, a moment later, a shock of agony crippled his toes as they began turning at an impossible angle. He let out a scream as the skin rolled back, exposing nerve and muscle, vein and bone, then slowly continued up his legs. The horror of what was happening crept through his brain, making it go numb as well.

He was turning inside out.

Khaddyr screamed again, a high wail of shuddering terror.

'Tell me,' the dark figures demanded again in one voice, man and dragon. 'Tell me or I will leave you like this, alive.' Khaddyr's kneecaps popped sickeningly as they inverted.

'Stop, I beg you,' Khaddyr moaned.

The man-shadow and its second nature, the shade of the dragon, walked slowly through the burning grass and over to Khaddyr until it stood directly above him, the vast shadow of the wyrm hovering over him in the smoky air. By the time man and dragon-shadow reached him he was writhing in agony, the long bones of his thighs exposed on the bloody grass. With another popping, then a crunching sound, the genitals and hipbones twisted inside the quivering muscle and skin, the large arteries pulsing hideously.

Khaddyr was muttering incoherently. With a ringing sweep Ashe drew Kirsdarke from the sheath across his back and pressed the point into the old man's throat. For a moment Khaddyr's eyes cleared, and he stared at the rippling waves of the weapon, surging blue-white like ocean currents, running down the length of the ancient blade.

'Please,' he whispered as his chest cavity turned inside out, exposing his racing heart and struggling lungs. The wheezing, squishing, and hideous tearing sounds almost swallowed his words. 'You'll need – me, Gwydion. A – healer. Rhapsody will – need—'

The sword point pressed deeper. 'What about Rhapsody?' Ashe demanded; the multitoned voice shook the burning leaves from the singed branches above them. 'What will Rhapsody need?'

'When – she—' Khaddyr panted. He turned and looked at his fingers, which had begun to turn inside themselves. 'When – she—'

From the depths of his exposed viscera a tiny root appeared. Within a heartbeat many others like it sprang forth and whipped around Khaddyr's vital organs. The vines thickened quickly, forming ropy strands pocked with thorns that drew taut around the would-be Invoker's heart and squeezed suddenly. A hideous stench billowed forth over the smell of the fire.

'What will Rhapsody need? Curse your soul, Khaddyr, *who is the F'dor?*'

Khaddyr let out a gurgling gasp, then turned one last time to Gwydion, his eyes glassy and sightless with pain.

'Kill me,' he whispered as beads of bloody sweat emerged from his brow. 'Mercy—'

The shadow-man bent down near enough so that the Invoker could hear him. 'Tell your master I am coming for him,' he said through gritted teeth.

The vine pulsed violently, and Khaddyr's heart exploded, sending streaks of bright blood into the air, where the raging fire illuminated it into showers of red light.

Ashe stepped back as the vine recoiled, flipping Khaddyr over onto his exposed stomach and entrails. Within moments dozens of other vines shot forth, encircling him completely. Then, with a snap, Khaddyr was dragged, slamming over burning brush and trunks of decimated trees, into a large mound of blazing fire. The stench grew overpowering as his body hit the flames, and Ashe had to shield his eyes from the explosion of black fire that ensued.

The F'dor was claiming its own.

For the second time that winter Ashe stood, spent, beneath the Tree amid the destruction of fire. The Filids moved about through the desolation like sleepwalkers, staring at the ruins of the tree palace, stepping in between the rubble, all that remained of the shining castle at the heart of the Circle.

At the edge of his senses Ashe could feel Gwen stepping carefully through the remains of the rooms she had once kept for his father, lost in the place she had once known better than any other. He closed his eyes and willed her presence from his mind; the dragon within his blood slept now, sated in its destructive rage. The awareness of his second nature stung, like a sore muscle.

The Filidic priests that remained loyal to Llauron stared dismally at the ruins of the holy circle of trees that ringed the Great White Tree. One of every known species had its place there before the fire, sometimes the last surviving specimen of a species. Now all that remained of the trees were blackened trunks and charred, ragged columns of ash pointing skyward like broken fingers.

Only the Great White Tree still stood, unscathed, undamaged, though it was stained with soot and ash. Its leafless boughs still gleamed in the diffuse sun, reached into the heavens despite the smoke that hung heavy in the air.

Fire shall not harm thee.

The wind picked up, tousling the red-gold curls of his hair. In its passing Ashe could hear his father's voice.

Thank you, old boy.

Ashe turned and walked into the smoldering forest, on his way to find Lark and the others.

58

Tyrian

Each of the hills in Tyrian City contained a piece of the sprawling royal complex, culminating with the throne room atop Tomingorllo. At the base of the first hill, Newydd Dda, were the main hall and some of the living quarters of the nonexistent monarch and his counselors. It was here that Rhapsody had arranged to meet with Rial, the Lord Protector of Tyrian.

She stood with Oelendra in the great rotunda, admiring the craftsmanship and architecture. Unlike the simple, austere design of the Great Hall atop Tomingorllo, the main palace at the base of Newydd Dda was the showpiece of Tyrian, the place where ambassadors were once housed and international business conducted. It was set within a vast courtyard, surrounded by a massive wall with stone guard towers, far outstripping even the grandeur of the keep of the Lord Roland in Bethany. Rhapsody's eyes, healing from the bitter, mistaken tears she had recently shed, took in the sights with wonder.

The rotunda itself contained an enormous circular hearth at its center, the fire of which warmed the expansive palace and its wings, keeping them at the perfect temperature year-round. The palace had been built around many tall trees that now grew within it, as did a wide variety of verdant plants and flowers, all of which were kept in a constant growing season by the heat circulating from the main hearth, imparting the feel of a conservatory.

A faceted crystal screen circled the hearth, and the prismatic reflections that bounced off it and around the main hall had a hypnotic effect on Rhapsody. She and Oelendra sat down on one of the cushioned wooden benches that faced the fire and waited for the Lord Protector to meet them.

Her eyes wandered over the intricately carved woodwork of the palace, polished to a mirrored shine for no one in particular. The floor was a giant mosaic of brightly colored marble, the patterns of which honored the formerly united factions of the Lirin, abstract representations of the sea, the plains, the forests, and the cities of Manosse. She had just returned from visiting two of these factions. The news was not promising.

Rhapsody looked up to see Rial striding toward them, smiling. The women rose as he approached, a fond look in his eyes. He took Rhapsody's hand and bent over it, then bowed to Oelendra, who returned the gesture.

'Welcome back, Rhapsody,' he said, gently pulling her hand into the crook of his arm. 'How was your visit to the plains?'

'Disturbing, I'm afraid,' she replied as the three of them walked toward Rial's offices within the eastern wing of the palace. 'The violence against the plains Lirin is apparently even worse than it is here; their lack of cover provides greater opportunity for random attack, as I expected. Their army is well trained but small; the incursions are escalating.'

'Did they ask for assistance?'

'No, they were uncomfortable requesting help from the forest, even though they were once part of Tyrian. An alliance makes perfect sense; Tyrian can spare some of its guards to reinforce the army of the plains, and in turn they can guard your southern border.'

'But will they agree?'

Rhapsody sighed. 'I don't know. I guess it depends on how compelling they find my proposal to reunite.' Rial held open the door to his tiny office, neatly kept but overflowing with manuscripts and scrolls.

Rhapsody looked around and shook her head. 'Rial, since there's no king currently, why don't you move into the huge office that was kept for the monarch? It doesn't make sense for you, the person who handles all the trade and ambassadorial agreements, to be wedged in here with a shoehorn like this when that big one across the hall is standing empty and has been for a hundred years.'

Rial offered the women the two chairs, leaning himself on the edge of the desk, and laughed. 'You know, Rhapsody, you may vaguely resemble the Orlandan Cymrians, but you certainly talk like a Lirin.'

Rhapsody smiled at him. The Lirin, in spite of their tradition of monarchy, were an egalitarian society. No marriage lottery existed; both men and women served in the army, as guards and ambassadors. Succession was granted to the oldest child, not the oldest son, and each monarch had to be confirmed by the joint Lirin council and by the diamond-shard crown itself. It was a monotheist and a monogamist society, one that fit Rhapsody's values perfectly.

'Thank you,' she said sincerely. Then a thought occurred to her. 'Interestingly enough, Lord Tristan Steward once informed me that, while I looked like a Cymrian, I had the manners of a Bolg.'

'Coming from a Cymrian, that's high praise, even if he doesn't know it,' observed Oelendra dryly. Rial and Rhapsody laughed.

'So how do you suggest we proceed?' Rial asked, settling into the chair behind his desk.

'Well, I think we should meet in the throne room in council with all the Lirin ambassadors. The power of the demon is growing because it is somehow able to temporarily bind soldiers of each faction to missions of murder they don't remember. I'm sure this is true of the human incursions into Lirin lands as well. So the first step is to resolve the petty differences between the various Lirin factions and bring them back together. That way the F'dor will have fewer camps it can divide against each other.'

'And then?'

'Second, we meet with Tristan Steward and his dukes. We form an alliance with Roland.'

Rial whistled. 'I'm afraid you don't understand the difficulty of what you are suggesting, my dear.'

'Yes, and that's precisely why she has the wisdom to want to try it,' Oelendra said, smiling at Rhapsody. 'Sometimes what's needed is a new eye that has not been informed of all the reasons why success is impossible.' Rial nodded.

'The Bolg and Roland already have a treaty; Sorbold has one with both of those lands, and with the Lirin as well. The Nonaligned States have their own problems, but the demon doesn't seem to be focusing too much there, though I predict they are next. Whoever is starting these incursions has access to the soldiers of each land. Once we are aligned we can flush that person out. It really can only be one of a handful of people, who can move from camp to camp, unchallenged.'

'Prostitutes? Merchants?'

'Perhaps,' Rhapsody said, nodding.

'What about Anborn ap Gwylliam?' asked Oelendra. 'He has the access you mention among all lands, even the Nonaligned States and the countries past the Hintervold. He has fought on and against all sides. Who better to pass among them unsuspected?'

Rhapsody thought of her rescue at the Kinsman's hands, his rough but careful ministrations to her after he had saved her from the storm. Her stomach tightened at the thought of his duplicity, but she couldn't deny its possibility. Then a more frightening thought occurred to her. If Anborn was the demon, she had slept alone in his hut, been vulnerable in his presence. Perhaps she herself had been bound, might be his thrall even now, unwittingly. The idea was too much to contemplate.

'We can't rule out anyone at this point,' she said, rising. 'Well, what do you say, Rial? Is it worth a diplomatic parlay?'

Rial smiled. 'It is, Rhapsody, if only for the opportunity to watch you wrap those hardboiled curmudgeons around your finger.'

Curmudgeonly was far too nice a word to describe the behavior of the Lirin ambassadors, Rhapsody decided many hours later as darkness came to the land. They had been arguing nonstop since the first two had arrived in the Great Hall at the top of Tomingorllo, and as each successive representative had joined the discussion it had become proportionally uglier. Finally she rapped on the wooden bench for their attention.

'This is ridiculous,' she said, exasperation in her voice. 'I can almost understand this kind of behavior in Roland; they have so many conflicting lines of succession, Cymrian and not, that it almost excuses them acting like children at a birthday party fighting over the extra sweetmeats.

'But you, ladies and gentlemen, confound me. You are Lirin, the longest-lived of all the races common in these lands. You have seen centuries of conflict and bloodshed. You have witnessed it yourselves, not through the words of legend, but through your own eyes, in the deaths of your own relatives. What is it going to take to awaken you to what's happening here? Soon it will be unnecessary for the enemy to destroy your lands; you will do it to yourselves! This should be the easiest group to convince, but you seem intent on arguing about nothing.

'The only thing you appear to agree on is that you don't trust Roland, and its Cymrian lineage, despite the fact that many of your own people are of that lineage, too. Very well, let me ask you this: if it was Anwyn who destroyed the Diamond, leaving your line of succession unclear, why would you want that to continue? The ancestors of Roland will keep you divided and weak forever. Rise above it! Choose one among you who can see these people not as plains Lirin, or sea Lirin, or forest Lirin, or Manossian Lirin, but Lirin! This should be simple.'

342

The ambassadors stared at her, dumbfounded. Finally Temberhal, the representative of Tyrian to Manosse, shook off his trance and addressed her politely.

'Precisely how would you propose we do that, m'lady?'

'First, agree to unite. Maintain your independent leadership under a ruler who agrees to recognize it, and swear loyalty to him or her. Can you all agree to that, at least in theory?' The ambassadors looked at each other, then nodded, one by one. 'Good. Next, each of you pledge that fealty on the crown. It had always been seen as a judge of wisdom before; ask its assistance in choosing a worthy candidate now. Agree to abide by its decision. Then go back to your various lands and return with anyone you know to be an appropriate possibility for High King or Queen of all the Lirin, and see who it chooses. Coronate him or her immediately. Fair enough?'

Silence hung over the throne room for a moment, then the ambassadors returned to their discussions. This time the conversations seemed constructive, however, and Rhapsody looked to Oelendra, who smiled and nodded slightly.

She let loose a sigh, and stared out the center opening in the ceiling at the stars as they appeared in the deepening sky. She had sung the greeting to them softly on the frosty hillside outside the Great Hall as the sun was setting, causing the first break in the arguments inside. When she and Oelendra had turned to go back into the building they found the ambassadors gawking at them from the doorway. The peace was temporary, however, and a few moments later their fighting resumed again. Now at least they were talking pleasantly.

Oelendra rose as the ambassadors' discussions continued and came over to her, sitting down next to her on the great circular bench.

'What's your next move? If they don't agree soon, that is?'

'I intend to starve them into compliance,' Rhapsody answered solemnly. 'I told Rial not to allow any food to be brought here, and not to feed any of them, until they agree. Hardly a good way to achieve consensus, but I'm running out of patience. Next I'm going to stop feeding the fireplace and freeze them until they comply.'

Oelendra chuckled, and Rhapsody shook her head. 'You know, Oelendra, this has been an eye-opening experience for me. I'm not sure what I expected to be able to assist with here, having no real place in this society myself, but whatever I had thought to accomplish I was wrong. I guess I'm not cut out for diplomacy or its facilitation.'

'Nonsense,' said Oelendra. 'First off, what you bring, in addition to your other skills, is the very fact that you are not aligned to any of these factions. You can't be seen as biased. In addition, you have no idea how remarkable it is that these people have even agreed to stay in the same room this long; it is undoubtedly a record. Whatever happens here, Rhapsody, that in itself is a tremendous accomplishment. It is not often that a warrior can act as a conciliator.'

'I don't think I qualify as either, actually,' Rhapsody said seriously.

'Now stop it,' Oelendra said sternly. 'We discussed this all the way to the court of the sea Lirin. You did not fail Llauron; he refused your service. The Iliachenva'ar needs to respect the customs of the religious leaders he or she protects, Rhapsody. There was nothing you could have done but what you did.'

Rhapsody looked away. She had not told her friend that Llauron was alive, despite her desire to confide the information to someone. She doubted she could even bring herself to tell Achmed or Grunthor, though she was certain Ashe would understand if she did. She rubbed her eyes, trying to soothe the headache pounding behind them. She was tired of carrying other people's secrets. Her own were heavy enough.

'M'lady?' Rhapsody looked up to see Temberhal standing over her, the other ambassadors behind him. The noble epithet he had addressed her with always caused her to grimace, as the title she had, Duchess of Elysian, was given to her as a joke.

'Yes?'

'We have reached consensus. We agree to unite.'

Her headache vanished at the words, and she stood immediately and embraced Oelendra.

'Wonderful,' she said, smiling at Temberhal and the others, whose faces reflected her grin immediately. 'Thank the stars. Now, first things first. Rial, let's eat. I'm starving.'

After the palace pages had cleared away the supper utensils, the ambassadors took their places around the crown. As Lord Protector it fell to Rial to invoke the pledge, and he stood, looking ecstatic and nervous, with his hand on the glass case that the crown rested beneath.

Rhapsody smiled at him, the excitement of the moment in his eyes. She hoped secretly that the crown would ultimately choose him; she felt his wisdom and kindness would go a long way to bringing the fractured Lirin people back together again. Then a thought occurred to her.

'Rial, may I call starlight upon the crown to bless it before you begin?' She looked at him, his grin growing broader as he nodded, then around to the others, who agreed as well.

Rhapsody drew Daystar Clarion and felt the rush of power as the sword savored the moment. A brilliant light flashed as it came forth from its black ivory scabbard, causing the ambassadors and even Oelendra to shield their eyes.

Rhapsody walked to the center of the room and raised the sword to the night sky, closing her eyes. She began to sing extemporaneously, calling to the stars to bless the crown of their children with light and ancient wisdom.

In response, a beam of intense brilliance descended from the heavens through the circular opening in the ceiling, bathing the crown and its pedestal, as well as the ambassadors who stood around it, in white

344

illumination brighter than the sun. With her eyes closed Rhapsody could feel its light, and a moment later heard a deep song begin within the throne room. It was the song of the crown, unheard for generations untold; its music reached into the hearts of all present, leaving them transfixed.

She opened her eyes, and stared at the diadem. It sparkled with the colors of a billion rainbows, each facet of every tiny fragment of the diamond glittering with prismatic brilliance. The light and color it generated lingered when the heavenly illumination brought forth by Daystar Clarion disappeared. The dark room became bright with the radiance of the crown. Rhapsody looked over to Oelendra. She was staring at the diadem with tears in her eyes. As the Singer looked around she found those tears mirrored in Rial's, and the eyes of the ambassadors as well.

A sudden awkwardness came over her, a feeling as though she was intruding on a moment that was sacred to the people of this land. She was not one of them, would probably never be, even though they had made her welcome, and heard her out when she was criticizing the way they chose to govern themselves. Rhapsody's face turned red in the darkness, unnoticed by the transfixed Lirin. Her half-caste status roared up within her, embarrassing her; she felt the urge to run. Knowing it would be disrespectful to the process she had herself begun, she backed slowly away until she was next to the bench near the wall and sat down quietly again.

After several minutes Rial blinked, and reached his hand slowly above the case. He touched the glass and as he did the other ambassadors followed his lead. Then he spoke solemnly, in a voice deep with emotion, the promise to join the Lirin together beneath a single ruler, and pledged his life in his or her defense. The ambassadors added their voices to the pledge, as did Oelendra, the Lirin champion. As the pledge ended they returned to silence.

Rial's eyes opened even wider, and he looked up across the room at Rhapsody. Her throat tightened under his stare.

'What have you done?' he asked in a scratchy voice when he could speak again.

Her palms began to sweat at the accusation. 'I – I don't know. What's wrong?'

Rial pointed to the crown. 'The diadem is not reflecting the starlight; it is generating this radiance on its own.' Rhapsody blinked and shook her head. 'Don't you understand? It is the fulfillment of the promise of Queen Terrell, under whose guidance the fragments of the Diamond were painstakingly collected and fashioned into the circlet. You have healed the Diamond, Rhapsody; you have returned the light of the stars to the stone.'

Rhapsody began to tremble. 'I – I'm sorry,' she stammered.

Rial turned to Oelendra. 'You are the only one among us who has ever seen the crown alive before,' he said to the Lirin champion. 'Is this as it looked in those days?'

The tears in the warrior's eyes spilled over and ran down her cheeks. 'No,' she said softly. 'The crown has never looked like this. Only the

Diamond in its original form held the light of the stars. Now the radiance of the crown surpasses the light it held when it was a single stone. If anything, its brilliance is magnified by its myriad pieces.'

The urge to take flight consumed Rhapsody. She stood slowly, as silently as she could, while the others were staring, enraptured, at the diadem, and backed quietly toward the door. She had turned and crossed the threshold when her mentor's voice sliced through the air in the room as it had in the spring during her training sessions.

'Stop. Where do you think you're going?' Reluctantly she turned around. 'Get back here, Rhapsody.'

Her trembling grew violent. 'Oelendra, I—'

'Don't be a coward.' Her mentor's words were harsh but her eyes smiled sympathetically. It was the smile of someone who had undertaken many tasks against her will in a cause greater than herself. 'Come over here.'

'I can't,' Rhapsody whispered. She could suddenly feel the call of the crown, stronger than that of the sword, coursing through her body. 'Please; I need to go home.'

Rial shook off his rapture and came to her, taking her hands gently in his own. 'M'lady, it would seem that you *are* home.' He smiled at her encouragingly. 'Don't be afraid. Do you doubt the wisdom of the crown?'

'No.' Her voice was so low as to be almost inaudible.

'Then subjugate yourself to its will. You are a child of the sky, Rhapsody. If the stars decide the Lirin need you, surely you would not turn your back on us? Your own people?'

'I've done all I know how to do,' she stammered, looking around at the ambassadors. They were all staring at her now, with varying degrees of delight on their faces. 'You don't understand. I'm a peasant.'

The ambassador from the sea Lirin, a woman named Marceline, left the display and approached her. 'You are the one who does not understand, m'lady,' she said gently. 'There is no such thing as a peasant among the Lirin. We are all children of the same sky that shelters us. You are as worthy as any to lead if you are called.'

'It would be rather hypocritical of you to refuse to take the crown, given what you were exhorting us to do, wouldn't it?' added Hymrehan, the minister from the plains.

Oelendra appeared at her side and took her elbow. 'Come,' she said, kindly but firmly. 'Let us see if the diadem has anything to add.' She steered Rhapsody over to the case, releasing her arm and resting her hand lightly on the Singer's back. 'Don't be frightened. Open the case and see what, if anything, happens. Perhaps you were only needed to bring the starlight back to the crown, and it will choose another to wear it.'

With hands that shook, Rhapsody opened the lid. Immediately the tiny stones of the diadem began to gleam even brighter, and, as if caught by the wind, swirled out of the case and above her head, circling like a halo of stars. The ambassadors took a step backward as the light from the glistening crown undulated over their faces, stinging their eyes for a moment, before it tempered into a glow above Rhapsody's head. In the brilliance Oelendra smiled and looked fondly at her student.

'Well, perhaps not.'

Rhapsody dissolved into tears. 'Please, please don't make me do this. I am pledged to serve, not to lead.'

Rial touched her arm. 'Don't be afraid, m'lady; we have all sworn to uphold you and help you in any way that we can, have we not, my friends?' The ambassadors nodded in unison, smiling. 'You have my promise of whatever assistance you need.'

'Now, what was your plan again?' said Temberhal seriously, his eyes twinkling. 'Agree to unite and swear our loyalty to a ruler who would recognize our independence. We did that. Pledge fealty to the crown and abide by its decision. We did that as well, I believe.'

'Yes,' said Jyllian, the ambassador from Manosse to the court of Tyrian. 'Then we were to see who the crown chose, and I believe we have. That just leaves the last step.'

'Yes,' said Hymrehan, smiling. 'And what was that again, Jyllian?'

'Coronate her immediately.'

59

The Patriarch's Manse, Sepulvarta

Four benisons of the Patrician faith crowded impatiently outside the intricately carved door of black walnut wood, awaiting their audience with the leader of their faith, the first they had been invited to in more than two years. They were all nervous, but Philabet Griswold was particularly agitated, as Nielash Mousa, the Blesser of Sorbold, had managed to arrange a private audience a few moments before, and now was in with the Patriarch, undoubtedly sowing the seeds for his own ascension to the Ring of Sepulvarta. Griswold was struggling to contain his rage, and losing the battle dismally.

'How much longer are we going to be consigned to this infernal hallway?' he snapped at Gregory, the Patriarch's sexton.

'Not one more moment, Your Grace,' Gregory replied dryly, taking hold of the door and opening it. 'The Patriarch will see you now. Please remember, Your Graces, that he is in very poor health and should not be upset or aggravated.'

Griswold glared at him, then strode rapidly into the room. The other three benisons nodded, and Lanacan Orlando patted Gregory on the arm as he walked past.

The room, customarily a cold place, had been heated, in the absence of a fireplace, with boiling water poured over piles of hot stones to keep the frail Patriarch from catching a chill. Clouds of steam rose and sank, passing like sky vapor over the silver star embossed in the floor, the room's only ornamentation.

In the heavy black walnut chair sitting atop a rise of marble stairs, looking frail and emaciated in his voluminous silver robes, sat the Patriarch, his bright blue eyes shining from within the prison of his failing body. In his clawlike hand, a hand which trembled violently, he was clutching a small scroll. He pointed to the five chairs that had been set up on the floor amid the rolling waves of steam, one of which was occupied by the Blesser of Sorbold.

'Please be seated, Your Graces,' he said. Despite his fragile appearance, his voice was clear, if thin. The benisons sat down, Griswold taking the seat farthest from Mousa with an undisguised scowl.

The eyes of the Patriarch went from one man to another, then to Gregory, who handed him a small white card.

'Thank you – all for coming so quickly. I have three things to tell you, my – brothers in Grace,' he said haltingly, consulting the card, then looking back to the benisons. 'As you probably – suspect, my time in this world grows short, and so I – wish to limit what I have to say to those things – that most need saying. Here they are.

'First, I have spoken – at length with – the Blesser of Sorbold regarding the terrible – tragedy at the solstice festival in – Navarne, and have read the missives – from the Crown Prince and the one – dictated by the Dowager Empress. I am convinced – that this was an inexplicable and – isolated act of violence, similar to all the – others that have taken place over the last – score of years, and not an attack – sanctioned by the crown of Sorbold – or its benison.' The Patriarch coughed deeply, then looked sharply at Philabet Griswold, who had begun to rise in protest. 'It is therefore the – position of the Ring that – Sorbold should not be punished in any – way for this incursion beyond – what they have already suffered.'

'Your Grace—' Griswold sputtered.

'Second,' the Patriarch continued, looking at his card, 'the Ring has received an – invitation, as I imagine have you all, to the – coronation in Tyrian of the new Lirin queen.' He looked up with a hint of a smile. 'I want to go. And I'd like – all of you to come with me.'

Ian Steward of Canderre-Yarim and Lanacan Orlando of Bethe Corbair looked at each other doubtfully. 'But Tyrian is an adherent to the faith of Gwynwood, Your Grace,' Steward said.

'Yes, which is under the – leadership of a new Invoker. But I have a great fondness for the – new queen; I owe her my life. And if there is not much more – of that life to be had, I wish – to spend it as I see fit. I invite you – to join me.' Each of the benisons nodded, Griswold curtly, while Nielash Mousa avoided his glance. The journey that the Patriarch proposed would mark the first time he had set foot outside of Sepulvarta since his investiture.

'Finally,' the Patriarch continued, 'I know you are – all very concerned with the issue of succession.' He wheezed harshly, causing Colin Abernathy and Ian Steward to jump. 'My decision – once it is made – will be recorded

348

on this – scroll. It is my hope that – you will not resort to – letting personal interest affect the aftermath of my passing. The Creator – speaks only to the one who – is invested as Patriarch with – a clear conscience and a willingness to submit to His will. Remember this.'

The hand holding the scroll began to tremble even more violently. The sexton stepped up to the throne and took the religious leader's hand.

'Do you wish to go back to the hospice now, Your Grace?' he asked as he held a cup of water to the Patriarch's lips. The Patriarch took a sip, then nodded. 'Very well, then, thank you, Your Graces, one and all. The coach departs in the morning at sunrise; I trust you can all be ready by then.'

'One moment, Your Grace,' Colin Abernathy called as the Patriarch rose to a shaky stand, ignoring the sexton's glare. 'I see you are not wearing the Ring of Wisdom this morning; is there a reason?'

The frail old man stood straighter, releasing for a moment his grip on the arm of the sexton. A mischievous light came into his eye.

'Indeed, Colin. One might think that – at my age and in my condition, undertaking – such a journey could *only* be done against the counsel of wisdom. It can only be – judged a very unwise idea, and detrimental to my health and continued existence.' He leaned forward a little and dropped his voice to a whisper.

'But I want to do it anyway!'

He took hold of Gregory's arm again, and took a few steps toward the marble stairs, then looked over his shoulder one last time on his way back to his sickbed.

'Please rest assured, Colin, and all of you, that the Ring will be there when the new Patriarch is ready to ascend the throne, whoever he may be.'

The Regent's Palace, Bethany

The office of the Lord Roland was cold, the coals of the fireplace having been allowed to burn down during the night. Tristan Steward sat before it, a glass of whiskey in one hand, the vellum invitation in the other, pondering his life and the next move in improving it.

The Lirin had chosen a queen for the first time in almost a century. Their choice came as no surprise to him.

He stared at the calligraphed missive and gulped the remaining liquid, clenching his teeth as it stung the length of his gullet. *What a colossal waste,* he mused, turning the invitation over in his hand idly. *I wed a beast to add Canderre to my holdings, when I could have married my heart's desire and gained sovereignty over Tyrian in the process,* something he knew had never been accomplished at any time in history. Sad.

Well, he had a year to make it right. To return Madeleine to her father's house and dissolve their union would surely cause tremendous uproar among the royal houses of Roland; Cedric Canderre would doubtless wish to have him ostracized from their mutual circles, even to the point of withdrawing his troops from the alliance. But one factor not currently in place would change everything; within the year he would be king.

Timing was everything.

The Lord Roland rose resolutely and shouted for his ambassador.

'Evans! *Evans!*'

When the old man appeared, still in his nightshirt, at the library door, Tristan Steward was already giving orders to scurrying servants. He paused long enough to look over his shoulder at the veteran ambassador.

'Evans, pack your court essentials. We have a coronation to attend.'

At the Phon River Crossing in Bethany

The Patriarch's massive coach rolled to an abrupt stop in the darkness.

The holy man sat up straighter as the small window in the front of the carriage opened, revealing the face of one of the four coachmen, and leaned forward, making a gesture for quiet to forestall the driver from wakening the Patriarch and the other four benisons who slept on the small couches that lined the carriage's inner walls.

'What is it, my son?' the holy man asked.

'The bridge is compromised, Your Grace; ice has broken through the main support brace. We are going to have to turn around and proceed north to Fisher's Landing; that's the closest place to cross the Phon.'

The holy man nodded, and the small window closed again.

He looked contemptuously around at the other men, snoring raggedly in disparate rhythms and varying degrees of glottal ugliness. Each of them was wrapped in the arms of sleep, something he had not experienced for as long as he could remember.

Since summer or perhaps before, he had found himself without the need of slumber, passing his days and nights in a state of heightened awareness, the human body he inhabited tiring occasionally, but never succumbing fully to unconsciousness. Instead his mind was adrift during quiet moments in a sort of meditation, a hazy pattern of thoughts and dreams that took the place of both sleep and true wakefulness. He was, in a way, a virtual sleepwalker, ever watchful, waiting for the day when sleep would end altogether.

And the nightmare would begin.

It was almost time.

60

Southwestern Navarne, at the Edge of The Forest of Tyrian

'I had no idea you made flutes,' remarked Grunthor as he watched the dying fire in the midst of their camp at the edge of Tyrian. 'You really are a man of hidden talents, sir.' He looked into the darkness of the forest and guessed that at their usual pace they would arrive a day ahead of the coronation.

Achmed slowly turned a sharply tapered auger deeper into the long, lacquered instrument he had found in a brass-bound chest in Gwylliam's treasure vault.

'I don't like the idea of being unarmed. This flute is a gift for Rhapsody, an antique, I think. And if it isn't one already, it'll look like one when I'm finished with it.' His voice clicked in a rhythm to match the cuts he made.

Understanding came into Grunthor's voice. 'Who do you expect a problem from at the coronation?'

'No one. Anyone. The Lirin take their "no weapons" rule very seriously. When I picked this up I felt it could serve as a staff, but I want to be ready in case of someone coming unannounced.' Grunthor nodded. 'Though I expect the Lirin to guard her well, I want to be prepared in case there is a slipup.'

'What kind of darts do you plan to use in your "flute"?'

'The heavy ones. That's why the inside needs to be grooved.'

'It'll sound like *hrekin*.'

'She won't care. It's the thought that counts. Particularly if it keeps her alive.'

The travelers worked at their respective tasks for a long while, finishing some time after the fire ring had gone completely dark. Grunthor fed the horses a few paces away and blanketed them for the night, then moved to the protected area between Achmed's watch position and the fire circle, preparing to go to sleep. He looked in the Firbolg king's direction and could almost see him. 'Is she going to know about the flute's other use?'

'No. And she won't need to if you can get the darts out of the bodies before she sees them.' Achmed moved slightly lower down on the ground. 'It's important that she doesn't. She's come into her own now, and if she's to win the life she wants then she has to feel she's on her own.'

An annoyed sigh came from where Grunthor lay, and a low growl was distinct in the giant's reply. 'I hate deceiving her. You all live with such lies, I don't know how you stand yourselves.'

'All of us except you, my friend; I know. The problem with telling the truth about some things is it would mean telling it about everything. The lies are how we *can* stand ourselves. I almost hope you live long enough to see what I mean.'

Grunthor, long accustomed to the sound of the startling voice, was already asleep.

The Lirin Palace at Newydd Dda

Rhapsody looked out the window of the balcony into the darkness of the courtyard. All day and far into the evening hours the preparations had been made, the trees of Tyrian's forest garlanded with winter flowers and wind chimes.

A dais had been built in the courtyard, making use of the existing reviewing stands and positioned so that the guests of honor could walk easily past the newly coronated queen. The persistent hammering and sawing outside her window made Rhapsody think of the sound of gallows being built, an apt image, given that, more than anything, she felt like a prisoner about to be executed in the morning.

She opened the large windowed doors to let in the night air now that the sounds of construction had abated. The curtains snapped in the breeze as the wind blew in, filling her bedroom with the sweet scent of a warm winter night. The leaves of the engilder trees that formed the canopy of the bed rustled above her as she sat down on it disconsolately, wishing she were back in Elysian.

The curtains billowed again in the wind, and a cloaked figure stepped out of the shadows on the balcony and came into the room. Rhapsody looked up, startled at the breach of security. Then her face broke into a broad smile of relief, and she jumped from her bed and ran to meet the intruder.

'You came! I was hoping you would. I'm so glad to see you I can't even begin to tell you.'

'Scaffold's almost done,' Achmed said with a wry smile. 'There's still time to escape.'

'Don't tempt me; I was hoping you would talk me out of making a break for it.' Rhapsody took his cloak and hung it in her closet.

'There are no more new worlds to run to,' Achmed said, helping himself to the decanter of brandy on the sideboard. He filled a heavy crystal glass.

Rhapsody shuddered. The memory of the Root was still strong, even all this time later. 'I thought you were here to cheer me up.'

'Window's open; we can go,' he said, dropping into one of the velvet wing chairs before the fire.

'So why are you getting comfortable?'

'Because it seems to me time to get comfortable.' Achmed looked at the fire; it was burning tentatively. 'You have to pick a place to live eventually; this seems as good as any for you.'

Rhapsody sighed. 'Wonderful. Now I'm being evicted from Elysian. Did you come all the way here to take my duchy back?'

'Of course not.' Achmed took a swallow. 'You'll need it now more than ever.'

Rhapsody went back to the window and closed the doors to the balcony. She turned and leaned against them, crossing her arms and regarding Achmed with a long look. 'Why does this feel so strange? Is this a sign that it's ill advised?'

'I'd be much more worried if it didn't feel strange to you,' he said. 'Your natural instincts would be clouded. If you are on edge that's a good sign that you are going into this with your eyes open at least.'

She came over to his chair and bent down next to him, taking his chin and making him look at her. 'Help me,' she said.

He stared at her unsympathetically. 'You don't need my help. You have everything under control. You have armies if you need protection. You have counselors if you need advice. You have a treasury if you need more clothes and baubles, though the gods only know why you would; you certainly depleted my coffers acquiring the ones you already have. What more help can I give you?'

'Tell me I'm doing the right thing.'

'No. You already know it. You're not receiving a crown tomorrow; you already have it whirling above your head. If you want to cancel the ceremony, call it off. Nobody sees a problem here but you.'

'That's it? That's your best advice?'

He chuckled. 'I gave you my best advice long ago: Tuck your chin; you're going to get hurt, so expect it and be ready; you may as well see it coming. It applies to more than battle and tactics.'

Against her will, Rhapsody smiled. 'I suppose. Can you stay?'

'A moment ago you were asking me why I was making myself comfortable.'

'That was because I was still hoping you would take me away with you.'

'You have to be the one to decide if you're going to stay or go. I won't do it for you.'

Rhapsody sighed again and walked back to the window. She stared out into the darkness of the courtyard, but could not make out the dais or the reviewing stand. She leaned her forehead against the coolness of the glass.

'I'll stay.'

Behind her back, Achmed smiled. 'Either way, whenever you're ready, just turn around. I will always be right behind you.'

'Uh, m'lady, may I trouble you for a moment?'

Rhapsody tied the belt on her silk dressing gown and opened the door to her chambers. 'Yes, Sylvia?' She shielded her eyes from the morning sun pouring through the window near the door.

The chamberlain, an older woman who Rhapsody liked immensely, was clutching her hands nervously. Her almond-shaped eyes, obsidian-black in the coloring of the Lirin of the cities, blinked rapidly in the morning light as she tried to speak in a calm voice.

'There's a – a gentleman here to see you, who says he's an invited member of your honor guard.'

Rhapsody took both of the woman's hands comfortingly. Perhaps it was Anborn; his gruffness often had an intimidating effect on people. 'What's the matter?'

'He's, well—' The chamberlain stammered anxiously. 'He's big, m'lady.'

A delighted smile broke over the queen-to-be's face. 'Oh, of course! Please show him in directly.'

Sylvia blanched. 'In here, m'lady?'

Rhapsody patted the woman's cheek. 'It's all right, Sylvia; he's an old friend, one of my dearest. Please bring him in.' Sylvia stared at her, then nodded and vanished. A moment later, the enormous grinning Firbolg came into her room. Rhapsody ran into his arms in delight.

'Grunthor! I'm so glad to see you.'

'The feeling's mutual, miss,' the Sergeant replied, returning her embrace. He set her down carefully and clicked his heels. 'I thank you for including me in the honor guard.'

'Including? They're under your command.'

Grunthor smirked in amusement. 'Oh, goody. I'm sure they'll *love* that.'

Rhapsody laughed. 'Well, it certainly will be fun to watch. There has to be *something* enjoyable about this godawful day.'

'Now, now, let's have none of that,' said Grunthor seriously. 'This is an important day, it is; I've thought you deserved something like this all along, after you got dragged away from home and all. Your forest certainly is a pretty one. Are you happy here?'

'As happy as I can be away from you and Achmed, I suppose,' Rhapsody said, offering him the breakfast tray. 'Are you hungry? Is there anything here that looks appealing?'

'Got any of the little Lirin-filled ones?' the Bolg asked solemnly as he poked one of the pastries with his claw. 'They're my favorite.'

'Not funny,' Rhapsody said even as she laughed again.

Grunthor surveyed the untouched tray, then helped himself to some of the delicacies. 'You haven't eaten a bite, Your Ladyship; now, come on, eat something. You'll faint in the middle of your own ceremony.'

'Good,' said Rhapsody, putting down the tray. 'Maybe they'll think I died suddenly and they'll crown someone else. Besides, I don't faint, unfortunately.' She picked up a biscuit and took a bite.

A knock sounded on the door. 'Are you ready, m'lady? The procession is forming.'

'Mllmckmt,' Rhapsody mumbled, her mouth full of pastry. She swallowed quickly. 'I'll be ready in a moment, Sylvia.' She stripped off her robe unselfconsciously in front of Grunthor, smoothed her petticoat, and ran to the closet. The exquisite gown that the seamstresses had worked on endlessly hung on a satin hanger. She eased it carefully down and stepped into it.

'Here, Grunthor, fasten that bottom stay, will you please?' She handed him the buttonhook. He was staring at it helplessly when Sylvia knocked and entered. She was holding a glistening strand of tiny pearls, a gift from the sea Lirin, to entwine in the intricate braid in Rhapsody's hair.

'Let me do that,' she said hurriedly, buttoning the bottom closures on Rhapsody's gown. 'Turn around, m'lady, and let's have a look at you.'

Rhapsody obeyed. Both the Firbolg giant and the small Lirin chamberlain looked at her in wonder. Her beautiful hair was delicately woven in the front into patterns resembling tiny golden flowers, pulling the front tresses back and exposing her exquisite face. The remainder was swept into a soft coil at the back of her head, secured with a pin that contained the sand-grain-sized pieces of the Diamond that had been too small to use in the making of the crown.

The dress itself was a wonder. It had been perfectly matched to her figure and coloring, shimmering iridescently, made from a silken fabric containing all the colors of the rainbow, yet at the same time glimmering white. The Lirin seamstresses knew how to dress a Lirin body better than any others did, and they had accentuated her form by tailoring the gown to her slender lines. The long sleeves pointed at the base of her wrists, the waistline dropped elegantly below her abdomen before flaring into a skirt that draped perfectly to the floor. A cape of white satin attached to the shoulders of the dress, both for ornament and to keep her warm in the winter chill. The toes of tiny matching slippers peeked out as she turned.

'You look great,' said Grunthor enthusiastically. 'Now let's get going. I've never been in charge of an honor regiment before. Don't want to be late.'

The coronation ceremony itself was attended only by the high-ranking Lirin from the forest, sea, plains, cities, and Manosse, and Rhapsody's closest friends and honor guard. Grunthor had been selected for that duty rather than as a guest because the guard were the only persons exempted from the weapons ban, and Rhapsody knew he would be lost without his weapons.

In addition to her giant Firbolg friend, she had asked Anborn, despite Oelendra's raised eyebrow, and Gwydion Navarne, the son of Lord Stephen, to serve in the honor guard as well. Anborn appeared delighted, in spite of the fact he was serving under a Bolg and with a lad of thirteen. He winked scandalously at Rhapsody when she entered the rotunda of the palace at Newydd Dda, making a rude curving gesture with his hands to indicate she looked appealing. Rhapsody laughed, grateful to him for breaking the solemnity that was threatening to make her bolt in panic.

She kissed Gwydion Navarne, her first adopted grandson, and watched as his face turned the color of Rial's scarlet cape. He was trembling with excitement, having been put in the company of the legendary Cymrian hero and the massive Sergeant-Major who had entertained him while they waited by showing him the proper way to pick nits from skinfolds and other private places. A silvery horn sounded, heralding the arrival of her sleigh.

The great doors of the low palace at Newydd Dda were thrown open. Rhapsody watched as four matching roans of irregular coloring pulled an ornate sledge of intricately carved wood in front of the doors and came to a precise halt there. Roans were steeds the Lirin valued highly, particularly those of especially mottled coloring, as they were well camouflaged in the forest and easily hidden. They were beautifully curried and braided, their breath forming clouds of steam and ice crystals in the frosty air.

Rial escorted her down the carpeted path and into the sleigh, helping her up onto the padded seat and straightening her cape for her. Then the procession was off, passing slowly over the snow and up the hill of Tomin-gorllo, climbing to the throne room, where the crown waited.

*

No clergyman or noble coronated the new queen, as there was no one in office to do so. The forestfolk of Tyrian were more closely aligned to the religion of Gwynwood than that of Sepulvarta, although several centuries before there had been representatives of both faiths serving there. Rhapsody had refused the suggestion of the Invoker as the one to bless her officially, giving no reason. It turned out to be unnecessary anyway, as the word had come a few days before the ceremony that Khaddyr, the new holder of that office, was missing and had not been seen in more than a fortnight since the great forest fire. The Lirin priests who had trained under Llauron offered to stand in at the general reception and were welcomed to do so.

Instead, as it had on the night she had called it to life, the diadem itself coronated the new queen. She stood before the silver pedestal and slowly opened the case. The sparkling gemstones roared to fiery life at her touch. The gleaming jewels became transparent and whirled out of the case and above her head, causing even those who had seen the sight before to stare in awe. When the radiance settled into a halo pattern of ethereal light, she looked up at Achmed and smiled, receiving a nod in return. Then she glanced at Oelendra and held her head high. The Lirin champion bowed slightly, an approving look in her eyes.

Rial knelt and spoke the ancient benediction, used in coronations that predated the arrival of the Cymrians to the continent.

'Inde arla tiron seth severim vur amasmet voirex.' May the stars give you their eyes and wisdom to lead us as they would if they could speak.

With the exception of the honor guard the assemblage knelt and repeated the words of the Lord Protector.

The sheer absurdity, the preposterousness of it all that Rhapsody had been secretly feeling melted away. She bowed her head and added her own prayer that she be worthy of these people who believed in her.

When the ceremony was over the assemblage dissolved into soft cheers and quiet applause, then laughter and embraces. Rhapsody hugged Oelendra first, then Rial, as she made her way across the circular room to where Achmed was waiting. She took his hands and kissed him on the cheek.

'Well, I survived, with your help,' she said, smiling at him.

'You prevailed, and on your own,' he answered pleasantly. 'I just kept you from escaping before you went ahead with what you wanted to do anyway.'

Her eyes went to the strange sunlike brooch on his robe. 'This is a nice pin,' she said absently. 'Is this a new Bolg emblem?' She reached out to examine it. Achmed took her hand quickly and kissed it. Rhapsody blinked in surprise.

'Don't touch,' he said chidingly.

'Your Majesty,' came Rial's voice from across the Great Hall, 'your guests are waiting below.'

61

The courtyard of Newydd Dda was filled past overflowing. Lirin citizens and the guests of state crowded the streets of Tyrian City, spilling into the vast forest clearing that surrounded the walls of the palace, hoping for an opportunity to view the newly crowned queen. Delegations of Lirin had come from each of the factional areas, from Manosse and the plains, from the cities in the Nonaligned States and the sea. Roland and Sorbold were represented, as were the Nonaligned States, Ylorc, and the lands beyond the Hintervold. Achmed was astonished; it seemed impossible that the word could even have reached those places so fast, and yet here they were, representatives from each, lining up to greet or bless Rhapsody.

He glanced back at her now, descending the hill in her heavily carved sleigh; a look of serenity was in her eyes that belied the panic he knew she felt at the sight of the throng below her. Grunthor rode before her; where the Lirin had found the horse they had given him for the procession he had no idea, but it was more than half the size of the sleigh itself.

He had managed to slip into the front of the procession as it came down the hill so as to afford himself as much time as possible to assess the crowd near where she would be standing. Assassination was not likely, given the number of trained Lirin guards that had secured the entire city, removing all weapons and potential instruments of damage. When he tried to enter the city that morning they had weighed the flute he carried as a gift for the new queen, leery of its heft. Only the intercession of Rhapsody herself had allowed his entry back into the city after he had left her room the night before. Despite the inconvenience, Achmed was pleased at the effectiveness of her protectors.

He leaned up against the palace wall and waited for Grunthor to pass. The Princes of Sorbold and Bethany were the first in line; Achmed smiled to himself at the irony. He would have been among them had he not been designated the equivalent of her family and invited to the private ceremony. Had he been in that company he would have been the most pleasant of the first three people to honor her.

Her antagonistic interaction with Tristan Steward was legendary throughout Ylorc, and the Prince of Sorbold was a hostile, dried-up old man who was waiting impatiently for his even-more-ancient mother to die so that he might finally succeed her. Rhapsody had met him only once, and she was too annoyed by his petulance to notice that he was utterly smitten with her. After she had left on her journey with Ashe to find Elynsynos the prince had sent emissaries to Achmed demanding her hand; the Bolg king had gloated at the prospect of sharing the news with her upon her return, knowing that the pyrotechnics display from her wrath would be worth inviting guests to watch. He had never told her.

Behind the princes were the Orlandan dukes, Martin Ivenstrand of Avonderre and Stephen Navarne, the Regents of Yarim and Bethe Corbair, and Cedric Canderre, who had nodded politely to him upon entering the courtyard, Stephen signaling his intent to meet up later. The dukes were followed by a small contingent from Gwynwood of Filidic priests of insignificant rank who had come in the effort to represent the religion in the apparent absence of Khaddyr the Invoker and his minions.

The priests were being repositioned by the chamberlain and her staff owing to the arrival a few moments before of another contingent. A gasp had gone up when the group had stepped forth from the enormous carriage that had been escorted under guard from the gates of Tyrian.

From the carriage had stepped the Orlandan benisons, Ian Steward of Canderre-Yarim, Lanacan Orlando, the Blesser of Bethe Corbair, and Colin Abernathy, whose See encompassed the Nonaligned States to the south of Tyrian. They were followed by the Blesser of Sorbold, Nielash Mousa, the only one in the robes of his country, colorful and striking in contrast to the pale holy garments of Roland. At length the Blesser of Avonderre-Navarne, Philabet Griswold, stepped out, a haughty smile on his face. He reached into the carriage and gently assisted a frail man in a tall miter and golden vestments. It was the Patriarch of Sepulvarta.

Though it was unlikely he had ever been seen by anyone present, the Patriarch's identity was obvious to all. It was his arrival that had caused the gasp to go up from the crowd. After a moment of shock, a smattering of applause began to ring out here and there, then swelled into a polite ripple, finally building into a wave that brought glad shouts with it.

As the Patriarch slowly tottered forward, his benisons and the Orlandan dukes stepped back to allow him access to the front of the receiving line. The two princes, who had been vying to be first, yielded their positions in the queue to him; if there was any resentment, it was well disguised. The Patriarch shook his head and bowed slightly, indicating that they should stay at the front of the line. Nielash Mousa and Philabet Griswold stepped to either side of him, assisting him up the steps of the reviewing stand. The other benisons fell in line behind him, followed by the dukes, then all the other guests of honor and the people of Tyrian.

The crowd swelled as Rhapsody's procession reached the edge of the city wall, waiting for the queen and her honor guard to emerge and ascend the dais to begin receiving the blessings and greetings of her well-wishers.

The honor guard was approaching the reviewing stand when suddenly the world shifted around Achmed. The exposed nerves and veins of his skin-web stung, then throbbed to pulsing life; the rhythm of his pulse began to pound in unison with another, one very close by. A moment later it was gone, then back again, moving.

He gulped a breath of the cold winter wind, hoping for clarity but instead breathed the air of the old world, of his life before, and it sickened him; it weighed in his lungs like stagnant water. He looked around, and for the first time in either life felt the crowd reel, felt it press against him like ocean waves; like he was adrift in strong surf. He had lost sight of Grunthor, of the wall he had been leaning on, of his whole awareness of existence in this land.

Just as suddenly, he came around. Instead of fighting the drowning feeling caused by the smell, he drew it in deeply. He opened his mouth and hands and eyes to the scent as he had in the old, hunting days, and it rushed into his mind like a flash fire:

F'dor.

He had come upon it. It was here. He shook his head to clear his mind and eyes, and found himself exactly in the spot he had been in before he detected his enemy. The shared blood rhythm pounded in his veins, beat in his chest like a drum of war, then moved again.

Grunthor had dismounted and was passing him at that moment on his way to the reviewing stand. Achmed touched him on the elbow. Without looking, the giant leant down to a practiced and discreet distance to hear his words.

'It's here, the Rakshas's master is here.'

Grunthor sought Achmed's eyes for an indication of direction, and saw them wide and taut, still scanning the crowd. He was looking with more than his eyes, breathing the particles of odor and breath and identity that wafted on the winter wind, matching them to the blood he had absorbed. The other two members of the honor guard passed him, Anborn eyeing Achmed suspiciously as he walked by. The scent, the malodor of burning human flesh in fire grew stronger, then vanished again as the breeze picked up.

Rhapsody was on the reviewing stand now; the dais had been built to allow her to enter from the back to avoid struggling through the crowd in front of her. Anborn, Gwydion Navarne, and Grunthor took their places behind her, the Bolg Sergeant immediately in back of her. His eyes went from Achmed to the crowd, awaiting the Dhracian's signal.

Achmed needed to get closer, but knew that if he could feel the demon's presence there was a chance the demon might feel his as well if he wasn't careful. He searched the courtyard for a good alcove in which he might be able to watch unobserved.

As he moved he wrapped a leather strap over the holes of the long flute and tied it off, hiding it in the moving folds of his cloak. The cold metal darts had been fashioned into an elaborate brooch that bounced dangerously, tantalizingly over his heart, the pin Rhapsody had commented on. He could feel the sharpness of the poisoned missiles sticking through the fine, thin Lirin ceremonial tunic he wore at Rial's insistence. As he moved closer to the dais, the scent of the regular air thinned and gave way to the acrid odor of the F'dor. It stood out in the open air of the courtyard much more vividly than it would have in any basilica.

Achmed drew the scent into his throat and across his palms. He closed his eyes and sought to match his heartbeat to that of the F'dor and hold it this time. At once he had it, beating in rhythm with his own, but it was still impossible to tell who it belonged to in the swelling crowd. The tension of the occasion mingled with the incense and the overabundance of rich fragrances worn by the emissaries from over a dozen different lands. He fought to tease out the ancient scent from all the ephemeral ones, to trust in his blood to feel the threads that tied the nightmares of this world to the horror of the last. Intently he tasted for that bitter tang and felt for the fearsome beat. He locked his own on to it.

Tristan Steward and the Prince of Sorbold had each kissed Rhapsody's hand and wished her well, moving off the platform and into the circle of their own guards. The Patriarch and his five benisons were approaching her now, each ready to bless her as well.

Suddenly Achmed's heart lurched, and he could see for a moment through the demon's eyes. It must be in the Patriarch's group, or near enough to her to touch her; only the other members of the honor guard were close enough.

At the same time his eyes melded with those of the F'dor he could see into its mind as well. There was no intent here to assassinate; it had come to bind the new queen to itself, to enchant her. He could feel it ready to spring, focused, hungry, to possess Rhapsody as it had bound the others. Given the choice, he knew she would have vastly preferred death.

Fear coursed through him and his momentary tie with the demon vanished; it was all Achmed could do to suppress a shout at Rhapsody to run, and take whatever risks would come from revealing themselves to it in this crowd of victims. It would be useless to do so, however; it was like trying to get a bride's attention from across a town square in the moments right after her wedding. He had to come up with another way to stop the F'dor from getting too close, preferably without letting it know he had discovered it.

He steadied himself, chasing the elusive threads of identity through the currents of air, over the landscape of the wind. The voice of the Grandmother, his Dhracian instructor in the thrall ritual, spoke in his mind.

Let your identity die.

Achmed nodded infinitesimally, willing his heartbeat to slow.

Within your mind, call to each of the four winds. Chant each name, then anchor it to one of your fingers.

Bien, Achmed thought. The north wind, the strongest. He opened his first throat and hummed the name; the sound echoed through his chest and the first chamber of his heart. He held up his index finger; the sensitive skin of its tip tingled as a draft of air wrapped around it.

Jahne, he whispered in his mind. The south wind, the most enduring. With his second throat he called to the next wind, committing the second heart chamber. Around his tallest finger he could sense the anchoring of another thread of air. When both vibrations were clear and strong he went on, opening the other two throats, the other two heart chambers. *Leuk.* The west wind, the wind of justice. *Thas.* The east wind. The wind of morning; the wind of death.

A net of wind.

Hear, O guardian, and look upon your destiny: The one who hunts also will stand guard, the one who sustains also will abandon, the one who heals also will kill, the Zephyr, the last Dhracian sage, had said in the last Dhracian prophecy. *Beware the Sleepwalker, for Blood will be the means to find that which hides from the wind.*

Time to stop hiding, Achmed thought silently. *Come out and play, you bastard.*

He cast the invisible net outward, toward the place where he had felt the demonic rhythm. Around him the sensitive nerves of his face felt the stinging breeze die down for a moment as the winds knotted together in a snare.

Then the scent, the heartbeat, the position all came together.

He had found the F'dor.

Now that he had finally identified the demon's host he knew he could get a clean shot off, but without any weapon to follow the first strike, it was likely there would not be a single survivor in this entire assemblage should he yield to the screams of his blood, his nature, and fire the blowgun into its back. His dart might be fatal to the human but it would not kill the demon. It would either flee the dying body of the host or turn and destroy everyone, starting with Rhapsody, unarmed in her beautiful gown. He tried to make eye contact with Grunthor as he raised the blowgun.

'Bye, Father,' he whispered as he put the flute to his lips.

Grunthor, for his part, had seen Achmed move, swinging the flute down out of sight. He was close enough to Rhapsody to touch her in one step; he could easily step between her and any threat he saw or sensed. Achmed's movement disturbed him, but he suspected he was the only one on the dais who had noticed. Rhapsody herself had only looked to her honor guard once, when the contingent from Gwynwood had approached.

The Sergeant tried to discern the nature of the threat and of whom Achmed was suspicious. He looked carefully at each of the two princes at the head of the line. They greeted the queen and stepped down without obvious incident. The next group was that of the Patriarch and a handful of his benisons.

Again, Grunthor tried to read the faces and movements of the guests, but saw no weapons or hostility evident. The Patriarch was a special favorite of Rhapsody's. He was very frail, and depended on many hands to keep his organization and himself alive. Rhapsody had defended him against the Rakshas some months back, and had said that she thought the F'dor might have been involved in the attack. It seemed unlikely that he was either himself possessed by the demon or able to detect it.

Grunthor looked quickly for Achmed again and could not find him.

Rhapsody was embracing the Patriarch emotionally; he was whispering a blessing into her ear.

Delight came over her face as she gently released him and their eyes met. They smiled at each other.

The Patriarch stepped back with the support of his benisons to let them make their personal greetings.

Suddenly he jerked sharply and collapsed into the benisons' arms.

A unified gasp rose from the crowd.

Grunthor reacted like lightning and interposed himself between Rhapsody and the commotion. He knew that men did not fall that way when something inside broke, and silently cursed Achmed's timing. Even though he could not see him, he knew the assassin's work.

'Step back, Your Majesty,' he said gently; he could feel her lifted off the ground as Anborn spun behind him and swung her to the back of the dais, adding his own body as a layer between her and the crowd. Grunthor, satisfied that she was out of the way, waded into the small flock of horrified benisons clustered around the body.

'Here,' he said roughly, 'let me.' Swiftly and effortlessly he lifted the dying Patriarch and moved him from the floor to a table several steps away where gifts of state had been set. With a sweeping action of his elbow the table was cleared and the old man settled on the surface like a feather coming to rest, the heavy dart from the back of his neck removed without a trace. As Grunthor had hoped, all of the benisons followed, praying for and ministering to their fallen leader as soon as they arrived, several of them in tears.

Lanacan Orlando, the Blesser of Bethe Corbair, was the first there, whispering words of comfort. He began immediately ministering to the dying man, checking his heart and wrists. Philabet Griswold and Nielash Mousa were next; both shoved the first benison aside and began immediately whispering in either of the dying man's ears, pleading with him to come to consciousness long enough to name his successor. Abernathy and Ian Steward stared blindly at the commotion, Abernathy muttering prayers under his breath.

Orlando angrily moved Mousa out of the way and went back to his ministrations. Frustration seemed to hamper his movements; his famed power of healing was not working. He checked the old man's breast, opened the robe particularly wide, felt his wrist, and became more agitated and irritated than resigned as the fact of imminent death became obvious.

'Stand back.' The voice, as clear as a bell, rang through the courtyard, sending the crowd into stunned silence. Rhapsody used Anborn to push through the benisons and moved directly to the Patriarch's side as he rested on the table. Grunthor quickly cut off any approach from the other side. She looked to her chamberlain.

'Sylvia, get my harp immediately.'

The chamberlain tapped a page on the shoulder and pointed; the young boy ran off at breakneck speed. The new queen bent over the frail man, who was curled like a baby bird fallen out of the nest, and took his hand.

'Your Grace, have you anything to say to these men?' She nodded at the benisons. The old man blinked his eyes; with great effort he shook his head. He reached shakily inside his robe and felt around awkwardly, then pulled out a parchment scroll and placed it in her hand. 'Very well; Anborn, please escort the various benisons to a place they can pray undisturbed.'

362

The Cymrian warrior stepped in front of the table and herded the benisons into a close, protesting mass. He walked forward, moving them out of the way, ignoring their arguments for access to their dying leader.

The Patriarch gestured wordlessly at the scroll in Rhapsody's hand. She held it up before his eyes.

'Do you want me to read this aloud?' she asked quietly. The Patriarch nodded.

'Very well,' she said. She gently released his hand that was clutching her own in the rictus of impending death and unrolled the scroll.

'Hear me,' she said; her voice carried the timbre of a Namer. 'I hereby herald the last missive of the Patriarch of Sepulvarta. It states: in the matter of succession, let the Ring and the Scales decide.'

The crowd began to murmur as the benisons, to a one, stood in shocked silence, turning alternate shades of angry red or ghostly pale. A moment later the page returned with Rhapsody's harp; he held it aloft and it was passed from hand to hand until it reached Anborn, who gave it to the queen.

'Grunthor, can you help me up here?' she asked, pointing to the table. The Bolg lifted her easily off the ground and onto the tabletop, where she sat and drew the Patriarch's head and shoulders into her lap. She made him as comfortable as she could and began to play softly, struggling to keep the tears out of her eyes. The old man smiled at her. At last he spoke.

'I – I'm sorry, my child,' he rasped, struggling to breathe. 'I didn't know it would – come now. I didn't – mean to ruin—'

'You've ruined nothing,' Rhapsody said reassuringly. 'Singing your dirge and witnessing your Last Words is an honor for me. I will herald them, and add them to the lore, so that they will live forever, and your memory through them. That we are together as you leave for the light is the best gift you could give me. Rest.' She stopped playing long enough to brush the shock of silver hair out of the eyes that were clouding over, reflecting the sun. Then she began plucking the strings of the harp again, crooning a sweet, wordless melody.

The Patriarch's breathing became labored. Rhapsody had seen enough death to know that it was at hand; she bent down to his ear and one tear fell from her glistening green eyes onto his face.

'My Last Words – speak them for me,' he whispered. 'You – know them.'

'Yes,' she said in return. She put her hand on the dying man's chest, and let his voice sound through her own, deep, rich and resonant as it must have sounded in his youth.

'Above all else, may you know joy.'

A blissful smile came over the cleric's face, and he closed his eyes. Rhapsody's song became stronger, and when he drew his last breath she began the Lirin Song of Passage, singing as sweetly as she could for the old man who loved the sound of the harp.

The cloudy day became slightly brighter as the bonds of the Earth loosened, just for a moment, long enough to allow the soul of the Patriarch to pass easily through. Except for the tiny surge of sunlight, the crowd was unaware of its passage, but Rhapsody could see it, and she blew a kiss skyward. Then she looked over at the benisons, standing in stunned silence off in the corner. Ian Steward and Colin Abernathy were clutching each other's hands, trembling and pale; Lanacan Orlando stood silent, his face a stoic mask, while Philabet Griswold and Nielash Mousa were barely in control of their rage.

'Your Graces, one and all, perhaps this would be a good time to lead us all in prayer.'

Achmed poured himself an extra-large glass of Canderian whiskey, and passed the bottle to Grunthor. The Sergeant looked at his king for a moment, then put the bottle to his bulbous lips and took a swig.

The day had been a nightmarish one. Rhapsody's skills as a Namer had served to keep the frightened assemblage calm, and she had stayed in the courtyard well past midnight, comforting those in mourning and greeting each of the well-wishers who had come to witness her coronation. Now she was taking a bath, hoping to wash away the effects of the chaos that had been her coronation ceremony. Her Firbolg friends sat before the fire in her chambers, discussing the next move before she came out again.

'You don't think she noticed the dart?' Achmed took another deep swallow, clenching his teeth as the burning liquid ripped down his gullet.

'Definitely not,' said Grunthor, taking another swig. 'She thinks the old goat dropped dead on his own, as he said he was going to months ago.'

'Good. Let's keep it that way. I doubt she would appreciate it if she knew her friend's death was a diversion.' He saw a scowl cross Grunthor's face, but the giant said nothing.

A moment later Rhapsody came into the main chamber in her dressing gown, her hair wet, with a drying cloth in her hand. She went to the fire, which crackled as she approached, and bent over before it, drying her hair with the drying cloth. Finally she shook her head, the semi-dry tresses falling around her face, rosy from the bath and the firelight. Then she came to Grunthor and took the bottle out of his hands, taking a swig and handing it back to him. She sat on his knee.

'Soon no one is going to want to come to any party I give,' she said. Grunthor chuckled; Achmed merely smiled. Her eyes darkened. 'Thank you both for all your help today. I would never have made it through without you.'

'It was a little worse than you think,' Achmed said, swallowing the rest of his whiskey and pouring himself another splash. 'Our friend from the Vault of the Underworld decided to come to your party.' Rhapsody looked at him questioningly. 'I discovered who the F'dor is today.'

Rhapsody sat straight up, almost falling off Grunthor's knee. 'Who?'

Achmed set his glass down. His face grew solemn in the firelight. 'Lanacan Orlando, the Blesser of Bethe Corbair.'

'Are you certain?' she asked, her eyes widening.

'Absolutely. I could smell him when the Patriarch's contingent got out of the carriage. I traced him and caught his heartbeat; it's him, the demonic knob.'

Rhapsody leaned back against Grunthor's shoulder, deep in thought. 'Well, that makes some sense. The Patriarch said Lanacan was the priest he would send to heal the injured and bless the armies; that gave him access to them when they were completely open to him. He could bind them as he was blessing them, planting the seed for them to erupt in murder later on, that bastard. Oelendra suspected Anborn because he had the very same kind of access.'

'He's been on our bloody doorstep all this time,' muttered Grunthor as Achmed took the whiskey bottle and poured another glass. 'No wonder he volunteered to be our personal cleric. Thank goodness we Bolg are godless pagans on our way to eternal damnation in the Afterlife.'

Achmed nodded. 'Well, the good news is that I don't believe he knows we're on to him. The Patriarch's timely, er, untimely demise covered my finding out, so we didn't have to move against him.'

'Yeah, what a coincidence,' muttered Grunthor. Achmed shot him an acid glance.

Rhapsody was looking puzzled. 'Something still doesn't make sense to me,' she said, taking another sip from the bottle. 'I know that the benison holds services every week in the basilica in Bethe Corbair. All the benisons do, each in his own See, except for Colin Abernathy, because the Nonaligned States don't have a basilica. Those basilicas are sanctified ground, blessed by the elements themselves; I can't believe it is within the power of even the mightiest demon to circumvent something like that. If he were to desecrate the holy ground in some way to allow himself to be able to even stand on it would be resanctified immediately by whatever element it is consecrated to.'

'Do you remember what element the basilica in Bethe Corbair is dedicated to?'

Rhapsody thought for a moment, retracing her conversation with Lord Stephen. 'I think it's the wind,' she said at last. 'Of course it is. Remember the sound of all those beautiful bells? You could hear them everywhere in the town.'

'It's hard to get around that,' Grunthor said. 'But, of course, nothing is impossible.'

'Right,' said Rhapsody. 'So what do we do now?'

'Well, Grunthor and I are leaving tonight or tomorrow to follow his caravan back,' said Achmed, downing his remaining whiskey. 'I asked Sylvia to let you know when and if the benisons take their leave; they should be easy to track.'

'What about me?' the new queen asked indignantly.

'You're to stay here for the moment and get established in your new kingdom. If you leave immediately after being coronated it will arouse suspicion. We will scout to see what is going on; then we'll come back here and plan the sortie to kill it. It should give you a few weeks to get things in order. Fair enough?'

'I suppose,' Rhapsody said, looking out the window. 'Let's not wait too long, though, all right? I don't want the body count of innocents to be any higher than it already is.'

Grunthor and Achmed exchanged a glance. It was one higher than she realized.

62

At the Eastern Edge of the Krevensfield Plain

The Blesser of Bethe Corbair was a patient man.

He had always been so. Even in the days before the Taking, in the time prior to becoming the host of the demon, Lanacan Orlando had been a patient man. Not suited by temperament or position to fight for dominance with Mousa or Griswold, he had instead chosen the path of long-suffering, humble service in the hope that the Patriarch would see the depth of his commitment to the All-God and to the Patriarch himself. Instead, the years passed; he repeatedly accepted the Patriarch's sincere thanks for taking on the most onerous of tasks, loyally serving as the healer to the festering wounded of the armies, the low-life populations of Bethe Corbair and the farming villages of the Krevensfield Plain, while the power and prestige were routinely reserved for the more assertive and combative benisons. Lanacan waited for the Patriarch, a soft-spoken man with a distaste for strife, to ultimately reward him for all his good works, his mild manner, but it never came to pass. His only thanks for all that patience was the Patriarch's good opinion.

When finally Lanacan Orlando made his deal with the demon, he discovered that it, too, was patient. Unlike most of the others of its race, intent on mayhem and chaos at all costs, lusting for power and the friction of destruction, the F'dor that took him on, came into him like breath, remaining in his lungs like heavy vapor, clinging thickly to his blood, had a long worldview, a plan it was willing to wait to implement until all the pieces were in place. Over the years, as he grew more and more demonic, it seemed as if the F'dor's avarice might have even been tempered somewhat by the patience he had possessed before it possessed him.

Now, spring was coming. He stood in the thin snow of the Krevensfield Plain, the anger from being thwarted at such an important juncture still unabated, growing more fierce and furious, like a spreading fire, by the moment.

The Patriarch had died in Tyrian, not in Sepulvarta. He had died without a successor, and, more important, without the Ring. Had he remained in Sepulvarta, where he had spent his entire life since investiture, the benison would have been the one to comfort him in his remaining days. To ease his transition from life to death, in Orlando's own time. To make sure all the pieces were in place for Orlando's ascension as the new Patriarch, which would give him the chance to crown his thrall King of Roland.

Well, no matter, he thought, trying to quell the screaming voice that burned in his ear. *He has the armies.*

Now, Tristan Steward, he whispered into the wind. *Begin.*

He waited until the command caught the west wind, then turned to his livery driver and the soldiers who served as his escort and smiled beneficently.

'Well, gentlemen, we are but a day from home. I can almost hear the sweet music of the bells of Bethe Corbair on the wind; shall we saddle up, then, and be off?'

Bethany

Tristan Steward swung open the door just as McVickers, the new knight marshal of the united army of Roland, was preparing to knock.

'Come in, McVickers,' he said thickly. The soldier stepped into the room and closed the door behind him. He stood at attention, waiting for the prince to speak, but Tristan merely returned to his desk and the enormous pile of parchment documents he had been paging through. After a few moments, McVickers spoke.

'What can I do to be of service, m'lord?'

'You can stand there quietly while I get the maps together, McVickers.' The prince's voice dripped with venom. The soldier inhaled deeply and remained at attention.

Finally Tristan found what he wanted. He spread the sheets out on the long table near the window and gestured impatiently to McVickers. The soldier came and stood by his side. He stared down at the maps that the prince was arranging on the table. Finally he spoke.

'Canrif, m'lord?'

'Yes,' Tristan answered, smoothing the corner of an ancient map that was attempting to reroll itself. 'The Bolglands.'

'Sir?'

Steward's eyes glittered impatiently. 'What is it you don't understand, McVickers? I've summoned Stephen Navarne and asked him to bring from his museum the drawings of the internal tunnels and mountain passes that were built in the Cymrian times; I doubt there has been much structural revision. Most of the changes will have been to the outer defenses, to the outposts and perhaps in the field tunnels known as the breastworks.'

'I – I don't understand, m'lord.' McVickers stammered as the enormity of what the prince was contemplating began to dawn on him. 'You – you aren't planning to – attack the Bolglands, are you, sir?'

The madness in Tristan's eyes shone brighter than the morning light outside the library window. He had been in a rage of sick disappointment ever since the coronation, when the Patriarch's untimely demise had caused a panic, and thereby prevented him from the private audience with the new Lirin queen he had been craving with anticipation. He had been forced to leave immediately with the benisons and the other provincial leaders, to return to Sepulvarta for the funeral. Rhapsody had not attended; she had already said her goodbyes.

But at least she was now ensconced in Tyrian.

Out of the Bolglands.

Out of harm's way.

'Yes, McVickers,' he said darkly. 'Yes, I am. It's only a shell at this point, anyway; a plague of some sort has destroyed the army and most of the populace. Those Bolg that remain must be contained to ensure that the disease does not spread to Roland. Now gather your generals, and begin a muster. I want to leave as soon as all the provinces have sent their soldiers, when the last troops arrive from Yarim two months hence.'

McVickers nodded, feeling the weight of an executioner on his neck as he did.

'Yes, m'lord.'

Lianta'ar, the Basilica of the Star, Sepulvarta

The sheer scope of the cathedral, its massive domed ceiling overarching a hall the length and breadth of several city streets, only served to unnerve Achmed even more.

He had surprised Grunthor to the point of speechlessness when the Bolg king announced that he wanted to stay near the basilica of the Star for a few moments after the benisons had left, along with the weeping faithful, as night fell on the conclusion of the funeral rites for the Patriarch. Lanacan Orlando, who had passed up the service itself to remain behind in the Patriarch's manse, comforting the grief-stricken abbot and ordinates, had already departed to return to Bethe Corbair. His coterie had headed north toward the crossroads of the trans-Orlandan thoroughfare, the roadway built in Cymrian times bisecting Roland from the seacoast to the edge of the Teeth. Achmed reasoned they could catch up with him easily by traveling overland.

You know why he stayed in the rectory? Achmed had asked.

Binding more thralls?

That, and he can't go into the basilica. It's blessed ground.

The giant Sergeant-Major stood, still befuddled, at the back door in the dark vestibule near the entrance to the nave, the largest part of the basilica, where the faithful stood or sat during services. He kicked his toe through the debris left behind from the funeral, scattered feathers that had been used in the ceremony by the congregation to help speed the Patriarch's soul to the Light, soiled with mudfilth from the soles of ten thousand feet amid a sea of candle drippings and torn flower petals. Idly he wondered if any of the ashes from the Patriarch's body, set alight on the great brazier that had been erected on the altar, were mixed in with the grime that marred the beautifully crafted mosaics on the floor beneath his boots.

Achmed looked over his shoulder for the fifth time, assuring himself that he was indeed still alone in the vast cathedral, then reluctantly made his way down one of the main aisles to the sanctuary where the pyre-altar stood atop a platform above a great number of stairs. Outside the cathedral the bells of the enormous tower known as the Spire were tolling the endless death knell. When he reached the foot of the stairs he stopped, then cleared his throat nervously in the haze of smoke that still hung heavy in the air.

'I hate priests,' he said aloud, his eyes fixed on the coals that had gone dark after being doused with holy water. He stared at the funeral brazier, from which a tendril of smoke rose questioningly.

Achmed rubbed the back of his neck as he spoke in the direction of the smoldering pile of brush and ash.

'I came to say that – I regret the way things came to pass,' he said quietly. 'I would have avoided it if there was any other way.'

The cathedral echoed with silence except for the reverberations from the endlessly tolling bells.

'Your death saved her life. Though we never met, given the choice, I think you would have wanted it that way, too.'

A sudden wave of discomfort flooded Achmed; he turned rapidly on his heel and hurried back down the aisle toward the shadowy vestibule. When he was almost at the end he turned once more to where the altar was now enveloped in darkness.

'Bye, Father,' he said.

63

Tyrian

Her workout at the lists that morning had been particularly tiring, and Rhapsody had embraced her bath with thankfulness. She came into her bedchamber, refreshed and dressed in one of the simple, artful gowns the Lirin seamstresses had fashioned for her. The clothing was a pleasure to wear, causing the body to feel unrestricted and light, and the color matched her eyes perfectly.

With a deep sigh she fell back onto the bed and stared up at the graceful engilder trees that served as bedposts, to their intertwined branches that served to form the canopy, lacy leaves casting sunlit shadows in dancing patterns on the bed and over her. The fire roared on the hearth, driving the chill from the room and warming the trees, keeping them in a false state of summer, even in winter.

In the courtyard below she heard the echoing sounds of distant commotion, and she rose and moved to the window, wiping away the frost and looking to see what was happening. Far off at the edge of the palace walls she could see amid a vast number of Lirin guards a large cavalcade of visitors forming an uneven line. The line swelled and grew larger as more joined, jostling and laughing, spiced with the occasional sound of argumentative confrontation. Their noise was unmuffled by the cold; steaming vapors rose from the distant conversations.

Rhapsody drew a soft cloak around herself, pulled on her boots, and left her chambers, seeking Rial, now her viceroy and chief advisor. Over the short time of her reign she had come to rely on him almost exclusively to explain the intricacies of the court, and advise her in matters of state. She was confident he would know what was going on.

She found him near the wall, very close to the convocation, watching grimly as guards and palace clerks catalogued the visitors and the items they seemed, without exception, to have brought with them. She slipped up next to him and touched him on the sleeve.

'Rial, what on Earth is going on?'

Rial turned to her and quickly took her arm, steering her hurriedly away from the crowd. They walked until they came to the curved wall of the guard tower. When they were out of sight of the throng he took her hand and kissed it.

'Good morning, m'lady.' He smiled down at her, his elderly face wrinkling into the kind expression Rhapsody had grown fond of. 'I thought you were away on the practice fields.' His breath formed an icy cloud in the air between them.

'I was, but there's only so much physical abuse I can take; Hiledraithe and Kelstrom took particular pleasure in beating me into submission today. What's happening? Who are these people?'

Rial sighed. 'Suitors, Your Majesty.'

'Suitors? Suitors for whom? I thought you told me that the Lirin did not have a marriage lottery, that women were free to choose their own mates.'

'They are, Your Majesty. These men are suing for your hand, or they are emissaries of lords who are.'

Rhapsody walked to the edge of the tower and peeked around. The line had grown even fuller, and the boisterous sounds were becoming deafening.

'You must be joking,' she said, staring at the crowd. 'There are scores of them.'

'Hundreds, actually, I would guess. I am very sorry, m'lady. I had hoped to spare you the sight of them.'

Rhapsody's face clouded over in dismay. 'I don't understand, Rial; why are they here, on such a cold day especially? I didn't say I was seeking a suitor, did I?'

Rial offered her his arm; as she took it he led her back to the palace. 'No, Rhapsody, but they are insidious. Normally within the first year we would have expected to see some of them, seeking to ally themselves with Tyrian by means of a marriage of state. Usually the first to arrive are the lords of the elder Lirin houses, since they have the early word when a new monarch is crowned; it was thus with Queen Terrell in the old times.

'My father was a page in those days and he described the scene to me often. Apparently a dozen or so of them came to the palace wall and waited all night after her coronation. The place was abuzz with excitement for days.

'That, however, cannot begin to compare to this. Many more of them out there are not Lirin. They are regents of other lands, some as far away as the Hintervold; undoubtedly they are looking to bind their kingdoms to yours. But if you would permit me to guess, I would say that word of you has spread for other reasons. I think it has more to do with you personally than with a desire to rule over Tyrian.'

'What do you mean? None of these people know me; at least I don't see anyone I recognize.'

Rial chucked. He was becoming used to her view of herself, and it amused him. 'I think it's possible that there are some things about you that might cause the word to spread faster than it normally would.'

Rhapsody shuddered. 'What are they bringing with them? Is it a brideprice?'

'Not exactly. They are gifts of state, similar to the others that came upon your coronation, but of greater worth. Traditionally, when you choose a mate, his gift is put on display in the Great Hall as a means of announcement. The others become part of your treasury, and Tyrian's. So you can imagine the competition that exists, trying to assure that a gift will suitably impress you, and will showcase the wealth of the suitor's lands, and his personal taste, to their best advantages.'

Rhapsody's face was becoming somber. 'Return them, please, Rial, and send these men away. I don't want to entertain any suitors at this time.'

As they entered the palace rotunda Rial stopped and took both of her hands, looking seriously into her face. 'I'd advise against that, Your Majesty,' he said gently, trying not to upset her. 'It would be perceived as a great insult. A better way is to accept the gifts and catalogue the requests, as the clerks are doing. Then they will return to their lands and await your invitation to those whose courtship you are willing to entertain. This way your desires can be accommodated, and the army will only have to fend off one or so at a time if they should become impatient.'

Even in the light of the roaring flames of the great hearth Rial could see her face go pale. 'What do you mean? Are you saying they might attack Tyrian if I don't accept suit?'

Rial stopped a page as she ran by. 'Bring Her Majesty some cider, please,' he said; the girl nodded and left. He brought the queen closer to the fire and sat with her on the wide bench before the hearth.

'It's always possible that, until you choose to marry and remove the possibility for other alliances, some of the regents will try and test your resolve by means of force. Do not worry, m'lady. This is unlikely, at least for a while, and the Lirin army, now that you have united all the factions, is a match for all of them.

'You not only have the loyalty of the soldiers, you have their hearts as well, and they will gladly protect your right to choose your time and your mate. Tyrian is a nightmare for invaders, and the casualties on their side will far outstrip our own. Someone will need to have a serious desire to make an issue of it before they will attempt to broach the forest. So please don't let it trouble you. Take your time; it's an important decision, and one I mean to see that you are able to make in peace.' The page returned with a heavy goblet and offered it to her. Rhapsody accepted it numbly.

With a polite gesture Rial dismissed the page, then looked into the face of the queen. He watched, fascinated, as the unguarded luster in her eyes receded and her face hardened into a resolute mask. She lifted the goblet and took a sip.

'I will follow your guidance, as always, Rial,' she said steadily. 'When you have a chance, please send a messenger to my offices. I have a missive I need to send.'

'That was a marvelous meal,' Anborn said, finishing the last of his wine and setting the goblet on the table. He cast a glance around the balcony at the bare, glistening trees that rose above the ornately carved railing. The day was brisk, but dining outside on the balcony had been pleasant, a refreshing change from the heavy smoke of the winter fires.

He was glad that he had responded in such a timely fashion to Rhapsody's invitation. Generally he made the issuers of such requests wait, just to be obnoxious. But he was pleased to have a chance to see her alone and assess her health and state of mind, which had been impossible to do at her coronation. She seemed much better than he could have imagined she would be after her experience in Sorbold and the forest, but then, she had been to the Rowans, and had undoubtedly passed far more time there than the rest of the world had marked.

When she had greeted him she was wearing the diadem, and he was fascinated to see it hovering above her head, whirling in a blazing halo of tiny starlike gems, transformed, it seemed, into glistening points of light. Once they had been left alone, however, she had removed it, and now was crowned only by her own resplendent hair, braided in the intricate patterns that none but skilled Lirin hands could weave. She was splendid lunchtime company, entertaining him with amusing stories and laughing unabashedly at his rude jokes. Even so, there was a reserve about her that he couldn't quite pinpoint; it was as if a piece of her were missing.

When the meal was finished she leaned forward, fixing him with as direct a look as he had ever seen.

'I was wondering if we might discuss something with the understanding that it's theoretical; that I'm proffering ideas to gauge your thoughts, but that neither of us is bound in any way by the discussion.'

Anborn wiped his mouth with the linen napkin and laid it, folded, beside his plate. 'Of course. What do you want to discuss?' He was intrigued by the look in her eyes; in previous meetings he had been struck by the remarkable openness of her face. Now her expression was guarded, and her bearing was even and cool, almost detached. Though her earlier beauty was enhanced by the excitement and mirth that shone in those eyes, there was an elegance and distance to her now that he found even more interesting.

'I was wondering if you ever contemplated marrying again,' she asked, looking at him levelly.

'No,' he answered. 'Why do you ask?'

'Well, if it is a possibility open for discussion, I would like to talk about it.'

Anborn leaned back in his chair, intrigued. 'I'm willing to talk about anything you'd like, m'lady,' he said, smiling slightly. 'Please, by all means tell me what's on your mind.'

'If it's not too unpleasant a concept to you, I wonder if you would consider marriage to me,' she said, still watching him keenly.

A small laugh escaped him, and he coughed into his hand as he sat forward. 'Sorry; I was just hearing the deafening sound of millions of hearts breaking all over the world. Did I hear you correctly? Are you proposing to me?'

'Not yet,' Rhapsody said calmly. 'As I said, I am gauging your interest. If you recall, we are discussing this openly with no obligations, right?'

'Right, of course,' Anborn replied, settling back in his chair. 'Well, on first consideration, let's say I'm intrigued. What would this entail? Why would you want to marry me?'

Rhapsody moved her plate out of the way and rested her arms, crossed, on the table before her. 'Well, I suppose the answer to that comes in two parts; why do I want to marry, and why you. First, why do I want to marry: I don't, actually. I would prefer not to, but then I would prefer not to be Queen of the Lirin, either. I don't seem to have much choice in either matter.' Anborn nodded, pleased by her candor.

'Unfortunately, since this has taken place I have been besieged by requests from the rulers of other lands seeking to parlay about a marriage of state. I have no desire to expand the lands of Tyrian, nor do I wish to be involved in the politics that would entail. I am also aware, however, that to remain a female ruler alone would be to invite constant testing of my resolve and the strength of my reign. I don't have the patience for that, nor the willingness to let anyone be injured or killed defending my honor for such a stupid reason. Therefore, I am resigned to the fact that I have to marry.'

A fragment of a smile crept into the considered expression Anborn was wearing. 'Somehow that doesn't seem like you, my dear,' he said dryly. 'I would have wagered a considerable sum that you would make a lioness's stand to the end against such threats.'

'You would be a far poorer man, then.' All traces of pleasantry disappeared from Rhapsody's face. She closed her eyes for a moment, fighting off the memory of the wyrm that slept within the bowels of the Earth. The vast tunnel wall she had once leaned against had been but a scale in its immense skin, its flesh a substantial part of the Earth's mass now. When she had banished the thought she opened her eyes again and looked directly at Anborn once more.

'Let us not mince words, General. We both know that war is coming; it draws closer with every passing moment. And while you have seen war firsthand, I have seen the adversary – or at least one of them. We will need everything we have, *everything*, to merely survive its awakening, let alone defeat it. I will waste neither the blood nor the time of the Lirin fending off a martial challenge over something so stupid as my betrothal. A marriage of convenience is an insignificant price to pay to keep Tyrian safe and at peace for as long as possible. We will need every living soul when the time comes. You once asked me if I was sworn to Llauron. I am sworn to the Lirin – I will do whatever I have to do to keep them safe, no matter how much it costs me.'

Anborn spun the stem of his wine goblet between his fingers, then nodded as his smile broadened. He raised the glass in a silent toast, drank quickly, then nodded as he set it down again.

'Pray continue.'

'Now, why might I ask you to be the one: you don't love me, and I don't want you to. I doubt that you ever will. I hope you won't be offended when I say that while I feel affectionately toward you, and might someday even be deeply fond of you, I don't think I could fall in love with you, either. That makes a marriage between us practical, and free from many of the problems that normally accompany the state.

'There is very little that I would ask of you: that you not embarrass me, or try to harm me or the Lirin people. Other than that, I make no demands. I don't expect you to be faithful to me, although I would appreciate your discretion. Of course, I would expect to have your loyalty in other matters. You would be free to come and go as you please.'

'Interesting,' said Anborn.

'Now, to the benefits. For me, aside from the beforementioned freedom from pursuit, I would have a husband I respect and like and whose reputation would frighten off potential problems. For you, I can't say what the benefits are. The Lirin army would be available in times of your need, though I would not commit them for unethical actions. There is some wealth and social stature to be had, even though obviously you are not without your own.

'Perhaps the reasons for you are not as strong as they are for me, and it might come down to doing me a favor. But you'd always have a place to come home to where you are welcome, honored, and appreciated. I would do the best I could to be good company and not to make demands of you. Anyway, that's what I am thinking. Do you have any questions for me?'

'Several.'

'By all means, please ask.'

'Well, let's see, what first – are children an expectation of yours?'

'No. Are they for you?'

'No. Actually, I prefer not.'

'I might, in fact, adopt one from time to time, but I think that would be seen as my child only, not yours. The Lirin are very understanding of this kind of thing.'

'I have no problem with that.'

'Very well. What else?'

'What about, er, conjugal relations? Is that a part of this agreement?'

Rhapsody didn't blink, and her face remained serene. 'That would be your decision,' she said. 'If it is an expectation of yours, it would be met. If not, that would be fine as well.' She smiled, and a hint of her old humor sparkled in her eyes. 'I believe you have seen enough to make an informed decision about this.'

Anborn shook his head and smiled in amazement. 'This is fascinating,' he said, an amused tone in his voice. 'I am sitting across from the most comely female that I have ever seen, a woman that has the male world prostrate at her feet, and she is discussing the possibility of our union with the same enthusiasm with which she might negotiate a land treaty or codification of technical law. It is almost surreal, Rhapsody. May I ask you one more question?'

'Certainly.'

'What happened to you? You are definitely not the girl I almost ran down on the road some time past.'

'No, I'm not,' she agreed.

His voice became uncharacteristically gentle. 'Was it whatever happened with the gladiator?'

'Oh, no. Not at all. It's just that I've grown up and come to understand what is attainable and what isn't, Anborn. I find that practicality costs me less than idealism did, and I've grown weary of wanting things I can't have. All I desire now is peace. And for the Earth to survive what is coming.'

Anborn rested his chin in his hand and studied her. 'What a shame,' he said at last. 'Although I will admit that I find you far easier to take like this, I have to say that I rather miss the other you. You are far too young and beautiful to sound so old and weary.'

'I am old and weary, Anborn; much older than you, by the way.'

'Only technically.'

'Point conceded. But I don't want you to think that I am always this pragmatic. There are still things I care deeply about, and I still have my music. As long as that remains I think I will not be too boring.'

Anborn watched her a long time; she did not avert her eyes or look uncomfortable, but lifted her goblet and finished her wine. Finally he spoke.

'No, I would guess not,' he said, with a slight smile. 'Well, without committing, since that was not part of the discussion, I would have to say that I am very interested. And honored, by the way. I think you would be almost the perfect wife for me, Rhapsody. As long as you allow me the freedom to come and go, I would enjoy the prospect of being your protector and guardian. I expect that we would share a good many interests. There are many things we could teach each other. And I know I certainly would relish a physical relationship with you – I'd have to be dead not to. You are right; love in a marital relationship is overrated and certainly not the most important factor.'

'I never said that,' Rhapsody said seriously. 'I just said I didn't think it was the most important factor for us.'

'Indeed; I stand corrected.' His eyes wandered over her face and upper body as if searching for something; a moment later he seemed to have found what he was looking for. 'The Lirin don't like me much, you know; an understandable hostility, left over from the war. Won't this be a problem for you?'

Rhapsody smiled. 'If the Lirin have a problem with it, I will abdicate gladly. One of the things I love best about Tyrian society, one of the main reasons I agreed to take the throne, is that they don't dictate who anyone marries. And perhaps we might be responsible for a small part of the healing process from that war, an undertaking that is long overdue.'

A look of frank admiration crept into his eyes. 'You are an amazing woman, Rhapsody – er, Your Majesty.'

She made a comically sour face. 'Oh, *please.*'

'And I am well and truly honored by your interest. So yes; if you decide you want a husband, and you are foolish enough to want that to be me, I would be interested in the position.'

'Thank you,' she said, smiling and sitting up. 'I will ponder what you've said, and I appreciate your candor.'

'If this is the sort of discussion topic I can expect whenever you invite me to lunch, I would like to make it a regular occurrence,' Anborn said, rising and bowing politely. 'I believe you know how to reach me if you come to a decision.'

'Yes,' she said, rising with him. 'Thank you for coming. I will walk with you to Oelendra's house. I have a few things I need to see her about.'

'Give her my best,' Anborn said, taking her arm in the crook of his own. 'By the way, have you discussed this with her yet?'

'Of course not,' Rhapsody answered. 'I felt you deserved to be the first to hear about it.'

Anborn laughed. 'We will get along just fine, Rhapsody,' he said, and together they strolled back to Oelendra's house.

At the crossroad path to the Lirin champion's cottage Anborn took Rhapsody's hand and kissed it.

'Goodbye, Your Majesty.' He nodded politely to Rial, who was coming up the path as well. The Lirin viceroy nodded coolly in return. 'Thank you for an interesting lunch. I will ponder what you said.'

'Thank you. Travel well.'

Rial waited until Anborn had disappeared into the forest, then came up to her.

'By your leave, Your Majesty—'

'Rhapsody, please.'

'Yes – sorry. There are a few matters I was hoping to consult you on.'

Rhapsody turned and continued to walk down the path toward Oelendra's house, motioning for him to follow. 'Such as?'

'The plains Lirin are asking for your aid in gaining tariff relief on their agricultural exports to Manosse and the Great Overward. Now that the realms are united, you are the controlling authority of—'

Rhapsody quickened her pace. 'Do you think I should grant the request, Rial?'

'Well, there are many good and—'

'So do I. Please take care of it. What else?'

'The battlements on the southern breastworks are in need of refitting.'

'Thank you for handling that as well.'

'The border patrols are requesting the building of two new longhouses—'

Rhapsody stopped walking. 'Rial, who took care of these things before I became queen?'

The elderly viceroy blinked. ' 'Twas I, Your – Rhapsody.'

'And, quite honestly, do you think I have any special knowledge of the details of refitting breastworks merely because I am a woman?'

Rial chuckled. 'No.'

'Surely you must be able to see that I am underqualified there as well, even if you are too polite to look directly. You were the Lord Protector of this kingdom for a hundred years before I came, Rial. You know far more about these things than I do. Continue to make those decisions on your own. Please don't take the time to make me feel important by asking me questions that you know the answers to and I don't.' A hoot followed by a round of raucous laughter went up near the outer gate from the place where the suitors were still gathered. Rhapsody looked off in the direction of the gate, then back at Rial.

'I have a few other things on my mind at the moment.'

'What a pleasant surprise,' Oelendra said, smiling, as she opened the door. 'It's always wonderful to see you, Your Majesty.'

'Oelendra, I love you, but if you don't stop calling me that I will have you beheaded.'

The older woman laughed. She spoke her reply in Ancient Lirin: 'With the help of what army?'

'Your own, actually,' Rhapsody replied in the same tongue, smiling.

Oelendra put an arm around Rhapsody's shoulders and led her inside, tossing her cloak over the edge of a chair. 'To what do I owe the pleasure of this visit?'

'I have a number of things to go over with you. Is this an inconvenient time?'

Oelendra sighed in mock despair. 'Rhapsody, you're the queen now. There is no such thing as an "inconvenient time" for someone where you're concerned.' She went to the fire and ladled out two mugs of *dol mwl*, then turned and handed one to Rhapsody. 'I take it you're still not enjoying the privileges of your new office?' Her smile faded as she looked in the Singer's eyes, and found a closed, distant look in them. 'What's wrong?'

'Nothing's wrong,' Rhapsody answered, sipping the mulled mead. 'Do you know Anborn ap Gwylliam by more than just reputation?'

'Aye,' Oelendra answered, settling into one of the chairs before the fire. 'Of Anwyn and Gwylliam's three sons, he's actually the only one I really do know. I attended all of their Naming ceremonies when they were infants, but they were only young men when the war began.

'I had seen them occasionally as children, but after the war Llauron spent much of his time at the Circle tending the Tree and leading the Filids, and I have not seen Edwyn Griffyth since before the war began. I hear he apprenticed in the forges of his father, and then went to sea. But as a child Anborn was always keen to learn the ways of the sword, so his mother sent him to me. I trained Anborn, and so know him rather well. Why do you ask?'

Rhapsody sat down in the chair opposite her and took another sip. 'I'm thinking of marrying him. Oh – he sends you his best, by the way.'

Oelendra looked her up and down a moment. 'Why?'

'Probably because he likes you.'

Oelendra snorted. 'Why are you thinking of marrying him?'

'To get rid of these incessant, stupid suitors, to put an end to the threat they bring. For all the reasons we've discussed before, Oelendra. Why not? Is there something wrong with Anborn?'

Oelendra put down her mug, leaned forward and regarded Rhapsody seriously. 'There is a rather obvious reason, I would think.'

'I can't think of any.'

'Don't be coy, Rhapsody; it doesn't suit you,' Oelendra retorted, her tone of voice becoming terse.

Rhapsody's tone matched her own. 'I'm not being coy,' she said, looking over at Oelendra with a look in her eyes that the warrior didn't recognize. 'Unless you have something about him of which I ought to be aware, I am thinking of finalizing the arrangements after the Cymrian Council.'

Oelendra watched her a moment longer, then drained the rest of her drink and put the mug down, her glance resting on the queen once more. 'What about Gwydion?' she finally asked, reluctant to have been the first to give ground.

Rhapsody regarded her levelly. 'What about him, Oelendra? He's married – doesn't that mean something to you? It certainly does to me.'

'So your response is to in turn marry his uncle? That's healthy. I don't care about Gwydion,' Oelendra replied, trying to make her vocal quality less intense. ' 'Tis you that has me worried. You are as you were when you first came here – ungrieved, unwept. You are carrying him in your heart, Rhapsody. There is no room there for anyone else yet, especially Anborn.'

'And it will be so for the rest of my days, Oelendra; so what of it? Anborn understands where he fits into my life, and I into his – if anything he may

378

respect my right not to care for him more than you do. This is a marriage of convenience, and we both know that. So what do you want of me? Am I supposed to mourn my life away, staying untrothed, and watch our soldiers meet and rebuff challenges for an alliance with their blood, their lives? How could you expect me to be so selfish, Oelendra? If anyone, I would think you would understand.' Her words became choked; she stopped speaking and glared at her mentor.

Oelendra rose and came to her, crouching on her heels before Rhapsody the way she did with children. With her hand she stroked Rhapsody's face.

'I do understand, darling, probably better than you do,' she said gently. 'You're wounded and in pain, and you're looking for a place to hide. Run to me, Rhapsody. I can protect you until you are healed.'

Rhapsody pushed her hand away. 'No, Oelendra, I can take care of myself. Gods, if I can't by now I should pack up and head back to Ylorc. Besides, you know as well as I do this nonsense isn't going to stop until something happens.'

Oelendra tried a different tack. 'So this is a marriage of convenience, and Anborn agrees?'

'Yes.'

'Then will you really live as man and wife? Alliance marriages aren't official until they're consummated.' She watched Rhapsody's face closely for signs of color as she usually saw during allusions to sex, but she saw none.

'Of course,' Rhapsody replied simply. 'I offered Anborn the choice, and he chose that one.'

'Are you surprised?'

'Not really.'

'And that's all right with you? You are going to let him make love to you?'

'Yes. It's part of the bargain.'

Oelendra shook her head sadly. 'I have lived too long. I would never have believed that I would hear you talk like this. Rhapsody, please consider what you are saying. You are going to sell yourself in marriage to a man you don't love, and defy the true feelings of your heart.' She stopped. The look on Rhapsody's face frightened her.

The queen was trembling with anger, or something like it; her eyes burned with green fire. 'I hate to disillusion you, Oelendra, but it won't be the first time. At least this time the reason is better – rather than just selling myself to survive, I will be selling myself so that Lirin soldiers will. It's a fair exchange, don't you think?

'I have been telling you all along that I didn't measure up to this position, but you wouldn't listen. So it shouldn't surprise you that water has found its own level again, and my reaction is to do the common thing – to resort to whoring as the path of least resistance. It's the only way I know, Oelendra. It's what I am. I guess you can crown a slut with ancient diadems and clothe her in as many silken gowns as you want, but blood will out, you see; she'll still lie on her back rather than stand and fight.

'And don't you dare throw Ashe up to me. He, at least, understood this. He, at least, knew me for what I was and accepted it. He didn't try to foist me off as someone worthy of respect, of leadership. He found someone he felt *was* worthy. He did the kingly thing, and I respect him for it. So please, don't pester me. Help me, Oelendra; this is hard enough for me as it is without you saying the things my mother would have. Thank Fate for taking her before she could live to see her daughter as the poorest excuse for a ruler the Lirin have ever had. Thank Fate she died without knowing me for the whore that I am.'

Before the last words had left her lips Rhapsody's head snapped sideways from a stinging slap delivered squarely across her face. She blinked, trying to absorb the physical and mental shock. As blood welled beneath her skin from the blow, she looked into Oelendra's silvery eyes and saw seething anger masked behind a calm facade.

'You have just insulted the honor of my queen, and more importantly, my friend,' Oelendra said in a cold, low voice. 'If you were anyone else, I would kill you where you stand for what you just said.'

Weary sympathy began to temper her fury. 'You may have mastered the sword, Rhapsody, but you are forgetting the more important lessons you learned here. I do not care what you were, or how you survived; we all do what we must when our backs are to the wall. I love you for who you are, and for what you can become.'

Rhapsody lowered her eyes as if ashamed. 'I'm sorry, Oelendra,' she said meekly. 'I can't help it; I know what I have to do, but it hurts so much that I'm afraid it's going to kill me. It's Anborn or Achmed; they are the only mates powerful enough to keep the others at bay. And I don't want to give Achmed access to Tyrian except in alliance. I love him, but I don't have any illusions about what he might do. Please help me do what I need to do, Oelendra. I can't bear to see anyone else die defending me. Please, Oelendra. I need your strength. If you love me, help me.'

Oelendra took her queen into her arms and held her as she began to weep. 'Listen, darling, we all need shoulders to cry on, and you are welcome to mine anytime. But you don't need my strength; you need to listen to what I've already told you, and heed your own heart.'

'No, I can't, Oelendra,' Rhapsody sobbed. 'My heart is selfish, and it can't have what it wants this time; that belongs to someone else now. So I have to listen to my gut, and it tells me that if any blood is shed defending my honor, which is a travesty anyway, that my soul will die.' Her tears subsided, and she fought to return to a state of calm. 'Help me, Oelendra. If anyone should understand, you should. You've stayed here, in this life, all this time when you could have been with your loved ones, out of a sense of duty to these people. How can you ask me to do anything less?

'If there is something you know about Anborn that makes him danger-ous, please tell me and I can talk to Achmed; perhaps we can reach an ironclad understanding. But don't make me live through this.' She gestured in the direction of the clamor that could be heard even from Oelendra's house; the suits were still being catalogued by weary clerks, four days after they had begun.

Oelendra listened for the first time, turning in the direction of the tumult outside her window. The laughter, the arguments, had receded considerably since the visitors had convened four days prior, but still the sound of catcalls and hooting merriment, bickering and ugly threats in myriad languages and dialects could be discerned. It was the sound of bloodsport, not unlike the noise heard outside the gladiatorial arenas in Sorbold and the far eastern provinces. Understanding came over her, and she turned back to Rhapsody, who wore the quietly panicked expression of a fox before the hunt.

Oelendra was filled with compassion for her friend and sovereign. *How awful it must be to embody such incomparable beauty and to have it bring nothing but despair,* she thought sadly. She ran her hand gently down the golden tresses, and then took Rhapsody by the shoulders, looking deeply into her eyes.

'Of course I will help you,' she said, smiling to give the trembling queen courage. 'You can depend on it, without question, always. As long as I live, I will help you. Not just because you are my queen, but for everything else you are to me as well. If you ever doubt that you are worthy of being the ruler of these people, remember the choice you were willing to make today. It shows ultimate leadership when one is willing to sacrifice what is most dear to her for the greater good of her subjects. The Lirin couldn't be in better hands. I will do whatever I can to end this, or I will help you through whatever difficult decision you need to make; you will not face this alone. But first you must give me some time. There are things I need to do, people I need to see. Do you trust me?'

'Yes, completely. But—'

'Good; then listen to me. Promise me you won't make a decision until I get back.'

'What if there is a demand or a martial challenge?'

'There won't be; I won't be gone that long. Have Rial send missives to each place represented, telling them you are considering the many attractive offers, and that you have gone into seclusion to weigh the value of each suitor.'

'I would have to do that, then. I don't want to lie about it.'

'Fine; you might learn some interesting things about your allies and enemies. Just don't race blindly into the arms of Achmed or Anborn until I've had a chance to do as you've asked. I will help you, but you must give me the time in which to do so.'

'Very well, I will. I promise. Take whatever time you need. Before I can deal with any of this, I have to confront and kill the F'dor. Achmed and Grunthor are coming any day now to plan the sortie and go after him. But I must ask you – what is it about Anborn that gives you pause? He seems like a good man.'

'There are many reasons, dearest. The Lirin hate Anborn. He fought very successfully against them in the war, and he was a brilliant general; his attacks on Tyrian strongholds were devastating.'

'That's the Past, Oelendra; I thought that you wanted me to help heal it and reconcile the people who hate each other. If the Lirin cannot accept him as my husband, I will step down.'

'Listen to what you are saying, Rhapsody; you're not thinking clearly. You are considering marrying Anborn in the first place because you are the Lirin queen and as such need a husband, even one you don't want or love, to stave off a challenge from your neighbors. Now you are saying that you are willing to abdicate if the Lirin object to your choice. What are you going to do then – marry Anborn anyway? Then you will have given yourself in marriage to a man you don't love, for no reason. That doesn't make any sense.

'You asked what was wrong with you marrying Anborn; what is most wrong is that you know very little about him. You are doing that deliberately; you think if you only know a part of him you can't care as much about him as you did about Gwydion. Muddled thinking again – there are things you might not want to see, but they are there nonetheless.

'Do not forget that even more than Llauron sided with his mother, Anborn sided with his father. He was Gwylliam's champion and his assassin; he is more like Achmed than you might care to recognize, Rhapsody. And he has a legitimate claim to the Cymrian Lordship, in some ways as legitimate a one as Gwydion does, at least with the Second and Third Fleets. By marrying him, you might just guarantee that Gwydion never ascends that throne, or that another war might come about. Think carefully, darling. And now, let me go look around. I won't be long.'

Rhapsody nodded, wiping the remnant of tears from her eyes. 'I love you, Oelendra,' she said gratefully. 'Thank you. Is there anything I can do for you?'

Oelendra was at the weapons rack, belting a sword and taking up the strange curving white bow. She blew Rhapsody a kiss as she took her high-collared gray cloak from its peg and opened the door onto the garden.

'Aye. You can be sure to lock up when you leave, Your Majesty.' She closed the door behind her.

Rhapsody wandered to the hearth, bending down to check the coals. A moment later Oelendra opened the door again, and entered the cottage, a scroll in her hand.

'Well, Oelendra, you're certainly a woman of your word; you weren't gone long at all.' Rhapsody's mild smile faded at the sight of Oelendra's face. 'What is it?'

Oelendra held out the scroll. ' 'Tis from Achmed.'

Rhapsody snatched the paper, broke the seal and unrolled it. The spidery script was unmistakable, the approximated spelling of the Firbolg language couched in their ancient code. The queen read the document as quickly as she could decipher it, then sat down on the couch before the fire.

'What is it?'

She did not look up. 'I'm to leave for Bethe Corbair in the morning.'

64

House of Remembrance, Navarne

Oelendra sat stirring the embers of the fire with a large stick, watching the sparks fly up into the sky. The chilly air hung heavy with moisture, causing her old wounds to ache, but she had grown used to such pains and ignored them. Instead she thought of the old outpost that had so recently stood in this clearing. Now all that remained of it was the burnt-out shell of the tower, and scattered timbers that had once held up its frame.

In what had been the central courtyard the Tree still stood, beautiful and undamaged by the smoke and destruction that had consumed the house. A small harp rested in the crook of its main boughs, still softly playing a repetitive melody. Oelendra's mind went back to when that tower was built, and the times it represented. She wandered down ancient pathways, and spoke to friends long dead. Distantly she asked the kings of old what had become of their noble line. She tossed the branch into the flames.

Her guest had arrived. He stood at the edge of the clearing, his visage hidden by his heavy mantle. In one hand he held a white wooden staff, in the other he carried Kirsdarke, the blue scrolled patterns visible in the ripples of its liquid blade even in the dark. Oelendra wondered how long he had been there. She smiled in welcome.

'Oelendra?' The voice of the shadowed figure was soft.

'You remember me, then?'

'No, not really,' Ashe admitted as he sheathed his sword and crossed to the fire. 'Not clearly, anyway. Just your strength, and your kindness. I have carried those things in my heart for many years. I owe you a great debt, but I'm afraid I don't remember much from those days aside from hazy, pain-filled dreams. I guessed who you were when I saw you. There are, after all, only so many people who know I am alive.'

'Until Rhapsody told me a short time ago, I was not one of them.'

Ashe sounded surprised. 'My father did not tell you?'

'Nay, nor did the Lord Rowan.'

He stepped into the light that ringed the air around the fire. As the young man entered the circle of warmth he pulled back his hood, revealing both the shock of his coppery hair and the small crystal globe he wore about his neck. *Crynella's candle*, Oelendra thought, the ancient melding of fire and water, created by a long-dead queen of Serendair for her seafaring lover, now adorning the throat of another lost sailor, by the hand of another Seren queen. It glimmered through the mantle of mist like a beacon through the fog. He was more handsome than Oelendra remembered, but she was not surprised. He had been at death's door when last they met.

'You look well,' Oelendra said as she gestured for him to take a seat. Her voice was terse; the smile of welcome had dimmed into one that was merely polite.

'You look worried.' He stepped over the trunk of a long-fallen tree and sat down on it, the firelight gleaming red-gold on his hair. 'What's wrong? Why did you call me here?'

'I thought the ruins of the old stronghold was a fitting, if ironic, place for us to meet.'

'Is there something I can do for you?'

The Lirin warrior looked him over thoughtfully. 'Perhaps. I have come in service of my queen.'

Ashe smiled, recalling the infamous words the legends said she had uttered to his grandmother long before his own birth. 'I thought you did not serve a monarch, but a people.'

'In my queen the two are united.'

He nodded. 'Good. Maybe it's a sign of changing times; it certainly would be a change for the better.'

'Indeed.' She took a drink from her water flask, then offered it to him. 'I see you are no longer hiding yourself. Is that a sign you are preparing to take the Lordship?'

Ashe shook his head, declining the drink. 'That title is granted, not taken.'

'That didn't stop your grandparents.'

'I am not my grandparents.'

The Lirin champion studied the man across the fire from her. She did not look at him directly; she knew better than to stare into the eyes of a dragon. She was a little surprised that he was not attempting to catch her gaze, as his grandmother always had. Oelendra had often wondered how much the power of the Seer's dragonesque eyes had to do with her selection as Lady. Anwyn had always looked people in the eye, always tried to draw them into herself, though few suspected it. Oelendra had been able to withstand that gaze, to endure both its beckoning and its hatred. She was pleased to see that he was not trying to put her will to the test, and looked away from him, turning once more to the fire.

'I hope so,' she answered after a time. 'But I will have to see that for myself.'

'You have the right to doubt my line,' Ashe said patiently. 'Certainly my family has never given you cause for confidence in it. I hope to prove myself to you by my own actions, if you are willing to judge me by them.' He blinked; her silvery eyes caught the light of the fire as they looked up at him directly, more than a trace of animosity in them. He waited for her to explain her hostile reaction, but she just watched him. He cleared his throat before speaking again.

'I have not come out of hiding to take the Lordship, but in the hope of flushing out the F'dor. The Rakshas is dead, Khaddyr is dead. Now all that remains is the last, the demon host itself. I hope that by walking openly I can draw it to me and kill it.'

'And you think you can do so alone? You certainly are sure of yourself.'

Ashe ran a hand down the back of his head to settle the hairs that had bristled at her tone. 'Yes; I'm confident, but I'm not foolish. My father is seldom far away, and I hope to rejoin Rhapsody soon. Between us and her Bolg companions I suspect we would be victorious over it.'

'Your father? I had wondered if he really was dead. Rhapsody had not said, but I suspected duplicity.'

'It was necessary.'

Oelendra laughed bitterly.

'All right,' Ashe acknowledged quietly, 'perhaps it would be more accurate to say it was necessary to him.'

'More accurate, and more honorable also, given who paid the price for that decision.'

Ashe looked away. 'You're right. But in one sense he did die. His human side is gone; he let it slip away to the rest it desired. I will not deceive you, however; in truth his death was a charade, designed to draw his enemies out into the open and allow him to come into his dragon nature through the elements of ether and fire, much like I did. Now he is seldom far from me. He stays in the shadows, watching, waiting for the F'dor to make its move. Still, tonight he is not here. I would not allow him attend this meeting.'

'Allow him? 'Tis a change.'

Ashe stared at her; her face was tight in the reflected light, her eyes intense. There had always been a similar edge to his father's voice when her name was mentioned, but he had not thought it particularly significant until now. He kept his voice steady, his expression mild.

'I suppose it is. It reflects a confidence in my own choices, something I learned from Rhapsody.'

'Did you learn that before or after you let her burn your father alive? Before she spread what she thought was the truth of his defeat at the hands of Khaddyr to the entirety of the Filidic order, and the nobility of Roland as well?'

Ashe's eyes narrowed, the dragon bristled in fury. 'Why are you doing this? Are you trying to goad me into something, Oelendra? You are treading on fragile ground.'

Oelendra leaned into the firelight. 'I am trying to decide whether or not I threw away the bond I had to Daystar Clarion, the piece of the star I gave the Rowans to sew within your sundered chest, on another manipulative spawn of Anwyn and Gwylliam. Make me understand, Gwydion. Explain why you would hurt the person I love as my own child like that; one whom you supposedly loved as well.'

Rage had begun to course through Ashe at her words; he struggled to control his temper, knowing in his heart she was right. 'Never doubt my love for her. *Never*,' he said, the fierce, multitoned voice of the dragon slipping into his words.

Oelendra didn't blink at the sound. 'If you loved her, why did you deceive her? Do you have any idea what the supposed death of your father, on top of everything else she has lost, did to her?'

Ashe's ire fled, replaced by deep sorrow at the memory of Rhapsody sitting before the dark fireplace, staring at nothing. His heart twisted as he remembered the way she had pulled aside her collar, moving her locket out of the way of the blow she expected from him.

Please; end it quickly.

'Yes,' he said hollowly. 'I think I know exactly what it did to her.'

'Then why did you do it? Why did you choose your father's scheme for power, knowing the devastation it would cause?'

Ashe looked off into the darkness. 'I didn't choose it. She did.'

The Lirin warrior's eyes tapered to slits of quicksilver in the firelight. 'What do you mean?'

Ashe continued to stare off into the night, his mind in the Teeth, remembering a woman in the wind. Finally he rose and looked back at her. 'I'm sorry, Oelendra,' he said, picking up the staff. 'If you came to find out if you wasted your piece of the star, the answer is yes.' He turned and walked out of the fire ring.

'Stop,' commanded the Lirin champion. Her tone had the ring of a voice that had commanded armies; he obeyed involuntarily. 'Come back here. I will decide that, not you. Sit down.' Ashe smiled in spite of himself, then returned to the log. 'All right, explain yourself. What was her choice?'

'An unfair one, I'm ashamed to say. The only thing she has ever asked of me is the truth; I felt I owed her that above all else. On the night before I left I told her everything, all of Llauron's plans and manipulations, among other things she needed to know.' His face grew darker with memory in the light of the fire. 'She understood that we were powerless to stop the plans that had already been set in motion. She knew if she didn't light the pyre that he would die, permanently, for nothing.

'That was all right as far as I was concerned; it was his own damned fault, not her responsibility to save him from the snare that was of his own making. But she decided to go ahead with it, knowing exactly what it would mean. Had I been the one to choose I would not have allowed it, but again, part of loving Rhapsody is respecting her right to make her own decisions about her life. I would have spared her if I could.' His voice broke.

Oelendra sat back and watched him thoughtfully, her anger dissipating a little. 'Why doesn't she remember this?'

Ashe looked back for the first time, his tone calmer. 'Part of the price of the truth, I'm afraid. We went to see Manwyn some time back; it was important to her, though she never had a chance to tell me why. I think now it must have been something to do with the children of the demon.

'During one of her insane ravings, the Oracle revealed part of Llauron's plot to her. It left Rhapsody with information that made her vulnerable; in a way, she would have been duplicitous in the scheme just by knowing about it. There was something else she needed to know, so on our last night together I took a pearl my father had given me with his image in it; it was meant to be a keepsake of him in his human form. I decided it could be put to better use, so I expelled the image and gave it to her, asking her to keep the memory of that night in it instead, with the proviso that she could take the memory back immediately once she knew the entire picture if she wanted to.

'Then I told her the whole sorry story. In the end, she decided that her knowledge would lead to eternal death for Llauron, and she sacrificed many things to prevent it, including the memory. He didn't deserve her.' He looked into the darkness again. 'I didn't deserve her.'

'Well, so far you're at least half-right,' said Oelendra. 'But I don't understand why Rhapsody's knowledge left her vulnerable. What else happened that night?'

Ashe sighed deeply. 'I'm afraid I can't tell you that, Oelendra, as much as I would like to. It's Rhapsody's memory too; she has the right to know it before anyone else does.'

'I suppose I can respect that. When do you intend to give it back to her?'

'The instant that it is safe to do so; once the F'dor is destroyed. I hid the pearl in Elysian for safekeeping in case I die in the process of bringing the demon out and killing it. So far I have been able to destroy its followers easily, but I have lost to this monster before, as you know better than anyone.

'I've been out of touch for a while, chasing down Lark and the other Filidic traitors. I am done with that now; I was on my way to Ylorc to see her when I received your call on the wind. Considering where you asked me to meet, I suspected the worst. Until I saw it was you, I thought I would be facing the F'dor again. That was the reason I came drawn; I don't usually come to meetings with sword in hand.'

'And yet you came without your father's protection?'

'He is not far away. He could be here in a moment if I summoned him. I am a great deal stronger than the last time I fought it. I might not be able to defeat the F'dor, but I could certainly hold it off until Llauron arrived. Together we would be quite formidable. Besides, Elynsynos is not far off, either, and I think that if I were to call, she would come as well.'

Oelendra stared into the fire, calculating something. When she looked up there was an expression of satisfaction on her face. 'Three dragons, Kirsdarke, and myself. Fair odds as a second strike.'

'Excuse me?'

She looked into Ashe's eyes. 'Achmed has identified the F'dor.' Automatically his muscles tensed, his hand went to the hilt of the sword. ' 'Tis Lanacan Orlando, the Blesser of Bethe Corbair.'

Ashe's eyes gleamed a brighter blue in the firelight, but outwardly all he did was nod. He released his sword and rested his elbows on his knees, intertwining his fingers, deep in thought. 'Of course. The saintly bastard. Humbly blessing the troops, turning them into thralls for his purposes. Bethe Corbair – gods, he was right on her doorstep.' He shuddered. 'No wonder the Rakshas could infiltrate Ylorc so easily – how disgusting. How many generations had the demon waited, readying itself for this? Blessing and binding armies. It would have taken Sepulvarta, Sorbold, and all of

Roland.' He shook off his meditations. 'Is that why you came? To tell me they are preparing to go after it?'

'They have already done so.'

He nodded and stood, excitement beginning to light his face. 'Where do they wish me to meet them?'

'They don't.'

Ashe stopped cold. 'What do you mean?'

' 'Tis their task, Gwydion; you would be of no help. Your soul still bears the scars of twenty years of domination. If you were to go, who knows what bonds that ancient evil might be able to lay upon you?'

Fury began to flush his face. '*I* know. There are none.'

'Perhaps. But even if that were the case, there is not time. They headed off to Bethe Corbair the day after I left Tyrian. If they traveled as they expected, the battle is probably raging as we speak.'

Ashe began to tremble, his voice shaking with anger. 'She went alone? With them? Without me?'

Oelendra looked at him oddly. 'Gwydion, 'tis their quest; 'tis their time, as was foretold centuries before your birth. You can be of no use there; this is what they were made for. Believe me, I wished to be there as well, more than you can imagine. But 'tis not our task to perform.' Her tone grew more solemn. 'Besides, if they do fail, then we must have a second line of defense. Between yourself and your father—' She stopped. Ashe was becoming frantic.

'They cannot fail,' he said in panic. 'I couldn't stand it if she were to – I couldn't bear it, not again. Why didn't you tell me before? Why didn't they send word? I have a right to be there!'

Oelendra's eyes opened wide in anger, and she rose to face him, unbridled rage in her voice. 'A *right*? *You* have a right? What right? If anyone has a right to slaughter that damnable beast it is me! I have endured more of its evil than anyone living. If I can pass up the right to slay it, who are you to claim it?'

His voice shook. 'That's not what I meant,' he said frenetically. 'I don't care who kills the blasted thing, as long as it dies. The right I meant was my right to be at Rhapsody's side when she faces it, in case – in case she fails.' His words trailed off into a whisper.

'Why?' Oelendra asked incredulously. 'What claim do you have on Rhapsody or her choices? You gave up those claims when you married another.'

He shook his head, burying his face in his hands, trying to calm himself. 'I have not given up those claims.'

The Lirin champion's voice grew cold. 'I believe I now have my answer to the second half of the question. You are more like your grandmother than I feared. Do you expect Rhapsody to be tied to you forever in spite of your marriage to someone else, someone highborn?' Ashe looked up at her. 'Obviously she would never tell you, but you have hurt her as much as the loss of your father, the loss of Jo, perhaps even as much as the loss of her home, her life before this. She loved you, and you threw that away for power; your own or your father's, it matters not. You are right; you didn't deserve her. You have driven her into a loveless marriage; that is really what I came here to tell you.'

His face went white. 'What?'

'You do know she is Queen of the Lirin now, don't you?'

'What?'

'You didn't hear? You didn't know?'

Ashe shook his head. 'No; I have been hunting down Lark, and Khaddyr's other followers, all the way to the far border of the Nonaligned States. I heard the Lirin had crowned a queen; I always hoped Rhapsody would take the crown, but I also heard—' His voice choked off.

'Heard what?'

'That the queen was accepting suit. I knew Rhapsody wouldn't do that. It's against everything she believes.' He closed his eyes in the pain of memory from a sweet summer night, a lifetime ago, in the old land. He could still see her, barely more than a child, crouched behind a row of barrels, hiding from the farm-lad suitors who were stalking her, hoping to win her in the village marriage lottery.

Doesn't this all seem, well, barbaric to you?

Well, yes, actually. Yes, it does.

Well, then, imagine how I feel.

Oelendra smiled grimly. 'What did you expect, that she would pine away for you, alone and unwed, forever? She has no choice but to marry, despite her wishes, just to placate the armies of her neighbors. Come, Gwydion, you know this drill; you were born into it. She needs a strong mate, and she has been left with a fairly grim choice, Anborn or Achmed. She has made that choice.'

The woods had grown very quiet. The air turned from chilly to cold. Oelendra looked into Ashe's eyes and saw an unnatural glint, a light she recognized as the soul of the dragon, but it did not appear angry or ready to strike.

It was frightened.

She allowed her eyes to wander over the rest of his face, and saw the devastation of the human side of him as well. She had seen that look before; it was the face of a man who just realized he had lost everything.

Ashe stared blankly ahead of him, trying to drive the unbearable image of Rhapsody in Achmed's arms from his mind. It was a picture that had haunted him every time she had made even a casual reference to the possibility.

You would never, well, mate with Achmed, would you? The thought has been churning my stomach for the last three hours.

You know, Ashe, I really don't like your attitude. And frankly, it's none of your business.

His stomach turned violently.

You never did answer my question about you and he.

What question?

About whether you would mate with Achmed – I mean marry him.

Maybe. As I told you, I don't expect to marry anyone, but if I were to live that long, he is probably my best prospect.

'She – she cannot,' he said, trying to keep from retching.

Oelendra looked at him ruefully. 'You have left her little choice. She needs an ally, a husband that none would dare to question. She has already spoken to Anborn and he has agreed. It will be a marriage with little love, a marriage of convenience. Unending agony for a woman like Rhapsody. Still, 'twill solve her political problems, though it might add to yours. After all, Anborn has as clear a claim on the Lordship as you do, at least the Lordship of the First and Third Fleets. With Rhapsody thrown into the mix, he might feel more eager to press those claims.'

'Anborn can have the blasted Lordship! It's Rhapsody I care about.'

Her voice was blistering. 'You should have thought of that before you married someone else.'

'I didn't marry anyone else.'

Oelendra blinked. 'You told Rhapsody you were married, why would you lie about something like that?'

Ashe began to pace in a frenzy of anxiety. 'I didn't lie. I couldn't lie, not to her. I just didn't tell her who I was married to. I couldn't, knowing that I was going to face Khaddyr. Not with the F'dor still out there, still knowing the taste of my soul. I have been using myself as bait to lure it into the open. What if I were to fail? What if I died? They could use that bond to find her, and they would take her. As long as Rhapsody doesn't know, the bonds of wedlock are not binding. If I am captured or killed, they can't use them against her. She will be safe.'

Oelendra put out her hands and stopped him in front of her. 'Are you telling me that the woman you are married to is Rhapsody?'

Ashe fought back tears. 'Yes. That night, that night in Elysian, when I told her of my father and his plans, that night when we discovered who we were, who we had been – we married that night. We stood together in the gazebo and took our vows and joined our souls forever. That was the other memory, the one I told you she had a right to know before others did. The memory of our marriage, our union.

'I have had to remain silent about it all this time, knowing that no one else alive knew of it, not even my wife, while all the time I was longing to tell the world. No one else knew. And now you tell me she has gone to face the F'dor? That she might never know who I am? What we were? That she might die, thinking that I wed another? That I abandoned her again? That I might lose her *again?*'

Oelendra shook him gently. Gwydion's eyes cleared slightly. 'What are you talking about?' she asked, a hint of compassion in her voice for the first time that night. 'What do you mean, abandon her again? Lose her again?'

He sat down disconsolately on the log and ran a hand over his shining hair, wet with frantic sweat. Oelendra sat next to him, gently patting his forearm to calm him. When he finally had control of himself again he told her the entire story of their meeting in the old world, of his grandmother's deception, and all that happened since. He related the tale in excruciating detail, with the minutiae that only a dragon could remember, the aspects that only a man deeply in love would care about. Oelendra listened sympathetically until suddenly realization came over her face. Her hand, resting gently on his wrist, became a clutching claw. Gwydion's tale ceased immediately, choked off by the look on her face.

'The old world? You met in the old world? You and she fell in love in the *old world?*' The elderly woman was trembling violently.

'Oelendra? What's wrong?'

The Lirin warrior rose, trembling, and stumbled blindly away from the fire ring. She ran to the first tree she reached in the darkness and rested her head against it, fighting the bile coming up from her stomach with the memory of herself and Llauron, standing before the Oracle with the mirrored eyes.

Beware, swordbearer! You may well destroy the one you seek, but if you go this night the risk is great. If you fail you will not die, but, as a piece of your heart and soul was ripped from you spiritually in the old land with the loss of your life's love, the same will happen again, but physically this time. And that piece it takes from you will haunt your days until you pray for death, for he will use it as his plaything, twisting it to his will, using it to accomplish his foul deeds, even producing children for him.

Oelendra felt her stomach rush into her mouth. As she retched she felt one strong hand at her neck, another supporting her back. She staggered away, Ashe still holding on to her, into the coolness of the air away from the campfire. The world spun hazily around her for a moment. Then she steadied herself and looked up into the face of the man smiling down at her kindly.

' 'Twas you,' she whispered. 'I thought she meant me, but 'twas you.'

His smile vanished. 'What are you talking about? Here, come sit down.' Ashe led her to a snowy patch under a great elm and lowered her gently to the ground. He decided to inject a note of levity.

'If that is the way all of Rhapsody's friends react to the news of our marriage, we won't be giving many dinner parties.'

The older woman did not smile in return, but rested her hand gently on his cheek. 'Forgive me, Gwydion,' she said softly. 'I am to blame for your torment at the hands of the F'dor. I am so sorry.'

Ashe stared at her in disbelief. 'What are you talking about? You saved my life.'

Oelendra shook her head, her eyes staring elsewhere, remembering different moments. Then she repeated the prophecy aloud, softly, to herself.

' "Beware, swordbearer," ' she whispered faintly. ' "You may well destroy the one you seek, but if you go this night the risk is great." '

'Is this a riddle?'

She nodded distantly. 'A terrible riddle. A prophecy from Manwyn from long ago.'

Ashe took her hand in both of his, trying to steady it. 'Was there more to it?'

Oelendra nodded again, her eyes locked on the crackling fire as it launched gleaming sparks into the cold night air. ' "If you fail, you will not die, but, as a piece of your heart and soul was ripped from you spiritually in the old land with the loss of your life's love, the same will happen again, but physically this time." ' She began to shake even more violently.

'Rhapsody told me about your husband, Pendaris,' Ashe said gently. 'I'm very sorry.'

' "And that piece it takes from you will haunt your days until you pray for death," ' she continued, ' "for he will use it as his plaything, twisting it to his will, using it to accomplish his foul deeds, even producing children for him." '

'Gods,' Ashe murmured. 'What a hideous prediction. No wonder you were terrified.'

Oelendra blinked. Finally she turned back and looked at Gwydion. 'Has your father ever told this augury to you?'

'No.' He was rubbing his arms as if to keep warm, but Oelendra could tell from the look in his eyes that he was coming to the same understanding she had.

'The ultimate vanity,' she said softly. 'I assumed that because Llauron was the only other person there with me in Manwyn's temple, and he does not bear a sword, that her curse was directed at me. But 'twas not me that she damned with her prophecy, Gwydion. 'Twas you. You were the sword bearer, the Kirsdarkenvar. I never even thought of you, nor anyone else save myself.'

'Of course you didn't.' Ashe smiled wryly. 'I've been the recipient of Manwyn's prophecies. She cannot lie, but she does not have to be clear in her rantings. She's insane. One of the last things my father said to me before he – he told me to beware of prophecies, because they do not always mean what they seem.' He patted her arm. 'He went with you, then? Why? I had always been under the assumption that you and my father did not get along, but I thought it was because he led Anwyn's army in the Great War, and you chose wisely to stay out of it. Such grudges seem to be common among the elder Cymrians who had lived through the war.'

The Lirin champion sighed. 'No, Gwydion. There was a time, long ago, when your father and I were quite cordial, before the war. He remained so to me despite the choice I made during it, though I can't say I've forgiven him completely for the horrors he visited upon our fellow Cymrians, whether or not it was his choice. When you hear the full tale, I'm sure you will understand our present enmity.' She looked into the starry sky as wisps of clouds, blown by a cold wind, raced in front of the twinkling lights, dimming them for a moment.

'It had been centuries since my first taste of the foul air of the F'dor on the wind. I had trained endless champions to search for it; none had ever returned. I had failed to find the F'dor in any other way. I was desperate. I knew the beast was growing stronger. Your father was one of the few who believed as I did, that the F'dor still lived, lurking somewhere, hiding within a human host, biding its time. So Llauron and I went to see Manwyn together, in the hope that she could tell us where the F'dor would be, so that we might kill it once and for all time.

'We had to phrase the question like that, because Manwyn can only see the Future, not the Past or Present. She was most cooperative. She told us the exact time it would be here, in the House of Remembrance, planning to despoil the sapling tree.' She pointed to the thriving oak, its glossy leaves gleaming in the light of the fire.

'Manwyn said we were to go there on the first night of summer, when the Patriarch would be consecrating the year in Sepulvarta, while the Filids observed their holy-night rituals in Gwynwood. 'Tis a night of great power, a night when the One-God's love is wrapped securely around His children.' Oelendra looked back into the fire as if looking into the Past. 'A night the beast would be vulnerable.

'Your father, being Invoker, would need to be with the Filids of his order, leading their worship, so we understood that I would have to go without him. But finally we had the information we needed to kill it. Llauron and I looked at each other, unable to speak for the import of what we had learned. 'Twas to be our deliverance from the hand of evil.

'But then, as we turned to leave Manwyn's temple, she spewed forth the other prophecy.' Oelendra's eyes dimmed in the memory. 'In my life I have never felt such fear as when I heard those words.

'For the first time I can remember in this world, I gave in totally to panic. You must understand, Gwydion, I had fought F'dor like this in the old world; they took from me everything that ever mattered, that I loved. My husband and I were captured by them; they killed him. They were not as kind to me.

'I misunderstood the prophecy. I took the sword bearer to be myself; it never occurred to me that it might be a sword other than Daystar Clarion. The prospect of bearing a demonic child—' Oelendra broke down, shuddering uncontrollably.

Ashe drew her into his arms, holding her against his chest to warm her. 'Sshh,' he said gently. 'Blot it from your mind. It's over.'

' 'Twill never be over,' Oelendra said hollowly. 'Never.

'Instead of using the information she gave me, taking my one chance to destroy it forever, I bolted; I hid. I waited until dawn had come, and then I went for a walk to clear my head of the accusations that were pounding in it. I could not escape them. 'Twas my duty as Iliachenva'ar to have gone, no matter the risk to myself. So I steeled my nerve and went to the House, hoping it was still there, though its power would no longer be on the wane.

'That's when I found you, Gwydion, broken and dying on the grass in the forest of Navarne. Llauron had said he might send reinforcements, but I had no idea 'twas you, or that you would go in alone when I didn't come.

'Twas my cowardice that destroyed your life; 'tis my fault that you have lived in the agony you have, hidden from your family and loved ones, dead in the eyes of the world these twenty years. Those children that the Rakshas sired, that is because of me.' Tears began to fall from the silver eyes.

Ashe held her against his shoulder, trying to think of something to say that would impart comfort to her in her despair. 'Rhapsody loves those children,' he said gently. 'They gave Achmed the weapon to find the benison. I never would have lived this long if I had not been required to hide, pretending to be dead. Given my lineage, I would have been among the first it assassinated anyway. It was my own father that sent me against the demon; how can I hate you, and not him? I prefer not to, if you don't mind. What is it you Liringlas say again? *Ryle hira*. Life is what it is. Forgive yourself; believe me, the world looks better when you do; I know. It is something Rhapsody and I learned together.'

At the mention of her name, his face changed, twisting into fear again. 'Rhapsody. She's probably fighting the F'dor now; gods, she may be dying, and I can do nothing to help her.' He began to tremble again.

Oelendra wiped her eyes. ''Tis difficult, is it not?' she said, resting her hand on his shoulder. ''Twas far easier facing my own death than to sit helplessly while someone I love faces hers. I wish I could go and do it for her, make certain she is safe. You have no idea how many men and women I have seen march off to meet their fate, Gwydion. One would think that after a time you would get used to it, but you never do. Not when 'tis someone you love.'

His voice was full of pain. 'How do you bear it?'

'The best way is to sit vigil with someone else who loves her. You can carry the burden together.'

Ashe looked up and Oelendra met his gaze. They took one another's hands and sat together, waiting. After a while they began to tell each other stories of Rhapsody, sharing their love for her, their memories of her. Eventually the worry became too strong, and they grew silent.

Finally Ashe looked at the sky; dawn was coming, the stars beginning to fade in the lightening horizon. 'Gods, it's over, don't you think?'

''Tis done.' Oelendra sighed, her eyes still on the darkness of the sky above her.

'It must be.'

They stood. Oelendra did so slowly, feeling the great aching pain in her knees. Ashe pulled up the hood of his cloak.

'I will go to Elysian and wait.'

'Do that,' Oelendra said, picking up her small pack. 'She will be happy to see you. And please, send word.'

'I will.' A grisly thought occurred to him. 'One way or another. If they didn't make it—'

'If they didn't, we will think of a way to lure the benison here, and then we will kill him.'

Ashe nodded silently and turned away.

'Gwydion,' Oelendra said as he stood at the edge of the clearing, 'you remind me more of the Kings of Serendair than you resemble the Lord of the Cymrians. I am glad to see that the star was well placed.'

Ashe smiled at the ancient woman. 'Thank you.' He took a step, then looked back again. 'And I am glad Rhapsody asked me to guide her to you. She is lucky to have you for a friend.'

Oelendra smiled. 'I suppose that makes me your friend-in-law.'

Ashe returned her smile, then walked away silently into the woods. Oelendra went back to the dying fire and absently kicked dirt over the remaining coals. She looked once more at the shell of the House of Remembrance and walked off into the forest.

65

South of Bethe Corbair

The wind over the Krevensfield Plain dipped low into the swale, causing the hidden fire to crackle and leap for a moment, sparks flying skyward, only to settle into a sullen smolder once more. The Three glanced around automatically, scanning the horizon for eyes that might have seen the embers. The two smaller travelers turned to the giant, who shook his head, then settled back and exhaled softly. Grunthor knew the earth; if there had been anyone upon it within sight, he would have felt him.

Rhapsody reached into the coals. '*Slypha*,' she said. *Extinguish*. The flames sank immediately into the ashes, taking the light with them.

'Get some sleep,' Achmed said to her, drawing the hooded cloak over his shoulders. 'You look tired.'

Grunthor put his arm around her and drew her against his chest. 'Nothing to worry about, darling. We can take him. Rest here now. It'll be like old times.' He grinned at her, tusks protruding from his jaw in a manner Rhapsody had come to find consummately endearing, though she knew a stranger would find the sight paralyzing.

He was reading her mind. The killing of the demon was ultimately to be her task; in the darkness in the middle of the open night, nothing but stars to witness the plans they had laid, she was feeling suddenly small and vulnerable. She did not fear her own death. It was the prospect of failure that had her shaking now from more than the cold.

Gratefully she came into the greatcoat that the Sergeant held open for her, closing warmth around her as he had within the Root long ago. She let loose a sigh full of memory. Aside from the dragons she had slept beside, Grunthor was the only one in the world that could keep her safe from her own dreams. She laid an arm across the broad waist, hoping desperately he would be alive to repeat the sleeping arrangement the next night. The knowledge that she had never been in a fight like the one they were facing on the morrow was terrifying to her.

The huge hand patted her head awkwardly and Rhapsody relaxed into sleep. Grunthor waited until the rhythmic pattern of her breathing indicated that the depth of her slumber was such that they could speak without fear of her hearing. Then he looked at Achmed.

'What's the fallback, sir?'

Achmed looked up into the sky, remembering a night beneath different stars long ago, broken by a summer rain. They were on the other side of the world now, seeking out a demon like the one they had run from then. His name was his own, no longer an invisible collar around his neck. And they were three, not two; an unluckier number according to the soothsayers, though it was hard to believe, given the addition to their team curled up in Grunthor's arms.

'Once it begins, it's her fight – and yours. I can only concentrate on the Thrall ritual,' he said softly, the natural sand in his voice growing even drier. 'As long as the Thrall ritual is intact, I will maintain it to the exclusion of all else. If she becomes unable to fight, take her sword and kill it if you can.' The Bolg nodded. 'If the Thrall ritual stops, the demon will have fled its present host. Kill whoever is still breathing.' Grunthor nodded again.

'She's up to the task, aren't you, Your Ladyship?' he said softly, rubbing his hand over her back. Rhapsody nodded in her sleep, whispering words that even she did not hear.

Achmed looked back up at the sky. 'I hope you're right.'

'Your Grace?'

Within the darkness of his study, the benison turned toward the solitary rectangle of light, shining through the open doorway.

'Yes?'

'Word has come from Sorbold that the Lirin queen has left Tyrian. She was seen ten days ago, riding alone across the bordering plains of their northern city-states.'

'Where was she headed?'

'They tracked her as far as the outer reaches of the Teeth, then lost her.'

From the doorway Gittleson could see nothing but the benison's silhouette in the chair. Then Lanacan Orlando opened his eyes, two points of white in the dim outline, rimmed in the color of blood. He smiled, causing a third patch of light to appear in the shadow, gleaming with amusement.

'Perhaps the bitch is in heat,' the specter said, his voice warm and sweet. 'Her stud of choice is chasing down poor Khaddyr's followers; perhaps she wants the Firbolg king to tumble her, eh?'

'Perhaps, Your Grace.'

The chair turned slowly away from him again. 'Don't be a fool, Gittleson. She is coming here.'

★

'The food in this place was wretched; why do you want to go back here?'

Rhapsody cuffed the Firbolg king affectionately. 'There was nothing wrong with this tavern's food,' she said sensibly. 'It was the company you objected to. This was where you first met Ashe.'

'That would explain it. Small wonder my stomach was writhing.' Achmed glanced around the street, but he didn't see Grunthor. The noon sun was casting shadows of unimpressive length; the Sergeant was probably still lurking in back alley doorways, waiting for more hospitable shade. He held a chair out for Rhapsody, watching her pull her hood more tightly around her face as she sat down. The wind was high and cold; they were the only customers of the pub who were sitting outdoors, the others taking comfort inside nearer to the fire and the ale.

The bells of the basilica were ringing wildly in the wind, sweet random music sweeping through the streets and over the buildings of Bethe Corbair. It was a sound that resonated in Rhapsody's soul, but the knowledge that somewhere beneath that bell tower lurked an unimaginable evil made the music in it feel off somehow. She bowed her head and averted her eyes as Achmed ordered rum and lamb for himself and soup for her, then looked over her shoulder at the church once more as the tavernkeeper hurried back inside.

Achmed closed his eyes. On his first scouting of the area near the basilica he had picked up nothing unusual in the vibrations around it, though the smell of the demon was unmistakable. Grunthor had immediately located the boundaries of the tainted ground. Their suspicions were right; the basilica had been desecrated in a way that was invisible to the eye and other regular senses, the contamination stretching several yards into the street around it. Thousands of unknowing churchgoers walked over the defiled earth every day, oblivious of its demonic possession. Achmed winced in the memory of his first sight of Ashe in the basilica's shadow. He had felt the taint then for a split second, and assumed Llauron's son to be its source; it was a mistaken association.

Rhapsody was listening intently to the music of the carillon. Her soup was delivered; it was left untouched as she sat, deep in thought, and absently watched it grow cold. Finally she looked up at him; unnatural light was gleaming in the emerald eyes, her face glowing.

'*Ela,*' she whispered. Excitement snapped in her eyes, and she reached out and took his hand in hers; it was trembling. '*Ela,*' she said again.

'What are you babbling about? I don't understand Ancient Lirin.'

'It's not Ancient Lirin, it's a musical term,' Rhapsody said softly. 'It's the last note in the old six-note scale, the way music was notated at the time the basilica was built centuries ago. *Ut, re, mi, fa, sol,* and *la,* or *ela*; it wasn't until hundreds of years later that they began using *ti,* the seventh note of the octave, and *do,* which is the same as *ut* but one scale higher. It also happens to be my Naming note, the note to which I am attuned.'

'Rhapsody, stop babbling at me. What has you so excited?'

'It's missing.'

'What's missing?'

'*Ela*. The last tone in the scale is missing from the carillon; it's only ringing five of the notes.'

'And how many bells does that affect?'

'Well, Lord Stephen said there were eight hundred seventy-six bells in the bell tower, one for every Cymrian ship that left the old world. If that's the case, and if they had set the bells up in equal sets, since they must have been using the six-note scale, then one hundred and forty or so of them would have been that one.'

'One hundred forty-six.'

'Right. I can discern the other groupings, and that many are missing. It's very subtle, and if the bells have been playing that way for a long time, no one except a Singer would even notice it, and then only if listening for it. Lanacan must have taken the clappers out of those bells, since removing the bells themselves would have been more than obvious, it would have been impossible to do without notice. The biggest one must weigh several tons.'

Achmed downed the last of his rum. 'He's a clever bastard; F'dor always are. So that's how he circumvented the wind sanctifying the ground. How can we fix it?'

Rhapsody smiled. 'I think I know. We had best find Grunthor; we have plans to make.'

She was alone in the marketplace buying arrows from the fletcher when Gittleson spotted her. She was hard to miss despite being disguised in the plain brown traveling clothes of a peasant; the smooth golden fall of her hair was neatly tied back in a simple black ribbon, and the afternoon sun reflected off it, drawing the eyes of the handful of townspeople braving the freezing wind of the square. She was lucky; it was only the weather that prevented her from being mobbed by the merchants who instead gazed at her from inside shops and from behind barrel fires next to their wares. Gittleson made careful note of the number and types of arrows she bought, primarily those with silvered points and made to hold flame, taking care not to let her see him.

Her next stop was the spice merchant, whose tents stretched half a city block and were open in the front. Huge burlap sacks of pods, roots, beans, peppercorns, and grains were set out along the street, along with bags of herbs and jars of spicy flakes. Rhapsody spent a great deal of time carefully examining the contents of each bag. Finally she bought several large heads of pungent garlic, two bunches each of horehound, mugwort, and datura, and three dozen long, fat vanilla beans, stuffing her purchases quickly into her sack and looking around hastily. Not satisfied, she gave a final glance to the bell tower rising above the rooftops before heading off into the shadows of the back alleys, losing her human shadow, who slunk off, back to the dark basilica, as dusk began to fall.

*

'How disappointing.' The robed figure in the vestry paused in front of a silvered mirror and checked his face. The countenance of an older man, a kindly man with sparse white hair and laugh lines around his eyes, looked back at him. It was the face of the quintessential grandfather, or the beloved village priest. 'What does she think I am, Gittleson, a *nosferatu*? Look in the glass; can you see my reflection?'

'Of course, Your Grace.'

'Yes, of course. And if you, Gittleson, even you know that, one would have hoped for more from the Iliachenva'ar. Garlic, mugwort, and silver arrows; really. Oh well, I guess I just expect too much. After two decades one would have thought that Oelendra could have come up with a brighter one, a better trained one, than the last, but alas, it is not to be. This will be far too easy. Are those the only things she acquired?'

Gittleson looked back down at the list he had made in the marketplace. Everything Rhapsody had bought he had already enumerated.

'Yes, Your Grace. Then she left the market and went off to the back alleys.'

'Ah, well. At least our little meeting will be brief, and then we can get down to the business of playing with her. Obviously I can't enjoy the full benefit of her – charms, but there's nothing to stop you, now is there, Gittleson? The Rakshas said she was lightning in a bottle, the eighth wonder of the world. Once she has her instructions, she's yours for the night.'

'Thank you, Your Grace.'

The benison turned in the vestry and put on his shawl. 'Don't drool, Gittleson; it's unbecoming.'

The giant Bolg shook his head vigorously. 'I still don't like it.'

Rhapsody patted his arm reassuringly. 'I know, I know you don't, Grunthor, but it's for the best. Tell him, Achmed.'

The mismatched eyes looked at her coolly. 'I never tell Grunthor what to think. You should know that by now.'

They had been arguing for the past ten minutes, the Sergeant objecting strenuously to the concept of Rhapsody going in first, alone. She sighed deeply. 'You'll be right there, outside the northern door, and Achmed will be right outside the vestry entrance on the south. I'll be fine.'

'You'll be alone too long in there—'

'What choice do we have?' she interrupted desperately. 'If you don't follow the plan, he'll know you're both here, and he'll put two and two together and get Three, if you take my meaning. I'll tell you what, Grunthor; I will stay on the floor of the nave until you get there. I won't even go near the stairs of the sanctuary until you have him. All right?'

The Bolg regarded her seriously. 'You promise?'

'I promise.'

'Nowhere near him? You'll stay far enough away that he won't be able to look in your pretty little face and turn you against us?'

Rhapsody stood on her toes while pulling his head down to her. She kissed the great green face. 'Nowhere near. I told you, I'll wait until you have him. I'm sure he can't possess me from across the basilica.'

Achmed smiled sourly. 'I had no idea you were such an expert on demons and their range of possession, Rhapsody. Let's hope your knowledge is more accurate than those arrows will be.' The two Bolg stepped into the shadows that had swallowed the cobbled alleys, checking the direction of the wind before heading up the streets to the center of the city, where the basilica stood, waiting for them in the night.

'Why? What's wrong with my arrows?' Rhapsody hurried to catch up, but her friends did not answer; they were as silent as the darkness into which they had melted.

66

When they reached the northern side of the basilica where the sexton routinely dumped the rubbish for the ashman, Rhapsody reached out and grabbed Grunthor by the elbow.

'There's something I have to tell you, Grunthor.'

The Sergeant looked down into the diminutive face and smiled broadly. He could tell what she was going to say by the look in her eyes; Rhapsody was as transparent to him as Canderian crystal.

'No,' he said gruffly, pulling his arm away. 'You had your chance; it'll have to wait till afterwards.'

'It can't,' she said anxiously. 'It's important, Grunthor.'

He smirked. 'I guess you'll just have to live through this, then, and tell me when we're done, eh, miss?' He ignored her tug on his sleeve and walked away, pausing long enough next to Achmed to allow a look to pass between them. As always, their communication transcended the spoken word. Then he strode away into the shadows that surrounded the pile of sand and ashes.

Rhapsody stared after him in dismay. For a moment she could pick him out, standing in front of the enormous mound of waste from the fires of the basilica. Then she was no longer sure she could discern in the dark what was earth and what was Grunthor. She blinked, and any vestige of differentiation was lost. He had blended into the dirt and ash as easily as he had into the darkness a moment before.

Grunthor's feet toed the line just outside the border of the tainted ground. He waited until he was securely standing on earth that had not been desecrated by the demon, and then became one with it, breathing in slow, measured breaths until even his body heat cooled to match the temperature of the street. He could feel the heartbeat of the Earth echoing through him, becoming his own.

Moments later two men hurried by, arguing in a congenial manner. They walked right past the giant Firbolg in front of the waste pile but did not give him as much as a glance. Rhapsody and Achmed turned to each other and smiled; *that was a first*, their shared grin seemed to say. Then he extended his hand, and she took it. Together they headed around the west end of the building, skirting the line of defilement that Grunthor had pointed out to them.

As they reached the southwestern corner of the basilica, Rhapsody pulled Achmed to a stop.

'Well, are you going to refuse to hear me out, too?'

A gloved hand came to rest on her face, then moved to her lips to silence her. Rhapsody marveled at the sensitivity of his touch, even through the thin leather sheath. *No wonder he can feel the vibrations of the wind and hide, undetected, within them,* she thought, smiling. His answer was soft.

'The time for words is past. We can't keep the bastard waiting.'

'All right, then I won't talk.' Her hand met his, and rested there; he looked at it, and then down at her, where their eyes met as well. Finally their lips met, softly; it was a first, too, as in the previous moment, a first that Rhapsody prayed did not also portend a last.

Her mouth clung to his a moment more, sharing a final breath; then she moved away. Achmed was already pulling up the hood of his cloak; it was the signal for her to round the corner.

She, in turn, pulled her hood down, and looked about the street. It was deserted, the night wind having picked up to a strong gale, blowing flecks of snow and debris in sheets of icy air across the dark city. Rhapsody turned the corner and walked quickly down the street along the southern side of the basilica, passing the vestry window, then turned the southeastern corner, heading for the main entrance into the eastern vestibule.

Gittleson watched out the small vestry window, unseen behind the heavy drape, his pale hands slick with nervous sweat, pallid in the half-light cast by the dimly glowing candles.

'She's coming, Your Grace.'

The benison was standing in the nave, the central part of the basilica amid the benches where the faithful sat. His elderly hands lovingly caressed the back of a lustrous wooden pew, his smile glittering in the half-light of the candles that burned in the chandeliers above him.

'Good,' he said softly. 'I'm ready.'

He walked down the side aisle to the polished marble steps that led up to the sanctuary where the stone altar stood and began to climb the stairs. Halfway up he turned and looked back at the vestry and the figure in the doorway, silhouetted against the light of the tiny dressing room.

'Close the door, Gittleson; you're letting the light in.'

A gloved hand reached out and shut the door.

The benison turned back once more and climbed the rest of the steps, smiling to himself.

★

Rhapsody pulled on the handle of the main basilica doors, finding a stubborn resistance; it was heavily wrought iron, engraved with the holy symbols she had seen in Sepulvarta. Panic coursed through her, starting at the roots of her hair. The possibility that the basilica might be locked had not figured into her plan.

She tugged a second time and the door opened easily, as if held by an unseen butler. She looked about the vestibule but saw nothing except the poor boxes and rows of intention candles, a few of which flickered in the wind when the door opened. She stepped inside.

The air in the basilica was heavy and menacing, as if it objected to her presence. She took a step and felt a burning sensation within the toe of her boot; the defiled ground did not want her on it any more than she wanted to be there. Even moving through the air itself was a struggle. Rhapsody steeled herself and pressed on, heading for the portals that led into the main section of the basilica. The central sanctuary was visible at the edge of her vision through the doors. She walked silently to the end of the vestibule and stopped before entering the nave.

The figure in the dark red robe at the altar did not turn. 'Come in, Your Majesty,' he said, a slight chuckle in his voice.

The air around her changed ever so slightly with the demon's invitation. It was as if the invisible bonds that were holding her back had been released, the tainted ground suddenly willing to accept her footsteps. Rhapsody hesitated, unsure about walking on the desecrated ground that was the benison's domain, then, in the absence of an alternative, stepped into the main part of the basilica.

It was vast and dark. Chandeliers of brass-bound oak hung from the towering ceiling, burning with the light of thousands of small, ineffectual candles. The basilica was austere, with benches of unadorned wood lining the nave. It was also windowless; the only aperture was the great opening in the ceiling beneath the lofty bell tower, the access to the wind that spiraled around the carillon. It rose in the darkness above the central altar.

A long balcony lined each of the four sides of the elevated section, led to by a circular staircase at each corner. The benches there were padded with dark fabric cushions, probably for the comfort of the hindquarters of the wealthier contributors among Bethe Corbair's faithful.

Rhapsody stopped midway down the aisle and looked up to the sanctuary where the benison stood, still with his back to her. The slate floor of the basilica led up to polished marble steps, similar to the ones in Sepulvarta but dark, with veins of white and silver running through the stone. The steps ended in the semicircular apse at their top, the back wall of which was carved from ancient mahogany in rising columns lined with carefully placed holes, a natural pipe organ. Rhapsody could tell that the wind had not reached the back of the sanctuary in many years.

Finally the benison turned away from the plain stone altar and looked out across the basilica at her. She could see his eyes, even as far away as she was, gleaming in the half-light.

'Welcome, my dear, don't stand on ceremony; approach, by all means. I have tea steeping for you here on the altar. When your two friends come they can share the pot as well.' He laughed softly at the look on her face. 'Of course I was expecting you. I haven't entertained one of Oelendra's trainees in several decades, so this is a rare treat for me.' He turned away for a moment, then turned back, holding a teacup, which he extended to her, just as he had in her dream about the Patriarch.

In response she drew her sword. The blade flashed in the darkness of the church; the flames burned angrily, billowing up the length of Daystar Clarion like a brushfire.

The benison laughed. 'Ah, yes, Daystar Clarion. Well, I am suitably impressed. I have to admit to being a little shocked at seeing you with it in Sepulvarta that night. None of Oelendra's other young champions were ever entrusted with it. How ever *did* you pry it loose from her craven grip? None of the others knew who or where I was, either, until it was too late. Is that why? Did she give it to you because you were able to discern my identity?' He fixed his gaze on her, the whites of his eyes darkening to red around the edges. 'Well, no matter. I assume you are aware that none of the four score or so of her noble knights ever returned to her, hmmm? They are some of my most prized possessions, if you will forgive the play on words.'

Rhapsody shook off the hypnotic effect of the sweet voice and came slowly down the aisle. A cold rage was building in her soul, and she tried to shake that off as well; it was interfering with her concentration. She was directly beneath the far side of the opening in the roof below the bell tower when his words made her stop again.

'But, then, you are intimately acquainted with the last one who tried, aren't you, my dear? Gwydion must have thanked the stars for you. Who would have believed that one of the Three would take pity on him, human wreckage that he was, and take him to her heart? To her bed, eh?' The benison shook his head and chuckled softly, then looked back at her; even halfway across the nave Rhapsody could see him wink mischievously at her, the leer remaining in his elderly eyes. 'Well, my dear, thanks to you, now he and I have some things in common. I give thanks for you, too; if not for you I would never have been able to confirm he was still alive, never would have found him again.'

Rhapsody closed her other hand around the sword's hilt and raised it until it was pointed at the benison. Lanacan Orlando laughed aloud.

'Oh, please do, my dear, come; try and take me on my own ground. It really will be amusing, if patently unfair to you. Surely you are not that much of a fool, are you? We have, after all, stood in these places before, one of us at the altar, the other in the back of the basilica, helpless to do anything. But this time the roles are reversed, aren't they, Your Majesty? It is you standing on my ground this time.'

'This is God's ground, Your Disgrace.'

Rhapsody lifted the sword above her head and spoke its name.

Blinding light lit the bell tower and spilled into the nave, the legacy of the daystar for which the weapon was named. A moment later a silver trumpet blast rocked the basilica, a clarion call that shook the carillon tower, setting the bells to ringing frantically in an earsplitting cacophony.

The benison merely smiled. 'Well, now, that was impressive.'

'Actually, it was a signal.'

The benison shrugged. 'Too late. By the time the townsfolk get here you will be mine, and apologizing for disturbing them so rudely. My turn, now. Come to me.'

The static air of the basilica shifted against her skin. Heat, deep and primal, enveloped her, then seeped through her clothes and into her bones, making her heart beat faster, her blood run hot. The demon's words of thrall, sweetly spoken in the benison's soothing voice, caressed her, stroked her soul like a mother caresses a child.

Rhapsody shook her head again and clenched her teeth until her ears rang. The lush voice tickled against her eardrums, the warm words wrapping soothingly around her neck, sending a shiver, a silver thrill, down her spine. She closed her eyes, trying to throw off the effects of the demon's words.

No, by the One-God, she thought to herself, anger mounting. *I'll not be your thrall. I am stronger than you, you piece of filth.* She summoned her will, shook her head once more, violently, and the warmth of the demon's thrall shattered like brittle sugar and dissipated into the crackling air. The red heat of anger flushed through her.

'I will come to you on my own terms,' she said evenly, struggling to keep her voice steady. 'And when I do, I will drive my sword into your miserable heart, rip it from your body, set it on fire, and watch it shrivel into ashes. I will snuff your twisted essence and burn your evil soul in the flames of elemental fire as it was before your kind blackened it.'

The benison chuckled.

'Really? Now *that* is a brave boast, though a trifle unpleasant and crass in the mouth of a queen. You disappoint me, Your Majesty, truly you do. You pick up an ancient weapon – little more than a flaming toothpick, really – and think that as a result you know something of elemental *fire*?' He laughed again, his expression one of genuine amusement that resolved a moment later into a more contemplative expression that turned darker before her eyes.

'Allow me,' he said flatly, 'to teach you a little of what you *don't* know about fire.'

He made an absent gesture with one hand. A ball of black fire appeared in his palm, and he tossed it her way. As it approached it grew in volume, hissing menacingly as it picked up speed and power from the evil-tainted air around them, soaring toward her. The flames spread out like a black-orange net, reaching for her with eager, ragged firefingers.

Rather than dodge, Rhapsody opened her mouth and softly sang the note *ela*, the last in the ancient scale, her own Naming note. Her voice held steady as the tiniest of the carillon bells picked up the note and began to

404

hum, unnoticed amid the others bells, still settling from the cacophony a moment before.

The air around her crackled and hissed with the sound, as if fighting it. She drew a quick circle in the air above her with the sword, trying to wrap the protection of the note, and the wind it called to, around herself. She did not fear the fire; it would not harm her.

The instant before the black fire impacted her, Rhapsody felt something shift within her. Fire had been her friend from the moment she had passed through it at the core of the Earth; it had absorbed into her soul itself, melding into her essence, tying her to the element irrevocably. From that time until this second she had not feared flame, because it had never sought to harm her, allowing her to pass, unscathed, through the hottest of infernos.

But in the fragment of a heartbeat before the fire hit her, Rhapsody felt her soul lurch. This was not fire, not really, not any fire that she knew, at least. It did not smell the same, mold the air as fire did; it was thin, acidic, evil, alive with malice and malevolence. It was the blinding, corrosive essence of hatred. And she knew, at that last moment, that she was not immune to its effects.

Slypka, she whispered.

The black fire dimmed slightly, but did not extinguish.

She had just enough time to avert her head to shield her eyes before the ball of black fire exploded, shattering the protection circle and igniting her clothing. With a gasp of pain Rhapsody staggered, patting herself frantically to snuff her smoking garments. The skin of her arms and legs stung violently from the contact and the searing flame.

Lanacan Orlando slowly closed his fist, his arm still outstretched, then twisted it suddenly. The acid from the black fire roared with anger, intensifying the heat, and against her will Rhapsody gasped again.

Pain shot through her, followed by cold shock. It had been so long since she had felt even hesitation, let alone caution, in the presence of fire, that she was caught totally off-guard by the damage it was doing to her. Still, at least a little of her immunity was in place; her skin stung deeply, but did not burn or blacken. Smoke poured out of her clothing, but her body still did not ignite.

The demon at the altar stared in amazement. Anger flooded his face, and once again he wrenched his hand, his eyes darkening to crimson at the edges. The elderly forehead of his human body furrowed; he clenched his fist even tighter, the muscles in his frail arm quivering, and twisted his arm once more.

A cry of agony was torn from Rhapsody's throat as she sank to her knees, struggling to hold on to the sword. *No*, she thought desperately. *No! I'm failing!* In the depths of her mind, she remembered the voice of the dragon in her dreams.

What if I fail?

You may.

She struggled to rise, resting one hand on the floor. Instantly the smooth slate gave way beneath her palm; a tendril of a vine, smooth as glass, black as night with veins of white running through it, shot forth with the recoil of a whip and encircled her forearm, tightening in a stranglehold.

In the alley outside the basilica, through the earth itself, Grunthor felt Rhapsody fall.

67

The benison laughed aloud as another corded vine broke forth from the floor and lashed around Rhapsody's leg, dragging her against the slate.

'Oh, my, won't the Lirin be disappointed,' he said with mock sympathy. 'After all that pageantry! So much effort went into the coronation, and indeed, it was a lovely event. Well, perhaps they will make a better choice next time.'

Rhapsody struggled in the grip of the demonic vines, kicking and pulling, with little result. Her skin prickled with cold fear as the memory of Jo's gruesome death, and Llauron's, came back to her; she could smell the hideous odor of the F'dor's excitement, even as far as she was from the altar, the sickening smell of burning flesh. From the floor in every direction tiny glass-like thorns were emerging, crawling through the seams in the paving stones like streams of roaches, evil seedlings that in a moment would be vines themselves, binding her hopelessly, strangling her.

Around her, Time seemed to slow; the magnitude of what loomed made her heart thud in a cadence that beat with the turning of the world. *Failure could bring about the end of Time,* she had said in the dream to Elynsynos. *I cannot even contemplate it.*

Another tendril grew in a sudden spurt, lunging for her neck. Rhapsody dodged out of the way, only to find her movements more severely restricted than she had imagined.

The vines bit deeper into her arm, into her leg, making her heart shudder and pulse arrhythmically. The dragon's words whispered in answer, fading in and out with the irregular beating of her heart.

You are at the place where the beginning of Time had its ending. Just as surely the ending of Time will have its beginning here, as well. You cannot change it, though you may delay its coming.

Fighting back the panic, she wrenched against the tension and rolled to her side, slashing at the vine that bound her other hand with Daystar Clarion.

The sword flashed angrily in the darkness of the basilica; the black candle flames in the chandeliers roared back in sinister response. The benison crossed his arms and leaned back against the altar.

'You put on a good show, Your Majesty. First rate amusement. I fear it will end far too soon.' The benison leaned forward a little. 'I am going to eat your soul, Rhapsody, and those of your Bolg friends who hover at the outer edges of my profane ground. Such a sweet soul it must be; I'm sure I will savor it. I think I will leave you alive while I do, so that you can watch each piece of it disappear down my throat and into the mouth of the Underworld.'

Focus, Rhapsody thought, *don't let him distract you.* She blotted the demon's words from her mind, honed her concentration, and, using her bound arm, pulled with all her might on the vine encircling it, stretching it as much as she could. With the other she struck the elongated binding with the fire sword, shattering it into a thousand shards.

Both hands free now, she dodged a serpent-like strike from the vine aiming for her neck, then slashed it at the base. A blast of pure fire from the sword issued forth as she hit the mark, a brilliant sunburst in a world of darkness, cauterizing the tendril, which withered within seconds to dust.

The snare around her foot tightened viciously and yanked, pulling her off balance on the roughened, broken floor. Rhapsody concentrated, taking the hilt in both hands, and brought the blade down on the vine with all her might. The spray of fragmenting slate stung her as the vine exploded in a hail of fire and stone.

As her pounding heart returned to a regular rhythm, she had a vision of Elynsynos, and a question she would one day ask her.

Why? Why me? Why was this onerous responsibility given to me?

Rhapsody struggled to stand, listening for the dragon's answer.

Because you are not alone.

A ferocious roar, a war-scream of horrific intensity, echoed through the dark, windowless basilica, causing the chandeliers to swing violently and the bells in the tower to pick up the cry and resound with it. The roar was followed by the sound of crashing objects and the heavy thudding of approaching footfalls.

In response, the benison raised his arms. The tainted ground burst forth into a sea of dark flame, leaping walls of blinding fire that surrounded the demon, engulfing the entire basilica.

A bellow of pain swelled from behind the fiery wall, clutching at Rhapsody's heart. It was Grunthor; she knew the sound of his agony in her soul, having heard it once before.

A wave of intense heat that crackled with menace washed over her. Adrift for a moment on the burning tide of fiery air, she shielded her eyes with her forearm, trying to catch a glimpse of Grunthor's shadow to the demon's left, where he was supposed to enter at the second signal. But everything was lost in a black inferno, the demon, her friend, the nave of the basilica. It was like being once more at the core of a very different Earth, an Earth where the F'dor had triumphed. Anger burned cold in her soul at the thought of how that possibility was now at hand.

The tide was about to come in; whether it would come in on a fair wind or a sea of blood.

Do you understand now what you are fighting for?

Life itself.

Yes, and more. The battle that is being waged is not just for this life, but for the Afterlife. In this you must not fail.

She stood straighter and changed her grip on Daystar Clarion a little, remembering how Achmed had once counseled her to do so.

First, however you initially grasp the sword, change your grip a little, so that you focus on how you're holding it. Don't take your weapon for granted.

The hilt of the weapon in her grip felt as if it was part of her hand, an extension of her body.

'Tis as it should be.

As Oelendra's voice rang in her mind, Rhapsody thought of her mentor, of all she had endured, and all the others before and after her, who had given their lives, their souls, their sanity in the age-old battle against this demon. This kindly benison brewing tea on the altar was nothing more than the most recent incarnation of an evil so ancient that it had existed prior to the races of man, to the formation of land masses, of cities, of nations; all of history crumbled next to the time it had existed, sowing lies, wreaking death, biding its time until it could release its fellows from the Vault of the Underworld, and awaken the Primal Wyrm, devouring all of Life itself in one horrific cataclysm of chaos. So many souls its victims, so many fallen in its wake. The distant voices of those who had stood against it, living and dead, cried out to her on the windless air, rang through the handle of the sword, echoing in her blood. Rhapsody's mouth opened of its own will, and from her lips came their words.

No more. No more.

A fireball of black flame was building in the inferno's rage, like an avalanche coming down upon her. Above the wailing howl of the fire she could hear the demon laughing.

Rhapsody swallowed, then closed her eyes against the approaching fireball, resting the flaming sword against her heart. The pure heat of the elemental fire warmed her soul, helping her clear her thoughts, even as death loomed. She took a deep breath, concentrating with the clarity derived from the sword, and softly sang a single note – *ela* – the note to which she was attuned, that all her life had given her wisdom, discernment in uncertainty. The clarity of it, pure and sweet, sounded over the fire's bellow, piercing the roar, silencing the laughter, as the smallest bells of the carillon began first to hum, then to ring, then to peal strongly, firmly. *No more,* they tolled, ringing without clappers, echoing with nothing more than the power of the Namer's voice. *No more.*

The rolling wall of fire was on her now. She could feel the acid of it stinging her eyelashes, the malevolence in its flames chanting in dark voices, distant, squealing in rage, in pain, in futile fury.

With a consistent crescendo she increased the power of the note, hearing more and more of the bells respond to her call. Strength swelled within her; with a powerful thrust she held the sword aloft, channeling the note through it with all her breath. As the black flames of the Underworld broke around her she heard the deepest and largest of the bells begin to vibrate and then to ring, clapperless, filling the basilica with harmonious music and instantly dispelling it of the demon's evil taint.

Rhapsody sheathed her sword. The wind blew in and down the tower, billowing her hair all around her as the fire disappeared.

The benison stood in furious silence and more than a little pain, absorbing the ringing of the one hundred forty-six bells that now sang with *ela*. The ground around him was no longer desecrated, but beginning to resanctify, and with it he could feel the draining of his power.

He opened his mouth to speak the words of damnation.

But couldn't find them in his memory.

Lanacan closed his eyes and concentrated. There was another sound here, a far older and more terrifying one. The bells in the tower grew quiet as the sword was sheathed, leaving the alien vibration humming alone. It was a sandy sound, one that had not been in his memory in this lifetime, in this world; it tugged at the back of his mind, scratching within his temples. It was growing louder; his head began to throb, as though his skull were no longer a sufficient container for the brain that was swelling in rhythm to the noise. It was a sound that whispered death.

Cold sweat prickled his skin. The bells must have cracked the braincase of this body somehow, broken his skull; the girl had found a tone to kill his host persona. He glared at her, standing straight in the darkness of the aisle below him, her arms at her sides. In the half-light she looked like the legends of the Windchild, with her golden tresses billowing around her. He burned the image into his mind. He would need to remember her when he found another body to become his new host, to find her and destroy her.

Then a more cheerful thought occurred to him.

She would make a marvelous host herself.

He fought the searing headache that blinded him intermittently, struggling to hold fast to the idea and to consciousness. If he could bind her, she would be the perfect instrument for his final ascension.

He had planned to take her as a thrall at her coronation, and would have tried, had the old fool not decided to die just then. But now, with the body he had inhabited for decades suddenly useless, failing as he stood there, he thought of what power would be at his feet as the Lirin Queen, the Iliachenva'ar, the possessor of a beauty so seraphic that it could blind nations with one look. He had inhabited women before, and found it disappointing to be socially less powerful than the male personas in which he had lived. But this woman was stronger than any host he had ever bound to, man or woman. Excitement coursed through him as he prepared to feign death, knowing that it would bring her near to investigate. He raised his hand before him and prepared for his spirit to escape its body.

The scratching sound suddenly extended into a six-note scale, hanging monotonously in the air to his right. Lanacan felt a clutching sensation in the air around him; it clenched like the grip of a fist, and his heart, lungs,

409

and chest were suddenly crushed in a viselike pressure. With great effort he turned toward the sound.

There stood a tall, hideous figure in black robes, singing the excruciating song. Its tongue was clicking with an insectoid buzz in the back of its throat, the noise issuing forth past the lips that were struggling not to smile. Its thin, gloved right hand rose slowly and stopped rigidly in front of him, palm up. The loosening of the bonds to his human body, which he had been metaphysically untying, as he had so many other times, stopped immediately.

The creature's left hand, similarly gloved, came up next to its side and extended out, its fingers pulsing in rhythm to the beating of his demon-human heart. Each jerking flick of the digits caused him horrific pain. Then the hand began to revolve, wrapping its metaphysical moorings around its palm like a kite string. The creature tugged, drawing the four winds into a strangling net around him, choking him with all the force the physical and metaphysical worlds could muster.

The benison screamed, unable to move, unable to flee. He was trapped.

'Let me guess; you've heard of Dhracians but you never met one before; right?'

Lanacan Orlando's eyes, the only part of his body still able to move, darted to his other side. Standing there, casting a shadow that covered the altar completely, was an enormous monster in mail, hilts, and polearms jutting from behind him. It was the queen's honor guard, the gigantic monster that had swept the Patriarch out of his way, preventing him from searching further for the missing Ring that held the dying man's office.

In two steps the great Bolg was upon him, twisting his human arms behind his back and locking him into an even more immobile position. The giant wrenched him off the ground, causing pain to roar through the host body that was now as ensnared as his demonic soul was.

'You know, in my not-so-limited experience, Dhracians think of demon-scum like you as appetizers,' said the Bolg cheerfully. 'But for me you'll be dessert.'

Fury raged through the benison's heart. The street urchin known as Jo, for a time in his thrall, had told the Rakshas about the giant and the king, but only that they were both Firbolg. Obviously she had never known of the existence of the Dhracian race, let alone been able to identify one, particularly one of mixed blood. There was something vaguely familiar about this particular Dhracian as well, a power that was beyond defiance.

To struggle was useless, Lanacan knew. His mind began rapidly scanning the situation, seeking a vulnerable area, a way to turn the tables. He looked down from the sanctuary at the small woman who was now approaching, coming down the aisle silently. Inwardly the benison smiled.

It was time to play the trump card.

'All right, now, miss,' his physical captor said to the Lirin queen as she came nearer to the square central sanctuary. 'Rip his heart out. I'm starving.'

410

*

Rhapsody untied the hood of her cloak. The tiny stars of the crown of the Lirin, hidden within the fabric of the hood, caught an updraft of the now-clean wind blowing down the bell tower all around her and whirled into place over her head. Even as far as she was from the benison, now tangled securely in Grunthor's crushing grip, she could see the light of the blazing diamond shards glitter in his eyes. F'dor feared diamonds, she knew, though somehow she could not convince herself that the gleam she saw in those eyes was terror. It looked more like excitement to her.

She walked slowly toward the apse, her heart pounding so loudly she was sure all three of the men could hear it.

The benison stared down at her from the sanctuary. His hand had been caught raised before him, frozen in midair, when the Thrall ritual began, doubtless with the intent of calling down black fire on her, an intention that would never come to pass.

The demon gestured slightly at her with one of his fingers.

'*Virack urg caz,*' he said in a warm, sweet voice that made no audible sound. 'Conceive.'

Deep within her abdomen Rhapsody felt a twitch, then a twinge of pain. The muscles of her belly contracted, and between her legs she felt a hideous burning sensation.

'*Merlus,*' he whispered. His lips did not move. 'Grow.'

She lurched forward from the cramp that erupted within her abdomen. Then her muscles relaxed and she felt a cold motion begin to seep through her, moving outward from her middle, spreading throughout the inner cavity. Rhapsody shook off the sensation and crossed to the altar steps.

'You only think you're angry at me, you know, my dear,' said the voice in her mind. 'It's really Gwydion you should despise. In a way it is he that handed you over to me, and you don't even know it yet.'

Rhapsody shoved the hateful words out of her mind as she continued in her path to the steps. She concentrated on Ashe, the warm twinkle of his dragonesque eyes, the gentleness of his smile. She tried not to think of the depths of his suffering at the benison's hands, because her fury would return, burning behind her eyes and blinding her to the higher cause of her mission. She set her foot on the first step.

'You think of him as my victim, don't you? You couldn't be more wrong. His soul was a willing captive. It really wasn't difficult to sway him at all, you know. Your lover is a very creative and ingenious man, although I'm sure I don't have to tell you that. Much of the Rakshas's proclivity for rape and ritual torture came from the inspiration of the soul it carried; did you know that? Being a celibate cleric, you certainly don't think *I* could have taught it that level of sexual knowledge, do you? No, that was all Gwydion.'

The eyes of the old man in Grunthor's grip sparkled wickedly.

'And such pleasure the twisted nature of his soul gave to my toy when it was alive. The Rakshas particularly enjoyed violating your sister. She was such a willing victim. She lay right down on the heath and opened her legs,

411

you know; she certainly didn't act like any of the others. She wanted him, my dear. At least that should bring you comfort as you mourn her untimely death. She relished her own rape.

'Of course, I don't even think you can accurately call it rape when the woman pulls the one who is ravaging her inside herself and rides him, now, do you? Obviously I'm no expert, but I would venture to say an unwilling woman doesn't rock her molester with her body, thrusting her hips and moaning his name, becoming frustrated when he slows down.

'I have to admit I became aroused myself listening to him talk about how he pleasured her with his tongue, drinking the juice of her excitement. You do know why she was aroused, don't you? It wasn't just his hands between her legs, his mouth on her breasts, Rhapsody. It was *you!* It was the belief that she was rutting with *your* lover! Who would have guessed that someone so close to you could hate you so much that she would give herself over to your paramour, let him seduce her willingly to get back at you, even at the expense of her own life?'

Hatred coursed through Rhapsody, flushing her face and making her blood run hot, but at the edge of her mind she felt a pang of doubt. She remembered the hard expression on Jo's face, the direct look in her eyes as she told her tale.

I'm not seeing anyone. Actually, you're seeing him.

Jo, what are you talking about?

It was Ashe. I had sex with Ashe. The night of the meeting, when I ran out of the council room, and he came after me – he found me on the heath. He didn't tell you, did he? I thought not. He probably told you he couldn't find me, didn't he? Scum. I tried to make him leave, but he wouldn't. And, well, we did it. Actually, although I enjoyed it a little at the time, it was pretty grisly overall. I don't think I'll ever get the image of his face as he was knobbing me out of my mind. Honestly, Rhaps, I don't know what you see in him. Don't you have anything better to do than let him rut on you?

Rhapsody's stomach knotted with the cold feeling of betrayal she had not felt at the time. She had been too worried about Jo, too concerned to think of anything but her sister, to even imagine the act itself. But now the picture came into her mind of the two of them together on the heath, pumping away in the highgrass, moaning in the throes of mutual orgasm.

Her heart twisted in sickening anger as she drew Daystar Clarion again with a ringing sweep and began to climb the steps of the altar, a murderous look on her face. The benison smiled when he saw it, and Rhapsody felt a click inside her. She could hear Oelendra's admonition ringing in her ears.

Let your hatred pass; he will use it against you. Your reason for destroying him should be the child's future, not her past. If you keep that fixed in your mind, you will do it because 'tis the right thing to do, not out of revenge. There is more power in the former than the latter. 'Tis something I cannot do; my hatred is too entrenched, but you, Rhapsody, you have the chance to set things right. Don't let the atrocity of his actions ruin your focus.

Rhapsody took a deep breath and relaxed. She stepped onto the sanctuary floor, crossing to position herself before the benison, and heard the voice in her head again.

'Don't be jealous, Rhapsody; the Rakshas liked it so much better with you than with your sister.'

Rhapsody stopped in midstride.

'What, you didn't know? Well, I'm not surprised. They did look identical, your two lovers. How fortunate for me that you fell in love with the son of Llauron; it made it so much easier for the Rakshas to have you. You don't think it was always Gwydion who took you, did you? Once your sister told my creation about the two of you, it was easy. It is, after all, very dark in the Teeth at night, isn't it, my dear?'

The silent voice in her mind laughed, and the sound echoed off her brain, making her head pound. Her stomach heaved as the memory of Jo's last night swam before her eyes, the shrieking wind on the mountain pass in the impenetrable dark, her blind climb up the crags to the sheltered arch.

It's probably just that my first time was a little, well, a little rough, a little violent.

The blood drained from her face as she remembered her desperate, almost violent lovemaking with Ashe that night against the mountain face, the usual tenderness lost to ferocious intensity and fierce pain. It was Ashe. Or was it? *It can't be,* she thought in panic, but the laughter in her mind grew louder as she realized she hadn't seen his face, and even if she had she might not have been able to discern the difference anyway in her despair and the howling wind.

What happened to Jo was not your fault. If anyone is to blame, it's me.

He had come to her from the darkness, after Ashe had left. Maybe he had been stalking the Teeth as he had been when he found Jo.

Khaddyr's smile was sickeningly knowing as he pointed at her abdomen.

Well, time will tell. We will see who is the whore of the demon.

The subsonic voice of the demon laughed once more. 'And to think, all this time you didn't know you were pregnant. Well, I suppose that's fair; the seed was planted a long time ago, but it was the word I just spoke that made it begin to grow. Surely you didn't think you were the only one with the ability of Naming, did you? No, certainly not – you're far too modest, aren't you, my dear? So charming. You will be a wonderful mother, Rhapsody, at least while the child is in your womb. It's a shame that you won't live through the delivery.'

The voice in her mind was replaced for a moment by Manwyn's voice in her memory.

I see an unnatural child born of an unnatural act. Rhapsody, you should beware of childbirth: the mother shall die, but the child shall live.

Her hands grew clammy, her grip on the sword loosened.

'Yes, my dear, it's true. You are carrying my child, like the others. Only yours will favor his father more, I think; having been held as a dormant seed for so long, it has had the chance to steep in my blood, like the tea here on the altar. The more time that passes before the mother's blood takes hold, the more its demonic nature gestates.'

Rhapsody began to tremble. Her time at the Rowans had been almost seven years; if there was any truth to the F'dor's words, the child would be totally demonic.

'And isn't it just a splendid irony: the beautiful star-mother, savior of lost children, patron saint of the demon-spawn, the Sky in the prophecy of the Three who comes from the Past itself to unite and heal the wounds of this orphaned population; you, Rhapsody, *you* will give birth to me again! It is *you* that will bring the F'dor back into this world. You are the doorway through which I will return, the one who will keep the evil alive. Oh, isn't this rich! What could be more perfect?'

The sword clattered to the floor.

Grunthor stared at her; Rhapsody's face was colorless, her eyes wide and staring blindly, almost the way Jo's had looked in the moment of her death. She shook uncontrollably, her hands moving to her abdomen.

He could feel the demon's strength growing as each second passed. He looked wildly over at Achmed, who was beginning to sweat from the exertion of maintaining the Thrall ritual. No sound came from the benison, but a smile was creeping over his elderly face, a face with eyes that burned like the fires of the Underworld, staring maniacally now at Rhapsody.

Beneath his feet the Earth began to tremble; when it began to scream Grunthor could feel it, its pain running like acid through his veins. He knew instinctually that something was very wrong; the tide was turning against them, and he didn't have any idea why.

The sleeves on his arms began to feel warm; within seconds they were on the verge on igniting into flame. Agony seared him, burning his skin where it was touching the monster. The old man had begun to *thicken*, it seemed; the fragile elderly body was becoming more tensile and ferociously strong as each second passed. The stench of the grave issued forth from the benison's mouth, choking him, burning his eyes.

Grunthor's heart was pounding loudly, its rhythm counterbalanced by a fear he had never experienced. He knew in a moment the beast would shatter his arms.

And then be free.

He grunted in pain as the cloth of his shirt began to smolder, trying to keep his eyes clear of the acrid smoke. He looked over at Achmed and gasped.

The Dhracian had sunk to his knees; blood was pouring from his nose and ears. His normally swarthy skin was pale as death, and his limbs trembled violently in the effort to maintain the Thrall ritual. He was gasping for air, the sounds from his shredded throats coming out gargled and unsteady. The veins in his neck vibrated, ready to explode. As panic began to consume him, his eyes darted back to Rhapsody.

She was staring at the benison, her face shiny with sweat, her eyes soulless, staring into another place.

Gods, he thought, *the bastard's enthralling her.*

'Your Ladyship?' he choked, trying to catch her eye. Rhapsody stared right past him, her eyes locked with the demon's. The metallic taste of blood was in his mouth.

He could feel his strength waning, knew that any second the demon would break free. His head was pounding with the sounds of dark voices chanting and the pressure of his own blood.

A thud and the sound of metal against stone; Achmed had fallen to the ground, prone, blood pooling beneath his chin. His chant had grown almost too weak to hear, his upraised hand trembled, threatening to close. His forehead was creased in chasms that throbbed visibly, ready to burst.

His last sight of Achmed vanished in a curtain of black as his own blood came to a boil; with the impact of a battering ram the demon broke free, tossing him across the basilica and slamming him into the sanctuary wall.

Woozily he put his hand to his head, trying to stanch the agony. He fought the unconsciousness that was threatening to close in, letting fury take its place. Grunthor reached into the part of his soul that was tied to the earth. The marble floor and the ground beneath it, so recently tainted, hummed in response.

Hold him for me, he thought.

Even from across the sanctuary he could feel the earth below the demon's feet soften. The pain in his head ebbed at the sight of the benison, now sinking into the mud that a moment before was marble, struggling to maintain his own concentration now. The maniacal gleam in his eye faltered, and the smile dimmed as he tried to pull free.

Grunthor inhaled deeply as the earth hardened again, trapping the demon. He could see that Achmed had only a few more moments in which he would be able to maintain the Thrall ritual.

He turned on his knees and crawled to a stand, using the wall, stained with his own blood, as support, then lumbered back to the inner sanctuary and grasped the benison's arms again.

The demon didn't even struggle. It turned its full gaze onto Rhapsody, its eyes boring holes in her soul.

The voice in her ear grew louder.

'Ah, Rhapsody, I can see you're happy; you've always loved children, haven't you? And to think you feared that you were barren, didn't you? I know what's in your heart, you know; I can see your deepest secrets, because I am in there, too. You really should be more careful for whom you spread your legs, my dear; sometimes what they leave behind is more than the momentary pleasure is worth.'

The warm voice sank even deeper into her ears.

Now, come to me.

Against her will, she took a step forward.

Her mind began to scream in agony. She fought the sound of the sweet voice, blinking to drive the words out from behind her eyes, but found her hands frozen. Involuntarily she took another step forward.

That's right, the benison's voice encouraged gently. *Come to me, Rhapsody.*

Within her heart the words resonated. There was a comfort there, a security. The benison would not harm her. She longed to obey his command. A desire, primal, almost sexual in nature, flushed through her, heating her blood. She took another step.

Come to me, dear one, the voice encouraged; the tone like that of a lover. Warmth surrounded her, like the darkness of a mutual bed. Rhapsody felt a thrill run up her spine, leaving her skin tingling.

Come to me, the father of your child, indeed, your child itself. I am both, your child and your child's father, and you love me. Together we have made this child. You would never hurt your own child, would you?

She shook her head.

No, of course not. Come, bring me the sword —

'STRIKE!' Grunthor bellowed, shattering the benison's words. 'Get your pretty head out of your arse and pay attention, or I'll rip it off and stick it on my poleaxe!'

The voice of her first trainer was like a beacon in the deepening darkness; it brought Rhapsody out of her trance and drove the silent utterances of the demon from her mind. An older, far more entrenched loyalty roared through her, evaporating the momentary possession the demon's words had anchored in her mind. The voice of the Sergeant rang through her clearly.

She was sworn to him. She had named him long ago.

The Lord of Deadly Weapons.

Her friend.

The Ultimate Authority, to Be Obeyed at All Costs.

She shook her head as if shaking off sleep, then looked to the floor next to her where Daystar Clarion lay, smoldering impotently. She bent and picked up the sword, then rose and strode purposefully across the marble floor of the sanctuary. The eyes of the benison widened in fear.

The blade of the sword sprang to life in her hand, and the shimmering flame leapt as she doubled her grip. Rhapsody raised the sword over her head, point down. The demon struggled against the bonds of Grunthor's massive arms, but it was a futile effort. Next to her, Rhapsody could hear the strange music of Achmed's Thrall ritual grow louder, and Grunthor's voice emerged from behind the benison.

'That's a girl; I've got him, Your Ladyship. A good clean blow, now.'

The demon looked into her face and saw no fear there, just a serene, deadly calm. As their eyes met, understanding passed between them.

I will see you soon, the benison said in her mind.

'Perhaps sooner than you think,' Rhapsody replied.

She drove the ancient sword, the weapon of kings and champions, the blade that had slain invincible enemies and united a nation, deep into the heart of the demon, and pulled it down with all her strength to split the chest and sever the base of the spine. The noxious, caustic stench of the F'dor billowed out of the benison's body as burning blood splashed the sanctuary steps.

Lying prone on the marble floor of the sanctuary, Achmed slowly raised his head. His upstretched hand, around which the net of the four winds was anchored, began to smoke as a spray of the burning, black-red blood spattered the palm. His thin lips pulled back in a grin despite his agony. A gurgling laugh mixed with the sound of the Thrall ritual.

Just as I have your blood on my hands now, one day I will have it so again.

The demon screamed; it sounded more of fury than pain, and it clawed wildly at Rhapsody as she twisted Daystar Clarion in its abdominal cavity and pulled it free. Grunthor strained from the exertion of holding it in place; the benison managed only to look up into Rhapsody's eyes with a glare of blistering cold before the giant Firbolg hoisted its bleeding body out of the marble floor of the basilica. He looked at her and they exchanged a nod. Then, with all his strength, Grunthor heaved the twitching carcass onto the altar beneath the opening in the ceiling.

At the same moment Rhapsody summoned starfire from the heavens through the open bell tower.

With a ferocious roar the ethereal flames descended onto the altar, blasting the Three back out of the sanctuary and consuming it. The screams of the demon were inaudible over the noise of the firestrike, but Rhapsody could feel them in her mind. The human form twisted and shriveled for a moment before disappearing in the blinding fire. Then, seconds later, everything was as it had been before, albeit blackened from the flame.

Rhapsody stared at the burned-out sanctuary, seeking any sign of survival, any piece that might have been spared by the starfire, but saw nothing but smoke and ash. In the distance the bells of the town began tolling urgently, and panicked voices could be heard in the night.

Grunthor opened his arms, and Rhapsody ran into his embrace, holding on to him with all her remaining strength. 'I'm sorry, I'm so sorry,' she gasped.

'Why? You did great, darling, just like I taught you. You lost focus for a moment, but that happens to the best of us, eh, sir?'

From the floor where he lay Achmed weakly raised his head. 'It certainly does.' He was watching her closely, even as Grunthor pulled him to a stand, then wrapped a supportive arm around him.

'Come on, Your Ladyship,' Grunthor urged, putting her down. He took her gently but insistently by the arm. Rhapsody stopped long enough to wipe the blood from the floor and the wall with her cloak, then followed them through the vestry, stepping over Gittleson's body and into the street, where they waited in the darkness to join the throng of townspeople hurrying to see what had happened in the basilica.

Many hours later, when the sexton had finally cleared the basilica and locked the doors, the Three emerged from the shadows to examine the sanctuary again. Rhapsody closed her eyes and listened for the music of the bells, which still tolled the all-clear that had been ringing for almost an hour. It was sweet and in tune, with a clarity she knew indicated that the wind was passing through the bell tower freely again.

'It's clear,' she said to her companions. 'The ground is being resanctified. How does it feel, Grunthor?'

'It's hard to tell yet, but the taint is definitely dissipating,' he said, bending to touch the floor. 'I'd say it's getting there; guess those bells need the clappers back to fix it totally properly. Now, you, miss; how are you doing? You had me worried for a moment, you know.'

She reached out her arms, and her gigantic friend lifted her off the ground in a relieved embrace. 'I'm fine. I really am,' she said, looking down into his amber eyes.

'I'm not sure I believe you.'

'Well, you should.' Rhapsody hugged Grunthor tightly for a few moments more, then reached up and kissed his monstrous cheek. 'Grunthor, will you go and see about an exit route now? I have to talk to Achmed alone.'

Grunthor looked at Achmed, who nodded. 'All right, Your Ladyship, I suppose I can take care of that if you want.' He set her down gently and patted her head, then headed down the marble steps of the sanctuary.

'Grunthor?'

He turned and looked back at her. 'Yes'm?'

'I love you.'

A wide smile crossed his broad face. 'The feeling's mutual, miss.' He clicked his heels and turned once more for the door of the basilica.

Rhapsody waited until the giant Bolg had left the church, then looked at the Firbolg king. There was a look of amusement on his face that vanished when she turned to him. She studied his eyes intently, and as she did the pain and fear she was feeling crept back into her own. Achmed saw it immediately.

He took her into his arms, and Rhapsody clung tightly to him, trembling. Wordlessly he passed his hand over her back, waiting for her to speak. She could tell without doing so that he understood fully the depths of her fright. He held her for a long time, and the immediacy of the panic passed.

'You know,' she said when she looked up again, 'we really are two sides of the same coin.'

'I know.'

She nodded, lost in thought for a moment. Then she looked into his face again.

'Is there a limit to what you would do for me if I asked?'

'No.'

'I didn't think so.' She moved out of his arms and down the steps of the sanctuary, her arms clutching her middle as she stared over the vast space of the basilica at the candelabras burning down into darkness. She sat on the step, to be joined by Achmed a moment later. They waited in silence for a long while, watching the basilica darken, listening to the noise of the crowd outside die down.

I just want it to be over. I just want to sleep peacefully again.

You want it to be over – it will never be over, Rhapsody.

Finally she looked at him, and her eyes were shining, but not with her customary emotions.

'In the old world, in the course of practicing your profession, did you ever have occasion to kill quickly, with little pain?'

'Yes. That was how I tried to do it most of the time.'

'Of course, it would be.' She looked away again and her eyes scanned the damage in the balcony and to the benches. 'I may have need of your services soon, after the Cymrian Council.'

Achmed nodded. 'For whom?'

Rhapsody looked him directly in the eye. 'Myself.'

Achmed nodded again. He understood.

68

The fire on the hearth in the council room behind the Great Hall of the Cauldron burned rambunctiously, smelling vastly better than it had in Grunthor's memory, thanks in large part to the three fat vanilla beans Rhapsody had tossed on it when they came in for supper. The meal had been a surprisingly quiet one, due in large part to the pensive look on the Singer's face and her lack of conversational patter, a signal to him that something was decidedly wrong.

It had been so all the way home from Bethe Corbair as well, his own celebratory mood not extending to either of his companions. He had cast a glance in Achmed's direction a moment before and had seen the warning look in his eye, so he did not ask, but rather attempted to lighten the mood with a pleasantry, or his approximation of one.

'Delicious meal, Duchess,' he said jovially, patting her roughly on the head. 'I don't remember your stew ever tasting that good before.'

'It's all that garlic from Bethe Corbair,' she replied, rising and taking his plate. 'I don't believe I've ever seen such plump, firm heads. I saved some to plant. Would you like more?'

'Yes, indeed.' Grunthor took a sip of the tea and made a face. 'And is this something you bought there as well?'

'Yes; that's the horehound. It's the same thing that was in the candy.' She smiled at his grimace. 'Don't like it, do you?'

Grunthor made an effort to look cheerful. 'Oh, it's lovely, darling.'

'Liar. That's all right, I'm used to people insulting my tea. That's the oil from the leaves; you said you had a sore throat. It's supposed to taste that way.'

The giant Bolg swallowed. 'I guess it's an acquired taste, eh? What are you going to do with all that demon stuff – the mugwort and datura? Isn't that poisonous?'

'I certainly hope so. I've painted all the cockroach nests with it.'

Achmed hid his smile. 'What are you going to do with all those arrows?'

'They're for my grandson, Gwydion Navarne. He's an archer, like his father, or at least is training to be. He'll love the ones that hold flame.'

'Don't let him practice with them near the keep or anything flammable you don't want incinerated. They're warped.'

Rhapsody's face clouded in dismay. 'They are? I didn't notice.'

The Firbolg king leaned back and crossed his feet. 'Of course you didn't. You were too busy concentrating on making sure Gittleson saw you in the market.'

'He was inept, wasn't he?'

'*Was* being the operative word.'

'The poor benny,' said Grunthor sympathetically. 'It's *so* hard to get good help these days.' He grinned when he saw a smile touch the corners of Rhapsody's mouth.

'Especially where he is now,' said Achmed, studying her as well. 'Actually, it's pretty hard to get anything good there.'

Rhapsody pushed her chair back. 'All right, stop watching me. I can't stand it.' She rose and went to the fire, staring into the billowing flames.

'You want to tell us what's wrong?' The deep voice was gentle; Grunthor saw the muscles of her back tense at his words, but otherwise could discern no reaction.

Rhapsody watched the fire a moment longer. Finally she turned and smiled slightly at both of them.

'I don't know for sure if anything's wrong at all, Grunthor,' she said quietly. 'I do have to go back to Tyrian, and it's making me sad to think about leaving you both again.'

'So stay,' said Achmed flatly.

She shook her head. 'I can't. It's time to call the Cymrian Council, and I have preparations in my own lands to make before I do. But after that I'll be back, and I'll have several months to wait before all the Cymrians show up. I have to stay within Canrif until they do, so we'll have some extended time together then.'

'I doubt it,' Grunthor mumbled gloomily. 'Just when we're having some fun, Old Waterboy will show up, and you'll be off with him.'

Rhapsody's face lost its smile. 'No, he won't,' she said decisively. 'He's out of the picture now, Grunthor. And if he does come, I don't want to see him anyway.' The Bolg looked at each other.

'Well, that's refreshing,' said Achmed. 'What do you need from us for the Council?'

'I have a list, actually. It mostly involves accommodations and security, no small task for a hundred thousand potential guests. There are some other things on it as well; I'll go to my room and get it.' She hurried out of the Council room and away from their watchful gaze.

After she was gone the two continued to stare out the door after her.

'What do you think's bothering her, sir?'

Achmed looked back at the fire. 'I think she's wrestling with her own internal demons now.'

Achmed rode with her as far as the Ylorc–nBethe Corbair border. They had shared a simple campfire supper and watched the stars come out in a sky that was darkening later at the approach of winter's end. They sat in silence, lost in their own thoughts. Finally, Rhapsody stood and prepared to leave.

'Thank you. For supper, and for everything else.' Achmed nodded. Her eyes became a little brighter, and she took his hand. 'Do you remember what you said to me the night before the coronation? About always being behind me?'

'Yes.'

Rhapsody smiled. 'When I was standing in the basilica, before you came in, I could feel you there, even though the demon couldn't.'

'I know.'

'It's the only reason I didn't turn and run right then.'

Achmed shook his head. 'No, it's not. But it doesn't matter; it will always be the case.'

'I know.' She hoisted the saddlebag over the back of her horse, then turned to face him again. 'Will you do something for me?'

'Of course.'

'Look in on Elysian while I'm gone. It's been such a long time since I've been there. My gardens are undoubtedly all dead, but I just want to know that the house is still standing.'

Achmed slung the other satchel on as well. 'All gardens die in the winter. It's almost spring. Your plantings will make it through; the hard part is almost over.'

Rhapsody studied him as he packed his own horse. 'Not necessarily,' she said. 'Sometimes the frost kills.'

He came back over to her and took her hand. 'Not when the garden is properly tended.'

She smiled at him again, then reached up and took his face in her hands. Gently she kissed him as she had in the street next to the basilica that night, allowing the warmth of her lips to linger on his for a moment. Then she stepped back and let her eyes wander over his face.

'I was afraid I would never get the chance to do that again,' she said softly.

'So was I,' he said. He walked with her to her horse and watched her mount. 'Travel well.'

'Thank you. You stay well, my friend.' She blew him another kiss, then rode off into the inky blackness of the night, toward the light of the rising moon.

As he rowed across Elysian's silent lake, Achmed muttered curses under his breath. He hated water. Only at Rhapsody's request would he be down here, sculling this loathsome boat across the giant pond.

He missed the mooring repeatedly and finally gave up in disgust, jumping into the knee-deep water and wading to shore. The moment his feet touched dry land he knew something was wrong with Elysian; there was an unwelcome vibration in the air.

Ashe was here somewhere.

As if in confirmation the front door opened. After a few moments Ashe appeared in the doorway, unshaven and wild-eyed. The look of abject panic on his face was clear even from several hundred feet away. Achmed took his time, removing his sodden boots and pouring the lake water out. Then he waded back into the lake and pulled the uncooperative craft to shore.

'Where is she?' Ashe's voice was right behind him.

'Yes, thanks, I certainly would like a hand,' Achmed said sarcastically. He tied the boat off and turned to face Llauron's son.

His consummate dislike and lack of trust abated momentarily; he was looking into a face contorted by stark fear and unrelenting worry. He had in fact only seen Ashe's face once or twice before, on the occasions of uncomfortable dinner parties here in Elysian the summer that the pest had been staying with Rhapsody. The air had been chokingly thick with tension as the two eyed each other suspiciously and exchanged barbs while Rhapsody went about serving the meal, pretending to be oblivious of it all.

Now his rival was at a disadvantage. He had obviously been waiting here for her to return; if he had been upworld anywhere he would have heard the news from Bethe Corbair about the benison. Panic had made his face look older than it had even when he was being hunted. Somewhere deep in his past Achmed remembered that feeling. It was hard to imagine that another, far worse, one existed, but clearly it did, and in that instant, for the first time in his memory, Achmed felt something that resembled compassion for the man whose presence he couldn't abide.

'She's alive,' he said, winding the rope and tossing it onto the beach. 'She's probably halfway to Tyrian by this time.'

Relief broke over Ashe's face, replaced a moment later by concern and another, more complex expression. 'Was she injured?'

'No. You can stop worrying about her now.'

'Why did she go to Tyrian?'

Achmed met his eyes with a characteristic stare. 'She lives there. Had no one told you?'

Ashe blinked uneasily. 'Yes. No. I mean, I thought she would come here first. She lives here, too.'

Achmed nodded, and turned to survey the gardens of Elysian. As she had predicted, they had gone dormant, frost withering their leaves and buds even underground. 'Then perhaps she had an inkling you might think that, and went to Tyrian to avoid you. She doesn't want to see you, Ashe.' He watched as Ashe's face flushed red.

'She said that?'

'Those very words.'

'I see.' Ashe turned away for a moment, running his hand through the implausibly copper hair. 'Is that why you came? To tell me that?'

Achmed snorted. 'Hardly. I am not your messenger. Rhapsody asked me to look in on the house and the gardens. She didn't have any idea that you would be here. Had she, I probably wouldn't have come.'

Ashe nodded. 'Well, thank you at least for giving me the news. Is the benison dead?'

'Yes.'

'Good; that's good.' He glanced around Elysian again; he looked as if he had no idea what to do next.

'Where will you go now, Ashe?'

Ashe turned around to face him again. A new calm had taken up residence on his face. 'I'm not certain. Tyrian, probably.'

Achmed smirked. 'You did hear me, didn't you?'

'Yes. But that doesn't mean I believe you, or want your advice.'

The Firbolg king chuckled. Being crossed made Rhapsody defiant, bordering on obstreperous; he wished he could see her face now, listening to this. 'Suit yourself. I assume the house is in order?'

Ashe colored a bit. 'It's in order, if not orderly.'

'I see. Well, be sure to clean up before you leave. I'd hate to have her any angrier at you than she already is.'

Ashe's face darkened. 'No, you wouldn't. You'd love to see us apart, wouldn't you?'

Achmed shrugged. 'You are apart, aren't you? Ashe, go find something to do. We've killed your demon for you; she's healed you and given you unbelievable power. You're the Invoker *and* the Patriarch now, both of which were her doing. What else do you want? Find a life and go lead it. If you stay in Elysian much longer I will have to assess you for residence taxes.' He picked up his still-soggy boots and headed back to the boat.

'Taxes? Do you charge them of Rhapsody as well? What kind of an account are you keeping for her expenses, and how do you expect to be paid?'

Achmed stopped and turned, leveling a sour look at Ashe. 'I would pretend you have the ability to understand, but why bother? You think you're a dragon, Ashe, but you are really just a giant leech. You're one to talk of payback. She has given you everything – what has she gotten in return? What have any of us seen as a return on our investment?

'Sooner or later you'll see her at the Cymrian Council, something she again will be responsible for calling, despite the fact that it was your bloody family's responsibility. When the arse-rags meet, you will undoubtedly be made Lord Cymrian, a role for which, I might add, you're perfect. Being worse than your grandfather would take some doing, and I don't think you have it in you. You aren't a wastrel, just a waste. You have the power to be the largest rock in history – all you have to do is fall into the pond – but you can't raise yourself to make the slightest ripple. Whatever your titles may be, don't flatter yourself to presume that you are her equal. She will outlive you, Ashe. We will all outlive you, like a blighted crop or a bad neighbor. Go away. We've already had to purify this island once.' He turned and walked back to the boat.

Awareness dawned, and Ashe saw past the barbed insults to what the Firbolg king was really saying. 'It was your way of being near her, coming here.'

Achmed kept walking, but slowed his pace. 'To be near her, all I'd have had to do was go with her to Tyrian. Stop assuming that everyone has the same motives you do.'

'You miss her, and you came down here to be with her, in a way, didn't you?'

'What you think has no bearing on anything, Ashe. Sooner or later you will figure that out.' Achmed tossed his boots into the boat as he approached it.

'You love her too, don't you?' Ashe's voice was mild, resonant with understanding.

Achmed stopped, but did not turn around. He was silent for several moments. When he spoke his voice was dry but contained none of his usual sarcasm.

'No, Ashe; *you* love her too. And do you want to hear something amusing? Killing the Rakshas? She still thinks I did it for you.' He climbed aboard the boat, fit the oars in the oarlocks, and rowed away out of sight.

By the time Ashe got to Tyrian, Rhapsody had already come and gone.

69

Oelendra was busy repairing a shield when the door to her cottage opened. Surprise, then delight, then dismay crossed her face when Rhapsody came in, hanging her cloak and weapons at the door. Oelendra stood up to embrace her queen, relief filling her soul and allowing her to breathe freely for the first time in weeks.

'Thank the stars,' she murmured, burying her face in the shining hair and pulling Rhapsody even tighter. 'You're all right. Thank the stars.'

'I have, twice daily, as usual,' Rhapsody answered, not pulling away. 'The F'dor is dead.'

'I know,' Oelendra said, drawing her over to the hearth and lowering her into the willow rocking chair she liked. 'The news has spread quickly; Rial came by yesterday with word from Roland, through Bethany. No one seemed to have any word of you, however.'

Rhapsody nodded, accepting the mug Oelendra held out to her. 'Good. We tried to be as anonymous as possible. What was said?'

'That Lanacan Orlando was in the midst of some rites in Ryles Cedelian, the basilica of Bethe Corbair, when the bell tower was struck by lightning. Poor soul, he was incinerated instantly, along with the sanctuary of the basilica.'

A wry smile came to rest on the queen's face. 'An amazingly lucky thing that the bell tower itself was undamaged, wouldn't you say?'

Oelendra laughed. 'I would. Now, what really happened?' Rhapsody related the details of the fight as Oelendra listened raptly, nodding from time to time, or wincing when the tale warranted it. When she had finished, Oelendra put down her own mug and crossed her arms over her knees.

'Though I must admit I am thrilled to see you, why did you come back here instead of going to Elysian?'

Rhapsody shuddered inwardly at the thought. 'Why would I go there? It's haunted with old memories.'

'Well,' Oelendra said awkwardly, 'one of those old memories is waiting for you there in desperate fear.' When Rhapsody looked puzzled, Oelendra sighed. 'Gwydion.'

'Ashe is in Elysian? How do you know?'

'I saw him not long ago; the very night you went against the demon, in fact.'

'What is he doing in Elysian?'

'By now I would say he is probably panicking,' Oelendra answered. 'He is waiting to see you, to assure himself that you survived the fight.'

'I doubt he is panicking any longer, then,' Rhapsody said, taking a sip of *dol mwl*. 'I asked Achmed to look in on Elysian when he got back, to make sure the house and gardens were all right and such. He'll let Ashe know I survived.'

'I think he would like to hear it from you,' said Oelendra. 'You should talk to him, Rhapsody.'

Rhapsody choked on her drink, then coughed. 'No, thank you, Oelendra, that is the last thing I need right now. I told Ashe I would see him at the Cymrian Council. That, by the way, is why I'm here.'

'The Cymrian Council?'

'Yes. It's time. I'm here in Tyrian to make preparations for being away for quite a while. If I understand the old manuscripts we found in Gwylliam's, they say the Summoner of the Council must stay within those lands from the time the Council horn is blown until the entire assemblage shows up, or the Cymrians can lose the compelling need that forces them to come.'

'Yes, that is how it works.'

'The gathering stage could take several months, so I need to have things in order here. I'd like to meet with you and Rial later today, if that's convenient.'

'As you wish. So you're going to summon the Cymrians?'

'Well, I'm going to try,' said Rhapsody, putting down her empty mug. She shook her head when Oelendra nodded toward the pot. 'No, thank you. It was just what I needed to calm my nerves.' She saw that Oelendra was examining her face; she rose quickly and turned away, walking to the window and looking out into the light of early spring.

It was too late. Oelendra had seen all she needed to. She decided to tread lightly. 'You should go to Elysian first, dearest. Go see Gwydion. Let him reassure himself at least.'

An ugly laugh escaped the queen. 'No. He'll have to be satisfied with getting word firsthand from Achmed, Oelendra. He is not a part of my life anymore, and frankly, I have a few more weighty things on my mind right now. I think it's abominable that he would leave his new wife alone to wait in Elysian, anyway.'

Oelendra coughed. 'I think he would agree with that statement whole-heartedly,' she said. 'But you should see him, darling. He is waiting to give you your memories back.'

Rhapsody looked at her in mild surprise. 'He told you that?'

'Aye. Don't be angry with him, Rhapsody; he was very upset when I saw him.'

Rhapsody looked back out the window. 'I don't want those memories back, Oelendra. He told me what some of them were the last time I saw him, and I don't think I can survive any more deception and lies. Did you know that Llauron is not dead?'

'Aye, Gwydion told me. I can't say I was surprised.'

'Well, believe me, I certainly was. Do you have any idea what it feels like to know that I, the woman who defended the Patriarch, called starfire down onto the Invoker, the head of the religion the people of Tyrian and I are more closely connected with, burning him alive? That the two men I have gone out of my way for more than anyone since I came to this land have used me in unspeakable ways to advance their own causes?' Rhapsody turned finally to face her mentor, and Oelendra's heart went cold at the expression in the queen's eyes. They were glowing with green fire, flickering with angry tears. 'You have no idea what this little demon hunt has cost me, Oelendra.'

Oelendra rose. 'I think I do.'

'No, you *don't*,' Rhapsody spat. She clutched the windowsill and tried to maintain control; she had much to get through before she could let her fear loose.

Oelendra came up behind her and took her by the shoulders. 'I do know what it is like to lose someone you love with all your heart to the F'dor, Rhapsody. I know you miss Jo, but Gwydion is still here. You must allow him to give you back your memories, no matter how painful, for without them you will never be whole.'

Rhapsody shook Oelendra's hands off her violently, and turned around slowly. The look of devastation in her eyes made the Lirin warrior's soul shudder.

'I will never be whole anyway, Oelendra. I can't see Ashe right now. Please, stop it. I told him I would not see him until the Cymrian Council, and I do not intend to break my word. Now leave me in peace.' She turned and walked to the door. 'Can I expect you this afternoon?'

'Tell me,' Oelendra said quietly. 'Tell me, Rhapsody.'

Rhapsody knew better than to dodge. 'I can't.'

'Can't, or are afraid to?'

'Both.'

Oelendra put her arms out silently. Rhapsody stood for a moment by the door, her hand on the latch. Then she shook her head. 'Don't, Oelendra, if you comfort me I will not make it through. I have to keep going until I can safely lay it down.'

'Then tell me from over there.' Oelendra went back to the fire and sat in her rocking chair, and pointed to a small wooden desk chair by the window. 'Tell me as if you are giving me a scouting report. Or like you're planning the spring festival, or as though you're updating me on plans for the children.' The queen's face turned white. 'Sit down, Rhapsody,' Oelendra said gently, but firmly. Numbly, Rhapsody sat. Oelendra waited patiently, and in silence.

Finally Rhapsody looked down into her lap, and squeezed her hands together until the blood left her knuckles. 'There is a possibility that I am pregnant,' she said hollowly, her voice barely above a whisper.

Oelendra let her breath out quietly. She hid her smile, knowing what joy the news would bring to Gwydion, and how thrilled Rhapsody would be once she knew the truth. She just needed to overcome the misconception that her husband was wed to another. 'All the more reason to tell him, darling,' she said sensibly. 'He has a right to know.'

'It's not his.'

Oelendra was thunderstruck, but outwardly all she did was blink. 'Oh? Who is the father, then?'

Rhapsody raised her eyes slowly and locked her gaze onto Oelendra's. 'The F'dor.' It was now her turn to watch her friend begin to shake uncontrollably. 'I'm sorry, Oelendra. You wanted to know.'

Oelendra rose from her chair and paced before the fireplace, trying to keep Rhapsody from seeing her face. When she had a modicum of control back she came to the queen and crouched down before her, taking her hands.

'Explain, Rhapsody. What's going on?'

Rhapsody looked away. 'I wish I knew for certain. The demon was able to speak to me from inside; Achmed and Grunthor couldn't hear him. He told me that the Rakshas had taken Ashe's place, and had – had – planted his seed inside me. He knew about a night when – when it could have happened. He knew a great many things he shouldn't have, Oelendra; and when he spoke the word that made the seed begin to grow, I could feel it. He said that it had steeped a long time in his blood, so now it was demonic, not human like the others.'

'You're taking his word for all this?'

'No, not absolutely,' Rhapsody answered quietly. 'But, as I said, it's hard to discount when he knows things that would be difficult to guess at.'

'But not impossible?'

She considered. 'No, I suppose not. But I have been nauseous and in pain ever since.'

'That could be nerves, or fear, or both. I know I have felt that way myself.'

Rhapsody was on the verge of losing her temper. 'Yes, Oelendra, it could be. It could also be that I am in the process of being the vehicle by which the F'dor returns to the Earth.' She stood and went to the coat peg, retrieving her cloak.

Oelendra could not watch her. 'Is it really possible, Rhapsody? Demons are expert liars. F'dor can take the smallest shred of the truth and build it into something terrifying, playing on your deepest fears. Could he have convinced you of this despite its impossibility?'

Rhapsody belted her sword, and came back to where Oelendra still crouched down, and bent beside her, resting her hand on the warrior's cheek. Oelendra turned after a moment and looked into her eyes, and cringed at what she saw there.

'I know you don't want to believe this, but it is definitely possible,' Rhapsody said softly. 'In fact, the more I reflect on it, the more I think it is likely. But it doesn't matter, Oelendra. I can't know the answer to it now. I can't, because if it is true, I won't be able to go on. So help me, please, as you always have.

'I need to get through the Council, and finish what we've started with the reunification and healing of the Cymrians. Before that, I have to be certain Tyrian is in good hands, which is where you can help. And when those two things are accomplished, I will seek out the truth. But I can assure you of the truth of one thing, Oelendra, on my word and my soul: if it is true, if I am carrying this demonic child, it will not be born. It will not revisit itself on this land. I will die first. I have already arranged it. Now, I'll see you with Rial later. Thank you for the *dol mwl*.' She kissed the older woman and stood, walking to the door.

'Rhapsody?'

She turned to see the ancient warrior staring out the window. 'Yes?'

Oelendra did not blink, looking into the distance. 'I love you as if you were my own daughter. I wish you were, more than you could ever know. Look after yourself.'

Rhapsody watched her for a moment, then left as quietly as she had come in.

70

With the knowledge that Tyrian was in good hands, Rhapsody headed northeast on her way to the Bolglands. The earth around her was beginning to stretch in the relief of the thaw that was coming, tufts of frozen grass and ground emerging here and there. The trees of the forests and the fields were starting to send forth tiny precursor buds heralding the new leaves that would arrive with spring, and the hardiest early snowdrops were blooming everywhere.

Rhapsody took in the sights with pensive eyes. She endeavored to make note of each of the things she had always found beautiful, cataloguing the memory of them in the knowledge that she might never see them again. Seeing them now was not the same as appreciating them as she once had; it was a joyless time.

Her abdomen, though still flat and lithe, cramped more each day, and what food she could occasionally force down often refused to stay there. In addition, her nightmares had grown violent and more intense than ever; visions of the benison laughing as the Rakshas violated her over and over again, speaking in Ashe's voice, then curling up inside her to await his abhorrent rebirth. Even the tamer dreams, images of Ashe and their time together, their gentle, reassuring love, would always end in his transformation into the construct of the F'dor.

Try as she might, she could not seem to shake the incubus that had attached itself to her. As a result, she had taken to sleeping only as long as she needed to sustain her life. She became haggard in appearance and in speech, occasionally unable to form coherent sentences or complete simple thoughts. Rial had grown alarmed and tried to keep her from going alone; Oelendra had volunteered to travel with her, but she had refused them both, saying only that she would sleep long and well soon.

Before she left she had made sure to say goodbye to the people in Tyrian that she loved, Sylvia and the pages in the palace, Rial, the townsfolk of Tyrian City, the soldiers and the Lirin children, as well as her adopted grandchildren, and most especially Oelendra. Her mentor refrained from all well-meaning advice and had stayed with her in silence or trivial conversation, watching the fire, sitting under the stars. The elderly warrior had held her hand and had sung Rhapsody's devotions for her when her voice would not come. On the night before she left, Rhapsody had opened the door of her chambers in Newydd Dda to find the ancient woman standing there, clutching a package. She had placed it hurriedly into Rhapsody's hands, refusing the invitation to come in.

'I want you to have this, darling,' she said in response to Rhapsody's questioning look. 'It was Pendaris's first gift to me, and there is more love in it than you can imagine. I hope it will bring you as much comfort as it did me. I will see you at the Council.' Rhapsody opened her mouth to protest, but before the words formed on her lips, Oelendra was gone.

Rhapsody went to the balcony of her room and watched as the warrior walked away, her broad shoulders bent as if carrying a great weight. She took the package to her bed and opened it. Inside was the red silk robe with the embroidered image of a dragon that Oelendra had left for her the first night she had stayed in the warrior's home. Her stomach turned; the image on it reminded her of Ashe. She hurriedly packed it up and placed it carefully out of sight in her satchel.

Anborn had come to see her, and had provided much useful information about the various Cymrian Houses and their leaders, as well as refreshing and brutally honest insight into the expected hostilities and bad blood between them. Rhapsody found him easy to talk to, as always. When he left he had taken her comfortably in his arms and warmly kissed her goodbye, then pulled back and regarded her with amusement.

'I suppose you are going to make me wait until after we are wed before going to bed with me.'

'Of course,' she had answered breezily. 'It's the only honorable thing for me to do. Otherwise, you might fear I was taking advantage of you, having my way with you to leave you, despondent and brokenhearted, at the altar. I know you would be consumed with worry.' His laughter had rung in her ears long after he had taken his leave that night.

Now, as she rode over the fields of Avonderre and western Navarne, she drove the thoughts of the people she cared about from her mind. The F'dor was dead, but she was now more afraid than ever.

Finally, after a week of hard riding, she found herself in the right place at sunset, in the secluded glade where she had come a year before, walking slowly around a quiet lake at the base of the hillside. When she could see the cave she felt the wind pick up, blowing her hair lovingly around her.

'Do you want to see me?' she whispered.

'I always want to see my friend,' came the multitone voice, warm and windy. 'Come in, Pretty.'

'I may be with child, and if I am, it is demon-spawn,' she whispered again in a tone so low that no one save the dragon could hear her. It was something she had given voice to only once before, and she choked on the words, her eyes filling with tears.

'Do not cry, Pretty,' the harmonious voice answered. 'I love you.'

Oelendra winced at the look on Ashe's face; he had obviously been to the palace and had been turned away. 'I'm sorry, dear,' she said gently, opening the door of her cottage wider to allow him entrance. 'She's gone. Do come in and rest awhile.'

Ashe looked away for a moment. 'No, thank you, Oelendra, I have to find her. Please tell me where she went so I can be on my way.'

'Come in,' Oelendra said firmly, in the same voice she had used to coerce Rhapsody's secret out of her. 'I have *dol mwl* on the fire; it's a beverage Rhapsody has loved since childhood. Perhaps it will ease your heart a little as well.'

Ashe sighed reluctantly and removed his hooded cape, then followed her into the house. He sat in the willow rocker before the fire as Oelendra ladled him out a mug of the steaming drink.

'You must go to the coast, Gwydion,' she said as she handed him the *dol mwl*. 'The Second Fleet will be arriving soon in response to the horn of the Council. It is your responsibility as head of the House of Newland to greet them and lead them into the Moot.'

Ashe's startlingly blue eyes opened wide in the hot vapor that rose from the mug. 'She's calling the Council?'

'Aye.' Oelendra studied his face. 'Is that disturbing to you?'

He took a deep drink, letting the soft flavor fill his mouth, then warm his throat as he swallowed. 'Only a little.'

'Why?'

Ashe looked into the fire. It was burning steadily, without an opinion, so unlike the way it did when Rhapsody was nearby. 'Because I expect the Council will change a great many things about her life, about our lives. All she wants more than anything in the world is to find a goat hut in the forest and live out her days in peace. If I could grant her anything, it would be that.

'But it will never happen now. Once the Cymrians see her they will idolize her. She will be sought after, harassed endlessly. I don't really want to share her with them, Oelendra; they don't deserve her any more than I do. For all I know I will be at the end of the line for her attention and her love.'

Oelendra nodded knowingly. 'It must be very difficult for you now.'

'Difficult?' His laugh was almost a bark. 'I'm afraid that doesn't even begin to describe it. Can you imagine what it is like being married to someone like her, and she doesn't even know it? She hates me, Oelendra.' His tone was more frightened than bitter.

'No, she doesn't, Gwydion. She loves you. She is under great pressure and false assumptions.'

Ashe nodded and took another sip, hoping it would loosen the choking knot in his throat. 'It probably doesn't help that she is being pursued mercilessly by every idiot in the world, slathering over her, locking their horns like stags in rut.'

'Undoubtedly not,' Oelendra said gravely. 'Are you behaving like one of them?'

Ashe set the mug down with a graceless thump. 'Of course; I never denied I was an idiot. So she has gone back to Ylorc; bloody *hrekin*, I just came from there. Well, at least I found all the shortcuts so the way back will be faster.'

'Gwydion, listen to me,' Oelendra said sternly. 'Do not go to Ylorc; go to the coast. She doesn't want to see you now; she won't see you now. Wait until after the Council is over; then everything will have been sorted out, and you'll know what you're dealing with.'

Ashe stood up. 'You expect me to wait for *months* to see my own wife? To

431

delay telling her that I love her, only her, and always have? Oelendra, I don't think you understand. I hid from the world for twenty years, believing that the next moment held my death and damnation; it was indescribable torture. But I would gladly go back to that state in a heartbeat rather than remain in the torment I am in now. By the time she finally consents to see me she'll have wed Anborn, or Achmed, gods forbid, or have been stolen away by one of her suitors against her will—'

'I doubt that,' Oelendra interjected.

He was already at the coat peg, retrieving his cloak. 'Perhaps not; I don't care. I can't let this go on any longer. I could carry this secret the rest of my life if I thought that the alternative was better, but it's not. She's going to find out someday what we promised to each other. If she has married another in that time, it will kill her; it will be like Llauron all over again, only worse.'

The ancient warrior sighed. 'Now you know why she hates lies so much, Gwydion. I will offer my advice to you once more, and it is yours to ignore if you choose: Forbear. Wait a little while longer. What's a few months to a man who is virtually immortal?'

'Too much to stand, that's what,' Ashe replied as he opened the door. 'Thank you, Oelendra. I'll give her your love.' He bowed politely and took his leave, closing the door quietly behind him.

Oelendra sighed sadly at the closed door. 'You won't even get to give her yours, I'm afraid.'

In the quiet of dreams they met in a misty place, a place of unreality, Rhapsody and the great dragon Elynsynos. All sound, all vibration, any signature of the world around them had been muted into silence, stilled by the wyrm matriarch's power over the elements. Rhapsody could barely see for all the steaming clouds of white, could hardly discern the great luminous eyes, their prismatic brilliance looking back at her through the hazy magic. She realized dimly that she was looking through the translucence of her own eyelids, seeing beyond her own tortured nightmares into the safe place the dragon had made for her between the dream world and the real one. And in that place she told the dragon her greatest worry.

What if I fail?

The warm, iridescent eyes of the wyrm disappeared in an extended blink. *You may.*

There was no fear, no panic in Rhapsody's heart at the answer; it was as if the dragon had removed all emotion in this ethereal place as well, leaving only words as they would be on a written page, not resonating within her heart.

I have lived through the death of one world. I do not wish to witness such a thing again.

I know. Through the haze the face of the dragon moved away, becoming more distant in the mist.

Rhapsody tried to look past the rolling clouds of vapor, straining to see through her closed eyelids, but only the faintest outline of the dragon remained.

Failure could bring about the end of Time, she whispered wordlessly. *I cannot even contemplate it.*

The warmth in the faraway eyes radiated through the mist. *You are at the place where the beginning of Time had its ending. Just as surely the ending of Time will have its beginning here, as well. You cannot change it, though you may delay its coming.*

Why? Why me? Why was this onerous responsibility given to me?

The filmy outline of the dragon vanished, leaving only a whisper of her voice in the mist.

Because you are not alone.

Rhapsody slept deeply and dreamlessly in the crook of Elynsynos's arm that night. She had awakened many hours later, refreshed but still distressed. The great wyrm had regarded her with sympathy and concern.

'There is something evil growing within you, Pretty,' she said seriously, fixing her multicolored gaze on Rhapsody's tearstained face. 'Right here.' The claw gently brushed her abdomen. 'It feels wrong, unnatural, but that is all I can tell.'

Rhapsody nodded. 'I know.' She struggled to stand up. 'I'll go now.'

The dragon shook her head, causing clouds of sand to spin around the cave, stinging Rhapsody's sore eyes. 'No; stay with me. Keep me company. What grows within you does not matter. Whatever must be done, I will help you.'

The Singer smiled. 'I know, I know you will. You already have. I haven't had as much sleep in weeks as I had last night; thank you.'

'It is strange to have a growing thing that is not of your own kind taking root inside you,' Elynsynos said, pulling Rhapsody into the crook of her arm again. 'When I carried Merithyn's children, it was a sad time for me. The body I was trapped in was so small, like yours, and they moved like moles within the earth, poking and kicking me, struggling to get out. It was horrible. I was so lonely, and I waited and watched each day, wishing he was here with me. He never came back, Pretty; he never knew he had made me with child.'

Rhapsody stroked the scaly forearm. 'It must have been awful. I'm so sorry, Elynsynos. I wish I could have been there for you. The Lirin have a song that they sing to women in the throes of childbirth to ease their pain.' Her eyes clouded over at the memory of Aria's birth; she shook her head to drive the ghastly image out of her mind. The irony of how her own fate was now tied up with that experience was too much to bear.

'But who will sing for you, Pretty?'

She forced back the tears that struggled to break free. 'No one,' she said softly. 'No one will.'

'That is why it is better to mate with a dragon,' Elynsynos said sensibly. 'Then perhaps you can just lay eggs, like normal beasts do. It hurts a little more when they come out, but it is over much more quickly.' Rhapsody laughed in spite of herself.

'I'll keep that in mind,' she said, blinking rapidly. 'Actually, if I live through this, I plan to. I've chosen a dragon for a mate, and he has agreed.' Anborn's face swam before her rapidly drying eyes.

The iridescent eyes twinkled. 'Good. Then perhaps I will have children to play with again that are of my own bloodline.'

'Perhaps.' Rhapsody looked away. She did not tell the dragon about her arrangement with Achmed.

Rhapsody stayed several days with Elynsynos, sleeping peacefully, growing strong again in the magical lair. She sang her the ocean songs the sea Lirin had taught her, getting drenched by the dragon's reminiscent tears. She also showed her the crown. Elynsynos was fascinated with the diadem, endeavoring to catch the whirling stars that spun around Rhapsody's head, entranced like an infant captivated by an especially shiny toy.

The dragon was delighted that she was about to call the Cymrian Council, and spent long hours telling her stories about the early days of the First Fleet. She had taken great pride in the accomplishments of the Cymrians in those times, despite mourning her loss of Merithyn, whom she spoke of often.

Rhapsody smiled each time Elynsynos repeated the same story. Merithyn and Elynsynos's time as lovers had been brief, and the dragon's lifetime long, so there were only so many tales to tell, each kept like a cherished treasure. When the prismatic eyes grew soft in memory, Rhapsody thought back to Anborn's cynical comments about his grandparents; obviously he had not gotten to know Elynsynos at all. Whatever else she felt toward anything, it was impossible to miss the depth of the love the dragon had felt for her lost sailor. Its poignancy made Rhapsody's heart ache.

The brimstone heat from the dragon's breath stirred her memory, and an image arose in her mind of another night, long ago, in the shadows of a crackling campfire.

So that's why I say you may have a problem, Ashe had said, hidden within the misty fold of his cloak, watching her intently from across the fire. *If you are a later-generation Cymrian, you will be extraordinarily long-lived, and you will undoubtedly face what others did: the prospect of watching those you love grow old and die in what seems like a brief moment in your life. And if you are a First Generation Cymrian, it will be even worse, because unless you are killed outright you will never die. Imagine losing people over and over, your lovers, your spouse, your children –*

Stop it.

As Ashe's words about immortality rang in her ears; Rhapsody wondered if she herself would be destined to endlessly relive the same few happy moments she had with him as well. Then she remembered the demon's words.

You will be a wonderful mother, Rhapsody, at least while the child is in your womb. It's a shame that you won't live through the delivery.

Perhaps a lonely immortality was not so much of a threat after all.

I doubt I will even live to see the end of what is coming now, let alone forever.

Achmed's voice spoke to her in the darkness of her memory.

He's damned, like the polluted Earth. She hurtles through the ether, bound even the gods don't know where, carrying inside, deep in her heart, the first and last Sleeping Child, the burden whose birth may be its mother's ending.

As am I, she thought morosely.

When finally Rhapsody left the lair of the lost sea to head off on her last mission to unite the people of this new land, Elynsynos wept.

After several weeks of furious, mindless travel, the rising sun found Rhapsody sitting on the crest of the *cwm*. The Great Moot of the Cymrian Council had once been a glacial lake, formed by the freezing and thawing of ice on the mountain faces of the Teeth when they were young. The glacier had carved the Bowl of the Moot as a vessel for the melting tears of the great wall of moving ice. As the land warmed, the lake had sunk into the earth or sent its water skyward, dried by the sun, leaving the amphitheater hewn into the mountainside. It was a place of deep power, and Rhapsody could feel it now as she sat on its brow, looking around the Bowl, watching the dawn fill the Moot with rosy light.

Spring had come while she was in the dragon's lair; she had emerged to find the snow all but gone, the trees in the advent of full bud. The desolate dust that was the floor of the Bowl in the height of summer was now green and lush, with new spring grass forming a verdant carpet along the floor and up into the terraced sides. It waited, having been deserted for centuries, as if in anticipation.

When the intense gold light of the top slice of the sun crested the horizon Rhapsody glanced behind her, having felt shadows fall on her shoulders. It was the other two-thirds of the Three; they had remembered to come.

They stood in silence behind her, looking around. She remained where she sat, watching the morning light come to the strange outcroppings of rocks that formed the natural features of the Moot. Gwylliam's manuscripts had mentioned the two most significant characteristics. The first was the Speaker's Rise, a towering pulpit sculpted from the limestone by what must have been a twisted blanket of ice millions of years before. As a result of the inconsistent erosion it had a curving natural pathway that spiraled to the top where a speaker could stand erect and be seen by the entire assemblage. In addition, that speaker could be heard clearly all around the Moot, owing to the intrinsic acoustics of the place.

The second attribute was known as the Summoner's Ledge. It was a long, wide horizontal sheet of slate, flat but for a vertical rock outcropping that resembled a pulpit, balanced between two great slabs of rock, at the summit of the tallest of the bordering hills around the Bowl. From this vantage point someone could see all of the vast Orlandan plain stretching out at his feet, as well as the entirety of the Bowl, with the shadow of the Teeth at his back. It

435

was the best possible point at which to sound a call that would echo over the land and beyond, vibrating within the earth itself, to reach the ears of those whose past and future was tied to the horn. Rhapsody shuddered; it was a long climb up to the unstable-looking place, and a longer fall down from it.

The Bowl itself was immense, larger than the gambling complex in Sorbold. What nature had not sculpted into the geologic bowl, the Cymrians had, although so many centuries had passed since it had been used as a gathering place that it was difficult to discern what was the work of natural forces and what was the work of man. A series of rising ledges had been hewn into the earth around the circumference of the Bowl, following the glacier's lines, to allow seating for tens of thousands. Enormous wedges had been cut from some areas of the Bowl's side to give access and egress from the arena. Though overgrown and forgotten by all but Time, it was the perfect place for a convocation. The air within it hung heavy with moisture and foreboding.

'Well? Are you ready, Duchess?' The low rumble of the Sergeant's voice rent the air and shattered the heavy silence.

'I suppose so,' she said, looking east to where the bottom rim of the sun was just clearing the mountain.

'That's inspiring,' said Achmed with a wry smile. 'You're acting as the Summoner, and you're not even certain you want to do it? Why are we bothering?'

'Because it's time,' said Rhapsody with a long sigh as she rose. 'Roland is a land ripe for war, as is Sorbold. The Lirin are united, but there is no one leader who can guarantee a treaty with them on behalf of the human realms. The only place not on the verge of bloodshed is Ylorc.'

'Ironic, isn't it?'

'I think it's sad,' said Grunthor with a melancholy tone in his voice. 'I've finally got myself an army to be proud of, and no one wants to come out and play.'

Rhapsody patted his shoulder. 'Well, think of it this way, Grunthor; if the Cymrians do select a Lord and Lady, and do as good a job of it as they did before, you should have lots of opportunity for armed conflict, and with a bigger, more powerful opponent; you'll have everyone in Roland, Sorbold, Tyrian, and possibly the Nonaligned States as well to play with.'

'Oh, goody.'

'Well, let's begin the show,' Achmed said. He handed Rhapsody the slim box that contained the Cymrian horn.

Rhapsody's eyes twinkled in the clear morning light. 'Now, that would be Doctor Achmed's Traveling Snake Show, if I'm not mistaken.' She cast a glance at Grunthor; it was a reference he had made on the Root long ago. The giant Bolg grinned.

She opened the box and carefully took out the horn, then began the slow, careful climb to the top of the Summoner's Ledge, its stone pulpit casting a long shadow in the morning light.

Achmed and Grunthor followed her up, and the Three stood in awe for a moment, mesmerized by the view from the Ledge. From the observatory at the top peak of the Teeth the world had appeared at their feet; now, as they stood on the high rim of the Bowl, it still stretched out below them, but it was impossible to feel distanced from it, as one did in the mountains. As far as the eye could see a fertile panorama swept out before them, the landscape turning from brown to chartreuse almost before their eyes. It was a stunning sight, and to Rhapsody a humbling one. A high wind blew across the plain below them and over the Ledge around them; it was a cleansing wind, strong and cold, carrying with it a scent of hope and destiny. She closed her eyes, raised the horn to her lips, and sounded it.

A silver blast, like a bugle call but richer, shattered the air and the stillness of the morning. It reverberated off the Teeth and the hills below, rolling in a wave of music over the land, spreading like the ripples in a pond. Rhapsody could feel the music ringing through her, forming a bond from her feet through the stone she stood on, which in turn echoed through the Bowl itself.

Suddenly she understood why she needed to remain within Canrif. The Summoner was the instrument through which the horn tapped into the power of the Moot. It was much like the call she had sent on the wind to Ashe long ago, the summons that brought him to Elysian, to her. The horn issued a compelling invitation, tied to the person who winded it. The Summoner was the directional point, much as the gazebo in Elysian had been. By the Summorer's remaining within the range of the Bowl the vibration was sustained, and the call held constant until all the Cymrians had arrived, an invisible thread they could follow to find Canrif again, wrapped inexorably around each of their hearts.

Rhapsody closed her eyes. She was tied to the call, and her mind followed it as it spread through the earth and the air, ringing across the Orlandan Plateau and into the hilly steppes and deserts of Sorbold. It sang through the current of the Tar'afel and into the forests of Gwynwood and Tyrian, washing over the sea and crashing with the ocean waves on the shores of Manosse, a thousand leagues away.

It spread like the touch of the king, back toward every soul that had made promise on that horn in the old land, before terrible voyages, before wandering in the wilderness, before the new empire, before death and war. The great horn sounded only at first on its own glory in the air; then it seemed to fade, as any blast will. But Rhapsody was carried at the beginning of its wave, and she heard it take new shapes, possess what the ancient magic must have deemed its own.

It moved from hand to hand in the spark of coins, in the drum of ax against tree, in the mule driver's call and snap of the whip. It rumbled through messengers' hoofbeats and whispered in hunters' arrows. It inhabited the creak of saddle and mast and axle, the grunt of livestock, the wheedle of merchants, the ring of smithies and whistle of sails, and carried the call of the builder king back to each drop of blood sworn in fealty to his exodus and venture more than a thousand years before. The call rolled and flew, reached over the entire conquered continent to drag and beckon fulfillment of the oath.

Every brick laid in his service, every nail driven, every artifact and monument echoed and hummed the call, so that when night fell, the imperative silence would make everything still, wolves, water, wind. The summons of Gwylliam's horn drove away the exhaustion of age-frozen survivors of those early voyages. Tired eyes suddenly shone their way out of dementia; breath of purpose entered the breasts of resigned patriarchs; ancient, stiffened fingers flexed for the feel of ancient swords.

Those who had made the vow originally felt rather than heard it, the king's presence. They stood first, interrupted their meals, their counsels, their baths. As if his scent and genius had entered, the sensation passed from father to son like a gesture, in a moment of silence to recall, reclaim the lost memory. It took the huge quietude to determine that they had been called to a pilgrimage.

Those who had no blood ties to the Cymrians were at a loss, wondering what had transpired to make the Earth, for one brief moment, stop in its path . . .

While Rhapsody's vision traveled at the front of the wave of sound, singing from goat bells, rasping in the purl of hoe pulling earth, Achmed was being driven mad feeling the air reconstructed around him. The thready curtains of wind he routinely saw and passed through thickened into ethereal kelp, entangling, pulling, adhering, leaving him short of breath, swimming where he should have been walking. The sound was not just a ripple, but a palpability, drawing in, as if the Moot had become a huge maw, a wyrm anglerfish drawing every particle in. Rhapsody was the luminescent center, the bait, and he reeled, unsteady, plankton-sized and drifting beneath the call of the Great Seal that reached perhaps beyond where the daylight touched.

Grunthor too felt rather than heard the sound, but he did not react to the airborne pulse of the call. He followed the echo through the earth. Like a tremor clawing its way from a wrenching fault, it crawled and twisted across the plains, a concentric serpent buried and on fire. It raged and pounded, blaring through the mountain behind them, stentorian and shrieking, as if every voice, every utterance had been peeled from the cave walls and released into the air again, but still with nowhere to go.

Rhapsody looked lost and distant; Achmed crouched, leaning against the stone of the platform, and Grunthor stood with his palms over his ears, his eyes shut tight, when the silence arrived. As disturbing and insistent as the shout of the horn had been, its wait for response pinched harder. It turned Achmed's vision of water to ice.

Across the sea at the farthest twilight soundrise of the call, Rhapsody felt the few hundreds of remaining Cymrians who had actually laid hands and oaths on the Great Seal stop breathing, stop living, as though they had been moving into the everyday futures of their lives when an invisible leash from their past had pulled them up short. Some few actually perished, from fear, or relief. The rest took up breathing again, but the conversations that had been interrupted would never resume. Each of the First Generation turned as a body to acknowledge the call and their debt. In a thousand years, this was only the second time they had heard it.

Those original Cymrians received the call first, but sons listening to fathers, daughters tending to mothers, felt their answer to the elders' moment of pause only momentarily later, in the time of a short intake of breath. Each of fifty generations felt it in their turn, as insistent as the need to slake thirst, satisfy hunger, make water, sleep, or yield to death. The straighter, purer family lines tasted the journey to come, moved in unison to prepare, and knew what might lie at the end. Some had even been told that the call might come, of how it had come to terror and ruin before, but how they were destined to answer it regardless, since what they had been offered for the ancient pledge was the only chance at life.

Bastard lines, deeply mixed genealogies, individuals with no lore and less concern about their heritage were compelled no less deeply. The first embers in the blood itched and scored vessel walls, struck like cloud-soft lightning, chewed delay and resolve so that a matter of hours or days perhaps stood between the unknowing descendant and his journey. All across the continent, men, women and children began the pilgrimage, thralls to a dead tyrant.

The youngest of all the Cymrian lines heard the call last. Being short-lived, most of them were a full fifty generations removed, but they possessed two advantages. The first was culture; nomads and scavengers by nature, they felt little resistance to the impulse to follow the call. The second was proximity; they already inhabited the catacombs beneath the Teeth.

Cymrian heritage was the dire and wonderful secret of the Finders. They had descended from those captured by the Bolg in the last days of Gwylliam's reign, their longevity, their blue eyes all historic traces of the blood of the unfortunate victims who could not get out of Canrif in time when the Bolg overran the mountain.

Deep within the tunnels near the Hand, or at the forges, the hospice, the caves in which they dwelt, the Finders felt the call like silver lightning shock through their bones. To a one the bastard children of the Cymrian line put away tools or food, turned away from tasks, and headed out into the sunlight of the foothills, blind fish, squinting and shading their eyes.

Hours after she had sounded the clarion, had opened the Great Seal, Rhapsody was still in the trance of following the call. Achmed had recovered his breath and bearings. He was free from the pull of the horn, but sensitive enough to its power that the vacuum it created to summon and guide the Cymrians made his ears pop.

Grunthor had been surprised by the volume and breadth of the instrument, but felt little disturbance until the summoned Cymrians began to answer. So deep was the debt, so overweening the oath, that even the faithful dead wished to comply. All around him, across and within the plain, throughout the mountain, scratched the hum and shiver of bones shifting in the earth. In the tremendous, immobile, windless hush, the giant's sense of the earth around him stretched like the view of a vast silent sea, where a single fin stands like a mast above the surface. Grunthor's awareness was teeming, crawling with myriad tiny ripples of the scrape of marrowless bones against the rags of their death shrouds and interments in mass graves, or picked driftwood-clean under dustings of sand and sod. For the first time he understood the scope of the slaughter that had ensured the Cymrian legacy. As his sense gave way to his real vision of stillness over the earth, resurrection seemingly beyond the power of this artifact, he did catch some movement on the crags out of the corner of his eye. He stared east into the blinding morning light.

'Hey, thanks a lot, Your Ladyship; you've given me an infernal headache.'

Rhapsody looked fondly at him as the rising sun touched his head, making him glow with radiant light like a mythic Firbolg god. 'Sorry, Grunthor. It'll go away soon.'

'How soon?'

She glanced around as the image of the distant shores of Manosse faded from her mind, followed by the seacoast of Avonderre and the Nonaligned States, then Tyrian and Gwynwood, the Orlandan Plateau and Sorbold, finally leaving her with just the vast panoramic view at her feet. She shrugged and set the horn on the stone pulpit.

'My best guess? About two months.'

71

At the blast of the horn that sounded over the Bolglands, the inhabitants of what had once been Canrif ran in fear, hiding in their huts and caves, certain that the age of death had returned. The Bolg scurried about in fright, getting ready to retreat back into the recesses of the mountains where they had hidden for the centuries prior to the arrival of Achmed and Grunthor. They waited for the armies of men to come and raze their villages, anticipating the long-awaited vengeance for defying the legions of Roland.

From her high vantage point above the Bowl and the Bolglands, Rhapsody watched in sadness. She witnessed the panic as the Firbolg scattered across the Heath, taking shelter in the caves of the Teeth in terror, and her heart went out to them. The last thing she had hoped to inspire by sounding the horn was fear.

Slowly, though, a few moments after the sound had died away, she could see shadows emerge from the caves below and walk into the bright sun as if transfixed. There was only a relative handful of them, a few hundred or so, drawn out by the sound of the horn, and they came slowly, looking around as if lost. All of them eventually turned toward the Bowl of the Moot and came there, trying to satiate the need that had risen in them to do so. They stood, bewildered and confused, looking dazed.

'What's going on?' Rhapsody asked Achmed, who was staring down at his subjects below. A glimmer formed in the Firbolg king's eye, and a smile crawled across his face.

'I believe your invited guests have arrived. Behold the first of the Cymrians to answer the call.' He glanced over at Rhapsody; their eyes met, and they shared a smile.

Grunthor had already begun to descend from the Ledge, and now the other two followed slowly, careful not to unbalance any of the rocks on the cliff. Once she arrived on the flat central floor of the Bowl Rhapsody waited while the king and the Sergeant-Major debriefed the dazed Firbolg, trying to determine why they had found the call compelling. There had been no record of any Bolg traveling from Serendair, so the likelihood of them being descendants from any Fleet seemed remote.

Finally Grunthor and Achmed returned. Rhapsody hurried to hear what they had discovered.

'Well? Why did they come?'

Achmed looked annoyed. 'I told you before, they're Cymrians, or at least descended from them. At the time the Bolg invaded Canrif there were still diehards that didn't want to give up Gwylliam's fortress or the lands they had fought to keep for seven centuries. In case you couldn't guess, when they went up against the Bolg they lost. These are the descendants of the Cymrians who were taken as slaves by the Bolg. I imagine the captives didn't live long past giving birth to the ancestors of these few stragglers.'

Rhapsody nodded.

'They call themselves the Finders, because they have an ancient directive that was spoken onto them. Apparently, as Gwylliam lay on the library floor, bleeding his life out behind a puzzle lock that none of them could open, the speaking tubes we used to subdue this mountain were open. Those Bolg of Cymrian blood knew that his voice was a command they could not disobey; their ancestors had sworn centuries before to come to the king in his time of need. But they couldn't find him; they couldn't find what he was asking for, because the horn was in the vault of the library with him. So all these years, all these generations, they have been waiting for the Voice to sound again, to tell them what to do. They also have a propensity to find Cymrian artifacts, hoping with each new one that it's what the Voice was calling for.'

'Well, perhaps they should be accorded guard duty, then, as both Firbolg and Cymrian; is that all right with you, Grunthor?'

'I think it would be an honor for them, Your Ladyship; I have to give them the "one false step and you're my dessert tonight" speech, though.'

'I think, for the time being, they should be the only Bolg visible when the Cymrians arrive,' Achmed noted. 'What do we need to do next?'

'We wait, I guess. I think I'll go and greet our first guests.'

The king nodded. 'I have a suggestion.'

Rhapsody had begun walking toward the Bolg. She stopped and turned for a moment. 'Yes?'

He looked her up and down; she was attired in her standard work clothes, a white cambric long-sleeved shirt, soft tan suede vest and brown pants. 'You complained that living in the Bolglands never afforded you the opportunity to wear any of those extravagantly expensive gowns of yours. Given the amount you depleted from my treasury to purchase the damned things, you may as well wear them; this seems as good a social occasion as any.'

Her face lit up. 'Oh, what fun! Which one do you think I ought to wear first?'

'I happen to like green or brown, but if I might, I suggest you stay away from red until there are more people here. You don't want any of the Bolg to think you're injured from a distance. Makes you a target.'

Rhapsody sighed. Suddenly she missed Tyrian, where, whatever anyone's opinion of her, they never thought of her as food.

Each day more travelers would arrive. Some rode into the Bowl on horseback or in carts, but by and large they were wanderers, like the disoriented Firbolg, without any idea where they were or why they felt compelled to come. They were part of the Cymrian Diaspora, the great group of disenfranchised descendants of the Cymrian Houses that had been divided by Anwyn and Gwylliam's war. *Another incalculable loss*, thought Rhapsody as she looked in their eyes, seeing the confusion and fear. How many generations of Cymrian children must have been separated from their Houses as a result of that conflict, yielding a population that never even knew its own lineage? She greeted them gently, and made them welcome, settling them into the tents and huts Achmed had erected at her request while she was in Tyrian.

A problem occurred almost immediately. For reasons Rhapsody couldn't understand, the flustered Cymrians seemed drawn to her as compulsively as they had been to the Moot. Upon meeting her they stood, slack-jawed and glassy-eyed, staring, unable to break their gaze. They followed her around ceaselessly, eventually forming large human herds, only able to tear themselves away when Grunthor interdicted. Achmed found it all extraordinarily amusing. She had rationalized it, as was her wont, into something that had nothing to do with her own charismatic charms, but rather had decided it was an effect of the horn she had sounded.

He had manipulated the situation himself. At his suggestion Rhapsody came each day dressed in a gown more stunning than the day before, dresses fashioned from shimmering silks, gleaming satins, and beautiful brushed linens from Sorbold and Canderre, places well known for their exquisite textiles and artistic dressmaking. The couture accentuated her beauty, and guaranteed that those who came into the Bowl were mesmerized by her. The crowning effect of the halo of whirling stars that the diadem became when placed on her head only made things worse. It was an interesting experiment in the harnessing of power for the Firbolg king, and a tool that he thought might come in handy should the Council meeting get ugly. He had no doubt that it would.

In addition, Achmed had recognized the power in the initial meeting. Rhapsody was the one who greeted each of the arrivals, made them welcome, and explained to most of them why they had come. It left a positive impression and a desire in each of the erstwhile Cymrians to belong to whatever people she might be part of, thus ensuring her success in her mission of uniting this irascible population. The Diaspora only comprised a small number of the entire Cymrian populace, however; as time went by it seemed as though only thirty thousand or so Houseless descendants showed up; that meant the overwhelming majority of the group was still to come.

The Houses of the First, Second, and Third Fleets were meeting outside the Teeth, re-forming their loose alliances. Undoubtedly each was waiting for the stragglers from their lines to arrive, for the purpose of entering the Bowl with as impressive a show of numbers as possible. From the beginning they camped on the Orlandan Plateau, their fires at night making them resemble an invading army. The comparison made Rhapsody uneasy, but did not seem to concern either Grunthor or Achmed.

'It's rather pathetic, in a way,' mused the giant Firbolg commander. 'It's like they think they're impressing someone who cares. Bloody childish, if you ask me.'

'Are you sure you really want to unite these idiots again?' Achmed asked Rhapsody incredulously.

'Why?'

'Well, the stupidity level is so high already with the convocation that we already have, it seems almost dangerous to tempt Fate by putting so many empty heads in one place at the same time. I'm afraid we're going to get sucked into a brainless vortex we won't be able to escape from.' Rhapsody laughed.

'The Cymrians aren't stupid, just obstreperous,' she said, cuffing him across the back of the head. 'Besides, they're here now. We have to make the best of it.'

'I doubt you'd like my suggestion for what to do with them,' said Grunthor gloomily.

'I'm afraid to ask.'

'Target practice, of course.'

72

Ylorc Border

It was a fine day to be alive, Tristan Steward observed as his war horse, chestnut coat and mane all but shielded from sight by its metal barding, crested a hilly swale in the steppes of the Orlandan Plateau. The wind was warm and sweet in summer's advent, the earth beneath him fragrantly verdant. Riding at the head of a force one hundred thousand strong, ten thousand mounted, was the headiest sensation he ever remembered feeling, an exhilaration that was powerful, almost sexual. He had the sense that the very earth was moving with him as he rode, surrounded in the fierce vibration, the deafening sound of his army on the move, blackening the landscape behind him.

The closer the contingent came to the Manteids, the more powerful his excitement grew. While a number of those riding with him, commanders and foot soldiers alike, were responding, as he was, to the summons of the Cymrian horn, the vast majority, not being of Seren ancestry, were in full muster, primed, they believed, to lay siege to the Bolglands.

It had initially been awkward to observe the confusion that the tiny minority of Cymrian soldiers was evidently experiencing. The great Moot, the legends said, was a place of deep power, where the very land itself enforced the laws of the Council, an agenda of minimal civility and contained behavior wherein the many factions of the Cymrian kingdom had been able to meet and conduct the business of keeping peace and planning the building of the empire. It was therefore distressing to those of Cymrian blood among his troops to be riding with a martial intent.

Along the trans-Orlandan thoroughfare where it crossed into the Bolglands Tristan had been pleased to note empty guard posts, way stations normally manned by the brutes who maintained the border. He had not, in fact, seen a single Firbolg since entering the steppes that led up to the mountain range. The desolate plain seemed even more bleak than he had expected.

Pandemic illness could be a wonderful weapon.

He turned to McVickers, his knight marshal, who rode beside him, a grim expression on his somber face.

'How much farther, McVickers?'

'We should be within sight of the Moot tomorrow, m'lord.'

'Excellent!' Tristan Steward said, patting his horse. 'We will encamp outside the Moot; those who are attending the Council will be dismissed in order to meet up with their Houses. Make certain all the troops know where to reassemble once the Council is over.'

'Yes, m'lord.'

Tristan sighed happily. He put his head back, letting the sun shine down on his face.

All in all, a fine day to be alive.

Finally, after months of arduous waiting, the day of the Council dawned. There could be no mistaking the appointed time; the night before, the air in the Moot had grown suddenly still, the clamorous sound of tens of thousands of voices slipping into deep silence.

The sunset had been particularly spectacular on this, the last night of spring, the fiery hues of nightfall spinning into one last blood-red cloud that softened to the gentlest shade of rose-pink before disappearing over the rim of the world into darkness. The sky dimmed to azure, then cobalt, then inky black; the stars appeared timidly, as if reluctantly summoned by Rhapsody's evensong. The Moot picked up the sound of her voice singing her vespers, as it had each night; this had become one of the only times during the long and noisy days that the assembled Cymrians routinely fell silent, listening raptly to the Singer greet the stars or the dawn.

On this night, as the last sweet note died away, a shower of shooting stars sped by overhead, drawing an astonished gasp from the crowd. Moments later, the collective intake of breath from the encampments on the other side of the Teeth could be heard; the Cymrian Houses had seen the omen as well, and acknowledged it. Deep within each breast, the understanding was clear. It was time to convene.

The night was a quiet one. Rhapsody eschewed her regular lodging within the Cauldron to sit vigil in the field, watching the smoldering fires of the exterior encampments be extinguished, one by one. Achmed and Grunthor had stayed with her, and she glanced over at them affectionately now. Grunthor was sitting with his enormous sword across his knees, his elbows resting on it, his chin in the tips of his clasped hands, musing intently. The burden of policing the small city-state that the Moot had become had fallen to him, and he had borne up under it without batting an amber eye, a particularly amazing feat, given that the only troops the king allowed him to use to police the plain were the soldiers who were Finders.

Achmed stood beside him, his gaze also targeted on the camp of the Cymrian Houses and the long caravan of travelers arriving to join them every day. His face was open to the wind, unhidden behind his usual veils, but it might as well have been for the lack of emotion on it. Nonetheless, Rhapsody knew at least part of what he was thinking.

It was this group of Cymrians that was responsible for his ugly attitude, this gathering that posed the threat of violence. These were the proud descendants of the ocean travelers, the city builders, the basilica architects, and the scholars of the Great Age of Civilization; they were also the children of the warring rulers, the marauding armies of rape and destruction, the silent conspirators, the traitors to humanity.

Despite Rhapsody's confidence in them as a people, he had his doubts as to the wisdom of bringing them back together again, to ascending their line to the throne once more. He did not trust this population, even though technically he was one of them, perhaps more ancient than any. Still,

Rhapsody had had aspirations just as unlikely for the Bolg, and, against all probability, she was being proved correct there. His words to her, and her answer, rang in his memory, words from a night long ago before she had gone off to help a desolate wanderer and had ended up in his arms.

It's probably better if you don't even try to understand it.

You're probably right. I think it's better for me to just decide how things are going to work out, and then they will.

It was Rhapsody who had made each of them what they were; she had called him the Pathfinder, and the gift of second sight was his. *Grunthor, strong and reliable as the earth itself,* she had said, the affection in her song marrying the Sergeant's soul to the land. She was the optimism to his own cynicism, the hope to his doubt. *We really are two sides of the same person,* she had said. Whatever came to pass as a result of the convocation the next morning, what they had been to each other must be sustained. What she didn't really know was that he had almost lost the memory of what his life had been like before she had come into it, renaming him and giving him the real key out of his past. He was unwilling to go back to that time.

Rhapsody was still awake and sitting vigil when the first ray of dawn broke. The sky had been lightening for some time, reversing the pattern of the blues that had come with the night; the inky darkness had given way to a rich cobalt, followed by the pale azure that signaled the coming of morning.

She closed her eyes and let the sunbeam touch her chest, filling her with the tone of its song. She smiled; it was *ela*. She quietly matched her voice to the note, then raised it in the aubade, the Liringlas love song of daybreak.

In the distance she heard a voice join hers, and even miles away she recognized it; Oelendra had come to the Moot. Then one by one she heard other voices take up the song, until more than ten thousand sang it, praising the sun as it rose in the sky. With Oelendra had come the Cymrian Lirin, some of Rhapsody's own subjects, the descendants of those who had gone to dwell with their ancient counterparts in Tyrian rather than live in Gwylliam and Anwyn's great cities. In her brief time as queen, Rhapsody had taught the aubade to Tyrian, and in turn the forest had taught it to them.

Farther off in the distance she could discern other voices, voices she had never heard before, take up the melody and add their own to it. Those faraway singers had a tone and inflection that matched Rhapsody's own perfectly, and her heart leapt in the realization that Liringlas had come as well, arriving from the shores of Manosse across the sea, or from lands beyond the Hintervold.

She had just absorbed the understanding of this when a final chorus went up from the end of the vast caravan making its way through the fields of Bethe Corbair and into Ylorc. The minstrelsy of these singers held an ancient harmony that reached down into Rhapsody's soul and made it ring as it never had. She turned away from the sun and shielded her eyes, trying to determine where the beautiful sound was coming from, but all she could see was an ocean of humanity wending its way to the Teeth, following a long, snaking procession.

When the last note finally died away, music of another sort began. Trumpets blasted across the plateau, and within the Bowl the sound of horns took up the call, heralding the arrival of the Cymrian Houses. It was a thrilling sound; the rich brass tones sent shivers up her spine, a feeling she had experienced only once before. The memory was an ancient one, from the old land, from the day that the youngest princess had been born in Elysian, the fortress of the Seren king.

Throughout the countryside, messengers had been sent to every small town to spread the glad news, and as they had approached her village they had sounded the great brass trumpet calls heralding the royal birth. Rhapsody had been a small child then, and had never heard such glorious music; she had dreamt about it for many weeks afterward, begging her parents for a horn of her own, waiting at the crest of the hill where she had seen the trumpeters in the hope that they would return again. They never had; Rhapsody's eyes stung with the memory, and she smiled.

She turned back in time to see the first House, the House of Faley, entering the Bowl. Five hundred strong, they were mostly human, with some Lirin blood evident as well. They came on foot and on horseback, some walking alone, many clustered in small family groups, adults and children, at the head of the great procession of Cymrians. Rhapsody greeted the head of the House with a bow, and he in turn waved back at her exuberantly. When the Cymrians had first begun arriving in the Moot, she had made a point of welcoming each one, often staying past midnight to be able to make sure they were comfortable and clear on their reason for being here. But the increasing tide of humanity had made it impossible to continue the individual greetings, and now she could only nod to the head of each House as they entered the Bowl.

Like a dam bursting, a sea of people spilled into the Moot, some shouting with glee and calling to people that they recognized, others nodding at old adversaries with an air that bristled with resentment. They followed behind enormous banners that proclaimed their lineage, or took the form of a mob of differing backgrounds. These were the greater and lesser Houses, the last vestiges of the Cymrian Age, the descendants of the Three Fleets who had maintained their ties after the end of the war, the political structure on which the Council had been formed twelve centuries before.

Some of the larger, more prestigious Houses were filled with the nobles of Roland, Sorbold, and the lands beyond these countries. Rhapsody dropped a deep curtsy to Tristan Steward, Prince of Bethany, riding behind Lord Cunliffe, a minor earl in his court, who was actually the head of his House, the House of Gylden.

Down in the human sea beneath her Rhapsody caught sight of frenetic movement. Lord Stephen Navarne and his children were at the end of the procession from the House of Gylden, and all three were waving furiously, Melisande from atop her father's shoulders. She smiled and waved back.

After the initial excitement that ensued with the entrance of the first Houses, the feeling in the air began to change. Groups began to sort themselves out not only by House but by the Fleet they or their ancestors had sailed with, or by race. When the Lirin processed in, they came directly to the foot of the Summoner's Ledge and stood with Rhapsody. She came down to meet them, embracing Oelendra and Rial and some of her closer friends from Tyrian; a moment later she could feel silence fall and the eyes of many of the other Cymrians on her.

Oelendra felt their notice too. 'Come,' she said, taking the queen's arm, 'let me help you with that gown Miresylle made for your welcome address.' Rhapsody agreed and led her off to the tent she had been occupying. Within the structure they could hear the noise pick up again, the occasional arguments growing heated and foul in the air as more and more of the Houses processed into the Bowl. Rhapsody sighed.

'The morning is young, there are still tens of thousands that have not entered yet, and already they're bickering like children,' she said, opening the cloth bag that held her dress. 'I hope they don't kill each other before everyone gets here.'

Oelendra took hold of the train and the hem of the skirt to keep it from dragging in the dirt. 'They won't fight, not at Council; it is strictly forbidden by the power of the Moot. Remember, Rhapsody, the last time many of these people saw each over was across a battlefield. They need to sort out their differences themselves; it is long past time for it. It is more important that as the Summoner you are seen as neutral; that is the only way you will be able to command the meeting.'

Rhapsody nodded, then stepped out of her existing garments to don the gown. Miresylle was her favorite Lirin seamstress, a grandmotherly woman who knew every plane and angle of Rhapsody's body perfectly, and could fit any garment to the queen without trying it on her.

This dress was fashioned from antique Cymrian silk left over from long before the war; it was silver with a gold cross-warp in the fabric, giving the gown the effect of either color, depending on the angle at which the person beholding her was standing. Miresylle had fashioned it with dozens of tiny buttons up the back and on the sleeves. Oelendra assisted Rhapsody in closing the dress and brushing out the swirling skirt before turning her around to observe the overall result. The Lirin champion inhaled involuntarily; the view was breathtaking. The ancient material glowed in the light from the diadem, which reflected in the queen's eyes, face, and shining golden hair. Oelendra's eyes teared at the sight, but dried a moment later at the look of consternation that had frozen on Rhapsody's face.

'What's the matter?'

Rhapsody turned away from her and slipped into her shoes. 'Nothing.'

'Tell me.'

The emerald eyes that met her silver ones were set in a calm face, but they held a depth of worry that vanished instantly and was replaced with serenity. 'It's nothing, Oelendra,' she repeated. 'The material across my abdomen is a little tight, that's all. Miresylle must have forgotten how my belly swells after I eat.'

Oelendra's face clouded over. 'When did you eat last, Rhapsody?'

'I had supper last night. Please don't worry, Oelendra. It's just off by a little; she hasn't seen me in a while. Perhaps she just forgot.'

Oelendra nodded, a practiced tranquillity taking its place on her face as well. 'Undoubtedly. Now, shall we get back to the Council?' Rhapsody belted on Daystar Clarion and took her hand, and they left the tent, embracing once more before Oelendra went to join the ranks of the Lirin. Rhapsody took her place again at the top of the Summoner's Ledge, looking down onto the growing gathering.

Most of the Cymrians assembled so far were human, or Lirin, or a combination of both, but occasionally she would notice people from other races she had not seen since she left Serendair, or had never seen before at all.

The first that she observed was a small figure wandering near the base of the Summoner's Ledge, looking around as if for shelter. It was a Gwaddi woman, not even four feet tall, with enormous green-gray eyes, a heart-shaped face with high cheekbones, and caramel-colored hair that was braided and hung long down her back. Her build was slender, like that of the other members of her race, with proportionally larger hands and long, narrow feet. She seemed ill at ease among the humans she was surrounded by, but before Rhapsody could call the Gwadd to her she was gone, lost in the crowd. Rhapsody choked up at the sight of her; she had feared the small, gentle people had been destroyed in the cataclysm or the Cymrian War and was greatly relieved to know her fears were at least partially unfounded.

After that she would note other races represented, men and women of unique build and features; tall, dark Lirinesque humans with eyes blacker than the previous night had been, willowy people with hair and skin that was gold like wheat in summer fields, squat, wide men with broad shoulders and long silver beards, a group of running children with silver-blue coloring that shone in the sun like light on the sea, all interspersed with humans and Lirin in the colorings of their nations. There was a uniqueness to them, a beauty that stirred Rhapsody's soul, making her feel protective of them as if she had known them all her life, though she was not one of them. She thought back to what Elynsynos had said to her about the Cymrians and smiled at the wisdom of the dragon.

They were magic; they had crossed the earth and made time stop in the process. In them all the elements found a manifestation, even if they didn't know how to use it. There were some of races that had never been seen in these parts, Gwadd and Liringlas and Gwenen and Nain, Ancient Seren and Dhracians and Mythlin, a human garden full of many different and beautiful kinds of flowers. They were special, Pretty, a unique people that deserved to be cherished and kept safe.

Rhapsody wondered where they had been hiding, these other races of people from a land that had been lost for a millennium. She didn't have time to muse on the question long, for from the east came a new blare of trumpets and hoofbeats heralding the arrival of a new group of Cymrians.

73

Grunthor watched the army of Roland come, his eyes shielded from the glare of the sun by the blade of his enormous poleax, Sal, short for Salutations.

If he was growing more unnerved by the seemingly endless march of wave upon wave of Orlandan soldiers blackening the hilly swales at the feet of the Teeth he gave no outward sign of it; instead he remained immobile, his face transfixed in an aspect of utter concentration. He was counting.

'At least ten thousand cavalry; another ten times that on foot,' he reported.

Achmed nodded. He stood, the newly finished cwellan of ancient Cymrian materials slung across his back, his arms folded, watching the forces of Roland spreading throughout the foothills around the Moot.

'Well, we knew it would come sooner or later,' he said dispassionately. 'I have to admit, I never thought Tristan had it in him to raise such a large force so fast, nor did I believe he was ambitious enough to risk the ire of the Cymrians by bringing it to the Council.' He spat on the ground, then looked south reflectively. 'Have you heard anything from your scouts concerning another incursion force coming from Sorbold?'

'No, sir.' Grunthor looked his way. 'You got a feeling we're in for more than this?'

Achmed nodded again. 'Vast and dangerous as a force this size will be, it doesn't seem to be enough to have inspired the vision Rhapsody had before we left for Yarim. She saw the mountain streams running red with blood, the earth black beneath the sky. I would think at least the Sorbold army would have to join the fray before we would be gravely outmatched enough for that sort of scenario to be brought about.'

'Roland has five squads of ballista, and five hundred catapults,' Grunthor said. 'We could be in for a rough time of it, depending on what they plan to do.'

The Bolg king spat on the ground again, trying to cleanse his mouth of the bitter taste of bile.

'Well, let's go call Tristan's bluff, and find out what exactly those plans are.'

The Prince of Bethany had just finished giving preliminary orders to his Lord Marshal and was briefing his generals when the scouts sent up the signal he had been waiting to hear.

The Firbolg king was approaching.

He tried to contain his excitement, but his hands were trembling with it. He had seen the monster standing on his lofty perch that morning as he processed with his House into the Moot for the opening of the Council. As the noise within the Moot swelled, signaling that the meeting would soon commence, he had slipped away for long enough to see to his army before the Summoner called the meeting to order.

And, as luck would have it, he had just enough time to break the spirit of the Bolg warlord who approached now with his enormous knight marshal, doubtless unnerved by the sight of the occupation army of Roland.

Tristan Steward stood defiantly, trying not to allow the smile of triumph he felt consistently spreading over his face from being seen. When the Bolg king was a few feet from him he came to a halt, the black robes of his garments snapping in the stiff wind. There was no fear in his mismatched eyes, only an insolent smirk. The Bolg king cast a condescending glance around the field behind Tristan.

'I hope you brought your own stores to feed your little friends. The invitation was only extended to Cymrians; it's bad enough to have to provide for that group of wastrels. I will not extend hospitality to taga-longs.'

Tristan Steward's mouth dropped open. He had long cherished the thought of the moment when he would arrive with his army at the gates of Ylorc, a hundred thousand strong, and wipe the smug smile off the nightmarish face of the creature that had threatened him so long ago. The smile did not appear to be moving. It appeared set in stone, in fact.

Abruptly he closed his mouth and studied the Bolg king's face. It was a face that had recently witnessed the devastation of his kingdom, had certainly borne the grimace of anguish while surveying the thousands of dead, the mass burials. He remembered his history lessons of endemic disease in Roland and Sorbold; one of his ancestors was said to have been driven mad and committed suicide in the wake of the plague that gutted his duchy.

Then again, the loss of a kingdom of monsters to the ravages of disease was doubtless not as devastating an experience as it would be were they actually human beings. Perhaps the Bolg king was pragmatic in his losses because he didn't value the lives of the Bolg any more than humans did. Easily won, easily lost.

'I wished to notify you, as a courtesy, what remains of your populace may evacuate peaceably before we take the mountain. When the Council is over I will be occupying Canrif.'

The fiendish smile grew broader. 'You personally? Canrif is a very large place, Tristan. You're a little fat around the middle, but I doubt even you would require an entire kingdom to house your corpulent body. I do have an extra-large hut I can make available to you, if you're finding your field accommodations uncomfortable. But I'm afraid all the guest suites are occupied. Rhapsody took care of those arrangements.'

At the mention of her name, Tristan Steward's face flushed; it was all

Achmed could do to keep from laughing aloud. He leaned forward conspiratorially.

'She assigned the ambassadorial quarters to the guests she felt most significant or of important status. I didn't see your name on the list – you aren't even the head of your House, are you? Even if you were, given what she thinks of you, I doubt you'd be assigned a room. But, as I said, I do have a large hut you can sleep in for the duration of the Council.'

A vein in the Lord Roland's forehead was pulsing so that Achmed thought it might burst. Tristan's nostrils flared; he took a step toward the Bolg king and dropped his voice to a murderous whisper.

'You arrogant bastard. I gave you a chance to spare your people from further bloodshed, and you insult me. I shall enjoy crushing you and every last one of your monstrous subjects beneath my heel. I will purge Canrif of every last vestige of you, down to the rancid air you have breathed into the mountain. I will make it fit for habitation by human beings once again, once every trace of your infestation is cleansed.'

He could see the man the Bolg called the Glowering Eye regarding him seriously through his veils.

'And with what precisely do you intend to enforce this threat?'

Tristan Steward stared at the Firbolg king for a moment as if he were daft. The swell of soldiers at the crest of each rolling rise of earth blackened the land. Perhaps the monster couldn't see properly in the glint of the sun radiating off their weapons and armor, a hundred thousand strong.

'I'm sorry,' he said with mock apology. 'Did I fail to introduce you to the united army of Roland?'

The mismatched eyes of the Bolg king continued to meet his gaze a moment longer, then broke away for a casual glance across the Krevensfield Plain. A hint of a smile took up residence on his lips.

'Nice of you to bring lunch,' he said dryly. 'You still haven't told me how you plan to force me to yield the mountain. It matters not. Go back to the Council, Tristan, and stop wasting my time.' Achmed turned and began to walk away.

The Lord Roland's nostrils flared in fury, and his hand went to the hilt of his sword. 'I'm warning you one last time, *monster*—'

Achmed spun around faster than Tristan's eyes could follow. The Lord Roland's longsword flew end over end into a patch of muddy grass. Tristan felt the sudden pain of the viselike grip that had encircled his wrist before he saw the Bolg king's eyes, smoldering with dark fury, a hairsbreadth away from his own. Behind him he heard the ring of swords as they were drawn, the creak of bowstrings as they were bent.

'Apparently neither of us is much for heeding the other's warnings, then,' he said; he voice was low and calm, and audible only to Tristan. 'If you recall, *I* warned *you* long ago in the quiet of your bedchamber, where I believed you might actually hear me, that if you crossed me you would learn what monsters are made of. Are you ready for the lesson now? Here, before your fellow imbecilic Cymrians? Are you ready to reenact the slaughter of

Bethe Corbair, or perhaps the evisceration of the fourth column, for the entertainment of your friends?'

Tristan dragged his arm from the Bolg king's clutches. 'You pathetic, subhuman brute. Your army is dead, your mountain empty. You couldn't defend your realm against the coming of night with lanternlight, let alone keep it from my soldiers.'

Beneath his ceremonial veils Achmed's smile was apparent. 'Really? An interesting theory. Shall we put it to the test?'

A silver blast of the horn rent the air, shattering the tangible tension that hung between them on the wind. Both men looked up to the rim of the Bowl to see Rhapsody on the Summoner's Rise, staring down at them, no more than a tiny sliver of silver light glinting in the sun, casting a long shadow. The gems of the crown whirled above her head, visible even in the distance.

Achmed smiled even more broadly, seeing Tristan's enraptured stare. 'The Summoner beckons us, Lord Regent,' he said humorously. 'Shall we ignore her call and have at it here, now? Or do you wish to baptize the Council by beginning it with the spilling of the blood of the poor, tattered remnants of my kingdom?'

He leaned forward confidentially. 'Rhapsody is our primary healer here in the Bolglands, you know. She suffers agony at the loss of every Firbolg soul, every stricken brat. These were her people as well, Lord Roland. You know how she came to you so long ago, seeking to spare the Bolg from further slaughter at your hands. Are you ready to make her watch it again? Is this what you and your army have come for – another Spring Cleaning?'

Tristan's eyes now held the gaze of the Bolg king. 'Kiernan!' he shouted to his general.

'M'lord?'

'Encamp. We shall proceed after the Council.'

'Yes, m'lord.'

Tristan turned his back and bent to pick up his longsword. He wiped it on his cloak, then sheathed it sharply. As the order to encamp rolled in waves through the multitude of soldiers, he turned back to Achmed once more.

'When this Council is over, it will not only be the army of Roland, but the power and strength of this assemblage under my command.'

'Even better. There'll be enough meat for supper.'

'I will have your lands before the next nightfall.' Tristan Steward signaled to his generals and his aides-de-camp, then strode through the great earthen gates of the Bowl of the Moot to join up with his House while the army settled in for siege.

Achmed watched until the Lord Roland had disappeared into the Moot, then turned to Grunthor.

'Good. I knew that her impossible beauty would come to some real use one day.' He glanced back at the mountains, cold and silent behind him. 'I'm hearing grumbling from the Cymrian ranks already about Tristan and his army; many of them are quite angry about him bringing them to a Council of Peace.'

'Yeah.' Grunthor cast an eye at the encamped force blackening the landscape around the Moot. 'Maybe they'll fight it out among themselves. Seems to be working out right nice.'

'Yes, it does. Well, then, let's go celebrate by torturing ourselves.'

Grunthor nodded, and together they climbed to the upper rim of the Bowl to take their places as hosts of the gathering beside the Summoner.

74

The cry of the horns might have been the first signal Rhapsody and the other Cymrians had to alert them to the next group's arrival, but Achmed had known of their coming for hours. His scouts and spies had warned him of their arrival, because when they first appeared on the horizon they had resembled an army more than a delegation, dressed as they were in uniform shining armor with banners flying high above them.

They were not human or Lirin; the men stood five to five and a half feet tall, with long flowing beards and well-muscled chests and shoulders as broad as that of a human man. The majority of the assemblage had never seen these people in their time, but had heard the old stories of the war and the Cymrian Age, and recognized them after a moment as the citizens who lived within and beyond the Night Mountain.

They were the earth dwellers, the Children of the Forge, the Nain who had come to the new world on the Cymrian ships but had chosen to live among others of their race far to the east. Much as Gwylliam had been taken to be the king of men, of both Cymrians and those who had occupied the lands before their arrival, so the leader of the Cymrian Nain had become the king of the Nain in the new world, and had remained so, maintaining the kingdom through the war until the two peoples blended. And he came as such now, Faedryth, king and Lord of the House of Alexander, both an ancient Cymrian of the First Generation, and the king of an indigenous people.

For centuries the Nain had lived in self-imposed isolation. They had fought in the war, primarily against the Lirin, had remained part of the Council but kept to themselves and the affairs of their own kingdom. The arrival of the Nain Houses caused a sudden silence, then a growing murmur as the repercussions of their attendance were widely discussed.

Once all of the delegation had arrived, the Nain positioned themselves across from the Lirin, whose Houses still stood together at the base of the Summoner's Ledge. A tension began to pick up in the air. The crowds were now sorting themselves out by House, race, or the fleet with which their ancestors had sailed. The Bolg Cymrians stood with Achmed, who had placed himself, as host, on the lip of the Bowl behind Rhapsody.

Then the tension in the air grew palpable. Some of the Houses had been claiming members from the Diaspora upon arrival, as some of their own recognized distant cousins or other family members in the crowd. Now others were seeming to adopt members more freely, without certain knowledge of their lineage, but with more political ends in mind. This padding of the numbers caused the outbreak of many arguments, with tempers flaring and the occasional drawing of weapons being witnessed, despite aggression within the Council being forbidden. Rhapsody was distressed when she saw that this was able to happen, but realized that until she called the Council to order, none of them were bound by the laws that they would be required to respect once it was in session. She decided to do so as soon as possible.

A great roar went up from the assemblage, and Rhapsody stood on her toes to see what was causing the commotion. A moment later, a path opened in the sea of people within the Bowl and a figure, resplendent in shining black armor and riding a barded black charger, rode through. Rhapsody recognized the horse immediately. When the man stopped before the Summoner's Ledge he removed his helmet and great cacophony ensued again; it was Anborn.

Even from as far away as he was, Rhapsody could see the smile that briefly crossed his face when their eyes met, and he winked at her. Then he dismounted and walked to the open center of the amphitheater and waited in silence. A crowd instantly began to form around him, some greeting him with quiet respect, others with open glee. Suddenly, more than ever before, she saw him as the general that he was, the great knight marshal of the Cymrians, rather than the surly dilettante she had gotten to know and like, and who might become her husband. He was a leader, born to it, and now she saw the command his presence drew. The Nain king crossed to him and clasped his hand in the gesture of old friends. Among the Lirin she could hear unpleasant rumblings and noticed glaring expressions and gestures of contempt.

With Anborn's arrival the Houses began to split loosely into their respective Waves, the remnants of the fleets in which they had sailed to their new home. Even within the fleets themselves was great disparity; although the Cymrian Lirin primarily stood with the First Fleet, there were also many Lirin numbered among the Third Fleet, acknowledging the Wave with which they had sailed more than the side they had taken in the war. The Nain positioned themselves between Anborn and the delegation of the Third Fleet, who had settled in the southern section of the Moot, though a few could be seen sprinkled here and there throughout the other factions. The diminutive races, like the Gwadd, had separated out and were clustering together, away from the larger groups. Some of the Diaspora, even those who had been welcomed into other Houses, had begun to separate from the rest, forming their own crowd off to the edges. Rhapsody was not sure if they did so out of confusion, out of an alliance that had formed while they had waited, or out of the desire not to be associated with the feuds and hostilities that were evidently brewing. The guests had not all arrived yet, and already a fight was in the offing. She glanced over to Oelendra, who was dressed in simple chain mail and a flowing blue cloak, and rolled her eyes. Oelendra laughed in return.

A moment later the attention of both of them was drawn to the next group entering the Bowl. With their entrance an uneasy silence fell. Some of the members of the procession were Lirin, or looked like Lirin but with darker skin and a more ancient mien to them. Others were giants, as tall as Grunthor, but with a thin, lithe build. Their skin was golden and their faces were ancient; the sight of them caused Rhapsody to hold her breath. Though she had never seen one in all her days on the Island, she recognized these people as Ancient Seren, the legendary Firstborn of Serendair, who had all but died out long before she was born. The darker Lirin she guessed were the Kith, another of the Firstborn of the Island, a mysterious people of the ancient woods and primeval forests. It was this House she had heard singing the final chorus of her morning aubade.

Neither of the Firstborn races led this House. At the head of the procession was a man, broadly built like Anborn, but portly and soft where the knight marshal was muscular and well defined. His lineage was strikingly evident, the hawklike nose, the silver hair: this was Edwyn Griffyth, the oldest son of Anwyn and Gwylliam, who had left at the advent of the war in disgust and gone to live on the island between the two continents, Gaematria, the Isle of the Sea Mages. At last Rhapsody understood the lineage of the Sea Mages, and why they held such power. They were made up of Firstborn and their descendants who had chosen to live apart from the other Cymrians even before the start of the war, and had therefore been untouched by it, allowing for a millennium of their growth and prosperity as a civilization. They avoided both fleets and formed a distinctly separate group.

As the last of the Sea Mages had taken his place, the Second Fleet arrived. Rhapsody's heart began to pound; Ashe was at their head, riding a gray stallion, leading the Houses into the Moot. Like the Nain they carried banners proclaiming their lineage, but they were wearing traveling clothes, not military garb. This last, largest fleet to arrive was the most heterogeneous of the three; all races were represented within its ranks, and there were substantial numbers of people of mixed blood. They took their place between the First and Third Fleets and did not mix ranks, though there were many greetings.

Ashe's arrival caused more of a stir than any other, undoubtedly because it was still widely believed that he was dead. A wave of recognition had begun outside the Bowl as he approached, cresting as he entered. Amid loud rumblings and cheers he rode into the inner circle, surrounded by his kinsmen from the House of Newland, and stopped before the Summoner's Ledge. He stared at Rhapsody for a moment, his face blank but a look of intense longing in his eyes. Rhapsody felt her heart tug as it had a year before when she looked out the window at him on the shore of Elysian's lake, after their first night as lovers, then it twisted in self-condemnation. She looked quickly to see if his wife was there as well; a number of young women were in the first line of the contigent that rode behind them, but it was impossible to distinguish one that might be the new Lady Newland. Ashe bowed to her, then returned to the center of the Second Fleet.

Once he was back in position it was easier for her to take notice of how he was attired. He carried the staff of the Invoker; Rhapsody took grim satisfaction in the understanding that Khaddyr had been removed from office. Across his back flowed the mantle of mist that had hidden him for so long. Instead of vaporous darkness, however, it now appeared like the rampant azure waves of the ocean, drawing the attention it had once averted. Around his neck Crynella's candle gleamed, illuminating the breastplate of armor of the Kirsdarkenvar, which glittered like blue-green fish scales in the golden radiance of the forenoon sun. But more than the armor, his hair caught the sunlight, and it made him look the quintessential picture of a great and noble lord, a king of ancient lineage. Rhapsody's eyes glittered in the light as well. It was easy to see why she had been unworthy of him.

Achmed, Grunthor, and the Cymrian Bolg had joined the Diaspora, and now formed a separate group. They stood on an elevated rise to the east of the Summoner's Ledge, assuming a position of honor as the hosts. Rhapsody turned to see how her friends were sizing up the most recent entrance and noticed fourteen cloaked and hooded figures grouped silently behind the Firbolg king. At first she felt her throat tighten with concern; she had not seen these Cymrians arrive, and had no idea which fleet, if any, they had come with. Then she noticed their thin hands, and the vague familiarity of their posture, so like Achmed's. Achmed smiled, and a look passed between the two of them. Instantly her consternation melted away; these were Dhracians. Rhapsody felt a flood of joy to know that Achmed's race was not extinguished after all.

A rumbling din removed the smile from her face. When her glance returned to the assemblage she found that the Bowl was in the throes of myriad arguments, disagreements, and outright hostilities. The fleets were bickering between and among themselves; a shouted exchange between the Nain and the Lirin was threatening to explode in violence. Rhapsody sighed in dismay; the Council had not even been called to order and already the Cymrians were on the verge of another war.

She took a deep breath and began to sing. With the same note as the Cymrian horn she intoned the ancient words of Gwylliam the Visionary that Merithyn had carved on the dragon's cave, that the Cymrians themselves had inscribed on every marker along the trail of their journey toward reunion with each other in the new world.

Cyme we inne frið, fram the grip of deaþ to lif inne ð is smylte land.

Like the ringing of the great bell of the carillon of Bethe Corbair, her song echoed through the Moot, the Bowl accentuating its resonance and drawing down the mutterings of discontent into silence. Two hundred thousand eyes fixed on her, standing on the Ledge above them, the star-crowned queen, the Namer, summoning the Cymrians and calling them to order. The assemblage stood, slack-jawed, staring at her in shock. The first to recover was Anborn, whose face broke rapidly into a broad smile; he sighed in relief, and with his exhale came tens of thousands of others. The tension in the air dissolved, and the silence became a respectful one.

'Well, wasn't that pretty?' A harsh voice, thick with power and elemental depth like the crashing of waves or a roaring bonfire, echoed through the Bowl, shattering the placid silence. A gasp went up from the Council; the sound made Rhapsody's blood run cold. She watched as the Cymrians moved rapidly away from the middle of the amphitheater.

At the center of the point of entry stood three figures. A path in the crowd had opened before them and had closed behind them; the hush that descended was fraught with fury and hatred. Three women stood at the core of the Bowl, tall as their father had been, holding themselves with silent dignity. The faces of the Cymrian assemblage were contorted with hate and fear.

Rhapsody recognized the first two of the sisters immediately. Rhonwyn was dressed in the black robe of her cloistered abbey; she was pale and fragile, and appeared lost in a dream. In contrast, Manwyn stood her ground defiantly, her flaming red hair streaming in the wind, her mirrored eyes reflecting the sunlight. But all attention was really on the third sister, a woman taller than Achmed or Ashe, not much smaller than Grunthor, with broad shoulders and a face that was intensely, almost painfully beautiful.

Anwyn's appearance was not at all what Rhapsody expected; she was stunning, and frightening. Her skin was golden, as her father's must have been; her face, though dazzling, was composed of features so hard they appeared to have been wrought in metal. And her hair was copper like Ashe's; the sun that beat down from directly overhead glinted off it, blinding many in the Bowl. She cast her dragonesque eyes around the assemblage, eyes of a blistering blue that cut through any who dared to look into them. Her displeasure was evident.

Achmed watched her with great interest, at the ready. Among the powerful and ancient people assembled here, Anwyn alone had a compelling perfection that rivaled Rhapsody's. He had watched the Cymrians, as a people, fall under Rhapsody's spell, becoming totally enchanted with one look at her, or one spoken word. But where Rhapsody inspired love and longing, Anwyn's appearance served to intimidate and spread fear. She knew it; it was obvious in the smile that came into her eyes a moment after she had surveyed the Council.

With the arrival of the Seers the assemblage was complete, and the Bowl became quiet. The deep timbre of the Nain king's voice rumbled from within his ranks, tinged with annoyance.

'Who has summoned us here? By what right has this Council, broken a thousand years, been called into being again?'

Achmed looked up at Rhapsody on the Summoner's Ledge. Her face was surprisingly serene, even with the arrival of the Seers, and her voice, when she answered him, was calm and sweet.

'I am the one who sounded the horn, Your Majesty.'

'By what right?' the ancient Nain demanded. 'We are a Council no more, and many of us have no wish to return to being one.'

From within the Lirin contingent at the edge of the First Fleet, Oelendra's voice rang out, cutting through the noise of the Bowl. 'She is the Lirin queen, and the Iliachenva'ar,' she declared. At once discussion broke out again, murmured and muttered, particularly among the Nain.

'Irrelevant,' shouted Anwyn; silence fell immediately. 'You have no right to have even touched that horn, girl. Those rights are reserved to the Lady or Lord Cymrian, as is the right to call this Council.'

'Nonsense,' Anborn bellowed from within the Third Fleet. 'That is the horn of the Cymrians, made for use in time of need or to summon the Council, as is the right of any Cymrian soul. No restrictions were put on its use, it is not your personal possession.' His brazen tone resulted in the assemblage taking a collective breath and holding it.

Anwyn's anger smoldered, and her eyes burned more brightly blue. 'You'd best be careful, Anborn; I disowned you centuries ago. Do you wish to challenge me here?' Anborn met her gaze without looking away, but said nothing. The air became slightly more static-filled, and overhead the sky began to darken as the wispy clouds thickened, heavy with unshed rain. A moment later Anwyn smiled. 'I thought not. In the presence of witnesses, it is usually best for a traitor to keep silent.'

'Traitor?' shouted one of the Lirin of the First Fleet. 'Who are you to accuse another of treachery?' Murmurs of agreement rose softly around the speaker. Anwyn turned slowly and glared at the man, who seemed to sink before her withering stare. He trembled in fear, unable to break the wyrmkin's serpentine gaze.

'Grandmother!' Ashe cried out, his voice clear in the silence that had returned. 'We are in Council! You are prohibited by the law of the Moot from assaulting another within the Bowl, you know that better than anyone!'

'Since when has Anwyn ever abided by the law?' muttered someone from the Second Fleet.

Anwyn ignored the comments and turned her glower on Ashe. 'Are you turning against me as well? Siding with him over me?'

'There is no need to take sides; I am only pointing out that you are on the verge of breaking your own rule. Whether you like it or not, the fact that we are all here proves we are officially in Council, and Her Majesty has called us to order.'

'If we are in Council, then this girl has no right to chair it,' Anwyn retorted, turning to Rhapsody once more. 'There can be no Council without the Lord or Lady to preside over it. There is now and always has been, and will ever be only one Lady Cymrian. I am the Lady of this Council! Stand down, wench.' She strode across the Bowl to the foot of the Speaker's Rise and began to climb the twisting path to the pulpit structure.

The Bowl erupted in turmoil. Words of condemnation and disbelief filled the air, drowning out all of Rhapsody's attempts to restore order. Achmed was certain that Anwyn's smile grew brighter as the outcry increased in intensity. Anborn was speaking strongly to Edwyn Griffyth, who in turn glared skyward and pointed in anger as Anwyn ascended the Speaker's Rise. The fleets and the Diaspora had dissolved into chaos, with foul shouts being heard and the shaking of fists seen everywhere. When she reached the first crest of the Rise, Anwyn stood tall and smiled proudly, reveling in the upheaval she had caused.

A moment later the air was rent by the blast of the horn. The assemblage froze, and even Anwyn's face blanched in shock. The last echo of the note died away, taking with it the resentful murmurs.

Rhapsody's face was calm as she lowered the horn from her lips. Achmed smiled at the grace with which she was comporting herself. He could tell by the color of her eyes that she was furious.

'There seems to be some dispute with your claim, Anwyn,' she said politely.

'What this rabble says is of no consequence,' Anwyn answered, unruffled by the silent hatred, rising in almost palpable waves, from the floor of the Moot. 'I am the Lady Cymrian. While I live, there can be no other.'

At once the air was filled with ugly shouted threats from volunteers offering to rectify that situation. Angry voices surged forth again, and Anwyn stared coldly down at the rabble calling for her to step away from the Rise. The sonorous voice of one of the ancient Seren could be heard above the others.

'Despite what you claim, you were cast out of this Council and stripped of your position. You no longer hold any title here.'

'I do not recognize the authority of the Council to perform such an act,' Anwyn replied icily.

'You do not recognize?' shouted Anborn, angrier than those about him had ever seen him. 'What makes you think you have the right to recognize *anything*? The Council named you Lady, and after you disgraced yourself and almost destroyed all of us, we threw you out!'

Anwyn drew herself up to her full height and glared at her estranged son, whose words had driven the mob back into silence again. 'You are a fine one to accuse another of disgrace, Nonentity. And my right to this land comes from a legacy far older than anyone here. My blood is the eldest in this land – I am the child of Merithyn the Explorer, and the dragon whose realm this was long before any of you came here. I am the bond! My very existence is the symbol of the tie between the Cymrians and this land, the union of the blood of the most ancient from the Island of Serendair with the Firstborn of this land as well. Which of you can claim that? Who can dispute my right?'

'Actually—' began Edwyn Griffyth, but his words were drowned by Anwyn's continuing tirade.

'I am the Seer of the Past, the child of the Ancient Ones, the living emblem of the unity of the people with the land. Without me you would have been cast back into the sea from which you crawled! You owed me your lives then, as you do now – who do you think is responsible for your longevity, your immortality? Who among you has the right to decry me?'

There was silence. As the echo of her voice died away unanswered, Anwyn looked down on the quiet throng with a victorious smile. She glanced around at the Cymrian assemblage, the piercing blue eyes taking in the people she had once ruled, once fought beside, once fought against. Her gaze came to rest for a moment on Oelendra, and the smile melted from her face, replaced by seething hatred. The Lirin warrior met her stare without blinking. Anwyn began to tremble with rage and raised her hand, pointing at her in accusation.

'I have the right to decry you.' Ashe's voice broke the silence, and all eyes turned immediately in his direction. 'You have betrayed your position as Seer. You lied to me.'

A low murmur swept through the crowd again, colored more with astonishment than anger.

Anwyn's golden face deepened to a shade approaching purple. 'Blasphemy! I told you no untruth.'

'No, you told me a half-truth! You manipulated what you saw and told me only what you wished me to know, not what I needed to, and not what I asked. That, Grandmother, is the same thing as lying. You betrayed the last shred of trust I had in you.

'Your lie broke my heart, but that is my suffering alone, and for that, perhaps, you could be forgiven. But in choosing to keep the truth from me, to keep me under your thumb, you hid the nature of the coming of the Three. Far too many have died because of that, Grandmother. It is yet another betrayal of the Cymrian people, and their champions, who were needlessly slaughtered seeking a demon we could have defeated without costing their lives! You will never find forgiveness now.'

His eyes turned to Rhapsody; the rest of the Council presumed he was yielding the floor, but Achmed, who stood slightly below her, facing the same direction she did, saw something more. He had no knowledge of what lie it was that Ashe was referring to, but it somehow seemed to have something to do with her. He glanced up in Rhapsody's direction; her face was blank. Obviously she had no idea what he was talking about, either, but the sudden attention brought a rosy blush to her cheeks.

He was not alone in his notice; Anwyn was staring at the Lirin queen, too. Her face grew hard, and she looked from Rhapsody to Oelendra and back again.

'Stand down, girl,' she commanded. 'These are my people, this is my Council. I am the Lady of the Cymrians, and I do not cede to you any right to act as the chair of this Council.'

461

Rhapsody smiled. There was a quiet but audible intake of breath among the assemblage, and they began to mutter angrily among themselves. In the time since the first to arrive had come, the Cymrian people had lost their hearts to the gentle Singer, the unassuming queen who behaved like a respectful peasant, and Achmed knew their devotion to her was strong.

A deeper anger was brewing within them now, an outrage at the insulting manner in which Anwyn was treating her. Achmed knew that Rhapsody understood this as well, and that was why she smiled. It was a way of defusing the situation before it exploded in a frenzy of loyal violence.

'I hardly think you should be referring to me as "girl," given that my birth predates yours by several centuries,' she said calmly.

A haughty sneer curled on the Seer's lip. 'What is that supposed to mean, *girl?*'

Achmed felt no such compunction to be polite. 'It means,' came the cool, sandy voice of the Firbolg king, cutting through the murmurs of the crowd like a slashing sword, 'that the girl doesn't like the way she is being addressed by the hag.'

Laughter mixed with gasps of shock rippled through the crowd. Anwyn's face contorted in rage, and Rhapsody looked horrified.

'Achmed, you're out of line,' she said reproachfully. 'Anwyn is not a hag.'

'Right you are,' came the furious voice of Grunthor. The assemblage turned toward the sound to see the giant Firbolg commander straining to control his wrath; he was losing the battle, and it was a horrific prospect. The outrage the Cymrians had felt on Rhapsody's behalf paled by comparison to the rage in the eyes of her dear friend. 'She's a bloody *harpy.* I'll thank you to keep a civil tongue in your flaming head, missus, and act more respectfully towards Her Ladyship, or I'll personally rip out whatever is where your heart ought to be and eat it raw.' There was another collective intake of breath from the Council. There was no way that could be perceived as an idle threat. Rhapsody gestured to Achmed, who stood beside the Sergeant, and he touched the giant's elbow.

Anwyn was livid. 'How dare you speak to me that way, you subhuman monster? You ill-begotten freak of nature? Your presence soils this noble ground. As your ruler I command you, leave this Moot at once, and if you ever dare to even raise your cannibalistic face in my presence, I will smite you down into the mudfilth from which you and your people sprang.' She shot him a look of hatred, the dragon-eye attack she had used on the Lirin spokesman earlier, that had reduced the man to a quivering mass on the floor of the Bowl.

Grunthor would have none of it. 'Have at me, then, you bitch!' he roared, his enraged cry echoing off the rockwalls of the Bowl and over the Teeth, where even the Bolg within the mountains heard it and trembled.

He scrambled down from the outcropping on which he stood and dashed toward the Speaker's Rise. The terrifying sight caused the assemblage to gasp. He was brute strength in motion, seven and a half feet of infuriated musculature single-mindedly intent on murder. He would have been at the foot of the Rise a moment later had Achmed not vaulted down in front of him and interposed his body between them. The path to the Seer was clear; the Lirin Cymrians who had been standing below Rhapsody on the Summoner's Ledge had moved back hastily when Grunthor's exchange with Anwyn had begun.

'Sergeant-Major, don't lower yourself,' Achmed said in a stern voice. 'She is not fit to wipe your boots; don't soil your hands by tearing out her throat, no matter how much she deserves it.' He looked into the giant's face; Grunthor was panting with rage, every muscle straining to avoid throwing Achmed out of his path. 'As your king I command it.'

'Not fit?' came the powerful trumpet-voice. Anwyn laughed, and the sound blasted the ears of the assemblage. 'I, the Lady Cymrian, the victor in the Great War, am not fit? So speaks the evidence that prophecies are generally a disappointment.' Manwyn bristled at her words and clenched her fists. 'My people, behold the Three, your purported saviors, the ones my sister said would rescue us all from the wrath of an invisible demon. Look at them in all their splendor. First, we have the giant freak, an animal that appears to have recently escaped from a traveling circus! Beside him his noble lord, the Purveyor of Death, the assassin who, like a whore, served whoever paid him, killing indiscriminately—'

'I believe she means me,' Achmed said to the crowd, raising his hand. He turned his face to Anwyn, whose speech had been choked off with his interruption. A mocking smile crossed his face. 'Oh, I'm sorry, Annie, that was presumptuous. Were you referring to yourself? Certainly you earned the title far better than I ever did. The Purveyor of Death? My trophies pale in comparison to yours. I can't claim, as only you can, to have annihilated a quarter of my own people over a domestic squabble. If only Gwylliam had slapped you harder, maybe he would have broken your bony neck and none of us would be here to have to endure your rantings now. Pity he didn't.

'And whore? Well, yes, I suppose that applies to you again. Who else would sell out her kingdom and that of her allies, the Lirin, to the same demon who once almost destroyed an entire nation? Would give it the opportunity to do so again? All to avenge herself on her fool of a husband? You are the consummate whore, Anwyn. Get off the Rise and out of my lands before I step away and let Grunthor remove your head from your shoulders and use your skull for a chamber pot.'

The silence in the Bowl was absolute; even the sounds of nature had died away. Anwyn's face had been frozen in amazement; over the span of her entire lifetime no one had ever dared to speak to her in that manner. Her eyes narrowed to slits for a moment as she formulated her response; when she had done so, she smiled cruelly.

'I thank you for granting me the title of Consummate Whore, but I'm afraid I can't accept it. That would belong to another in this assemblage.' She turned toward Rhapsody. 'Step forward, Your Majesty, and—'

'*Enough!*' Ashe's voice thundered over the Moot, ringing with the multitoned echoes of the dragon in his blood. He knew what was coming, and would sooner die, or kill Anwyn where she stood, than allow it. He turned toward the Seer of the Present. 'Rhonwyn, who is the Lady Cymrian?'

The fragile Seer looked toward the sky as the eyes of the throng locked onto her. 'There is no Lady Cymrian,' she said as if in a dream, lost inside herself.

'Thus says the Seer of the Present, the indisputable authority!' Ashe cried. 'My fellows, as of this moment, there is no Lady Cymrian! Your claim is rejected, Grandmother!'

75

After a moment of silence, the Bowl erupted in hoots and cheers. Anwyn was thunderstruck; she glared at Achmed and Ashe, who were exchanging the glance of inadvertent co-conspirators.

'Silence!' she snarled, and the thunderous applause diminished. 'You are a leaderless rabble, unable to even discern the difference between royal blood and the self-aggrandizing opportunist who took over a realm of monsters and called himself King.'

'You're wrong there,' said Oelendra in a commanding voice. 'I believe everyone here is able to discern who the self-aggrandizing opportunist is. Give up, Anwyn; spare yourself any further humiliation. This Council has come together to build up what you have destroyed, to fix the trust that you and Gwylliam shattered. The Three have rid this land of the demon you are solely responsible for. Had you been any kind of ruler at all, you would not have sold us to the F'dor for your own petty purposes. Leave and go back to your cave. You are a thing of the Past, in all senses of the word.'

Anwyn turned slowly in the direction of Oelendra's voice. Unlike the others that had decried her, this particular shout had caught her attention, and the deliberation with which she moved to face her accuser was apparent to the assemblage. The Council grew quiet as the Seer looked down into the Lirin warrior's eyes, an expression of undisguised hatred disfiguring her face.

'Thus speaks the so-called Lirin champion,' Anwyn said in a mocking voice; she laughed derisively as Oelendra's nostrils flared and her eyes began to gleam with an antipathy that matched the Seer's. 'Well, well. How very interesting. Given the subject is treachery and self-serving behavior, I would think that you would have chosen to remain silent, Oelendra, to try and avoid scrutiny of your own actions. I guess you are as much a fool as you are a coward.'

Loud shouts of angry protest issued forth, mostly from the First Fleet and Lirin encampments, but the sound was swallowed almost instantly by a vibration within the Bowl of the Moot. Anwyn had the floor, and she knew it. Triumph began to shine in her eyes, as she strode farther up the rocky outcropping to the west of the Summoner's Ledge.

When she got to the summit of the Speaker's Rise, she reached out her long arms to the sky in a gesture of celebration, as though she was gathering power to herself. Then she pointed at Oelendra and laughed, a loud, nasty laugh that echoed off the rockwalls of the Moot.

'You pathetic hypocrite,' Anwyn said, staring down at Oelendra. Unconsciously the crowd around the Lirin champion began to peel away slightly, leaving space. Though Oelendra was surrounded by her contingent still, she was alone in the circle. Rhapsody's blood boiled, and she tried to step away from the Summoner's Ledge; if no one else would stand by Oelendra, she would. But her feet were frozen where she stood; she could not leave the Ledge.

'There she stands, the Holy Warrior, the sworn enemy of the mythical demon. You've made quite a reputation for yourself, haven't you, Oelendra? The passionate crusader, singular in her quest to deliver us all from the evil that Gwylliam unwittingly brought with him. Refusing the leadership, refusing the power, to concentrate on ridding the world of the F'dor. Aren't you noble. How many have come to you, seeking to make your quest their own, to be ridden mercilessly, trained obsessively, then sent without exception to their deaths? Do you still weep for them, Oelendra? Do you mourn the loss of the flower of the Cymrians? When the power was yours all along to prevent it yourself?'

The silence in the Bowl grew heavier. Even as far away as he was from her, Ashe could see Oelendra's jaw clench tighter, and the look of hate in her eyes grew more intense.

'Tell them, Oelendra, while you have them all here. Tell them how you knew, you knew the appointed time and place to kill it *decades ago*. Manwyn told you, in the presence of my son, exactly when and where you would need to be in order to destroy the demon, back when it was still weak enough to do so without the aid of the Three. Do you deny it?' Her eyes flashed and her voice grew harsher. *'Do you?'*

Two hundred thousand eyes turned to Oelendra. Her head was still erect, her back and shoulders straight, but something had left her eyes. 'No,' she answered. Her voice was barely audible.

A sickening smile of victory crawled over Anwyn's face. 'I don't think anyone heard you, Oelendra,' she taunted, drawing herself up straighter. 'What did you say?'

Oelendra sighed inaudibly; Rhapsody could see the light go out of her face. 'No,' she repeated. The breaking of her spirit was visible.

Murmurs of disbelief began to whisper through the Bowl, and there were mutterings on all sides. Anwyn was smiling gloriously at the humiliation of her longtime adversary.

'You knew it, and you refused to go. You shirked your responsibilities as Iliachenva'ar, not to mention those of the grand and glorious Lirin champion! Admit it, Oelendra; you were *afraid*, the state of which you allow no one else the benefit. You heard the warning, and the risk was too great, wasn't it? So instead you allowed another to go in your place, another worth a thousand of yourself, to stand in your stead and endure the consequences. My grandson, the hope of the Cymrian peoples, an innocent, suffered indescribable agony, the loss of his very soul, because of your cowardice. Your inaction delivered him into its clutches! Do you admit it?'

'Stop it!' shouted Ashe. 'Who are you to taunt her? You, who destroyed the Purity Diamond, our one weapon against it? I went alone against the demon; it was my decision. If I don't hold her responsible for my fate, why should you?'

'Why?' Anwyn asked contemptuously. 'Shall I tell him why, Oelendra? Perhaps he would be interested to know that he is not the only one you have delivered thus. Shall I tell him, tell all of them, of Pendaris?' Oelendra's brow furrowed in disbelief. 'Yes, Oelendra, perhaps you should tell them instead. Tell them how your husband died; tell them whether it would have happened had it not been for you.'

Oelendra's face went white. Even from across the Bowl in his position at the head of the Second Fleet, Ashe could feel the breath leave her body, and he knew that this accusation was a new one, one that caused a fresh, deep wound. Anwyn let loose a crow of delight, and pointed at the warrior again. 'This is why I should retain the title of Lady; I alone understand the Past, the history of the Cymrians! I alone know your secrets. Well, Oelendra? Tell them! Tell them who you have delivered to the F'dor in the Past; shall you deliver all of us to similar fates as well in the Future?'

The assemblage was now beginning to break into arguments and mutter loudly, far more bitterly and violently than they had before. Ashe looked across to Achmed and their eyes met. Between them a thought passed instantaneously: a riot was about to start. They both looked up to the Summoner's Ledge at Rhapsody, but she was bent over, obscured from their view. When she stood again they could see she was rummaging through her pack. Her face was calm, and when her eyes met Achmed's, she smiled.

Rhapsody took out her harp and began to play. Ashe instantly recognized the tune; it was the song she had used during his renaming ceremony. The melody echoed off the walls of the Moot, the vibration increasing with each bounce. Wherever it touched, the earth began to shimmer.

'Anwyn,' she said. Her word, spoken softly, drowned out all other sound in the Moot. The Seer turned to her with wrath in her eyes at the interruption. 'Anwyn,' she repeated, 'be silent.'

Anwyn's mouth opened in shock; seconds later she recovered, and her face burned with rage, her body coiling like a serpent ready to strike. The muscles of her throat tensed as she prepared to reply, and her eyes met Rhapsody's own with a hate unlike any the Singer had ever seen.

Rhapsody returned her gaze unblinkingly. Her face was serene, even glowing; the only sign that she was at all intent was the striking shade her eyes had turned. They were the color of spring grass, blazing with a light that caused even the Seer to hesitate for a moment. Then Anwyn spoke, or tried to; her mouth moved, but no words, no sound, came out.

Pity came into Rhapsody's eyes as Anwyn clutched at her throat; otherwise her face remained serene. The woman roiled in rage, curling down into herself with a silent scream that had no echo; when she looked back at Rhapsody her anger was replaced with a fierce look of fear.

'You have yielded the floor by repeatedly demanding that another answer your questions; indeed, you have violated your office as Seer of the Past by demanding an answer for the Future. Anwyn ap Merithyn, tuatha Elynsynos, I rename you The Past. Your actions are out of balance. Henceforth your tongue will only serve to speak of the realm into which your eyes alone were given entry. That which is the domain of your sisters, the Present and the Future, you will be unable to utter. No one shall seek you out for any other reason, so may you choose to convey your knowledge better this time, lest you be forgotten altogether.'

She began to sing, and the faces of the throng of Cymrians went slack with wonder. Her voice was sweet but smoky, filled with sorrow, and her song spoke of their history, in all its horror and pain. The lyrics were Ancient Lirin, so not everyone in the gathering understood them, but those who did began to weep. The tears were not theirs exclusively, though; understanding of the words was not necessary to comprehend the message of the song.

The song told of war, the war of their homeland, and their flight in desperation to escape its destruction. It built to a terrible crescendo, then resolved into a sea aire, the story of their voyage to the new world, through the Great Storm, and the wonder of the discovery.

Ashe, himself weeping in awe, felt a smile come over his face as the song changed yet again. He realized that the song was a rhapsody, with movements unique to each tale in the legend; somehow the thought delighted him. He listened raptly as she sang of the wonder of finding the White Tree, of meeting the inhabitants, of reuniting the Three Fleets, and all the glory days of the Cymrian Age that built great cities, sought deep knowledge, and strove for the betterment of their people. Then, as the hearts of the masses were floating in poignant remembrance, their faces transfixed in proud memory, the tune changed again.

It became an insidious melody, secretive and dread, with discordant notes indicating breakdowns of the dreamlike aire that had preceded it. The light in the faces of the Cymrians faded, and their eyes darkened along with the music as she told of the Great War, of the destruction of Tomingorllo and the Lirin stronghold of Haner Til, the rout of the Third Fleet and the slaughter in Canrif and Bethe Corbair, and other stories of devastation and genocide that marked the blackest moments of the seven hundred years of senseless bloodshed. The pain in the song reflected in the faces of the people, and many of the tears turned to shuddering sobs. The tune became grueling, relentless, like the war itself, and just as it was about to break the spirit of the assembled Cymrians it resolved down into stillness, sustained by one long, vibrating note.

From that one note soft harmonics blossomed, then simple strains, building into a concerto countered by a deep chant; the dark, simple mantra played on the harp lent depth to the fresh, springlike descant she sang over it. It was a symphony of rebuilding, of change and vigilance, of assimilation and staunch maintenance of tradition; it was the perfect portrait of the Cymrians as they were now. And as that became apparent, Rhonwyn, the frail sister, began to smile, and spoke.

'We are here,' she said, her eyes focusing for the first time. 'It is now.'

Rhapsody's music abruptly ceased. 'You're right,' she said to Rhonwyn with a smile of unsurpassed gentleness. 'And so we must stop, for this is not your time, Anwyn.'

'What of the Future?!' a voice from the assemblage cried out. 'Tell us! Give us hope!' The cry was taken up by the crowd; tens of thousands of voices calling for the rest of the song. The voices were as an earthquake rocking through the Moot.

'Tarry a moment,' Rhapsody answered them. 'That belongs to us, not to her. Give Anwyn her due. She is leaving.'

The hate in Anwyn's eyes was gone for the moment, replaced by tears of sorrow and marvel. She tried to speak again, but could not. She looked at Rhapsody's face, a face that contained no gloat, no victory, just peace. The awfulness of her realization that she was no longer the only Cymrian Lady who understood their Past was clear to all who saw her; so was her amazement that the one who did had not lived it. For the first time in the memory of the Cymrian people, she bowed her head.

'My tribute to you is ended. Go now, m'lady of the Past,' Rhapsody said kindly. 'Go and sort out your memories. We will be making grand new ones for you to count soon.'

Anwyn looked balefully at Rhapsody once more, then strode out of the Moot and disappeared.

Rhapsody's eyes searched for Oelendra, and when they found her she smiled. She held her harp aloft like a weapon, and a look of singular understanding passed between them: *This is what I meant,* she was saying. *There are many kinds of weapons, and all of them are powerful in their way and time.* Oelendra did not return the smile; she nodded, turned, and disappeared into the crowd.

The roar that issued forth from the multitude swept over Rhapsody like a tidal wave. It resonated through her body and her soul, and in that moment, for the first time since she arrived, she felt completely one with them.

She looked out over the crowd for faces she recognized, and her eyes came to rest on Ashe. Sunlight had cracked through the cloud-blanketed sky, illuminating the red-gold hair until it burned like a raging fire. The searing blue eyes were visible even from a great distance, and she could see them focused on her, burning with an intensity that made her flush.

She felt suddenly awkward, suddenly too visible, and she glanced around for a place to recede to. But the stare on Ashe's face was the same one worn by most of the crowd; everywhere she looked they gazed on her thus, making her long to disappear from the dais.

The clamor grew louder with each of the beats of her heart; they were calling for resumption of her song, pleading to hear the rest, imploring to know the Future. Rhapsody cleared her throat, surreptitiously wiping the perspiration from her palms.

'Don't pass so quickly over the Present,' she said to the clamoring crowd. 'Before you can determine what will be, it is necessary to determine what is now. I was about to answer your question about why you were all called, Your Majesty, when that minor interruption occurred.' A titter of laughter rolled through the noisy throng as she bowed to Faedryth, the Nain king, who smiled and nodded at her in return. 'If you put any stock in the prophecy, you know that the death of the demon is the omen of unity and peace being restored to this land and to the Cymrian people. The demon is dead. It is time you put aside your differences and became one people again.'

A voice, filled with sadness, spoke up from the delegation of the Sea Mages. 'How can you even hope that we might, after what we have just witnessed? Even before the she-devil came into our midst there was derision and hostility among this gathering. Is it not best that we just live among the people who were here before, become part of them and forget what we once were?' Murmurs of agreement and dissent swelled all around.

'But you have,' Rhapsody said. 'The Cymrians do live among the people of their various lands. When you first arrived in this world you were a people set apart, refugees, a kingdom unto yourselves. That is no longer the case. Centuries of war and assimilation have changed all that. Look around you. Almost half of you here today came in answer to a summons you did not understand, unaware of who you were, and yet the power to call you as Cymrians, and the need to do so, is still strong. You – we – are part of the land in which we live, people of different nations, different races, kings and queens, princes and lords, standing here as equals, as Cymrians. If any good came from the horror of Anwyn and Gwylliam's war, it is that we are no longer refugees but part of this land.'

'And why should we not just stay that way?' asked a small man within the group of Gwadd that stood in front of the Second Fleet. 'We have endured so much warfare and bloodshed.'

'That is precisely why,' Rhapsody answered. 'The Great War was horrific, but it is not really over. All around there are incursions and murderous raids that have brought this land to the brink of war again, only this time it will be much worse. Instead of fighting for the honor of honorless leaders, you will be fighting out of hate and prejudice; the seeds have been sown for four hundred years or more. You have the opportunity to form a Council now that recognizes the sovereignty of its various member kingdoms, yet works to maintain peaceful relations across the continent. Do you not owe this new land, the land that took you in when you were but storm-tossed refugees, at least that much? After all this place has given you? After all the horror you visited upon it?

'If I have one message for you it is this: The Past is gone. Learn from it and let it go.' Rhapsody swallowed hard to quell the knot that was constricting her throat and the tears that were filling her eyes; she was learning this lesson herself as she spoke to the people gathered below her.

She looked down at Anborn, smiling broadly at her from the center of the Bowl, a look of encouragement shining on his weathered face. 'We must forgive each other. We must forgive ourselves. Only then will there be a true peace.' She glanced around for Oelendra but could not find her in the multitude; instead her gaze came to rest on Ashe, staring at her with an intensity that caused her heart to pound. 'I know I am not one of you; I did not sail with any of the fleets, I left Serendair before a war there and arrived here after one. I have not suffered as you have, but even I have borne more than I can endure anymore. The Lirin have taken me in, made me at home, and I am honored to represent them to you.

'This Council can be a place where the nations of Tyrian and Sorbold and Roland can meet and confer, under the guidance of a Lord and Lady who recognize their independence, but have their sworn allegiance as High King and Queen. It would be their responsibility to guard a lasting peace. As it is, each of those countries is ruled by Cymrian stock now, as are the realm of the Nain, Manosse, and the Isle of the Sea Mages.

'I propose to you this: Keep your lands under their present stewardship, and unite as a Cymrian empire under a High Lord and Lady. Meet in Council to avoid war, promote peace, and make the nations great once more. Be one people, diverse in your makeup while united in your goals again as you were when you came to this land, but live up to Gwylliam's words this time. If you will do this, I vow that the Lirin will fulfill the words of Queen Terrell and join you as another loyal nation-state in the next Cymrian Age.'

Again the roar of the throng swept over her; she struggled to bear up under it as though standing in the face of the winds of a hurricane. The assemblage was cheering now, applauding and calling out in assent. The rock ledge below her feet hummed as if alive with power, and in her soul she felt the collective agreement of the Cymrians confirmed by the earth itself from which the Bowl was carved. She laughed aloud in amazement; the Moot was a device by which the wisdom of the people was made obvious to the person chairing the Council, channeled up through the Summoner's Ledge. The entire assemblage could make a choice without the need for ballots to be cast or counting to take place. A more sobering thought wiped the smile from her face a moment later; Anwyn and Gwylliam must have known when they stood on the Ledge the desires and wishes of their people. Apparently they were willing to subvert what they knew in order to get what they wanted. It was one more betrayal, and one that turned her stomach.

The assemblage had dissolved into excited chatter as the Cymrians began debating among themselves the next actions to take. Rhapsody held her hand aloft, blinking in shock at the complete and instantaneous silence that ensued.

'I am finished here now,' she said. 'I have called you together; now you must work on your goals under more appropriate leadership. Is there one among you, or several, who are willing to take over the responsibility for chairing the Council now?' A hundred thousand pairs of eyes blinked at her words. 'Come now,' Rhapsody said, a little more anxiously, 'you have much work to do, many differences to resolve, and you can't do it one hundred thousand at a time. Please; will someone at least take on the roles of speakers for each of the Three Fleets? And perhaps the regents of each principality or the sovereigns of the different countries can step forward and take the helm now? Those people can remain behind after the general session is complete and work on the specifics of the new alliance.'

The Cymrians in the assembled throng looked at each other. Achmed stepped forward.

'I will speak for the Firbolg,' he said, 'both those of Cymrian descent, and the entire nation, as a potential member of the alliance.'

'And I for the Nain,' said Faedryth. Voices began to rise in agreement.

'I will represent the principalities of Roland,' came the voice of Tristan Steward, and there was general acclaim to his statement.

One by one, speakers stepped forward to represent various lands, races, and historical assemblies. Rhapsody looked around, trying to find Oelendra, but she was nowhere to be seen. Finally she nominated Rial to speak for the Lirin, citing his knowledge of the details of the war and his current status as viceroy of Tyrian. Ashe, as Chief of the House of Newland, was chosen to speak for the Second Fleet and the Cymrians of Manosse.

At last speakers had been nominated and confirmed for all groups but the other two Cymrian fleets. The cry went up from the Third Fleet.

'Anborn! We nominate Anborn ap Gwylliam!' The Bowl resonated with the agreement of the members of the fleet, though many from the First Fleet stared on in stony silence.

'Do you agree to this?' Rhapsody asked the Third Fleet as a point of procedure.

'We do,' came the answer in unison. The Lord Marshal stepped forward without a trace of his usual arrogance. As had each of the speakers before him, he bowed to the Summoner, but as he stood erect again Rhapsody saw him wink surreptitiously at her, and the reluctance she had felt about their impending marriage began to fade. Their relationship would be enjoyable, and uncomplicated. She was, in fact, growing to like him a great deal. She had not met Ashe's eye when it had been his turn.

Finally came the last and most difficult question: who would speak for the First Fleet, the Cymrians who had fought for Anwyn, and their descendants? The largest number of survivors of the war were part of this group, though many had chosen to define themselves in other manners with other groups, as citizens of a specific country, or by race. There were many whispers and much muttering as the question was debated on the floor of the Bowl. Rhapsody stood patiently and waited for an answer, all the while wishing she had chosen more comfortable shoes. Then a shout came forth from a group of humans.

'I put forward Gwydion ap Llauron as speaker of the First Fleet as well.' The multitude began to clamor among itself again, the nomination attracting much discussion and support. Rhapsody stepped forward to ask the same confirming question of the First Fleet as she had of the Third, when Anborn interrupted in a voice that silenced the throng.

'I object,' he said.

76

Anborn turned to Ashe as the crowd began to rumble with voices again.

'Sorry, boy; I don't mean it as a personal attack. It's a little more complicated than that, I'm afraid.' Ashe nodded brusquely, and looked to Rhapsody again. *Far more complicated*, he thought ruefully.

Arguments began to break out, not the violent threats of before, but debate as to who was the appropriate leader of the First Fleet. An occasional voice could be heard above the rabble.

'The right to the First Fleet belongs to Edwyn Griffyth, as Anwyn's eldest son,' said Hyllion, a Lirin noble who had put forth a suit for Rhapsody's hand. The First Fleet began to call for him.

'Lead us, Edwyn Griffyth!'

'Leave me out of this,' snarled Edwyn Griffyth, and the crowd grew silent for a moment. It was the first time the assemblage had heard him speak. 'I would be far too tempted to lead you to the end of the Earth and push you off. A moment ago I almost believed, however foolishly, that there was hope for you all. But you are doing it again, the same blind servitude that led you to follow my mother to your devastation in the first place! Choose someone who speaks for you, not to whom you were sworn because of which ship your bloody ancestors crossed on! Save your oath of allegiance for the new Lord and Lady.' The assembled Cymrians began to murmur again.

'Oelendra, then,' suggested another voice, and there was a change in the tone of the rumblings. 'She led us after the storm that took Merithyn, brought us safely to this land and established us in here in peace.' The crowd began to mutter in agreement, then took up her name as a chant.

'I decline,' came a quiet voice from the hillside away from the assemblage. Rhapsody looked up to see the ancient warrior standing apart from the others on the lip of the Bowl. She turned and began to walk away.

Rhapsody's heart sank. She knew as Summoner it was her duty to remain neutral, but the words of encouragement were about to spill out anyway. She glanced down at Grunthor and smiled.

'We must forgive ourselves,' she repeated softly; her words echoed around the Bowl.

'Right,' said the giant Firbolg. 'None of my business, of course, but I think you're the perfect choice. If the fleet had listened to you, they never would have gotten into the stupid war in the first place. And if the Lirin had listened to you, neither would they, eh? And if old Annie had listened to you, we'd all be home having supper and not trying to put a bloody continent back together, now, wouldn't we? So what do you say, miss? Give them one last chance to get it right this time.'

After a moment of stunned silence at the Sergeant's speech, the First Fleet burst into cheers and began proclaiming her name even louder. Rhapsody blew Grunthor a kiss, then turned to Oelendra for her answer. Even as far away as she was Rhapsody could see a glint of tears in the warrior's eyes.

'Very well,' she said, and the cheers turned to shouts of acclamation.

'Good,' said Rhapsody, blinking back tears herself. 'Now, I suggest that the various speakers come together in one of the meeting rooms of Ylorc while the rest of us make merry and get to know each other. Perhaps that will engender goodwill enough to keep us through the next several days of session, through the selection of the new Lord and Lady, and the other work of rebuilding. You asked of the Future; we are making it here.' She picked up her harp again; there was a collective intake of breath from the Council.

'I'm not Manwyn, you know,' Rhapsody said, a glint of humor returning to her eyes. 'I can only tell you what I think is possible; it's your choice to make it true or not.'

She signaled to a small, golden-haired child within the Lirin delegation.

'Aric – you are the Future. Come and sing with me.' The child ran to the foot of the Summoner's Rise.

She began to play again, this time a trippingly melodic tune. It was a Gwadd song from the old land called 'Bright Flows the Meadow Stream,' a love song to the rolling hills and pasturelands that were the home of the diminutive folk. As she sang, a number of them came forward beside the golden-haired boy, along with the other smaller races with which they had interbred, and stood, transfixed, listening to her, a few endeavoring to sing along. The tiny pointed faces shone, the large, angular eyes glittered, and the slender forms of the Gwadd cast long shadows in the afternoon sun.

When the song had been taken up by that contingent she wove into it another, the only Nain song she had ever learned, which was a mining chant that was sung within the caverns as the people of the Night Mountain went about their endless labor, uncovering the treasures of the earth. The chant was picked up instantly by ten thousand Nain voices, voices deep and rich as the earth in which they lived. Rhapsody had chosen a key that would blend harmoniously with the Gwadd song, and as they sang together their voices resonated through the Moot, echoing through the bones of the gathered Cymrians.

One by one she added the songs of other lands, anthems and hymns, the simple farming songs the Filids sang while working in the fields, the sea chanteys of Serendair, joined by the voices of each group that recognized it as its own. The rhapsody of the Past she had sung in tribute to Anwyn had become a glorious symphony, its movements diverse as the people who stood in the Bowl before her, but beautiful in their unity. The faces of the Cymrians mirrored the brilliance of the afternoon sun that was sinking low beyond the Teeth, and in her heart, for the second time, she felt one with them, and the love she shared with Elynsynos for them as a people. It was like looking for one last time at the Patchworks in her homeland, the fields of grass and grain making a beautiful quilt in the landscape below the sky.

At last the opus was finished, and silence took root in the Bowl as Rhapsody put her harp away. The gleaming aura of hypnotic power that had surrounded her since she braved the Fire at the Earth's core seemed to be gone; now it hovered in the air of the Moot, brightening each of the souls that had heard the song, tying them together in a common bond.

She turned toward the west and began her vespers, singing to the setting sun and the evening star that glimmered above the tallest crag of Achmed's mountains.

The evensong was picked up by tens of thousands of Lirin voices, many from the Tyrian contingent, but others from the various fleets, Roland and the Isle of the Sea Mages. It rang to the evening sky, echoing through the Bowl and over the Orlandan plains, through the Teeth and over the heath and beyond. They sang the sun down as the sky filled with glorious ribbons of orange and red, entwining through the azure blue of the western horizon, which reached out its arms into the fading darkness as if reluctant to leave.

When the echo of the last note had died away, Rhapsody shouldered her pack. 'My service to you has now ended,' she said to the assemblage. 'If you will have me among your ranks, I will be glad to join you now and leave the leadership of this Council to those whom you have chosen from among you.'

At the crest of the rising wave of acclamation, Ashe leapt forward from his place in the crowd and signaled to the departing Summoner.

'Your Majesty, may I have the floor?'

Rhapsody sighed wearily; she had been standing all day and her feet were sore. 'You certainly may,' she said, grateful for the break. She sat down on a carved rock that functioned well as a stool near the back of the Ledge.

Ashe broke from the ranks of the Manossian contingent and ran to the Speaker's Rise. He climbed to the highest crest and looked down at the sea of his fellow Cymrians, the red light of the setting sun making his hair gleam as though crowned with fire.

'As Speaker of the Second Fleet, I ask that we turn our attention at once to the matter of our leadership as a Council. As Anwyn said, with no Lord or Lady, we are not a Council. Gwylliam is dead, and I feel it is clear that though she still lives, Anwyn has proven herself unfit time and again to be our leader.'

To this there was a general murmur of consent. Even those present who had voted to keep her as Lady at the end of the war could not now agree to it. Time and Anwyn's earlier behavior had guaranteed it.

'So,' Ashe continued in a louder voice, 'to that end, I nominate Her Majesty, Rhapsody, Queen of the Lirin, as Lady Cymrian!' He had to shout to be heard over the commotion that erupted. 'She is of the First Generation, but sailed with no fleet, and therefore has no preference for any one group over another. She is one of the Three of whom Manwyn spoke. Indeed, she is the Sky in the prophecy, the Liringlas, the one who encompasses all, that cannot be divided; the only means by which peace will come and unity will result. She has killed the F'dor, the ancient enemy of our people and bringer of so much woe since our flight from Serendair. She has united the Lirin and brought peace between them and the principality of Bethany, with whom they were on the verge of war. She has helped the Bolg enter a new age of peace and prosperity. As with the last of the kings of Serendair, she is of mixed blood, signifying a new unity between the races. She is foretold to be our Lady, Anwyn's opposite, the one who can bring us together where Anwyn drove us asunder. And if that is not enough, she has managed to silence my grandmother, which by itself is an act worthy of high praise.'

Consternation had come into Rhapsody's eyes at his initial words, but she was unable to interrupt him; she had recognized him and had yielded him the floor. As the throng began to laugh at his final words and cheer his suggestion she leapt to her feet, shock blanching her face.

'Are you out of your—'

'I second the nomination,' shouted Anborn, and the groundswell of roaring approval grew louder.

'Wait,' Rhapsody said, panic setting in. 'I object.'

'Rhapsody, you are out of order,' said Ashe, a humorously wicked look in his eyes. 'A motion has been made and seconded. As Summoner it is your responsibility to make sure that motion is put before the entire Council for a vote; now, kindly do so.'

Rhapsody glared at him in fury. Then she turned to the Council, and tried to keep the desperation she felt from showing through in her voice.

'Are there any more nominations?' The Council resolved into silence. 'Any at all?' The stillness was broken only by a few quiet murmurs and whispered statements. 'What about objections? Doesn't anybody else object?'

'Apparently not, m'lady,' came Ashe's voice again. 'As a Council it seems we are of one mind; united as in the prophecy. Am I right?'

A thunderstrike of assent roared across the valley, and Rhapsody could feel the rock ledge she stood on vibrate with power as the cheering rumbled through the Bowl and up through her feet. She felt a surge, a strengthening of her soul and building of her body the like of which she had not experienced since she had passed through the fires of the earth. It was as though the Moot, responding to the unanimous voice of the Cymrian Council, was granting her the wisdom and fortitude she would need as their leader, a new bond with the people and the land. She finally understood what it meant to have a granted power: she was the Lady Cymrian. It was not what she had wanted, or expected; only the wisdom she had received from the joy of the assemblage prevented her from bursting into bitter tears.

'My friends,' roared Edwyn Griffyth, 'let us celebrate!'

Ashe saw the look on Rhapsody's face and felt his stomach twist. He turned to the crowd again.

'I can see that His Majesty, the Firbolg king, our host, has arranged a banquet on the field,' he said, pointing outside the Bowl to the tents Achmed's forces had erected. 'Let us break bread and return for the final session of the night when the moon has risen above the Teeth.' There was enthusiastic agreement, and the throng began to dissolve into chattering groups, mixing within each of the factions. Old friends met and wept, old enemies clasped hands, all in joyous celebration of the possibilities brought about by the new Cymrian Age, the new Council, the new Lady. He turned to look again at Rhapsody, to gauge how she was accustoming herself to the idea of her new role, but she was gone.

Bright torches and dim lanterns had been staked and strung across the wide fields at the foot of the Teeth, bringing a cheery light into the darkness of the early night. Tables laden with food had been set out, wine was passed around freely, and merry laughter resounded through the mountains and echoed over the heath above. The Cymrians had not gathered together in celebration since the wedding of Anwyn and Gwylliam, and the festive mood was infectious, goodwill roaring through the crowd like a strong wind.

Ashe looked around for Rhapsody at the supper. He could feel her presence there, and just as certainly felt her displeasure at what had transpired. When initially he had decided to make her Lady – it had been confirmed by the Patriarch's ring on Midsummer's Night the previous year, but he had actually determined it long before – he knew that her ingrained belief in an antiquated system of nobility would make it difficult for her to adjust to being royal. He fervently believed she would adapt, as she had to being the Lirin queen, but now, sensing the bile that she was carrying in her stomach and throat made him worry that perhaps he was wrong.

He had been unable to reach her during the meal. His fellow Manossians, and many members of the other fleets and the courts of Roland, stopped him at every turn, exclaiming with joy in the knowledge that he was still alive, welcoming him back. Comrades in arms from the battles he had fought in, as well as friends from long ago, and especially Lord Stephen, expected him to regale him with his exploits and fill in the gaps of the past twenty years for them. Rhapsody herself was swarmed with admirers; leaders of every principality, the nation of Sorbold, and the Nonaligned States sought a moment with her to establish ties even before she was coronated. Her face was serene and pleasant on the rare occasions when Ashe could catch a glimpse of it, but he knew her calm countenance belied the building agitation she was really feeling. Her eyes bore the signs of a deer in thrall or a cornered rabbit.

Finally the moon crested the tallest crag of the Teeth, and the horn sounded, summoning the Cymrians back to the business at hand. It took almost an hour for the assemblage to be called to order again, so insistent was the merriment. Rhapsody looked out over the Cymrian populace, the sea of diverse faces shining up at her in the glow of the full moon ascendant now above them. When the sun had risen on this day she had hoped to become one of them, this refugee population from her homeland, and now she was their sovereign; it was surreal to the point of bordering on the absurd.

She took a deep breath, and exhaled slowly, willing herself to remain calm. She was addressing them now not as the Summoner but as their Lady; as a result when she moved forward to speak, silence fell like a curtain almost instantaneously.

'What shall we address first?' she asked the crowd. The question roared forth in many different phrasings, but the intention was universally the same.

'Who, then, shall be our Lord?'

Her selection and confirmation as the Cymrian's choice of Lady had given Rhapsody a new understanding of the Cymrian people, and as a result she could discern their comments more clearly than she had before. Previously their shouts had seemed nothing more than the noise of a rabble; now they came forth as the spoken thoughts of individuals, crashing on her brain like waves on a beach. *This must be a little like having dragon sense,* she thought. Ashe had described it as being acutely aware of the minutiae around him all the time; in a way she felt the same thing.

'The real question is, who holds the right?' asked a Nain warrior named Gar.

'The right lies with each of us; anyone can be Lord,' answered someone from the First Wave.

'But the Lord Cymrian was Gwylliam, a descendent of the ancient Seren kings. Should we not choose again from that House? It was the House that led us safely from the Island,' said Calthrop, another of the Nain contingent.

'And it was also that line that led us into warfare,' said Harklerode, one of the soldiers in the army of Canderre.

'The mistakes of one man should not condemn his descendants.'

'Nor should the glory of one's ancestors decide one's worthiness.'

'The Lady is First Generation. Should not the Lord have been born in these lands? With the blood of these people in his veins? Is that not why we chose to follow the Lord and Lady before? Because he was of the old line and she of the new?'

'But they were married, should not we have the Lord and Lady married once more?'

'The Lord and Lady were married to ensure a reunification and alliance.'

'It was the marriage that caused the war, if you remember.'

'We must have a married Lady and Lord. No one with the wisdom necessary to be selected Lord by this Council would be fool enough to strike our chosen Lady, as Gwylliam did; he'd have the entire population demanding his blood.'

'Besides, she's the Iliachenva'ar. If she can take down the demon, it seems likely she can defend herself.'

'Well said. It makes sense that they be married, then, particularly because it solves the issue of succession.'

'Hold.'

The voice of the newly named Lady rang throughout the Moot. It had deserted her in the tumult that had led to her being confirmed into a position she felt unqualified for; now it had returned with a vengeance as her blood boiled.

'Aren't you all very presumptuous. How dare you speak about me as if I were a brood mare? Do you think that you own me now, that you suddenly have the right to decide my destiny in all aspects of my life? I find it extremely offensive that you would instinctively assume that I am even available for an arranged marriage. How do you know that I am not married now? No one asked my marital status. And even if you had, how do you know whether or not I have promised myself already? For all your potential, you can be a most infuriating people. If you feel the need to make this choice for your Lady, she will not be me. I gladly will yield my title before any more discussion of this nature ensues.'

Rhapsody strode to the end of the Summoner's Ledge and tried to climb down. As before, when Anwyn was attacking Oelendra, she found herself unable to leave the rock ledge as shouts of dissent rose all around her.

'No!' came the cry from the Moot; the repeated calls modulated on the wind, resembling the sound of booing at the Sorboldian arena. The clamor receded as Anborn hurried to the top of the Speaker's Rise.

'Forgive us, m'lady,' he said, smiling; the tone in his voice was commanding, ringing with the timbre of one who had long been accustomed to addressing an army. 'In the excitement of being a united people again we fell into our old pigheaded, arrogant ways. The Third Fleet, and I believe our fellow Cymrians, humbly recognize your right to make this choice yourself.' He turned to the crowd. 'Am I right?'

The roar of agreement would have unbalanced Rhapsody and possibly knocked her off the ledge if she had been able to leave it. She struggled to stand upright and looked at Anborn. He was still grinning at her, and she returned his smile uncertainly; there was something in his expression that unsettled her. Within herself she felt a strange tug, and she looked around the crowd in the torchlight to find Ashe staring wildly at her. His face was frozen in an emotion that resembled panic; it was painful to see. She looked away quickly.

'Atta girl, Your Ladyship,' Rhapsody heard Grunthor whisper in the crowd. She turned his way and summoned a smile.

'All right, then,' she said, clearing her throat. 'Let's try this again.'

77

The tiresome arguments went on until almost midnight. Rhapsody's head throbbed at the monotony of the speakers from throughout the Council repeating and refuting each other.

'Why not have two Ladies and no Lord?'

'Equal representation of the sexes in the seat of power, I believe.'

'I have no desire to be ruled by a Nain Lord!' yelled one of the Lirin during the point when Faedryth was being considered for the Lordship.

'And I have no desire to sit in the flower garden of an all-Lirin court!' responded an annoyed Nain.

'Then we must find someone with ties to all the races,' Oelendra said.

'And someone whose birth lies on this side of the world, not the other,' said one of the tall golden people with Edwyn Griffyth. 'Otherwise the union of the people with the new land will not be symbolized.'

'I would leap from this Ledge to my death if I could,' Rhapsody sighed. 'I want the Lord Cymrian to be someone who can fix this stupid thing so I can leave when I want to.'

The Cymrians looked up at their new Lady in horror, then decided she was throwing in a joke to break the mood. They laughed uproariously before going back to their monotonous debate. *They don't know me very well,* Rhapsody thought. She looked around the Bowl absently and caught the eye of Ashe, who was smiling up at her sympathetically. She turned her attention promptly back to the Council.

'There is only one line that holds the ties between the old world and the new one, and that is the line of Anwyn,' Oelendra was saying. Her statement had caused a shocked silence; her enmity with Anwyn was well known and recently demonstrated. 'What other blood binds the ancient peoples of Serendair, oldest of the old world, with the blood of the dragon whose essence was inured in this land? Firstborn mixed with Firstborn. What is more, that line carries the Right of Kings through the blood of Gwylliam. He was the descendant of the Seren high king, lord of all the races.'

'Then you are saying to trust once more in the line that has brought us to ruin?' asked Nielsen, a Sorboldian duke.

'I am saying that they are the only House which has bonds to us all, and that perhaps they, more than any other, might learn from the wrongs of their ancestors,' Oelendra answered.

'But who then?'

'The Right of Kings went from eldest son to eldest son,' a human from the Third Wave said. 'That would mean Edwyn Griffyth.'

'Apparently you haven't been listening,' the High Sea Mage said, his silver eyebrows drawing together. 'I have no desire to rule anyone or anything. If I am selected, I will flee to the highest mountain or deepest sea and hide from you until you go off and kill yourselves again. I will never –

let me repeat that for the conveniently deaf among you – *never* accept the title of Lord Cymrian.'

Rhapsody sighed inwardly. Not being born to rulership, she had had no idea that outright refusal was an option. She would have to make note of that.

'Then the title would have fallen to Llauron, but, of course, he is dead,' said the same man who had proposed the elder brother.

'Well, in a way that's true,' said a deep, cultured voice resonating from the rock all around that formed the Bowl. It could be felt in the feet of everyone standing within the Moot, and caused the debates to choke off into stunned silence. 'But I came anyway; I hope no one minds. I heard the call as well, after all.'

'What kind of stupid trickery is this?' demanded Gaerhart of the Second Fleet.

'No trickery whatsoever, I assure you,' came the answer. From within the living earth itself a great iridescent gray shape emerged; a moment later it took the form of a vaporous serpent over a hundred feet long. Huge wings unfolded from its sides, and the glitter of silver and copper shone in its scales. Its size was hard to determine, being coiled, but as it raised its immense head Rhapsody could tell that its mass was close to that of Elynsynos. Enormous arms lifted its forebody off the ground as it rose and surveyed the Cymrian assemblage, all but a handful of whom had fallen back in utter panic at the sight of it. A great hot wind blasted them as it spoke, and they closed their eyes, trembling in fear.

In response the dragon opened its own eyes to reveal two vast orbs that shone like blue fire. The Cymrians fell to the ground in fear, all except the Three and the heirs of Anwyn.

'You become more like Mother every time I see you,' Anborn said to Llauron with a smile. Edwyn Griffyth eyed his middle brother in contempt.

'Good to see you, too,' the dragon replied. 'Glad you could make it to the Council, Ed.'

'I am regretting it more by the moment,' answered Edwyn Griffyth, making no attempt to disguise the disgust in his voice. 'Hasn't anyone bothered to tell you that grand entrances are only for court occasions?'

'And I consider this one. I am here to express my best wishes to the new Lady Cymrian, and my congratulations to the assemblage for their wisdom in selecting so well.' The giant wyrm made a bow in Rhapsody's general direction, but the Lirin queen and new Lady Cymrian did not respond; instead she stared straight at the dragon without comment, all the while avoiding looking directly into his eyes. The dragon cleared its massive throat, a sound that sent shivers up a hundred thousand spines.

'Ahem, yes, well, let it be known to all present that I am, or at least was, Llauron, son of Anwyn and formerly the Invoker of the Filids.'

'Are you here to claim the Lordship, then?' asked Edwyn Griffyth.

'Goodness, no,' said the dragon. 'That would be rather silly, now, wouldn't it? None of the crowns or robes of state would fit. No, whatever rights or claims on that sort of thing I gave up when I gave up my humanity. I am here to let you know that I have passed those rights and claims on to my son, who has earned them on his own through his acts of selfless bravery in defending the members of all the fleets against the treachery of the F'dor, and by avenging my, er, death at the hands of the traitor Khaddyr, who was in league with that demon. Is that acceptable to the assemblage?'

'Do you expect an honest answer while you look like that?' asked Anborn, unimpressed.

'Oh. Well, this is what I am now, but your point is well taken.' With that the great serpent began to diminish until he no longer filled the Bowl with his presence. The ethereal glow of his former state vanished and he became solid, appearing in the form of a dragonlike lizard of fifteen or so feet in length. He crawled over the floor of the Moot, causing the Cymrians to scatter in all directions, and took his place by Ashe's feet, where he settled down in the grassy dirt and got comfortable. He glanced up in amusement at his son, who looked mortified.

'Sorry, my boy, it's a family tradition: parents in our line live solely to be an embarrassment to their sons.' Ashe sighed.

'Which is why Anborn and I have no heirs,' said Edwyn Griffyth testily.

Rhapsody watched as the Cymrians slowly made their way back to the center of the Bowl, leaving a wide circle around Ashe and the attendant dragon at his feet. She felt a smile come over her face at the sight in spite of herself, and Ashe looked up and met the smile with his own. It was just the sort of situation they would have taken great pleasure in laughing about together, nestled under the covers of her bed in Elysian, whispering and giggling outrageously in the shadows of the firelight. The shared thought caused them both to lose their smiles a moment later and look away, albeit for different reasons.

The discussion resumed again. For a while the alternatives to the House of Gwylliam came up again, different factions putting forth many different candidates for the Lordship until Rhapsody was sure they were further away from reaching a decision than they had ever been. Eventually even Achmed and Grunthor were brought up as possibilities, which confirmed her assessment.

It was perhaps Achmed's nomination as a prospect that brought the conversation back on course. He stated emphatically to the Council that, if selected as Lord, he would cede the power back to Rhapsody; he saw no reason to have a Lord at all.

'You've selected a leader, and now you want to subordinate her to another,' he said disdainfully. 'There is no such thing as a successfully shared authority. If the Lord and Lady disagree, who traditionally has the final word?'

'The Lord,' answered Longinotta, a Gwaddi woman of the First Generation who had served as sergeant-at-arms in the court of Anwyn and Gwylliam.

Achmed nodded. 'You see? If she is your choice, respect her enough to let her lead you. Why complicate things unnecessarily?'

'Nonsense.' The voice of Tristan Steward echoed through the Moot, breaking the debate and bringing all conversation to a halt. 'You are missing an obvious choice, someone who has experience at sharing power equitably and successfully.' He stared at the assemblage pointedly.

'And who would that be, Tristan?' Stephen Navarne asked guardedly. The expression on his face indicated that he feared he already knew the answer.

Tristan turned to Lord Cunliffe, the head of his House, and nodded. Lord Cunliffe cleared his throat.

'It seems – well, appropriate that we select Tristan as the new Lord Cymrian,' Cunliffe said haltingly. 'He has done a marvelous job as the Regent of Bethany, providing leadership in a leaderless time, making the army strong again.' Tristan Steward leaned over and murmured something in Lord Cunliffe's ear. 'Right, of course. In addition to all his other sterling virtues, the Lord Roland would be a fine match for the new Lady Cymrian, respecting her authority and helping her to make the right decisions. He is a man of great integrity. Tristan Steward should be the Lord Cymrian.'

'Tristan Steward should be devoured by weasels!' thundered Edwyn Griffyth in a booming voice that echoed off the Moot. 'Tristan Steward is a man of great *integrity?* Tristan Steward is a jackass!' Not a sound could be heard as Gwylliam's eldest son rose to a stand and pointed his staff at the trembling Lord Roland.

'How dare you bring an army, any army, not to mention a force of that size, to this place? Are you just the most arrogant man in history, or are you merely an idiot of titanic proportions? This is a place of peace, of Council. Every Cymrian, even those not extensively schooled in our history as you must have been, knows the law of the Moot. Aggression is strictly forbidden in this place! How dare you come as if to lay siege? I denounce you, man. I would rather take the lordship myself than see it in your hands, and I believe I've been clear about how much I want that to happen. Step back, you fool. Make ready to break camp and crawl back to Roland as soon as the Lady dismisses the Council.'

A wave of hooting laughter and applause swelled through the Moot and crested, then vanished as the Lady Cymrian stood up.

'Stop that,' she said severely. 'The Lord Roland has been elected the Speaker for the provinces of Roland, a rather significant piece of the new Cymrian Alliance. His role is an important one, and I will be listening very carefully to his counsel during the meetings with the Speakers after the general session concludes. I look forward to meeting with him after he has sent his army home. And I don't want to hear of *anyone* consigned to be devoured by weasels.' She stared with exaggerated severity at Edwyn Griffyth; the Sea Mage chuckled and bowed deferentially. Rhapsody sat back down.

Edwyn Griffyth's comments sparked an entirely new debate, the result of which was the determination, by general consensus, that the Lordship should go to one of Anwyn and Gwylliam's heirs. Grunthor walked out of the talks in disappointment, but Achmed merely shrugged. He looked up at Rhapsody, who was lying on her stomach on the Ledge, her head cradled in her arms.

'You are exhausting the Lady Cymrian,' Rial said angrily. 'Let us either call an end to this session unresolved, or make a choice. This is ridiculous.' A general murmur of consent rippled through the crowd.

'If we are going to follow the Right of Kings, the Heir Presumptive is Edwyn Griffyth,' said Longinotta. 'He has refused the title, is that right, m'lord?'

'I'm not sure what more I can do to make that any clearer,' said the leader of the Sea Mages with an annoyed growl.

'The Right then goes to the remaining heirs, without regard to order,' Longinotta continued. 'That would leave Llauron—'

Llauron had grown weary of the discussion and had stretched out, partially coiled, behind his son at the head of the delegation from the Second Fleet, under the banner of the House of Newland. To all appearances he seemed asleep, yet when his name was suggested his eyelid opened a crack, sending an eerie blue light across the floor of the Bowl as the fire of his eye settled on the tiny sergeant-at-arms. The metallic scraping of scales could be heard as he stretched out on the ground, uncoiling slightly, and his voice, dignified but cold and reptilian, issued forth. It sent shivers down the spines of almost all who heard it.

'You *must* be joking,' he said. He closed his eye again and shifted into a more comfortable sleeping position.

'Your point is taken,' said Rhapsody hastily, and the Council seemed to agree.

It took a moment before Longinotta could continue. Finally she spoke again. 'That leaves Gwydion, son of Llauron, who now holds the rights to direct descendancy as his father would, and Anborn ap Gwylliam. The choice is between these two, without a clear favor going to either.' Instantly debate broke out all around the floor of the Bowl, the sound of arguments and discussions filling the air with noise.

'But Anborn led the armies against the First Fleet!'

'As Llauron did against the Third Fleet, is his heir any better?'

'Should not each person be judged on his own actions?'

'Anborn burned the outer forest of Tyrian! How can we be expected to forgive that?'

'And Anborn saved the Lirin in the attack of the Khadazian pirate fleet not seventy years afterward – or has that also been forgotten?'

'The favor of the Nain lies with Anborn,' said Faedryth with ringing authority, and much of the Moot fell silent. Then another voice spoke up.

'Not the Nain of Manosse. We stand by Gwydion.'

'We need a sign. Perhaps the Lady should consult the stars.'

'The stars tell me I should have been in bed hours ago,' muttered Rhapsody, and the multitude laughed uneasily.

'The Gwadd support Gwydion as well, he has always protected us, even while he was walking the world unseen.'

'Though admittedly, Anborn did save the Gwaddi village of Finidel fifteen years ago—'

'If we want the Lady to marry the Lord, perhaps we should ask her which one she likes better.'

'Again I tell you that Anborn holds the political and military—'

'Aren't we doing this to avoid the use of military—'

'Of course Gwydion did serve well in the battle of—'

Rhapsody closed her ears to the discussions; she couldn't stand them anymore. Despair welled in her heart and found its way into her eyes. Her gaze fell on Ashe, or Gwydion, as he was now being called. He was standing quietly, avoiding being drawn into the discussions of his worthiness. He had the same slightly sad expression on his face as she did, coupled with a look of complete indifference to the outcome of the discussions. Understanding dawned on her: he didn't care for the position any more than she did.

Then, as she watched him, he looked up at her and smiled, and inadvertently she smiled back. His metallic hair reflected the torchlight, and his blue eyes gleamed at her. As in their days together, the look in those eyes caused her heart to leap. His scaled armor glistened in the soft misty light of Crynella's candle, looking for all the world like moonlight on the ocean waves. In his left hand he held the white staff of the Invoker, the same hand that wore the ring of the Patriarch, and her words of long ago came back to her now.

Are you aware that the original religion was a combination of the practices of Gwynwood and Sepulvarta, and that it was the Cymrian split that forced the schism? If you are planning to heal the rift in the governance of the Cymrian people, why not heal the religious rift as well? I've witnessed holy rites in both churches, and they are much closer to each other than you may believe. Who needs a Patriarch and an Invoker? Why can't you be both? Or why can't the Lord Cymrian be the governing head of both sects, and leave the ecclesiastical rule to the leaders of each faction? Recognize the right for people to have different belief systems, but still be united as one monotheistic people.

He no longer looked to her as he had when they were lovers. Even knowing his face, she would not have recognized him as the cloaked vagrant that she had met on the streets of Bethe Corbair that morning, or as the lonely forester who had served as her guide and traveling companion. Indeed, now he looked to her every inch a king, a lordly figure standing at the head of his House, power radiating from him, a dragon at his feet; his image belonged on a crest or a shield, or in a court painting. Despite his obvious suitability, in a tiny corner of her soul she hoped he would be passed over, only because she did not wish to be forced to be near him.

She cast a furtive glance around for his wife, the woman he had been telling her about for almost a year, but saw no one standing near him.

Rhapsody drove the selfish thought from her mind. He was the clear choice, and she knew it.

She felt eyes on her now, and looked up to see Anborn watching her intently. He, too, had been silent through the discussion of the Lordship, calmly watching the discourse. He had the appearance of a king as well, and he had seen her watching Ashe, she was sure of it. A calculating smile, with almost a hint of cruelty to it, came over his face. The look sent shivers down her spine. She had begun to recognize that reptilian expression on the faces of each member of the family; it was the look their faces took on when they were about to strike. The blood drained from her face as Anborn suddenly stood up and strode to the Speaker's Rise. In the absence of another speaker, he took control of the floor.

'People of the Council!' he intoned loudly, causing the crowd to fall immediately silent. 'I have heard countless recriminations cast on me for my role in the Great War, and I wish to spare my supporters any more effort defending me. To those charges I acknowledge my guilt. I was the general of Gwylliam's armies; I did sack the Lirin wood and killed countless members of the First Fleet. And yet the loudest accusations I hear come from faces I saw across the fields of battle, guilty themselves, though perhaps not as talented at dispensing death as I. It was a war, a terrible war. Which of you who would find fault with me played no part in it yourselves?'

The silence of the Bowl remained unbroken. Anborn smiled; it was a victorious smile that sobered a moment later into a serious expression. 'I performed my duty, not out of love for my father or hatred of my mother, but for the same reason my brother and all of you did: because I wanted to defend what I believed was worth defending. Caught up in the madness, I undoubtedly overstepped my bounds, and for that reason I apologize. To the Lirin and their new queen, I apologize the most, not only for the siege of their cities, but for the wrong done to them by my mother and father. It was not their war, but they suffered greatly for it all the same.

'In addition to our acts of cruelty in that war, however, there were countless tales of compassion, and I think that is because, in truth, we were only trying to serve what we loved and were loyal to. The only participants of which this is not true were Anwyn and Gwylliam themselves. We have heard much recrimination of my mother this night, and seemingly let my father's crimes pass, but I tell you now, as his chosen heir and general, Gwylliam bore as much guilt for this war as my mother did. In truth it was he who started it, and his own pride allowed it to escalate as it did. So, as his heir and the speaker for the Third Fleet, his army, I apologize on his behalf to the First Fleet as well, for our crimes against them.'

A moment of awkward silence followed. Then Oelendra stepped forward.

'As speaker for the First Fleet, I accept your apology, and offer ours to the Third Fleet as well.' A rolling wave of acclamation went up, breaking as it crested into cheers and whistles. Anborn held the Council spellbound, and he knew it. He cleared his throat and continued.

'As our new Lady has said, we must forgive ourselves. I have tried to make up for those crimes by serving as best I could in the new countries and lands that have formed since the war. In Roland and Dronsdale, in the Nain realms and Sorbold, and many other kingdoms, I am known as a soldier and a leader of men. I speak to you as such tonight, not as Gwylliam's heir or the Speaker of the Third Fleet, but as a man who has lived among more of the peoples of this country than any other. As such, there are several truths that have become apparent to me tonight.

'The first is that the responsibility for bringing the peoples of the new world together lies with us, for this is the new world no longer, but our home, and we are as responsible for its politics and peace as we were for the war that tore it asunder. And the people of this land do need a peace to be invoked, a peace that can only be brought to them by Cymrians. And we can only lead this land to peace if we are led ourselves by one who has lived among them as I have.'

Rhapsody's throat began to constrict; Anborn was taking the Lordship before her eyes. There was nothing she could say.

'It has also been said that my House alone can provide that leader, and that is also true, for we hold the tie between the races and kingdoms. Only in the children of Anwyn and Gwylliam are the bonds of the old and new world united; only in the House of the Seren kings have the races been brought together. Only one man here knows armies and hospices, peasants and kings as if he were one of them. Only one man is descended of all the fleets, and holds both the offices of Invoker and Patriarch. He is descended not only of the First and Third Fleet, but of the Second as well. And so I, Anborn ap Gwylliam, son of Anwyn, do nominate Lord Gwydion ap Llauron ap Gwylliam, of the House of Newland, Speaker of the Second Fleet, son of Anwyn's chosen heir, Kirsdarkenvar, to be the Lord Cymrian. He served no part in the war, but has served his whole life selflessly to heal the rift that it caused. Can any but he fulfill this role?'

A roar of agreement swelled through the Bowl and spilled out over the fields. It rolled up the Teeth and into the caves of the Bolg, disturbing their sleep yet again. It rang over the army of Roland, sending silver shivers of hope for peace through them, even as they lay encamped for war.

Through the Summoner's Ledge Rhapsody could feel the Moot taking stock of the appellations and determining that Gwydion was in fact the overwhelming choice for the Lordship, and acclaimed him as such. But Ashe was staring at Anborn in shock. His uncle just smiled and held out his arms to him as though presenting him to the multitude.

'The House of Fergus abstains!' shouted someone from within the Second Fleet, and that group burst into laughter; apparently it was an old rivalry and more a joke than anything else. 'Well, at least they didn't object,' someone said to Ashe in a blaring, jovial voice.

The cheering grew louder, and a moment later the frenzied crowd swept Gwydion onto their shoulders and into a sea of celebration. Likewise, even more of them stormed the Ledge where Rhapsody stood, hoping to talk to her or touch her.

Rhapsody bolted. She ran down the ridge that led to the Summoner's Ledge and threw herself into Grunthor's waiting arms.

'Get me out of here,' she gasped.

The giant Firbolg nodded and carried her over the rocky outcroppings, shouldering his way through the crowd. When they got to a spot the Cymrians had not reached he put her down and walked beside her, blocking her from view. They headed together in quick step for the exit of the Moot that bordered on the entrance to the Cauldron.

As she made her way out of the Bowl, Rhapsody heard a voice calling her name; there was an urgency in it she could not ignore. She turned to see a woman, Liringlas, running to her, arms open. She was about the age her mother had been when she last saw her, and, though she looked nothing like her, Rhapsody felt her throat tighten all the same.

When she got within arms' reach she held out both her hands, and Rhapsody took them, still having no idea who she was. The woman stared at her in amazement, but with none of the awe that made her feel freakish. There were tears in the woman's eyes, and they glistened in the dark as they rolled over the fine lines that etched the rosy skin of her face.

'Do you remember me?' she asked softly. There was something familiar about her, but after a moment of study, Rhapsody still could not place her. The crowd of excited Cymrians was coming nearer.

'No, I'm afraid I don't; I'm sorry,' she answered.

'It's me – Analise,' the woman said, and she began to cry harder.

Rhapsody thought for a moment, and her eyes widened in amazement. It was the child Michael the Wind of Death had called Petunia, the one she had wrested from him. The last she had seen of her was on the day they had ventured together into the Wide Meadows, under the protection of Nana's guards, to search out the leader of the Lirin that lived there. It had been a sad parting, but not the first or last time Rhapsody would say goodbye to someone she loved for his or her own sake. The Lirin had taken the child in warmly, and Rhapsody had long comforted herself with the image of her, sitting before the leader on her horse, waving goodbye and smiling, both she and Analise knowing that she would be well cared for.

Tears welled in her own eyes, and the women embraced tightly. Rhapsody's tears turned to sobbing as she realized this was the first person from the Island that she had known who survived, aside from her two Bolg friends, someone who knew her in the first life. Rhapsody caught Grunthor's eye, and drew Analise aside as he stepped between the two of them and the crowd pressing toward her, giving them some privacy.

In their ancient language they caught each other up; at least, Analise told Rhapsody her story and answered the questions the Lirin queen could not hold back. She had sailed with the Second Fleet, and had settled in Manosse, living quite happily and avoiding the war that had destroyed so much of the other two fleets. She had heard of the new queen's coronation, and had determined to make the voyage anyway as a gesture of respect when she felt the call of the horn. She was astonished to find that the queen and the Rhapsody she knew were one and the same.

'I will never forget what you did for me,' she said, her face breaking under the weight of emotion.

Rhapsody shuddered. 'Please do; I have tried to.'

'I can't,' Analise said, her smile returning. 'You saved me from a far worse fate than I could even imagine, Rhapsody. Because of you I found a happy life, and survived the war on the Island; I'm content in Manosse, and I have a family of my own now. I shall have to bring my grandchildren to see you later, to meet the woman to whom they owe their existence.'

Rhapsody looked embarrassed. 'Please, Analise, don't tell them that; I would love to see them, though. You are welcome in Tyrian any time you wish to come.' Exhaustion was setting in, and sadness was beginning to call to her soul again. She gave Analise a kiss, with the promise they would meet up the next day, and, when she was sure none of the celebrating Cymrians could see her, she tried to slip away in all haste for Elysian.

It didn't work. There were thousands now, primed with wine and in the mood to celebrate, calling her name, cheering her. Rhapsody thought she had spoken at supper with the major people, but, looking around, she saw no end in sight of well-wishers and important heads of state. To greet them all would be impossible, and to deal with just the heads of House would take long past dawn. She had to get out of there.

The crush of admiring subjects was beginning to make Rhapsody nauseated. She felt trapped, and panic was coursing through her, causing her palms to sweat and her heart to race. As the wall of humanity began to rush toward her, she saw a coppery glint out of the corner of her eye; Ashe, who himself was surrounded by well-wishers, was attempting, as politely as he could, to make his way to her side. He caught her glance and signaled to her, then moved a little more through the crowd.

The prospect of speaking to him was more than Rhapsody could stand. She bolted again, and ran straight for Rial, whom she could see on the other side of the exit. As she approached him a broad smile appeared that was quickly replaced by a look of concern when he saw the expression on her face. He held his hands out to her and she ran into his arms.

'M'lady, what's the matter?' He gave her a comforting squeeze, then pulled back from her to look into her eyes again.

'Please, Rial,' she gasped, more from anxiety than exertion, 'get me out of here. Please; I'm going to break down if you don't.'

Understanding took root in her viceroy immediately, and he executed a quick half-turn, pulling her under his arm as he did. His long red cape swung behind them both as they walked, and he spoke to her in a comforting tone, much like the one she used with frightened children.

'There, now, m'lady, don't worry. You've had an exhausting day, and everyone will understand. I believe you put in enough time at the feast to be polite; we'll get you away from here, and I'll make your apologies to the assemblage.' He patted her hand gently as they walked, and she clutched his, hanging on for her sanity.

78

Ashe struggled to remain upright, such was the swell of the crowd. He endeavored to smile at each person who grabbed his shoulder, took his hand, or clapped him on the back. He knew Rhapsody would expect as much from him, and it was only her potential disapproval that kept him from drawing his sword and slashing a path clear to her through the annoying jackasses that barred his way.

The cacophony of voices and cheers was giving him a headache; he could not wait to be rid of this place and in her arms. It was a moment that he had waited for more than half a year, and if he was kept from it one moment longer, he was afraid of what might ensue.

As he broke free of another pocket of humanity he looked to where Rhapsody had been. She was gone.

He whirled around and let his dragon sense loose, but he couldn't feel her. He knew immediately she must have returned to Elysian, but then a chill swept over him as he realized this might not be the case. Rhapsody had been to many strange places in their time apart, and had learned techniques to hide herself even from him. Maybe she wasn't there at all.

At any rate, he didn't have the time to misguess, as he had after Llauron's pretended death; if he should take the time to track her to the wrong place, the night would be gone before he caught up with her, and the Council would resume before he had given her memory back. He could not allow that to happen.

His eyes scanned around for clues and came perchance upon Oelendra. She had made her way out of the crowd and was walking slowly on the rim toward the night. He dashed for her and caught her arm, the words exploding before he could engage in any polite pleasantries.

'Where is she?'

Oelendra looked at him regretfully. 'Congratulations, my Lord Cymrian. My best wishes to you for every good thing—'

'Where is Rhapsody? Oelendra, tell me, or by the gods, I'll—'

Oelendra's eyes narrowed. 'Or you'll what? Don't start out on the wrong foot, m'lord.'

'I'm sorry, Oelendra,' Gwydion replied, subdued. 'With one notable exception, there is no one I owe more to than you. But if you think I am going to be kept from my wife for one more second—'

'Did you ask her before you named her Lady?'

Gwydion's face froze. 'What do you mean?'

'Did you bother to ask her, or even tell her about what you planned to do?'

'When?' he asked incredulously. 'I haven't even bloody *seen* her for three months, Oelendra. I have gone slowly insane, waiting for permission to talk to my own wife, and it has never come.'

'Perhaps there's a reason for that.'

'There are undoubtedly many reasons, but none of them matter. I have to see her, Oelendra, I have to see her right now. Before anything else goes wrong, before Anborn presses his claim to her, or Achmed; gods, I have to tell her the truth. Please, please help me. Did she go back to the Cauldron? Or did she go to Elysian?'

Oelendra looked into his eyes; they were already touched by new wisdom, the look of a true king. But deeper, and more encompassing, was the look of utter fear and despair of a frightened husband; the look of a man about to lose his soul. Her heart went out to him, but her honor stood between him and the information he needed.

Ashe knew her dilemma. 'Oelendra, I know and admire your loyalty to Rhapsody, but you must know that the decisions she is making she is deciding in the dark, without some very important information. Instead of doing what she asked of you, please consider doing what she would want you to do if she had all the facts. Don't you think it will hurt her more if she takes any action that will compromise what she decided on that night six months ago? What do you think will happen to her when she eventually finds out what we have promised each other, if she has married another in the meantime?'

Oelendra got the point. Ashe watched the conflict in her eyes, holding his breath. Finally he saw her decision register.

'Where do you think she would go to hide, to find comfort, where no one else might find her?'

Ashe understood. 'She's in Elysian.'

Oelendra smiled. 'I wish you luck, m'lord.'

As she crossed the edge of the plain that led into the pass to the Cauldron, Rhapsody glanced through the flickering light of distant torches and saw a dark figure packing up a dark horse. The man looked up at her and smiled broadly. Even in her desire to escape from the Bowl unnoticed, she felt compelled to stop and walked over to him, looking around to be sure the Cymrians hadn't followed. They hadn't; the wine was flowing now, along with the stronger spirits of the distilleries of Ylorc and Canderre, and loud drunken singing could be heard echoing off the Bowl.

Anborn stopped his packing for a moment and looked at her intently. 'They certainly know how to celebrate, don't they?'

'I suppose it comes from all those years of needing a reason to,' Rhapsody said, her eyes glittering in the dark. 'Why did you do it?'

'Do what?' He withered under her knowing glance. 'Oh, Gwydion? I meant what I said; he is the most suited to lead them. The gods know he has far more patience for that sort of nonsense than I do. Besides, I could envision us all spending the rest of our lives in that damned Moot. The First Fleet would have felt compelled to argue at least a hundred years before they would agree to listen to anything I had to say, and frankly, I have better things to do.'

Rhapsody's hand came to rest on his arm. 'Why do I think it was more than that?'

Anborn sighed and threw his saddlebag over the horse's back. 'Because, despite your tendency to put yourself in extraordinarily stupid situations, you are actually an extremely wise woman, one wise enough not to ask any more than she really needs to know.' He looked directly into her eyes and smiled; she understood what he was saying.

'You're not staying for the rest of the meeting?'

Anborn shook his head. 'I'm not the head of my House, and besides, I think I've done enough here, don't you?' They both laughed. Then Anborn took her hands as his face grew serious.

'I have to ask something of you, something that will be harder than anything I ever remember doing.' His eyes twinkled within the serious expression. 'Knowing my history as you do, you know that's saying a great deal about how difficult this will be.'

Rhapsody's face grew solemn. 'Ask anything of me; it's yours, without question or hesitation.'

'Ah, ah, careful, my dear; I warned you a long time ago about making promises rashly, especially to someone who has wanted you from the moment he laid eyes on you. I could take you here quite easily; the ground is soft and relatively warm.' Blood rushed to her face, and Anborn laughed. 'I'm sorry, Rhapsody, that was rude. This is what I have to tell you: I must ask you to release me from my promise to wed.'

Rhapsody's face went blank for a moment, and the blood that had flushed her face spread throughout her body, leaving her weak and feeling a little sick. 'All right,' she said reluctantly. 'May I ask you why?'

The great warrior gave her hands a gentle squeeze. 'For three reasons. First, the Cymrians have chosen you for their Lady, and the truth is I passed up the Lordship because it would be a bore. As you know, the thing I cherish most in this world is my freedom. I might have had that as your husband, but if I had to fulfill a role of my own, that freedom would disappear under a hill of responsibilities and duties. I couldn't allow that, Rhapsody, not even for you.'

She nodded. 'I understand,' she said, her eyes filled with respect for his honesty. 'Will you tell me the other reasons?'

Anborn sighed and examined the ground. 'Well, as much as I agreed to the terms and understandings we set forth, I have to admit I don't think I'd much like being wed to someone who is in love with another man. You have done a good job of hiding it, my dear; I doubt anyone else knows. But I can tell; it's in your eyes. And, as much as I hate to admit it, I think I would be very jealous.'

Rhapsody's face went red again, but the expression she found in Anborn's eyes was mild and understanding. The tension broke and they smiled at each other again.

'And the last?'

Anborn hesitated, then spoke. 'I'm afraid I cannot live up to even the first condition you asked for. If I recall, the main reason you chose me is that I didn't love you.' He looked away, and Rhapsody felt a tinge of pain rise in his throat.

She put her arms around him in a warm embrace. 'That's ironic,' she said softly. 'I guess I can't live up to the terms myself.'

Anborn laughed and returned her clasp. 'Words a man could die happy upon hearing from you,' he said. He pulled back and looked down at her; the roughness of his features softened for a moment, and he knelt down before her. 'You have my allegiance, Rhapsody – my *sworn* allegiance, whether as Lady Cymrian or the Lady of the Lirin, or just as a lady. My sword and life are yours for your protection and need.'

Rhapsody understood the significance of this pledge. 'I am well and truly honored,' she said softly, as she helped him rise. 'Thank you, Anborn.'

'And now, if you'll allow me, I'd like to kiss my almost-wife goodbye and be on my way before I give in to my baser nature and change my mind.' Rhapsody smiled and came into his arms; they were strong and rough, as he was, and yet gentle as they wound around her waist.

His lips took hers warmly, gently at first, then with more insistence. She felt the heat from the fire inside her begin to rise and fill the spaces within herself that were reaching out, calling for him. The feeling shocked her, but she gave into it, sad in the knowledge that it would never come to pass. She could never be in love with him, or any man again, but she had grown accustomed to the prospect of living as his wife in comfortable friendship. She would miss him.

The kiss grew intimate, and she could feel Anborn's heart begin to race. He pressed her closer, then abruptly pushed her away.

'Not a good idea,' he muttered to himself. 'Will make for uncomfortable riding. Goodbye, m'lady. You know how to reach me on the wind if you should ever be in need of me.'

'Please remember that it works both ways,' she said, giving him one more heart-melting smile. 'Don't be a stranger.'

Anborn laughed. 'You needn't fear that, my dear. Goodbye, and enjoy your newly conferred royalty.' He mounted his great black charger; the horse snorted and danced in place as he turned to look at her once more.

'Oh, and by the way, Rhapsody, welcome to the family.' He gave her a rakish wink and galloped off toward the west, leaving her staring at him in bewilderment as he rode out of sight.

Across the plain a mile away, still trapped within the rim of the Bowl by the circulating crowd, Ashe felt her lips press against Anborn's, and he let out a shriek of despair that caused the Cymrians standing near him to part hastily and make a path for him. He ran through it and blindly into the night, hurrying, as she now did, for Elysian.

79

The Elysian gardens were in full bloom, overgrown from neglect, wild with the sweetness of maturity. Rhapsody had spent the last month before the Council with Achmed and Grunthor in Ylorc, sleeping at night alone in her solitary, windowless quarters within the Cauldron, across the hall from where Jo's room had been.

She hated it, but she felt protected there. In a close call she had returned to Elysian from the Bowl one day, after greeting and accommodating some of the later arrivals, to find a loving note and a bouquet of winter flowers on the dining-room table. Apparently Ashe could still infiltrate the Heath, but he couldn't broach the security of the Teeth and the Cauldron. So Rhapsody had stayed there, knowing it would keep him away.

She opened the door of the dark house, feeling the scent of spicy herbs and dried flowers rise up to greet her. Despite its vulnerability and bad associations, Elysian had a comforting feel to it, a sense of home like none she had ever owned.

Rhapsody hung up the satin cape and pulled off the matching shoes, the soles worn and split from hours of standing on the rock ledge. With a tired hand she rubbed her foot and then made her way in the dark up the stairs to her bedroom. She opened the door and found it as she had left it, the bed still made.

She crouched before the bedroom fireplace; it was clean and fuel for a fire had been laid, though not lit. Today she was grateful, whether to Ashe or Achmed; she didn't have the heart to build a new one. She spoke a single word, and the fire kindled, the tiny twigs snapping and hissing as they came to life for a moment, only to disappear in smoke and dissolve into ash.

Rhapsody looked around her bedroom as the light began to take hold. The fireshadows swept across the beloved furnishings and into familiar corners, bringing memories up from her soul, memories whose beauty stung as they touched the surface of her heart. As much as she loved Elysian, as much as she had missed it when in Tyrian, she knew she would not be able to stay here long; it was just too painful.

As the darkness receded and the room became bright, a glimpse of white caught her eye. Hanging over the folded dressing screen in the corner of the room was the white shirt, the shirt she had intended to ask Ashe for the night he confiscated her memories. Obviously she had remembered to do so, and he had complied. Rhapsody went to the painted screen and took down the shirt. She examined it for a moment, then brushed it against her cheek. It still carried his scent, clean and windy, with a touch of the smell of salty ocean spray. The scent brought tears to her eyes; she cursed herself for being vulnerable to it. Even the guilt that followed the tears into her eyes couldn't make her put it down.

Rhapsody stood for a long time, caressing her face with the garment. Then, as the warmth in the room grew, she felt exhaustion and sadness begin to take her over. She slung the shirt over one shoulder and went into the bathroom. She pumped a basin full of icy water and touched it, raising its temperature to a comfortable level, then washed her face vigorously, as if to rub off the invisible tearstains and the serene face she had worn as a mask most of the day.

She stared at her reflection in the glass; it was a human face, unremarkable to her eyes, with a weariness that permeated the pores of the skin made pale by exhaustion. Not a beautiful face; she could not for the life of her understand the reaction she was getting. *Must be the crown,* she thought. *I guess a blinding halo of circling stars will make anyone stare in awe.*

With a detachment caused by increasing tiredness she pulled the combs from her hair and brushed it slowly, trying to sort out the events of the day. She brushed her teeth and rinsed her mouth with a tonic made with anise and peppermint, hoping to banish the bitter taste in it, but it was no use; the acidity was coming from deeper inside her. With a final shake of her head to relax her long tresses, she went back into the bedroom.

The fire was burning steadily now, and leapt in welcome as she came back into the room. Rhapsody tossed the shirt onto the bed, went to her closet, and rummaged for her buttonhook. Oelendra had helped her dress that morning, but now she was alone to struggle with the numerous tiny buttons that ran down the back of her gown. When Ashe was there she never had need of a buttonhook; the assistance in dressing was one more thing she would have to get used to being without, although more often than not his help was detrimental to her attempts to become clothed anyway. She laughed to herself at the picture of the Lirin queen, the new Lady Cymrian, crawling around on the floor searching for tools to pry her body loose from its garments.

Finally she located it on the floor behind some hatboxes – Ashe had had a detrimental effect on the organization of her closet as well. She slid the buttonhook down her back, unfastening the stays with a familiar ability that came back from her days alone; there was some comfort in knowing she could go back to being by herself and life would still go on. The gown slipped off her shoulders and she stepped out of it; Rhapsody stared at it a moment, and then, for the first time in her life when alone, left her clothes in a heap on the floor.

She pulled her camisole over her head, tossed it into the pile for good measure, and returned to the bed. She lifted the shirt and stared at it; the cuffs were frayed at the ends, and there was still a tiny white wine stain on it where he had spilled his glass at dinner that night. *He must have been nervous,* she mused, the memory of his handsome face coloring with laughter. How she had loved to see and hear him laugh.

Loss welled up in her throat again, and she hugged the shirt to her naked chest, trying to dispel the pain. The sensation of the linen against her skin was a pale reminder of holding him in her arms; clothed in nothing but her lower undergarments, she put the shirt on and hugged herself, trying to re-create the feeling.

It didn't work, but his scent filled her lungs, and she rolled up the sleeves, enormously long on her. The shirt itself hung down almost to her knees; it was a little like an embrace. Rhapsody knew it was all she had left of him, and it would have to suffice. She pulled back the flowered coverlet and turned down the sheets, crawling in between them in her odd nightwear. Then she gave herself over to tears of despair, hoping that if she let them all out she would cleanse her heart of him once and for all.

It was thus that he found her, curled up on the bed, under the quilt, wrapped in his shirt, sobbing as though her heart would break. She hadn't even heard him come in, nor had she sensed his presence. He was wearing his mist cloak and so had passed undetected, and in her misery she didn't notice until he was almost upon her.

'Aria? Are you all right?'

Like an arrow from the string Rhapsody shot out of the bed, a look of shock and horror on her face. She darted behind the dressing screen, her tears stanched by the surprise.

'Ashe! What in blazes are you doing here? Gods; get out! Please.'

A jumble of emotions swept over Gwydion as she ran past; pain for her suffering, amusement at her reaction, longing to hold her, desire at the sight of her, particularly attired as she was. He struggled to wipe the smile off his face and hold a serious tone.

'Sorry. I guess I should have knocked first.'

'No, you just shouldn't be here. Gods, what were you *thinking*? I don't care if you are the Lord Cymrian. Please leave immediately.'

Ashe removed the mist cloak and hung it on the coatrack near the door, then took a large, glowing pearl from the top drawer of the dresser and set it on top. He went and sat in one of the wing chairs by the fire, where he had a better view of the dressing screen. He put his feet up, then looked at the crumpled clothes on the floor, and laughed aloud.

'Why, Rhapsody; I'm rubbing off on you! You're becoming a slob.'

'Get out,' she ordered more forcefully. 'What do you think you're doing, coming here?'

'Introducing you to my wife,' he replied, his amusement mounting. 'If you recall, I told you I would do so after the Cymrian Council.'

Rhapsody gasped aloud in panic. '*What?!* You brought her *here*? Gods, what's the matter with you? The Council isn't even over yet. I thought you meant some time after, like days, weeks—'

'Months, years – I know you did, and I didn't trust that you would stay put long enough for me to make the introduction. You forget, I know you very well, Rhapsody.' His eyes sparkled in the firelight; he was relishing the joys of domestic conflict.

'How dare you,' she whispered, angry tears reappearing in her eyes. 'You have no right to tell me what I will and will not do. This is my house, in case you've forgotten. Now get out.'

Gwydion leapt to his feet. 'Wait; don't say it,' he said seriously, knowing her next words: *You're not welcome here.* The last thing he needed was to have her Naming lore make that true. 'I'm sorry. Please, just come out and we'll talk.'

Rhapsody was beginning to panic. 'Where is she? I can't even feel her presence in my house. Oh no. Oh no. Please, Ashe, please just leave now. We'll talk tomorrow at the council; I promise. We have to deal with each other eventually, anyway. Now, please go, both of you.'

'I'm not going anywhere until you come out and talk to me. And there is no one else here; we're alone. Now, come on. Face this as you do everything else, Rhapsody; it's not like you to hide.'

Her anger deepened. 'It is no concern of yours what I'm like, or what I do from now on, Ashe, in any arena but the political one.'

'Wrong. Come out. I'm not leaving.'

'And I'm not appropriately dressed.'

'I noticed; all the better. Come out. Please.'

She looked out at him from behind the screen. Her facial kaleidoscope shifted from anger, to shock, to fury, and Gwydion laughed uproariously at the comical permutations her beautiful countenance was undertaking. Rhapsody picked up a book from the shelf built into the wall by the fireplace, and hurled it at him, smacking him squarely on the head.

'What is it about your family?' she asked in amazed rage. 'They name you Lord Cymrian, and instantly you turn into horses' arses.'

'Hey!' Gwydion shouted in mock annoyance. 'Is that any way to speak to your Lord and fellow sovereign?' The screech of wrath from behind the screen reminded him of a whistling teakettle, and he doubled over in merriment.

'Get out!'

'All right, all right, Rhapsody,' he said, bringing his mirth under control. 'I'll make a bargain with you: You come out and hear what I have to say; then, if you still want me to leave, I will do so immediately, without another word. I promise. Fair enough?'

'No. I'm not dressed.'

'You look fine. Now come out.'

'Gods, you're a married man; have you no shame?'

'Not one bit. Now, come out right now or I'll demand the return of that shirt immediately.' He moved closer, positioning himself between her and the closet.

For a moment no sound came from behind the screen. Then he heard a deep, sad sigh, and she finally came out, abject humiliation on her face.

Gwydion's heart wrenched. 'Oh, Rhapsody, I'm sorry,' he said, coming to her and taking her hand. He walked her to the chair he had occupied and handed her one of her quilts to cover up with. He sighed himself as the exquisite legs disappeared beneath the blanket.

She stared at the fire, saying nothing. Gwydion could see the toll the months of sorrow had taken on her spirit, and he cursed himself for playing with her feelings.

He sat on the floor at her feet, exactly as she had the first day she called him to this place. From his pocket he drew forth a small box and opened it, looking inside for a moment. Then he turned it toward her.

'Do you remember this, Aria?' he asked her, his voice gentle.

Rhapsody glanced at it, then her gaze returned immediately to the fire. 'No.'

'Look at it more carefully,' he urged, trying to draw her attention back. 'Is it familiar at all?'

She looked down into the box again. It held a tiny ring, composed of infinitesimal fragments of the Lirin diadem's gemstones, with a small, perfect emerald in the center. She took the box to get a closer look, and at her touch the diamonds blazed with fire, sparkling to life the way the crown had. The emerald caught their light and shone like a star-sprinkled sea.

'It's beautiful,' she said, handing it back to him. 'But no, I don't remember it.'

Gwydion sighed. 'Oh. Well, put it on.'

Rhapsody's brows drew together in a frown. 'Don't be ridiculous.'

'I've never been more serious in my life. Please put it on.'

'Neither have I. No.'

He had not anticipated this. 'Rhapsody, in order—'

She rose, clinging to the blanket. 'All right, I've heard what you had to say. Now I want you to leave. Immediately, and without another word. That was what you promised.'

'Ar—'

'Ah, ah,' she interrupted, holding up her hand, 'stop right there. You have just assumed the lordship of the united Cymrian peoples; it would not do to break your word within a day's time. You promised; now go. I will speak with you in the morning, or at least some time during the Council, assuming we don't have another riot on our hands.'

He stared at her in utter disbelief. His joking humor had been his defense against his overwhelming need to seize her and never let go again. For three interminable months he had roiled in agony, man and dragon, missing her magic, missing her love – just missing her. He had counted impatiently through every day, stalking the edges of the Teeth, hoping for a glimpse of her. Finally he had put as much distance as he could between them, comforting himself with the knowledge that this moment was coming.

And now that it was here, she was afraid of him, embarrassed in his presence. He had foolishly believed that it would be as simple as putting the ring back on her finger. He had tried to ease her back into it, taking it as slowly as he could stand, to avoid overwhelming her with so much conflicting information. And for his pains he had just banished himself from her company for at least another day, during which he expected she would find reasons to talk to him, but, for propriety's sake, never alone.

Tears welled in his eyes, and rolled down his cheeks. He tried to maintain his composure, but he couldn't. He turned from her and walked to the coatrack, grabbed his mist cloak, and ran down the stairs. He cursed himself again for laughing at her tears a moment before; now she surely was unmoved by his own.

As Gwydion reached the threshold of the front door he heard her call from upstairs.

'Ashe?'

He turned and walked back to the bottom of the steps, looking up at her. Her eyes were wide with alarm, and her hair, mussed and glistening, tumbled around her shoulders. She was still clothed only in his shirt, looking like Man's ultimate fantasy in distress.

She came down the stairs slowly, and when she stood a few steps above him her hand, hidden by the cuff of a sleeve much too long, moved to the collar of the shirt she wore, her graceful neck with its golden necklace widely exposed by the largeness of the garment. Her motions were hesitant, but her eyes were filled with sympathy.

'I release you from your promise,' she said. 'What did you want to tell me?'

'I love you,' he said. The words came, unbidden, from the loneliest place in his heart, and though it was not what he would have said given but one chance, it was the most truthful answer to her question, and the only thing he could bring himself to say. The words resonated with longing, and depth, and all the pain that the oceans together would be stretched to contain. They spanned two worlds, two lifetimes, and their poignancy filled Rhapsody's heart with sorrow and her eyes with tears again.

'You should go,' she said gently.

He barely saw her tears through his own. 'Are you telling me you don't love me anymore, Aria?'

She looked at the floor. 'No,' she said to her feet. 'I told you I always would. Always. That will never change. But it doesn't matter.'

'That's where you're wrong, Rhapsody; it's the only thing that does matter. The *only* thing.' He sighed and felt the pain abate a little, and warmth begin to return to his soul. 'Please; I know I have no right to ask this of you again, but will you trust me just once more? Will you just listen to what I need to say? Until the end this time?'

Rhapsody recognized the intensity in his eyes. 'All right,' she said reluctantly. 'But then will you please go?'

'Yes; if you still want me to, I will go. I promise.'

A unwilling smile came over her face. 'You know, you should stop promising things you really don't want to do.'

'More than you would ever believe,' he said. 'Can we go back upstairs? I don't think the stairwell is the best place for this conversation.'

Rhapsody blushed. 'I suppose so,' she said, looking embarrassed again. 'Can I at least put on a robe?' She looked down at her bare legs, and color flooded the rest of her body. She turned and started up the stairs.

'Why bother?' he asked, a hint of the old humor returning. 'I may be leaving in a moment; it's hardly worth the effort.'

Rhapsody returned to the chair, and drew the blanket back over herself. Gwydion sat on the floor again, and pulled the ring box out once more.

'Now, where were we? Oh yes, I had asked you to put this on. You see, Rhapsody, if you do, you will understand everything. It will save us hours of arguing. And though I admit I enjoyed the conflict, I could live without being brained by a book again. So please; humor me, your fellow reluctant monarch. I swear to you, my wife will not be compromised in any way by your doing so.'

Rhapsody smiled in spite of herself. 'All right,' she said, and she took the ring from the box. In her hand the gems sparkled with a brilliance that reflected in his eyes; it made her think of other eyes and a night sky in another lifetime. She squeezed it for a moment, feeling the music that came forth from the ring; the whole of Elysian seemed to be tuned to it, humming softly as if preparing for the overture of an imminent symphony.

'Left hand,' Gwydion instructed gently. She looked askance at him. 'Please. Just trust me.'

Rhapsody slipped the ring on her finger. For a moment she stared at it, waiting for a great revelation, but none came. Across the room, the glowing pearl began to hum. The sparkling of the diamonds and emerald in the ring intensified, and she had to look away. When she did, Gwydion raised up onto one knee and leaned over her, kissing her lovingly in the radiant glow of the ring.

The music she had heard grew louder, and each note was joined, one after another, by the next harmonic tone; it swelled, filling the room, then the house, then the island, then the grotto and finally the whole of the underground duchy that was Elysian with the most beautiful song she had ever heard. It built to a thundering crescendo, and diminished into the slightest of sounds, maintaining its harmony. Then, as a flag released from its tether in a high wind, it broke free and soared off, dancing in the air and throughout the lake, touching every corner of the cavern with gladness.

Her eyes returned to Gwydion, who was watching her intently, and as she looked into his face she saw it again in her mind's eye, vague pictures of him from the lost night returning to be recalled, varying expressions gracing his countenance, all of them joyful. She was ill prepared for the onslaught of memories that caught her off-guard, blowing her backward. She reached for him; he caught her as she swayed in the chair, her eyes pleading for help before they rolled back and the world went dark in the roar of the flood.

80

'You know, I would never take you for the fainting type, but you certainly do a lot of it lately.'

Gwydion's voice broke through the fog that surrounded her jumbled thoughts, clear in its tone. The other voices she was hearing were occluded by memory, fighting for dominance in her understanding. Rhapsody struggled for consciousness, but succeeded only in determining she was lying down on her bed, because her cheek brushed the stiff lace that trimmed the flannel pillowcase. She lost her battle to hang on to the Present, and succumbed to the contradictory, confusing voices and images from the Past.

She could hear the words of their wedding vows, beautiful in the way that only a Singer of her power and a dragon who had loved someone through two lifetimes could speak them. She had committed the song the vows created to the grotto, so that Elysian itself would bear witness to the love promised there. The song rang there still, now that the memory was returned, lighting the cavern with gladness.

Then the image shifted, and she saw other faces, heard other voices. *I'm not seeing your son anymore, Llauron. I've done as you asked; we've parted company.*

What a shame, and after I specifically gave him my blessing. A shame; I am sorry, my dear.

Rhapsody pitched from side to side in her coma-like state. *They are all liars,* Achmed had insisted. *At least in the old world you knew who the bad guys were because they professed what they stood for. Here the allegedly good ones are calculating users; the ancient evils could never wreak the level of havoc that the Lord and Lady Cymrian did. And you want to hand yourself over to the potentially biggest liar of all on a silver platter.*

Well, if I do, it is my choice to do so. I will take the risk, and live or die by my own volition.

Wrong. We may all suffer that fate, because you aren't just compromising yourself, you are throwing all of our neutrality into the pot, and if you overbet your hand, we all lose.

She could feel hot tears on her neck, and arms holding her tightly, but gently. *It's all right, Sam. You won't hurt me. Really. It will be all right.*

Emily, I would never, never hurt you on purpose; I hope you know that.

Rhapsody? Rhapsody, please say something. Please.

Is your temper tantrum over?

I'm sorry; gods, I'm so sorry –

The hair that had fallen into her eyes was brushed back gently. *I say we kill him. And if we're wrong, and another one shows up, we kill him too.*

You can't go around killing people if you're not sure whether you're right.

And why not? Always worked for us before. Seriously, miss, this is too big to take chances with, if you're not sure.

The shooting lighttone had touched the newly blooming flowers of her garden, absorbing their colors and spinning them skyward, exploding into shimmering fireworks as it impacted with the dome of the firmament. Ashe's face smiled down at her in her memory.

Are you sure?

I'm sure.

Hazily she slapped away the hand that caressed her forehead. *You seem to have appointed yourself the guardian of my heart, Rhapsody. Why don't you make me the protector of yours? I promise I will keep it safe.*

It was a hoax; Llauron is not dead; you were used. I'm sorry, I wish I could tell you in a more gentle way.

Please be what you seem. Please, please don't hurt me.

I am. And I never will.

Please understand I would rather die at this moment than tell you what I am about to.

Why?

Because I know what I am going to tell you will hurt you.

He had picked her up from the spot where he had married her and carried her carefully over the threshold and up the stairs to their nuptial bed. He trembled as he leaned over to kiss her, and when he looked down into her eyes she saw the same boy she had fallen in love with a world before, on a moonlit summer night under the lacy shadows of a willow tree.

She could hear her father's voice: *When you find the one thing in your life you believe in above anything else, you owe it to yourself to stand by it – it will never come again, child. And if you believe in it unwaveringly, the world has no other choice but to see it as you do, eventually. For who knows it better than you? Don't be afraid to take a difficult stand, darling. Find the one thing that matters – everything else will resolve itself.*

Rhapsody opened her eyes. Gwydion was looking down into her face, worry on his own. When he saw her awake he grinned in relief; then his grin dimmed to one tempered with concern, and more than a touch of fear.

'Welcome back. Are you all right?'

She closed her eyes and put the heel of the hand to her forehead, endeavoring to drive the pounding headache out of her skull. 'I don't know; what happens now?'

'I guess that depends on how you're feeling,' Gwydion said, a hint of nervousness in his voice. 'If you'd like my vote, I say we find a goat hut and go live happily ever after.' A look of undiluted love washed over his face for a moment, then was tempered by her uncertainty. 'I love you, Aria; gods, I've been dying to tell you this for so long. But I don't want to overwhelm you; I know you've had enough of that state to last a lifetime. So I'll follow your lead. Tell me what you need to know, or what you're feeling. Please, tell me what's in your heart.'

Rhapsody looked into his face and studied his eyes. They were free from deception, or so she thought, with hope brimming beneath the surface; he seemed to be holding his breath, waiting for her answer. In her mind she tied up all her feelings of betrayal and resentment into a large mound and set them aside for a moment to be better able to discern how she really felt. That she still loved him she knew, had known all along; it seemed apparent that he still loved her, too. But there was something she had to learn before she could decide anything else. She sat up with great difficulty and a little help from Gwydion.

501

'I need to know something, but I am afraid to hear the answer, more than I have ever been afraid of anything in my life,' she said. She tried to give voice to the question, but after many moments of opening her mouth and then closing it again, she began to cry. 'I can't even bring myself to ask you,' she wept.

Gwydion took her in his arms and cradled her. 'Let me see if I can both ask and answer it for you, so you don't have to. Are we really married? Yes.'

Rhapsody's tears ceased, but her face grew paler as she pulled away from him. 'That's not it,' she said.

'Very well, then, am I really your Sam, and are you really my darling Emily? Yes.'

'Ashe—'

'Not that one, either? All right. Do I still love you? Impossible to express how much, but yes.'

'Please—'

'Am I, or have I ever been, married to or in love with anyone else? No.'

'Will you *shut up?*' Rhapsody snarled. Gwydion was taken aback, and dropped his hands from her arms. The pain on his face twisted Rhapsody's heart, and tears sprang to her eyes again. 'I'm sorry, Sam,' she whispered. 'I didn't mean to say that. Please, just let me think a minute.'

Gwydion nodded numbly. She knew how long he had waited to set things right, how much he wanted their life back, but until she could answer one last question that was not possible. She closed her eyes and thought back to the words she had struggled so hard to drive from her mind.

Don't be jealous, Rhapsody; the Rakshas liked it so much better with you than with your sister. What, you didn't know? Well, I'm not surprised. They did look identical, your two lovers. How fortunate for me that you fell in love with the son of Llauron; it made it so much easier for the Rakshas to have you. You don't think it was always Gwydion who took you, did you? Once your sister told my creation about the two of you, it was easy. It is, after all, very dark in the Teeth at night, isn't it, my dear?

Rhapsody grew pale and began to tremble, and the fear in her eyes went straight to Gwydion's heart. 'Just ask, Emily; whatever it is, I swear to you, I will tell you the truth.'

'I know you will,' she said, trying to remain calm. 'All right. Do you remember the night in the Cauldron when I told you about Jo and the Rakshas?'

Gwydion shuddered. 'How could I forget? Yes, unfortunately.'

'Tell me what happened after you left the Cauldron.'

He looked confused. 'After I left? How would I know?'

Desperation came into Rhapsody's eyes. 'I don't mean in the Cauldron, what happened to *you?*'

'I went off, at our mutual instigation, and left for the coast. Is this about my not being there for you when you were hurt, Aria?'

'No,' she said, beginning to shake. 'Please, stay focused. Exactly what happened that night? You're a dragon; I want a reasonable level of detail.'

'I walked across the barricades and out into the Teeth, and made my way up the crag face to the steppes. I got past the rock ridge and was on my way down the slope when I heard you calling me; I thought it was the wind.'

'And what did you do?'

'I came back and found you in the sheltered arch, wearing next to nothing – we have to talk about this little proclivity of yours, by the way. I love the idea of you naked or next to it, but not outside in winter.'

Rhapsody almost assaulted him. 'Keep going!'

Ashe shrugged. 'You had come crawling out in the dark to make me swear I would not track the Rakshas, and, against my better judgment, I agreed. And then we made love; it was not the way I wished it could have been, sort of helpless and desperate, and I feared through it all I was hurting you, but I couldn't stop myself; we were both in so much pain that I—' His voice came to a grinding halt as relief broke over her face and she began to weep aloud with joy. 'What? Now I'm really confused.'

Rhapsody continued to sob, but now her weeping was mixed with glorious laughter. As if shattered, the pain that had gripped her abdomen unclenched, and she threw her arms around Gwydion, startling and delighting him at the same time.

'All right,' he said as he pulled her closer. 'I don't understand this, but I can get used to it.'

Rhapsody dried her eyes on the sleeves of his shirt. 'No, don't do that,' she said, wiping the tears away and breaking into a smile. 'I don't ever want to be this relieved again as long as I live, because I never want to be that frightened again.'

Gwydion caressed her cheek. 'Can you tell me about it?'

Rhapsody nodded as she reached into the pocket of his cloak for his handkerchief. Gwydion smiled and sighed in relief himself at the gesture; the old Rhapsody was coming back. After she blew her nose she told him the details of the intervening time, and what had happened with the demon. He blanched when he learned the extent of the pain she had been carrying around; he knew even his own agony at the loss of the piece of his soul could barely match the fear she must have felt. He pulled her into his arms again.

'Gods, Aria, why didn't you come to me? Why didn't you let me see you? I would have told you that it was me that night in the Teeth, and you wouldn't have had to suffer like this.'

'Well, obviously because your answer could have been different,' Rhapsody answered calmly. 'And if what the demon said had turned out to be true, I would have broken down; I never would have been able to get through this blasted Council.'

'You carried this fear for the sake of the Cymrians?' Gwydion asked incredulously. 'They certainly don't deserve it.'

'Be that as it may, for the sake of everyone who shares the world with them, they needed to be called and united. Speaking of which, I have a bone to pick with you.'

'Oh?' His eyes twinkled. 'I'm all yours. My attention, as well as the rest.'

She looked at him seriously. 'What did you think you were doing, naming me Lady of that Council? Are you insane?'

'Why?'

'We have been having this discussion since the first night we, well, since our first night as lovers,' she said. 'You know my rank; why did you put me in this position? I don't want to be Lady Cymrian. You know my birth status. I'm not qualified.'

Gwydion laughed. 'Obviously the Council doesn't agree with you, since you were elected unanimously. Must be nice; they argued about my suitability for hours.' Rhapsody's face grew hot and she looked down into her lap. Ashe stopped laughing and took her hands. 'Rhapsody, I've been trying to tell you all along, there is no one who could make even as good a leader for these people as you; certainly there is no one better.'

'That's a sad statement.'

'Beware,' Gwydion said seriously. 'You are talking about my Lady, as well as the woman I love. Didn't you once tell me that we had a responsibility to help in whatever way we could? Who but you could have calmed that rabble, got them to talk to each other civilly for the first time in centuries, perhaps ever? The members of the First and Third Fleets were hanging on each other like old friends, toasting your health and reign mutually. Can you fathom the significance of that? Who but you could silence Anwyn, could banish her back to where she belongs, without a hint of rancor, then sing a tribute to her? Could make her cry for love of you?'

'I seriously doubt that Anwyn would agree with your assessment of her feelings.'

He took her face in his hands and regarded her seriously. 'Who would have carried the hideous belief that you have, a possibility you would have died because of, in order to make it through for people to whom you felt an obligation, even though you had no vested interest in power over them? Gods, Aria, if that doesn't prove your worthiness, I don't know what could. I did not make you my wife so that you would be the Lady Cymrian, nor did I make you the Lady Cymrian so that you would be my wife. I did it because, for each of the roles, there is no other possible candidate; none whatsoever. And I am here to help you. I will handle, at least initially, while teaching you about, the annual fisherman's catch rights, and planting cycles, and taxation rates on oxen in the Orlandan provinces, and armament procurements—'

Rhapsody sighed comically. 'I can't wait. I don't already have enough of that nonsense in Tyrian.'

His face became solemn. 'Rhapsody, are you going to forgive me? Can you find it in your heart to take me back? Neither of us could foresee what would happen since the night we married; I knew you would face terrible pain, but I had no idea how much. Do you still love me?'

She sighed. 'Yes. Always.'

'And is that enough for you?'

She regarded him seriously. The pain had been excoriating, the lies had almost destroyed them both. But the lies had not been theirs, and now they were the leaders, the ones to decide how the power would be used. The memory of their wedding came flooding back unbidden, the incredible happiness she had felt and seen in his eyes as they promised themselves to one another; the tenderness of their lovemaking as their souls touched and were joined completely in the total knowledge of who they were; the giddiness of unabashed laughter beneath the covers, sharing secrets and plans that night; the hopes they told each other of. It had been her first taste of true and utter joy, and that realization brought back another voice of wisdom to her. She could see the smile on the face of the Patriarch in her memory.

Above all else, may you know joy.

It became a simple decision. In her mind she pictured the bundle of negative feelings and set them ablaze with imaginary fire, burning them quickly into ash, leaving nothing but those things that were sacred to her. *Ryle hira.* 'Yes,' she said, watching his face begin to glow with the happiness she had not seen for half a year. 'Yes, I think you taught me that. It's enough. In fact, it's more; it's something to be humbly grateful for, and I am.'

'Then you will take me back?'

Rhapsody laughed. 'I don't think I ever gave you away, but of course I will. I may even forgive you for making me Lady Cymrian someday, but don't count on it.'

'Well, lest you forget, you made me Lord, or planned to, so we're even.'

'Wrong. We will never be even.' Rhapsody paused, then she smiled at him. 'You will always be much taller; I admit it.'

'Just as long as you are clear in your understanding that I am your devoted husband; there is and never was anyone but you.'

'I've got that, I think.'

'And there is one little comment you made that I have felt the need to clear up for the last six months.'

'Really?'

'Absolutely. Do you remember, on the night of our wedding, after I proposed but before I went all scaly on you, that you were telling me about our time in the old land? Not knowing who I was yet?'

'Yes.'

'And I believe you referred to our lovemaking under the starry Serendair sky, our first time, our mutual deflowerment, as "one night of meaningless sex in a pasture"; is that right?' His eyes twinkled as his face set in a scowl of mock annoyance.

Rhapsody laughed even as her own face colored in embarrassment. 'I believe that was the term I used, yes; I think you're right.'

'Oh, I am right,' he said, amusement threatening to drive away his pretense of irritation. 'That was a beautiful, sacred moment to me, Emily.'

Her laughter diminished into a serious smile. 'It was for me, too, Sam,' she said sincerely, speaking with her lore. 'It felt like the consummation of a marriage that had already been blessed.'

'Exactly! Exactly what I felt. I don't even remember proposing to you; it was as though we just mutually decided that we were to be married.'

'Yes. I agree.'

'Well, since that is the case, I believe I hold the record for marital abstinence, having gone approximately a hundred and forty years between episodes of carnal knowledge with you; vastly more if you count it in your time. Then it would be calculated in centuries; millennia, even.'

Rhapsody laughed again. 'Congratulations! Now, there's an accomplishment to be proud of.'

'And now, now that we've been married, with vows and rings and everything, I have waited six months, *six months*, Rhapsody. No man who has ever seen you or heard about you could believe that kind of connubial celibacy was possible.'

'And no one who knew me, unless they also knew I was unaware of the opportunity. It isn't easy for me, either, Sam.'

'But I am becoming the Lord of Forbearance, don't you think?'

'Definitely. I've already admired your restraint; what else do you want?'

'That is a silly question.'

'Let me guess; you're going for a new abstinence record?'

'That's not funny.' Despite his statement, he chuckled.

Rhapsody grinned at him. 'Does this mean you expect me to somehow make this up to you?'

'Yes.'

'Oh. Well, I don't think mathematically it is possible for me to do so tonight; I'm sorry.'

He leaned over her and rested his forehead on hers, his eyes looking deeply into her own. 'You could at least try.'

'I suppose. I don't have to be anywhere until sunrise.'

'Forget sunrise. The Cymrians are still drinking to us, even now. They won't be able to move until noon or later.'

Rhapsody's eyes sparkled. 'Oh, all right.' She put her arms around his neck.

Gwydion stayed nose-to-nose with her; he climbed up onto the bed and positioned himself over her on his knuckles and knees. 'And, after this blasted council is over, your dance card is completely filled for the next six months.'

'Six months? I don't think so, Sam. Two weeks, maybe. I've been away from Tyrian an awfully long time.'

A dragonlike growl came forth.

'I'm sorry; if you want me to yourself, you're going to have to marry me publicly; otherwise—'

'Say no more. It's done.'

'Good.'

'Then you are mine exclusively for as long as you can stand me. Right?'

Her eyes glittered in the darkness. 'Right.'

A dazzling smile spread over his face. 'Good. Now give me back my shirt.'

The bonfires had spread throughout the Moot and the surrounding fields; there were tens of thousands of them now, with one vast inferno blazing in the center of the Bowl's floor. The billowing flames lighted the night sky, making it gleam orange through the thick waves of black smoke that turned from gray to white as they wafted to the stars.

The considerable stores of wine and spirits that Achmed had provisioned for the gathering were exhausted within the first hours, leaving a very inebriated, very happy populace still in the frenzy of glorious celebration. Loud choruses of drunken singing swelled over the mountains and foothills, frightening the Bolg in Canrif as the anthems grew in volume.

When the moon set, Achmed, who was watching the festivities with sober interest, offered to replenish the alcohol from his stores near Grivven Post, a recommendation that was seized upon gladly. Faedryth and his aide-de-camp, Therion, began rounding up volunteers to assist in the transportation of the new supplies, finding the Nain to be one of the few groups among the revelers still able to stand erect, let alone locomote or carry anything valuable.

Within a few moments a small squadron of the volunteers accompanied the Firbolg king out of the Bowl, gathered wagons, and lurched unsteadily across the steppes toward where the king had directed, following the Bolg Cymrians in charge of the detail.

Achmed stood at the entrance of the Moot as they disappeared into the night, absorbing the screeching of the wagon wheels, the sound of singing and music of a thousand different types and origins, all playing simultaneously, the roar of merry laughter thundering against his skin-web, the sensitive network of exposed nerve and vein that made up his epidermal layer.

It was a clamor the like of which he had never experienced before, even in war. Grunthor had once said that the most frightening thing about battle was the sound of it, the thunderous noise of horses and mounted weapons being positioned, the murderous sound of fury and destruction, the wailing, the sound men made when they were exploding inside.

This noise was different; there was something far more fascinating and disturbing to him about it. It was an amalgamation of shrieking laughter and song, crackling flames, splintering wood and shouting, the sound of jubilation and years of pain mixed into one unholy roar. It had an effect on him similar to that of the sea, masking individual sounds by blending them into this hideous anti-symphony that was as ugly to his ears as Rhapsody's song had been beautiful.

The inconstant light of the bonfires swept over him, flickering with blinding brightness one moment, going dark with smoke and flying cinders the next. When the darkness lingered for a longer-than-usual moment Achmed looked up and saw his Sergeant-Major standing beside him; the

507

din had been enough to mask Grunthor's pulse, which until this Council had been one of only two he still could perceive. Now he was drowning in the noise of all of the heartbeats of the First Generation; it was a surprisingly comfortable sensation, and made him feel almost nostalgic.

Grunthor handed him a battered tankard overflowing with cheap ale.

'Got to give it to them; they know how to throw a party, eh, sir?'

Achmed said nothing, but raised the mug to his lips and drank deeply.

The rim of the Bowl at the edge of the Summoner's Rise was cloaked in thick smoke from the roaring bonfires, shrouded intermittently in blinding light and darkness. No one could have made out the figure standing there, silently watching the merrymaking, not even the Bolg guards who flanked the Rise, passing a wineskin between them.

No one saw that figure turn after a moment, blending into the smoke like a shadow from the Past. In darkness it crept to the pulpit, picked up the Cymrian horn, and walked away into the night amid the clouds of fire ash.

81

The sweet scent of warm cinnamon and cardamom tickled his nose, followed by richer, deeper aromas that gently forced Gwydion's eyes open. He focused his gaze on his glowing wife, who sat at his side on the edge of the bed, holding a breakfast tray on her lap. She was waving her hand, wafting the rising steam in his direction and smiling at him.

'Good morning, m'lord,' she said in her very best serving girl voice. 'Would you care for a small repast before returning to Council?'

'I certainly would, but it got out of bed already. And it hates being reminded that it's small.' He grinned at her in his fog, succumbing to the aromatic symphony. 'Gods, what a heavenly smell.'

'I'm glad you like it. The cinnamon and sweeter spices are like the flutes and piccolos, teasing the edges of your nose, while the—'

'I was not referring to the food,' he said wickedly. 'And who gave you permission to leave the royal arms?'

Rhapsody looked down at her own. 'Leave them where? They're still attached.'

'Oh, that's right, I'd forgotten; you get to use the royal "we" too, don't you? You are the Lady Cymrian, after all.'

'Don't remind me,' she said with mock grimness. 'It's all your fault.'

'Guilty, and I admit it with delight. It's probably the only thing the Cymrian assemblage will ever thank me for.'

'Don't count on it,' she said. 'Now eat your breakfast. There are cinnamon buttocks—' His laugh almost unbalanced the tray. 'Hie there, careful. And I made you that nasty coffee you like; ugh.'

'Oh, bless you.' Gwydion took the proffered cup eagerly, and held it while she topped it with cream. He took a sip and grinned. 'It's marvelous. Thank you.'

She sighed in mock despair. 'He hates my tea, but at least he loves my coffee.'

'He loves your tea, too; he told you that ages ago. He loves everything about you. I guess this means it's my turn to make you breakfast tomorrow?'

'That's right,' she said seriously. 'I figure we should trade off every morning, and that way each of us will get a chance to sleep in.'

He took another sip. 'Who are you kidding? You never sleep in; you're too busy tidying or singing or whatever it is you do during the three hours you get up before me. This is a case in point; you're up and dressed, it's two hours before dawn – it's still *dark* outside, Emily.'

She crossed her wrist over her knee. 'Well, a few more nights like last night, and that will never happen again. I almost expected to wake up with a large smoking crevasse running down the bed. I'll need to sleep in just to survive.' She watched his face redden behind the cup. 'Coffee too hot?'

'No, it's fine, thank you.'

Her laugh pealed like bells; the vibration rang through the whole of Elysian. 'Why, Sam! You're blushing!'

Gwydion put the empty cup back on the tray. 'Yes, in every place on my body. Want to see?' She laughed and slapped his hand away from her knee. 'Here, put that down, m'lady,' he said, smiling at her evilly. As soon as she did she rose, ignoring his outstretched arms.

'No, sorry,' she said, moving away. 'We have to be at Council very soon, and I know this ploy.'

'This is no ploy; it's a royal edict.'

'Well, I hate to disappoint your – edict,' she said, 'but there are a hundred thousand people waiting, and I think they might notice us missing.'

Ashe ran a hand over his unkempt hair. 'Sheesh, no wonder Anwyn didn't have a chance against you,' he said. 'You're tough. Please, Emily, come back to bed. The Council be hanged; I'll be in a ugly mood if you don't.'

'Sorry,' she repeated, but her smile was sympathetic. 'The way I see it, an ugly mood at the Council is almost unavoidable; I know mine was. But I'm about to take my bath – excuse me, the royal bath. Would you like to join me?'

'Yes!' There was a dramatic pause. 'I hope you mean that literally.'

'You really are naughty. Come on.' She took his hand and pulled him out of the bed.

He put his arm around her as they walked to the bathroom. 'Naughty? What an awful thing to say, m'lady. I assure you, my intentions are—'

'Purely honorable; I've heard this before. Do you want to get a book to read before we go in?'

'Not a bad idea,' he said, looking thoughtful. He stooped and picked up the volume that she had bounced off his head the night before, and tucked it under his arm. 'I'll be safer this way.' Rhapsody laughed, pulled it from beneath his elbow, and tossed it into the growing pile of rumpled clothes.

'Come on,' he said, his eyes sparkling mischievously. 'Let's go make our own version of Crynella's candle.'

'Hmmm?'

His lips brushed her hair as he held the door for her. 'You know; water within fire.'

Gwydion lay back in the tepid tub and sighed. The water was disappearing through the drain in the bathtub's base, one of Gwylliam's marvelous designs, leaving his chest and waist exposed to the warm air of the bathroom, heavy with vapor. With the water the anxiety and loneliness of the past half-year was draining, too; he looked over at his wife on the other side of the bathroom and sighed again. He was happy.

Rhapsody stood unclothed before the long silvered looking glass, examining herself from different angles. Her eyes seemed fixed on the area of her abdomen, and her face was thoughtful, almost pensive. Gwydion gripped the sides of the tub and raised himself, still dripping, out of the cooling water. He went up behind her and took her in his arms, laughing as she squirmed away.

'Iiiiggggggghhhhh, get a towel.' She kissed him, then turned back to the mirror again.

He drew her closer and nuzzled her neck. 'No, I prefer to dry myself by the *fire*,' he said teasingly, enjoying the feel of the warm skin of her back on his chest. Her attention was still on the mirror, something he had never seen before. 'What are you looking at?'

Rhapsody stared a moment more before answering. 'I'm trying to figure out why my abdomen felt as if it were expanding, why Elynsynos thought there was something evil growing inside me, if it really was you in the Teeth that night – it was you, wasn't it? I didn't dream that?'

Gwydion ran his hands over her hair soothingly as her eyes widened in concern. 'Yes, yes,' he said hurriedly, then turned her around and took her into his arms. 'That was me, Aria, every clumsy, inept moment. And prior to that inelegant assignation, I didn't leave your side for a moment from the time we became lovers, so unless you made love to someone who looked like me after I left that night, the demon definitely was lying.'

Rhapsody's face, pressed up against the hard muscles of his chest and shoulder, took on a half-smile. There was a question in his voice that she knew he would never ask her, so she answered it for him. 'I didn't make love to anyone at all after you left, Sam. I would have thought that was obvious last night. But that still doesn't explain why I have felt those sensations in my abdomen, and what Elynsynos noticed.'

Gwydion looked her over thoughtfully, then took her hand and led her back into the bedroom and over to the bed. 'Here, lie down,' he said soothingly, 'let me see if I can detect anything.' She climbed on top of the coverlet and lay back on the pillows while he sat down beside her, resting his hand on her flat stomach. There was no hint of swelling whatsoever.

He took his time, checking her over carefully with every divining sense of his dragon nature, but it only confirmed what he had known from the beginning; she was unaltered. He had memorized every detail of her, to the core of her essence as only a dragon could, and knew irrefutably that she was not pregnant or carrying anything living inside her. There was, however, an infinitesimal trace of something tainted in her blood, growing less with each beat of her heart, as if the endless circulation of her blood was dissolving it. In addition, there was a glow within her that he couldn't identify, a diffuse energy; perhaps it was her tie to the element of fire. He smiled reassuringly at her, hoping to dispel the look of uncertainty in her eyes.

'Tell me what the demon said when this happened,' he said gently.

She thought for a moment. *'Virack urg caz,'* she said, shuddering at the memory. 'Then he said, "conceive." After that, he said *'Merlus,'* or something like it, and then said, "grow."'

A shiver ran momentarily down Ashe's back. 'All right, darling, let me assure you, there is nothing growing inside you anymore.'

Rhapsody began to tremble. 'Anymore?'

Gwydion stroked her arm. 'Well, there never was anything real there at all. You know that there are various ways that the F'dor can possess someone, like the soldiers who only did its bidding once and didn't remember?' She nodded. 'The demon undoubtedly knew it was trapped, and that it was dying, so in a last effort to save itself it planted a seed, not the seed of a child, but the seed of a doubt. It had been priming you, talking to you all along; it knew the vibrations of your brain and what it would take to make you believe something; F'dor, as you know, invented deception. But you see, Rhapsody, because you are a Namer, you are particularly vulnerable to something like that. How many times have you told me that you prefer to believe what you want and then make it happen, rather than accept what is?'

It's probably better if you don't even try to understand it.

You're probably right. I think it's better for me to just decide how things are going to work out, and then they will.

'Yes,' she admitted reluctantly.

Gwydion caressed her face. 'In a way, you invited him in, and you didn't even know it,' he said gently, trying to ease the frightened look out of her face. 'Once you believed he might be telling the truth, you gave him entry, and then, in a way, he *was* telling the truth. He possessed a small piece of you, and the more you believed it, the more he owned. The seeds of doubt were growing. Eventually, if you had stopped wondering and decided it was true for certain, he would have possessed your soul; you would have been his completely.'

He stroked her stomach as he saw it begin to clench. 'The good news is, now that the belief has been eradicated, so has the possession. In a way, your hope, or faith, saved you. And ever since you've discovered the truth, each breath you've taken, each beat of your heart, has cleansed your body of the vestiges of that possession. Now you're free of it. You belong totally to yourself again.'

Rhapsody smiled. She took his hand and kissed it. 'Not true,' she said. 'I belong totally to you.'

Gwydion grinned. 'I was hoping you'd say that,' he said mischievously, leaning over her. 'Why do you think I had you lie down on the bed?'

She pulled him to her and kissed him, encircling him with a slender leg. 'Let me see if I can guess.'

82

Even as far from the Moot as she was, she could still hear the sounds of shrieking and merrymaking, could still see the bonfire's roaring flames flickering against the dark sky in the distance. The wind that blew around the rise of the swale on which she stood carried with it the smell of embers and the taste of a bitter Past made sweet again by hope.

Anwyn stared down at the horn in her hands. Even in the absence of the moon's light it gleamed, like a luminous pearl in the darkness. Its metal was still warm, doubtless residual heat from the woman who had usurped its usage, had pressed her perfect mouth to it and summoned Anwyn's own people to her feet. Of course they had been compelled to come. None that sailed from Serendair, nor those of their blood who came after them, could resist the command of the horn; Gwylliam had made certain of it.

It was no excuse, not for the betrayal she had suffered.

No excuse whatsoever.

She closed her eyes and held the horn aloft, stretching out her arms to the starlit darkness of the sky.

The words of the upstart wench came back to her now, blowing in the laughing wind of night, drunk with celebration.

Anwyn ap Merithyn, tuatha Elynsynos, I rename you The Past. Your actions are out of balance. Henceforth your tongue will only serve to speak of the realm into which your eyes alone were given entry. That which is the domain of your sisters, the Present and the Future, you will be unable to utter. No one shall seek you out for any other reason, so may you choose to convey your knowledge better this time, lest you be forgotten altogether.

The Seer began to laugh. At first the mirth came forth as a chuckle, then a gasp. Then she threw her head back and roared with merriment, maniacal as her sister Manwyn, but far more insidious. She laughed until it would have been impossible to tell if she were screeching with glee or shrieking in madness, though no living soul could hear her above the bellowing of the bonfires that still filled the Moot with dancing light.

Henceforth your tongue will only serve to speak of the realm into which your eyes alone were given entry.

Anwyn clutched the horn even tighter, her searing blue eyes gleaming in the darkness as they opened.

'Very well,' she said aloud. 'As you command, Your Majesty.'

I need your memories, the demon-spirit had whispered from within the fire. Her own reply blended into the bristling wind.

'I understand,' she said.

Anborn was in an unusually good mood as he rode west across the foothills to the broad expanse of the Krevensfield Plain. Considering the way the day had started, and what had transpired, it was a refreshing surprise to see how well things had turned out.

It had been many centuries since the Lord Marshal could remember feeling so free, so burdenless. The wind was high, the night clear and starry, the damp air of near-morning filled with the fresh scent of summer tinged with the sharp odor of smoke from distant bonfires. Anborn pulled the helmet from his head and set it before him, running his hands through his streaming hair. The smooth gait of the horse, the pounding against the earth beneath them – there were still things in life to be cherished after all.

After so many centuries of disillusionment, the vault of stone around his heart had shattered at last. Anborn had been an idealist in youth; he remembered the intensity with which he had once lived life, the deathless vows he had made early in his martial training to uphold the statutes of the Kinsmen, the ancient brotherhood of warriors to which he sought inclusion. All of that impassioned commitment had died on the battlefields of the Great War, along with his soul – or so he had presumed.

He remembered the words of his instructor in the sword, Oelendra Andaris. *I serve no Lord, no Lady, only a people,* she had said. *When those that would lead would also serve, then shall I swear fealty to a crown. Only then.* For both of them, Anborn and Oelendra, both Kinsmen, both irreparably scarred by a war, the time had come to believe again. Like the coming dawn, perhaps peace was on the horizon.

His mind went to Rhapsody, as it often did when he was not concentrating on anything in particular. Anborn wondered what she was doing at that moment, then squelched the thought. He had caught the look between her and Gwydion. Unless his nephew was an utter fool, he had a fairly good idea what she was probably in the process of undertaking, and it would not be gentlemanly to speculate about it further.

He laughed aloud, delighted in the turn of events and the promise of a new beginning. Good cheer broke over him like a wave, racing through his hair like the wind that flapped his cloak behind him. His spirits were high as the starry sky above him, around him, all the way to the endless horizon just beginning to lighten at the approach of morning.

★

Anwyn brought the horn to her lips and sounded it.

The blast that issued forth was not heard in this time, nor by any living soul. It echoed instead through the realm of the Past, as it had so many centuries before, swelling from the silvery horn and hovering on the heavy air of ancient memory.

Then, after a long reverberation, it rained slowly down from the air and settled into the earth.

Anwyn smiled and closed her eyes. In a voice hollow with memory she began the chant.

The raid on Farrow's Down.
The siege of Bethe Corbair.
The Death March of the Cymrian Nain.
The burning of the western villages.
Kesel Tai.
Tomingorllo.
Lingen Swale.
The slaughter at Wynnarth Keep.
The rape of the Yarimese water camp.
The assault on the southeastern Face.
The evisceration of the fourth column.
The mass execution of the First Fleet farming settlements.
The Battle of Canderian Fields.

One by one, ever so patiently, she recounted each grim history, each bloody event in the Great War, a conflict ignited by the F'dor but brought about by simpler factors – rage, betrayal, jealousy, lust for power. Hatred, even older than the Before-Time.

When she had recited all the great losses of the war she moved on, to each conflict since, each place where men fell at the manipulation of the demon-spirit.

Finally, when the litany was complete, she raised the horn to her lips again and sounded it.

Anwyn opened her eyes. She smiled.

As Anborn crested the rise of a great swale his stallion reared in fright. Anborn brought him to heel, gentling the animal down, then cast a glance over his shoulder to see what had spooked the horse.

For a moment, he could see nothing in the dark. Then, as his vision sharpened, the blood of the dragon within his veins roared like fire with panic.

'Sweet Creator,' he murmured. The words caught in the back of his throat.

The darkness at his feet was shifting.

The wide expanse of the Krevensfield Plain was moving.

Without taking a second breath Anborn dragged his horse back from the brim of the swale and bolted, galloping back toward the Moot, as the ground beneath him split asunder.

83

A haze hung over the Moot; it was not merely the vaporous mist that collected in the Bowl each morning, owing to its low-lying topography, but a cloud of thickheadedness enhanced by the excessive intake and absorption of alcohol. The Great Cymrian Fog, as it was later jokingly known, lifted, as Ashe had predicted, around the same time as the sun came into position directly overhead, forcing even the most resilient of day-sleepers to squint and rise, to make ready for the second session of the Council.

'What a waste,' Rhapsody whispered to Gwydion as they surveyed the human wreckage stumbling and groaning below them in the Bowl as the attendant Cymrians set about becoming functional again. 'I can think of a much nicer form of debauchery than drinking oneself into a stupor.'

'Hold that thought,' Gwydion replied, patting her 'muffins.'

Rhapsody had sought out Oelendra and privately told her the upcoming news. The Lirin champion's eyes filled with tears and she hugged her queen with an embrace more maternal than any Rhapsody had experienced since she left home. The new Lady Cymrian's throat tightened for a moment, and when she pulled away, her eyes glimmered like those of her ancient friend.

She had dressed for the occasion in a gown of azure silk, fitted at the waist and sleeves before flaring into a full skirt, on which she had belted Daystar Clarion in a waist scabbard. Gwydion's eyes had twinkled when beholding her in it, and he had brushed a kiss on her cheek.

'What a beautiful dress; very royal.'

Rhapsody shook her head. 'It's camouflage. I'm hoping to blend in with the sky. Maybe they won't see me and will leave me alone.'

The ovation that greeted the new Lord and Lady was more subdued than it had been the night before upon their selection, owing mostly to the headaches that excessive applause and whistling might cause the assemblage. The atmosphere seemed to clear up quickly, however, when Ashe took to the Rise and presented his Lady, then asked for a moment of attention for a portentous announcement.

'It is with great joy and consummate humility that I proclaim to you the wonderful news that the Lady Cymrian has graciously consented to be my wife.'

The Cymrian multitude was silent for a moment; then a wave of excitement swept through the Bowl, swelling into a roar of approval. Applause and acclamations in myriad languages rang out. The Mountain Knives, the contingent of Nain that Ashe had described on Midsummer's Night the previous year, sent up a war whoop that rocked the Moot, causing the heads of many of their fellow Cymrians to feel as if they had split. Rhapsody smiled at the cheering crowd, the sun glinting off their armor and banners, gleaming with a radiance that bespoke hope for the new age.

A voice, recognizable to her from the day before as a heckler from the House of McLeod, shouted above the gleeful din.

'Gwydion ap Llauron, grandson of Gwylliam the Abuser and Anwyn the Manipulator; how did you gain this Lady? She is unlike your line, which is why she was so well affirmed. Can you assure this assemblage that no violence or coercion was used to reach this agreement?'

The roaring throng fell silent. Gwydion's face turned white and his hands began to shake with a mounting fury. The joy that had been in his eyes a moment before disappeared in the wake of the insult, replaced by a dark, reptilian aspect. He had endured many affronts and slurs the day before on behalf of his family and his House, and had taken them all with goodwill, but the suggestion that he would raise a hand to his bride was more than he could endure. Before he could speak, Rhapsody took his hand.

'Well, I can,' she said, and her words bore the stamp of true speaking, as well as a hint of humor. 'I'm happy to say that no, I didn't have to resort to anything like that – he agreed pretty willingly, actually. So I guess I brought the sword and the thumbscrews for nothing.'

The crowd absorbed her words, then burst forth into gales of laughter and applause that rocked the sides of the Moot and echoed off the Teeth. It washed over Gwydion, sweeping his wrath away with it. He blinked as his anger passed, and looked down at Rhapsody; she was smiling up at him with a look of pure trust and confidence making her beautiful countenance ethereal. A grin crept back over his face, and Rhapsody took it in her hands, reaching up to kiss him before the eyes of the Council.

He drew her into his arms, and the cheering rabble faded into obscurity; it was as if they were the only two people there. Their lips met softly, then with more warmth, and as his body began to tremble Gwydion was aware again of the thunderous clamor from the assemblage; the tumult was shaking the ground beneath them. At least he thought it was the noise of the multitude; he knew it would have felt the same kissing her alone on the heath above Elysian.

The sweet scent of Rhapsody's skin, the joy that permeated him in having her finally back in his arms, was perhaps responsible for the obscurement of his senses, the happy haze the shielded him from the growing rumble within the earth, counterbalanced by the eerie silence that had swept over the crowd and swallowed the cheering.

By the time he realized what was happening it was too late.

84

The first to feel the change was Grunthor.

Like the sensation that occurred within the ear while climbing a high mountain, the pressure in his head expanded, then popped as the earth beneath his feet turned ill.

Achmed looked to his friend questioningly. There was no mistaking the change that had come over the Sergeant-Major; the amber eyes were wide and growing glassy; his bruise-colored skin was flushing, his enormous nostrils flaring as his heart pumped great volumes of blood. He stared off to the west for a moment, and then his muscles coiled as he vaulted off the rim of the Moot and down toward the tentative gathering below.

'Down from the rise!' he roared to Rhapsody, then bolted down the face of Bowl into the crowd of confused Cymrians, who only a moment before had been in the throes of joyous celebration. 'Move! Move!' His voice rumbled through the air and over the bewildered populace, frozen in fright as he charged them; then he was shoving them in any direction away from the sloping rise at the center of the Moot which no one but the giant Bolg had felt shaking.

Rhapsody had broken from Gwydion's embrace at Grunthor's shout, and turned to look down into the blank faces of the throng of Cymrians. The crowd was quickly parting in Grunthor's path, scattering out of his way, though the noise of fear had not come forth yet; everything was eerily silent. Her eyes went back to the pulpit, then widened in horror.

'The horn is gone,' she said to Gwydion, then turned and shouted to Achmed. 'The horn is gone!'

Achmed nodded, not turning; he at that moment heard an alarm go up from his lookouts and Tristan's forces on the western face of the Moot. He spun quickly and shielded his eyes from the bright light of noon.

A rider was galloping across the Krevensfield Plain, spurring his horse mercilessly. Even as far away as he was the Bolg king could hear him shouting hoarsely, sounding an alarm. The Orlandan army, encamped now, began rising unsteadily, cautiously gathering arms and armaments, when another shout went up.

'It's Anborn! Open the gate!'

Behind him the sky was rolling black, clouds of smoke billowing as though a volcano in the sky had erupted. As Anborn approached, the black smoke roared closer; it had the breadth of a grass fire of continental proportions driving ahead of a purposeful wind, but as it approached it became clear that there was no flame, but rather the earth itself, ripping violently from the wide plain, dust and grit vaulted skyward by the sheer force that disturbed it.

In the shadow of the darkness came an army. For a moment it appeared to be legions of beasts, as much of it did not walk erect, but rather moved across the land as if being dragged by some unseen force. Rhapsody gasped and clutched Gwydion's arm, recalling the vision from the observatory tower.

'It's the Cymrian dead, the Fallen, slaughtered in the Great War.' Her words came out in a half-whisper. 'Anwyn has summoned them from the Past.'

The sea of walking bodies crested the horizon, staining the rim of the world black with their number. The shell of every corpse that had perished

517

on the plain or in the mountain, any body that had not been immolated or otherwise fully consumed, had been reanimated by the sheer force of memory and had crawled or staggered or slid toward the Moot; now they stood, amid a sea of the dead, of decay and disease and human fragments magnetized to Anwyn's wrath.

From the peaks of the Teeth came a roar like captured thunder moving through the mountains. Avalanches of rock and soil rolled from the crags, starting at Grivven and then rumbling through Canrif and all of the peaks that rimmed the foothills, until the shale began to rain down on the Moot, a pelting hail of sharp dust. From those hillsides rose more soldiers in Anwyn's force, animated bodies of Nain and Lirin, human and demi-human, adults and children, all the victims of Anwyn and Gwylliam's great folly, crawling forth from the vaults of the dead to answer the call of the horn as they once had long ago.

Outside the Moot, the army of Roland, one hundred thousand strong, began massing into legions and columns. Rhapsody shuddered at the sight. Where before they had seemed a numerous force, one that by its sheer number threatened to challenge Achmed's hold on the mountain, now they were suddenly and overwhelmingly dwarfed, outnumbered perhaps a hundred to one, perhaps more. She didn't have time to count.

From the belly of the Moot a thundering rumble issued forth. The ground bubbled and broke open an instant later, crushing, overwhelming, swallowing Cymrians from every fleet who had been unable to move out of the way. Amid screams of terror more soldiers of the dead crawled forth, from ancient and forgotten mass graves, swords and rotting spears in their hands wrapped in burial cloths or shroud-rags. Their sightless eyes turned to the scattering masses that fled before them like crows before a storm.

Grunthor and a small band he had conscripted and armed from his personal arsenal had managed to interpose themselves between the crush of fleeing pilgrims and the grisly approach of what seemed thousands of the disinterred. He was simultaneously screaming orders to the ramparts to mobilize the hiding army of the Bolg.

In the panic of the earthen tremors Rhapsody felt a sense of calm settle on her, muting the anger that was burning behind her eyes. Quickly she cast her gaze around the Moot, erupting now beneath the sea of the living, foaming and cresting like an earthen sea, filling it with waves of the dead.

A group of children, mostly human, had been separated in the initial cataclysm, torn from their family groups when the ground sundered. Their cries of panic were only slightly louder than those of the adults struggling to get to them. From her place on the rim above, Rhapsody could see a river of as-yet-undisturbed earth that might serve as a bridge between them.

Gwydion squeezed her hand, then loosed it as they exchanged a nod. 'Open the gate!' he shouted to the swirling mass of panicking people nearest the Moot's great earthen doors. He darted down the side of the Bowl toward the entrance gates while Rhapsody hurried in the opposite direction, to the chasm between the children and adults, where the ground was rumbling in the advent of another schism.

'Here! Here! Follow the unbroken ground!' she called. Her voice, clear with royal timbre and full of a Namer's authority, rang over the cacophony below, cutting through the noise like a diamond through glass. The children turned immediately and sighted on her. 'Come – come to me.' Rhapsody held out her arms, beckoning the panicking children over the rise of earth.

Across the Bowl Gwydion's eyes had sighted on an answer as well.

'Stephen!' he shouted from one of the Moot's lower rims. The Duke of Navarne spun amid the maelstrom of Cymrians, living and dead, hearing his friend's call. 'Stephen – open the gates! Clear the Moot!' Gwydion could see understanding take root in his eyes; Stephen nodded that understanding, then passed his screaming daughter to the outstretched arms of a nearby guardsman and broke through the crowd, heading toward the earthen gates.

Gwydion turned to see the masses of panicking people raining down the sides of the Moot into its floor, toppling and smashing into one another in their fright. The rocky causeways and rims of earthen seats shuddered, both from the disturbance below the ground and from the flood of evacuees crawling and tumbling from the higher sides of the Bowl. He grabbed the arm of a half-Lirin woman as she fell, then interposed himself in the stream of evacuees.

'Settle, be calm!' he said authoritatively, the rumble and threat of wyrmflame barely beneath the surface. 'I command you, slow your pace and egress carefully.' The crowd swelled, then stopped. The new Lord Cymrian lifted the supine woman and hauled her easily over the broken mounds of earth, guiding her toward the exit, then turned to the mass behind him. 'Slowly,' he commanded. 'Be cautious.' He pulled the first man forward and assisted him through the dust from where the earth had been rent, hovering in the air over the newly formed rise, then signaled to the others to follow.

On the center rise of the Moot's floor, Grunthor was counting troops and victims, grimly revising his estimates moment by moment as more of the disinterred poured forth from the hillsides, broke up from the valleys, and clawed up from the earth. The Cymrians, powerful and long-lived as they might be, were unprepared for any sort of battle. With the exception of Tristan's army, now preparing to engage the coming tidal wave of the dead, the attendees of the Council had come dressed and equipped for a pilgrimage rather than a campaign. The Sergeant-Major knew that if he was fast, and very, very lucky, he might be able to choose which groups had to be sacrificed, instead of leaving that choice to Anwyn.

'Should have torn that bitch's head from her shoulders when I had the chance,' he muttered darkly, then shielded his eyes from the blinding brightness of the sun and the hailstorm of gravel and dust mixed with blood, fresh and long-dried.

His stomach roiled as he edged his thin troop of volunteers into an arc to protect those Rhapsody was guiding away. The Earth itself was filling his ears with screams, like the anguished protest of a brutal rapist's victim, a mother bewailing the slaughter of her children before her eyes. Against his will his mouth opened and roared in answer, a war scream of ferocity and threat that rose above the din for a moment, then was swallowed in the noise of terror and panic around him.

Rhapsody heard the sound, and it turned her blood to ice. She passed the last of the children over the buckling bridge of land beneath her in the center of the Bowl's floor and crawled over the slab of buckled earth, struggling to make her way to Grunthor, dodging the clutching sea of bony hands emerging from the tomb of memory.

The light of the sun above disappeared into the roiling clouds of blackness swirling like the sea in a tempest. As the darkness of noon fell over the Moot the scattered Cymrian assemblage fell into wary silence. Then a shout went up and rolled in a wave through the shattered Moot, only pieces of words sounding over the din.

'The gates! The gates are open!'

By now the tide of the Disinterred had surged in a monstrous wave, swallowing the earth and those who stood upon it. The shambling army streamed down from the mountain passes like rivers of gore, making the shining waterfalls run red with the red clay of disgorged earth. The ground within the Moot continued to spew them forth, and all the while the horizon continued to darken with their approach as the soldiers of the Past answered Anwyn's call, filling the air with the scent of the grave.

Ripples of blue light caught Rhapsody's eye. She turned to see Ashe, Kirsdarke boiling in his hands, swinging the water sword in sweeping arcs, driving back a phalanx of fallen, holding a stand of unbroken high ground. He had rallied a number of ancient warriors to the cause, and with him they beat the corpses back with staves, lanterns, any object that could be employed as a weapon, fighting by the side of the new Lord, the grandson of those who had brought this calamity upon them. The Lord Cymrian remained in the place his grandparents had once reigned, holding back the tide of the dead as best he could.

'Aria!' he shouted over the din. 'Lead them out of here!'

She turned again; behind him was a huge cluster of trembling people, Gwadd and human mostly, trapped between the blistering ground and the oncoming tide of the dead. A tiny sliver of unbroken ground was all that remained between them and the great gaping hole that barred the gate, occluded in darkness – the frightened Cymrians either could not see the land bridge, or were too panicked to try to cross the chasm.

Quickly she drew Daystar Clarion. The blade of elemental fire and starlight roared forth from its sheath, ringing its call across the growling roar of the Moot. Those huddled in panic heard the sound, saw the bright flash of light, and shied away, then squinted.

In her mind she could hear the voice of Oelendra, her mentor, instructing her patiently.

Iliachenva'ar; the word means 'bringer of light into a dark place.'

Or from one.

Yes.

Rhapsody held the sword aloft, a great burning beacon that cut through the gritty darkness of death that hung heavy in the air.

'Come!' she shouted. Her voice reverberated in the air.

She leapt down from the mound on which she was standing onto the sliver of earth, holding the sword up in front of her, then began to back across the land bridge over the chasm, toward the gate, praying that the army Tristan had brought to threaten Achmed was now holding the ground outside the Moot. The light from the sword splashed over the land bridge; the flames cast a bright, uneven glow, illuminating the path.

The masses that had been standing in terror began to follow her slowly. She kept up the pace, occasionally striking at a fleshless hand or head that rose up from the ground beneath her feet, leading the cluster of terrified souls closer and closer to the doors of the collapsing Moot. In the distance she could still see the blazing blue light of Ashe's sword, driving back the waves of darkness that still emerged from the belly of the Earth.

Then behind her the crowd swelled, and she was carried along on a surge of speed as they passed through the broken gate, torn open by Stephen and his forces, who now were somewhere in the fields surrounding the Moot. The Cymrians, having escaped the certain death of being trapped within the Moot, now faced the oncoming army. All around, from every mountainside, every swale of earth, bodies clashed in combat, some who still lived, some who had lived and died long before, locked in the embrace of mutual destruction.

Outside the Moot, the powerlessness vanished, but desperation was beginning to take hold. Women and men fought with flagpoles, food baskets, bare hands, whatever was available to them, joining the fray from which they had once cowered. The leaders of the provinces, Stephen Navarne, Quentin Baldasarre, and Martin Invenstrand, had rallied large groups of them, setting up a secondary front behind the soldiers of Roland. Stephen turned to Tristan, who had managed to escape the Moot in the last swell.

'Well, cousin,' he panted, drawing his sword, 'I don't know for what purpose you really brought the army to a gathering of peace, but a stroke of luck it was.' Tristan, his garments torn and blackened with the dried blood of his ancestors, only nodded.

'Look well on them one last time,' Baldasarre said, fingering the hilt of his sword. 'Trapped with the Teeth behind them, the dead before and all around them, they have no chance – none whatsoever.'

'Gods,' Invenstrand whispered, coming up alongside of them. The approaching army of the Fallen was now within range of the soldiers of Roland. The Orlandan army had employed every ballista, every catapult, flinging burning pitch into the advancing bulwark of the dead, but to no avail. They were vastly outnumbered; it was as if the tide of victims of the heinous battles of the Great War were endless, like the tides of the sea, crashing ever onward in waves, bent only on the destruction Anwyn savored to avenge her humiliation.

From the midst of the fray, Achmed had cleared the Ledge of emerging corpses. He caught the eye of his Sergeant-Major, standing atop a rise in the ruins of the Moot. The giant Bolg nodded, and the Firbolg king nodded in return.

Grunthor threw back his head and roared. The sound carried over the din below; it vibrated in the Earth itself, shaking loose shale from the mountains, rumbling through the rocks. In the heat of battle raging on the fields surrounding the Moot and on the Krevensfield Plain the combatants felt the tremors from the Sergeant's call; even the disinterred dead, the war-fallen, seemed to pause at the sound.

A moment later great fissures opened in the Teeth; the battlements and guard towers tore open. The mountainsides ran black as the Firbolg army roared forth, swelling down the cliff faces and onto the steppes below.

Grunthor's war cry was picked up by half a million voices, chanted across the peaks, screamed in the descent to the fields, rattling the very earth. The soldiers of Roland, embroiled in the conflict with the dead, felt them come, much as they had a year before, only this time to engage a common enemy. The swirling maelstrom of battle blackened further as the Bolg spilled forth, joining the men in common warfare, seeking to drive the dead back into their graves.

Martin Ivenstrand clutched at Tristan Steward's arm as the ocean of Firbolg rolled like a tidal wave down onto the Krevensfield Plain.

'I though you said they had been decimated!' he shouted above the deafening clamor.

'They – they were,' the Lord Roland mumbled. 'They—'

The dukes had just enough opportunity to run for cover as a column of Bolg soldiers stampeded through where they had been standing, screaming a war cadence, bent on destruction.

Rhapsody stood at the top of a torn swale on the plain. All around her cacophony reigned. The ground rumbled with the vibration of war, the thundering of horses; it was all she could do to remain upright in the fray. Amid the shrieking and clashing that filled the air she could hear a frighteningly familiar tattoo, a cadence of horrifying crescendo coming ever closer.

She looked up, trembling. In the near distance a swirling storm of dust and black clods of earth blasted skyward into the air beneath a tangle of galloping hooves, moving closer with each passing second. From within that approaching storm the bloodstained warrior of her nightmares was riding down on her, blue eyes gleaming ferociously, beating his straining mount with merciless urgency. The veins in his neck and forehead protruded from a face clenched in grim concentration.

It was Anborn.

He was shouting something, screaming really, but Rhapsody couldn't hear him over the din. He leaned slightly off the saddle to the right, stretching his arm out to her. Behind him the horizon was black with motion too distant and frenetic to discern. Rhapsody held out her arms, preparing to be swept up and onto the horse before him.

As she did the sky above and around her darkened, the searing heat of battle suddenly purged by a rush of wind that chilled her to the bone. As if time had slowed, she saw the veins in Anborn's neck stiffen, his teeth bare, as he opened his mouth in a great war scream, drowned out by the noise all around her. His eyes had moved from her face to the sky above her.

She looked up just as the slashing claw of the dragon that blotted out the sun above struck with blinding speed, snatching her from the ground, crushing her in its talons, taking her into the sky in the twinkling of an eye, like the helpless prey of a raptor.

85

Ashe was standing on the rise of a broken hillside, urging the remaining Cymrians out of the ruins of the Moot, when he felt Anwyn appear in the sky.

A great blast of energy shocked the air, leaving it dry, almost brittle, in his nostrils. A rolling wave of heat followed by the dark blotting out of sunlight appeared above him a moment later; the dragon had been hanging, formless, in the ether overhead, preparing to strike, and when she took shape the action sucked all the elemental lore that was extant in the air into the creation of her shimmering form. Great jointed wings as wide as two oxcarts each and claws like curved swords appeared first, most solidly, followed by the mistier, wyrmlike body of the beast, which glided over his head, then struck like a snake at the ground on which Rhapsody had been standing. A split second later the serpent took to the sky, the ground beneath her bare and unoccupied. Anborn galloped through the space where she had been, then reined his mount to a crashing halt, staring around wildly.

A word from the past, an agonizing scream of the soul, tore from Ashe's throat.

Nooooooooooo.

From deep within him, in the place where the Rowans had carefully sewn a piece of a star to save his life, the birthplace of his dual nature, the awakening of his own dragon spirit, Ashe felt the change begin. The wyrm within his blood rushed forth like a brushfire, bellowing as it came.

'Here!' it screamed in his voice and its own, the primal, multitoned sound of the wind within his gullet. *'ANWYN! Here!'*

Grunthor, his face bleeding, the cheekbone partially visible, tore his way to Ashe, who was focusing on the objects in the sky and roaring menace and revenge in some wordless wyrm speech that caused every vein to protrude. The giant thought he could see a shift beginning to be visible even beneath Ashe's armor and the cloak of mist that roared now, rampant, like the crashing waves of the sea.

He grabbed the smaller man's shoulder and a clump of the copper hair, and pulled him free of the sliding shale of the crumbling Moot, holding him suspended at eye level. Ashe's eyes did not meet his. He was instead wrenching his body to keep his target in view, writhing, slithering in Grunthor's grasp, and growing heavier as each second passed, his body turning almost vaporous.

'ANWYN! Here! HERE!'

'Hear!' Grunthor roared in Ashe's face. The Lord Cymrian's eyes, vertical pupils slit in the madness of his wyrm rage, struggled to break free from the Sergeant's grasp; when the Bolg did not drop him he reached for his sword.

Grunthor had had enough. He released the hair and wrapped his whole arm around Ashe, putting his claws firmly into the Lord Cymrian's throat.

'Be still! Stop your rampage. Be a man! Be a king, or I'll rip you apart right here!'

Ashe blinked. He looked up at the stern visage of the Bolg commander, and felt the dragon's hold within him break. He swallowed, trying to force his voice.

'I have to get to her. I can't fail her again.'

Grunthor, face-to-face with the man, found himself staring into eyes blue as a glacier, could see the deep vertical pupils contracting in fear. In the same heartbeat he knew that the Cymrian lord's terror was only for Rhapsody. And in that moment his anger melted away in the face of the same fear he felt for the same beloved woman.

He set his jaw, grasped Ashe's forearm roughly, and held the Ring of Wisdom up before the Lord Cymrian's dragonesque eyes. 'What does it tell you?' he demanded above the sounds of anguish and panic flooding over them in the caustic wind that rose, heavy with burning cinders, from the floor of the Bowl.

Ashe's face went slack, the aspects of the rampant dragon's rise diminishing somewhat from his features. His brow unfurrowed, and he looked from the ring to the black sky above, then back to Grunthor's expectantly solemn face.

'If I take on Anwyn in an air battle, Rhapsody will die,' he said, calm returning to his voice.

Grunthor growled brusquely. 'What else?'

'Anwyn no longer cares. If I attack her and hold back to spare Rhapsody, we will both die.'

'Right. So be the lord we named you. If she's to die, let her last sight of you be more man than dragon. Command them.' He gestured impatiently at the swirling mass of panicking humanity below them. 'It's what Her Ladyship would want.'

Ashe stared at the Firbolg giant one moment more, then nodded. 'Yes,' he said heavily. 'It's what she would want.' He turned back to the Moot below him, the crowds still pressing blindly in the panic to exit. He saw a cluster of Nain near the egress and shouted to them, his voice carrying over the clamor.

'Men of the Forge!' he shouted in their language. 'Hold this rise!'

The Nain, hearing the ringing command, turned from their flight and stared up at their new High King, waving now at a group of peasants, directing them ahead toward a break in the wall. The Mountain Knives fell in, attacking the sea of dead warriors with a vengeance, steeling themselves against the likelihood that some of the rotting corpses were those of their own ancestors.

In desolation Ashe looked up into the sky.

A sickening rush of air slapped Rhapsody hard as the dragon banked, dangling her over the Krevensfield Plain, bloody and pockmarked as a leper's face.

Her arms were squeezed against her sides in the grip of the wyrm's talons, cutting off her access to the sword. It dangled impotently from her swelling wrist; she could feel the fire lapping at her leg and skirt as it brushed against her. Dangling above her head, out of reach and wrapped around the first knuckle of the dragon, was the Cymrian horn, its housing cracked.

Anwyn clenched her fist, grinding the air from Rhapsody's lungs, bruising her ribs.

'A pretty sight, isn't it, m'lady?' The harsh voice of the dragon scratched her ears. 'Look well on your people – see where you have brought them. Child of the Sky! How do you like the view from up here?'

Another sudden turn of air; Rhapsody struggled to maintain consciousness as the dragon beat her wings and spun, making the world go black for a moment.

The dragon's great strength was too much for her. She fought futilely to break free, even to move a tiny bit, within the clutch of the talons, to no avail.

'Damn your soul, Anwyn!' she shouted, wrenching her shoulder in an attempt to free the sword.

'Too late.' The wyrm matriarch chuckled, a deep, throaty laugh that carried with it the sound of grinding glass and bone.

'End it,' Rhapsody choked as the beast swooped teasingly near the ground, then dove into the sky again. 'They were – your – people – serve them! Save – them.'

'They betrayed me,' the dragon hissed, hovering over the fray where man and Bolg fought the remnants of men and Bolg. 'All of them, at one time or another, they all betrayed me. Just as you have. And—'

A whirr of silver sound, three times. Bright blood, acid red, splashed across Rhapsody's face. The beast gave a sickening lurch, and loosed a scream of pain and rage. Rhapsody felt Anwyn's grip slacken as a severed talon dangled from a single tendon, then tore off, spinning as it plummeted to the earth below, along with the silver horn, freeing Rhapsody's sword arm.

She grabbed on to the bony forearm above her to keep from falling herself. There, wedged in the knuckle, was the back end of a glossy blue cwellan disk, buried up to the middle, behind two others, no doubt; Achmed's weapon discharged its ammunition in threes.

The dragon screamed again, shaking its leg violently, flying in sickening spirals and strafing the ground, vomiting fire.

Rhapsody wrapped her arm tighter around the leg, then thrust the sword into the webbing between the bones of the dragon's wing. The burning blade slipped into the wyrm's flesh as if it were canvas, tearing a blackened hole. Anwyn roared in agony, and began to flex her claw and beat the injured wing violently, trying to dislodge the prey that was now her tormentor.

Rhapsody's stomach rushed into her mouth as the great beast spun in the air again, making her vision go black. She knew she could not survive the fall from the sky, and now thought that the longer she could keep the dragon away from the fray, the farther from the battlefield they could be when they finally fell, the safer those on the ground would be. In her hazy mind, the answer came to her, the thing the dragon would fear most.

She summoned her breath and began to shout.

'Anwyn ap Merithyn, tuatha Elynsynos, I rename you the Empty Past, the *Forgotten* Past. I consign your memory to those who have gone before you, wretched beast!'

'No!' the dragon screamed.

From his perch atop the broken rise, Achmed reloaded the cwellan, his thin hands sweating as he pulled back on the spring, reset the heavy rysin blades that had been designed centuries before by Gwylliam expressly for the purpose he was about to employ. He waited until the dragon was on the downswing of her dive, as close to the ground as possible. He signaled to Anborn, who galloped beneath the dragon as she banked and hovered in the air above, dodging to avoid being scorched by the erratic firefall of her breath.

Anborn spurred his horse.

Achmed aimed for the prismatic eye, blue as the fire at the heart of the Earth. He sighted the weapon, made allowances for the speed at which the wyrm was traveling, and spoke a small prayer to whatever was holy.

Then he fired.

The recoil from the cwellan made a sickening *crack* against his shoulder, sending waves of pain through his body.

Even from a distance he could feel the slice of air, the ripping of eye tissue.

Could see the dragon rear up, roiling in agony.

Saw the blazing blade in distant hands, tiny against the black smoke of the sky, disappear as Rhapsody drove Daystar Clarion once more into the beast, this time beneath the upstretched wing. The great claw opened, and her body fell out. She rolled down the monster's armored stomach, dragging the sword through its flesh along with her as she tumbled through the air, then pitched downward to the ground below, the sword falling far away, like a burning ember from the sky.

Anborn spurred the horse again mercilessly. Man and animal were locked in a death race, a desperate dash to interdict the hurtling body that fell from the sky. In his ears he heard the words of Manwyn, the Seer of the Future, spoken at Council so long ago, could hear them repeated in the voice of Rhonwyn, as the Future became the Present.

If you seek to mend the rift, General, guard the Sky, lest it fall.

Guard the Sky, lest it fall.

Lest it fall.

He could see Rhapsody's body tumbling to Earth, almost within his grasp; the Bolg king had timed his shot well. With one last kick he urged the horse forward as she hurtled into his arms, catching her, plucking her from the air, rolling with her, man and horse, amid the sound of grisly snapping and waves of shock that resolved a moment later into pain that blinded him with its intensity, bringing with it the sweet relief of unconsciousness.

Distantly Rhapsody could hear Grunthor's voice bellowing her name. Disoriented, she tried to move, but found she was trapped, crouched on her hands and knees, with heavy weight, weight far too burdensome for her to breathe beneath, let alone lift, draped across her back and shoulders.

The voice got louder, came nearer. She felt the shifting of weight, the moving of the burden, then was lifted up in the air into arms, warm and familiar. She opened her eyes to see the great green face of her friend staring down at her in panic.

'Your Ladyship? You all right? You alive there?'

She nodded, unable to catch her breath. Her body ached with the shock of her head moving.

'Thank the gods,' Grunthor murmured, leaning his forehead against hers.

A blast of fire erupted behind them, and the giant dove beneath a mound of torn earth. The dragon, injured and angry, was flying in great circles now, bleeding acidic gore onto the earth, raining her furious breath down on them.

Rhapsody's blood boiled.

'Enough of this,' she said, angrily brushing the clods of earth and brambles from her tattered dress. 'Where's Achmed?'

'Behind you,' came the sandy voice. 'As I always will be.'

Rhapsody turned to see the Firbolg king coming to her side. She opened her arms and embraced him quickly, then pointed to a broken rise at the edge of the Moot.

'Come,' she said to her two friends, scanning the sky angrily. 'We've got one more bloody prophecy to fulfill, damn it all.'

'*Hrekin,*' said Achmed sullenly. 'This had better be the last one.'

86

The sounds of battle strife rent the air as the Three crawled over the broken chasms that had once been the smooth green fields of the steppes leading to the Krevensfield Plain. Bodies of the long-dead and those more newly in the state littered the ground. The light from the sun was gone now, obliterated by the fall of night and the death that hung, like bitter earth, in the air and on the wind that swept the battlefield.

Rhapsody had found her sword by its glow not far from where she fell and sheathed it; now the Three crept in darkness through the ruins of the Great Moot, the broken symbol of Gwylliam's dream of peace, the place where a once-great nation had met in Council, planning and building an empire that had stood for a moment, shining brightly in the history of man, only to fade and crumble like sand beneath the selfish lust for power and dominion.

Within the Moot Ashe still stood, fending off the remains of the fallen, holding back the tide of death while his people escaped. He was surrounded and alone, as he had been that day on the Krevensfield Plain when he stood to defend Shrike.

Achmed slung the cwellan and sighted it on the grisly remains of soldiers that were attacking the Lord Cymrian.

'Ashe!' he shouted across the Bowl of the Moot.

Ashe turned and looked at him.

'Want help this time?'

Between swings of the sword, the Lord Cymrian nodded.

Achmed fired. The bright disks whirled like firesparks through the air, slicing across the gusts of wind and into the tattered necks of the corpses on Ashe. In the wink of an eye Achmed had reloaded again, and again, sending a hailstorm of cwellan disks whizzing around Ashe, causing the bodies to fall like chaff to the ground.

Then the Three hurried back behind a rocky outcropping as the dragon strafed through, bleeding and spinning, roaring in anger that shook the base of the mountains. The sky blazed with orange light as the fire from her breath struck the ground, blasting shards of rock and dust into the night. Rhapsody stamped out Grunthor's greatcloak, which had ignited in the blast.

'Ashe!' she shouted as they climbed toward the Summoner's Rise. 'Get out of the Moot!'

She followed the Bolg up the rock ledges, over the rubble that had once been seats carved into the earth, scraping her bare knees and the tatters of her gown on the boulders that still supported the long, flat ledge of granite from which she had called the Council into being.

When they reached the top Rhapsody stared in dismay at the distant fields, roiling still in battle. The Firbolg army had joined forces with the soldiers of Roland, and they, along with every living Cymrian soul, were still battling, still dodging the dragon's wrath, still holding the land that had been in their blood for centuries, beating back the nightmares of the Past.

She looked down into the fractured Moot, split in twain from the emergence of the fallen. A great rift bisected the floor of the gathering place where only this morning the Cymrians had been celebrating the dawn of their new era. She turned to Achmed and Grunthor.

'There?' she asked.

The two Bolg nodded in answer.

Behind her she heard the crumbling of stone, the rushing of panting breath. Achmed swung the cwellan and pointed into the shadows. A moment later Ashe appeared, bloody and torn, with the black earth of the grave smeared on him. Rhapsody's eyes filled with tears; tattered as he was, he was every inch the Lord they had named him.

He took her into his arms, but she pushed away quickly, her eyes still scanning the sky for the dragon. She could see Anwyn, circling in the distance, raining fiery death down on the fields at the Bolg, searching for her, and anger began to burn furiously behind her eyes.

She drew Daystar Clarion, its flame burning bright as a brand in a black night, roaring with righteous fury, ringing like a chime, swallowing all other sound.

'Anwyn!' she shouted. Her voice rocked the earth, causing shale to slide and the echo to rumble over the Teeth and the plain below them. 'Anwyn, you coward! Here I am!'

In the distant sky the dragon turned, hovering in a haze of bloody fire for a moment, then streaked toward the Moot.

Rhapsody held the sword aloft; Grunthor and Achmed grasped the hilt together, helping her hold it even higher. She searched the sky for a star, finding after a moment Carendrill, the tiny, blue-white star beneath which the Lirin signed peace accords.

'Are you ready?' she asked, struggling to keep the sword steady. 'This is the moment that has been awaited since the end of the First Age. Our words will carry power – we must use them carefully.' The two Bolg looked off into the sky at the approaching dragon and nodded.

Over the billowing flames of the sword Achmed could hear silence fall, and the beating of his heart begin to echo, thudding heavily in his ears. Within his veins his blood ran hot, humming with life, with portent, the blood that had been tied in the old life to that of his kinsmen, the refugees of Serendair. All of those kinsmen that remained in this world huddled on the fields below, seeking shelter from the dragon's wrath. He could feel their terror in his veins, their blood united in common history, in hope for the future. The closest thing to a prayer he had ever uttered came forth from his lips.

'Not one more drop of blood will be shed here,' he said simply.

Child of Blood.

The amber eyes of the giant who stood silently beside him were filled with tears of sorrow. Those eyes were no stranger to the tragedies of war or mass destruction; they had looked unblinkingly on the death of nations, on the ravages of the deepest depravity without flinching, but this moment was somehow different. From deep within his soul, through the bond that had formed long ago as he traveled along the Axis Mundi, Grunthor felt the pain of the Earth, the abject horror that so many fallen had been dragged from the peace they had found within Her arms, ripped from their rest, unwillingly rallied by a soulless woman to the madness that was now rending fallow fields asunder. Tears streamed down his cheeks, not for those who were cowering from death, but for those who had embraced it centuries ago, and now, through no fault of their own, were being forced to brave the agony of the sun, of battle, after so long at rest in the peaceful darkness of their Mother's embrace.

'Open, Earth, and take back your children,' he said.

Child of Earth.

Alone among the Three, Rhapsody was fighting back anger. Her body, aching a moment before from the shock of falling, of the injuries she had sustained, was whole again for the time being, sustained by the power of the sword, the fire and the stars to which it was tied. *Enough*, she thought bitterly, trying to rein in her hatred as the beast roared closer. *You despoil the Sky. It is meant to shelter the world, not to rain destruction down upon it. The Sky is the collective soul of the universe, and, as you've said, you have no soul.* She inhaled and let her breath out slowly, watching the dragon's approach.

'If there is to be fire from the Sky, it shall not serve your hateful will, Anwyn. Let any fire that would rain down from the Sky bring the end of strife, and seal the beginning of a new era of peace.'

Child of the Sky.

Below them, in the Bowl of the Moot, the enormous rift in the ground rumbled and widened, splitting deeply. The bodies of the Fallen crumbled and rolled into the opening grave like pebbles rolling down a hillside.

The light from the dragon's fiery breath splashed over the four standing on the Summoner's Rise. The sound of rage, ancient, more powerful than the ages, screamed in the air around them. The beast, bleeding from one eye and the severed claw, surged through the air, soaring over the Moot; she inhaled, drawing in breath like the wind of a hurricane, preparing to discharge her fire in the direction of the Summoner's Rise.

At that moment, Rhapsody spoke the name of the star.

The blast that descended shook the Rise, and the Moot itself. With an unearthly roar the fire of the star, the pure, unbridled element of ether that preceded the birth of all other elements, rained down from the sky and struck the dragon as she hovered in the air, poised to strike. The beast arched, illuminated by a light brighter than the sun, then fell, spiraling, into the rift of earth in the Moot floor, the grave that had erupted like a spider pustule with the Disinterred and which Grunthor had widened.

As Anwyn sank beneath the crust of earth Grunthor closed his eyes and shrugged, pushing his hands together as though molding ethereal clay. The floor of the Moot shuddered, then closed rapidly, filling in the place where Anwyn had fallen. The crumbled sides of the Moot gave way, tumbling in upon themselves, forming a great mound of earth and rock in the middle of the floor of the Bowl.

Rhapsody spoke the name of the star again; this time light, clear and pure, descended from the star, washing over the Moot, sealing the ground beneath which the dragon lay.

In the distance she was aware of the thundering noise of war dimming to silence. As the starlight faded she looked across the dusky sky and saw that the Fallen had slipped, tumbling back into the Earth, back to the Past, leaving behind confusion but no more battle.

She turned to Gwydion and threw her arms around him, holding tight as he returned her embrace, then in turn embraced both of her companions, two men who shared her history, her life, and her future.

'It's over,' she said simply. 'Now the work begins.'

As the night passed Achmed and Grunthor sorted through the rubble of the fields with Rhapsody and Ashe, reassigning troops, destroying ghoulish remains that still quivered with malice, assigning healing units, working to calm the populace that was still in shock.

In the glow of the thousands of campfires now burning amid the devastation, Achmed came upon Tristan Steward. The Lord Roland was uninjured but silent, gazing into the distance at the Moot, his sobbing wife leaning on his arm for support.

The Firbolg king stared down at the regent, an expression close to pity in his eyes. Tristan Steward finally looked up at him.

'Do either of you require medical assistance?' Achmed asked. The Lord Roland shook his head. The Firbolg nodded, then turned to leave.

'Wait,' Tristan Steward said. His voice came out in a weak whisper. Achmed stood silently as the regent rose shakily, then brushed the grime from his hands. He stared at the Firbolg king without speaking. Finally Achmed grew impatient.

'Well?'

'The – the army – my army—'

'Yes?'

The Lord Roland lapsed into silence.

'It was inspired that you brought them here in a gesture of goodwill,' Achmed said as pleasantly as he could. 'Now that, like my army, their allegiance is to Rhapsody, it was good that they were here to witness her investiture. Is that what you were trying to say?'

Tristan Steward's mouth dropped open, then shut resolutely.

'Yes,' he said.

'I thought so. Excuse me,' Achmed said. He turned and walked off into the night with Grunthor and his aides-de-camp.

Rhapsody moved among the injured with Krinsel, the Finder midwife, tending to the wounds of both human and Bolg alike. The Cymrians had largely been spared, thanks to the armies of Roland and Ylorc, and the work of Ashe and the soldiers he had enlisted to hold back the Fallen while the rest escaped.

She was tying up the broken arm of a dark Cymrian, a man of the race known as Kith, when Rial appeared at her side, a somber expression on his face.

'M'lady?'

Rhapsody glanced up at her viceroy and smiled, the expression draining from her face at the look in his eyes.

'What is it?'

Rial extended his hand. 'Come, please, m'lady.'

She took his hand and followed him in the dark over the broken field to a place where the body of a beautiful black stallion lay, twisted back upon itself. At the stallion's side bent Faedryth, the Nain king, beside Oelendra, also crouched on the ground. Rhapsody stared at the dead horse and began to tremble.

'No,' she whispered. 'Oh, gods, no. Anborn.'

The king of the Nain looked up at her, blood oozing from a gash to his forehead. 'He's alive still, barely,' Faedryth said sadly. 'His back is broken.'

'No,' she said again as she stepped over Faedryth's legs and bent between him and Oelendra. 'Anborn? Gods, what have I done to you?'

The Cymrian general was propped up against the chest of his friend, the Nain king, covered with Rial's red cloak. His face was ghostly white beneath the dark hair of his beard, but he managed to feebly strain his arm toward her. She reached to take his hand.

'You've – redeemed me,' he said, his voice soft and ragged. 'Through you Manwyn's prophecy has – been fulfilled. I have found the – slightest of my kinsmen. I caught the sky when it fell. You have helped me – mend both the rift within – myself, and the one I caused – so long – ago – among my fellow Cymrians. See? I am tended by both Lirin and Nain; who – would have thought it possible?'

Tears streamed down her face as she tenderly took the rugged hand between her own and rested her cheek on it. Anborn reached out with some pain and stroked her hair.

'I would gladly give my life – or my legs – in your service, m'lady,' he said with great effort. 'It is my honor to be – sworn to you.'

'Rhapsody! *Rhapsody!*'

Ashe's voice sounded over the crackle of the fire, the whine of the wind, carrying with it the sound of desperation and fear.

Anborn patted the side of her face.

'Go – to him,' he said.

'When I come back I will tend to you,' she said, rising. 'I will employ every skill I have as a Singer to heal you.'

Anborn smiled and waved her off.

'Go,' he said.

Rhapsody looked over the fields of injured and dying, great splits of earth where the field had once been fallow. She followed Ashe's voice on the wind, back toward the doors of the Moot where only a day before the Cymrians had processed in with so much hope.

Lying beyond the doors, in a place where many had fallen, Ashe was bent over the broken body of Lord Stephen Navarne, his best friend. Rhapsody hurried to his side.

'Help him – Aria, please; don't let me lose him again,' Ashe choked. He patted Stephen's face, trying to revive the duke, whose blue-green eyes stared into the next world.

Rhapsody sank to her knees on the gory earth next to the men. Her eyes went from Lord Stephen's pale face to the hill above where he lay. Gwydion Navarne, her oldest grandchild, stood, a look of forced bravery on his face, his arms around his sister, Melisande, who wept as if her heart would break. Rosella stood with her arms around both of them, a look of terror in her eyes.

Rhapsody laid a hand on the duke's chest, feeling for the beating of his heart.

'M'lord?'

There was no response; the skin beneath her hand was cold. Her fingers went to his throat.

'M'lord?'

The pulse was as weak as she had ever felt on a living man, in his eyes she could see the distant reflection of the mist from the Veil of Hoen.

'Aria – please—'

'Daddy?'

The sound of Melisande's voice brought a memory back to Rhapsody. The last time she had spoken with Lord Stephen was outside of Haguefort, in the arms of a bitter wind, as she heralded Llauron's supposed death. He had smiled in the way he always did, causing the corners of his eyes to crinkle affectionately.

You know, Rhapsody, we're practically family. Do you think there will ever be a time when you might address me just by my first name?

No, m'lord.

Rhapsody sat up straighter, thinking. She had once sung Grunthor back from the brink of death, though as far as she could see Stephen was even more grievously injured.

'Stephen,' she sang, leaving her hand over his heart. 'Stephen; stay here, with us.' She turned to Ashe, whose eyes were gleaming. 'What is his name, Sam? His full name?'

'Stephen ap Wayan ap Hague, thuatha Judyth.'

She repeated the name, singing in tune with the fragile beating of the duke's heart. *Stay your hand from him, m'Lord Rowan,* she thought, singing with all the powers of her Naming ability. *Leave him here, in this place, just a little while longer.*

She chanted his name over and over again, singing until the sun rose, her voice hoarse and tattered. As the sword tip of dawn pricked the horizon, she focused straight into it, trying to draw the warmth of the sun into Stephen to keep his body from cooling, to keep his brightness with her in the world she knew. In that sliver of blindness Rhapsody caught the silhouette of the Lord Rowan. For her, he might wait, stay his hand, however broken and torn Stephen was, commute the death sentence of any of the Cymrians who had traveled from their lives in the present to face the resurrected feud. She could mend them, repair, rename, and spare them all. And she turned away in relief, to see still scattered among the wounded, being carried off like bits of firewood, the thousands that had been pulled from rest by Anwyn.

Her ministrations would be wholly different, could raise them to life for peace, resurrect them to higher service. She imagined them smiling, imagined Stephen at the door of the museum.

And wept at the temptation, and at the incalculable loss.

'No,' she said between her tears. 'I can't do it, Sam. I can't. He will have to cast his own lot, make his own passage through the Gate, or choose to stay on this side of it. I can sing him to the path, but he has to choose it. If Death has decided to take him, I have no more right to try and dissuade it than Anwyn did.'

'Aria—'

'No,' she said, her voice stronger. 'I can't call him back through the Gate. He has those he loves on both sides of it. If he chooses to slip away to that rest, who am I to force him to remain? He has reason to stay, and reason to go. We must be humble and reverent in the face of whatever choice he and Death make between them.'

She took Ashe's hand, and he bowed his head over it in grief. They stood watch, hoping that Stephen would begin to breathe again, to inhale the color of the sunrise into his cheeks. But as each moment passed, his skin grew more alabaster, his hands colder.

As dawn crested the clouds, the light left the duke's eyes. Rhapsody looked to the horizon, and thought she saw a brief glint of a smile within the shadow from beyond the Veil of Hoen.

'Receive him kindly, m'Lord Rowan,' she whispered into the morning wind. Beside her Ashe began to weep.

Rhapsody looked over her shoulder at the white faces of Rosella and the children. She put her hands out to them.

'Quick! Come quickly!'

Gwydion Navarne's hand was icy as she grasped it and pulled him and Melisande in front of her, wrapping her arms around them, pointing off into the rising sun.

In the shadow of golden light edging over the horizon they could see the outline of their friend, their lord, their father, standing straight again, broken no more. His shadow, long and black before the sunrise, stretched out to them. The radiance of the morning light caused his hair to shine, golden.

Beside him was another shadow, slighter, darker, backlit by daybreak.

'Who is that?' Melisande asked, shielding her eyes.

Rhapsody pulled her closer, smiling through her tears. 'Your mother.'

Softly she began to sing the Lirin Song of Passage, weaving his name – *Stephen* – into the ancient dirge. The growing light of dawn seemed to stop brightening, holding steady for a moment.

Ashe recognized what she was doing. He reached out and touched Melisande's face, then rested his hand on Gwydion Navarne's shoulder.

'Bid him farewell,' he said to the children. His voice had regained its strength; there was wisdom in its tone. Gwydion Navarne raised his head and stared off at the horizon.

'Goodbye, Father,' the boy said softly. Melisande waved, unable to speak. Behind them, Rosella dissolved into grief.

In the depths of memory Gwydion recalled his father's words at the passing of Talthea, the Gracious One.

Time holds on to us all, Gwydion. Like all mortal men subject to the whims of Time, he struggles to stave off death as long as possible, because he does not know it for the blessing it sometimes can be. For you, and for me, Time goes on.

Gwydion raised his hand to the rising sun.

Numbly Rhapsody sang, light spilling into her eyes now, her head buzzing, her heart frozen, a dam against the pain she knew was to come. She wondered if the wisdom that the Moot had granted her was giving her the strength to maintain calm for the sake of Stephen's children, for the sake of the Cymrian people. For Ashe's sake.

For her own sake.

Behind the fading shadow in the sun she could see others, scores of them, standing in the distant light of a glade, peaceful and green, behind the Veil of Hoen.

She brought the dirge to its end.

'Goodbye, Stephen,' she said. 'I'll take care of them for you.'

In a burst of glory, the sun crested the horizon fully, illuminating the sky to a brilliant blue. The wind came up, the wind of morning, dispersing the smoke from the smoldering ashes.

Rhapsody looked around at the dawn shining hazily through the desolation and smoke of the fields around the ruin of the Great Moot. The soldiers of Roland and of Ylorc were moving among the Cymrians like living men among sleepwalkers.

The Lord Cymrian stood and offered her his hand.

'Come,' he said. 'Let's finish this.'

From the remains of the Summoner's Rise, the new Lord and Lady

Cymrian looked over the morning valley at the base of the Teeth, down on the people who had sworn fealty to them only the day before. The pain and loss were unmistakable, but so was the hope – even as Firbolg soldiers joined with the army of Roland in rebuilding and rescue, the refugees of Serendair and their descendants put aside old animosities and reached across the chasms of bitter years to begin rebuilding a new alliance of peace.

Rhapsody stared down at the horn in her hands. The casing was cracked, the magic that bound the storm-tossed survivors in promise broken, drained from it like the shine from tarnished metal. Still, there was good cheer in the air that surrounded it, a sense of hope and survival that had lasted through the death of the Island, the horror of the Great War, and even the rising of the Dead, to stand firm, a bellwether of a future that was strong and bright.

She raised the horn to her lips and sounded it; it was not a martial call, a call to battle, but rather a call of victory.

In return, the Cymrians below roared in affirmation, filling the summer air with the sound of their cheers.

She yielded the floor to Gwydion, who stood by her side, commending those who had fought bravely, blessing those who had been lost, and returning to the announcements he had been in the process of making when the Earth had sundered beneath them.

He hurried through his proclamations: the speakers for each representative group, and any other interested parties, were invited to stay to plan the merging and rebuilding of the Cymrian states. The rest of the group was excused, invited to return in a year's time for the next Council, which would convene every third year thereafter. The wedding would take place three months hence, on the first day of autumn, at the sapling tree of the Oak of Deep Roots, growing in what had once been the House of Remembrance. He thanked the Cymrians for their attendance and participation, then seized Rhapsody's hand and led her speedily off the rise before the crowd of well-wishers could sweep them away as they had tried two nights before.

On her way down the side of the rockwall Rhapsody looked up to see Achmed and Grunthor watching her. She smiled at them hesitantly: Grunthor stared at her, straight-faced, but Achmed gave her the hint of a knowing smile in return. Then she was gone, pulled out of the way of the swelling crowd.

From her hiding place on the lower ledge Rhapsody watched as the crowds slowly made their way out of the remains of the Bowl. It would take many days for the fields around the Moot to empty, she knew, between the reunions among Houses and old friends who tarried behind, renewing their ties, and the sheer logistics of moving a hundred thousand people and their belongings. She sighed; Achmed had handled things for her without complaint; she felt guilty at the prospect of leaving him with such a tremendous mess to clean up. She had sought him out before the announcement, securing his permission to have annual access to the

Moot, but had been pulled away without forewarning him about her engagement. The dismay she had felt was still palpable.

She sensed a strange tingle on the surface of her skin, a static charge that buzzed in the strands of her hair and made her fingertips itch. Then she heard the voice, and a frown spread over her face.

'I hope you will allow me to extend my heartfelt congratulations, my dear, both on your appointment and your engagement.' The statement issued forth from the earth itself, or the air; she was uncertain as to which.

'Thank you,' she said, not knowing what to turn away from. 'Please leave me alone, Llauron. I have nothing to say to you.'

A deep chuckle resonated in the ground, and she felt the wind pick up, as it did when she had visited Elynsynos. But instead of it lovingly caressing her hair, the way it had in the quiet glen outside the hidden cave, it blew her tresses around her face with a confident strength.

'Now, somehow I doubt that is the truth, my dear.'

She tried to keep from losing her temper. 'You're right; let me rephrase that. I have many unpleasant things I could undoubtedly say to you at this point, Llauron, but I'd rather not. Go away and leave me alone.'

'That's better. I am sorry you're so angry, Rhapsody; of course you have every right to be. I was just hoping you might be willing to extend some of your famous forgiveness to your father-in-law-to-be. I can't very well ask your pardon if you won't hear me out. You did say, after all, that we must forgive one another.'

'There are somethings that are unforgivable.' Gwydion's voice came from behind her, its tone harsh, startling her. 'Leave the Lady alone, Father; you have no right to speak to her after what you've done.'

Rhapsody reached out for him. 'Sam—'

'He's right, of course,' said the warm, cultured voice. 'I certainly have no right to anything where either of you are concerned anymore. I was merely asking your indulgence.'

'Sam, why don't you see if Achmed and Grunthor need any help with the crowd,' Rhapsody said gently. 'I can take care of myself. Go on. Please.' Gwydion looked at her doubtfully, then reread her intention and walked away with a sigh of annoyance.

'He's very angry still, and grieving,' Llauron said; it was as if the air and the earth both contained the sound of his voice. 'I hope you can help him let go of his wrath, my dear.'

'I'm not sure I should,' she answered. 'Perhaps it is better for us both to remember it.'

A deep chuckle rumbled through the earth. 'You may think you want to, Rhapsody, but you don't. You don't have the stomach for it. I suspect you've had enough bad feeling to last you a lifetime. Given your life expectancy, that's a lot of pain. You don't seem the type to hold a grudge.'

'Well, if I ever have difficulty remembering why I don't speak to you I can just conjure up the image of today, of Anborn crippled trying to save me, of Stephen dying so that the Cymrians could get out of the Moot, of the horrors that Anwyn visited upon us – I think I can remember. Time will tell if I am the type to hold a grudge.'

The voice in the wind seemed genuinely perplexed. 'Why are you so angry with me? What have I done?'

She slapped her hand into the wind in exasperation. 'Where were you? Why didn't you help? You could have spared so many, these Cymrians you have claimed to revere, to cherish – why didn't you take on Anwyn yourself? Surely you were in a better position than any.'

The wind sighed around her.

'She was my mother, Rhapsody.'

'Gwydion is your son. Anborn is your brother. Stephen was your friend. Those are your people. It hardly seems a worthy excuse.'

'Gwydion has you. Anborn has the friendship of many. Stephen, may the Creator bless him, had the love of a woman, two marvelous children, and everyone who ever met him. The Cymrians had each other, and many in their lives to give them meaning, connection. Anwyn had only me.' The wind blew warm through her hair. 'I hope one day you will understand, and will extend me your forgiveness. I do hope one day to see my grandchildren. Surely you won't deny me that, will you?'

'I doubt I will ever understand why you did any of the things that you did, but I don't have to, Llauron,' Rhapsody replied. 'You are in your own world now. One day, if we have children, and if they want to see you, that may come to pass.' Then her eyes turned a darker green. 'But not if you try to manipulate us in any way ever again.'

'Understood. I think our worlds are separate enough to assure that won't happen.'

'Let's hope you're right.'

The sonorous voice sighed in the wind. 'Rhapsody, I must ask you to remember something.'

She looked over the rise at the Cymrian stragglers, standing about the Bowl in small groups, talking. 'Yes?'

'Whether you realize it now or not, for all that you hated our last interaction, you will be faced one day with the same situation again.'

Her attention snapped back to Llauron, invisible around her. 'What does that mean?'

'It means,' said the elemental voice of the wyrm, 'that when you marry a man who is also a dragon, one day you will find that he is in need of becoming one or the other. If he chooses to let his human side win, you will eventually understand the pain of being widowed, as I have. And if he takes the path I chose, well, you have had a window into what both of you must do. I don't mean to impinge on your happiness in any way, my dear, but these are the realities of the family you are about to marry into. I just don't want you to wake up one day and feel you were misled.'

Rhapsody felt sour pain rise in her throat. The truth of his words, despite her desire to ignore them, was undeniable. His reasons for telling her were less clear; it was impossible to discern whether he was forewarning her of what she was to face, or trying to discourage her from entering into the situation in which she would have to do so.

She looked across the field at the base of the Bowl again, to where Gwydion knelt, surrounded by old friends, consoling the children of Stephen Navarne and Rosella.

'Goodbye, Llauron,' she said, gathering her skirts. 'I'll see you at the wedding, I expect, or at least feel your presence.' She climbed down from the rocks and hurried across the Moot where her husband waited.

87

In the Great Hall of Tyrian atop Tomingorllo, amid the glad sound of silver trumpets, a solemn procession carried the chosen gift of suit to the display pedestal where the diadem had rested. It was carefully set in place, and revealed with great respect.

Out of all the rich gifts of state that were presented for the Lirin queen's approval, gifts whose incalculable wealth showcased the treasuries and artistry of the nations whose leaders sought her hand, she had chosen a simple scroll, bound with a black velvet ribbon. It was sealed with an odd, thirteen-sided copper signet, said to be one of only two in the entire world.

The scroll was rumored to be a song unlike any other. As the queen was a musician unparalleled, it was widely believed to be beautiful to the point of magical if she had been moved to choose it above all other offerings. The plate beneath it, by way of announcement, bore the name *GWYDION OF MAN OSSE, LORD CYMRIAN*.

During this meaningful and joyous ceremony, the queen, by custom, was absent; at least she was not noticed, lying on her stomach on the floor of the Grand Balcony, looking down and watching it all from underneath Gwydion's mist cloak with him. It was a struggle for them both to refrain from giggling like maniacs as they had when, straight-faced, she had presented her betrothal choice to Rial and left his offices in a dead run before her composure collapsed.

The song was a gift for the eyes of the bride-to-be only. Gwydion had threatened to have the scroll hold the tender lyrics to one of Grunthor's bawdy marching songs. Instead, when she opened it she found he had been putting the music instruction she had given him to good use; the carefully graphed staff carried the notes that spelled out *Sam and Emily Always* without a single error.

The bouquet of winterflowers he had presented her with at the same time remained in Elysian, opening a little more day by day, revealing petals of deeper red with each new layer. The bouquet was held in stasis by the magic of the place, and did not fade, remaining permanently suspended in glorious bloom. It was a true marvel, but one the queen did not feel the inclination to share with any other eye. *Proof of being selfish again*, she had told her chosen suitor, who had only smiled.

'But who is there to marry us publicly?' Rhapsody asked Gwydion as they strolled in the garden of Tomingorllo. 'You hold the offices of Invoker and Patriarch; there is no one above you in the religious hierarchy.'

Gwydion smiled. 'You are not current in your information,' he said, kissing her hand as they walked. 'While you were refusing to see me, I had to do something to keep from going insane, so I set about delegating some of those responsibilities.'

Rhapsody laughed. 'Pretty certain of yourself, aren't you? I thought you didn't know if you would be confirmed as Lord Cymrian or not.'

'I didn't. I still believed there should be others leading the religious factions directly. Besides, if you had married Anborn or Achmed I would have thrown myself into the sea anyway, so it wouldn't have mattered.'

'So do you intend to remain the titular head of the order?'

'Yes, but I am nominating leaders of both factions who I think will be able to work together toward reunification. And even if it doesn't happen, I believe there will still be a harmonious coexistence of both faiths.'

'Excellent. And whom did you choose to take on the office of Invoker?'

Ashe stopped and looked off into the distance. 'Gavin. And I believe there is my candidate for Patriarch now, though of course the Scales of Jierna Tal will have to weigh him and find him worthy. He seemed mildly amused at the prospect. I asked him to come to Tyrian after the Cymrian Council so you could meet him; he's new in the faith, but very wise. Come, let me introduce him to you.'

Rhapsody took his hand and followed him across the garden to where an older man was waiting. His beard was long enough to curl upward at the edges, with streaks of white and silver winning the battle for control within it over the insistent white-blond. Despite being somewhat advanced in years he was tall and broad-shouldered, and had a smile that Rhapsody could swear she had seen before, though from a distance she did not recognize him.

'Was he at the Council?' she asked as Gwydion picked up the pace.

'Yes; he was part of the Diaspora. I met him a few days before the Second Fleet arrived at the Moot. I asked him where he had come from, and all he would say was that it was both near and farther away than anyplace in the known world. We camped out together a few nights, and I was astounded at his wisdom and vision, and his extraordinary powers of healing. While we were there he tended to several people in the throes of great illness or pain, with amazing skill. He radiates great peace; I resolved to offer him the post if I was ever in a position to grant it to him. He seems to know of you; he asked if I knew you, but of course I couldn't tell him anything except that I did. I think you'll be pleasantly surprised.'

Rhapsody stopped still on the forest path, staring at the robed man. His lined face was wreathed in a smile that made her flush hot and cold with memories simultaneously.

'Constantin!'

He held out his hands to her, hands marred by time and the life he had led, and she hurried to him and took both of them in her own, kissing his cheek. Warmth flooded her face, as she thought back to their myriad, and occasionally unpleasant, experiences. His eyes were serene, however, and he looked at her knowingly and just smiled.

'Hello, m'lady,' he said in the deep voice she remembered. 'I'm honored that you remember me.'

Rhapsody reached up, as if unable to stop herself, and touched his wrinkled cheek. *I was gone behind the Veil of Hoen for seven years, and when I came out the snow had barely covered the hilt of the sword,* she thought poignantly. *I've been back now half a year. Gods, I'm amazed he's still alive.*

'I told you I would never forget you,' she said gently, 'and I haven't.'

Constantin kissed her hand. 'Nor I you. Best wishes on your engagement. The Lord Cymrian is a lucky man.'

'Thank you,' Rhapsody and Gwydion said simultaneously. The Lord Cymrian drew her closer to his side.

'Constantin has agreed, if the Scales confirm him, to accept the office of Patriarch on Midsummer's Night,' Ashe said. 'And as such he will be the one to marry us, if you agree, Aria, in a joint ceremony with Gavin.'

Rhapsody smiled. 'I certainly do. Thank you, Constantin.' She studied his face intently for a moment. 'What made you decide to leave?'

His eyes darkened, and he looked deep into hers. 'It was time,' was all he said.

Rhapsody remembered what Anborn had said about the wisdom not to ask more than she really needed to know. She turned to the Lord Cymrian, who was watching their interaction with surprise. 'I am delighted in your choice of a Patriarch, darling. He has studied with the best possible instructors and I know for a fact there's not a drop of evil in him.' Her eyes sparkled wickedly and Constantin laughed. Gwydion looked puzzled.

'Come along, Sam,' Rhapsody said, pulling at her groom's hand. 'Let's find His Grace somewhere to rest; he's come from farther away than you think. And we'll tell you the whole story. You may be surprised to learn how the new Patriarch had a hand in killing the F'dor.'

Gwydion stared at her in amazement before following them up the path. 'You know, Rhapsody, you certainly know how to ruin a surprise.'

True to her word, Rhapsody had requested a simple dress, as she told Gwydion she would after the royal wedding in Bethany. It had only enough train to brush the ground two or so feet behind her, and left her shoulders open to the sun for the wedding taking place on the first day after the season dedicated to it had passed.

Despite the dress's seeming simplicity, the seamstresses of Tyrian had worked endlessly on it. Miresylle had found a bolt of Canderian brushed silk, white with a gleaming blush undertone that touched off the sunrise coloring of Rhapsody's rosy golden skin perfectly. It was trimmed judiciously, sparingly, a sign of true craftsmanship, as Rhapsody had explained to her incredulous groom, who wondered rudely aloud why she was having a seventh fitting for this allegedly simple dress.

'It's not all covered with beadwork and lace; many seamstresses use that stuff to hide the imperfections in the fabric or the workmanship. Miresylle's a perfectionist.'

Gwydion had taken his bride into his arms and kissed her. 'I'm sure. And I'm sure I'll like the dress, despite it being responsible for keeping you away from me so much.'

'You're so time-greedy,' she scowled at him jokingly. 'You'd probably prefer I didn't wear anything at all.'

'How right you are.'

Gwydion himself had been faced with a sartorial dilemma. Though the design for his wedding garment was easy enough to come by, he had been besieged with gifts from the various family factions, fighting units, and political groups to which he had belonged over his lifetime, each an emblem or a symbol of his honored status, conferred on him with the expectation that he would wear each of them at his wedding. Rhapsody had gone into a giggling fit as he indignantly displayed them, spread out on the vast meeting table in the Great Hall of Tyrian. The table was over twenty feet in length, and every inch of it was covered with some sort of item he needed to exhibit somewhere on his person.

'You had better start eating; you'll need to add to your size ten times over,' she laughed, her eyes taking in the hundreds of hats, daggers, staves, ceremonial swords, crowns, and codpieces littering the table. She picked up one of the twenty-one signet rings in a pile in the middle of the spread. 'Now let's see; one on each finger, one on each toe, and one on your—'

'Don't say it,' he threatened jokingly. 'That might be even more uncomfortable for you later that night, my dear. I might choose the one with the biggest prongs.'

'This gift is my very favorite,' Rhapsody said, lifting a hideous Nain war mask. 'Do they really wear these things in battle?'

'Yes, and worse.' He looked around the table and sighed in dismay. 'I'll look ridiculous if I wear any of these emblems, Aria. If I wear some of them, I risk offending anyone whose symbol I didn't choose. And if I wear none of them, I will offend everyone. What am I going to do? Is it too late to elope?'

'We did that already, remember? This is just the official ceremony; you and I already did the important one alone.' She smiled at him, hoping to ease his distress. 'Here, I'll take care of it. Let's sort through these things together, and you can tell me who they're from and what they represent.'

A month later, on the morning before the wedding rehearsal, she presented him with a velvet-covered box.

'This is for all your patience with the endless fittings of my wedding dress,' she said as he kissed her. 'Open it and see if it solves your dilemma.'

In the box was a segmented necklace of state, a chain-like series of uniform hexagonal pieces wrought in red-gold, jointed together to a length that would drape about the neck and shoulders, inlaid with the symbols of each of the groups that had presented him with emblems to wear. Even the hideous war mask of the Nain of the Sardonyx Mountain had been painstakingly rendered in tiny gems and enameled scrolling on one of the small segments; Gwydion had burst out laughing at the thought of the jeweler working long hours to find a colored stone the same hue as the mucus dripping from the miniature war mask's nostrils.

'As with everything about you, it's perfect,' he said, drawing her close.

'Oh, good. So does this mean I'm to be spared from those big prongs now?'

'All but one.'

Gwydion lugged the bucket to the door of the hidden room behind the waterfall and heaved the cleaning water outside into the grass. *How does she do this?* he wondered incredulously as he sank into his comfortable old chair with a groan. He had helped her clean house in Elysian, but somehow that had been a pleasure. Gwydion shook his head and laughed. Being branded with a hot iron might be a pleasure, as long as she was there to hold his hand.

The memory of drowsy summer mornings a year before came back to him, the scent of coffee brewing and spicy aromas floating by, accompanied by the smell of soap and the sweet sound of singing. She had always been up before dawn, tidying Elysian, pressing clothes, tending her gardens, long before normal people had cracked an eyelid; it was the farm girl in her, she had said as he protested, pulling her back into bed if she came close by. These memories of simple domesticity were among his favorite, images of normalcy and sanity in a world run amok. He sighed, anticipating the return of those days with glee.

He looked around his room and felt a sense of satisfaction. The messy man-cottage was spotless, the new double bed gleaming under the fresh satin bedspread he had bought for her in Navarne. He had carted all the new furnishings here himself by night to maintain the hidden room's security, a sort of western Elysian, a place they could be alone when in these provinces.

This place needs a woman's oversight – or a maid, she had said. The first he had provided by duplicating many of the comfortable accessories and ornaments she had used in decorating Elysian; even now the cottage was unrecognizable in its warmth and charm. The second he had assured by spending four hours on the day before his wedding sprucing up the place; it had taken her about half an hour to produce better results that day a year and a half before, but he knew she would appreciate the effort.

Gwydion rose with a creak and made a final inspection. The wine was in the chilling bucket, the crystal goblets on the table, the fire laid with sweet-smelling spices, waiting to be set ablaze. He would need to build a room with a tub if they were to use this place in winter, even though the prospect of Rhapsody's warmth heating the waterfall's pool amid the snow was tantalizing. He pulled out the finishing touch, a sackful of pink and white rose petals he had convinced her to work her magic on without telling her why. She had spoken the words to preserve their freshness and given him an odd look; he imagined the expression on her face the next night as he scattered them across the bed and the floor, leading to the threshold.

A romantic dragon; isn't that a contradiction in terms?

Yes. Do you love me anyway?

Always.

When the bed was covered with the petals he took one more look around. Then he left the cabin and locked the door carefully, whistling all the way back to where he had hidden the horse and cart.

House of Remembrance, Navarne

The Lirin had decorated the forestlands of Tyrian and Gwynwood in the traditional manner for the wedding, with bells, reed flutes, and windchimes dangling from the trees, through which bright streamers had been laced. Maypoles had been erected in the forest along the way from the Lirin city to the Great Tree, also tied with ribbons that were peppered with thousands of crystals, a gift from the Cymrian Nain. As a result, the forest was bathed in colored light, casting a rainbow glow on the setting and, eventually, the guests.

And, as improbable as it was, the morning of the wedding the grounds and gardens of the House of Remembrance bloomed in a vast scarlet carpet of winterflowers, a gift from a Child that slept, safe now, in the arms of her mother the Earth.

In addition to the traditional decorations, Ashe had sought the aid of some of the palace servants in tying muslin love knots about the bed-chamber of the Lady Cymrian and throughout the halls of Stephen's keep where she was staying. With the excruciating detail born of a dragon's memory he re-created the scene in which they had met, that simple, beautiful summer night at the foreharvest dance. Rhapsody awoke on the morning of her wedding to a room full of fresh-cut pine and fir boughs and sprays of late-summer flowers, many of which were of the same kinds that had adorned the tables and barrels that night. She sat up in bed and blinked in amazement at the accuracy with which he had duplicated the adornments that the people of her farming village had used in the old land, then laughed aloud. In the night he must have stolen into the room himself; she was covered by his cloak, and her bed was strewn with willow leaves. On top of the cloak rested a thin black velvet ribbon in which was tied a heart-shaped silver button.

Oelendra sat on a chair in the bedchamber of the bride and watched the flurry of preparations in amusement. Rhapsody was sitting on the floor in her undergarments, patiently adjusting the hem of Melisande Navarne's dress, while the Lirin chambermaids sat on the bed behind her, plaiting pearls into her hair and looking disconcerted every time she moved. Sylvia had positioned herself near the door, as deliveries were arriving every few minutes, all the while swatting at the queen's Firbolg grandchildren, who were busy leaping from couch to couch and scattering her belongings across the room.

'They're eating the flowers from the hair wreaths, m'lady,' the chamberlain said.

Rhapsody nodded. 'I know. Please try to keep them from getting the ribbons stuck between their teeth.'

When her eldest child attendant was finally turned out properly, Rhapsody rose. Her hair had been intricately braided in tiny patterns, pulled back off her face, but hung in a long fall down the back, sectioned intermittently with tiny white flowers and sprigs of rosemary for wisdom. She gave Oelendra a flustered grin, then followed the chattering chambermaids to the place where the wedding gown hung. Miresylle, the dressmaker, helped her into it with a look on her face that matched that of a midwife delivering a royal infant. Finally, after many adjustments, the queen stood erect and turned, and the Lirin attendants stepped back in awe. Oelendra's amused smile grew warmer. She had not believed that anything could make Rhapsody any more beautiful than she already was, but she now saw that she was mistaken. She set her mind to the puzzle of whether the enhancement came from the perfect dress, gleaming white with a hint of blush rose shining through, or from the look of happiness that shone in the bride's eyes.

Sylvia clapped her hands decisively. 'All right, out with you all, now,' she said to the children and the chambermaids. The resulting flurry allowed Oelendra the moment she had been awaiting. She went up behind Rhapsody, who was attaching her earrings in front of the looking glass, and rested her hands on her shoulders.

The bride smiled at her friend in the glass, then turned to embrace her. Oelendra held her tightly for a moment, then moved to the dressing table and dropped a key on it. Rhapsody gave her a puzzled smile.

'What's that?'

'The key to my house,' Oelendra said, adjusting the neckline of her own gown. 'I told you that it was your house now as well.'

Rhapsody nodded. 'But why would I need a key? I would only come there when you're home.'

Oelendra kissed her cheek and went to the door. 'Just in case you want to spend some time alone with your husband, away from the palace. You look beautiful, darling; and happy. I will remember this sight and treasure it always. Now, don't tarry; your groom awaits.' She smiled, then took her place in the procession.

Rhapsody brushed out her skirt once more and looked around her. She was surrounded by the people she loved, and would be more so momentarily. Her grandchildren – the Navarnes, the children of Hoen, and the Firbolg – were decked out identically in white silk and adorned with flowers. Rial was in her procession, as was Oelendra, who was standing as her witness. Achmed and Grunthor stood, dressed in full regalia, ready to escort her down the aisle. Anborn, on his litter borne by two Nain soldiers, waited to be carried in. And glimmering in the ether, hanging within the air and unseen by any but herself, were two great dragon shapes, multicolored eyes glittering at her lovingly. She thought how Jo would have laughed at the sight and blew her sister a kiss, knowing she was there too, unseen.

'All right,' she said to the strange assemblage. 'Here is where we begin.'

'This is perverse.'

Lady Madeleine Steward, wife of the Lord Roland, stepped quickly out of the way of the wedding procession to avoid continued contact with the grinning child who had patted her jewel-encrusted gown as he passed by. The hairy little face was grisly beneath its floral wreath; in the Lady's opinion there was something obscene about dressing Firbolg brats in wedding finery, not to mention including them in a royal ceremony.

The Lady Roland had not been very happy for the past three months, ever since her husband had accompanied her home from the Cymrian Council, blithering happily about ceding his sovereignty to the new Lord and Lady. It had been a matter of pride for Madeleine that she had married into the highest House in the land, and now that was being subordinated to an admittedly handsome man with metal hair and a woman who was escorted down the aisle on the arms of a monster and the rudest creature she had ever met. Her world was capsizing, and Lady Madeleine could only sit helplessly by and observe the nightmare.

Tristan Steward scowled at his wife. 'Shhhh,' he whispered fiercely, then turned back to watch the Lady Cymrian's face take on the same glow as the Lord's as they pledged their union.

The wedding, by royal standards, was a small one. Though it was strange to be standing in the open air beneath the Sagian Oak in what was once the courtyard of the House of Remembrance rather than in the basilica in Bethany or Sepulvarta, there was something charming about the ceremony. He smiled sadly as he watched the new Patriarch bless the marriage with the Invoker of the Filids.

It was impossible to keep his gaze on Madeleine's face, twisted in the throes of disapproving disgust, when he could be looking at Rhapsody's. He turned back to look at it again. Certainly there were all the regular features that made her countenance well worthy of appreciation, even at the risk of his own wife's irritation, but it was really the way she looked at the Lord Cymrian that made it impossible to take his eyes off her. The expression on her face was unguarded, and was fixed in the aspect of a woman utterly in love and consummately happy.

Tristan sighed. He wished someone would once look that way at him, if only just once more. He knew that now that Prudence was gone, it would never happen, and it made the day darker for a moment, even as the merry bells in the trees and from the newly rebuilt tower pealed in celebration when the pair were united in a kiss.

Rhapsody was talking to Constantin under the shade of the towering engilder trees when she felt someone's intense gaze come to rest on her back. Out of the corner of her eye she saw a vertical white line standing totally still, focusing on her. Rhapsody turned to give the image clearer attention and broke into a warm smile; it was Oelendra. The Lirin warrior had discarded the gown she had worn earlier at the wedding and redressed in a white robe of undyed wool, one much like the priests at the Tree wore. Oelendra smiled in return, but there was a look of significance in her eye that made Rhapsody's other thoughts come to a halt.

'Will you excuse me?' she asked Constantin.

The bright blue eyes in the wrinkled face smiled. 'Of course, m'lady.'

Rhapsody lifted the hem of her wedding gown and stepped over the rocks that bordered the forest path on which she stood. As she did, the figure in the distance shook her head and held up her hand, bringing Rhapsody to an abrupt stop. Oelendra waved, and then walked off slowly into the woods, in the direction of the Veil of Hoen. She turned once more and smiled at the bride, bathing her with a loving look of unsurpassed warmth. Then she walked away into the forest and disappeared from view.

'Rhapsody? What's wrong, darling?' Ashe's voice spoke warmly next to her ear.

Rhapsody turned to her husband and smiled up at him, unaware of the tears that rolled down her cheeks. 'Nothing, Sam. Nothing is wrong at all.'

Gwydion looked off into the distance, then closed his eyes for a moment. 'Was that Oelendra? I can barely make her out.'

'Yes. Look as well as you can, Sam; I don't expect you will see her again, at least not in this world.'

Gwydion brushed the tears from her cheeks. 'Are you all right?'

Rhapsody nodded. 'Of course. How can I help but be happy for her? Tonight she'll sleep beside Pendaris again.'

Achmed stood under the leafy boughs of an ancient oak tree, uphill from the dance floor that had been cleared in the gardens of the House of Remembrance. The members of a small but skilled orchestra from Navarne had positioned themselves across from where he stood musing, and they had set about filling the air with cheerful music, providing a welcome and appreciated break for the musicians of Tyrian. The Lord and Lady had taken almost immediately to the floor, to be joined by hundreds of their guests, and now, hours later, the forest still rang with the glad sound of celebrating people moving gracefully to the rhythmic strains of the music.

Grunthor came over, grinning, winded from his turn on the dance floor with the bride. 'Watch out for her, sir, she's a demon at the waltz,' he said, mopping his gigantic brow. 'I've got the method figured out, though; you let her stand right on your feet – it doesn't hurt, she doesn't weigh any more than a feather – and that way you can avoid tromping on her gown. She does look most vexed at you if you do that.'

Achmed took a sip of his brandy and smiled. 'Thanks for the tip.'

Grunthor tucked the handkerchief into the pocket of his dress uniform, and rubbed the back of his neck as they both turned to watch the dancing. It was hard to miss Rhapsody, small as she was, even in the enormous crowd of revelers. Her face was shining with an ethereal light, and her laughter rang like the bells in the trees of Tyrian and the forest of the White Tree; those dancing within ten or so feet of her routinely stopped just to watch her as if entranced. She was being waltzed around by Rial now, but when, from time to time, her husband managed to steal her for a turn, her face outshone the sun.

'She looks happy, eh?'

'Yes, she does.'

Grunthor looked down at his friend. 'How are you holding up?'

'What do you mean?'

'Well,' said the Bolg, 'I always got the impression you had a soft spot for her, if you take my point.'

Achmed took another drink, saying nothing.

'Course, it's none of my business, sir, but what are you going to do about it? I mean, why did you just let her go?'

Achmed smiled as the waltz ended and Rhapsody made a deep bow to her partner, who looked startled for a moment, then joined her in merry laughter. Edwyn Griffyth swept Gwydion aside jokingly and took her into his arms for the next dance as the orchestra shifted into the Lirin *pennafar*, a traditional dance of celebration. 'Who said I am going to just let her go?'

Grunthor's brow wrinkled as he looked down at the Firbolg king. 'I think you might be a little late, don't you?'

'No, actually, I'm early.'

'How do you figure?'

Achmed leaned against the tree they were standing under. 'All this is temporary. Ashe is a dragon, and of Cymrian blood, so he is very long-lived, but he is not immortal like the three of us. And as his longevity stems from his dragon blood, sooner or later he will confront the same problem Llauron did. He will grow more and more wyrmlike, until he eventually turns his back on his humanity, including his beloved wife, and goes off to commune with the elements.'

Understanding was beginning to dawn on Grunthor. 'And then she's yours?'

Achmed glanced up at him. 'What none of you understand is that, in a very important way, she is already. She's the only other one who knows it.'

'She does?'

'Yes.' He drained the last of his brandy. 'Now, if you'll excuse me, I believe it's my turn to dance with the bride.'

Grunthor shook his head as Achmed made his way down the hill. He was standing beside Rhapsody just as the dance ended, and the Sergeant watched in amusement as she looked up at the Firbolg king and smiled broadly, nodding in delight and taking his hand. He wasn't sure what was more amusing: the sight of Achmed dancing the mazurka, or the look on Gwydion's face as Achmed nimbly swept his bride out from in front of him and danced her away.

As the first star appeared it was greeted by a chorus of Lirinsong, then by a tempest of fireworks lighting the heavens around it. Gwydion watched the display from the top of a hilly rise beneath a willow tree, his beautiful, finally official wife leaning on his shoulder and watching the sky with him. She sighed deeply and looked up at him, her eyes gleaming with the memory of another starry night, another willow tree.

'You know, I've decided something, m'lady,' he said as he leaned over and kissed her.

'Yes, m'lord?'

'The only way I intend to watch the stars from now on is by seeing their reflection in your eyes.' He kissed her again as a new shower of sparks went up, lighting her face and gleaming in her hair.

'As you wish.' The clamor from down the hill grew; the wedding guests were growing impatient, waiting for the next round of toasting and music. Rhapsody sighed again. 'How much longer is this supposed to go on? We've been celebrating all day.'

Gwydion stood and pulled her up with him. 'The nice thing about being in charge is that you get to say when you can leave,' he said, smiling down at her and remembering the rose-petal-strewn bed waiting for them in the room behind the waterfall. 'Let's go drink to our collective happiness, and then depart to start experiencing some of our own. Does that sound good to you?'

'Very good.'

Above them a golden shower of sparks ignited, brightening the darkness, to fall a moment later, slowly, drifting to earth on the warm wind. Rhapsody put out her hands with childlike delight and tried to catch some as they fell; tiny star-like embers coming to rest in her palms, gleaming between her fingers, like the dream she had had so long ago, on the other side of the world, and of Time. The light sparkled brilliantly on the diamonds of her wedding ring. The significance of the moment was lost on all but one, the one who had been with her there, under those stars, half a world away, who waited with her now, smiling, as the tiny lights gleamed brightly in her hands before burning out.

She turned to him and saw the last few floating sparks reflected in the deep chasms of the vertical pupils of his eyes, then reached up and kissed him, setting off a roar of applause from the bottom of the hill. 'Ryle hira,' she whispered to him. *Life is what it is.*

'Nol hira viendrax,' he answered, smiling. *And I am grateful for what it is.*

They hurried down the hill, hand in hand in the starry darkness, running excitedly to begin the rest of their lives.

Epilogue

Meridion stopped the frame. The image on the Time Editor's screen froze, hovering fuzzily in the air and dusty light projected onto the curved, clear wall of the observatory. He leaned forward over the instrument panel, resting his chin on his hands, gazing thoughtfully at the picture of his parents, captured eternally in a moment of true happiness, frozen in Time, laughing as they ran through the starry night. His timing, however inadvertent, was fortuitous.

Meridion rose from the Editor. His aurelay, which he had formed into a chairlike seat while he worked, dissolved and reabsorbed into his translucent body as he stepped away from the machine. He walked slowly over to the glass wall and came to a stop in front of the blurry image of his mother; the projection undulated as he moved, causing the lines and shadows to stretch and wave as if dancing on an unnoticed breeze.

How happy you look, he thought, crossing his arms in front of him as he stared at the projection from the lorestrand. *I am glad. Even if this is the end for me now, even if the new tapestry of Time that has just been woven turns out no better than the first, at least there is this moment of happiness for you. Far better than what had gone before, for certain. I am glad.*

His eyes wandered over the picture of his father, a man he had seen but never met, utterly unrecognizable in the vigor of youth and health. *By this time in the old life you had sunk irretrievably into madness, broken in both body and mind,* Meridion thought, watching the way the currents of air within his glass globe observatory made the image look as if Gwydion were running even now, caught forever in jubilant motion. *Again, I am glad for you.*

How strange it was, he mused as he returned to the machine, to feel such sentiment, such a connection, to people he had never met.

Time thudded heavy around his ears. Meridion finally worked up the courage to look out through the glass panes of the observatory at the world below. He inhaled slowly, letting his breath out in increments.

The fire had receded, disappeared in fact from the surface of the distant Earth; now clouds gathered over the blue-green seas, swirling on the wind, racing around the mountain ranges, obscuring his view. *As it should be,* he thought, fighting off the melancholy that was surging within his heart. *No man should have so clear a view of the world if he is going to live in it.*

He bent down on the floor next to the Time Editor and carefully gathered the scorched scraps of timefilm, shredded into burnt confetti and stripped ribbons at his feet. Meticulously he searched until he came upon a fragment that he had seen fall not long before, as the new history replaced the old, like a rerouted riverbed, or a tapestry rewoven from the same silken threads into different patterns. The brittle scraps were growing dim, dissolving on the floor, gone now from Time, from history. Soon they would disappear altogether, leaving nothing, not even memory, for in reality they were now only the remains of a Past that never was.

Meridion held the filmstrand up to the light. Satisfied, he draped it over a secondary lamp on the Editor's instrument panel, and focused it on the wall next to the screen that held the picture of his parents.

In the dim light he could barely make out the image, a small, elderly figure in pale robes woven in the symbology of the ancient Namers, her long hair white as snow, braided and bound simply back in a black ribbon. Her face was lined and scarred, her body bent under the weight of age, though held steady in the grace of a strong will. In the crook of her arms she cradled a white birthing cloth, a garment used to catch a child as it emerged from the womb. Her hands reached aloft, as if in supplication.

It was the moment of his birth in the old life.

He avoided looking at the next frames of film fragment that lay across the panel, coiled in a tattered spiral. Within those next few moments of time had been great agony, gruesome death. Though he had never known his mother, upon coming into existence he had still felt her love, even in those last moments of her life, and in the wake of her hideous demise. He had changed Time, and probably her fate, but he still could not bear to witness what had happened to her again.

The reel that held the film of the new history caught Meridion's eye, resting patiently on its pinion. Idly he took the end and unspooled it, holding it up to the ambient light of the observatory. Unlike the shards of fading Past that were melting before his eyes, this new thread was clean and strong, vivid.

He spun it out farther, looking for moments that had been particularly rewarding to witness: the meeting of Emily and Gwydion, the boy she had called Sam, in a green summer meadow; the Three emerging from the Root into the air of a new world they otherwise would never have seen; the moment Achmed took the throne, and the destiny, of the Bolg, as his own; the reunion of his parents; the victory over the demon; the rebuilding of the new world. *Yes*, he thought, running the smooth, thick film along the edge of his finger, *it was worth it indeed.*

But what of the Past as it had been? There needed to be a reverence for its loss. The outcome of events in that course of Time that had led ultimately to failure had been disastrous, for certain, but there had been moments of glory, too, heroism and brave acts of selflessness, choices, both wise and foolish, and love. He looked again at the frame of Achmed watching his parents' wedding and smiled wryly. Certainly there had been love.

An overwhelming impulse seized him. Before he even had time to process the thought his hand darted out and swept the fragment of timefilm from the lamp, gathering it up from the floor with the last remaining scraps of the old life, the first history, the rewritten Past. He laid the disappearing snippets on a glass panel, the bottom half of a slide that rested on the Time Editor, and snatched a bottle of fixative from the whirling prismatic disk hovering in the air beside the machine. Feverishly he doused the shards with the glimmering potion, preserving them. His eyes blinked rapidly as he pressed them carefully between the glass panel and a cover plate.

He opened a drawer in the Time Editor, lifted the slide he had just created, and slowly slid the panes of glass into the depth of the cabinet, then closed the door softly. He breathed shallowly, trying to regain his calm.

A sense of great dread coupled with relief washed over him. He had no idea what other moments of the rewritten Past he had just rescued; it might be as much a dire action as a good one, but it had been as strong an impulse as he had ever experienced. Since he did not know what lay ahead for him now, he decided he was right to trust the compulsion.

A shadow on the wall caught his eye. He looked up to where the last image had been projected to see shadows of it still there, as if burned into the glass. The outline of the elderly woman's body was dimmer now, her hands reaching up into diffuse light and gray patches. Meridion put his hot forehead down on the cool surface of the Time Editor and tried to summon the courage to take the next step.

Even though his body was formed only of thought, lore, and pure will, his consciousness unhindered by the limitations of human flesh, Meridion was still capable of feeling the pain of imminent physical loss, the sting of tired hands, the delayed weariness after so much despair. He struggled not to be swept up in the choking fear of the unknown that faced him now.

The events that had brought him into being had been inexorably altered, shredded into scraps of amber film, gone now except for the few random fragments he had rescued along with the record of his birth. The steps he had taken in manipulating Time had produced the result he had prayed for, it seemed. The world beneath him was turning, sailing slowly through the ether, blue and whole and covered with swirling currents of air that danced across its surface, heedless that there had ever been any destruction looming. His meddling in the Past had worked. The disaster he had sought to avert had been averted.

At the same time he knew that the events his intervention had put into place had disrupted his own story, had negated the circumstances under which he had been conceived. He did not know if the new path Time was now taking would lead to his own rebirth somewhere in it.

Or not.

Contemplation, both now and before he undertook to alter the Past, had led him to believe against it. He had been brought to life, conceived as a concept, not really as a child, by two scarred individuals, one aged, one made old beyond his years by circumstance, who gave of their lives, their lore, to fulfill a prophecy different from any that now existed in the rewritten history. At least the first part was different; Meridion had been surprised to see Manwyn utter some of the same prophecy in the new history, in Time as it was now. In the old history it had foretold his birth:

I see an unnatural child born of an unnatural act. Rhapsody, you should beware of childbirth: the mother shall die, but the child shall live.

Why did the Seer utter it again, in the rewritten history? he wondered, cradling his head in his hands. Would the magical sacrifice that Rhapsody, the elderly Liringlas Namer, and Gwydion of Manosse, a broken man dead in the eyes of the world, had undertaken to bring him into the world still be necessary in the Future? With the F'dor destroyed and the war averted, it hardly seemed so. And yet now that the Past had been erased and re-formed, the Future was unfathomable.

Instead of meeting as they had, in the new world, solely for the purpose of forming him to fulfill the warning of a prophecy, his parents had instead met in their mutual youth, had fallen in love and joined their souls of their own free will. Everything they had endured had brought them together again; it seemed little enough to hope for, that they might eventually bring him into existence by the mere happenstance that every other living soul comes out of. Meridion knew that this was merely wishful thinking, however. Just bringing lives together did not guarantee how they would be put to use. It was an observation he had made many times while watching the Past unspool itself as it was being altered. Time was fragile, and subject to change.

It's your destiny.

Hogwash. We make our own destiny.

Yes, Meridion thought, bitterly amused. *Yes, yes, we do.*

For now his life hung, suspended in Time, within the glass globe of his observatory, powered by the ethereal fire of Seren, the star for which his mother's homeland had been named. When the Time Editor shut down, the film of Time would begin to run again, endless and uninterrupted. And he would then come to his ending, winking out like a candleflame.

Have I made all the amends, begged all the forgiveness I need? he wondered dully, running through a list of people in his mind, hoping that absolution would come in any case for whomever he had inadvertently harmed with his intervention. He thought mostly of Achmed, and what the changes in Time had cost him. *Forgive me*, he thought in silent prayer to a man he had also never met. *In my place, I think you would have done the same.* He remembered the words of contrition that the Bolg King had offered up to the Patriarch in the new history and smiled wanly. *Given the choice, I think you would have wanted it that way, too.*

His ultimate goal, of course, had been paramount; all sacrifices, all changes that had occurred between one history and the other had been worth the cost. Whatever detriments had come from the revision were to be added into the balance sheet and weighed off against the result, just as all more fortuitous outcomes were merely coincidence. Meridion looked up once more at the image of his mother in happy events of the new history and exhaled. Had he not sliced his father out of Time in his youth and grafted him back into the Past for the purpose of meeting her, she would never have followed him, never would have journeyed with Achmed and

Grunthor, never would have had this moment, and any other happy ones that might follow. And the world would have been consumed in fire. *I didn't do it for you*, he thought, staring at the projection. *But I am still glad.*

Before his eyes the darker image of his birth faded and disappeared into oblivion.

I am fading, too.

Slowly Meridion reached over and shut off the Time Editor's switch, separating the machine from the light of Seren. The glowing instrumentality vanished into utter darkness. He closed his eyes as the remains of the timefilm he had known ignited on their reels, dissipating like the smoke from the last embers of a long-dead fire.

The circular glass walls of his observatory melted away in a heartbeat.

The last words he heard as the world fell down around him were spoken in the voice of the man who had guarded him from birth, who stood with him until the moment he entered the Time Editor's enclosure, had comforted him in his own awkward way.

Will I die? Meridion had asked his guardian, knowing that the answer could not impact his undertaking. He heard the reply again now as the air from the circular glass room left, rushing into the dark vacuum of space. The words reverberated against the disappearing glass of the windowpanes in fading echoes.

Can one experience death if one is not really alive? You, like the rest of the world, have nothing to lose.

Amid the horrific noise and swirling vortex that consumed his life energy, Meridion felt the translucent form that had been his body expand, stretched infinitely out over the vastness of Time and space, then explode in a burst of agony. His diminished awareness ebbed, then grew, only to flash around the outer reaches of the sky, an incandescent beam of light, until it fell like a blazing stone through the windswept clouds, hurtling to the Earth below.

The last fragments of his conscious thought screamed with the anguish of death, howled with the pain of birth, tumbled, blind, through the flashing images of a Past he didn't recognize, of a future he could barely see, until it stopped, became aware again, like awakening from a dream-filled sleep.

Meridion opened his eyes.

The first thing he saw was the familiar, smoothly polished stone and thick glass windows of the high tower around him. He felt the coldness of the marble chair on which he sat, chilling the muscles of his body, a body that had pleasurable heft and weight to it. He was glad to note the reunion of his conscious mind with his physical form; he remembered that the first few times he had meditated, traveling back or forth in Time, he had been petrified there would be nowhere for him to return, but had eventually reconciled himself to the risk.

It was reassuring to step out of Time and back into himself, into his memories, the history he knew both from the old tales, and from seeing it himself.

Whatever he had been seeking on this journey had eluded him. He had always had a sense that there was something different about Time than the way it appeared, but could never find the link, the evidence, that any other reality had ever existed than the one he knew, and could see in his mind's eye. It seemed to him for some reason that his memories, and the history he was able to view, were somehow *new*, fresher than one might think they should be.

Sometimes in his dreams there were flashes, fragments that seemed to belong to some other time, some other reality, filled with images of strange lights and darkness and spools of something that looked like thread, suspended as if hanging among the stars. Always in these dreams there was a sense of dread, an urgency that he could not escape, from which he would wake, panting, fearful, to the bright sun of morning that did little to warm the chill from his soul. He had tried to explain the strange misgivings he felt to his mother, who herself had been prescient, but she had never really been able to grasp what he was trying to convey.

The door in the tower room opened, and she came in; Meridion watched her out of the corner of his eye as she set the tray she was carrying down on the table next to him. He smiled at her, then turned in his seat and regarded her thoughtfully. Many years had passed since the day of her wedding, and she still looked exactly the same, although her face held a look of wisdom that had not been there in her youth. His father still had the appearance of youth about him also, though time had etched a few more lines around his eyes, visible when he smiled.

'All finished?' Rhapsody asked, handing Meridion a mug of *dol mwl*. He took the cup of steaming liquid gratefully and nodded, sipping the rosy amber drink they both liked. His father drank it on occasion, but had never really developed a taste for it. Meridion swallowed.

'Yes,' he said. 'Thank you.'

She came behind him and slid her arms around his shoulders. 'Where did you go today – forward or back?'

Meridion thought back to the only image he remembered, the hazy picture of his parents running through a starry night. 'Back,' he said, taking another sip. 'I think I attended your wedding, but I don't remember much. Your gown was beautiful.'

'Miresylle would have been glad to hear that you thought so,' his mother said, picking up her own mug. 'She worked for two months straight on it.' Her emerald eyes gleamed. 'Did you see Oelendra, my mentor, at the wedding?'

He thought for a moment, searching his memory. 'Yes, but not this time. This is only one of many times I've gone to watch the wedding, because the fireworks were spectacular. I don't remember seeing her this time. Or the fireworks, for that matter.' He lifted the mug to his lips, unwilling to reveal that he remembered nothing but the one image from the journey. Everything else was blank.

555

Rhapsody blinked quickly and nodded. 'I wish you could have known her, Meridion; she was very special.'

Meridion smiled. 'I did know her, in a way,' he said. 'You didn't notice on the day you first came to Tyrian, but I was one of the children in her swordplay class.'

Rhapsody laughed and tousled his hair, leaving her hand resting on the wiry golden curls a moment afterward. 'You really have been all over in Time, haven't you? I remember you from the fountain in Easton; you used to ask me to play the same song over and over.'

Meridion nodded and took a sip of the *dol mwl*. 'I came to witness the Cymrian Council, too, but I was an adult then.'

'It's a great treasure you've been given, you know, this gift of Time, and the ability to step in and out of it at will.'

'It is.' Meridion set the mug back on the tray and picked up a pastry from the plate on it. 'But it's a little frustrating, being able to see events in the Past and the Future, but having no ability to affect them. I have the strange feeling that I should be able to make some sort of an impact, but alas, when I step into the Past I am only an observer, and on rare occasions a commentator – I had to work very hard just to make you hear me when I asked you to play that song.' He chuckled. 'It's most likely for the best that I'm just an image and not really there. If I could affect Time I'd probably make a botch of it.'

Rhapsody took a sip from the steaming mug, then looked at her son seriously. 'I think anyone would. It seems to me that being able to see into the Past or the Future, which is a family trait in your case, causes nothing but trouble. The visions I have had gave me horrific nightmares, and as for your great-grandmother and her sisters – their lore certainly cost them their sanity, especially Manwyn; the power of seeing the Future must be the most dangerous.' Her eyes narrowed slightly as she saw something come over her son's face. 'Meridion, what are you thinking?'

He shrugged and lifted the mug to his lips again.

'Do you have any idea where Manwyn gets her information about the Future?'

Meridion laughed. 'Well, she gets some of it from *me*. I stop by for tea and a good gossip with her every now and then. She is my great-great-aunt, after all, and no one else visits her without seeking something from her. I'm more than an image to her; I actually have some physical presence when I'm with Manwyn. Sometimes she lets me use Merithyn's sextant to look into the Future. She's a lot of fun, once you get to know her, in a crazy sort of way.'

'Really?' His mother untangled a nest of curls in his hair. 'That's odd. You're a Namer, Meridion. If she gets her prophecies from you, then why is she so mysterious about them? And so seldom right when she relates them to the world?'

His smile faded, and he looked away to see a lark gliding past one of the tower windows, the sun on its wings. 'Well, she is somewhat deaf, after all.'

'Is that the extent of it?'

Meridion exhaled slowly, still watching the bird until it banked away to even greater heights. 'Who said she was wrong?'

'Isn't she, on occasion?'

He shook his head, not looking at her. 'No. She's mad, and crafty, and hard of hearing, but never wrong.' Finally he turned and met her gaze. 'Do you remember what Jo told you in the place of the Rowans about not being able to understand about the Afterlife until you are in it?'

Rhapsody put down her mug. 'Yes.'

'It's true of knowledge of the Future as well. Manwyn may see it, but that doesn't mean she understands it.' *Any more than you do*, he thought with a touch of melancholy.

'But you do?'

He leaned toward the window, hoping to see the bird again. 'Most of the time.'

'Hmmm.' Rhapsody followed his gaze out the window, the autumn sunlight spilling into the tower room. When she looked back again she was smiling.

'Have you ever determined where this ability of yours came from? I understand why the three Seers have their gifts; their father was born in the birthplace of Time's beginning, their mother at its end, both of them of ancient races. Why you, then, Meridion?'

He took a bite of the pastry. 'Good cookies,' he said. Her question hung heavy in the air, unanswered.

After a few moments of uncomfortable silence, Meridion began to fidget. Finally he sighed. 'Like the Seers, it certainly helps for me to have parents from opposite sides of the Prime Meridian, but who both spent time in each world.' *And to have had one's soul conceived in one, and carried throughout Time, ungestated, to be born in the other*, he thought.

He averted his eyes, avoiding her clear green gaze. He had never really found a good way to explain to her that it was the presence of his unborn soul inside her, the bridge across Time, the bond between his mother and father conceived that night in the green meadow, that had given her visions into the Future throughout her life, visions that had ceased upon his birth, mostly because he was not entirely certain himself of how it had all come about. He had often looked in his journeys for the answer to his greatest question, how his father had been plucked for an instant from Time and sent back to the moment where his parents had joined their souls, making the beginnings of him in the process, but he had never found it.

Rhapsody looked fondly at him in return. 'The Prime Meridian isn't where your name comes from, just in case you're wondering. You were named for your father and Merithyn.'

'I know; I heard the speeches at my naming ceremony when I was a newborn. You named me, after all. You do have a habit of inadvertently bestowing powers with the names you give.' Meridion slid off the marble chair. 'Can I go and play now?'

'Of course.' Rhapsody regarded her son indulgently. 'My, you're getting so big. You'll be as tall as me soon.'

'In three years, three months, and seventeen days,' answered Meridion, stuffing the remains of the cookie in his mouth. 'Bye, Mama.' He kissed her cheek as she bent to embrace him, the strange vertical slits of his blue eyes sparkling warmly. Then he ran out the door, down the stairs, and into the clear autumn air.